Revelation

C. J. SANSOM was educated at Birmingham University,
where he took a BA and then a PhD in history. After working in
a variety of jobs, he retrained as a solicitor and practised in Sussex,
until becoming a full-time writer. *Revelation* is the fourth novel
in his acclaimed Shardlake series. He lives in Sussex.

C. J. SANSOM

Revelation

§

MACMILLAN

First published 2008 by Macmillan

This edition published 2008 by Macmillan
an imprint of Pan Macmillan Ltd
Pan Macmillan, 20 New Wharf Road, London N1 9RR
Basingstoke and Oxford
Associated companies throughout the world
www.panmacmillan.com

ISBN 978-0-230-73623-8

1 3 5 7 9 8 6 4 2

A CIP catalogue record for this book is available from
the British Library.

Map artwork by Neil Gower

Typeset by SetSystems Ltd, Saffron Walden, Essex
Printed in the UK by CPI Mackays, Chatham ME5 8TD

Visit *www.panmacmillan.com* to read more about all our books
and to buy them. You will also find features, author interviews and
news of any author events, and you can sign up for e-newsletters
so that you're always first to hear about our new releases.

Revelation

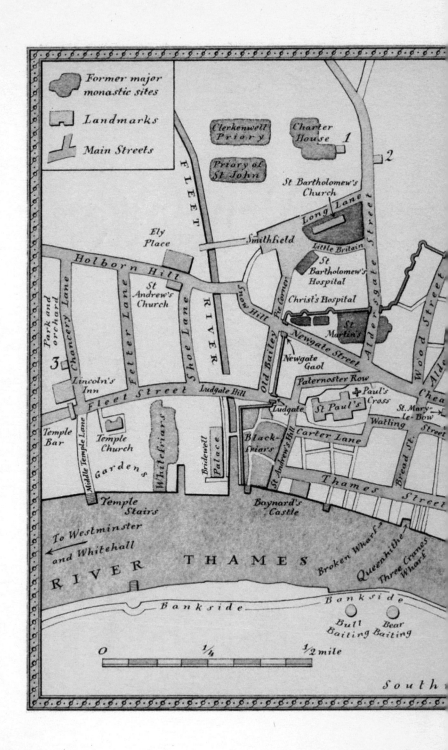

Former major monastic sites

Landmarks

Main Streets

Clerkenwell Priory

Charter House   1

2

Priory of St John

St Bartholomew's Church

Long Lane

Smithfield

Little Britain

Ely Place

Aldersgate Street

Holborn Hill

St Andrew's Church

St Bartholomew's Hospital

Snow Hill

Christ's Hospital

Pie Corner

Park and orchard

Chancery Lane

Fetter Lane

Shoe Lane

RIVER

FLEET

St Martin's

Wood Street

Old Bailey

Newgate Street

Alde

3

Lincoln's Inn

Newgate Gaol

Paternoster Row

Cheap

Fleet Street

Ludgate Hill

Paul's Cross

St Mary-le-Bow

Temple Bar

Middle Temple Lane

Temple Church

Whitefriars

Bridewell Palace

Ludgate

St Paul's

Watling

Street

St Andrew's Hill

Carter Lane

Black-friars

Gardens

Baynard's Castle

Bread St.

Thames

Street

Temple Stairs

To Westminster and Whitehall

Broken Wharf

Queenhithe

Three Cranes Wharf

RIVER   THAMES

Bankside

Bankside

Bull Baiting

Bear Baiting

0   ¼   ½ mile

South

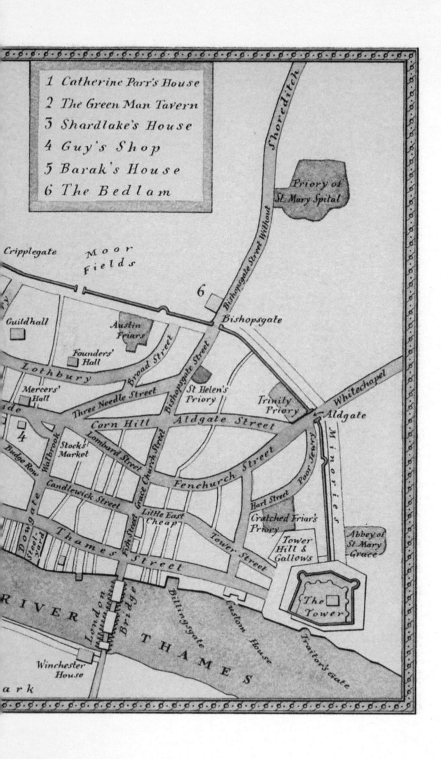

1 Catherine Parr's House
2 The Green Man Tavern
3 Shardlake's House
4 Guy's Shop
5 Barak's House
6 The Bedlam

Shoreditch

Priory of
St. Mary Spital

Bishopsgate Street Without

Cripplegate

M o o r
F i e l d s

6

Bishopsgate

Guildhall

Austin
Friars

Broad Street

Founders'
Hall

Lothbury

Bishopsgate Street

St Helen's
Priory

Whitechapel

Mercers'
Hall

Three Needle Street

Trinity
Priory

Aldgate

ide

Corn Hill

Aldgate Street

4

Stocks'
Market

Lombard Street

Grace Church Street

Fenchurch Street

Poor Jewry

Minories

Bulge Row

Walbrook

Candlewick Street

Hart Street

Cratched Friar's
Priory

Abbey of
St. Mary
Grace

Dowgate

Steel-
yard

Thames

Street

Fish Street

Little East
Cheap

Tower Street

Tower
Hill &
Gallows

London

Bridge

Billingsgate

Custom
House

The
Tower

Winchester
House

R I V E R

T H A M E S

Traitor's Gate

ark

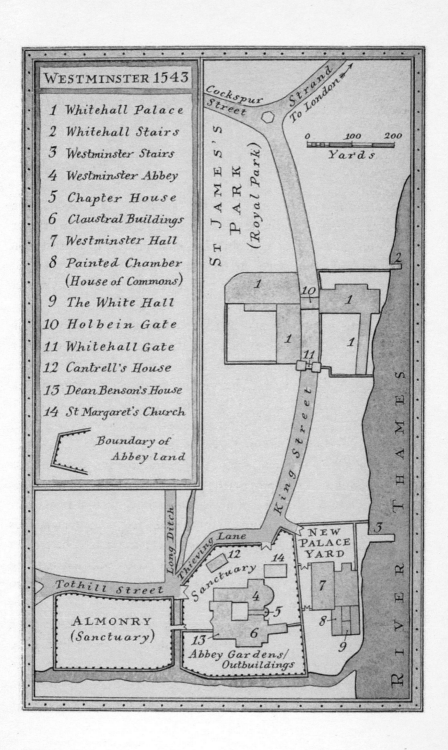

WESTMINSTER 1543

1 Whitehall Palace
2 Whitehall Stairs
3 Westminster Stairs
4 Westminster Abbey
5 Chapter House
6 Claustral Buildings
7 Westminster Hall
8 Painted Chamber
  (House of Commons)
9 The White Hall
10 Holbein Gate
11 Whitehall Gate
12 Cantrell's House
13 Dean Benson's House
14 St Margaret's Church

Boundary of
Abbey land

Cockspur Street

Strand
To London

St James's Park (Royal Park)

0   100   200
Yards

King Street

Long Ditch

Thieving Lane

Tothill Street

ALMONNY
(Sanctuary)

Sanctuary

NEW PALACE YARD

RIVER THAMES

Abbey Gardens/
Outbuildings

Chapter One

THE HIGH CHANDELIERS in the Great Hall of Lincoln's Inn were ablaze with candles, for it was late afternoon when the play began. Most members of Lincoln's Inn were present, the barristers in their robes and their wives in their best costumes. After an hour standing watching, my back was starting to ache, and I envied the few elderly and infirm members who had brought stools.

The performance of a play at Lincoln's Inn, traditionally held in March, had been cancelled earlier in the month because of heavy snow; late in the month now, it was still unseasonably cold, the breath of actors and audience visible, wafting up like smoke to the high roof-beams. The play that year was a new Interlude, *The Trial of Treasure*, a heavy-handed moral fable with the gorgeously robed actors portraying the vices and virtues of mankind. As the actor playing Virtue, resplendent in pale robes and a long, white, false beard, lectured Dissimulation on his deceitful ways – appropriately, perhaps, to an audience of lawyers – my attention wandered. I cast my eyes over the shadowed faces of the audience. Treasurer Rowland, a thin-faced, acerbic old man, was eyeing the actors as though wondering whether it might have been better hiring a troupe with less expensive costumes even if this play required no elaborate scenery. Across from me I saw my old enemy Stephen Bealknap, his greedy pale blue eyes studying his fellow lawyers. Those eyes were never still, would never meet yours, and as he saw me looking at him his gaze slid away. He was perhaps the crookedest lawyer I had ever come across; it still smarted that eighteen months before I had been forced to abandon a case against him through the ruthless machinations of his patron, Richard Rich. It struck me that he looked tired, ill.

I

Some distance away my friend Roger Elliard, to whose house I was invited to a dinner afterwards, held his wife's hand. A new scene had begun; Lust had made a pact of fellowship with Inclination To Evil. Embracing him, Lust was suddenly seized with pain and crouched on his knees.

> Out alas, what sudden passion is this,
> I am so taken that I cannot stand,
> the cramp, the cramp has touched me,
> I shall die without remedy now out of hand.

The actor, struck down by divine judgement, stretched out a trembling hand to the audience. I saw Bealknap look at him with a sort of puzzled contempt; Roger, though, turned suddenly away. I knew why; I would talk to him later.

At last the play ended; the players bowed, the audience clapped, and we got our cold limbs into motion and stepped out into Gate-house Court. The sun was just setting, illuminating the redbrick buildings and the melting snow in the courtyard with an umber light. People walked away to the gate, or if they lived at Lincoln's Inn stepped homewards, wrapping their coats around them. I waited in the doorway for the Elliards, nodding to acquaintances. The audi-ence were the only ones abroad, for it was a Saturday out of law term, Palm Sunday Eve. I looked across to the Elliards' lodgings. All the windows were lit and servants could be seen within, bustling with trays. Dorothy's dinners were well known around the Inn, and even at the end of Lent, with red meat forbidden, I knew that she would have large tabling and good belly cheer for the group they had invited.

Despite the cold I felt relaxed, more peaceful than I had for a long time. In just over a week it would be Easter Sunday, and also the twenty-fifth of March, the official start of the New Year of 1543. Sometimes in recent years I had wondered at this time what grim events the coming year might bring. But I reflected that now I had only good and interesting work, and times with good friends, to look forward to. That morning while dressing I had paused to study my face in the steel mirror in my bedroom; something I seldom did, for the sight of my humped back still distressed me. I saw streaks of grey in my hair, deepening lines on my face. Yet I thought perhaps they gave me something of a distinguished look; and I had passed forty the previous year, I could no longer expect to look young.

That afternoon, before the performance, I had walked down to the Thames, for I had heard the ice was breaking up at last after the long, bitter winter. I stood at Temple Stairs and looked down at the river. True enough, huge chunks of ice tumbled against each other with great crashes and creaks amid roiling grey waters. I walked back through soft, melting snow, thinking that perhaps spring was coming at last.

Standing in the doorway of the Hall, I shivered suddenly despite my heavy fur-lined coat, for though the air was definitely warmer today it was still chill and I had never put back the flesh I lost in my bad fever eighteen months before. I jumped slightly as someone clapped me on the shoulder. It was Roger, his slim form swathed in a heavy coat. Beside him his wife Dorothy, her plump cheeks red with cold, smiled at me. Her brown hair was gathered under a round French hood set with pearls.

'You were in a brown study, Matthew,' Roger said. 'Reflecting on the high moral sentiments of the play?'

'High as a house but heavy as a horse,' Dorothy said.

'That they were,' I agreed. 'Who chose it?'

'The Treasurer.' Roger looked to where Rowland was talking to an ancient judge, nodding his head gravely. Roger lowered his voice. 'He wanted something that wasn't politically contentious. Wise in these days. But an Italian comedy would have been better.'

We walked across the courtyard together. I noticed the snow on the Gatehouse Court fountain, which had been frozen this last three months, was almost gone, revealing patches of grey ice. Soon perhaps the fountain would be working again, its gentle plashing sounding across the court. A few coins were exposed on the ice; even with the fountain frozen people still threw money in with a prayer for victory in a case or luck in an affair of the heart; for though they might deny it, lawyers were as superstitious as other men.

✝

ROGER'S STEWARD, an old man called Elias who had been with the family for years, greeted us at the door and took me upstairs to wash my hands. Then I went into the parlour, where fat candles cast a warm buttery light on the chairs and cushions. A dozen guests, all barristers and their wives, already sat or lounged, served with wine by Elias and a boy. A roaring fire warmed the room, bringing sweet smells from the scented herbs on the wooden floor, its light glinting on the silverware on the cloth-covered table. The walls were decorated with framed portraits in the new fashion, mostly of biblical characters. Above the large fireplace stood one of the best pieces of furniture in Lincoln's Inn, Roger's pride and joy. It was a large, carved wooden frieze of intricate design, the branches of trees in full leaf interlaced with flowers and fruits, the heads of animals peering through, deer and boar and even a unicorn. Roger stood beside it, talking to Ambrose Loder from my chambers. His slim form was animated, his fine hands waving as he made some point to the plump barrister, who stood immobile, a sceptical look on his red face.

Dorothy stood beside him, wearing an expression of good-natured amusement, her colourful clothes a contrast to the black robes of the two lawyers. She wore a green damask dress with gold piping down the front, and a high collar open at the throat; it suited her well. Seeing me, she excused herself and came across.

I had known Dorothy near twenty years. She was the daughter of a serjeant in my first chambers. We had both been in our early twenties then and I had at once been attracted to Dorothy's elegance, wit and kind nature – a rare combination. She seemed to like my company too, never seemed to mind my bent back, and we became good friends. After a while I dared to think of trying to turn friendship into something more. I had given no signs of my real feelings, though, and therefore had only myself to blame when I learned that Roger, my friend and colleague, had already proposed marriage and been accepted. He later said – and I believed him – that he had not realized my feelings for Dorothy. She had guessed, though, and tried to sweeten the pill by saying she had had a difficult choice to make. I had found that hard to believe, for Roger was handsome as well as clever, with a quicksilver, energetic grace to his movements.

Dorothy was, like me, past forty now; though apart from little wrinkles visible around her eyes she looked a good deal younger. I bent and kissed her on her full cheeks.

'A merry Palm Sunday to you, Dorothy.'

'And to you, Matthew.' She squeezed my hand. 'How is your health?'

'Good these days.' My back had often given me trouble, but these last months I had been conscientious in the exercises my physician friend Guy had prescribed, and had felt much better.

'You look well.'

'And you look younger each New Year, Dorothy. May this one bring peace and prosperity.'

'I hope so. Though there has been a strange portent, have you heard? Two huge fish washed up by the Thames. Great grey things half the size of a house. They must have been under the ice.' The twinkle in her eyes told me she found the story, like so much in the world, delightfully absurd.

'Were they alive?'

'No. They lie on the mudbanks over at Greenwich. People have been crossing London Bridge in hundreds to see them. Everyone says that coming the day before Palm Sunday it portends some terrible happening.'

'People are always finding portents these days. It is a passion now among the busy Bible-men of London.'

'True.' She gave me a searching look, perhaps catching a bitter note in my reply. Twenty years ago Dorothy and Roger and I had all been reformers, hoping for a new Christian fellowship in the world. They still did. But though many of their guests had also been reformers in the early days, most had now retreated to a quiet professional life, frightened and disillusioned by the tides of religious conflict and repression that had flowed ever higher in the decade since the King's break with Rome. I wondered if Dorothy guessed that, for me, faith was almost gone.

She changed the subject. 'For us at least the news has been good. We had a letter from Samuel today. The roads to Bristol must be open again.' She raised her dark eyebrows. 'And reading between the lines, I think he has a girl.'

Samuel was Roger and Dorothy's only child, the apple of their eye. Some years before, the family had moved to Bristol, Roger's home town, where he had obtained the post of City Recorder. He had returned to practise at Lincoln's Inn a year before, but Samuel, now eighteen and apprenticed to a cloth merchant, had decided to stay behind; to the sorrow of both his parents, I knew.

I smiled gently. 'Are you sure you are not reading your wishes into his letter?'

'No, he mentions a name. Elizabeth. A merchant's daughter.'

'He will not be able to marry till after his apprenticeship.'

'Good. That will allow time to see if they are suited.' She smiled roguishly. 'And perhaps for me to send some spy to Bristol. Your assistant Barak, perhaps. I hear he is good at such jobs.'

I laughed. 'Barak is busy with my work. You must find another spy.'

'I like that sharp humour of his. Does he well?'

'He and his wife lost a child last year. It hit him hard, though he does not show it.'

'And she?'

'I have not seen Tamasin. I keep meaning to call on them at home. I must do it. She was kind to me when I had my fever.'

'The Court of Requests keeps you busy, then. And a serjeant. I always knew you would reach that eminence one day.'

'Ay.' I smiled. 'And it is good work.' It was over a year now since Archbishop Cranmer had nominated me as one of the two barristers appointed to plead before the Court of Requests where poor men's pleas were heard. A serjeancy, the status of a senior barrister, had come with the post.

'I have never enjoyed my work so much,' I continued. 'Though the caseload is large and some of the clients – well, poverty does not make men good, or easy.'

'Nor should it,' Dorothy replied vigorously. 'It is a curse.'

'I do not complain. The work is varied.' I paused. 'I have a new case, a boy who has been put in the Bedlam. I am meeting with his parents tomorrow.'

'On Palm Sunday?'

'There is some urgency.'

'A mad client.'

'Whether he is truly mad or not is the issue. He was put there on the Privy Council's orders. It is one of the strangest matters I have ever come across. Interesting, though I wish I did not have to tangle with a Council matter.'

'You will see justice done, that I do not doubt.' She laid her hand on my arm.

'Matthew!' Roger had appeared beside me. He shook my hand vigorously. He was small and wiry, with a thin but well-favoured face, searching blue eyes and black hair starting to recede. He was as full of energy as ever. Despite his winning of Dorothy all those years before, I still had the strongest affection for him.

'I hear Samuel has written,' I said.

'Ay, the imp. At last!'

'I must go to the kitchen,' Dorothy said. 'I will see you shortly, Matthew. Talk to Roger, he has had an interesting idea.'

I bowed as she left, then turned back to Roger.

'How have you been?' I asked quietly.

He lowered his voice. 'It has not come on me again. But I will be glad when I have seen your doctor friend.'

'I saw you look away when Lust was suddenly struck down during the play.'

'Ay. It frightens me, Matthew.' Suddenly he looked vulnerable, like a little boy. I pressed his arm.

In recent weeks Roger had several times unexpectedly lost his balance and fallen over, for no apparent reason. He feared he was developing the falling sickness, that terrible affliction where a man or woman, quite healthy in other ways, will periodically collapse on the ground, out of their senses, writhing and grunting. The illness, which was untreatable, was regarded by some as a kind of temporary madness and by others as evidence of possession by an evil spirit. The fact that spectacular symptoms could erupt at any moment meant people avoided sufferers. It would mean the end of a lawyer's career.

I pressed his arm. 'Guy will find the truth of it, I promise.' Roger had unburdened himself to me over lunch the week before, and I had arranged for him to see my physician friend as soon as possible – in four days' time.

Roger smiled crookedly. 'Let us hope it is news I shall care to hear.' He lowered his voice. 'I have told Dorothy I have been having stomach pains. I think it best. Women only worry.'

'So do we, Roger.' I smiled. 'And sometimes without cause. There could be many reasons for this falling over; and remember; you have had no seizures.'

'I know. 'Tis true.'

'Dorothy tells me you have had some new idea,' I said, to distract him.

'Yes.' He smiled wryly. 'I was telling friend Loder about it, but he seems little interested.' He glanced over his guests. 'None of us here is poor,' he said quietly.

He took my arm, leading me away a little. 'I have been reading Roderick Mors' new book, the *Lamentation of a Christian against the City of London.*'

'You should be careful. Some call it seditious.'

'The truth affrights them.' Roger's tones were quiet but intense. 'By Jesu, Mors' book is an indictment of our city. It shows how all the wealth of the monasteries has gone to the King or his courtiers.

The monastic schools and hospitals closed down, the sick left to fend for themselves. The monks' care was niggardly enough but now they have nothing. It shames us all, the legions of miserable people lying in the streets, sick and half dead. I saw a boy in a doorway in Cheapside yesterday, his bare feet half rotted away with frostbite. I gave him sixpence, but it was a hospital he needed, Matthew.'

'But as you say, most have been closed.'

'Which is why I am going to canvass for a hospital funded by the Inns of Court. With an initial subscription, then a fund for bequests and donations from the lawyers.'

'Have you spoken to the Treasurer?'

'Not yet.' Roger smiled again. 'I am honing my arguments on these fellows.' He nodded towards the plump form of Loder. 'Ambrose there said the poor offend every passer-by with their dangerous stinks and vapours; he might pay money to have the streets cleared. Others complain of importunate beggars calling everywhere for God's penny. I promise them a quiet life. There are arguments to persuade those who lack charity.' He smiled, then looked at me seriously. 'Will you help?'

I considered a moment. 'Even if you succeed, what can one hospital do in the face of the misery all around?'

'Relieve a few poor souls.'

'I will help you if I can.' If anyone could accomplish this task it was Roger. His energy and quick wits would count for much. 'I will subscribe to your hospital, and help you raise subscriptions, if you like.'

Roger squeezed my arm. 'I knew you would help me. Soon I will organize a committee—'

'Another committee?' Dorothy had returned, red-faced from the heat of the kitchen. She looked quizzically at her husband. Roger put his arm round her waist.

'For the hospital, sweetheart.'

'People will be hard to persuade. Their purses smart from all the King's taxes.'

'And may suffer more,' I said. 'They say this new Parliament will

9

be asked to grant yet more money for the King to go to war with France.'

'The waste,' Roger said bitterly. 'When one thinks of how the money could be used. But yes, he will see this as the right time for such an enterprise. With the Scotch King dead and this baby girl on their throne, they cannot intervene on the French side.'

I nodded agreement. 'The King has sent the Scotch lords captured after Solway Moss back home; it is said they have sworn oaths to bring a marriage between Prince Edward and the baby Mary.'

'You are well informed as ever, Matthew,' Dorothy said. 'Does Barak still bring gossip from his friends among the court servants?'

'He does.'

'I have heard that the King is after a new wife.'

'They have been saying that since Catherine Howard was executed,' Roger said. 'Who is it supposed to be now?'

'Lady Latimer,' Dorothy replied. 'Her husband died last week. There is to be a great funeral the day after tomorrow. 'Tis said the King has had a fancy for her for some years, and that he will move now.'

I had not heard that rumour. 'Poor woman,' I said. I lowered my voice. 'She needs fear for her head.'

'Yes.' Dorothy nodded, was quiet for a second, then raised her voice and clapped her hands. 'Dinner is ready, my friends.'

We all walked through to the dining room. The long old oaken dining table was set with plates of silver, and servants were laying out dishes of food under Elias' supervision. Pride of place went to four large chickens; as it was still Lent the law would normally have allowed only fish to be eaten at this time, but the freezing of the river that winter had made fish prohibitively expensive and the King had given permission for people to eat white meat.

We took our places. I sat between Loder, with whom Roger had been arguing earlier, and James Ryprose, an elderly barrister with bristly whiskers framing a face as wrinkled as an old apple-john.

Opposite us sat Dorothy and Roger and Mrs Loder, who was as plump and contented-looking as her husband. She smiled at me, showing a full set of white teeth, and then to my surprise reached into her mouth and pulled out both rows. I saw the teeth were fixed into two dentures of wood, cut to fit over the few grey stumps that were all that was left of her own teeth.

'They look good, do they not?' she asked, catching my stare. 'A barber-surgeon in Cheapside made them up for me. I cannot eat with them, of course.'

'Put them away, Johanna,' her husband said. 'The company does not want to stare at those while we eat.' Johanna pouted, so far as an almost toothless woman can, and deposited the teeth in a little box which she put away in the folds of her dress. I repressed a shudder. I found the French fashion some in the upper classes had adopted for wearing mouthfuls of teeth taken from dead people, rather gruesome.

Roger began talking about his hospital again, addressing his arguments this time to old Ryprose. 'Think of the sick and helpless people we could take from the streets, maybe cure.'

'Ay, that would be a worthwhile thing,' the old man agreed. 'But what of all the fit sturdy beggars that infest the streets, pestering one for money, sometimes with threats? What is to be done with them? I am an old man and sometimes fear to walk out alone.'

'Very true.' Brother Loder leaned across me to voice his agreement. 'Those two that robbed and killed poor Brother Goodcole by the gates last November were masterless servants from the monasteries. And they would not have been caught had they not gone bragging of what they had done in the taverns where they spent poor Goodcole's money, and had an honest inn-keeper not raised the constable.'

'Ay, ay.' Ryprose nodded vigorously. 'No wonder masterless men beg and rob with impunity, when all the city has to ensure our safety are a few constables, most nearly as old as me.'

'The city council should appoint some strong men to whip them out of the city,' Loder said.

'But, Ambrose,' his wife said quietly. 'Why be so harsh? When you were younger you used to argue the workless poor had a right to be given employment, the city should pay them to do useful things like pave the streets. You were always quoting Erasmus and Juan Vives on the duties of a Christian Commonwealth towards the unfortunate.' She smiled at him sweetly, gaining revenge perhaps for his curt remark about her teeth.

'So you were, Ambrose,' Roger said. 'I remember it well.'

'And I,' Dorothy agreed. 'You used to wax most fiercely about the duties of the King towards the poor.'

'Well, there's no interest from that quarter, so I don't see what we're supposed to do.' Loder frowned at his wife. 'Take ten thousand scabby beggars into the Inn and feed them at High Table?'

'No,' Roger answered gently. 'Merely use our status as wealthy men to help a few. Till better times come, perhaps.'

'It's not just the beggars that make walking the streets a misery,' old Ryprose added gloomily. 'There's all these ranting Bible-men springing up everywhere. There's one at the bottom of Newgate Street, stands there all day, barking and railing that the Apocalypse is coming.'

There were murmurs of agreement up and down the table. In the years since Thomas Cromwell's fall, the King's patronage of the reformers who had encouraged him to break with Rome had ended. He had never fully endorsed Lutheran beliefs, and now he was moving gradually back to the old forms of religion, a sort of Catholicism without the Pope, with increasingly repressive measures against dissentients; to deny that the bread and wine of the sacrament were transformed into the actual body and blood of Jesus Christ was now a heresy attracting the death penalty. Even the doctrine of purgatory was becoming respectable again. All this was anathema to the radicals, for whom the only truth was to be found in the Bible. The persecution had only driven many reformers towards the radical fringes, and in London especially they were daring and vocal.

'Do you know what I saw in the street today?' another guest said. 'Outside one church people were laying branches in the snow for the

Palm Sunday ceremonies tomorrow. Then a rabble of apprentices appeared and kicked the branches away, calling out that it was a papist ceremony and the Pope was the Antichrist!'

'This religious radicalism gives apprentices another excuse to run wild,' Loder observed gloomily.

'There could be trouble tomorrow,' Roger said.

I nodded. On Palm Sunday the traditional churches would be having the usual ceremonies, the churchwardens dressed as prophets and a child riding in on a donkey, while the radical preachers in their churches would be calling it papist blasphemy.

'There'll be another purge,' someone said gloomily. 'I've heard rumours Bishop Bonner is going to crack down hard on the Bible-men.'

'Not more burnings,' Dorothy said quietly.

'The city wouldn't stand for that,' Loder said. 'People don't like the radicals, but they like burnings less. Bonner won't go that far.'

'Won't he?' Roger said quietly. 'Isn't he a fanatic too, on the other side? Isn't the whole city becoming divided?'

'Most people only want a quiet life,' I said. 'Even those of us who were once radicals.' I smiled wryly at Roger. He nodded in acknow-ledgement.

'Fanatics on both sides,' old Ryprose said gloomily. 'And all we poor ordinary folk in the middle. Sometimes I fear they will bring death to us all.'

✝

THE COMPANY broke up late, and I was one of the last to leave. I stepped out into a night that had become colder again, refrozen slush crunching under my boots. My mood was much less cheerful after the conversation round the dinner table. It was true that London was full of both beggars and fanatics now, an unhappy city. And a purge would make things worse. There was, too, something I had not told the company; the parents of the boy in the Bedlam were members of a radical Protestant congregation, and their son's mental problems were religious in nature. I wished I had not had to take the case, but

I was obliged to deal with the Requests cases that were allocated to me. And his parents wanted their son released.

I paused. A quiet footstep, crunching on the slush behind me. I turned, frowning. The precincts of Lincoln's Inn were supposed to be secure, but there were places where entry could be gained. The night was dark, the moon half hidden by clouds, and at this hour only a few lighted windows cast squares of light on the snow.

'Who's that!' I called.

There was no reply, but I heard the slush crackling again as someone walked rapidly away. Frowning, I followed. The sound came from the far end of the building where the Elliards lived; it adjoined the rear wall of Lincoln's Inn. I put my hand to my dagger as I rounded the corner of the building. The outer wall was ahead of me. Whoever was there was trapped. But no one was there. The little square of ground between the buildings and the twelve-foot-high rear wall, lit by the windows of the Elliards' apartment, was quite empty. A shiver trickled down my spine.

Then I saw the snow on top of the wall had been disturbed. Whoever it was had climbed over. I stood and stared; to scale that wall would require a good deal of strength and agility. I was not sure I would have said it was possible, but the empty yard and the disturbed snow told their own tale. I frowned and turned away; I would tell the watchman that broken glass should be set atop the wall.

Chapter Two

NEXT MORNING I set out early for my chambers; the parents of the boy who had been put in the Bedlam were due at nine. The details the Court of Requests had sent me were sketchy, but enough to be worrying. The Privy Council itself had put him there, 'for blaspheming true religion in his madcap frenzy', as their resolution put it, without even an indictment in the bishop's court. The matter was therefore political, and dangerous. I tried to reassure myself again that any involvement I had would be in a purely legal capacity, but cursed the luck that had sent this case to me rather than to my fellow-pleader.

The papers described the boy, Adam Kite, as the son of a master stonemason and a communicant at St Martin's church, Creek Lane. I had got Barak to investigate and he had reported back that the vicar was, as he put it, a 'great railer and thunderer'.

This was unwelcome news. In the dealings I had had with the godly men I had found them difficult to deal with, crude hard men who drove at you with biblical verses like a carpenter hammering in nails.

I was jerked from my worrisome thoughts as I slipped on a patch of slush and almost fell over. Somebody laughed.

All over the city, church bells were ringing for the Palm Sunday services. These days I only went to church when it was expected; next Sunday I would have to take Mass and make my annual confession. I was not looking forward to it. The topsy-turvy weather was warmer again, and Chancery Lane was muddy as a farmyard. As I passed under Lincoln's Inn Gatehouse I wondered if the Treasurer would do anything to secure that wall. I had told the gatekeeper to inform him of my near-encounter last night.

I felt something wet hit my face; another drop followed and I realized it was raining, the first rain after two months of snow. By the time I reached my chambers it was coming on heavily and my cap was soaked. To my surprise, Barak was already in the outer office. He had lit the fire and sat at the big table, getting papers in order for tomorrow's court session. Plaints, affidavits and statements were piled around him. His handsome, impish features looked tired, his eyes bloodshot. And his face was stubbly.

'You need to get a shave, or the judge will be calling you out for a disrespectful demeanour.' Though I spoke roughly, Barak and I had a fast friendship. We had originally come together on an assign-ment for Barak's late master, the King's Minister Thomas Cromwell. After Cromwell's execution three years before, Barak had come to work for me, an unorthodox assistant but an efficient one.

'All right,' he said grumpily. 'The madwag's parents are due soon.'

'Don't call him that,' I said as I looked through the papers he had prepared. Everything was in order, annotations made in Barak's spidery handwriting. 'In on Sunday?' I asked. 'You were here yesterday too? You are neglecting poor Tamasin.'

'She's all right.' Barak rose and began filing away books and papers. I looked at his broad back, wondering what was wrong between him and his wife that he should thus drag out his time at work and, by the look of him, stay out all night. Tamasin was a pretty girl, as spirited as Barak, and he had been happy to marry her last year even though they had been forced into a speedy wedding by her pregnancy. Their son had died the day he was born and in the months since, though Barak had been as cheerfully irreverent as ever, there was often something forced about his banter, at times something haunted in his eyes. I knew the loss of a child could bring some couples closer, but drive others apart.

'You saw Adam Kite's parents yesterday when they called to make their appointment,' I said. 'Goodman Kite and his wife. What are they like?'

He turned back to me. 'Working people, he's a stonemason. He started on about God's mercy in allowing them to take their case to Requests, how He doesn't abandon the true faithful.' Barak wrinkled his nose. 'They look like some of the busy Bible folk to me. Though the godly folk I have seen mostly seem very satisfied with themselves, and the Kites looked like a pair of squished cats.'

'Not surprising given what's happened.'

'I know.' Barak hesitated. 'Will you have to go there, among all the lunatics tearing their clothes and clanking their chains?'

'Probably.' I looked again at the papers. 'The boy is seventeen. Brought before the Council on the third of March for frantic and lewd behaviour at the Preaching Cross in St Paul's churchyard, railing there "with strange moans and shrieks". Committed to the Bedlam in the hope of a cure. No further order. No examination by a doctor or jury of his state of health. That's improper.'

Barak looked at me seriously. 'He's lucky they didn't arraign him for a heretic. Remember what happened to Richard Mekins and John Collins.'

'The Council are more careful now.'

Mekins was a fifteen-year-old apprentice who eighteen months before had been burned alive at Smithfield for denying the presence of Jesus in the Eucharist. The case of John Collins had been worse still, a youth who had shot an arrow at a statue of Christ inside a church. Many had also thought him insane; but the previous year the King had passed an act to allow insane persons to be executed, and Collins too was burned to death. The cruelty of these cases had turned the populace against Bishop Bonner's harsh religious rule of the city. There had been no burnings since.

'They say Bonner's after the radicals again,' Barak observed.

'So people were saying at dinner last night. What do you think's going on, Jack?' Barak still had friends among those who worked on the more shady fringes of the King's court, those who frequented the taverns and alehouses and reported back on the state of public opinion. I had gained the impression that recently he had spent a lot of time drinking with these disreputable old friends.

He looked at me seriously again. 'The word is that now Scotland has been removed as a threat, the King wants to make an alliance with Spain and go to war against France. But to be acceptable to the Emperor Charles he'll have to be seen to be hard on heretics. They say he's going to try and get a law through this Parliament banning women and common folk from reading the Bible, and give Bishop Bonner encouragement to crack down on the London Bible-men. That's what they're saying at Whitehall, anyway. So I'd be careful in handling this one.'

'I see. Thank you.' This only made matters more delicate. I essayed a smile. 'The other thing they were gossiping about last night is that the King is after a new wife. Lady Latimer.'

'That's true as well, from what I'm told. But he's having trouble this time. The lady doesn't want him.'

'She has refused him?' I asked, surprised.

'So they say. Can't blame her. The King's got ulcers on both legs now, they have to carry him around Whitehall in a cart half the time. They say he gets fatter every month, and worse tempered. They say she is interested in someone else too.'

'Who?'

'That's not spoken of.' He hesitated. 'This Adam Kite looby might be better off if he stays in the Bedlam. So might you, rather than tangle with the Privy Council again.'

I sighed. 'I'm only acting as a lawyer.'

'You can't hide behind the law once these people get involved. You know that.' I could see Barak was as worried as I of going near some of the mighty enemies we had made in the past. The Duke of Norfolk and Richard Rich both sat on the Privy Council.

'It's ill luck they passed this to me instead of Herriott to deal with,' I said. 'But I've got it now, so I'll just have to handle it with care. I'll take tomorrow's papers through. Send the Kites in directly when they arrive.'

I went to my inner office and closed the door. Barak's words had unsettled me. I crossed to the mullioned window. The rain was coming down harder, splashing on the pane and distorting my view of Gatehouse Court. I shivered a little, for the sound of hard rain always brought back the terrible night eighteen months before, when for the first and only time I had killed a man. If I had not he would certainly have murdered me, yet even now his awful drowning gasps haunted me. I sighed deeply, ruefully recalling my good mood the evening before. Had my acknowledgement that I felt happy tempted a malign fate?

Bedlam, I thought. The very name brought fear and disgust in London. For a long time the Bethlehem Hospital had been the only hospital in London that treated the insane, and although mad folks were a common enough sight begging in the streets, and many people knew some friend or family member who had been touched by sickness of the mind, people avoided the mad. For not only were they feared as dangerous or even possessed, but they reminded folk that madness could strike anyone suddenly, and in a variety of terrible forms. That was why Roger feared the falling sickness so, for the fits that attended it were a fearful sight. The Bedlam, I knew, housed only severe cases of lunacy, some of them patients from rich families, others supported by charity. Occasionally, some like Adam Kite who were a nuisance to the powers that be were deposited there out of the way.

There was a knock on the door, and Barak ushered in a middle-aged couple. I was disconcerted to see that a third person accompanied them, a clergyman in a long cassock. He was tall and spare, with bushy eyebrows, thick, iron-grey hair and a red, choleric face. The middle-aged couple were dressed in sober black, and both looked deeply dejected; the woman close to tears. She was small and thin, birdlike; her husband tall and broad with a craggy face. He bowed, and his wife curtsied deeply. The cleric gave me a bold, appraising stare, not at all intimidated by being in Lincoln's Inn, or by the sight of me in my robe, in my office full of law books.

'I am Serjeant Shardlake. You must be Master and Mistress Kite.' I smiled at the nervous couple to put them at their ease, concentrating my attention on them. I knew from long experience that when clients are accompanied by a third party, the supporter is usually far more aggressive than the client. I guessed the clergyman was their vicar, and that he would be a problem.

'Daniel Kite, at your service,' the man said, bowing. 'This is my wife, Minnie.' The woman curtsied again, and smiled uncertainly. 'It is good of you to see us on a Sunday,' Daniel Kite added.

'Palm Sunday,' the clergyman said with distaste. 'At least if we are here, we do not have to see those papist ceremonies.' He gave me a challenging look. 'I am Samuel Meaphon. This afflicted family are of my congregation.'

'Please sit,' I said. They sat in a row on a bench, Meaphon in the middle. Minnie fiddled nervously with the folds of her dress. 'I have seen the papers the court forwarded,' I told them, 'but they tell only a bare story. I would like you to tell me what happened to your son, from the beginning.'

Daniel Kite cast a nervous look at Meaphon.

'I would prefer to hear it from you and your wife, sir,' I added quickly. 'No disrespect to the good reverend, but first-hand evidence is best.' Meaphon frowned slightly, but nodded for Master Kite to continue.

'Our son Adam was a good boy until six months ago,' the father began in a sad, heavy voice. 'A lively, strapping lad. Our blessing from the Lord, for we have no other children. I had him as apprentice in my workshop, out by Billingsgate.'

'You are a stonemason?'

'Master stonemason, sir.' Despite his distress, there was a note of pride in his voice. I looked at his hands: big, callused, a mass of little scars. 'I hoped Adam might follow me into the business. He was a hard worker; and a faithful attender at our church.'

'That he was.' Reverend Meaphon nodded emphatically.

'We are true Bible folk, sir.' A slight note of challenge crept into Kite's voice.

'However the sinful world may look on us,' Meaphon added, looking at me with fierce eyes under those bushy brows.

'Whatever you tell me of your beliefs will be held in confidence,' I said.

'You do not believe as we do, I see.' There was sorrow rather than anger in Daniel Kite's voice.

'It is not my beliefs that are at issue,' I replied with what I knew was a strained smile.

Meaphon's eyes swept over me. 'I see that God has seen fit to afflict you, sir. But he has done so only that you may turn to Him for succour.'

I felt myself flush with anger that this stranger should take it on himself to refer thus to my hunched back. Minnie Kite interrupted hastily. 'We only want you to help our poor boy, sir, to tell us if the law may help us.'

'Then tell me what happened, from the beginning, straight and simple.'

Minnie quailed at the sharp note in my voice. Her husband hesitated, then continued his story.

'I told you Adam was a fine boy. But about six months ago he started to become very quiet, withdrawn into himself, sad-seeming. It worried us both. Then one day I had to leave him in the shop; I came back and found him crouched on his knees in a corner. He was praying, begging the Lord to forgive him for his sins. I said, "How now, Adam. God has ordained a time for prayer and a time for work." He obeyed me then, though I remember he rose to his feet with a great sigh like I'd never heard.'

'We've heard it often enough since,' Minnie added.

'That was the start of it. We've always encouraged Adam to pray, but from then on he – he wouldn't stop.' Kite's voice broke, and I sensed the fear in him. 'Any time of day, in the workshop or even in company, he'd just drop to his knees and start praying, frantically, for God to forgive his sins and let him know he was saved. It got so he wouldn't eat, he'd lie crouched in the corner and we'd have to pull him to his feet while he resisted, made himself a dead weight. And when we made him stand, always that terrible sigh.'

'The despair in it,' Minnie added quietly. She lowered her head, but not before I saw tears in her eyes. Kite looked at me. 'He is certain that he is damned, sir.'

I looked at the three of them. I knew that the religious radicals believed with Luther that God had divided humanity into the saved and the damned, that only those who came to Him through the Bible would be saved at the Day of Judgement. The rest of humanity were condemned to burn in Hell, for ever. And they believed that the Day of Judgement, the end of the world foretold in the Book of Revelation, would soon be upon us all. I did not know how to reply. I was almost grateful to Meaphon for ending the silence.

'These good people brought their son to me,' he said. 'I spoke with Adam, tried to reassure him, told him God sometimes sends doubt to those he loves most, to try their spirits. I stayed for two whole days with him, fasting and praying, but I could not break through to him.' He shook his head. 'He resisted me sorely.'

Minnie looked up at me. Her face was bleak, bereft. 'By then, Adam was naught but skin and bone. I had to feed him with a spoon while my husband held on to him to prevent him sinking to the floor. "I must pray," he kept on. "I am not saved!" To think I should dread to hear prayer or salvation mentioned.'

'What sins does Adam believe he has committed?' I asked quietly.

'He does not say. He seems to think he has committed every sin there is. Before this he was just an ordinary cheerful boy, sometimes noisy and thoughtless, but no more than that. He has never done anything wicked.'

'Then he started leaving the house,' Daniel Kite said. 'Running away to alleyways and corners where he could pray unhindered. We had to go chasing after him.'

'We feared he would die in the cold,' Minnie added. 'He would slip away without putting on his coat and we would follow his footprints in the snow.' She banged a little fist into her lap with sudden anger. 'Oh, that he should treat his parents so. *That* is a sin.'

Her husband laid a work-roughened hand on hers. 'Now, Minnie, have faith. God will send an answer.' He turned back to me. 'Ten days ago, in that snowy weather when no one was going abroad unless they had to, Adam disappeared. I had him in my workshop where I could keep an eye on him, but he's become crafty as a monkey and when my back was turned he sneaked off, unlocked the door and disappeared. We went searching up and down but could not find him. Then that afternoon an official from Bishop Bonner came to see us. He said Adam had been found on his knees in the snow before the Preaching Cross in St Paul's churchyard, begging God for a sign he was saved, that he would be allowed into heaven as one of the elect. He screamed that the end of the world was coming, begged God and Jesus not to take him down to Hell at the Last Judgement.'

Minnie began to cry, and her husband stopped and bowed his head, overcome with emotion as well. The depth of the simple couple's suffering was terrible to contemplate. And what their son had done was deeply dangerous. Only licensed preachers were allowed at St Paul's, and the King's doctrine was firm that faith alone, *sola fide*, did not suffice to bring a man to heaven. Even less orthodox was the doctrine of mankind divided between God's elect and the damned. I looked at Meaphon. He was frowning, running his hand over the top of his thick hair.

'So then Adam was brought before the Council,' I prompted Daniel gently.

'Yes. From the bishop's jail where they put him. I was summoned to appear. I went to Whitehall Palace, to a room where four men all dressed in rich robes sat at a table in a great room.' His voice shook and a sheen of sweat appeared on his forehead at the memory. 'Adam was there, chained and with a gaoler.' He glanced at his vicar. 'Reverend Meaphon came too but they wouldn't let him speak.'

'No, they would not hear me,' Meaphon said. 'I did not expect them to,' he added with scorn.

That was probably just as well, I thought. 'Who were the men?'

'One in white robes was Archbishop Cranmer; I've seen him preach at St Paul's. There was another cleric, a big angry-looking man with brown hair. I think the two others wore robes with fur and jewels. One was a little pale man, he had a sharp voice. The other had a long brown beard and a thin face.'

I nodded slowly. The little pale man would be Sir Richard Rich, Thomas Cromwell's former protégé who had joined the conservatives when Cromwell fell; a ruthless, vicious opportunist. The other man resembled descriptions I had heard of Lord Hertford, brother of the late Queen Jane and a reformer. And the angry-looking cleric was almost certainly Bishop Bonner of London.

'What did they say to you?'

'They asked me how Adam had got into the state he was and I answered them honestly. The pale man said it sounded like heresy and the boy should be burned. But just then Adam slipped off his chair and before his guard could grab him he was down on the floor frantically asking God to save him. The councillors ordered him to rise but he took no more notice of them than if they were flies. Then the Archbishop said Adam was clearly out of his wits and he should be sent to the Bedlam to see if they could find a cure. The pale man still wanted him accused as a heretic but the other two wouldn't agree.'

'I see.' Rich, I guessed, would think having another radical Protestant burned would raise him in the favour of the traditionalists. But Cranmer, as well as being naturally merciful, would not want to further inflame London. Having Adam shut away in the Bedlam would dispose of the problem, for a while at least.

I nodded slowly. 'That raises the crucial issue.' I looked at them. 'Is Adam in fact mad?'

'I think he must be,' Minnie replied.

'If he is not mad, sir,' Daniel Kite said, 'we fear the case may be something even worse.'

'Worse?' I asked.

'Possession,' Meaphon said starkly. 'That is my fear. That a demon has hold of him and is urging him to mock God's mercy in public. And if that is so, then only by praying with Adam mightily, wrestling with the devil, can I save him.'

'Is that what you believe?' I asked the stonemason.

He looked at Meaphon, then buried his head in his big hands. 'I do not know, sir. God save my son if that should be true.'

'I think Adam is only in great confusion and fear.' Minnie looked up and met Meaphon's eye, and I realized that she was the stronger of the pair. She turned to me. 'But whatever the truth, being in the Bedlam will kill him. Adam lies in the chamber they have locked him in. It is cold, no fire. He will do nothing for himself, he just crouches there, praying, praying. And they only allow us to visit for an hour a day. They ask us for three shillings a month in fees, more than we can afford, yet they will not make him eat nor take care of himself. The keeper will be happy if he dies.' She looked at me imploringly. 'They are afraid of him.'

'Because of the fear he is possessed?'

She nodded.

'And you doubt he is?'

'I don't know, I don't know. But if he stays in the Bedlam he will die.'

'He should be released to my care,' Meaphon said. 'But they will not do that. Not the backsliders and papists on the Council.'

'Then on one thing you are all agreed,' I said. 'That he should not be in the Bedlam.'

'Ay, ay.' The boy's father nodded eagerly, relieved to find some common ground.

I thought hard a moment, then spoke quietly. 'There are two problems with this case. One is jurisdiction. Anyone who cannot afford a lawyer may bring his case before the Court of Requests, but the judge may say the matter is one of state, and should go back before the Privy Council. However, if you cannot afford the fees they charge in the Bedlam, the court may ask the Council to pay. And the court may intervene to stop poor treatment. But the matter of releasing Adam is much more difficult.' I took a deep breath. 'And what if he were released? If he were to escape again, if there were a repeat of what happened at St Paul's, he might find himself accused of heresy after all. If we could get his conditions improved, in all honesty the Bedlam may be the safest place for him, unless he can be brought to his right mind. To tangle with the Privy Council could be very dangerous.' I had not mentioned poor John Collins, but I could tell from their faces that they remembered the horror of what had happened to him.

'He must be released from that place,' Meaphon said. 'The only cure is for Adam to understand that God has sent him this trial, and he must not doubt His grace. Whether a devil has entered into him or his mind is stricken from some other cause, only I can help him, with aid from fellow ministers.' The minister looked at Adam's parents. Daniel Kite said 'Amen,' but Minnie looked down at her lap.

'His release will not happen unless the Council become convinced that he is sane,' I said. 'But there is one thing we can do. I know a physician, a clever man, who would be able to assess Adam, might even be able to help him.'

Daniel Kite shook his head firmly. 'Physicians are godless men.'

'This physician is most godly.' I thought it better not to tell them my friend Guy was a former monk, still at heart a Catholic.

Kite still looked dubious, but Minnie grasped eagerly at the straw. 'Bring him in, sir, we will try anything. But we have no money to pay him . . .'

'I am sure some arrangement can be made.'

She looked at her husband. He hesitated, looked at Meaphon and said, 'It can do no harm, sir, surely.' Meaphon looked as though he was about to disagree, and I jumped in. 'I have no doubt that is the sensible thing to do, from the point of view of Adam's interests. And in the meantime I will apply to have Adam's care monitored, and the fees remitted. There are so many cases in Requests just now that the judge is sitting out of term to clear the backlog. With luck an urgent application might be heard in a week or so.'

'Thank you, sir,' Minnie said.

'But I would not even like to try and list the matter of release without some change in Adam to report.' I looked at Meaphon. 'Such a request would simply fail.'

'Then it seems we must wait and see what the doctor says.' He spoke quietly, but his eyes were hostile.

'And I think I ought to visit the Bedlam, perhaps put some fear into this keeper. And see Adam.'

The Kites exchanged uncomfortable glances. 'That would be good of you, sir,' Daniel Kite said. 'But I must tell you, my poor boy's dismal frenzy is a terrible thing to behold.'

'I have seen many sad things in my career,' I said, though in truth I quailed at the thought of this visit.

'We are going to see Adam tomorrow, at nine, sir,' Minnie said. 'Could you come then?'

'Yes, I will have time before court.'

'Do you know how to get there? Go through the Bishopsgate, sir, then look for the Bedlam gates.'

'I will be there.' I smiled at her and stood up. 'I will do what I can. But this is a most difficult matter.'

I showed them out. Meaphon hung back in the doorway after the Kites passed into the outer office. 'I do not think this doctor will have success,' he said quietly. 'God moves in strange and marvellous ways, and for all their trials and persecutions in this world, He will lead true Christians into his peace at last. Including Adam.' The grey eyes burned beneath his shaggy brows; yet it struck me that there was something oddly actorish about him, as though he were playing Virtue in a play whose audience was all London.

'Indeed,' I answered. 'I pray the poor boy may find peace.'

'We are going to our church service now,' he said. 'We shall pray hard for him.'

After they had gone I returned to my desk, looked again at the papers. Then I went and stared out at the rain-drenched court. The Kites passed the window, holding on to their caps as they bent their heads against the driving rain. 'He is not one of us,' I heard Meaphon say. '*He* will not be saved at the end-time.'

I watched them as they crossed to the gate. One thing I was certain of in my own mind. Adam Kite was my responsibility now. I had to judge what was in his best interests, and I doubted very much whether an early release from the Bedlam would serve those, whatever Meaphon might say. Minnie Kite, I felt sure, would put her son's interests first and listen to me.

I went back to the outer office. Barak was sitting at the table, looking into the fire, a serious expression on his face. He jumped when I called his name.

'You look thoughtful,' I said.

'I was just wondering whether to go for a shave now or see if the rain stops. That vicar gave me a nasty look as he went by.'

'Recognized you for a godless fellow, no doubt. I overheard him kindly condemning me to eternal fire as they passed my window.' I sighed. 'Apparently he stuck Adam Kite in a room and prayed with him for two days. Made the boy fast as well, though he was already skin and bone. I almost wonder if Bonner purging the lot of them might not be a good thing. All right,' I added, as Barak looked at me in surprise. 'I didn't mean that.' I sighed. 'But I begin to wonder whether these people are the future, whether they are what religious reform is turning into. And that thought frightens me.'

'But you're taking the case?'

'I must. But I shall be very careful, do not worry about that. I want Guy to see the boy. But first I must visit him myself.'

'At the Bedlam?'

I sighed. 'Yes, tomorrow.'

'Can I come?'

'No. I should go alone. But thank you.'

'Pity,' Barak said. 'I'd like to see if it's true the groans and shrieks can be heard across the streets, making folk scurry by.'

Chapter Three

LATER THAT MORNING the rain eased off. The sun came out and the weather grew clear and cold again. My meeting with the Kites had given me much food for thought and I decided to go for a walk. Everything seemed sharper in the clear air; the naked branches of the trees were outlined against a blue sky, patches of snow were still visible in the corners of the bare brown fields behind the houses. I walked through the nearby suburbs, along Holborn and down Shoe Lane. The Palm Sunday services were under way now, and I noted as I passed how some churches had garlands on the lychgates and church doors, and greenery spread in the street outside, while others presented only their normal aspect. In one churchyard an outdoor service was taking place, a choir of white-surpliced boys singing a hymn before a garlanded cross, where three men stood dressed as prophets in long robes, with false white beards and brightly decorated headgear. I was reminded of yesterday's play.

I remembered the guest at Roger's table talking of apprentices disrupting a palm-laying ceremony. There were many stories of the religious divisions in London's forest of tiny parishes: a radical vicar in one church whitewashing over ancient wall paintings and replacing them with texts from the Bible, a conservative in another insisting on the full Latin Mass. I had recently heard of radical congregants in one church talking loudly while the sacring bell sounded, causing the traditionalist priest to lose his temper and shriek 'Heretics! Faggots! Fire!' at them. Was it any wonder that many, like myself, stayed away from church these days? Next weekend it would be Easter, when everyone was supposed by law to take confession. In London those who failed to attend were reported to Bishop Bonner, but illness or urgent pressure of business were accepted as excuses, and I decided I would argue the latter. I could not bear the thought of confessing my sins to my parish priest, a time-server whose only principle in the doctrinal struggle was to follow the wind and preserve his position. And if I were to confess, I knew that one of my sins was a long-growing, half-buried doubt whether God existed at all. That was the paradox – the vicious struggle between papists and sacramentaries was driving many away from faith altogether. Christ said, by their fruits shall you know them, and the fruits of the faithful of both sides looked more rotten each year.

As I walked down Shoe Lane, one set of decorated church doors opened and the congregation stepped out, the service over. These were very different people from those I had seen in the churchyard, the women in dark dresses, the men's doublets and coats all sober black, their manner severely reverent. Meaphon's church would be like this, the congregation a tight-knit group of radicals, for some people would up sticks and move house to find a parish where the vicar agreed with their views. If Bishop Bonner were to try to enforce all the old practices on these churches there would be serious trouble, rioting even. But he was tightening his net; a new index of prohibited books had recently been published, unlicensed preachers were being arrested. And if harsh measures were successfully enforced, I thought, what then? The radicals would only go underground; already groups of them held illegal meetings in people's houses to discuss the Bible and bolster their radical beliefs.

I was tired when I arrived back at my house in Chancery Lane, a little way up from Lincoln's Inn. The smell of broiling fish from the kitchen where my housekeeper Joan was preparing lunch was welcome, although I looked forward to the end of Lent next week when it would be legal to eat meat again. I went into my parlour and sat down by the fire, but even my welcoming hearth could not dispel the tension I felt, not just because the case of Adam Kite had drawn me into the threatening doctrinal currents washing through the city, but because they made it hard for me to avoid awareness of my own deepening unbelief.

✝

EARLY NEXT MORNING I set out for the Bedlam. Under my coat I wore my best robe, and I also put on my serjeant's coif. It would do no harm to impress the warden. I confess that I was nervous at the thought of going to the asylum. I knew next to nothing of madness; I was fortunate enough never to have encountered it among my family or friends. I knew only the doctors divided the brain-sick between those suffering from mania, who often engaged in wild and frenzied behaviour, and the melancholics who withdrew from the world into sadness. Melancholy was more common, and usually less serious; I knew I had a melancholic turn of mind myself. And Adam Kite, I thought. Which is he? What is he?

The inconstant weather had turned bitter again; during the night there had been another dusting of snow, which glittered in the cold sunlight. I rode out on my good horse Genesis. I was sorry to take him from his stable but the streets were too slippery to make for easy walking and the Bedlam was on the other side of the city.

I passed under London Wall at Newgate and rode along Newgate Street to the market. Traders were setting up their stalls under the looming bulk of the abandoned church of the dissolved St Martin's friary, a few white-coifed goodwives already looking over the produce as it was laid out. As I rode past the market I heard someone shouting. On the corner where Newgate Market met the Shambles, a man in a dark doublet, coatless despite the cold, stood on an empty box waving a large black Testament at the passers-by, who mostly averted their eyes. This must be the ranter old Ryprose had mentioned at the dinner. I looked at the man: a young fellow, his face red with passion.

The butchers in the slaughterhouses behind the Shambles had already started work. Lent would be over on Thursday and already they were killing sheep and cattle. Trails of blood were trickling from the yards to the sewer channel in the centre of the frosty street. The preacher pointed to them with his Bible. 'So it will be for mankind in the last days of the world!' he shouted in a deep voice. 'Their eyeballs will melt, the skin will drop from their bones, all that will be left is their blood, deep as a horse's bridle for two hundred miles! So it is foretold in Revelation!' As I rode off down the Shambles I heard him cry, 'Only turn to God, and you will know the sweet joy of his salvation!' If the constables took him he would be in serious trouble for preaching without a licence.

Along Cheapside the blue-coated apprentices were setting up their masters' shops for the day's trade, erecting brightly coloured awnings, their breath steaming in the cold. Some were ordering away the beggars who had sought shelter in the doorways overnight, with kicks and blows if they did not move fast enough. A host of destitute men and women had already limped over to the Great Conduit to beg from those who came for water, huddling against each other on the steps that surrounded it like a flock of starveling crows. As I passed I looked into their pinched, chapped faces. One, an old man with a shock of grey hair, drooling and trembling, caught my eye. He held out a hand and called, 'Help an old monk of Glastonbury, sir. They hanged my master the abbot!' I threw a sixpence to him, and he dived for it with a sudden turn of speed, before others could.

So many homeless in the streets now. To live in London since the monasteries were dissolved was to be inured to pitiful scenes everywhere. Most people simply looked away, made the sufferers invisible. Many beggars were former monastic servants, others poor folk who had come in from the countryside where much land was being enclosed to pasture sheep, their villages demolished. And the sick who had once been able to find at least temporary shelter at the monastic hospitals now lay in the streets, and often died there. I thought, I will help Roger with his hospital scheme; I shall at least do something.

I passed under the city wall again and rode up the Bishopsgate

Street. The hospital was beyond the city walls, where new houses encroached more every year. I had gone back to Lincoln's Inn the previous afternoon, and read what I could find about the Bedlam in the library. It had been a monastic foundation, but had survived the Dissolution since some of its patients came from families of means and it was therefore a potential source of profit. The King appointed the warden, currently a courtier named Metwys, who in turn appointed a full-time keeper. The man, his parents believed, who hoped that Adam Kite would die.

☩

NEAR BISHOPSGATE I was held up. A rich man's funeral train was passing, black horses, black carriages and poor men dressed in black following behind, singing psalms. A dignified-looking old man walked at the head of the procession carrying a white stick – the steward of the dead man's household carrying the symbolic staff of office he would break and cast into the grave. From its great size I guessed this must be the funeral of Lord Latimer, whose wife the King apparently coveted. I took off my cap. A large carriage passed; the shutters were open. A woman looked out, her face framed by a jet-black hood. She was about thirty; a receding chin and small mouth made a face that otherwise would have been pretty, merely striking. She stared at the crowd with wide, unseeing eyes as she was borne along. It seemed to me that there was fear in them.

The carriage rumbled past, and the Lady Catherine Parr disappeared from view.

☩

AT BISHOPSGATE I passed under London Wall. A little beyond I came to a pair of large wooden gates in a high wall. They were open, and riding through I found myself in a wide, earthen courtyard, stippled with snow, a chapel at its centre. The backs of houses formed three sides of the yard; a long, two-storied building of grey stone, which looked very old, made up the fourth. Some of the unpainted wooden shutters on the windows were open. People were passing to and fro across the yard, and I saw a couple of narrow lanes running between the houses. The Bedlam was not, then, a closed prison. And I heard no shrieks or rattling of chains.

I rode to a large door at one end. My knock was answered by a thickset man with a hard, sardonic face, who wore a dirty grey smock. A big key-ring dangled from his greasy leather belt.

'I am Master Shardlake,' I said. 'I have an appointment to see Adam Kite.'

The man studied my robe. 'Lawyer, sir?'

'Yes. Are you Keeper Shawms?'

'No, sir. He's out, though he's due back soon. I'm another of the keepers, Hob Gebons.'

'Are young Kite's parents here?'

'No.'

'I will wait.'

He stood aside to let me enter. 'Welcome to the chamber of the mad,' he said as he closed the door. 'You think you can get Adam Kite released?'

'I hope so.'

'We'd be glad to see him go, he makes the other lunatics nervous. We keep him shut away. Some think him possessed,' he added in a low voice.

'What do you think, Gebons?'

He shrugged. 'Not for me to think.' The man leaned close. 'If you've a bit of time, sir, I could show you some of our prize specimens. King Commode and the Chained Scholar. For a shilling.'

I hesitated, then handed over the coin. The more I knew about what went on here, the better.

✟

GEBONS LED ME along a whitewashed corridor running the length of the building, windows on one side and a row of green-painted wooden doors on the other. It was cold and there was a faint smell of ordure.

'How many patients do you have?'

'Thirty, sir. They're a mixed lot.'

I saw that viewing-hatches had been cut in the green doors, at eye height. Another grey-smocked attendant stood in an open doorway, looking in.

'Is that my washing water, Stephen?' I heard a woman's voice call.

'Ay, Alice. Shall I take your pisspot?'

The scene appeared civilized enough, almost domestic. Gebons smiled at me. 'Alice is sane enough most of the time. But she has the falling sickness bad, she can be on the floor foaming and spitting in the wink of an eye.'

I looked at Gebons, thinking of Roger.

'She's allowed to come and go. Unlike this fellow.' The warder had stopped at a closed door with a heavy bolt on it. He grinned at me, showing broken grey teeth. 'Behold His Majesty.'

He opened the viewing hatch, and stood aside to let me look. I saw a square cell, the windows shuttered, a candle guttering in an old bottle on the floor. The sight within made me gasp and step back. An old man, large and enormously fat, sat on a commode that had been painted white. He had a short beard cut in the same way that the King's was depicted on the coins. An extraordinary, multi-coloured robe, made of odds and ends of cloth patched together, swathed his heavy form. He was holding a walking stick with a wooden ball jammed on the end to resemble a sceptre. On his bald head was a paper crown, painted yellow.

'How are you today, Your Majesty?' Hob asked.

'Well enough, fellow. You may bring my subject in, I will receive him.'

'Maybe later, sire. I have to clean the jakes first!'

'You insolent fellow—'

Gebons closed the hatch, cutting him off. He turned to me, laughing hoarsely.

'He's convinced he's the king. He used to be a schoolteacher. Not a good one, his charges used to mock him, play football in his classes. Then he decided he was the king and his mind flew away from all his troubles.'

'Mocking the King,' I said. 'That's dangerous.'

Gebons nodded. 'That's why his family put him here, out of the way. Many lunatics proclaim many dangerous things, being loobies they forget you must be careful what you say these days. Now,' he grinned again and raised his eyebrows. 'Come and see our Chained Scholar. He's two doors down. A fine educated fellow.' He looked at my robe, mockery in his smile. 'A doctor of common law from Cambridge. Failed to get a post there that he wanted, and attacked his college principal, half killed him. He's all right with the likes of me, but hates seeing anyone educated. You should see his rage then. If you went into his room he'd leap at you and scratch your face off. He's one we keep locked up carefully. But I could open the hatch up for you to have a look.'

'No, thank you.'

'He loves drawing maps and plans, he's redesigning the sewers for us. You'll note there's a stink in here.'

'Indeed, a bad one.'

I heard voices nearby, and recognized Daniel Kite's, raised in anger.

'Where is he?' I asked.

'The parlour. They must have come in the back way. Sure you don't want to see the scholar?' he added, the mockery now clear in his voice.

'No,' I answered curtly. 'Take me to the Kites.'

Gebons led me into a small room with cheap stools set around, a scuffed table and a fire lit in the grate. The walls were bare. Minnie Kite sat on a stool, looking utterly dejected, while her husband argued with a plump, surly-faced man in a black jerkin.

'You could try to make him eat!' Daniel was shouting.

'Oh, ay. Get one of my keepers to force him to his feet then another to force the food into his mouth. They haven't the time, and they don't like doing it, he frightens them. And by Mary he's frightening enough the way he lays there gobbling and muttering and calling God's name, no wonder half my keepers say he's possessed! The food's put in there and he can eat it or no as he wills.'

'Is there a problem?' I asked quietly. 'You must be Keeper Shawms,' I added as the fat man turned. 'I am Master Shardlake, the Kites' lawyer.'

Shawms looked between me and the Kites. 'How come you can afford a lawyer, when you say you can't afford my fees?' he asked them in a bullying voice.

'I have been appointed by the Court of Requests,' I said.

'Oh,' he sneered. 'Poor man's lawyer, then, for all your fancy rig.'

'Who can apply to the court to have your fees waived, and any question of mistreatment considered,' I replied sharply. 'Tomorrow, if I am unsatisfied with what I see today.'

Shawms looked at me from deep-set piggy eyes. 'That boy's hard to take care of . . .'

'He only needs feeding,' Minnie said. 'And someone to put a blanket round his shoulders when it slips off.' She turned to me. 'It's so cold in there, and this wretch won't lay a fire—'

'Fires cost money!'

I turned back to the Kites. 'Perhaps I could see Adam.'

'We were about to go in.'

'See him if you want to,' Shawms said. 'You'll get no sense from him.' He glared at me. I realized that for him Adam was a troublesome nuisance; he would not be sorry if he died. Nor would the Council; for them it would be a problem solved.

'And afterwards, Master Shawms,' I said, 'I would like a word.'

'All right. Come on then. I've no time to waste.'

✞

WE WERE LED to another of the green doors. It was locked; Shawms unlocked it and glanced in. 'He's all yours,' he said, and walked away.

I followed Daniel Kite into the room. It was light, whitewashed, the shutters partly open. As Minnie had said, it was bitterly cold. There was a dreadful stench, a mixture of ordure and unwashed skin. The place was furnished only with a truckle bed and a stool.

A tall teenage boy with filthy black hair knelt in a corner, his face to the wall, whispering to himself, the words coming so fast they were hard to follow. 'I repent my sins I repent please listen please listen in Jesu's name . . .'

He was dressed in a food-stained shirt and leather jerkin. A large dark stain on his hose showed he had soiled himself. There was a fetter round his ankle, a chain running from there to an iron ring in the floor. Minnie approached and knelt by her son, putting an arm round his shoulders. He took no notice at all.

'The chain's to stop him running out to the churchyards,' Daniel Kite said quietly. He did not approach Adam, merely stood beside him with his head bowed.

I took a deep breath and went over to the boy, noticing he was a broad-shouldered lad, though reduced now to skin and bone. I bent to look at Adam's face. It was a pitiful sight. The boy might once have been handsome, but now his features showed such misery as I had never seen. His brows were contorted into an agonized frown, his wide terrified eyes stared unseeingly at the wall, and his mouth worked frantically, strings of spittle dripping on his chin. 'Tell me I am saved,' he went on. 'Let me feel Your grace.' He stopped for a moment, as though listening for something, then went on, more desperately than ever. 'Jesu! Please!'

'Adam,' his mother said in a pleading voice. 'You are dirty. I have brought you new clothes.' She tried to pull him to his feet, but he resisted, squeezing himself into the corner. 'Leave me!' he said, not even looking at her. 'I must pray!'

'Is he like this all the time?' I asked Minnie.

'Always, now.' She relinquished her hold, and we both stood up. 'He never wants to rise. His sighs of despair when he is forced to stand are piteous.'

'I will get my physician friend to call,' I said quietly. 'Though – in truth, while he is like this, if I can make sure he is cared for he may be better off here.'

'He must be cared for,' she said. 'Or he will die.'

'I can see that. I will talk to Keeper Shawms.'

'If you would leave us, sir, I will try and clean him a little. Come, Daniel, help me lift him.'

Her husband moved to join her.

'I will speak to the keeper now,' I said. 'I will meet you in the parlour when you are finished.'

'Thank you, sir,' Minnie gave me a trembling smile. Her husband was still avoiding my eye. I left them and went in search of Shawms, full of anger at the way Adam had been left to wallow in his own shit. The horror of what his broken mind was experiencing was beyond my understanding, but lazy, venal officials I could deal with.

✝

SHAWMS WAS in a little room of his own, sitting drinking beer and looking into a large fire. He stared at me truculently.

'I want that boy fed,' I snapped. 'By force if need be. His mother is changing his clothes and I want to see he is kept clean. I shall be applying to the court for an order that his welfare is properly attended to, and that the Council be responsible for his fees.'

'And till then who's to pay for all this work my keepers will be put to with him, to say nothing of calming the patients who fear they have a possessed man in their midst?'

'The Bedlam's own funds. By the way, do you have a doctor in attendance?'

'Ay. Dr Frith comes once a fortnight. He's a great one for his own potions, but they do no good. There was a herb-woman used to call, some of the patients liked her but Dr Frith sent her away. I don't appoint the doctors, that's for Warden Metwys.'

'Does a priest come?'

'The post is vacant since the old priest died. The warden hasn't got round to dealing with it.'

I looked into his fat red face, angry at the thought of the helpless mad being left to such as he and the lazy warden.

'I want a fire made up in that room,' I said.

'You go too far now, sir.' Shawms protested. 'Fires are extra, I won't pay for those out of the Bedlam funds. Warden Metwys would have my job.'

'Then I'll apply for the fees to be waived, not for the Council to pay them.'

Shawms glowered at me. 'You take liberties, crouchback.'

'Fewer than you. Well?'

'I'll order a fire set.'

'See you do.' I turned and left him without another word.

☦

I RETURNED to the parlour, and sat there, deep in thought. Adam Kite had shaken me; whatever ailed him so terribly, there was no question of applying to the court for a declaration he was *compos mentis*. My only hope was that Guy could help him in some way.

I looked up as the door opened. A white-haired woman was led in by a younger woman in a keeper's grey smock. I was surprised to see a woman keeper, but guessed they would be needed if the female patients were to preserve any modesty. The white-haired woman's head was cast down, and she walked with a leaden tread as the keeper guided her to a chair by the window. She slumped there, heavy and lifeless as a sack of cabbages. Seeing me, the woman keeper curtsied. She had an arresting face, too long-featured to be pretty but full of character and with keen, dark blue eyes. The hair round the sides of her white coif was dark brown. She looked to be somewhere in her thirties.

'I would like Cissy to sit here for a while, sir,' she said.

'Of course.'

'She's very mopish today and I want her out of her room. I've brought you some sewing, Cissy, you like making the smocks whole again.' It was strange to see her speak to the much older woman as though she were a child. Cissy raised dull eyes as the keeper took a sewing bag and a torn smock she had been carrying in the crook of her elbow. She laid the smock on Cissy's knees and placed a threaded needle in her plump hand. 'Come on, Cissy, you're a wonderful needlewoman. Show me what you can do.' Reluctantly, Cissy took the needle.

'She won't be any trouble.' The woman curtsied and left me with Cissy, who began sewing, never looking up at me. So not all the keepers are brutes, I thought. Shortly after, the Kites returned. I rose and told them of my conversation with Shawms.

'So Adam must stay here?' Minnie asked.

'This is the safest place for him, until he can be brought to his right mind.'

'Perhaps this is meant,' Daniel Kite said. He looked at me with sudden defiance. 'Sometimes God visits the most terrible trials on those he loves most, like Job, Reverend Meaphon says.'

'This may be a warning, to remind folk the end-time is coming, that they must give up their sinful ways. Perhaps that is why Adam frightens folk, he reminds them that they too should pray for salvation.'

'No!' Minnie rounded on her husband. 'God would not try a poor believer so.'

'Who are you to say what God may do in His wisdom?' he snapped. 'If this is not God's work, it is Satan's, and he is possessed as some people say.'

They were both at breaking point, I saw. 'He is ill,' I said gently.

'You would say so,' Daniel Kite replied. 'You are not a right believer!' He looked between his wife and me, then turned and went out.

'Do not be angry with him, sir,' Minnie said. 'He casts around in desperation for answers. He loves our boy.'

'I understand, mistress. I promise I will do all I can. Adam will be looked after now and I will see what can be done for his poor mind. I will be in touch again very soon. And tell me at once if his care does not improve.'

'I will. We visit every day.' She curtsied, and went out after her husband. I turned to see Cissy looking at me, a spark of curiosity in her dull eyes, but when I met her gaze she dropped her head to her sewing. I heard footsteps, and the woman keeper came in, looking concerned.

'I heard raised voices,' she said. 'Is Cissy all right?'

'Yes.' I smiled ruefully. 'It was only my clients.'

She went and looked at Cissy's sewing. 'This is good work, t'will be as good as new.' She was rewarded by a fleeting smile from the old woman. She turned to me again.

'You have been visiting Adam Kite, sir?'

'Ay.'

'His poor parents.' She hesitated, glancing at the open door. Then she said quietly, 'Many here are afraid of Adam, fear he is possessed. And Keeper Shawms hopes that without care he will waste away and die.' She frowned. 'He is a bad man.'

'I have just given Keeper Shawms a warning. He will find himself in trouble with the courts if he does not give Adam proper care. Thank you for your information.' I smiled at her. 'What is your name?'

'Ellen Fettiplace, sir.' She hesitated, then added, 'What ails poor young Adam, sir? I have never heard of a case like his.'

'Nor I. I am having a doctor come to look at him. A good man.'

'Dr Frith is no use.'

'I am glad to see at least one keeper here cares for her patients.'

She blushed. 'You are kind, sir.'

'How did you come to work here, Ellen?'

She looked at me, then smiled sadly. 'I used to be a patient.'

'Oh,' I said, taken aback. She had seemed the sanest person I had met there today.

'They offered me a position as an under-keeper when I was – was better.'

'You did not want to leave?'

The sad smile again. 'I can never leave here, sir,' she said. 'I have not been outside in ten years. I will die in the Bedlam.'

Chapter Four

I WAS BUSY in court over the next two days, but Thursday afternoon was free and I had arranged to take Roger to see Guy. It was Maundy Thursday, the day before Easter, and as I walked back from the court at Westminster to Lincoln's Inn I saw the churches were again full. Tomorrow the great veil that shrouded the chancels during Lent would be removed, and those who cleaved to the old traditions would creep to the Cross on their knees. After Mass the altars would be stripped of their vestments in commemoration of Christ's betrayal after the Last Supper, while down at Whitehall the King would wash the feet of twelve poor men. I felt sad at how little any of it meant to me now. There were four days' holidays to come, but to me they would be empty and dull. At least when Lent was over Joan, my housekeeper, had promised me roast saddle of beef.

The weather was still cold, the sky iron-grey although there had been no more snow. I called in at my chambers before going to fetch Roger, and was pleased to see that a large fire had been lit. Barak and my junior clerk, Skelly, were both busy at their desks. Barak looked up as I took off my fur-edged coat and warmed my hands before the fire. He had had a shave on Sunday, but I noticed his brown doublet had a button missing, and there was what looked like a beer stain on the chest. I wondered if he had been out all night, and thought again about Tamasin. The two lived quite near Guy's shop, and I resolved that on the way back from taking Roger I would call in on them, as though by chance.

'I called at the court office,' Barak said. 'They're going to hear

44

Adam Kite's application next Tuesday, at the same time as the Collins case.'

'Good.' I was tempted to tell him to get his doublet cleaned up, but did not want to sound like an old woman. And he knew enough not to come carelessly dressed to court. I looked quickly through a couple of new briefs that had come in, then donned my coat again.

'I am going to take Master Elliard to Guy,' I said.

Barak had risen and was looking out of the window. 'What's wrong with that rogue Bealknap?' he said curiously.

'Bealknap?' I rose and joined him.

'Looks like he's about to peg out.'

Through the window I saw my old rival sitting on a bench next to the still-frozen fountain. A knapsack lay on the snow beside him. Even at this distance, his lean face looked an unhealthy white.

'What's the matter with him?' I said.

'They say he's been faint and ill for weeks,' Skelly said, looking at us earnestly from his table.

'I thought he looked under the weather at the play.'

'Let's hope it's nothing minor,' Barak said.

I smiled enigmatically. 'I must go.'

I left them and walked back into Gatehouse Court. I had to pass the fountain to get to Roger's rooms. Bealknap had not moved. His thin form was swathed in an expensive coat lined with marten, but even so this was not weather to be sitting outside. I hesitated as I passed him.

'Brother Bealknap,' I asked. 'Are you all right?'

He looked at me quickly, then glanced away. He could never meet anyone's eye. 'Perfectly, brother,' he snapped. 'I just sat down for a moment.'

'You have dropped your knapsack. It will get wet.'

He bent and picked it up. I saw his hand trembled. 'Go away!' he said.

I was surprised to see that he looked frightened. 'I only wished to help,' I said stiffly.

'You, help me!' He gave a snort of mocking laughter, then forced himself to his feet and stumbled off towards his lodgings. I shook my head and passed on.

✝

ROGER WAS in his outer office. A candle had been lit against the gloomy afternoon and he stood before it, an affidavit in his long fingers.

'A moment, Matthew,' he said with a smile. His head moved rapidly, scanning the document, then he passed it to the clerk with a nod. 'Well done, Bartlett,' he said. 'A very fair draft. Now, Matthew, let us go and see this leech.' He smiled nervously. 'I see you have your riding boots. Sensible. I will get mine, these shoes would be ruined in the slush.'

He collected his boots, strong old leather ones he often wore, and we walked to the stables. 'No more sudden falls?' I asked him quietly.

'No, thank God.' He sighed deeply; I could see he was still worried.

'Have you much work on?' I asked, to distract him.

'More than I can handle.' Roger was an excellent litigator, and since returning to London had built up a formidable reputation. 'And I have to go and see a new *pro bono* client tonight, after we have been to the doctor's.'

A voice calling Roger's name made us turn. Dorothy was hurrying towards us, an amused expression on her face, carrying a package wrapped in oilskin. 'You forgot this,' she said.

Her husband reddened as he took the package. 'His urine bottle for the physician,' Dorothy explained.

Roger gave me a wry smile. 'What would I do without her?' he asked.

'Forget your head, husband.' Dorothy smiled again, then shivered, for she wore only an indoor dress.

'Go back in, sweetheart,' Roger said, 'or you will have need of a doctor too.'

'I will. Good luck, my love. Goodbye, Matthew. Come to supper next week.' She turned and walked away, hugging herself against the cold.

'I hate deceiving her,' Roger said. 'She still thinks I have a bad stomach. But I would not worry her.'

'I know. Now come, and take care you do not drop that package.'

✝

ROGER WAS PREOCCUPIED, saying little as we rode along Cheapside. The traders were packing up their stalls and we had to pick our way between the few late shoppers and the discarded wooden boxes thrown in the road. A pair of barefoot children in rags darted perilously close to the horses' hooves, picking up rotten vegetables, the dregs of last year's produce which the traders had thrown away. The beggars were crowded around the Conduit again, and one was waving a stick with a piece of rotten bacon on the end, shouting maniacally from the steps. 'Help Tom o'Bedlam! Help a poor man out of his wits! See my broken heart here, on the end of this rod!'

'He's probably never been anywhere near the Bedlam,' I said to Roger. 'If all the beggars who say they've been there had truly been patients, the place would be the size of Westminster Hall.'

'How is your client that has been put there?'

'Grievous sick in his mind. It is harrowing to see. I wish to ask Guy to visit him, and I hope he can make sense of it, for I cannot.'

'Dr Malton specializes in madness, then?' Roger gave me an anxious look.

'Not at all,' I answered reassuringly. 'But he has been practising medicine for nearly forty years and has seen every type of illness there is. And he is a good doctor, not like so many physicians who know of no remedies save bleeding and purging. 'Tis but your own fear that tells you you might have the falling sickness. Symptoms of falling over can have a hundred causes. And you have never had a ghost of a fit.'

'I have seen those fits, though. I once had a client who suffered from them and he fell down in my office, gibbering and foaming with only the whites of his eyes showing.' He shook his head. 'It was a dreadful sight. And it came on this man late in life.'

'You experience these falls and fix your mind on the most frightening thing you have seen. If I did not know you for a clever lawyer I would call you a noddle.'

He smiled. 'Ay, perhaps.'

To take his mind from his worries I told him the story of the preacher who had stood at Newgate promising great rivers of blood. 'Can a man who preaches such things possibly be a good man, a Christian man?' I asked. 'Even though the next minute he was proclaiming the joys of salvation.'

He shook his head. 'We are in a mad and furious world, Matthew. *Mundus furiosus.* Each side railing against the other, preach-ing full of rage and hatred. The radicals foretelling the end of the world. To the conversion of some, and the confusion of many.' He looked at me, smiling with great sadness. 'Remember when we were young, how we read Erasmus on the foolishness of Indulgences granted by the church for money, the endless ceremonial and Latin Masses that stood between ordinary people and the understanding of Christ's message?'

'Ay. That reading group we had. Remember Juan Vives' books, about how the Christian prince could end unemployment by sponsor-ing public works, building hospitals and schools for the poor. But we were young,' I added bitterly. 'And we dreamed.'

'A Christian commonwealth living in gentle harmony.' Roger sighed. 'You realized it was all going rotten before I did.'

'I worked for Thomas Cromwell.'

'And I was always more radical than you.' He turned to me. 'Yet I still believe that a church and state no longer bound to the Pope can be made into something good and Christian, despite the corruption of our leaders, and all these new fanatics.'

I did not reply.

'And you, Matthew?' he asked. 'What do you believe now? You never say.'

'I no longer know, Roger,' I said quietly. 'But come, we turn down here. Let's change the subject. The buildings are close together here, the voices echo, and we must be careful what we say in public these days.'

✝

THE SUN WAS SETTING as we rode into the narrow alley in Bucklersbury where Guy lived and worked. It was full of apothecary's shops, and Roger's face became uneasy as he saw the stuffed alli-gators and other strange wonders displayed in the windows. As we dismounted and tied our horses to a rail, he looked relieved to see that Guy's window contained only a selection of ornate apothecary's jars.

'Why does he practise in this godforsaken place if he is a physician?' Roger asked, retrieving his sample from his horse's pannier.

'Guy was only admitted to the College of Physicians last year, after saving a rich alderman's leg. Before that his dark skin and his being an ex-monk kept him out, despite his French medical degree. He could only practise as an apothecary.'

'But why stay here now?' Roger's face wrinkled in distaste at the sight of a baby monkey in a jar of brine in the adjacent window.

'He says he has grown used to living here.'

'Among these monsters?'

'They are just poor dead creatures.' I smiled reassuringly. 'Some apothecaries claim their powdered body parts can work wonders. Guy is not of that opinion.'

I knocked at his door. It was opened almost at once by a boy in an apprentice's blue coat. Piers Hubberdyne was an apprentice apothecary whom Guy had taken on the year before. He was a tall, dark-haired lad in his late teens, with features of such unusual comeliness that he turned women's heads in the streets. Guy said he was hard-working and conscientious, a rarity among London's notoriously unruly apprentices. He bowed deeply to us.

'Good evening, Master Shardlake. And Master Elliard?'

'Yes.'

'Is that your sample, sir? May I take it?'

Roger handed it over with relief, and Piers ushered us into the shop. 'I will fetch Dr Malton,' he said, and left us. I inhaled the sweet, musky scent of herbs that pervaded Guy's consulting room. Roger looked up at the neatly labelled jars on the shelves. Little bunches of herbs were laid out on a table beside a mortar and pestle and a tiny goldsmith's weighing balance. Above the table was a diagram of the four elements and the types of human nature to which they correspond: melancholic, phlegmatic, cheerful and choleric. Roger studied it.

'Dorothy says I am a man of air, cheerful and light,' he observed.

'With a touch of the phlegmatic, surely. If your temperament was all air, you could not work as you do.'

'And you, Matthew, were always melancholic. Your dark colouring and spare frame mark you out.'

'I was not so spare before my fever eighteen months ago.' I gave him a serious look. 'I think that would have carried me off without Guy's care. Do not worry, Roger, he will help you.'

I turned with relief as Guy entered the room. He was sixty now and his curly hair, black when first I knew him, was white, making the dark brown hue of his lean features even more striking by contrast. I saw that he was beginning to develop an aged man's stoop. When we had first become friends six years before, Guy had been a monastic infirmarian; the monasteries had housed many foreigners and Guy came originally from Granada in Spain, where his forebears had been Muslims. Having abandoned a Benedictine habit for an apothecary's robe, he had now in turn exchanged that for the black high-collared gown of a physician.

When he came in I thought his dark face seemed a little drawn, as though he had worries. Then he looked at us and smiled broadly.

'Good day, Matthew,' he said. His quiet voice still carried an exotic lilt. 'And you must be Master Elliard.' His penetrating dark eyes studied Roger closely.

'Ay.' Roger shuffled nervously.

'Come through to my examination room, let us see what the problem is.'

'I have brought some urine, as you asked. I gave it to the boy.'

'I will look at that.' He smiled. 'However, unlike some of my colleagues, I do not place entire reliance on the urine. Let us first examine you. Can you wait here a while, Matthew?'

'Of course.'

They left me. I sat on a stool by the window. The light was growing dim, the jars and bottles casting long shadows on the floor. I thought again of Adam Kite, and wondered uneasily whether Guy, still secretly loyal to the old church, might also say Adam was possessed. I had found myself thinking too over the last few days about the dark-haired woman keeper. What had she meant by saying she could never leave the Bedlam? Was she under some permanent order of detention?

The door opened and the boy Piers entered, carrying a candle and with a large book under his arm. He placed the book on a high shelf with several others, then went and lit the candles in a tall sconce. Yellow light flickered around the room, adding the smell of wax to the scent of herbs.

He turned to me. 'Do you mind if I continue my work, sir?' he asked.

'Please do.'

He sat at the table, took a handful of herbs and began grinding them. He rolled back the sleeves of his robe, revealing strong arms, the muscles bunching as he crushed the herbs.

'How long have you been with Dr Malton now?' I asked.

'Just a year, sir.' He turned and smiled, showing sparkling white teeth.

'Your old master died, did he not?'

'Ay, sir. He lived in the next street. Dr Malton took me on when he died suddenly. I am lucky, he is a man of rare knowledge. And kind.'

'That he is,' I agreed. Piers turned back to his work. How different he was from most apprentices, noisy lewd lads forever looking for trouble. His self-possessed, confident manner was that of a man, not a boy.

✝

It was an hour before Guy and Roger returned. It had grown dark, and Piers had to bend closely to his work, a candle beside him. Guy put a hand on his shoulder. 'Enough for tonight, lad. Go and get some supper, but first bring us some beer.'

'Yes, sir.' Piers bowed to us and left. I looked at Roger, delighted to see an expression of profound relief on his face.

'I do not have the falling sickness,' he said and beamed.

Guy smiled gently. 'The strangest matters may have a simple resolution. I always like to start by looking for the simplest possible explanation, which William of Ockham taught is most likely to be the true one. So I began with Master Elliard's feet.'

'He had me standing barefoot,' Roger said, 'then measured my legs, laid me on his couch and bent my feet to and fro. I confess I was surprised. I came expecting a learned disquisition on my urine.'

'We did not need that in the end.' Guy smiled triumphantly. 'I found the right foot turns markedly to the right, the cause being that Master Elliard's left leg is very slightly longer. It is a problem that has been building up for years. The remedy is a special shoe, with a wooden insert that will correct the gait. I will get young Piers to make it, he is skilled with his hands.'

'I am more grateful than I can say, sir,' Roger said warmly.

There was a knock, and Piers returned with three pewter goblets on a tray which he laid on the table.

'Let us drink to celebrate Master Elliard's liberation from falling over.' Guy took a stool and passed another to Roger.

'Roger is thinking of starting a subscription for a hospital,' I told Guy.

Guy shook his head sadly. 'Hospitals are sorely needed in this city. That would be a good and Christian thing. Perhaps I could help, advise.'

'That would be kind, sir.'

'Roger still holds to the ideals of Erasmus,' I said.

Guy nodded. 'I once studied Erasmus too. He was in high favour when I first came to England. I thought when he said the church was too rich, too devoted to ceremony, he had something – though most of my fellow monks did not, they said he wrote with a wanton pen.' His face grew sombre. 'Perhaps they saw clearer than I that talk of reform would lead to the destruction of the monasteries. And of so much else. And for what?' he asked bitterly. 'A reign of greed and terror.'

Roger looked a little uncomfortable at Guy's defence of the monks. I looked from one to the other of them. Guy who was still a Catholic at heart, Roger the radical reformer turned moderate. I was not so much between them as outside the whole argument. A lonely place to be.

'I have a case I wanted to ask your advice about, Guy,' I said to change the subject. 'A case of religious madness, or at least *perhaps* that is what it is.' I told him Adam's story. 'So the Privy Council have put him in the Bedlam to get him out of the way,' I concluded. 'His parents want me to get him released, but I am not sure that is a good idea.'

'I have known of obsessive lovers,' Roger said, 'but obsessive praying – I have never heard of such a thing.'

'I have,' Guy said, and we both turned to look at his dark grave face. 'It is a new form of brain-sickness, something Martin Luther has added to the store of human misery.'

'What do you mean?' I asked.

'There have always been some people who hate themselves, who torture themselves with guilt for real or imagined offences. I saw such cases sometimes as an infirmarian. Then we could tell people that God promises salvation to any who repent their sins, because He places no one outside His mercy and charity.' He looked up, a rare anger in his face. 'But now some tell us that God has decided, as though from caprice, to save some and damn others to perpetual torment; and if God does not give you the assurance of His Grace you are doomed. That is one of Luther's central doctrines. I know, I have read him. Luther may have felt himself a worthless creature saved by God's grace, but did he ever stop to think what his philosophy might mean for those without his inner strength, his arrogance?'

'If that were true,' Roger said, 'surely half the population would be running mad?'

'Do you believe you are saved?' Guy asked suddenly. 'That you have God's grace?'

'I hope so. I try to live well and hope I may be saved.'

'Yes. Most, like you, or I, are content with the hope of salvation and leave matters in God's hands. But now there are some who are utterly certain they are saved. They can be dangerous because they believe themselves special, above other people. But just as every coin has two sides, so there are others who crave the certainty, yet are convinced they are unworthy, and that can end in the piteous condition of this young man. I have heard it called salvation panic, though the term hardly does justice to the agonies of those who suffer it.' He paused. 'The question perhaps is why the boy became consumed with guilt in the first place.'

'Maybe he has committed some great sin,' I said. I was glad to see Guy shake his head.

'No, usually in such cases their sins are small, it is something in the workings of their minds that brings them to this pass.'

'Will you help me try to find what it is, Guy? Some in the Bedlam think Adam is possessed. I fear they may do him harm.'

'I will come and see him, Matthew,' Guy said. 'I will go as a doctor, of course, not an ex-monk, or he would probably fear he was indeed in the hands of the devil.' Suddenly my friend looked old and tired.

'Thank you,' I said. 'Young Piers seems a hard worker,' I observed.

'Yes, he is. A good apprentice. Perhaps better than I deserve,' he added quietly.

'How so?' I asked, puzzled.

He did not answer. 'Piers is very clever, too. His understanding is marvellous quick.' Guy gave a sudden smile that transformed his face. 'Let me show you something I have been discussing with Piers, something new in the world of healing, that many of my fellow physicians disapprove of.' He rose and crossed to his shelf of books. He took down the big volume that Piers had replaced earlier. He cleared a space on the table and placed it there carefully. Roger and I went over to join him.

'*De Humani Corpora Fabrica*,' Guy said quietly. 'The workings of the human body. Just published, a German merchant friend brought it over for me. It is by Andreas Vesalius, a Dutch physician working in Italy. They have been allowed to practise dissection of bodies there for years, though it has been forbidden here till recently.'

'The old church disapproved,' Roger said.

'They did, and they were wrong. Vesalius is the first man to dissect human bodies on a large scale for centuries, perhaps ever. And you know what he has found? That the ancients, Hippocrates and Galen, the ultimate authorities whom a physician may not question without risking expulsion from the College of Physicians, were *wrong*.' He turned to us, a gleam in his dark eyes. 'Vesalius has shown that the ancients erred in many of their descriptions of the inner form of the body. He concludes they too were not allowed to dissect bodies, and that their descriptions came from studies not of men but of animals.' He laughed. 'This book will cause a great stir. The college will try to have it discredited, even suppressed.'

'But how can we know Vesalius is right, and the ancients wrong?' I asked.

'By comparing his descriptions and drawings here with what we can see for ourselves when a body is opened. Four bodies of hanged criminals the barber-surgeons' college is allowed now, for public dissection.' I quailed a little as his words, for I was ever of a squeamish disposition, but he went on. 'And there is another way I have been able to see for myself.'

'How so?' Roger asked.

'A London coroner can call for a body to be opened and examined if it is needed to find out how a man died. Most physicians think the work beneath them and the pay is not great, but I have offered my services and already I have been able to test Vesalius' claims for myself. And he is right.' Guy opened the book slowly and almost reverentially. It was in Latin, illustrated with drawings that were marvellously executed but with something mocking and even cruel about them; as Guy flicked over the pages I saw a skeleton leaning on a table in the pose of a thinker, a flayed body hanging from a gibbet, all its innards exposed. In the corner of a drawing of exposed bowels, a little cherub sat passing a turd and smiling at the reader.

Guy laid the book open at a picture of a human heart cut open on a table. 'There,' he said. 'Do you see? The heart has four chambers, *four*, not the three we have always been taught.'

I nodded, though all I could see was a horrible tangle of valves and tissue. I glanced at Roger. He was looking a little pale. I said, 'That is very interesting, Guy, but a little beyond us, I fear. And we must be getting back to Lincoln's Inn.'

'Oh. Very well.' Guy, normally the most sensitive of men, did not seem to realize the book had disturbed us. He smiled. 'Perhaps this new year heralds in a time of wonders. I hear a Polish scholar has published a book proving by observation of the planets that the earth goes round the sun, not the other way around. I have asked my friend to bring me a copy. This new year of 1543 may find us on the threshold of a new world.'

'Do you know many foreign merchants?' Roger asked curiously.

'We of alien looks or words must stick together.' Guy smiled sadly. He brought our coats, and Roger left his fee of a mark. Guy promised the inserts for his shoes would be ready in a couple of weeks at most.

We left, Roger thanking Guy again profusely for his help. When the door was closed Roger clasped my arm. 'I cannot tell you how grateful I am for your guiding me to Dr Malton. I will ever be in your debt.'

'There are no debts between friends,' I said with a smile. 'I am glad to have helped.'

'I could have done without the dissection book, though,' he added as we rode away.

✝

WE RODE ON, up Bucklersbury. We passed the ancient mansion from Henry III's time, the Old Barge, long converted into a warren of crumbling tenements. Barak and Tamasin lived there.

'Roger, do you mind if I leave you to go on?' I asked. 'There is a visit I would like to pay.'

He looked up at the Barge, raising his eyebrows. 'Not some doxy?' he asked. 'I hear many live there.'

'No, my clerk and his wife.'

'And I should go and see my new client.'

'What is the case?'

'I do not know yet. A solicitor has sent me a letter about a client of his, who has some property dispute over in Southwark. His client is too poor to pay for a barrister, but he says the case is a worthy one and asked if I will act *pro bono*. It is all a bit vague, but I agreed to go and meet the client.'

'Who's the solicitor?'

'A man called Nantwich. I've never heard of him. But there are so many jobbing solicitors looking for work around the Inns these days.' He drew his coat round him. 'It is cold for riding, I would rather go home and quietly celebrate the end of my fears.' He turned his horse, then paused. The air was heavy with woodsmoke and chill with frost. 'Where is spring?' he asked, then waved a hand in farewell and rode off into the dark night. I dismounted, and walked towards the lighted windows of the Old Barge.

Chapter Five

I HAD VISITED Barak's tenement in the days before he married Tamasin, and remembered which of the several unpainted street doors to take. It gave on to a staircase leading to the ramshackle apartments into which the crumbling old mansion was divided. The stairs creaked loudly in the pitch-black, and I recalled thinking on my previous visit that the whole place seemed ready to fall down.

I remembered Barak's apartment as a typical young man's lodging: dirty plates piled on the table, clothes strewn about the floor and mouse droppings in the corners. I had been glad when he announced, on marrying Tamasin, that they would move to a little house somewhere near Lincoln's Inn, and sorry when the plan was abandoned. The Old Barge was no place for a young girl, especially one as fond of domesticity as Tamasin.

On the second floor I knocked on the door of their tenement. After a minute the door opened a fraction, and I saw a coiffed head dimly outlined against the candlelight within.

'Who is it?' she asked nervously.

''Tis I. Master Shardlake.'

'Ah, sir. Come in.' Tamasin opened the door and I followed her into the big room that served as dining-room, bedroom and parlour. She had been at work here; everything was clean, the plates stacked in a scuffed old dresser, the bed tidily made. But the place stank of damp, and patches of black mould spotted the wall around the window. Rags had been stuffed between the rotting shutters to keep out the wind. Attempts had been made to clean the wall, but the mould was spreading again. Barak, I saw, was absent.

'Will you sit, sir?' Tamasin indicated a chair at the table. 'May I take your coat? I am afraid Jack is out.'

'I will keep it. I – er – will not be long.' In truth it was so cold in the fireless apartment that I did not want to remove it. I sat and took a proper look at Tamasin. She was a very pretty young woman, still in her early twenties, with high cheekbones, wide blue eyes and a full mouth. Before her marriage she had taken pride in dressing as well as her purse would allow; perhaps a little better. But now she wore a shapeless grey dress with a threadbare white apron over it, and her blonde hair was swept under a large, white housewife coif. She smiled at me cheerfully but I saw how her shoulders were slumped, her eyes dull.

'It has been a long time since I saw you, sir,' she said.

'Near six months. How are you faring, Tamasin?'

'Oh, well enough. I am sorry Jack is not here.'

'No matter. I was passing on my way from taking a friend to consult Dr Malton.'

'Would you like a cup of beer, sir?'

'I would, Tamasin. But perhaps I should go . . .' I was breaking the proprieties in being with her alone.

'No, sir, stay,' she said. 'We are old friends, are we not?'

'I hope so.'

'I should like a little company.' She went and poured some beer from a jug on the dresser and brought it over, taking a stool opposite me. 'Was Dr Malton able to help your friend?'

I took a draught of the beer, which was pleasantly strong. 'Yes. He had taken to falling over without warning, he thought he was taking the falling sickness, but it turns out he only has something amiss with his foot.'

Tamasin smiled, something like her old warm smile. 'I should think he is mightily relieved.'

'He is. I imagine when he gets home he will be dancing round his lodgings, bad foot and all.'

'Dr Malton is a good man. I believe he saved you when you had that fever the winter before last.'

'Yes. I think he did.'

'But he could not help my poor little Georgie.'

'I know.'

She stared at an empty spot against the far wall. 'He was born dead, laid dead in his little cot over there that we had made.' She turned to me, her eyes full of pain. 'Afterwards I did not want Jack to take the crib away, it was as though some part of Georgie remained while it was there. But he hated the reminder.'

'I am sorry I did not come to see you after the baby died, Tamasin. I wanted to, but Jack said you were both better alone.'

'I used to get upset a lot. Jack would not want you to see.' She sighed, frowning a little. 'And you, are you in good health, sir?'

'Yes. Working hard and doing well, with Jack's help.' I smiled.

'He looks up to you, sir. Always saying how Master Shardlake managed to win this case by undermining the opposition, that one by turning up new evidence.'

'Does he?' I laughed. 'Sometimes the way he talks, I feel he thinks I am a noddle.'

'That is just his way.'

'Yes.' I smiled at her. When we first met two years before, on the King's Great Progress to York, I had been suspicious of Tamasin's confidence and lively personality, which had seemed unwomanly. But in the course of shared perils I had developed an almost fatherly affection for her. Looking at the tired housewife before me, I thought, where has all that spirit gone?

Something of my thoughts must have shown in my face, for her mouth trembled, then two large tears rolled down Tamasin's cheeks. She lowered her head.

'Tamasin,' I said, half rising. 'What is the matter? Is it still the poor child?'

'I am sorry, sir.'

'Come, after all we went through in Yorkshire a few tears are nothing. Tell me what ails you.'

She took a shuddering breath and wiped her eyes on her sleeve before turning her tear-stained face to me. 'It began with the child,' she said quietly. 'His death was a shock to Jack as well as me. They say when a child dies his mother will always have him quick in her heart, but he is in Jack's too. Oh, he is so *angry*.'

'With you?'

'With everything. With God himself, he felt it cruel of Him to take his child. He was never much of a churchgoer but now he does not want to go at all. It is Easter tomorrow, but he has refused to go to service or confession.'

'Will you go?'

'Yes, though – though I feel the faith has been squeezed from me too. But you know me,' she added with a touch of her old humour. 'I prefer to keep on the right side of the powers that be.'

'That is wise these days.'

'Jack says I only go to show off my best clothes.' She looked down at her apron. 'Well, 'tis true that after wearing these things all week I like to go out in something nice. But I fear if Jack absents himself continually, questions will be asked, he could be in trouble with the churchwardens. Especially as he is known to have Jewish blood.' She set her lips. 'He wanted to carry on his bloodline through our child. It comes out when he is drunk.'

'Is he drunk often?' I remembered his dishevelled look that morning.

'More and more. He goes out with his old friends and sometimes does not come back all night. That will be where he is now. And I think he goes with other women too.'

I was shocked. 'Who?'

'I do not know. Perhaps with female neighbours. You know what some of them are here.'

'Can you be sure?'

She gave me a direct look. 'From the smell of him some mornings, yes.'

I sighed. 'Is there no sign of – another child?'

'No. Perhaps I am like old Queen Catherine of Aragon, and cannot produce healthy children.'

'But it is only – what – six months since your baby died. That is no time, Tamasin.'

'Time enough for Jack to turn away. Sometimes when he is drunk he says that I would rule him, make him into some weak domesticated creature.' She looked around the room. 'As though you could domesticate anyone in this place.'

'Sometimes Jack can be insensitive. Even cruel.'

'Well, at least he does not beat me. Many husbands do.'

'Tamasin—'

'Oh, he apologizes when he is sober again, he is loving then, calls me his chick and says he did not mean his words, it is only his fury that God took our child. That I can share. Why does God *do* such cruel things?' she asked, in sudden anger.

I shook my head. 'I am not the man to answer that, Tamasin. It puzzles me too.'

'Sir,' she said, sitting up and looking at me. 'Can you speak to Jack, find out what is in his mind? He is so unpredictable these days, I do not know whether – whether he still wants me at all.'

'Oh, Tamasin,' I said. 'I am sure he does. And talking to him of such matters would be no easy thing. If he even discovers you have been talking to me of his marriage he will be angry with us both.'

'Yes. He is proud. But if you could try to find out somehow.' She looked at me beseechingly. 'I know you have a way of making people talk. And I have no one else to ask.'

'I will try, Tamasin. But I will have to pick my time carefully.'

She nodded gratefully. 'Thank you.'

I stood up. 'And now I should go. If he were to come in now and find you telling me your sorrows he would certainly be cross.' I laid a hand on hers. 'But if things become too much, or you want someone to talk to, a note to my house will bring me.'

'You are kind, sir. Some days I just sit staring mopishly at that damp patch for hours, I have no energy and wonder what is wrong with me. The mould will not go away. However I clean it the black spots are soon creeping over the wall again.' She sighed. 'It is not like the old days, when I worked in poor Queen Catherine Howard's household. Oh, I was only the lowest of servants, but there was always something of interest to see.'

'Danger, too,' I said with a smile. 'As it turned out.'

'I know.' She paused. 'They say there will be a new queen soon. A widow. Catherine, Lady Latimer. She will be the sixth. Fantastic, is it not?'

'Strange indeed.'

She shook her head wonderingly. 'Was there ever such a king?'

I left her. As I descended the dark staircase, I remembered when Barak and Tamasin had married, on a fine spring day the year before. I had felt envious of their content. A single man can easily assume all marriages are blissful, the couple devoted like Roger and Dorothy. But tonight I had seen the sad things that could lurk beneath the surface. I had been right to guess something was amiss, but had not known things were as bad as this. 'Damn Barak!' I said aloud as I stepped out on to the road, startling a gentleman going into the Barge, perhaps to see one of the prostitutes.

✝

I SPENT MOST OF Good Friday and Easter Saturday at home, working on papers. I did not go to church on Easter Sunday. The weather remained unseasonably cold, with a further light fall of snow. I was in an unsettled, restless mood. On Saturday I even took out my pencils and drawing pad; this last year I had gone back to my old hobby of painting and sketching, but that day I could think of noth⁄ing to draw. I looked at the blank paper but nothing came to mind but vague circles and dark lines and a sane man could hardly make a drawing of those. I went to bed but could not sleep. I lay thinking how I might broach the subject of Tamasin to Barak without making matters worse. Then when I did get to sleep I dreamed of poor mad

Adam Kite. I came into his wretched room at the Bedlam to find him crouched on the floor, praying desperately. But as I approached I realized it was not God's name nor Jesus' that he was invoking, but mine – it was 'Master Shardlake' that he was begging for salvation. I woke with a start.

It was still dark, but dawn was not far off and I thought I might as well go into work, even though it was Easter Sunday. There was more paperwork to do in chambers. My housekeeper was already up, chivvying the boy, Peter, to light the fire and bring some heat to the cold morning. I breakfasted, then donned my robe and wrapped myself in my coat to walk up Chancery Lane to Lincoln's Inn.

As I turned out of my gate I fancied it was less cold again, the remaining snow turning once more to muddy slush. I looked back at my house. The tall chimneys rising from the tiled roof were outlined against a strange-coloured sky, streaks of faint blue interspersed with banks of cloud tinged pink underneath by the rising sun. I set off, turning my mind to the cases to be heard on Tuesday, including Adam Kite's. I passed under the Great Gate, past the still-shuttered porter's lodge, and walked across the slushy yard towards my chambers.

It was not yet full day. Almost all the windows were unlit, but to my surprise I saw a light in my own chambers; Barak must have come straight here from wherever he had been last night, not gone home at all. Damn the wretch, I thought.

Then I jumped at the sound of a cry. A man's voice, yelling out in terror. I made out two figures standing by the fountain, looking into the water. 'Oh God!' one cried.

I turned and crossed to them. I saw the ice was broken into pieces. The water under the ice was red, bright red. My heart began thumping painfully.

By their short black robes, the two young men standing staring into the fountain were students. One was short and thickset, the other tall and thin. They looked red-eyed, probably returning to their quarters from some all-night roister.

'What is it?' I asked sharply. 'What is happening?'

The thickset student turned to me. 'There's — there's a man in the fountain,' he said in a trembling voice.

The other student pointed at something sticking out of the water. 'That — that's a foot.'

I looked at them sharply, wondering if this was some prank. But as I stepped close I saw in the growing light that a man's booted leg was sticking out between the chunks of ice. Taking a deep breath, I leaned over. I made out the shape of a long dark robe billowing out in that bright red water. This was a lawyer. I felt a moment's giddiness, then pulled myself together and turned to the students. 'Help me get him out,' I said sharply. The one who had spoken shrank back but the tall thin one approached.

'You'll have to pull on that leg,' I said. 'Then I'll take hold of him.'

The student crossed himself, then grabbed the leg by the ankle, took a deep breath, and pulled. The ice heaved up in big fragments as the leg emerged, then the body. The other student joined me in seizing hold of the stone-cold corpse.

We hauled it out, then laid it on the slushy ground. The gown had ridden up over the head, hiding the man's face. I looked at the body: a small, thin man.

'Look at that water.' The tall student spoke in a whisper. It was almost full light now, showing a bright vermilion circle.

'It's full of blood,' the other said. 'Sweet Jesus.'

I turned back to the body. I was shivering, and not just from the cold water that had soaked me as we pulled the body out. I crouched down, took the hem of the robe and pulled it away from the face.

'Oh Christ Jesus!' one of the students cried out. He turned away and I heard a retching sound. But I sat transfixed by what was, for me, a double horror. The first was the great gaping wound in the man's throat, red against the dead-white skin and stretching almost from ear to ear. The second was the face. It was Roger.

Chapter Six

For a few moments I stood transfixed, staring at that awful corpse, the terrible wound in the throat. Roger's eyes were closed, the alabaster face looked peaceful. I thought, surely his face should be contorted with horror as he suffered that appalling death? For a second, in the shadowy early morning light, I hoped madly that the thing on the ground might not be Roger at all, but a plaster figure some crazed artist had created as an evil joke. But even as I watched, some dark blood from the ripped neck seeped on to the snow.

'Please, sir, cover him!' the stocky student called in a shrill voice. I removed my coat and bent down to the body. Suddenly I was overcome by emotion. 'Oh, my poor friend!' I cried out, tears starting to my eyes as I gently touched Roger's face. It was icy cold. I covered it with my coat and knelt by him, letting the tears come.

A hand on my shoulder made me jump. I looked up at the anxious face of the tall student who had helped me. 'Please, sir,' he asked tremulously. 'What shall we do? People will be coming in soon.'

I rose shakily to my feet and took a deep breath. 'Go and tell the gatekeeper to rouse the constable, who must fetch the coroner. Can you do that, lad?'

'Yes, sir.' The boy nodded and ran off towards the lodge. I turned and stared again at that great stone bowl of bright red water. The sun was almost fully risen now, bringing an unaccustomed warmth but showing the corpse and the fountain in their full horror. The other boy, who was leaning against the fountain, his back to that awful red water, was shivering violently. 'You,' I said, 'will you run across the court to my chambers — see, there where there is already a light? My assistant is there; tell him to come at once. His name is Barak.'

The boy gulped, nodded and staggered away. I looked up at the windows of the Elliards' quarters. There were no lights; I prayed Dorothy was still abed. I realized with sinking heart that I would have to tell her that Roger was dead. I could not leave that task to some stranger.

Moments later, to my relief, I saw Barak running towards me; the student was following more slowly. His mouth fell open when he saw the body by the fountain.

'Judas' bowels! What the devil's happened here?' He looked red-eyed and smelled of drink; he must have been out all night again. But for all that there was no one I would rather have by me now. 'Roger Elliard is dead,' I said, my voice shaking. 'He has been murdered.'

'Here?' Barak asked disbelievingly.

'During the night. Someone cut his throat and put him in the fountain.'

'Jesu.' Barak bent gently, twitched back the corner of my coat and stared at the dead face. He quickly replaced the coat. He looked at the fountain. 'His throat must have been cut in there. There's no blood on the ground.' He frowned, puzzled. 'And no signs of a struggle in the snow. Unless . . .' he hesitated.

'What?'

'Unless he did it himself. Didn't you say he feared he was ill?'

'He wasn't ill, not seriously. I took him to Guy on Thursday. Do you think anyone would kill himself like this, in the middle of Gatehouse Court?' I heard my voice rising. 'Don't be so stupid! Roger was as content as any man I know. He had everything to live for! He was planning a campaign to build a hospital, he was happily married to the best of women—' I realized I was shouting, and broke off. I put one hand to my damp brow and raised the other in a gesture of apology.

'I am sorry, Jack.'

'It's all right,' he said quietly. 'You've had a shock.'

'No,' I said, and heard my voice tremble. 'I am *angry*. This was meant as a terrible display.'

Barak thought for a moment. 'Yes,' he said slowly. 'If those students hadn't come by, he would have been found when the resident barristers left chambers to go to the Easter services.'

I looked again at the body. I clenched my fists. 'Who could do such a monstrous thing to a good and peaceful man, cut his throat and let him to bleed to death in there? On Easter day. And why?'

I heard a murmur of voices. Three or four barristers had emerged from their quarters and were approaching. Perhaps they had heard my shouting. At the sight of the body one cried, 'By Our Lady!'

A tall elderly man in a silk robe pushed through. I was relieved to see the Treasurer, Rowland. His unbrushed white hair stuck up over his head.

'Brother Shardlake?' he asked. 'What is going on? The porter roused me—' He broke off, looked at the covered body, then his eyes bulged in horror at the red fountain.

I told him what I knew. He took a deep breath, then bent and uncovered Roger's face again. I fought an urge to tell him to leave him alone. There was a murmur of horror from the onlookers, a dozen of them now. I saw Bealknap among them. Normally eager for scandal, he stood looking on silently, still pale and sick-looking. I thought, Dorothy will hear their gabbling, I must tell her. Then Barak spoke quietly at my elbow. 'There is something you should see. Over here.'

'I must tell Roger's wife—' I said.

'You should see now.'

I stood undecided for a moment, then nodded. 'Master treasurer,' I said. 'Could you excuse me for a moment?'

'Where are you going?' he asked crossly. 'You and those boys, you were the first finders, you must stay for the coroner.'

'I will be back in a minute. Then I will tell Mistress Elliard what has happened. I am a friend.'

The old man turned as he saw, out of the corner of his eye, a newly arrived student approaching the body. 'Get back, you crawling clerk!' he shouted. I took the chance to get away.

Barak led me to a point twenty feet away. 'See these footprints?' he asked.

I looked down. Around the fountain the students and I had churned the snow to slush, and the onlookers had left a mess of prints converging on the murder scene. But Barak was pointing to a separate double trail, one approaching and another leading away from the fountain, that went round the side of the building where the Elliards lived. It was the spot where I had heard the unknown intruder a week before.

Barak bent to study the footprints. 'Look how deep the ones leading to the fountain are. Deeper than the ones returning. Like he was carrying something heavy.'

'I heard someone there on New Year's Night,' I breathed. 'He got over the wall—'

'Let's follow the prints.'

'I have to tell Dorothy—'

'These will melt soon.' In truth the morning sun had brought the first real warmth of spring; I could hear meltwater dripping from the eaves. I hesitated, then followed Barak round the side of the building.

'They look like prints of a man of ordinary size,' Barak said.

'Bigger than Roger, anyway.'

The footprints went up to the wall, then turned sharply right. They ended at a heavy wooden door. 'He got through here,' Barak said.

'He came over the wall last time. If it was him the other night.'

'He wasn't carrying a body then.' Barak tried the gate. 'It's locked,' he said.

'Only the barristers have keys. The orchard is on the other side, then Lincoln's Inn Fields. I've got a key, but it's in chambers.'

'Help me up,' Barak said. I made a stirrup of my hands and Barak climbed up, resting his elbows on top of the wall. 'The footsteps go on into the orchard,' he said. He jumped down. 'He carried poor Master Elliard in from the orchard? Jesu, he must be strong. Tell me which drawer the key's in and I'll run and get it.'

I hesitated. 'I should go back. It should be me that tells Dorothy. The fountain is visible from her window—'

'I'll go by myself. But I must go now, before the footprints melt.'

'You don't know what you may find at the other end,' I cautioned.

'He's long gone. But I'll follow the footsteps as far as they go. We need to find out all we can. You know as well as I that if a murderer is not taken quickly, he is often never found.' He took a deep breath. 'And this is no normal killing, done for money or lust. The killer knocked him unconscious then carried him into Lincoln's Inn and put him in the fountain. He was still alive when his throat was cut or he wouldn't have bled. He must have knocked him out hard enough to keep him unconscious for a good time but not hard enough to kill him. That's very chancy. What if he had woken and started struggling? It looks like some sort of awful vengeance.'

'Roger hadn't an enemy in the world. Was it another barrister? Only a member of Lincoln's Inn would have a key to that door.'

'We should go now, sir.' Barak looked at me seriously. 'If you are to tell the lady.'

I nodded, biting my lip. Barak squeezed my arm, an unexpected gesture, then began running back to Gatehouse Court. I followed more slowly. As I rounded the corner I heard a woman's scream. I felt a violent shiver down my spine as I started to run.

I was too late. In the middle of the growing crowd around the fountain, Dorothy, dressed in a nightgown, was kneeling on the wet ground by her husband's body, wailing piteously, a howl of utter desolation. My coat had been removed from Roger's head; she had seen that awful face. She wailed again.

✞

I RAN TO HER, knelt and grasped her by the shoulders. Under the thin material her skin was cold. She lifted her face to me; she looked utterly stricken, her eyes wide, mouth hanging open, her brown hair wildly disordered.

'Matthew?' she choked.

'Yes. Dorothy – oh, you should not have come out, they should not have let you see . . .' I glared accusingly at the crowd. People shuffled their feet, looking embarrassed.

'I could not stop her,' Treasurer Rowland said stiffly.

'You could have tried!'

'That is no way to talk to me—'

'Shut up,' I snapped, anger bursting out again. The Treasurer's mouth fell open. I lifted Dorothy up. As soon as she stood she began trembling. 'Come inside, Dorothy, come—'

'No!' She fought me, trying to break loose. 'I cannot leave Roger lying there.' Her voice rose again.

'We must,' I said soothingly. 'For the coroner.'

'Who – killed him?' She stared at me, as though trying to seize hold of something to make sense of the horror around her.

'We will find out. Now come inside. Treasurer Rowland will ensure no one does anything disrespectful. Will you not, sir?'

'Yes, of course.' The old man actually looked sheepish. Dorothy allowed me to lead her inside, where Roger's clerk, Bartlett, stood in his office doorway, looking shocked. He was a conscientious middle-aged man who had come with Roger from Bristol.

'Sir?' he asked in a whisper. 'What – what has happened? They say the master is murdered.'

'I fear so. Listen, I will come down to you later and see what should be done with his work.'

'Yes, sir.'

Dorothy was staring at Bartlett as though she had never seen him before. Again I took hold of her arms, leading her gently up the wide staircase to their rooms. Old Elias stood in the open doorway, half dressed, his white hair standing on end. A young maid in a white apron and coif stood beside him.

'Oh, my lady,' the maid said in an Irish accent. She turned her tearful face to me. 'She had just got up, sir, she must have gone through to the front and looked from the window. She screamed and ran out and—'

'All right.' I studied the girl. She was plump and dark-haired. She seemed sensible, and genuinely upset for her mistress. Dorothy would have to rely on her much in the days to come. 'What is your name?' I asked.

'Margaret, sir.'

'Do you have some strong wine, Margaret?'

'I've some aqua vitae sir. I'll get it. Sir – out there – is it truly the master?'

'Yes, I am afraid it is. Now please, get the aqua vitae. And fetch your mistress a thicker gown. She must not get cold.'

I led Dorothy into the parlour and sat her in a chair before the fire. I looked round, remembering my pleasant evening there a week before. Dorothy sat trembling. She had passed, I realized, from horror to shock.

The maid returned, draped a warm gown round Dorothy's shoulders and passed her a glass of spirits, but Dorothy's hand trembled so much I took it from her fingers.

'Stay,' I said to Margaret. 'In case she needs anything.'

'The poor master . . .' Margaret brought a stool to her mistress's side and sat on it heavily, herself shocked.

'Come,' I said gently to Dorothy. 'Drink this, it will help you.' She did not resist as I held the glass to her lips, helping her drink as though she was a child. Her face was pale, her plump cheeks sagging. I had told her at the banquet that she looked years younger than her age. Now she was suddenly haggard and old. I wondered with sorrow if her warm, impish smile would ever return.

Her face grew pink from the spirit and she seemed to come slowly back to herself, though she still trembled.

'Matthew,' she said quietly. 'They said you found Roger.'

'Some students did. I came on them, helped them lift the body out.'

'I came into the parlour and heard a noise outside.' She frowned, as though remembering something from a long time ago. 'I saw the fountain all red, the people standing there, and I thought, what on earth has happened? Then I saw the body on the ground. I knew it was Roger. I recognized his boots. His old leather boots.' She gulped and I thought she would start crying but instead she looked at me with eyes full of anger.

'Who *did* this?' she asked. 'Who did this cruel wicked thing? And why?'

'I do not know. Dorothy, where was Roger yesterday evening?'

'He – he was out. His new *pro bono* client.'

'The same client he went to see on Thursday? When I left him after we had visited Dr Malton he said he was going to see a *pro bono* client. He said he had had a letter about the case.'

'Yes, yes.' She gulped. 'It came on Tuesday, from some solicitor. Yes. I remember. A man called Nantwich.'

'Did Roger say where he was writing from?'

'Somewhere by Newgate, I think. You know those jobbing solicitors, half of them haven't even got proper offices. He had heard Roger did free work for poor people. He asked if Roger could meet his client at a tavern in Wych Street on Thursday evening, as the man worked during the day.'

'Did you see the letter?'

'I did not ask to. I thought it odd, asking to meet in a tavern, but Roger was curious about it, and you know how good-natured he is.' She stopped dead and gave a sobbing gasp. For a second, talking, she had forgotten Roger was dead and the horror hit her with renewed force. She stared at me wildly. I clutched her hand. It felt cold.

'Dorothy. I am so sorry. But I must ask. What happened at the meeting?'

'Nothing. The man never turned up. But then another letter arrived, pushed through the door on Good Friday, apologizing that the client had not been able to get to the tavern and asking Roger to meet him yesterday night, at the same place. I did not see that letter either,' she added in a small voice.

'And Roger went, of course.' I smiled sadly. 'I would not have done.' Something struck me. 'It was cold last night. He would have worn a coat.'

'Yes. He did.'

'Then where is it?' I frowned.

'I do not know.' Dorothy was silent for a moment, then went on. 'I was surprised when it got to ten o'clock and he had not returned. But you know how he would get caught up in something and stay talking for hours.' Would, not will. It had sunk in properly now. 'I was tired, I went to bed early. I expected him to come in. But I drifted off to sleep. I woke in the small hours, and when he wasn't beside me I thought he had bedded down in the other bedroom. He does that if he comes in late, so as not to disturb me. And all the time—' She broke down then, burying her head in her hands and sobbing loudly. I tried to think. The client had asked to meet Roger at Wych Street, on the other side of Lincoln's Inn Fields. The easiest way to get there was to go through the orchard. So he would have taken his key to the orchard door. But why had the man not turned up on Thursday? My heart sank at the thought that Roger, like any barrister, would have taken his letter of instruction with him. There was little chance it would have been left on the body, and the coat he would have worn was gone. But at least we had the name, Nantwich. An uncommon one.

I looked at Dorothy, my heart full of pity. Her sobs ceased. She glanced at me and I saw an anger in her eyes that reflected my own.

'Who has done this?' she asked quietly. 'Roger did not have an enemy in the world. Who is this devil?'

'I will see him caught, Dorothy. I promise you.'

'You will make sure?'

'I will. On my oath.'

She scrabbled for my hand, gripped it fiercely. 'You must help me with things now, Matthew. Please. I am alone.'

'I will.'

Her face crumpled suddenly. 'Oh, Roger!' And then the tears came again, great racking sobs. Margaret put an arm round her mistress, while I held her hand. We were still there, like some pitiful tableau, when Elias came in to say the coroner was below, and must see me at once.

✝

ARCHIBALD BROWNE, the Middlesex coroner, was an old man and a sour one. He was one of the old corrupt breed, who would leave a body lying stinking in the street for days till someone paid them to hold an inquest, not one of the more competent paid officials the Tudors had brought in. Small, bald and squat, his round face was pitted with smallpox scars. When I came out he was standing beside the Treasurer, arms in the pockets of his thick coat, looking down at Roger's body. Passers-by stopping to stare were being moved on with curt gestures from Treasurer Rowland. I saw the sun had melted most of the snow now. I wondered wearily where Barak was.

Rowland gestured to me. 'This is Brother Matthew Shardlake,' he told Browne. 'He had the constable roused.'

'I hope I'll get more sense out of him than those two lads.' Coroner Browne grunted. He turned bleary eyes on me. 'You've spoken with the widow?'

'Yes, sir.'

'How is she?'

'Weeping,' I said shortly.

'I'll have to question her. You can come with me if you know her. Now, tell me what in Jesu's name has happened.'

I told him about finding Roger's body, about Barak following the footprints and what Dorothy had told me about the strange client.

'Nantwich?' Treasurer Rowland frowned. 'I've never heard of him. I thought I knew most of the solicitors.'

Browne's eyes narrowed as he studied me. 'Shardlake, I know

that name.' He grinned. 'You're the Lincoln's Inn man the King made mock of at York a couple of years ago, aren't you? I recognize the description.'

Of a hunchback, I thought. That story would haunt me, I knew, till I died. 'We need to find out who Roger was meeting,' I said coldly.

Browne looked down at Roger's face, then he stirred the awful head with his toe. I clenched my hands with anger. 'This is a dreadful business,' he went on. 'Putting him in the fountain. He looks very calm. Couldn't have cut his own throat, could he?'

'No. He was a happy man.'

'Then it's a strange one.' He shook his head. 'A fountain turned to blood.' He addressed the Treasurer. 'You should get that drained.'

I frowned. That phrase, a fountain turned to blood. I had heard it before somewhere, I was sure.

'Where's this man of yours who went to follow the prints?' Browne asked.

'I don't know. He set off half an hour ago.'

'Well, have him report to me when he comes back. I shall have to visit the King's coroner before impanelling a jury.' I recalled that the King was at Whitehall now, and cursed the fact. Any murder within twelve miles of the royal residence and outside the City of London boundary – even just outside, like Lincoln's Inn – came under the authority of the King's coroner. He would have to be involved along with Browne.

'That will cause delay,' I said.

Browne shrugged. 'Can't be helped.'

'How long will it take to impanel a jury?'

'Depends if the King's coroner agrees to impanel a jury of lawyers. And it's Easter Sunday. Doubt we'll get an inquest before the middle of the week.'

I set my lips. It was vital in any murder to investigate at once, before the trail went cold. As Barak had said, most murders were solved quickly or not at all.

'I think the lawyers of the Inn will want the inquest to be held as soon as possible,' I said. 'As one of their own is involved.'

Treasurer Rowland nodded in agreement. 'Yes, we shall want an inquest soon.'

'We need to hunt this solicitor Nantwich. Could you do that, sir – just a general query under the Treasurer's authority?'

Rowland nodded. 'Yes. That must be done.'

'And if I may suggest something else,' I said to the coroner, pressing home my advantage. 'The manner of his death is so strange, apparently knocked unconscious and kept that way till he was put in the fountain, it might be good to have the body opened.' It was a grim thought, but Guy might find something that would help us. 'I know Dr Malton, who does that duty for the London coroner. His fees are low. I could send him to you.'

'Oh, that old Moor.' Browne grunted. 'And who's to pay?'

'I will, if need be. Roger Elliard was my friend. And could I please ask' – my voice rising – 'to have him covered up?'

'All right.' The coroner casually pulled my coat back over Roger's face, then turned to me, rubbing his pudgy hands together.

'What was the deceased's name again?'

'Roger Elliard.'

'Right. I'll see the widow. That body can be taken away now. Master treasurer, have a cart take it to my shed.'

✟

DOROTHY HAD somewhat recovered her composure when old Elias, dressed now but stricken-faced, led us to her parlour. She sat by the fire, staring into it as she held the maid Margaret's hand.

'Dorothy,' I said gently. 'This is Coroner Browne. He would ask you some questions, if you feel able.'

The coroner looked at the frieze above the fireplace, the carved animals peering through the branches. 'My, that is a fine thing,' he said.

Dorothy stared at it. 'A piece got broken off when we moved back here,' she said dully. 'Roger got it replaced but it was badly done.' I noticed a corner of the frieze was rather poorly executed, a slightly different colour.

'It is still fine,' Browne said, clumsily trying to put Dorothy at her ease. 'May I sit?'

Dorothy waved him to the chair where I had sat. He repeated the questions about the *pro bono* client, and asked about Roger's recent movements, in which nothing else unusual was revealed. I saw the coroner was not taking notes, which worried me. He did not look like a man with great powers of memory.

'Had your husband any enemies?' Browne asked.

'None. He had barristers he did not like particularly, whom he had won or lost against in court. But that is true of every barrister in London, and they do not murder their fellows in' – her voice faltered – 'this ghastly, wicked way.'

'And no question he could have done it himself?'

The bluntness of the question appalled me, but it brought out the best in Dorothy. 'No, master coroner, none at all. Anyone would tell you the idea he did this to himself is nonsensical. I wish you had had the grace to talk to others before baldly asking me if my husband might have cut his own throat.' I felt admiration for her; her spirit was returning.

Browne reddened. He rose from his chair. 'Very well,' he said stiffly. 'That will do for now. I must go to the palace, see the King's coroner.'

He bowed to us stiffly, then left. His heavy footsteps clumped slowly down the stairs.

'Old fat fustilugs!' Margaret said warmly.

Dorothy looked up at me. Her red-rimmed eyes were despairing. 'He does not seem to care,' she said. 'My poor Roger.'

'This is just one more job to him,' I said. 'But I promise you, I will be at his heels.'

'Thank you.' She laid a hand on my arm.

'And now I will go down to Roger's chambers. I will take on what work of his I can. If you wish.'

'Yes, please. Oh, and someone must write to our son. Tell Samuel.' Her eyes filled with tears again.

'Would you like me to?' I asked gently.

'I should not ask. I—'

'No. I will do all I can, Dorothy. For you. For Roger.'

☦

OUTSIDE, TO MY RELIEF, I saw Barak watching as Roger's body was loaded on to a cart, my coat wrapped round it. He looked downcast. I saw he was carrying a dark coat that I recognized.

'You found Roger's coat?'

'Yes. In the orchard. I thought it must be his, from the size.'

I shivered, missing my own coat. 'Did you follow the prints?'

'As far as I could. They led through the orchard into Lincoln's Inn Fields, but the snow there was pretty well gone.'

'Was there anything in the pockets?'

'A set of house keys. The killer must have kept the key to the orchard. And his purse, he left his purse, with near two pounds in it.'

'Were there any papers? Any notes?'

'Nothing.'

'He went to meet a new client at an inn in Wych Lane last night.'

Barak looked over at the wall. 'Taken somewhere in Lincoln's Inn Fields, then. That's a hell of a way to haul a body.' He looked at me, frowning. 'What on earth is going on?'

Chapter Seven

TWO DAYS LATER, on the Tuesday after Easter, Barak and I walked down to the river to catch a boat to Westminster. I had on a new coat; I had left my old coat with the coroner; stained as it was with Roger's blood, I could never wear it again. I had a busy day ahead, five poor men's pleas to be heard before the Master of Requests. I hoped I would also get a date for hearing Adam Kite's application.

The morning had a real touch of spring at last, the breeze gentle and moist. Normally that would have lifted my spirits; but not with what lay on my heart now. As we crossed Fleet Street on our way down to Temple Bar, we saw a penitent heretic being led along to St Paul's. He was dressed in a grey smock and carried a faggot of birch twigs in trembling hands. Ashes had been tipped over his head and shoulders, turning his hair and face grey. A rope was round his neck, and he was led along by one of Bishop Bonner's men. Three halberdiers followed, wearing swords, the little procession led by a man beating a drum. Passers-by stopped, some jeering and others looking serious. Someone called, 'Courage, brother!' and the soldiers looked round angrily. I was taken aback to see that the tethered man was the wild preacher from Newgate market; he must have been taken for unlicensed preaching. He would be brought to St Paul's Cross where Bonner would preach to him of the evils of heresy. If he were caught again he could burn.

The ice had quite gone from the river now, which was high, the grey water flowing rapidly. The wherrymen had had a hard winter, as always when the river froze, and the man at the oars of the boat we took at Temple Stairs had a pinched, hungry look. I told him to make for Westminster.

'The stairs there are broken, sir. The ice has crushed the supports, they'll have to be replaced.'

'Whitehall Stairs, then,' I said with a sigh, not relishing a walk through the Westminster crowds. The man pulled out. I sat staring over the river. I had spent much of the previous day looking through Roger's cases and giving instructions to his clerk. Then I had written a letter to young Samuel Elliard in Bristol. When I went up to see his mother again in the evening, I found she had retreated into herself and sat staring into the fire, her maid holding her hand. At length she was persuaded away to bed.

''Eard about those great fish?' the wherryman asked, interrupting my sad thoughts.

'What? Oh, yes.'

'Just bobbed up from under the ice. Almost as big as houses they are.' He nodded and smiled. 'I've seen 'em.'

'What are they like?' Barak asked curiously

'Grey, with huge heads full of the strangest teeth you ever saw. They're starting to stink now. They're cutting them open to get the fish oil, though some say they're cursed. My vicar claims they are the Leviathan, the great monster from the deep whose appearance portends the Second Coming.'

'Maybe they're whales,' I said. 'A kind of giant fish that lives in the deep sea. Fishermen speak of them.'

'This ain't the deep sea, sir. And they're bigger than any fish could be. Giant heads they've got. I've seen them, like half London.'

The boat pulled up at Whitehall Stairs. We walked under the Holbein Gate and down into King Street. I kept a hand on my purse, for Westminster was as disorderly a place as could be found in England. Ahead of us loomed the vast bulk of Westminster Abbey, dwarfing even its neighbour, Westminster Hall, where most of the courts sat. Behind Westminster Hall lay a warren of buildings, those which had survived the fire a generation ago that destroyed much of the old Westminster Palace. The House of Commons met in the Painted Chamber there, and the Court of Requests was near by.

Around Westminster Hall and the abbey was a chaos of buildings, shops, inns and taverns, serving the lawyers and churchmen and MPs who came to Westminster. Pedlars, hucksters and prostitutes always thronged the streets, and the presence of the Sanctuary at Westminster had long drawn rogues to the area. Westminster's government was chaotic, for the requests of rich citizens to have it incorporated as a city had always been rejected, and now that the abbey had been dissolved, the old secular powers of the abbot had gone.

✝

PARLIAMENT WAS in session, and King Street was even more crowded and colourful than usual. Shops and houses were set higgledy-piggledy along the road, the large houses of rich traders with their overhanging top stories next to run-down hovels. The street stank of the many tanneries and of the brickworks on the outskirts. I remembered the complaints the judges had made last year, that during their robed annual procession to Westminster Hall they had had to squeeze their way past sheep and cattle being led to the market.

We jostled our way down to Palace Yard, past shopkeepers calling their wares. There were innumerable pedlars, some calling from donkey carts, others with trays of cheap, skimble-skamble stuff round their necks. Barak waved them off if they approached. I saw a gang of ragged but muscular young men watching as a haughty-looking middle-aged man dressed in a long sable-lined coat and a fine doublet slashed to show the silk lining, walked slowly along. An MP up from the country, probably, who knew no better than to parade his wealth in King Street. Had it been after dark, I would not have given much for his chances.

'The inquest is tomorrow,' I told Barak. I had a message first thing. 'I am sorry, I forgot to tell you.'

'Will I need to be there?'

'Yes. Dorothy too, poor woman. It will be terrible for her. They were devoted.'

'Will she be up to the inquest?'

'I hope so. She is strong. I went in to see her first thing. She is still very quiet, white as a sheet.' I bit my lip. 'I hope the pamphleteers do not get hold of the story and start spreading it round the city.'

'They would love it.'

'I know. God's death, that coroner Browne is useless. The inquest should have been yesterday. The killer could be in another county by now.' I shook my head. 'I am taking it on myself to visit Guy later, see what he has found about the state of the body.'

A ragged pedlar with a tray of cheap trinkets round his neck stepped into my path. 'Rings and brooches, sir, for your lady, straight from Venice—' I sidestepped him. We were almost at New Palace Yard now; the great gate that led to Westminster Abbey precinct was just ahead. The crowds were thicker and as I walked under the gate I almost tripped over a card sharper sitting beside it with his marked cards, calling people to try their luck. We passed into Westminster Yard, the wide space already busy with lawyers. The big clock tower showed half past nine. We were in time, almost.

'Tammy says you called in a few nights ago,' Barak said. 'Came to visit us.'

So she had told him. Was that to pressure me into speaking to him? This was not the time. I made my voice light. 'I passed the Old Barge on the way home from Guy's. That tenement of yours is very damp.'

He shrugged, looked sullen. 'I'd have moved if the baby lived. But it didn't.'

'Tamasin seemed a little – downcast.'

'She should get over the baby, I've had to.' His voice went hard. 'She's full of womanish weakness. I don't know where her old spirit's gone.' He did not meet my eyes as he spoke, which was rare for him. I saw that the domed fountain in the centre of the yard, frozen through the winter, was working again, water splashing merrily. I remembered the fountain at Lincoln's Inn, and closed my eyes for a moment.

✝

THE WHITE HALL was a small chamber. A crowded little entrance hall was set with benches along the walls. There plaintiffs sat huddled, watching the lawyers talking in the body of the hall. Poor folk from all over the country came to have their suits pleaded here, by me and my fellow state-funded barrister, and many wore the homespun clothes of country gruffs. Most seemed overwhelmed to find themselves among these great old buildings, though some had determined expressions. I saw my first client sitting there: Gib Rooke, a short stocky man in his thirties with a square face. He wore a red surcoat, far too gaudy for court. He was frowning at two men who stood talking in the body of the hall. One was a tall, expensively dressed man; the other, to my surprise, was Bealknap. I saw that my old rival looked gaunt in his black gown as he fiddled with some papers in his knapsack. The tall man did not look pleased with him.

'How now, Gib,' Barak said, sitting beside Rooke. 'You're richly dressed for it.'

Rooke nodded to Barak, then looked up at me. 'Good day, Master Shardlake. Ready for the fight?'

I gave him a stern look. Having their own barrister went to some of my clients' heads, and they would take the chance to strut and mock; to their own detriment, for the courts demand sober respect. 'I am ready,' I said. 'We have a good case. If we lose, it may be because the court judges you insolent. So watch your words in there. Dressing like a peacock is a bad start.'

Gib reddened. He was one of the many cottars who had set up market gardens on the Lambeth marshes across the river over the last fifteen years; the growth of London meant an endless demand for food in the city. Draining patches of empty bogland, the cottars squatted there without permission from the owners, who had never developed the land and might live far away. Recently, however, the landlords had realized there were profits to be made, and sought to use the manor courts to turn the cottars out and reap the benefits of their work. Gib had applied to Requests against eviction, citing ancient laws, for which I had been able to find rather shadowy precedents, that if a man occupied land under two acres in extent for a dozen years unchallenged, he could remain.

Gib nodded at Bealknap. 'That old swine Sir Geoffrey seems unhappy with his lawyer.'

'I know Bealknap. Don't underestimate him.' And, in truth, he was a clever lawyer. Today, though, he seemed to have a problem with his papers; he was searching frantically through his bag now. Raising his head briefly and seeing me, he whispered to his client, Gib's landlord, and they moved away.

I sat on the other side of Gib. He looked at me, eyes greedy with curiosity. 'They say there's been a terrible murder at Lincoln's Inn,' he said. 'A lawyer found in the fountain with his throat cut. On Easter Sunday.'

It was as I had feared, the story was spreading. 'The killer will be rooted out,' I said.

Gib shook his head. 'They say they don't know who it is. What a way to kill someone. Ah well, 'tis the times.'

'I suppose you mean signs and portents,' I said wearily, remembering the boatman.

Gib shrugged. 'I don't know about that. But there have been some nasty killings lately. One of the marsh cottars was found murdered horribly in January. That was another strange one. I wouldn't be surprised if his landlord killed him,' he added loudly. People turned to look.

'If you don't control your mouth you'll lose this case,' I snapped at him.

'Here's trouble,' Barak whispered. Bealknap had left his client and come over to us.

'May I speak with you, Brother Shardlake?' he asked. I noticed he was sweating, though the unheated hall was cold.

I stood. 'Very well.'

We stepped away a few paces. 'Your client should not make

insulting remarks about landlords in the precincts of the court,' he said pompously.

I raised my eyebrows. 'Is that all you have to say?'

'No – no . . .' Bealknap hesitated, bit his lip, then took a deep breath. 'There is a problem, Brother Shardlake. I have not filed my client's title to the land.'

I stared at him, astonished. The most routine piece of a lawyer's work was to ensure the paperwork was properly filed in court. Many were the stories of junior barristers who failed to get their proper paperwork in on time and found their cases thrown out. But Bealknap had been a lawyer twenty years. For once he actually looked straight at me with his light blue eyes. I saw panic there. 'Assist me, Brother Shardlake,' he whispered desperately. 'Assist a fellow-lawyer. Get the case adjourned. I can file the deeds then.'

'If you file them now the judge might hear you. The plaints office is open.'

'I have *lost* them,' Bealknap said, a sudden frantic blurt. 'I appeal to you, Shardlake. I was going to bring them today, I thought they were in my bag. I have been ill! Dr Archer has purged me again and all last night my arse was in a bloody sweat—'

Many lawyers would have helped him for the sake of the fellowship of the bar; but I had always set my face against such arrangements at a client's expense.

'I am sorry, Bealknap,' I said quietly. 'My duty is to my client.'

Bealknap let out a sound between a sigh and a groan. Then he leaned forward, almost hissing. 'I knew you would not help me, you – you bent-backed toad. I won't forget this!'

I saw his client, standing a little way off, eyeing Bealknap curiously. Without a word I turned and went back to Barak and Gib Rooke.

'What was that about?' Barak asked. 'He looked ready to fly at you.'

'He hasn't filed proof of title. He's lost the deeds somewhere.'

Barak whistled. 'Then he's in the shit.' I set my lips. Bealknap's insult only strengthened my determination to stand by Gib Rooke, who for all his bravado was a mere child in the face of the law.

'What?' he asked eagerly. 'What's happened?'

I explained. 'If he'd make a clean breast of it, the judge might agree an adjournment if he's in a good mood. But Bealknap will lie and fudge.'

'Sir Geoffrey's done for, then?'

'He may be.'

Bealknap was crouched on the floor now, looking through his pannier again, frantically, hopelessly. His arms were shaking as he rifled through the bag. Then the usher appeared in the doorway of the courtroom.

'Let all who have business before His Majesty's Court of Requests step forward . . .'

Bealknap looked at him in despair. Then he rose and joined the crowd as everyone stepped forward into the old white-painted hall with its high dirty windows, the judge on his bench in his scarlet robes the only splash of colour.

✟

SIR STEPHEN AINSWORTH, Judge of Requests, was fair but sharp-tongued. As soon as he came to our case he said the court record was incomplete. As I had expected, Bealknap rose and said he had filed the deeds but the court clerk must have lost them, asking quickly for an adjournment.

'Where is your receipt for the deeds?' Ainsworth asked.

'I left it with my clerk, but he has the key to the office and has not arrived. I had to leave early to get here, the Westminster stairs being down—' I had to give Bealknap credit for quick thinking. But Ainsworth turned to the usher.

'Have the Clerk of Requests brought here,' he said.

Bealknap looked ready to collapse as the clerk was brought and confirmed the deeds had never been lodged. 'I suspect you lied to me there, Brother Bealknap,' Ainsworth said coldly. 'Be very careful, sir. Your client's claim against Gilbert Rooke is dismissed for lack of title. Goodman Rooke, you may remain on your land. You have been lucky.'

Gib grinned from ear to ear. Bealknap sat down, his face grey. His client leaned close and began whispering fiercely, his face furious. I caught the gleam of white teeth, brown wood above. Another who had taken to false teeth.

'Brother Shardlake,' Ainsworth continued. 'I am told you have filed an application in the case of a boy sent to the Bedlam by the Privy Council.'

'Yes, your honour.'

He tapped his quill on his table, frowning thoughtfully. 'Do I have the jurisdiction to hear this?'

'The issue, your honour, is that no enquiry has been made into the boy's state of mental health. That should be done before a person is deprived of their freedom. It is a matter of due process.' I took a deep breath. 'I propose to get a doctor to examine him, sir. But in the meantime, if you will consent to hear the matter, there is also the issue of who should pay the fees they charge in the Bedlam, and of the need to report on his progress. The boy's parents are poor.'

'Those at least I can deal with. Very well, the court will set an early date for a hearing. But, Master Shardlake – ' He looked at me seriously. 'These are deep waters. Politics and madness.'

'I know, your honour.'

'Tread carefully, for your client's sake as well as your own.'

✝

GIB WAS delighted at the result; his arrogance had gone and he was tearful with relief. He promised me undying gratitude and almost danced from the courtroom. The cases continued; it was a good day for me, I won all the cases I had listed. The court rose at four thirty, and as the day's victors and vanquished walked away, I stood on the steps with Barak.

'Bealknap looked sick,' I said.

'Sicker still after his case was thrown out.'

'He has always been such a crafty rogue, but today he was pitiable. He will be a greater enemy than ever now.'

We looked across the quadrangle to the Painted Hall, where the Commons of Parliament were sitting. Candles had been lit, yellow flashes of light visible through the high windows. Barak grunted.

'They say every bill the King has put before them is being passed this session.' He spat on the ground. 'Those members not in the King's pocket already can be bought off with bribes and threats.'

I was silent, for I could not disagree.

'Adam Kite's folks will be pleased he has a hearing,' he said.

'Yes. Judge Ainsworth was nervous of taking on the Council, but he is an honest man. That reminds me, I did not tell you, I saw Lord Latimer's funeral passing the day I went to the Bedlam. I saw the Lady Catherine Parr, or at the least I think it was her. She was in a big carriage.'

'What was she like?' Barak asked curiously.

'Not a great beauty. But something arresting about her. I thought she looked frightened.'

'Afraid to say yes to the King, perhaps, and afraid to say no.'

I nodded sadly, for the woman's fear had impressed itself on me.

'Well,' I said. 'I must catch a boat to Guy's, learn what he has found. Will you go to Lincoln's Inn and draw the orders for today's cases? And write to the Kites, asking them to come and see me tomorrow?'

We walked back to Whitehall Stairs. A row of brightly made up whores had taken places by the gate into New Palace Yard, standing in a row to catch the eye of the MPs walking past when the house rose. As I passed two bent forward to show me ample cleavages.

'They're bold,' I said. 'They'll be whipped at the cart's tail if the authorities catch them.'

'That won't happen.' Barak smiled wickedly. 'The MPs would

object. The chance of a bit of sport in the stewhouses is all that makes those long debates worthwhile for some.'

'Maybe that is why they are granting all the King wants so quickly.'

☦

IT WAS DARK by the time I arrived at Guy's. His shop was closed, but he answered my knock. He invited me gravely to sit down. He sat opposite me in the consulting room, clasped his hands together and looked at me seriously. The candlelight emphasized the lines in his dark face.

'How is poor Mistress Elliard?' he asked.

'Distraught. We are no further forward in investigating Roger's murder. We can find no solicitor by the name of Nantwich, which was the name in the letters Roger was sent. It begins to look as though the killer sent them.'

'And you? You look strained, Matthew. And recently you have seemed so well. You are still doing your back exercises?'

'Yes. I cope, Guy. I always cope.' I took a deep breath. 'And I will try to have the stomach for whatever you have to tell me of your investigation of Roger's body. But the less detail the better, please.'

'I visited the place where the body is stored this morning. I took Piers—'

I frowned. The idea of Guy opening Roger, examining his innards, was horrible enough. But a stranger, a mere boy . . .

'I am training him, Matthew. The licence I have to open bodies offers a unique chance to study human anatomy. He may be able to use it to help others in the future.'

I still did not like the notion. 'What did you find?' I asked.

'So far as I could see, Master Elliard's health at the time of his death was good.'

'It always was. Till someone knocked him out and cut his throat.'

'I don't think he was knocked out,' Guy said in the same grave, even tones. 'Not as we understand that phrase.'

I looked at him, appalled. 'You mean he was *conscious* when he went in there?'

'Not that either. Have you ever heard of dwale?'

I shook my head.

'There is no reason you should. It is a liquid compound of opium and certain other elements, such as vinegar and pig's bile, which induces unconsciousness. Depending on how much is used it can bring relaxation, unconsciousness – or death. It has been used on and off for hundreds of years to render people unconscious before surgery.'

'Then why have I never heard of it? That would save terrible pain.'

He shook his head. 'There is a severe problem with it. The correct dose is very hard to determine, very hard indeed. It depends on many factors: the age of the ingredients, the size and age and health of the patient. It is very easy to give the patient too much and then the physician is left with a corpse. For that reason very few use it now. But I think Master Elliard's killer did.'

'Why?'

'Let me show you something.' He left the room, returning a moment later. I feared what dreadful thing he might return with, but it was only one of Roger's boots. He laid it across his knee and brought the candle to it, illuminating a large dark stain.

'This boot was dry, it must have been on the leg that was sticking out of the water. When I saw that stain I smelt it, then put my finger to it and tasted. The taste of dwale is quite distinctive.' He looked at me. 'The first stage after it is taken is nearly always a sense of euphoria, then unconsciousness. That explains your poor friend's peaceful look.'

'You said it is out of use now. So who *would* use it?'

'Very few physicians or surgeons, because of the risks. Some of the unlicensed healers.' He hesitated. 'And there was a tradition of its use in certain monasteries.'

There was a moment's silence. Then I said, 'You used it, didn't you?'

He nodded slowly. 'Only when I thought the shock of severe surgery might kill a patient. And I have a long skill in determining dosages. But though it is not used now, the formula is well known among practitioners. It is no secret.'

'But needs great skill to administer.'

He nodded. 'The killer would not have wanted to give Roger a fatal dose. He meant to make that terrible display in the fountain. Drugged him so he would not wake even when his throat was cut.'

'Did the body tell you anything else?'

'No. The organs were otherwise all healthy. They might have been those of a younger man.'

'You make it sound very impersonal, Guy.'

'I have to be impersonal, Matthew. How else would I cope with the things I see?'

'I cannot be impersonal. Not with this.'

'Then perhaps it should be left to others to investigate.'

'I have given Dorothy a promise. I am committed.'

'Very well.' For a moment Guy's face took on that tired, strained look I had seen when I brought Roger to see him. 'There was one thing, a lump on the back of his head. I think whoever your friend went to meet that night knocked him out. When he came round he was forced – somehow – to drink dwale. He passed out, and the killer brought him to Lincoln's Inn.'

'Across the fields and through the orchard door.' I told him about the footprints Barak had followed. 'Roger was a small man, but this brute must still be very strong.'

'And determined. And vicious.'

I shook my head. 'And an educated man. From what you say he has knowledge of the medical profession and perhaps the legal world too, if he could fake a letter from a solicitor well enough to take Roger in, which it seems likely he did. But why? Why kill a man who has harmed no one, and leave that terrible spectacle?'

'He had no enemies?'

'None.' I looked at Roger's boot again, and suddenly it was all too much. My stomach lurched violently.

'Your privy, Guy—' I gasped.

'You know the way.'

I went to the privy at the rear of the house, the usual wooden shack over a cesspit, yet less noisome than most, something scented in the air to minimize the stinks. There I was violently sick. As I walked back to the house I felt weak, my legs shaking.

Low voices came from the consulting room. The door was open and I saw Guy and the boy Piers sitting close together at the table. They had brought the candle over and were looking, rapt, at an open book. I recognized Vesalius' horribly illustrated anatomy book. Piers brushed a lick of dark hair from his face and pointed to the drawing. 'See,' he said eagerly. 'That illustration is just like Elliard's heart.' Piers broke off suddenly, his face reddening, as he saw me. 'Master Shardlake! I – I did not know you were still here. I brought in the book—'

'I saw,' I said curtly. 'Poor Roger. I wonder what he would have thought if he knew the intimate details of his body would become chatter for apprentices. Well, perhaps he would have been amused, though I cannot say I am.' I looked with distaste at the picture, a human abdomen torn open, all the organs exposed.

''Tis only to gain better knowledge, sir,' Piers mumbled. I gave him a cold look, thinking Guy gave him far too much latitude.

'No, Piers, it was my fault.' Guy for once looked discomfited.

'You will be giving evidence at the inquest tomorrow morning?' I asked him.

'Yes. Of course.'

'And Adam? Do you know when you may be able to visit him? I ought to come too. The court is not sitting on Friday morning, if that would be convenient for you.'

He brought a little leather-bound notebook from his pocket and studied it. 'Yes, Friday at noon?'

'Then I will leave you,' I said, with an angry glance at the book, which still lay open on the desk, and at Piers, who still stood quietly at his master's side. Guy raised a hand.

'No, Matthew, stay, please.' I hesitated. Guy closed the Vesalius book and handed it up to Piers. 'Take it out, my boy, and bring some wine. Then continue studying the book if you wish.'

'Yes, sir.'

Guy patted Piers' shoulder in an affectionate gesture, and he left the room. 'I am so sorry, Matthew,' he said. 'We meant no disrespect to Roger Elliard. It is just – the implications of Vesalius for the practice of medicine are so great – but Matthew, even as I investigated how your friend died, as you asked me to do, I prayed for his departed soul.'

I smiled. I knew Guy too well, knew his goodness, to be angry for long. 'Is Vesalius so very remarkable, then?' I asked.

'Oh yes, yes. It is a change of approach that is much needed, study based on observation, not merely acceptance of blind doc-trine.'

'It will not be popular among physicians, then.'

'No. It challenges their monopoly of arcane knowledge. And who knows where it may end?' He looked at the chart on his wall. 'The very doctrine of the humours itself could be challenged and tested.'

I followed his gaze to the chart, with its complex equations and symbols. The notion that the human body was composed of four humours, black bile, yellow bile, phlegm and blood, corresponding to the four elements of earth, fire, water and air that made up everything in the world, was so universally accepted I could not imagine it ever being challenged: nor the doctrine that every human ailment was caused by imbalances between the four elements in the individual body. I remembered discussing our respective humours with Roger, on the last evening I saw him.

'Then I will not be recommended to eat salad when I am low in spirits,' I said. 'To moisten the dryness of black bile. That would be a relief.'

Guy smiled sadly. 'I would rather recommend attending a musical evening, or a long walk over Lincoln's Inn Fields.'

'Not Lincoln's Inn Fields, Guy. It seems that was probably where Roger met his assailant.'

Piers knocked at the door and brought in a large jug of wine and two glasses. When he had gone I said, 'I have promised Dorothy to find the killer, but I do not know how he can be caught.'

'You have resolved such matters before, as I know better than anyone. You underestimate yourself. I know that too.'

'I would be a fool to underestimate the difficulties of this case. And because of Easter and the wretched politics of the coroner's offices, the inquest will be four days after the murder. Four days with no official investigation. I thought the royal coroner might hurry things up, but he has not. Ten to one the murderer is out of London now; though for all the chance we have of finding him he could still be in the city, laughing at the coroners and the constables and their stupidity.' I shook my head.

'If he is an educated man, that must limit the numbers. You know as well as I that both the law and medicine are closed worlds, their practitioners seeking to keep their secrets to themselves.'

'Perhaps. But many of our class have some knowledge of both. Though the knowledge of dwale is unusual.'

'And how to administer it. Wait until the inquest tomorrow, see if anything more is revealed.'

I nodded, took a drink of wine from my cup. I saw that Guy had finished his already, which surprised me for he was a believer in moderation in all things.

'Thank you for taking on Adam Kite,' I said.

He nodded slowly. 'Salvation panic. A strange obsession. How prone people are to become fixated on ideas, or religion, or people. And of course fanatic religion is everywhere. Perhaps the surprise is there are not more people like Adam.' He turned his cup in his hand pensively.

'A wherryman told me today that those huge fish they found in the river are the Leviathans, and foretell the second coming of Christ, the end of the world.'

Guy shook his head. 'There was only one Leviathan.'

'So I thought.'

'It has become a world of black and white, Matthew, a Manichean world where preachers encourage everyone to rush towards a conflict between good and evil. Each knowing, of course, that their own side is entirely in the right.'

I smiled, inclined my head. 'Protestants and Catholics alike?'

'Yes. Do not forget my parents were *moriscos*, Moorish Spaniards made to leave Spain by the Inquisition. I too have seen the wildness that follows when fanatics without self-doubt gain power.' He looked at me gravely. 'But mark this. Whatever wrongs it has done, the Catholic Church has always believed in free will, that men by their actions as well as their faith may choose to come to God. This new Protestant radicalism will not allow for that, everyone is either saved or damned through God's will, not free will. They may pray to be saved once and for all, may feel they are saved once and for all, but for them it is God's decision, not man's. And so we have Adam Kite, who thinks that God will not have him.'

'And his wretched vicar, because he cannot cure him, believes he is possessed.'

'It is a way of explaining failure.'

'I never supported Luther on predestination, Guy. I was on Erasmus' side in their debate on free will.' I looked at him seriously. 'I saw a nonlicensed preacher taken to St Paul's in sackcloth and ashes this morning. Bonner is going to crack down on the Protestants, and they will not take it quietly. It is not going to be a good time for outsiders.'

'Yes, you are right. With my dark face and monkish past, I am best to keep quiet and stay indoors when I can. And not talk too widely about the discoveries of Vesalius, still less this Polish scholar who says the earth goes round the sun. But what peace of mind is there even at home?' he added, so quietly I barely heard him. His face was suddenly full of pain and sadness.

'Are you all right, Guy?' I asked quietly. 'Have you some trouble of your own?'

'No.' He smiled. 'Only the aches and pains of old age. And I have had enough of wine and should go to bed.' He rose. 'Good-night.'

'I shall tell Adam Kite's parents you will see them. They will be relieved.'

We shook hands and I left. I was glad we had parted on good terms after all. But I did not believe him when he said nothing was wrong.

Chapter Eight

NEXT MORNING I went to fetch Dorothy to accompany her to the inquest. She had not been out of doors since Roger's death, and I was worried about how she would cope. Crossing Gatehouse Court I saw that as at Westminster the fountain's underground valve had been turned and the water had come on; it splashed merrily into the huge bowl. The weather was still mild, the birds chirking in the trees. The world of nature was being reborn, though I could take no pleasure in it.

Dorothy sat in her chair by the fire, the faithful Margaret beside her. Both were dressed in deepest black and wore coifs with long black wings behind, the pale oval of Dorothy's face staring out starkly. I was reminded of that other mourner I had recently seen, Catherine Parr. Dorothy gave me a brave smile.

'Is it time? Yes. I see from your expression that it is.' She sighed, looking at the frieze above the fireplace. I followed her gaze. A weasel looked out at me from between thick wooden vines. 'How lifelike that is,' I said.

'Ay, Roger was so fond of it. He was displeased with the repair of that corner after it was damaged.'

'Are you sure you can bear this?' I asked, looking at her white face and sunken cheeks.

'Yes,' she said with a touch of her old firmness. 'I must see Roger's killer caught.'

'I will do the identification of the body, if you wish.'

'Thank you. That — that might be too much.'

'We shall take the boat to the Guildhall.'

'Good.' She hesitated, then asked suddenly, 'What are they saying, in the streets?'

'Just that there was a nasty murder here.'

'If I hear anyone speak badly of Roger I shall fly at them.'

'That's the way, mistress,' Margaret said approvingly. She helped Dorothy rise to her feet.

✝

THE GREAT PILLARED vestibule of the London Guildhall was as busy as usual. Unusually, a pair of constables in city livery were posted by the door. Within, council and guild officials scuttled to and fro. Some glanced curiously at a large group of black-robed lawyers gathered in a corner. I recognized the stern face of Treasurer Rowland; the others were all Lincoln's Inn barristers – the jury. I was surprised that apart from Treasurer Rowland they were all very young; there was no one else there of any seniority. Some looked distinctly uneasy, as did the two students who had found the body and who stood on the fringe of the group. Guy stood a little apart, talking to Barak.

Dorothy looked at the crowd, hesitated, then moved to a bench by the wall. She sat, signalling Margaret to join her. 'We will wait here until the court opens,' she told me. 'I cannot face talking to anyone.'

'Very well.'

I crossed to Barak and Guy. 'Good day, Matthew,' Guy said. He looked across at Dorothy. 'Is that the poor widow? She is very pale.'

'It has cost her much to come today. But she is brave.'

'Yes, one senses strength beneath her suffering.' He nodded at Barak. 'Jack here has noticed something strange.'

'What?'

Barak looked red-eyed, a little bilious. Had he had yet another night in the taverns? He leaned close; his breath was sour.

'A spectacular death like this,' he said, 'you'd think there'd be a crowd here to fill the public gallery. But those constables are turning folk away.'

'Really?' That would be good for Dorothy, but it was unheard of; the coroner's court, like all jury courts, was supposed to be public.

'Brother Shardlake, a word.' Treasurer Rowland appeared at my elbow. I followed him away from the group.

'My clerk tells me no spectators have been allowed in,' I said.

'The usher says the coroners have decided the hearing is to be private, to prevent idle babble. I have never heard of such a thing.'

We were interrupted by a black-robed usher calling from a doorway. I went back to Dorothy. She rose to her feet; lips set, a spot of red in each cheek. 'Take my hand, Margaret,' she said quietly. The jurors parted to let her enter the courtroom.

✟

WE HAD BEEN GIVEN one of the meeting rooms. Rows of benches faced the table where the two coroners already sat. The usher guided me, along with the other witnesses, to the front row and the jurors took the two rows behind. The rows where the public would have sat were empty. I studied the two coroners sitting at the table facing us. Browne slouched with his plump hands folded across his ample stomach. Next to him sat a very different man: in his early forties, short but strongly made, with a square face. Thick brown hair curled beneath his black cap and he had a short, neat beard just starting to go grey. He met my look; the gaze from his bright blue eyes was sharp, appraising.

'That's Sir Gregory Harsnet,' Barak whispered. 'The King's assistant coroner. He used to be in Lord Cromwell's camp, he's one of the few reformers who's kept his place.'

Browne let out a little belch; Harsnet frowned at him and he turned another belch into a cough and sat up straight. No doubt who was master here. The doors were closed.

'We will come to order, please.' Harsnet spoke in a clear, quiet voice with a west country accent, his eyes roving round the room. 'We are here today to adjudicate on the sudden and dreadful death of Roger Elliard, barrister of Lincoln's Inn. As the jurors are all lawyers

I do not need to tell you that today we shall view the body, hear the evidence and decide whether we can come to a verdict.'

The jury was sworn in, the young barristers stepping up to take the Testament from the usher. Then Harsnet addressed us again.

'Before we view the body I would call Dr Guy Malton, who has been charged with examining it, to tell us what he found.'

Guy stood and recited his impressive medical qualifications, the jurors staring curiously at his brown skin. He spoke of how he believed Roger had been rendered unconscious using the drug called dwale, then carried to the fountain where his throat had been cut.

'He was alive when he went in,' he said. 'He died from a massive loss of blood, not drowning. That means' – he hesitated – 'that means his throat was cut, then he was held over the fountain until he died, and then was thrown in.'

There was silence in the courtroom for a moment, as the full horror of the scene Guy described sank in. Then Harsnet asked, 'How long was he dead before he was found?'

'Some hours. Rigor mortis would be delayed by the cold.' He looked at me. 'And I believe a skin of ice had had time to re-form on the fountain.'

'It had,' I said.

I glanced across Barak to Dorothy, who sat with Margaret on Guy's other side. She was quite still, her face expressionless. She seemed smaller somehow, as though shrinking into those heavy black clothes.

Harsnet frowned at Guy. 'What object could anyone have in creating such a terrible spectacle? A man dead in a fountain of blood.'

Guy spread his hands. 'I cannot say.' Again I thought, that phrase is familiar. A fountain of blood. But from where?

'A ghastly thing.' Harsnet shook his head; he looked troubled. He then rose slowly. 'Jurors,' he said quietly, 'you will now accompany me to view the body. Dr Malton, please come too in case there are questions. I see a Brother Shardlake is to identify the body.' He looked at me. 'That is you?'

'Yes, master coroner.'

He gave me a long, considering stare. 'How long did you know the deceased?'

'Twenty years. I wished to spare his widow.'

Harsnet looked at Dorothy. 'Very well,' he said quietly, and rose to lead us out.

✟

THE JURORS HAD little to say when the sheet was drawn back from Roger's corpse. The incense someone had set to burn in the room could not hide the rising smell of decay. I closed my eyes at the sight of Roger's poor face and though I did not pray often now I begged that his killer be caught, that I be given strength to play my part, and that this time at least God might listen to my plea. I opened my eyes to see one or two of the jurors looking green. Guy showed us the terrible wounds, explained the mechanisms of death again. No one had any questions, and we trooped back to the inquest room. Harsnet looked at us seriously.

'What we have to determine today is how Roger Elliard died. Murder, clearly, but by whom? I would like to call Jack Barak.'

He asked Barak a series of questions about the footprints he had followed.

'The footsteps led to the fountain and then went back in the opposite direction.' Barak said. 'He was carrying something on the way in, not on the way back. The snow was melting fast but the impressions were quite clear.'

Harsnet looked at him. 'No ordinary man, surely, could carry an unconscious body as far as you have suggested.'

'A very strong and determined man could.'

'You used to work for Lord Cromwell, I believe?' I wondered, how did Harsnet know that?

'I did. Before I became a law clerk.'

'In what capacity?'

'This and that,' Barak answered cheerfully. 'As my master commanded.'

'Sit down,' Harsnet said coldly, clearly not liking Barak's attitude. Beside him, Coroner Browne gave a little smirk. He was taking no part in the proceedings, his presence evidently a mere formality.

Other witnesses were called: the two boys, then I, to attest to the time and circumstances of the body's discovery, then Treasurer Rowland. Asked about Roger's state of mind, he replied clearly and precisely that he was a happy, cheerful man, respected in the profession, with many friends and no enemies anyone knew of.

'He had one enemy,' Harsnet said. 'A vicious and clever one. This killing was planned, with patience and cunning.' I looked at him. He was no fool. 'Someone hated Roger Elliard,' he continued. He turned to Rowland.

'What about this solicitor who wrote to Master Elliard?'

'Fictitious, sir. No one knows anything of a solicitor with the unusual name of Nantwich. I have made enquiries at all the Inns of Court. As no one else seemed to be doing so,' he added, pointedly glancing at Browne. Harsnet frowned at him, but the crotchety old man was hard as teak and his eyes did not waver.

'If I may remind the court of something?' Guy stood and spoke quietly.

'Yes,' Harsnet snapped. I was puzzled. I could understand the coroner becoming a little annoyed by witnesses who kept speaking up, but Rowland's point was not trivial, and Guy's was unlikely to be.

'Sir, even the most skilled physician would find it hard to gauge the dose of this drug. This man has at least a degree of specialized knowledge.'

'He may have,' Harsnet said. 'But unfortunately that does not take us any further. In a case of savage vengeance such as this, I would expect there to be an obvious culprit, yet there seems to be none. With the delays necessitated by Easter, I find it hard to see how this murderer can be quickly caught.'

I looked at him in surprise. It was not for a coroner to discourage investigation like this. I sensed he was uneasy with what he was saying. Browne gave a slight smirk, as though he had expected this outcome.

'We must be realistic,' Harsnet went on. 'I foresee a verdict of murder by person or persons unknown, and I fear that they may remain unknown.'

I was astonished. This was blatant leading of the jury. Yet none of the young men who had been selected dared speak up.

Then I heard a swish of skirts. Dorothy had risen to her feet and stood facing the King's coroner.

'I have not been asked to speak, sir, but if anyone has that right it is me. I will see my husband's murderer caught, though it costs me all. With the help of faithful friends, I will.' She was shaking from head to toe but her voice, though quiet, cut the air like a knife. With her last words she turned to me. I gave her a vigorous nod. She sat down.

I expected some sort of explosion from Harsnet, but he merely sat with his lips pressed into a narrow line. His face had reddened. Browne was grinning at his discomfiture; I would have liked to rise and wipe that smirk from his froggy face. At length, Harsnet spoke.

'I can make allowances for Mistress Elliard's state of mind, I will not censure her. Perhaps we need more evidence before the jury can deliver a verdict. Therefore I will not ask it to deliver a verdict now; the matter will be left open while I undertake an investigation myself—'

I rose to my feet. 'With the help of the jury, sir, I take it. As is normal?'

'A coroner may investigate without a jury if he feels it appropriate; as I do here. The jurors, like the deceased, are all lawyers. Less heat and more light will be generated if I act alone. Now sit down, sir.'

I sat, but glared at him.

'And now all of you note something, and note it well.' Harsnet looked over the room. He spoke slowly, his accent noticeable. 'I will not have the details of this case hawked around London. There is a royal order going out today banning the printing of any pamphlets on the subject. Everyone here is ordered to keep these matters secret, and discourage those who come to pry, as they will. There is too much loose talk in London now. That is my order, as the King's deputy coroner, and anyone who disobeys it will be punished.' Then he rose, Browne heaving himself to his feet beside him. 'This inquest is adjourned *sine die*. It will be recalled when I have more evidence. Good morning, gentlemen.' The usher opened the door, and the coroners left. There was an immediate babble of talk.

'This has to be the devil's work. Such a dreadful display, on a Sunday. This killer was possessed—'

I stared round at the young fool of a juror who had spoken. Loose talk, indeed.

'His unnatural strength. That is always seen in cases of possession—'

Margaret turned to me. 'We should get my mistress out of here.' And indeed Dorothy looked as though she might faint. I rose and helped Margaret steer her out of the room. Her arm felt light as a bird's; I wondered if she was eating. We led her to a bench and sat her down. Barak and Guy followed. Treasurer Rowland emerged, looking angry. I hoped he might come and offer some words of encouragement to Dorothy but he only gave me a nod and swept away, shoes clicking on the tiles; his concern was with the Inn's reputation and power, not a grieving widow. Turning back to her, I reflected the Inn would want her out of her lodgings before long.

She had closed her eyes, but now she opened them and heaved herself upright. She looked at each of us in turn: me, Margaret, Barak and Guy.

'Thank you for your help, all of you, and for refusing to be swayed from the truth.' She turned to me. 'They won't investigate, will they? They think the killer has got away, and it will be too much trouble.'

'There's something going on. Harsnet wanted the matter kept entirely to himself.'

'Who *is* that man?'

'I know nothing of him.'

'They want it buried,' she said bitterly. 'Don't they?'

'Well . . .'

'Come, Matthew, I was not married to Roger near twenty years without learning a good deal about the law. They want this dropped and forgotten.'

'It looks like it.' I shook my head. 'If we waste more time the killer may never be found.'

'Will you help me, Matthew, please? I am a woman, they will take no notice of me.'

'I give you my word. I will start by talking to Coroner Harsnet. Guy, will you wait with Dorothy?' I sensed she was holding on by her fingertips. He nodded.

'Then come, Barak.'

'You've taken something on there,' Barak said as he followed me to the Guildhall steps. 'Seems to me finding the killer is all she has to hold on to. I don't know what would happen to her if we fail.'

'We will *not* fail,' I said firmly.

Outside in the paved square I saw the black-robed figure of Harsnet. He was talking to a tall, strongly built man in his thirties with a long, copper-coloured beard, richly dressed in a green jerkin with gold piping, a shirt decorated with intricate Spanish lacework showing beneath, and a red cap with a white feather worn at a jaunty angle. The scabbard for the sword he wore at his waist was leather decorated with gold. He carried a heavy coat. Normally I would have hesitated in challenging a royal official in public, especially when he was engaged with a man of obviously high status; but I was fired by anger as seldom before in my life.

The two men turned to us as we approached. The bearded man, whose long face was handsome yet with something harsh about it, turned to Harsnet with a smile. 'He was right,' he said. 'Here he is.'

I looked from one to the other, noticing the younger man was sunburned. 'What do you mean, sir?' I asked. 'I do not understand. Who told you what?'

Harsnet took a deep breath. Close to, he looked strained, burdened. 'I was told you might to be unhappy with the verdict, Brother Shardlake.'

'Told? By whom?'

The young man waved at Barak. 'Get rid of your minion and we'll tell you.'

Barak gave him a nasty look, but I nodded. 'Jack, tell Dorothy I may be some time, she had best go home. I will visit her later. Go back with them.'

He went reluctantly back to the Guildhall. I turned to Harsnet, who eyed me keenly. So did his friend. I began to feel uneasy.

'I dare say you have come to ask why I adjourned the hearing,' Harsnet said quietly.

'Yes.' I took a deep breath. 'It seems you do not want the killer discovered.'

The tall man laughed bitterly. 'Oh, you mistake us there, lawyer.' He spoke in a deep, musical voice. 'There is nothing in this world we want more.'

'Then why . . . ?'

'Because this matter has political implications,' Harsnet said. He glanced round to ensure nobody was in earshot. 'I was told you would contest my decision. By Archbishop Cranmer.'

'What?'

He fixed those keen blue eyes on me. 'Do you truly seek to find Master Elliard's killer, above all else?'

A chill had run down my back at Cranmer's name. Somehow Roger's death was involved with high politics, which I had sworn never to involve myself in again. But then I remembered Roger's brutalized corpse, Dorothy's ravaged face.

'Yes,' I said.

The richly dressed man laughed. 'There, Gregory, he has courage after all.'

'Who are you, sir?' I asked boldly. He frowned at my insolence.

'This is Sir Thomas Seymour,' Harsnet said. 'Brother of the late Queen Jane.'

'So watch your manners, churl,' Seymour growled.

I was lost for words for a moment. 'If you questioned my actions,' Harsnet continued, almost apologetic, 'my instructions were to bring you to Archbishop Cranmer.'

'What is this about?'

'Much more than the death of Master Elliard.' He looked me in the eye. 'Something truly dark and terrible. But come, we have a wherry waiting to go to Lambeth Palace.'

Chapter Nine

ONE OF ARCHBISHOP Cranmer's own boats was waiting for us at Three Cranes Stairs, four oarsmen in the Archbishop's white livery in their places. Harsnet told the men to row fast for Lambeth Palace.

After the thaw the river was thronged with white sails as wherries carried customers to and fro; heavy barges pulled upriver, blowing horns to warn smaller craft out of the way, all under a pale blue sky, the river breeze light and cool. But I thought of the depths beneath us that had spewed up those giant fish.

Behind us I saw London Bridge with its crowds of houses and shops, the great bulk of the Tower looming beyond. Atop the arch at the south end of the bridge long stakes thrust into the sky, the heads of those who had defied or angered the King set atop them mercifully indistinct. Among them, still, those of my old master Thomas Cromwell and those of Dereham and Culpeper, alleged lovers of the executed Queen Catherine Howard. I remembered Thomas Culpeper at York, in all his peacock pride and beauty, and shuddered at the thought that now I was sailing back into the world of the King's court.

'Ay, 'tis still cold,' Seymour said, mistaking my tremor. He had wrapped his heavy coat around him. I studied him covertly. I knew he was the younger brother of Henry's third queen, Jane Seymour, who died giving birth to his heir Prince Edward. It was said she was the only one of his five wives that Henry mourned. Seymour's older brother, Edward, Earl of Hertford, held high office at court, and had been appointed Lord Admiral of the Navy. Barak had told me that

Sir Thomas was something of an adventurer; he would never be trusted with a place on the Privy Council, but he had been awarded a number of lucrative monopolies and had recently been ambassador in Austria where the emperor was fighting the Turks. Lord Hertford, with Cranmer, was one of the few serious reformers to have survived on the Privy Council after Cromwell's fall three years before. He was known as a serious and capable politician, and a successful military commander who had led the campaign against Scotland the previous autumn; his brother Thomas, though, had the reputation of an irresponsible ladies' man. Looking at his handsome face I could believe it: the way he wrapped his coat round himself, gently stroking the long fur collar while his eyes roved over the water, the full lips held in a half-smile under the heavy, fashionably long brown beard, all spoke of a sensualist. Harsnet, with his rugged features, serious eyes and worried expression, was an entire contrast. As the boat bobbed through the choppy water of mid-river I wondered fearfully what Thomas Seymour could have to do with poor Roger.

We reached the far bank in silence and sculled quickly down to Lambeth Palace. We pulled past the empty niche where the statue of St Thomas Becket had stood, that all the London boatmen bowed to; that image of an archbishop who had defied a king now removed and destroyed. We passed the Lollards' Tower where heretics were held. I recalled Cranmer's brutal gaoler whom I had met in York, and shuddered anew. Cranmer, knowing Cromwell had trusted me, had forced me into undertaking a dangerous mission there; yet his conscience had pricked him afterwards and led him to find me my position at Requests. Now, it seemed, I would meet that passionate, troubled, God-haunted man again.

✝

I REMEMBERED the plain oaken door of Cranmer's study from my last visit. Harsnet knocked and entered, and I followed him and Seymour inside.

The Archbishop of Canterbury sat behind a large desk, wearing a white robe with a black stole, his head with its greying dark hair bare. He looked strained and worried. The twin furrows on his cheeks had deepened in the last year, drawing the corners of his full mouth downward. Cranmer was far from an extreme reformer, but he was always under threat from the conservatives at court. Many of them would have had him burned if they could. The King's long affection for him was all that kept him safe. His large blue eyes were as I remembered, full of passion and conflict.

Another man stood beside him, wearing a plain but expensive dark robe. His prominent nose, long face and athletic frame were so like Thomas Seymour's that it could only be his brother. Yet where Thomas was handsome, the same elements, slightly recast, made Lord Hertford an ugly man. His eyes were large and protuberant, the face too long and thin, the long beard straggly. Yet I sensed a depth of character and purpose in the plainly dressed Hertford that his brother lacked. I recalled that it was he who, with Cranmer, had sent Adam Kite to the Bedlam when Richard Rich wanted a worse fate for him. Sir Thomas removed his cap with a flourish and seized his brother's hand. 'It is good to see you, Edward.' He turned to Cranmer and bowed. 'My lord. As you see, we have brought him.'

'Yes, Thomas.' Cranmer's tones were weary, and there was dislike in the look he gave the younger Seymour. He turned to me and gave me one of his characteristic sad smiles.

'Well, Matthew Shardlake, we meet once again on strange business. Serjeant Shardlake,' he added, reminding me of the rank I had gained through his patronage.

He turned to Harsnet. 'Is it as we feared?'

Harsnet nodded. 'Yes, my lord. Exactly the same as the other.'

Cranmer exchanged a look with Lord Hertford, then stared for a moment into the dancing flames of the wood fire burning in the grate. These, I realized, were worried men. The two most powerful reformers at court, working together. Cranmer turned to me, forcing a smile. 'Well, Matthew, how is the Court of Requests?'

'It flourishes, my lord. I thank you again for helping me to that post.'

'You were owed it.' He stared at me again. I was conscious that they were all looking at me: Cranmer, Harsnet and Lord Hertford seriously, Sir Thomas with a cynical smile. I shifted uneasily. It was Sir Thomas who broke the silence.

'Well, can we trust the hunchback?'

'Do not call him that!' Cranmer looked genuinely angry. 'I am sorry, Matthew.' He turned to Sir Thomas. 'Yes, I believe we can.'

'He was after us like a rabid dog when the coroner adjourned the hearing.'

Cranmer looked at me intently. 'Matthew,' he said quietly, 'you found the body, and you were a close friend of Lawyer Elliard and his widow, I believe. How deep are you in this?'

'I promised Mistress Elliard to find her husband's killer,' I said.

'Would you do that for yourself, or for her?' The question came from Hertford. I turned and met his eye.

'For both, my lord. But what I have promised Mistress Elliard is a debt of honour.'

'And would you still work to redeem that debt, even if it turned out to be a matter of politics?' Cranmer asked. 'Think carefully before you answer, Matthew, for you once told me you wished never to be involved in such matters again. Yet you must be, if you are to help us fish out the bottom of this.'

I hesitated. Thomas Seymour gave a bark of laughter. 'He has not the stomach for it! And you said he failed you last time, he never found those papers.'

I bowed my head. I did not want him reading my expression; in fact, that time I had not failed, only decided to keep secret the things I had found out. My heart beat faster, remembering what these men could do to me.

'You have a fine mind, and much experience,' Cranmer said. 'And discretion.'

I took a deep breath. For a second I saw Roger's face in my mind; smiling, animated, full of life. I faced the Archbishop. 'If I can help you in this, my lord, I am yours.' And now I had a sense of bridges crashing in flames behind me.

Cranmer looked at the other three. Harsnet and Lord Hertford nodded; Thomas Seymour shrugged. Cranmer frowned at him. 'You are only here, Thomas, because your household may be useful and because of your particular association with – her.' Seymour reddened and for a moment looked ready to burst out angrily. He looked at his brother.

'The Archbishop is right, Thomas,' Lord Hertford said seriously.

Sir Thomas set his lips, but nodded.

Cranmer turned to me.

'You will wonder, Matthew, what the political link is to your friend's murder.'

'Yes, my lord.'

He took a long breath, holding in his secrets for a last second, then said, 'Your friend was not the first to be killed in that terrible manner.'

My mouth fell open. 'Another? The same?'

'In every horrid detail. It was kept secret because of who the victim was.' The Archbishop nodded to Harsnet. 'Tell him, Gregory.'

Harsnet looked at me. 'One morning a month ago, in late February, a labourer was walking to work along the river, past the mudbanks over on the Lambeth shore.' He paused. 'There was snow on the banks then, and the river was frozen a yard deep; but the tide still ebbed and flowed underneath the ice into the tidal pools along the south bank. That morning the labourer saw that one of the pools was red, with something floating in it.' My eyes widened. Harsnet nodded seriously. 'Yes. He found a man lying there with his throat cut. Exactly as Elliard was in that fountain, and again in a public place where he was bound to be discovered.'

'Dear God.'

'Our labourer went to the constable, who fetched the coroner.' Harsnet's look at me now was keen, probing. 'My colleague the Surrey coroner is a good reformer and he keeps himself up on court news. When he realized who the man was, he came to me, as he knew of my connection with the Archbishop.'

'Has there been an inquest?' I asked.

'No.' It was Lord Hertford who answered. 'It was vital the matter be kept secret.' He looked at me firmly with those protuberant eyes. 'It still is.'

Harsnet spoke again. 'The dead man was a physician, Dr Paul Gurney. An eminent man.' He paused. 'And physician to Lord Latimer, late husband of Lady Catherine Parr. Dr Gurney had attended Lord Latimer since he sickened last autumn, and visited him constantly at his home by the Charterhouse.'

So that was the connection. 'They say the King is courting Lady Latimer,' I ventured.

'They say right,' Cranmer agreed.

'We can't tell him all,' Thomas Seymour burst in. 'If this leaks out it could be to the peril of that good lady.'

'Matthew will not break a confidence,' Cranmer said. 'If he gives me his word to keep secret all we tell him, he will not break it. And I think he will have some sympathy for our position. Will you swear, Matthew, to say nothing of this matter, except to us? Remember, it means that if the killer is found you may not be able to tell your friend's widow the circumstances.'

I hesitated, then said, 'May I tell her the killer is caught and dealt with?'

'Yes. And he will be,' Lord Hertford said grimly. I caught a sense of this dour man's strength, and ruthlessness.

'Then I swear, my lord.'

Cranmer leaned back, satisfied. 'Then continue, Gregory. Tell him everything. All.'

'I investigated, quietly,' Harsnet said. 'But I found no clues. As with Master Elliard, Dr Gurney was a man respected in his profession, with many friends and no enemies. He was a childless widower, and we had his friends told he had died suddenly in his sleep. Diligent enquiry has offered no clues as to who killed him, or why. Nothing. According to discreet enquiries, he had left Lord Latimer's house late the evening before. He was staying there, for Latimer was near his end – he had a great growth on his back. He told the steward he had an urgent "errand of mercy" somewhere in the town.'

'Was a note delivered to him? As with Roger?'

'Not that we know of, though one may have been. Dr Gurney too helped poor people in need of his advice. And died for it, perhaps.'

'Was the body examined?'

'No. Perhaps I should have had that done.' Harsnet frowned. 'That Moor gave us an important clue today, about the drug. It means we should look for someone with medical connections.'

'Legal, too. A man of wide knowledge.'

Cranmer spoke again. 'I consulted Lord Hertford, and we decided it was vital as few people knew as possible. Catherine Parr had been married to Lord Latimer for ten years. Both were well-known figures at court, and the King has long had an eye on her. When it became known in January that Lord Latimer would die soon, the King let his interest be known. He has now proposed marriage.'

'Another older husband.' Thomas Seymour spoke with bitterness in his voice. I recalled Barak saying there was a rumour that someone else was interested in Catherine Parr. Could it be Seymour? He and she would be of a similar age. 'Latimer was past forty.'

Cranmer clasped his hands together. 'This would be a sensible, safe marriage and Jesu knows we have had few of those.' He hesitated before explaining his remarks, then continued, looking straight at me. 'The Lady Catherine has an interest in religious reform. She has kept it quiet, for Lord Latimer was a conservative. And God knows we need an ally now. Bishop Gardiner of Winchester is back in the King's councils working with Bishop Bonner of London to crush the reformers.' He looked at me. 'Even I may not be safe.'

Hertford gave Cranmer a quick shake of the head, but the

Archbishop raised a beringed hand. 'No, Edward, if we are to tell him we should tell him all. And it will be public soon enough, heaven knows. Matthew, the conservatives are moving on a number of fronts. Bishop Bonner's campaign against the London Bible-men will soon escalate. And a bill will be laid before Parliament shortly, restricting reading of the Bible to nobles and gentlemen only. No common folk, and no women.'

He hesitated. Harsnet interjected, quietly but bitterly. 'They will pluck Christ's holy word from the people.' I looked at him; the phraseology was that of a radical. Cranmer frowned slightly.

'And finally,' he continued, 'they seek to attack me. Lord Hertford too perhaps, but principally me. There have already been arrests of radicals among my staff at Canterbury, and among some of the junior courtiers at Windsor. They will be charged with heresy. Young men with foolish tongues, who may end by bringing me down.' His cheek twitched uncontrollably, and I saw the Archbishop was afraid. He collected himself, looked at me again.

Lord Hertford spoke, quietly and seriously. 'What protects us more than anything is that the King still has moderate reformers in his household, men he trusts. His physician, Dr Butts. His new secretary, William Paget. When those like Gardiner and Norfolk whisper venom in his ear, their private access to the King means they can counter it. A Queen of reformist sympathies could help us more than anyone.'

'But would this marriage be safe for *her*?' Thomas Seymour interjected. 'Anne Boleyn pressed the King too far on religion and was executed. And Catherine Howard was beheaded not much more than a year ago.' I remembered again that glimpse of Catherine Parr I had caught in the funeral procession, her expression of fear.

Cranmer nodded. 'Yes. It is no wonder she has not yet accepted. For the first time, Matthew, a prospective wife has refused the King's proposal. But he wants a companion in his old age. Lady Catherine has placed her decision in God's hands, I know. The situation could not be more delicate. An extraordinarily brutal murder close to her, still more now there has been a second, would worry the King, for he is a superstitious man. Two of these shocking pointless deaths. People will start to say this murderer is possessed.'

'They are already,' Harsnet said. 'At first we feared the killer's purpose was to make a scandal that would imperil these marriage negotiations. But if so, why strike again?'

'To make a spectacle that would be linked firmly to the doctor's death?' I suggested.

'It has not been so far,' Cranmer said. 'And it must not be. That is why we wished to send Master Elliard's death officially to sleep. *Unofficially* I will leave no stone unturned to find the killer. And Catherine Parr, like the rest, thinks Dr Gurney had a sudden seizure.'

Now I understood the strain in their faces. The King did not look kindly on those who kept secrets from him. I realized I was involved again in something that could get me in bad odour with the King. Something dangerous. A second time, I might not survive. Yet I had sworn; there was nothing to do but go on.

'The manner of these deaths was monstrous,' Cranmer said, fingering the silver pectoral cross that hung round his neck.

Thomas Seymour laughed scornfully. 'No more than the things I have seen in Hungary.' He laid a hand on his gold-embroidered scabbard. 'I saw the Emperor's defeated army returning from Budapest. They failed to take it from the Turks, but they brought back as a trophy a great cart full of the heads of slain Turks, with one live Turk on top, slipping and rolling, covered with blood and bits of rag from the dead men's turbans. Everyone laughed as the cart tail was opened and the Turk rolled out screaming among all his comrades' heads.' Sir Thomas smiled; he had laughed too.

'That was war,' his brother said. 'Cruel but honourable.'

I looked at Hertford, wondering what he might have seen and done in Scotland.

'Well, Matthew,' Cranmer said. 'You come fresh to this matter, and you knew poor Elliard well. Where do you think we should go next?'

They all looked at me. I squared my shoulders. 'I would suggest we find out whether Roger and Dr Gurney had any acquaintances, or any clients, in common. Though it would be strange for someone to hate *two* men so viciously.'

'I have made an extensive list of Dr Gurney's patients and friends,' Harsnet said.

'And I can do the same for Roger.' I looked at them. 'With his widow's help.'

'Very well.' Cranmer nodded. 'But she is to know nothing of Gurney.' I hated the thought of not being frank with Dorothy, but saw it must be so.

'How old was Dr Gurney?' I asked.

'Old. Past fifty.'

'And his build?'

'His build?' Harsnet looked puzzled. 'He was a small, spare man, by the look of his body.'

'As was Roger. Our killer had to carry Roger to the Lincoln's Inn fountain, and no doubt Gurney to the marshes. Almost as if he chose small men to kill, men he could carry.'

'What were Master Elliard's views on religion?' Harsnet asked.

'He was a reformer.'

'As was Dr Gurney. A safely moderate one, though, these days.' He sounded almost disapproving.

'So was Roger. There seem to be more and more things in common between them.'

'Which encourages the view that this has been done by the papists to scotch the King's marriage,' Harsnet said. 'Jesu, they are capable of anything. They would devour poor Protestants as beasts eat grass.'

'And you, Master Shardlake,' Hertford asked quietly. 'What are your religious views? They say you are a Laodicean, a man of little faith.'

'Matthew would not harm our cause,' Cranmer interposed. 'So long as he thought our methods just, eh?' That sad smile of his again. 'That will not be a problem here.'

'Who is he to tell us what is just?' Thomas Seymour scoffed. 'A crookback lawyer.'

His brother turned on him with sudden anger. 'God's wounds, Thomas, I will have you kept out of this if you say another word! I'll warrant this man will be far more help than you!'

Thomas Seymour looked chastened at the fresh reminder of where the power lay. Cranmer turned to me. 'Matthew, I apologize again for Sir Thomas.'

'It does not matter, my lord.' Though it did. Why was this foolish boor involved? 'If I may,' I went on, 'I would like to talk to the labourer who found the first body, and visit the scene. These correspondences with Roger's death are so close, they may help us.'

Cranmer looked at Harsnet. 'Where is the man now, Gregory?'

'I had him locked up for a few days to impress the need for silence on him. He's back home now, I'll have him sent for.'

'Thank you, coroner.'

'I want you and Gregory to work together on this,' Cranmer said.

'Might I bring in my man Barak? He could be of much use.'

Cranmer smiled. 'Ah, yes, him. Yes, I know Lord Cromwell trusted him. But no one else. And not that ex-monk doctor. He cannot help us over Dr Gurney; he has been buried for weeks.'

'I understand.'

'You will keep me closely informed. Contact me here and only through my secretary, Ralph Morice. I trust no one else.'

'Yes, my lord.'

Cranmer stood up. Harsnet and I followed, bowing low.

'Gregory, Matthew,' Cranmer said, 'I pray to Our Saviour you may be able to resolve this.'

'Amen, my lord,' Harsnet answered feelingly.

'I believe you have put Adam Kite's case into the Court of Requests?' Cranmer asked me suddenly.

'Yes, my lord. I have applied to have his fees remitted, and to make sure he is cared for. And I am having a physician examine the question of his sanity.'

'I will see the Privy Council does not stand in your way,' he said. 'So far as Kite's fees and his care are concerned, it was mentioned yesterday, and your name was a provocation to Sir Richard Rich. Who is the doctor you have instructed – Dr Malton?'

'Yes, my lord.'

Cranmer nodded, considering, then looked at me again seriously. 'Neither Lord Hertford nor I would want the boy released, unless he was cured to the extent that it was certain there would be no more crazed public demonstrations. He must be kept secure.'

'In times of trial, Christians must show the wisdom of serpents as well as the innocence of doves,' Hertford said. He looked sad for a moment.

'I understand, my lord.'

Cranmer smiled. 'Good. Make sure that old ex-monk does not turn him papist.' I looked at him. So he knew about Guy's past, he had probably had enquiries made about him. Lord Hertford, over-hearing, looked at me curiously as he stepped past me. He bowed and swept away, leaving me alone with Harsnet in the corridor. We walked away together. Harsnet seemed a little uneasy with me. He seemed to ponder a moment, then said, 'I am sorry for the way I had to conduct the inquest. I hope you understand now why that was necessary.'

'I understand why you did it, sir,' I answered neutrally. I looked at him, wondering what he would be like to work with. A clever man, but a religious radical, I guessed. When the King had defied the Pope to marry Anne Boleyn ten years before, he had allowed Thomas Cromwell to install in the Royal household men who were far more radical reformers than he was – even Lutherans. Since Cromwell's fall, the King was steadily moving back towards the old religious practices, and most reformers bent to the wind, at least in public. But some radicals remained, clinging on to their posts through ability and cunning.

'I fear for the Lady Catherine Parr,' he said. 'I have met her, a good, sweet lady. I hope the killer did not get to the doctor through someone in her household.'

'That is not how he got to Roger.'

'No. But then what is the connection?' He looked me seriously. 'We must find it, Serjeant Shardlake. I agree it would be useful for you to talk to the man who found Dr Gurney. I will arrange that, send the message to your house. And you will prepare a list of everyone that Master Elliard knew — clients, friends, possible enemies.'

'Yes I will speak to his clerk.' I took a deep breath. 'And his widow.' I looked at him. 'What of the body? May it be released for the funeral?'

'Of course.' Harsnet looked uncomfortable again.

'Thank you.'

Somewhere a clock struck one. I had an appointment with the Kites that afternoon at Lincoln's Inn, and I had to see Dorothy.

We passed into Lambeth Palace yard, where the sweet smell of wet grass met us, unfamiliar after those weeks of snow. I turned to Harsnet. 'I do not understand Sir Thomas Seymour's involvement. He seems—'

'Unreliable? A foolish braggart?' The coroner smiled wryly. 'He is all that and more. A man of proud conceit, born to mischief. An elbow-hanger on his brother. But we are stuck with him.'

'Why?'

'Thomas Seymour wished to marry Catherine Parr. And she was in love with him. Heaven knows why, though even sensible women may have their heads turned. He has had to step aside for the King. But he has made his brother involve him in this. To protect her interests, he says. If Lord Hertford has one weakness, it is devotion to Thomas. But Thomas is something even worse than a papist.'

'What?'

I saw disgust in Harsnet's look. 'An atheist,' he said. 'A man who denies God.'

Chapter Ten

HARSNET LEFT ME at the river, where I caught a wherry back to Temple Stairs and walked up to Lincoln's Inn. The fierce anger I felt after the inquest had been replaced by sober fear; as I thought of the mighty men in that room my stomach twisted and knotted with anxiety. Yet I told myself that at least this time there was no ambiguity, we were all clearly on the same side in wanting this killer caught.

It was a relief to find Barak in chambers, working at his desk beside young Skelly. I inclined my head to Barak that he should follow me to my room. Skelly looked at us through the glasses he wore for his weak sight, his expression sad. I guessed he felt excluded, left out of the events whirling round Lincoln's Inn. Well, he was safer out of it all.

I told Barak all that had transpired at Lambeth Palace. I had expected him to show pleasure at the prospect of some excitement, but he heard me in silence and then sat frowning. 'That Thomas Seymour's a dangerous character,' he said. 'Lord Cromwell distrusted him and blocked his advancement, though he respected his brother.'

'His romantic interest in Catherine Parr complicates matters.'

'He's known as an indiscreet woman-chaser. Sounds like an indiscreet man is the last thing this business needs, if Cranmer's keeping this from the King.'

'I know. But I am bound to assist them, I promised Dorothy.' I looked at him. 'But you do not need to be involved if you do not wish,' I said. 'There is no reason for you to place yourself in danger.'

'No,' he said. 'I'll help.' But he still looked uneasy. 'Though I don't understand any of it. One man killed as your friend is strange enough, but *two*?'

'Could the killer be mad? Someone who conceived a wild hatred for Roger and that doctor, perhaps developed a belief they had wronged him?'

'A mad person couldn't have organized and carried through something like these murders.'

'No. The killer tricked Roger cleverly with those letters. Maybe did something similar with the doctor. Took them to a lonely spot, drugged them somehow, then carried them to the fountain and the tidal pool, and slit their throats.' I shuddered.

'That time you disturbed an intruder near the Elliards' lodgings, maybe he was looking over Gatehouse Court? Preparing the way.'

'That would mean he was unfamiliar with Lincoln's Inn. Yet he knew enough about the law to fake a solicitor's letter for Roger, and enough about medicine to be able to make dwale.' I shook my head. It occurred to me that if I had come out from Roger and Dorothy's a little earlier that night I might have encountered the killer. Would he have killed me too, lest I identify him later?

'I don't understand how this arsehole got to know them,' Barak said. 'And he must have done.'

'Yes. And who could possibly have hated Roger enough to make that ghastly display in the fountain?' I looked at him seriously. 'It was a display, wasn't it? He was meant to be found like that, in a public place. And by the sound of it, Dr Gurney too.'

Barak nodded slowly. 'I came across some strange things when I worked for Lord Cromwell, some grim things. But I never heard of anything like this before, never.'

'Nor I.' We said nothing for a moment, then I roused myself. 'Come, we do not know enough yet to speculate. We must think of practical steps.'

'All right. Where do we start?'

'First I am going to prepare a list of Roger's clients and acquaintances, to see if he had any in common with Dr Gurney. I will go across now and speak to Roger's clerk, and to Dorothy. How was she on the journey back?'

'Quiet. But you could see she was upset at how the inquest went.'

'Yes.' I sighed. 'I must be careful how much I tell her. I should like you to come with me to meet the man who found the doctor's body, out by the river. Harsnet is arranging it.'

'What's Harsnet like on closer acquaintance?'

'One of the pure Bible-men, I think. But his feet are on the ground. Clever, efficient.' Something struck me. 'But many coroners are not. And we are at the junction of four coroners' jurisdictions – Surrey, Kent, Middlesex and London. I think Harsnet should check there have been no other killings like this in the other jurisdictions. I'll suggest it to him.'

'Gib Rooke said a cottar had been killed horribly.'

'Not in the same way as Roger, or he would have said. But it might be worth talking to him. Good idea. Thank you, Barak,' I added encouragingly. 'See how you help me?'

'Glad I help someone,' he said gloomily.

I hesitated, then said, 'Is that aimed at Tamasin?'

He shrugged. 'She's been complaining I go out too much. I won't be told where I can and can't go by a woman.'

'Maybe she worries about who you might be seeing.' I ventured.

'She'd do better to stop her complaining and mopishness. Then her company might be worth cultivating.'

'She is still suffering the loss of the child, Barak,' I said quietly. 'As I think you are. Surely that is something you could share?'

I saw from the anger that leaped into his face that I had gone too far. 'That's our business,' he said roughly. 'If you are going across to see Mistress Elliard, sir, remember Adam Kite's parents will be here at three.' With that, he turned and left the room.

✝

AS I WALKED ACROSS Gatehouse Court I got curious looks from the passing lawyers. News of the adjourned inquest would have been brought by the jurors, some of whom had seen me leave with Harsnet and Seymour. Well, their curiosity would have to go unsatisfied. I went into Roger's chambers and greeted his clerk.

'Good day, Bartlett,' I said. 'How are things here?'

'We're coping, sir,' he replied in his Bristol burr. 'Mistress Elliard has asked me to arrange the funeral. Can the body be released now?'

'Yes. The coroner has approved it.'

'And there's two cases in court this week.'

I bit my lip. I would have little enough time for my own work now, let alone Roger's. 'I think we must pass his cases on,' I said. 'To barristers we can trust to pay for work Roger has already done. I can give you some names.'

'And I will chase them and see they do pay, sir.'

'Thank you.' I smiled gratefully.

'Master Elliard was always good to me. He was a fine man.' The clerk blinked back tears.

'Yes, he was.' I hesitated. 'But a lawyer always makes enemies. Could there possibly have been someone, a client perhaps, or even a lawyer he had bested, who might have taken against him?'

'I can't think of anyone, sir. No one at all. Everyone liked Master Elliard, sir.'

'I know. But can you make me a list of all the clients and lawyers he had professional dealings with since he came back from Bristol? Can you have that for me by this evening?'

'I'll set to it, sir.' He hesitated. 'If I may ask, what is to happen now? The inquest was adjourned, they say.'

'There is to be an investigation, and I am part of it. That is all I can say now, Bartlett. That list may help.' I looked at his honest face. 'What will you do now? Go back to Bristol?'

'I'd as soon stay in London, all my family are with me here.'

'Then I'll see if I can get you a job in another chambers when Roger's work is wound up.'

His face lit up. 'Thank you. You — you are a good man, sir.'
'I hope so, Bartlett. Though not all would agree.'

✝

I MOUNTED the stairs to the rooms above. Old Elias answered my knock and bowed me in. He still looked stricken. Margaret came out of the parlour. 'How is your mistress?' I asked in a whisper.

'Quiet, sir. She was so angry after that hearing I thought she'd break down, but she hasn't. She's sitting in her usual place by the fire.' She hesitated. 'She's been hoping you would bring news.'

'Thank you, Margaret. I will go to her.' I noticed the girl's full cheeks were pale. The servants' lives had been turned upside down too, their futures suddenly uncertain.

Dorothy was sitting in her chair under the frieze. She looked up and ventured a smile, but her white face was tight with anger.

'What happened?' she asked. 'Why did you go off with that coroner?'

'To discuss the investigation. There will be one, Dorothy, and I will be part of it. I promise you. And I will get the body released tomorrow. You can arrange the funeral.'

She stared at me intently. 'If they know he was murdered, why that — performance?'

'Politics. I may not say more. I wish I could.'

Her eyes widened. 'Dear God. But Roger had naught to do with politics. He despised all courtiers.'

'I know. But there must be some link to — this political matter. I have undertaken to help find it.'

'Undertaken to whom, Matthew?'

'Cranmer. And I have already told you more than I should.'

'But you hate politics as much as Roger did. You have said so often.'

'But working with these people is the only way I can ensure Roger's killer is found. They and I want the same thing.' I hesitated. 'I will be working with Coroner Harsnet.'

'That man. The way he tried to twist things.'

'That was to get the case adjourned, out of the public gaze. For what it is worth, I do not think he enjoyed deceiving you.'

She looked at me with sad, exhausted eyes. 'What if I free you from your promise to find Roger's killer, Matthew? I know you fear those great men, as anyone should with any sense.'

I smiled sadly. 'I have promised Cranmer, Dorothy. It is out of our hands now.'

'I am become a burden,' she said flatly. 'As a middle-aged woman alone will always be.'

I leaned forward and ventured to take her hand. 'No, Dorothy. You are a strong woman. Just now it is all too much to bear, I know, but you will regain your strength. In time.'

'I have heard people say that when a loved one has died they feel them near in spirit. I have been sitting here waiting, hoping, but – there is nothing. I feel only that Roger is gone, ripped out of all existence.'

'Time, Dorothy, you will need time to grieve.'

'I have years of empty time now.'

I felt my heart clench at her suffering. 'Dorothy,' I said quietly, 'there is something I must ask you. This is not the best time, but it is urgent. We need to see if Roger and – this other man who died – knew anyone in common. Bartlett is preparing a list of professional contacts. Can you make me a list of anyone else he knew? Any non-lawyer friends—'

'We had none. The law was Roger's life.'

'Then tradesmen, his barber, his tailor. Your servants – have you dismissed any recently?'

'No. There is no one.'

'Anyway, a list may help.'

'Then I will prepare it now,' she said.

I got Margaret to fetch some paper, and Dorothy sat thinking, then wrote down the names of everyone Roger had known in London. She passed the list to me.

'That is them all,' she said.

I looked at it. 'Good, that will help.'

'Anything else I can help with, come at any time. The funeral must wait till next week. Samuel will be here from Bristol, I have had a letter. And afterwards, Matthew, come and eat with us. Let us sit and remember Roger then, in peace.'

'I shall be glad to.'

☩

I HASTENED BACK across Gatehouse Court to my chambers, for it was now near three o'clock. I was hungry, I had missed lunch. Among those passing to and fro I saw, at a little distance, Bealknap. He was walking slowly, his long thin body hunched and stooped. Feeling eyes upon him he turned, gave me a look of concentrated fury, and walked on. I thought, Roger may not have had an enemy, but I have, all the more now. I dismissed the wretched man from my mind.

Daniel and Minnie Kite were waiting in my outer office. Meaphon sat beside them in his cassock, frowning. Today he held a copy of the New Testament in his lap. 'Good day,' I said to Daniel and Minnie, pointedly ignoring Meaphon.

'I have had word from the Requests Office,' Skelly called over from his desk. 'Master Kite's hearing will be on the fourth of April.' He handed me a paper. I looked at it as I led the Kites and Meaphon into my office.

'Good news,' I said, when all were seated. 'My request to have Adam's care supervised by the court, and his fees remitted, will be heard in nine days. And I have arranged for the doctor I spoke of to attend him. On Friday. I will go too.'

'We saw Adam yesterday,' Daniel Kite said. 'He is no better.'

'He spoke to me,' Minnie said. 'It was the first time my son spoke to me since they put him in that place. And do you know what he said? He said he could smell the fire, feel the sharp pricks of the devil's imps scratching at his arms. It was only lice, he is crawling with them, but that is what he made of it.' She shook her head, setting her lips into a tight line, trying not to cry.

'Minnie,' Daniel said.

'This is why I do not want him released from the Bedlam till there is some sign of a cure,' I said gently. 'He could get into deadly trouble. If his welfare is taken care of he is better there for now. Not all the keepers are bad.' I thought again of the kindly woman Ellen and her strange statement that she could never leave the Bedlam. I glanced at Meaphon, expecting opposition, but to my surprise he nodded, patting his thick hair.

'Perhaps, after all, that is best. The papist wolves are abroad once more. Honest preachers have been arrested, one was paraded as a heretic only yesterday.'

'I saw,' I said.

'But if I could be allowed to spend time with Adam, if I could try again to persuade him to accept that he can and will be saved—'

'We should see what the doctor says,' I said, temporizing.

'Doctors,' he said contemptuously. 'What if he *is* possessed? That is my fear, more and more.'

'What if they report to the Privy Council that you have been there?' Minnie spoke up. 'What if they have spies there, and they report you are preaching doctrine they do not approve?'

Meaphon shook his head. 'I should do what I can to save Adam.' He gripped the Testament in his hands tightly, like an icon, a talisman.

'My wife is right.' Daniel spoke up. 'Were Adam to leave he might – do something dangerous. And he is in no fit state to choose martyrdom.' He looked at me. 'We shall see what the doctor says. That is what we must do next.' He looked at Meaphon.

'Am I to meet with uncertain heart in my own congregation that I may not go and pray with him?' Meaphon asked bitterly. This time both Daniel and Minnie met his gaze, though both reddened.

'I will tell you what the doctor says,' I told them, rising. I felt an unprofessional degree of pleasure at their defiance of Meaphon, despite his raising again the dread idea of possession. It was a small victory, but a victory nonetheless.

Chapter Eleven

T HE FOLLOWING DAY a letter arrived from Harsnet. It came by a fast rider from Whitehall, reminding me that the coroner commanded sizeable resources. He asked me to meet him by the Southwark bear pits at eight the next morning.

I set off early on Friday to ride through the city to London Bridge, where I had arranged to meet Barak. Though I had slept I felt tired, weighed down, as I had since Roger's death. There was a cool breeze and high clouds scudded rapidly across the blue sky. I saw a patch of budding crocuses had appeared in a grassy corner by Newgate Market under the great shadow of St Paul's.

There were few people about as yet, and as I walked down the Shambles, avoiding the butcher's offal in the piss-channel in the middle of the road, my attention was drawn by the sound of a scuffle. On the corner of Bladder Lane a burly man in a bloodstained apron was struggling with three London constables. A plump woman in a smock had hold of the arm of one of them and was trying to pull him off. Three small children ran howling and screaming around the adults' feet. As I watched, the constable shook himself free and pushed the goodwife over. She landed in a filthy puddle, skirts billowing and the wings of her coif hanging loose. The children ran to her, yelling.

'Now come quietly,' one of the constables shouted at the man, who ceased struggling and allowed himself to be manhandled away. I hesitated, then went to the woman, who was rising slowly to her feet, covered in filth, the children milling around her.

'Are you all right, madam?'

She gave me a suspicious look. 'I'm not hurt.'

'What happened?'

'They say my husband was selling meat in Lent, they're taking him to Bishop Bonner.' She looked at my robe. 'A lawyer won't help if they prosecute him, and we've no money anyway. You must seek trade elsewhere!' And with that she limped into a shop followed by the children. One of them, emboldened by his mother's tone, looked round and shouted 'Crookback' at me as she shepherded them in.

I walked on, angry for I had only wished to help. But if her husband was guilty, he might face the rope. I remembered what Cranmer had said about Bonner working to crush the reformers.

Barak was waiting at London Bridge. He looked bright and alert, no sign of a hangover today, and he greeted me cheerfully enough. He had put on his sword, I saw.

'Well, let's see what awaits us over the river,' he said with a touch of his old swagger.

'Some answers, I hope.'

We walked across London Bridge to the Southwark waterfront where Harsnet was to meet us. He was already there, wearing a coat lined with marten fur over his lawyer's robe, looking every inch the royal official. I saw that he had donned sturdy riding boots in anticipation of walking through the tidal mud.

Harsnet was staring up to where the great circular structure of the bear-baiting ring reared over the rooftops. He turned to us with a sombre expression on his face.

'Good day, Master Shardlake. And you are Barak, yes.' Barak bowed to him. Harsnet looked up at the bear ring again, and sighed. 'Is it not sad that we make merry with the bleeding miseries of those poor harmless beasts?'

'Harmless?' Barak said, looking at me. He was recalling the time I had been attacked and nearly killed by an escaped bear. But in fact I agreed with Harsnet.

'Yes,' I said. 'It is a cruel sport. I never go.'

He nodded approvingly. 'Did you bring the list of those known to Master Elliard?'

I produced the list from my coat. 'Master Elliard's wife and clerk helped me. They knew of none who wished him harm.'

'Dr Gurney had no enemies either. I have his list.' He produced a paper from his coat and we stood together to read. Dr Gurney had some courtiers and prominent London merchants among his patients, I saw. Lord and Lady Latimer's names were there. It was as comprehensive a list as mine, but there were no names that matched.

'Nothing.' Harsnet frowned. 'If I may keep your list?'

'Of course.'

He rolled both documents up, putting them in his coat. 'Yet those men had so much in common – religion, professional status, even their size. What made this monster choose them?'

'I do not know. But I wondered—'

'Yes?' His look was eager, anxious.

'Whether there might have been any other killings. We are on the borders of Kent and Surrey here. The coroners do not always liaise and are not always efficient. Like Coroner Browne.'

Harsnet nodded agreement. 'You are right, sir, thank you.' He gave me an approving look. 'I will speak to the other coroners.'

'I know of at least one strange killing this side of the river recently. One of my clients told me. I thought I might ask him for details.'

'Yes. Good idea. Thank you.' He raised his eyebrows, took a long deep breath. 'And now we must walk over to Lambeth. The man who found the body will meet us there.'

✝

WE WALKED ALONG the south bank. Soon the houses gave way to wide marshes, high green reeds waving in the breeze among deep stagnant pools. Here and there patches of higher ground were cultivated, fields of vegetables laid out beside little mud-and-daub houses the cottars had built. It must be a lonely life out here.

'Archbishop Cranmer speaks highly of you,' Harsnet said. 'He said that but for a treacherous servant you might have saved Lord Cromwell from falling, three years ago.'

'That is kind of him. Though I prefer to avoid such matters these days.'

'You do this for your friend, for honour.' He nodded. 'Well, that is a godly thing. There is little honour among the circles I move in, at court.'

I found I was warming to him despite our bad beginning. 'Have you been the King's coroner long?' I ventured.

'Only the assistant. Most of my work is with deaths in London. I got my post six years ago.' He looked at me seriously. 'In Lord Cromwell's time, God rest him. These days are hard for reformers. We hang on by our fingertips.'

'I saw a butcher taken into custody on the way here. His wife said it was for selling meat in Lent.'

He nodded slowly, and I saw he looked worried. 'The order went out to the constables this morning to seize all butchers suspected of selling meat in Lent. They will be asked, none too gently, to inform on their customers. So those who place their faith in the word of God rather than ancient dietary rules will find themselves under arrest. That is how Bonner will prosecute us this time.' He gave a harsh smile that made his face look unpleasant. 'Though they may find some fish caught in their net they would rather not swallow. The Earl of Surrey is charged with Lent-breaking, the Duke of Norfolk's son. Have you read any of his poetry?'

'I fear not.' I knew though that the son of a principal figure in the conservative faction was a religious radical as well as a poet.

'He has written a new poem in prison. About London.' Harsnet quoted:

> Oh member of false Babylon!
> The shop of craft! The den of ire!
> Thy dreadful doom draws fast upon
> Thy martyr's blood, by sword and fire.

I thought of Roger, quoting Roderick Mors. For a second his face appeared to me again. I sighed and looked at Harsnet. 'Surrey sees London as the Babylon referred to in the Book of Revelation, then?'

'Which will be destroyed when God comes to judge the world.' He studied me, watching for my response.

'I thought people said Babylon was Rome. But I was never able to make much sense of Revelation.'

Harsnet inclined his head. 'If you study it properly, you see that God does not just foretell how the world will end, but when.' When I did not respond he smiled again, sadly.

'It's quiet here,' Barak said, breaking the silence that followed.

I nodded. The path was empty apart from us; to our left the river was at low tide, occasional gurgles and pops coming from the mud. To our right the wind hissed and clacked in the reeds. Across the river, the wharves and houses of London, Surrey's 'den of ire'.

'It will be busy enough when the working day gets going,' Harsnet observed. 'People will be walking and riding on this path all day.' He turned to me again. 'The Archbishop said you were acting for Adam Kite. How is he?'

'Very disturbed in his mind. You know of the case?'

'I have met the family once or twice at meetings. His vicar and mine are friends. They seemed sober, honest folk.'

'They are.' I wondered if he meant illegal Bible-study meetings.

'I know Reverend Meaphon fears Master Kite may be possessed,' Harsnet said seriously. 'In any event, I think he is better where he is. If he were to make a spectacle of himself again, Bonner might make a spectacle of *him*. On top of a fire.'

'There, sir,' I answered feelingly, 'I agree.'

✝

WE WERE NOW coming to where the river turned south to Westminster. On the river the wherries had begun work, white sails bobbing on the grey Thames. A bank of cloud had risen, covering the sun. On our side, the low mudbanks were dotted increasingly with pools of water left by the tide. Ahead, standing in the mud by a small pool, we saw a lonely figure outlined against the sky: an elderly labouring man in a grey smock, a wide leathern hat on his head. As we approached he studied us with narrow, frightened eyes set in a weatherbeaten face. Harsnet stepped down from the path into the mud. It quivered as his boots sank in six inches.

'Careful, sir!' Barak called. 'That mud can suck you in!' We followed him carefully to where the old man stood. The pool beside him was circular, shallow, perhaps twenty feet in diameter.

'How now, Wheelows,' the coroner said. 'Have you been here long?'

The labourer bowed low, wincing as he rose. Trouble with his back, I thought sympathetically. 'Half an hour, sir. I don't like it here. It reminds me. And I keep feeling I'm being watched.' He cast scared eyes over the reedbanks on the other side of the path. It was indeed a dismal spot.

'Well, we won't need to trouble you again after this,' Harsnet said. He indicated in my direction. 'This gentleman is helping my investigation. I want you to tell him exactly what happened when you found Dr Gurney's body.'

A look of irritation crossed Wheelows' face. 'I've told the story so many times—'

'Then tell it once more,' Harsnet said, smiling but firmly.

'It was three weeks back, when the snow was still thick on the ground. I was going to Southwark to work, there's new houses going up along the Croydon Road—'

'Where do you live?' I asked.

'Westminster village. I was coming along the path at first light. The river was frozen but the tide still ran and would seep out under the ice and make tidal pools as usual. I was walking along and something caught my eye. One of the pools was a strange colour. I looked and saw it was red, bright red. I couldn't believe it at first. Then I saw a dark shape floating in it, and I went down to look.'

'Were there footprints?' Barak asked.

'Ay.'

'What were they like? Large, or small?'

'Quite large, I'd say.' He shook his head. 'That red pool, standing out against the white snow, it was like something from a nightmare. It turned my stomach.'

'The pool is much larger than the fountain,' I observed. 'Yet it was stained red.'

'You'd be surprised how little blood it takes to turn water red,' Barak said.

Harsnet looked at him in surprise. 'That is strange knowledge for a law clerk. But of course, you worked for Lord Cromwell.'

'So I did,' Barak answered. I saw old Wheelows narrow his eyes. Cromwell's name could still bring fear, even now.

'So he walked here with the body, dumped it and walked back,' I said.

Wheelows looked frightened. 'I heard there was another one, similar, over at Lincoln's Inn.'

'You must keep your mouth shut about that,' Harsnet said sternly.

'I know I must, master,' Wheelows answered resentfully. 'Or end in Marshalsea Prison. You told me.'

'Then carry on with your story.'

'There was a place beside the pool where all the snow was churned up. There was blood there too,' Wheelows said. Where he cut the doctor's throat, I thought. I looked at the pool. The wind made little ripples on the surface.

'What did you do next?' I asked the old labourer gently.

'I went into the pool, turned the body over. I saw it was a gentleman by his clothes. His face was white as bone, was no blood left in him. I saw what had been done to his throat.'

'What was the expression on his face?'

Wheelows gave me a sharp look. 'No one's asked me that before. But it was strange. He looked peaceful, as if he was asleep.'

Dwale, I thought. 'So, what did you do then?'

'I ran to Southwark, to find the coroner. I know that's what you must do if you find a body.' He glanced at Harsnet. 'Then ever since I've had gentlemen questioning me, pressing me to keep it all a secret.'

'There is good reason,' I said.

'So make sure you do as you're told.' Harsnet took a shilling from his pocket and passed it to Wheelows. 'All right, you can go.'

The old man bowed quickly to us, cast a last frightened look over at the marshes, then clambered grunting through the mud to the path. He walked rapidly off towards Westminster. Harsnet watched him go. 'I didn't like locking him up,' he said. 'But we had to scare him to keep him silent.'

I nodded, then stared into the tidal pool. 'It's just like Roger. The doctor was lured to a meeting with someone, drugged, then carried out here. His throat was slit and he was dumped in the pool. People walk along this path every day, more when the river was frozen and the wherries weren't running. If the old man hadn't come on the body early it would have made another—' I hesitated – 'spectacle.'

Harsnet looked down the path. 'But how could he drag the body out here? Dr Gurney wouldn't have met anyone on this path at night, surely.'

I nodded at the river. 'People were walking across the ice then. It was very thick. I would guess the killer met Dr Gurney on the far bank, drugged him there and hauled him over here.' I shook my head. 'The killings identical, the men so similar in many ways. What *is* it that links them?'

'He must have timed it right at low tide,' Barak said. 'Like now. When the sea tide rose under the ice the bloodied water would have leaked out underneath and covered the shore, and the pool.'

Sea tide. Water turned to blood. Words snagged at my mind, as had the Treasurer's about a fountain turned to blood. I knew those phrases. But from where?

Then Barak leaned in close to us. 'Don't look round, but there's someone watching. On a patch of higher ground behind us. I saw a head outlined against the sky, just for a second. The old man was right.'

'Are you sure?' I asked.

'I'm going after him.' The light of excitement was back in his eyes.

I put a hand on his arm. 'It's all marsh. You don't know how deep the mud and water are.'

'I'll risk that,' Barak turned, ran across the path and plunged into the reeds. There was a great splashing and the water came up to his thighs, but he ploughed on. Harsnet and I stared. About fifty yards away a green-covered knoll rose from the reeds. For the merest second I saw a head outlined against the grey sky, then it was gone.

'I'm going to follow,' Harsnet said. I had to admire the way the coroner threw himself into the reeds after Barak, mud splashing on his fine coat. I followed in his wake, gasping at the chill of the muddy water against my legs.

Ahead, we saw Barak step on to dry land. He stood outlined against the sky, looking around. 'Shit!' he said loudly.

I followed Harsnet up on to the small knoll. Barak was looking out over the marshes. It was dotted with cottars' cottages in the distance but between us and them lay a wide bare expanse of waving reeds.

'I thought if I got up here and he ran, I could see where he went,' Barak said. 'But he's vanished.'

'But where to?' Harsnet stared out across the wide empty land-scape. 'It's not been a few minutes, we should see him running.'

'I'd guess he's lain down somewhere in those reeds,' I said. 'They're perfect cover.'

'Then we wait,' Harsnet said in clipped tones. 'No man could stand lying out among those reeds for long. The water's freezing.'

'Look at this.' Barak was pointing at something on the ground. A rough pallet of straw. He put his hand to it.

'It's still warm,' he said. 'He's been lying here watching us.'

Harsnet frowned. 'Then he knew we were coming. But how? How?' His eyes roved over the marshes, looking for movement. But there was nothing. I shivered. Was the killer lying out there in the freezing mud and water, watching us? Harsnet took a deep breath. 'I will not stir from this spot till dusk. He has to move sooner or later.' He looked at Barak. 'Good, you brought your sword.'

Barak looked at the sky, a deeper grey now. 'I think it will rain.'

'All the better to drive him out.'

The three of us waited, watching the marshland below. Occasion-ally a waterbird started up with a clatter of wings, but otherwise we saw no movement, even when a heavy shower came and soaked us all. I was becoming uncomfortable and my back hurt. How much worse the discomfort must be for someone lying down out there.

Harsnet looked at me, probably thinking I would be of little use in a tussle. 'You go,' he said. 'Barak and I can deal with this.' Barak was sitting down on the pallet, but the coroner stood like a rock.

'Do you want me to fetch some more men?' I asked. 'Search the reeds?'

'No. He could be anywhere in there. It could take hours. We will wait till he moves. If Barak might stay here.'

'Of course.'

I left them to their vigil, wading back to the path. A couple of early passers-by stared in astonishment as I appeared, my robe and boots mud-spattered. I cast a look back at the little knoll, where Harsnet stood outlined against the sky, a waiting, avenging angel.

Chapter Twelve

AN HOUR LATER I walked through the Bedlam gates and approached the long building. This time, from somewhere within I heard two people shouting, the words indistinguishable. I did not want to enter. A monstrous killer and a deranged boy; it seemed as though this past fortnight I had left the world of normal behaviour, normal passions, behind, and entered a strange, terrifying new country. I remembered the companionable warmth of that last dinner with Roger and Dorothy. Now Roger was dead and Dorothy a shadow of herself, leaden with grief. I worried about her constantly. I thought of Barak and Harsnet waiting out there in Lambeth marshes, and prayed they would catch Roger's killer. It had been somehow terrifying, the contrast between the violence of the second identical, horrible death and the still emptiness of the marsh where the killer lay – unless it was some stranger who had chosen to camp on that knoll; but that seemed implausible.

On the doorstep of the madhouse I took a deep breath, then knocked. Keeper Shawms himself answered; perhaps he had been watching my approach from a window. He had a grim expression on his hard face. The shouting was louder now. 'Let me go, let me go, you churls.' There was a clash of chains.

'Oh, you're here, then,' he said. 'I've had notification of a hearing at the Court of Requests, about my care of Adam Kite. It's next week, the fourth.'

'Good,' I said. 'They've let you know. It is to ask you to report on him regularly.'

'I've got no time to go running to courts. You're saying I don't take care of him.'

I bent close to him, catching an odour of foul breath and drink. 'Nor do you, rogue. But the court order will ensure you will. Now let me in, I have to see my client.'

He stood back, surprised by the anger in my voice. I stepped past him, feeling the better for snapping. The shouting was louder now.

'There's a man who says he's a doctor waiting for you,' Shawms said. 'Skin as dark as coal. As if it's not enough having that madwag boy upsetting everyone, now you have to bring a blackamoor here to affright Christian folk. The Chained Scholar saw him pass, though, in that robe of his. Thought it was the Cambridge don who denied him a post, burned black in Hell and returned from the grave to torment him.' He paused, and then said, 'Come and see, sir, see what I have to contend with!'

He stumped off down the corridor. I followed him, reluctantly, but thought again that I should know as much as possible about what went on here.

A viewing hatch was open in one of the last rooms in the corridor. Through it I saw Hob Gebons and another keeper strug, gling to chain a middle-aged man in a dirty white shirt and black hose. He had a long, ascetic face beneath thinning brown hair. He was quiet now, panting with exhaustion. The two keepers had shackled his hands together before him, and one was manacling his ankle to a chain on the floor. I shuddered, for the sight brought back my brief but terrifying experience of the Tower of London.

'Is this necessary?' I asked Shawms.

There was a clinking sound as the man turned to look at us. His eyes widened as he saw the lawyer's robe beneath my coat. In a second his face went wild, and he tried to break free of the warders and fly at me. 'A lawyer now,' he yelled. 'First Pellman's ghost and now the devil sends a lawyer to torment me!'

'Stay still,' Gebons growled. 'Madwag!' He turned to the door. 'Please close the hatch, Master Shawms.' Shawms nodded, closed the door and turned to me. 'You see what I have to deal with? He'd scratch your face off if he could. His family pay for him to be kept here, or God knows what he would do. Now, I'll take you to see Dr Malton. I put him in the parlour so the patients could have a gawp at him. The ones in there are all right,' he added. 'They're not violent.' I followed him, still shocked by the scholar's savage lunge.

✝

THE PARLOUR was full today. The old woman Cissy sat in her corner sewing, while a man and two women played cards at a table. It was a normal enough scene. The keeper Ellen, who had been with Cissy before and had said she would never leave the Bedlam, was not there. I was disappointed, for she had intrigued me. Guy sat on a stool by the fire, ignoring the curious looks Cissy and the card-players gave him, his brown hands folded in his lap. He seemed, as he occasionally did in company which might be hostile, to have retreated quietly into himself.

'Guy,' I said. 'Thank you for coming. Have I kept you waiting?'

He stood up. 'I got here early.' He smiled gently. 'The residents seem to find me interesting.'

'Let us go and see Adam.' I stepped to the door, keen to get Guy away from those curious eyes. Then one of the card-players, a tall woman in her forties, jumped to her feet, sending her chair crashing over, making me start violently.

'Jane—' The other woman grabbed her arm, but she shook herself free, and stood before us. To my amazement she bent, took the hem of her skirt and lifted it up, revealing her privy parts, a bush of greying hair against white skin. She leered at us.

'Shouldn't go without seeing this.' She laughed wildly.

'Oh, shame, wicked shame,' Cissy cried from the corner. The other card-players seized Jane's arms so that her skirt fell back into place. She began laughing hysterically.

Guy laid a hand on my arm. 'Come,' he said. We stepped outside.

'Dear God,' I said.

From behind us Jane's wild laughter turned to tears as the others remonstrated with her, calling her wicked, a base whore. Guy shook his head. 'I could feel the suffering in that room while I waited, behind those people's curious eyes.'

'You're about to see worse. Shawms!' I called out.

The keeper did not reappear, but the woman Ellen emerged from a nearby room. A bunch of keys dangled from the belt of her grey smock. She stared at Guy for a moment, then turned to me.

'What is it, sir? What's that noise in the parlour?'

'One of the women made—' I felt myself reddening—'made an exhibition . . .'

'Jane, I expect.' She sighed. 'Are you here to see Adam Kite? I'll let you in, then I must go to the parlour.'

She led us to Adam's cell, opening the viewing hatch and looking in before unlocking and opening the door. I heard the rapid murmur of prayer from within.

'He's as usual, sir,' she said. 'And now, I must see to the others.' With a quick curtsy, she turned and walked to the parlour, cutting off a hubbub of noise as she closed the door. The Chained Scholar seemed to have gone quiet.

'A woman keeper,' Guy said. 'Remarkable.'

'She at least seems to be kind to the patients. She warned me against Shawms. But now, we must go inside. I warn you, this is – bad.'

'I am ready,' he answered quietly.

I led the way in. The notice from the court had had an effect: the room smelt better, there was a small fire in the grate, fresh rushes were on the floor, and Adam wore clean clothes. But he was as before, a creature of skin and bone crouched in a corner, his back to us, praying quickly, desperately. 'God, please tell me I am *saved, saved* by Your grace . . .'

Guy looked at Adam for a second, then hitched up his robe and crouched down beside him with a litheness remarkable in a man of his age. He looked into Adam's face. Adam gave him a quick sidelong look. His eyes widened a little as he registered Guy's unusual colour, but only for a moment, then he turned his head away and began praying again.

Guy twisted his head to try and look into the boy's eyes. He waited till Adam paused for breath, and asked softly, 'Adam, why do you believe God has abandoned you?'

Something flickered in Adam's eyes, and I saw that a connection had been made. 'No,' he whispered fiercely. 'If I pray, abase myself before Him, He will show me I am *saved*!'

'Will you not rise? I would like to talk to you and I am too old to squat on a stone floor.' Gently, he reached out to take Adam's arm. At once the boy's face set hard, he clenched his teeth and curled his body tighter. Guy released him. 'All right,' he said quietly. 'The poor old man will just have to crouch.'

'Who are you?' A whisper from Adam, the first words I had heard from him that were not frantic entreaties to the Deity.

'I am a doctor. I want to find out why you think God has abandoned you.'

'He has *not*,' Adam said fiercely.

'But He will not give you assurance you are saved?'

'Not yet. I have read the Bible and I pray, I pray.' Tears came to his eyes. 'But his assurance will not come.'

'That is hard.'

'Reverend Meaphon prayed with me for days, he fasted me as the Book prescribes. But I only fainted.'

'You pray so hard,' Guy asked gently, 'would you hear God if He answered you?'

Adam frowned, looked at Guy suspiciously. 'How could I not hear Him?'

'Because of your fear that is so strong it drowns everything. Is it Hell you fear?'

'The eternal burning,' Adam whispered, so low Guy had to bend close to him. 'Last night I had a dream.'

'What was it?'

'I was in a coach, such as rich persons are driven in. A black coach, four black horses pulling it. We were driving along a country lane, the fields brown and the trees bare. I wondered where I was being taken. Then we passed through a village and the people came out to their doorsteps and said, "He is being driven deeper into Hell. Deeper and deeper. Woe for the pains he will suffer, he is so bad he must be taken to the very depths!" I looked ahead and I saw a red glow on the horizon, felt a sulphurous heat.'

'Who was driving the coach?' Guy asked.

'I cannot remember.' Suddenly Adam broke down, sobbing desperately, tears running down his dirty face. Guy laid a hand on his shoulder. 'Cry,' he said. 'Yes.' And I saw deep sadness in his own eyes, Guy who had been so coldly rational about Roger, who had discussed his corpse's innards with his apprentice. I felt an unreasoning stab of anger.

At length Adam's tears subsided. Again Guy tried to coax him to his feet, but still the boy resisted. 'I must pray,' he said, in tones of desperate exhaustion. 'Please, I have wasted time talking, I have to pray.'

'Very well. But let me ask you a question. Why do you think God visits this suffering upon you? Do you think He has singled you out?'

'No.' Adam shook his head vigorously, though he looked at the wall, not at Guy. 'All should fear the pains of Hell as I do. Burning, in agony, for ever and ever. In our church we know the truth, that is what awaits those who are not *saved*, who sin.'

'And the other believers, Reverend Meaphon's congregation, are they sinners too?'

'Yes, but they have all received God's assurance that they are forgiven, they are among the elect, the saved.'

'But not you?'

'No.' He turned full-face to Guy. 'I know I am not saved. Reverend Meaphon says it is a devil inside me. I must ask God, beg Him to release me from it. Save me. Now leave me. *Leave me!*' His sudden shriek made me jump. Adam turned back to the wall, began his dreadful intoning again. 'God hear my prayer I beseech You hear me . . .'

Guy rose and inclined his head to me. I followed him outside. His expression was very angry.

'Will you fetch the keeper here?' he asked me. 'The woman, not that oaf who is in charge?'

'Very well.' I went up the corridor to the parlour. Here all was quiet again, Cissy sewing and the card-players gaming. Ellen had joined them at the table. I saw that Jane's face was red with tears. When she saw me she buried her head in her hands.

'Mistress Ellen, Dr Malton would like a word,' I said awkwardly. The keeper rose, keys jangling at her waist, and led me outside.

'I am sorry for Jane's exhibition,' she said, looking at me seriously. 'She is sorry now. But I am afraid the patients' disturbing ways are a penalty of being a visitor.'

'I understand.'

'We will have to watch her today, or she may hurt herself.'

Guy was in the corridor, looking through the viewing hatch. He turned to Ellen with a smile. 'My friend says you have been kind to Adam.'

Ellen reddened. 'I try to be.'

'He is very ill.'

'I know that, sir.'

'It is vital he is kept locked up, he must not get out or he would make another exhibition of himself. But it is very important he is kept clean, and made to take food even if he struggles. And try, but only very gently, to distract him with practicalities, the need to eat and keep warm and so forth.'

'As though he were mopish or melancholy, and needed to be lifted from his dumps? But it is much worse than that with Adam, sir.'

'I know. But can you do that? Will the other keepers help you?'

'Some will and some won't, sir. But I'll tell Keeper Shawms

those are your instructions.' She smiled sardonically. 'He is afraid of Serjeant Shardlake.'

'Good. Thank you.' Guy clapped me on the shoulder. 'Now come, Matthew, let us find somewhere to talk. For once I feel in need of strong drink.'

✝

We found a tavern nearby. I went to the bar-hatch and returned with a bottle of wine and two mugs. Guy was sitting frowning, preoccupied. 'That boy Adam noticed my colouring,' he said sud-denly. 'There was a flicker of surprise in his eyes.'

'Yes. I saw that.'

'That gives me hope, that and getting him to talk, even if only for the shortest while. Because it shows he *can* be distracted from that praying.'

'It is terrible seeing him. That story of being driven into Hell . . .'

'He is suffering as much as anyone I have ever seen. Despair.' He frowned.

'That place . . .' I shook my head.

'Some, if they have no family to take care of them, are better off in the Bedlam. Otherwise they would beg in the cities or roam as wild men in the woods. Enough do. And Adam would be in danger outside.'

'What did you think of him? His case seems desperate. Hopeless.'

Guy pondered again. Then he said, 'Let me ask you something. What do you think Adam Kite feels about himself?'

'That he is abandoned by God.'

'That is what he feels about God. But about himself?'

'That he is unworthy of God's love.'

'Yes. He is a self-hater. And there have been self-haters since the world began, people who believe they are unlovable.'

'We must fight such notions with reason,' I said.

'Oh, come, Matthew.' Guy smiled. 'If only it were so simple.

Our minds are ruled by passions more than reason. And sometimes they run out of control.' His eyes went blank for a moment, as they had been when he was sitting in the parlour, as though he were looking inward. He frowned, then continued. 'And why? Sometimes we learn to hate ourselves from early on.'

'I suppose so.' As I had learned, through insults and rejection as a child, that to many my form was frightening and shameful.

'And these radical churchmen must hate themselves more than anyone. Despite their ranting, they feel they are quite unworthy. If they are saved from Hell it is only through God's mysterious grace.'

'When the end of the world comes. Any minute now, a lot of them say.'

'There have always been churchmen forecasting the imminent Apocalypse. Though many more now amongst the radical congregations. And Adam was brought up in that setting. How did his parents say his illness started?'

I told him what the Kites had related to me, that Adam had been a happy, outgoing child, until a while ago he became increasingly preoccupied, and thus descended to his present state. 'They are good folk,' I concluded. 'They are under the sway of their minister, a canting dogmatist called Meaphon, but concern for their son is leading them towards an independent stand, especially Adam's mother.'

'I should like to meet them.' Guy stroked his chin. 'Something happened, something specific brought this on, I am sure. His dream is a clue. The people he saw from that coach said, "He is so bad, he is being taken to the depths." And I think he did know who was driving that coach in his dream. If I can find out who that was, that may help us on the path to saving him.'

'You can set too much store by dreams, Guy.'

'They are a guide to understanding. A way.' He shook his head. 'Strange to hear that poor pallid creature was once a strong, happy youth. But madness can distort the body as well as the mind.'

'Will you visit him again?' I asked.

'If you and his parents wish.'

'Yes.' I looked at him curiously. 'I did not know that you had worked with the mad.'

'It was part of an infirmarian's duties. And diseases of the mind have always interested me. Perhaps because there are so many different types, and no clear view as to what they are. There are those who say they are caused by an imbalance in the humours, a rush of bad humours to the brain.'

'Like corrupted black bile rising to the brain and causing melancholy?'

'Yes. Others see mental illness as caused by physical disorders in the brain, though no one has ever found any that I know of, apart from tumours, which kill.' He took a deep breath. 'And then there are those, like your friend Meaphon, who see some madness as possession by devils, which must be driven out.'

'And which school do you incline to?'

'I belong to another tradition, Matthew. The tradition of Vesalius, although he has had many intellectual forebears. An approach that starts not with the theory but with the disorder; examines it, studies it, tries to understand what it is. The crazy words and actions of the mad may hold secret clues to what is happening in their minds. And even with the mad one can sometimes use reason, commonsense.'

'That old woman we saw in the parlour, Cissy, Ellen seems to treat her in that way, trying to bring her from her inner world into the everyday one, giving her simple sewing tasks to do.'

'Yes, that may help with melancholics. Forcing the mind away from dark thoughts, into the everyday.'

'I wonder,' I said, 'whether Roger's killer may be suffering some form of madness. To kill someone so brutally, apparently pointlessly.' Twice, I thought, but did not say, for I knew it could be dangerous for us both if I breached Cranmer's injunction not to tell Guy about Dr Gurney.

'It is possible,' Guy said. 'Unless Master Elliard gave someone cause to take such a terrible revenge, which having met him, I doubt.'

'That is impossible.' There *was* something I could ask him about, I realized. I took a draught of wine.

'Guy, you said some of the monastic infirmarians used dwale. Do you know of any infirmarians in London who might have?'

'I did not know them, Matthew. Remember I came to London from Sussex when my old monastery was dissolved.' He looked me. 'You are thinking of those monks who were driven out of their wits when they were thrown out of the monasteries?'

'Yes,' I admitted.

'Then I should tell you that the use of dwale was mainly restricted to the Benedictines. And the only Benedictine foundation that had an infirmary in London was Westminster Abbey. But as I said before, its use is not a secret.'

'Its expert use?'

'There may be many healers who still use it.' I could see that Guy found the whole idea of Roger's killer being an ex-monk distasteful as well as improbable.

'Its basis is opium, is it not? Poppies would need to be grown and cultivated. Whoever it is would need to have a garden.'

'True. Though many grow poppies in their gardens for their bright colour. And I myself grow them in my herb garden to make opium.'

I wished I could tell him this was not just a matter of finding someone with the motive to kill Roger. Again, I hoped fervently that Barak and Harsnet had caught him already.

'How is Mistress Elliard?' Guy asked.

'Bereft.'

'You are fond of her.'

'She has always been my friend.'

'A woman of courage, I think.'

'Yes, she is.' I thought, with frustration, I cannot tell Dorothy the full story either. I drained my wine.

'I have to go,' I said. 'Thank you, Guy, for seeing Adam. I will arrange for you to see him again, and meet his parents. Will you come to the court hearing next week, give evidence as to his state of mind, asking that he be kept in the Bedlam for now?'

'Yes, I will. May I bring Piers?' I gave him a look of surprise. 'I want the boy to see all aspects of the physician's work. I know he is only an apprentice apothecary, but he has a very good mind. I am thinking of sponsoring him to study as a physician.'

'Could you afford that?'

'It would not be easy. But my earnings are growing since I have been accepted as a physician myself, and I still have my pension as an ex-monk. And poor people with ability deserve to find sponsors, to find patrons, do they not?' His look was challenging.

I was taken aback. That would be a huge investment for Guy. I met his look, realizing to my shame that I was jealous. For a long time I had been Guy's only friend.

✝

I HURRIED HOME through the busy streets, for it would soon be curfew-time. Barak was waiting for me in chambers. He was towelling his hair, which like his clothes was soaking wet. Skelly had gone home.

'No luck?' I asked.

'We waited till it got dark, then came away. That bastard was crouching in those reeds all day, he's got away now.' He frowned. 'How did you know?'

'Just a feeling.'

'Harsnet's furious with himself, said he should have left us two there to watch and roused some of the Westminster constables to flush him out. He hadn't believed anyone could have sat it out in those cold marshes all day.' He raised his eyebrows. 'He said it was as though the man was spirited away by a devil.'

'That's all we need.'

'He's right that it would take something to lie out there all day without making a noise. I couldn't do it.'

'We know how determined this creature is,' I said. 'But how did he know we would be there to look at where Dr Gurney was found? That is what worries me.'

'And me,' Barak said with feeling.

We sat silent for a minute, then Barak asked, 'How was Adam Kite?'

'Mad. I hope Guy can help him, but I don't know.'

'Well, I've some news at least. I sent word to Gib Rooke, and he sent a reply, at once, by one of his children. He'll meet us at his house tomorrow, tell us about that killing in Lambeth last winter.'

Out on those marshes again. But the news lifted me, it was something positive to do after a day of horrors. 'Thank you, Jack,' I said. 'You should get off home. Tamasin will be worried about you.'

'I'm seeing some old friends for a drink tonight,' he said brusquely.

When he had gone I went into my room. Poor Tamasin, I thought. And poor Dorothy, I must look in on her before I went home. I saw a sheaf of papers with the Court of Common Pleas seal on my desk, more work. Outside the rain had begun again, pattering on the windows.

Chapter Thirteen

NEXT MORNING Barak and I set out once again for the marshes. We took the horses; it was bright and sunny, a truly springlike day, and they were skittish, Barak's black mare Sukey sniffing the air and tossing her fine head. As we rode through the city I saw crocuses and snowdrops springing up everywhere, even among the tumbled stones of the dissolved Blackfriars monastery. At Cheapside conduit I looked at the beggars gathered round. The Bedlam man was there, singing a nonsensical song to himself, snowdrops stuck in his wild hair. He had a sharp eye on the crowd though, hoping to catch someone's eye and shame them into casting him a coin.

We rode across London Bridge and through Southwark. Gib's child had left directions with Barak; we were to take a path on the far side of Southwark village, where a church stood on the edge of the marshes, and follow it through the marshes to the cottars' dwellings. We found the church easily enough, a square little Norman building perched on the edge of the reedbeds. Beside it a wide track led through the marshes, twisting and turning to follow the higher ground. We passed a group of men shoring up a muddy, sunken stretch of path with cinders and branches. They stepped aside and bowed. I wondered if the cottars had widened and maintained this stretch themselves, to bring their produce to market. They were bringing a whole new area into development; no wonder the landlords were keen to filch the product of their labours.

'Our local butcher's been arrested,' Barak told me.

'Him too?' I looked at him sharply. 'You haven't been buying meat in Lent?'

'No. I would have, left to myself, but Tamasin is too careful.'

'She always had a sensible head on her shoulders.'

'If it's right that Catherine Parr has reformist sympathies,' Barak said, changing the subject, 'she's stepping into a dangerous position if she marries the King. Gardiner and Bonner will be after her, watching every word she says, hoping she'll let slip some reformist opinion they can run and tell the King about.'

'They will. But it will take courage to turn down a proposal from the King.'

Barak looked across the marshes. 'Were those two killings to do with her? Someone who wants to stop the marriage?'

'Thomas Seymour would have a motive,' I said.

'I can't see Sir Thomas lying flat in a bog for most of a cold day. He'd damage his fine clothes.' Barak spoke lightly, yet there was an uneasy note in his voice as he steered a way through the reeds, all around us now.

Cottages began to appear beside the path, surrounded by little market gardens; Gib's was the fifth along, a mud-and-daub cottage like the rest, smoke curling through a hole in the thatched roof. Gib was working in his patch, loosening the heavy soil with a spade. A woman and several small children were also at work digging and sowing. Barak called out Gib's name and he came across, his wife and children following. They gathered round as we dismounted, the children staring at me wide-eyed.

'My barrister,' Gib introduced me proudly. 'He seeks my help on a certain matter.'

His wife, a thin, tired-looking woman, curtsied then smiled at me warmly. 'We are so grateful, sir, for what you did. We won't ever forget.'

'Thank you.' Like all lawyers, I was delighted by gratitude. It happened so rarely.

Gib clapped his hands. 'Come on. Maisie, children, back to work! Master Shardlake and I have confidential matters to discuss.' Barak winked at me. The family returned to their labours, the children casting glances over their shoulders at us.

'I don't want them to hear about this bad business,' Gib said, suddenly serious. 'Tie your horses to this post, sir, and come inside.'

We followed him into the cottage, which smelt of damp and smoke. A few poor sticks of furniture stood about, and a fire burning in the hearth in the middle of the floor provided some warmth. The single window was unglazed, the crude shutters open. I looked out at the view of his market garden, the marshes stretching out beyond.

'Ay, it's a doleful spot,' Gib said.

'It must have been lonely this past winter, with all the snow.'

'It was. Bitterly cold too. At least now we can get busy with the sowing. Sit down on that settle.'

He brought some weak beer and sat on a stool opposite us. 'Now then,' he said, looking at us seriously. 'You've questions about poor Wilf Tupholme?'

'He was the man who was murdered?'

'Yes.' He paused, remembering. 'He was found in January. They are after Welsh Elizabeth, that he lived with. A Bankside whore.' He spat in the fire. Barak and I looked at each other. This sounded as though we were on the wrong track.

'Are they sure she did it?' I asked.

'Sure enough to issue a warrant against her. She and Wilf had been living together a few months, but they were always fighting. Both liked the drink too much. He turfed her out in December, then he was found dead a month later. The coroner's trying to trace her but the other whores say she's gone back to Wales. She'll go to earth there, they won't find her.'

'But there was no direct evidence?'

'Well, whoever did that to him must have hated him.' He looked at us curiously. 'Are you saying it was someone else?'

'We don't know. At Westminster you said his landlord probably killed him.'

Gib grinned. 'That was just to annoy Sir Geoffrey.' He looked at us with great curiosity, but saw that we were not going to tell him anything more.

'So what happened?' Barak asked. 'You said he was killed most horribly.'

'So he was. I'll tell you on the way to his house. His neighbour has the key, I thought you might like to look.' He inclined his head to the window and I saw that one of the children, a girl of ten or so, had edged close to the window as she walked up and down the vegetable patch, sowing. 'Little pigs have big ears,' he said quietly.

I glanced at Barak, who shrugged slightly. It did not sound as though this killing had anything to do with our investigation, but we might as well hear the full tale. 'Very well,' I said, 'let us go.'

✠

GIB LED US eastward along the path. The cottages became fewer as the ground became marshier, water squelching under our feet and large pools standing among the reeds. An early pair of swallows, the first I had seen that year, dived and glided above them.

'What happened to Tupholme, then?' Barak asked.

'Wilf was a strange man,' Gib said. 'He was always bad-tempered and surly, seemed to prefer living alone in his isolated cottage. We'd only see him at market. A couple of years ago he became a hot-gospeller, telling everyone that the end-time was nigh. Plagues and earthquakes and Jesus coming to judge us all. He'd talk about the joys of being saved, in a smug way as though secretly enjoying that the rest of us poor cottars weren't saved. He went across the river to some hot-gospelling church in the city. But you know how it is with these folk, often it doesn't last long. Last autumn he took up with Welsh Elizabeth and she moved in. They'd get drunk and argue, like I said. You could hear them way out over the marshes. Then Wilf booted Elizabeth out. He was surly after that, you'd find him stumbling drunk around the lanes. Then he disappeared, his neighbour saw his cottage was locked up. After a while his neighbour thought, if he's gone, I'll take the land over before it goes back to marsh. So he broke open a shutter to take a look inside. Said the smell nearly felled him.'

Gib looked sombre. 'Wilf was inside on the floor, tied up, dead. He was gagged. They said his staring eyes were terrible to see. Someone had cut him badly all over, then tied him up. His thigh had this great sore on it, all black and crawling with maggots. There was a rag in his mouth to stop him shouting. Whether his diseased leg got him, or cold and hunger, nobody knows.'

We were silent. This death was even worse than Roger's. Tupholme would have died in slow agony.

'If his leg went bad that would probably kill him first,' Barak said.

'Welsh Elizabeth deserves to hang,' Gib said with sudden fierce-ness.

I looked at Barak and he shook his head slightly. Horrific as this killing was, its manner was nothing like those of Roger and Dr Gurney.

Gib led us up a side-path to where an isolated cottage stood, as poor as the others. No smoke came from the roof. The shutters were closed, and the door had a heavy padlock. The wood of one shutter had been splintered at one end where the neighbour had broken in. Gib stared at the house, then quickly crossed himself. 'I'll get the key,' he said. 'Gib's neighbour has it. I won't be long.'

He walked back to the main path, the reeds soon hiding him. I looked at the cultivated land around the cottage. It was already going to seed, new grass coming up among the little furrows.

'This is a dead end,' Barak said.

'It seems so. And yet . . .'

'What?'

'Gib described a great sore. I know that phrase, or one like it. People keep using phrases that I know somehow. Treasurer Rowland talked of a fountain of blood. The man who found Dr Gurney said something too – water turned to blood.'

'We've got enough to worry about without word mysteries,' Barak said irritably. 'Look, when he comes back, let's just say we don't need to go inside; it seems clear enough this Welsh whore did it for spite.'

'That's a huge amount of spite.'

Gib returned in a few minutes. 'Pete Lammas has given me the key, the coroner left him responsible for the house. He doesn't want to go in again, though.' He paused. 'Look, sir,' he said. 'I'd rather not go in either. I've heard enough of what it was like. Can I leave you to bring me back the key?'

'All right,' I agreed.

Gib handed the key to Barak, bowed to us and left. I was still lost in thought, those phrases jostling in my head.

'I'll be the one to open the door, then, shall I?' Barak asked with heavy sarcasm. He unlocked the padlock and pushed at the door. It was stiff, scraping along the ground as it opened. Barak and I both stepped backwards at the smell that hit us, a butcher's shop stink overlaid with the stench of sweat and dirt. And a great buzzing, as from a swarm of flies.

'Jesu!' Barak said.

We stepped carefully into the dark interior. I saw the shapes of chairs, a table and what looked like heaps of rubbish scattered around. Despite the season blowflies were everywhere, buzzing around the room, slow and disoriented in the cool weather. We batted them away from our faces. The earthen floor was spotted with dead ones. Barak went across to the shutters and opened them.

In the light that fell into the room we saw the place was filthy, stinking old rushes on the floor, a full chamber pot in one corner and rags everywhere. The disturbed blowflies began to settle again, on the rags and the pot; a few flew out of the window.

'Gib said his leg was a mass of maggots,' Barak said. 'They must have hatched. There's enough filth in here for them to feed on.' He lifted one of the rags with his foot, and a couple of flies buzzed upward. 'This is his upper hose, I think. There's a tear in it, look, it's stiff with dried blood. Jesus, to cut someone up and leave them to die of infected wounds. That's some revenge.'

I stood in the middle of the foul room, looking round. 'The coroners' men probably cut the clothes off the body and then left everything here as it was,' I said. 'Look, there are some fragments of cut rope over there.'

'It must have been filthy enough here even before the poor arsehole was killed.'

I looked at a truckle bed in the corner, the sheets grey with dirt. A cheap wooden cross was nailed to the mud wall above the bed. A relic of the man's hot-gospelling past?

'Let's get out of here,' Barak said. 'There's nothing but filth and rags.'

'Not yet.' I would have liked to sit down, my back was aching from so long on my feet. 'This is a lonely spot and he was unpopular. If Wilf Tupholme's killer knew him, he would know that in the depths of winter if he was tied up and left to die it might be weeks before anyone opened the place up.'

'Why do you say, he? Surely it was his woman.'

'I wonder.' I looked at a dark bloodstain on the floor by the long-dead fire. 'He was overpowered, perhaps knocked out, then tied up, a rag put in his mouth, then laid down here. Finally his leg was slashed open. Surely a drunken whore he'd kicked out would be more likely to knock him on the head.'

'She wanted to ensure a slow death,' Barak answered grimly.

'And if it wasn't her?'

'Who else could it have been?'

'Someone who kills skilfully, carefully, to make an evil spectacle.' A few dozy bugs still crawled over the bloodstain. 'Jesu, how he must have suffered,' I said.

'This has nothing in common with those others,' Barak said impatiently. He stirred the rags with his foot. 'Hullo, what's this?'

Something among the rubbish had made a metallic chink. Barak bent and, wrinkling his nose, felt among the scraps of clothing. He came up with a large tin badge, showing the painted image of an arched stone structure. I took it from Barak's hand.

'A pilgrim badge,' he said. 'From St Edward the Confessor's

shrine at Westminster. That's an odd thing for a hot-gospeller to have. Don't they see shrines as papist images?'

'Maybe one of the constables dropped it while they were clearing the body out,' Barak suggested.

'Unlikely. People don't wear pilgrim badges these days, in case they're taken for papists. But someone dropped it here. Look through the rest of that stuff, Jack, see what else you can find.'

'I do get the nice jobs, don't I?' Barak began turning over all the filthy clothes and other rubbish. 'There's nothing else here,' he said at length. He looked at the cross on the wall, then at the bloodstained spot by the fire. 'Poor bastard,' he said. 'I wonder if he repented him of his fornication as lay watching the maggots eat his leg.'

I gave a start. 'What did you say?'

'I said I wondered if he regretted his time with the whore—'

'No, no, you said "repented him of his fornication". Why did you use that phrase?'

He looked at me as though I had lost my senses. 'I don't know, it just came into my head. It's from the Bible, isn't it?'

I clapped him on the shoulder. 'Yes, it is. Phrases from the Bible, they are what we hear everywhere now, are they not? In the pulpit, in the streets. They have become part of our daily language. That's why those other phrases snagged at my mind.' I stood in that terrible place, thinking. 'Is it possible?'

'Is what possible?'

'Oh, Jesu,' I said quietly. 'I hope I am wrong. Come.'

'Right about what? You talk in riddles—'

'We must get to a church. That one on the edge of the marshes will do.'

I led the way out of the cottage and began walking rapidly down the path. Barak locked it and came after me, for once having to run to keep up as I led the way back to Gib's place. He was back at work. I left Barak to hand over the key, while I unhitched the horses and used a tree trunk as a mounting block.

'What's the hurry?' Gib called out as Barak ran back to me, his face alive with curiosity. 'What did you find?'

'Nothing!' Barak called back as he swung into Sukey's saddle. 'He has to go to church, that's all!'

☩

THE DOOR OF the church was open, and we stepped into the cool interior. It was, I saw, still decorated in the old style, the walls painted in bright colours, worn patterned tiles on the floor. Candles burned everywhere and there was a smell of incense, although the niches where reliquaries and statues of saints once stood were bare. On a lectern beside the richly decorated altar lay a Bible, fixed to it by a chain. The English Bible, ordered by Lord Cromwell to be set in every church, the year before his fall. This particular church, I reflected, was a faithful image of what the King wished to see: saints and relics gone, but otherwise everything as it was before the break with Rome. Here, at least, everything was conformity.

'Why are we here?' Barak asked, following me down the aisle.

'I want to look at that Bible. Sit down in a pew while I seek what I want.'

'But what *do* you want?'

I turned to face him. 'We've been talking about the hot-gospellers, the end-timers who say Armageddon will soon be here. They preach their message everywhere these days, that's why Bishop Bonner is so keen to stop them. But where do they get their message from, which part of the Bible?'

'The Book of Revelation, isn't it?'

'Yes, the Apocalypse of St John the Divine. That's where most of their religious quotes come from. The last book of the Bible; full of wild, fiery, cruel language, hard to understand, unlike anything else in the New Testament. Erasmus and Luther both doubted whether Revelation was really the word of God, though Luther at least calls it inspirational now.'

'You're saying that's where these phrases you remember come from? But how does—'

'I think they come from a specific part of the Book of Revelation. But please, sit quiet a minute, don't distract me.' I spoke somewhat unfairly, as I had been doing the talking.

With a shake of his head, Barak sat down on the thick-cushioned pew of a rich family in the front row. I mounted the lectern and opened the great blue-bound Bible. I paused at the frontispiece: the King on his throne, underneath him Cromwell and Cranmer passing the Bible down to richly dressed lords, who in turn passed it down to those of lower degree. Then I turned the heavy pages until I came to the very end, to Revelation. I found the part I was seeking and read slowly, following the text with my finger. At length I stood up. 'Barak,' I said quietly. 'Come up here.'

He joined me. 'Look,' I said. 'This is the part of the Book of Revelation where St John is shown the seven angels who pour the seven vials of wrath upon the earth.'

'I remember our vicar reading about that once. I couldn't follow it, it sounded like a mad dream.'

'A mad dream. Yes, well put. Here, look at this, in Chapter 2.' I quoted: '*And I gave her space to repent of her fornication; and she repented not.* When you used that phrase, or a version of it, I realized where all these other gobbets that had stuck in my mind came from. Here.' I turned several pages, until I came to a heading: *The angels pour out their vials of wrath.* 'Now, listen to this,' I said. 'Chapter 16:

'*And I heard a great voice out of the temple saying to the seven angels, Go your ways, pour out your vials of wrath upon the earth.*

'*And the first went, and poured out his vial upon the earth; and there fell a noisome and grievous sore upon the men which had the mark of the beast, and upon them which worshipped his image.* A noisome and grievous sore. Gib said "a great sore". Poor Wilf Tupholme was murdered in the manner of the victims of the first vial. And he was a believer who had lapsed into fornication. Many would say that meant he had the mark of the beast on him.'

Barak frowned. 'Aren't you making what happened to the cottar fit what's in here?' he asked dubiously. 'Like the hot-gospellers try to fit everything that happened into these prophecies? He didn't have any mark on him, of the beast or anything else. What is the mark anyway?'

'The number 666. But it's not clear from Revelation whether that is an actual mark on the body.'

'And if all apostate hot-gospellers were to be killed there'd be men dead of grievous sores all over London.'

'The one death may be symbolic. Barak, if it was only this one reference I would agree with you. But listen to this:

'*And the second angel poured out his vial upon the sea; and it turned as it were into the blood of a dead man: and every living thing died in the sea.* If Wilf Tupholme was the first to die, that means Dr Gurney was the second. He died in salt water, a tidal pool, turned to blood.'

Barak frowned, read the passage for himself. I had given even his sceptical mind food for thought. 'And it continues,' I went on quietly. '*And the third angel shed out his vial upon the rivers and fountains of waters; and they turned to blood.* Roger Elliard died in a fountain turned to blood.' Suddenly overcome with emotion, I gripped the sides of the lectern. 'Poor Roger. This is a blasphemy.'

'Dr Gurney and Master Elliard were said to be good people, though,' Barak said.

'Yes, they were. It looks as if they did something sinful; or the brute that killed them thought they had.' I took a long deep breath. 'And Roger, like Tupholme, had once been a radical but abandoned that path. I wonder if Dr Gurney did too.' I looked at Barak. 'Well, do you agree with me? Someone is killing people in accordance with the prophecy of the vials of wrath?'

'To fulfil the prophecy,' Barak said slowly.

'Yes. Symbolically.'

'Jesus.' He looked truly shocked. He was silent for a moment, then said, 'That means four more murders.'

'Yes.'

'What happens next?'

I looked at Revelation again. '*And the fourth angel poured out his vial upon the sun; and power was given unto him to burn men with heat of fire.*'

'Shit,' Barak said. 'People left to rot, dead in water; and burned with fire next.'

'I do not think this is to do with Catherine Parr,' I said. 'This is not politics after all, Barak; it is religion. Mad, debased religion.'

Barak looked at the pages, turned them over. 'What happens after the seven vials have been spilled? Where does it end?'

I laughed, heard the half-hysterical sound echo round the old church. 'What do you think? This is the Book of Revelation, Barak. It ends with the destruction of the whole world.'

Chapter Fourteen

WE WENT AT ONCE to Lambeth Palace, riding fast along the Thames-side path, sending up spatters of mud and attracting stares from passers-by. When we arrived at the palace I asked at once for Cranmer's secretary. Morice quickly appeared, a little pale-faced man in a black robe who looked at us dubiously. I told him who I was and that I had urgent news, and he scuttled away, leaving us standing in the Great Hall. He returned a few minutes later and told us in hushed tones that the Archbishop had sent across to Whitehall for the others involved in the matter. He showed us into a comfortable little room to await their arrival.

'One thing,' I asked him. 'Could you please fetch me a copy of the New Testament in English?'

'I will have one brought.' He looked at us in puzzlement, then smiled before bowing himself out.

'Are you sure about this notion?' Barak asked when the door was closed. 'It seems fantastic. I don't know what Cranmer and the others will make of it.'

'You saw the chapter. It speaks for itself, surely.'

'But it talked of thousands being killed by each vial of wrath, not just one man each time.'

'I think this is some sort of devilish, perverted symbolism—' I broke off as a servant appeared bearing a copy of the Testament. I laid it on the table and again I pored over the text of Revelation, Barak peering over my shoulder. I was only too well aware that if I had misread, or misunderstood something, my reception from the great men now being gathered from Whitehall was likely to be unpleasant.

'This book makes no sense,' Barak said at length. 'It tells the same story in different ways, different versions of how the world will end, angels and wars and vials. There is no . . .'

'Narrative? I know. It is the only book in the New Testament that is so obscure.'

'It's powerful stuff though. Fixes itself inside your head somehow.' He read. '*The smoke of their torment ascendeth up for ever and ever, and they have no rest day or night, who worship the beast and his image.* The beast being the devil?'

'Yes, though some say it is the Church of Rome. There are as many interpretations of Revelation as there are interpreters, each one saying his understanding is the true one. And most are ill-educated fanatics. This book is causing much trouble in the world.'

'You know your Bible well.' Barak eyed me curiously.

'Not Revelation especially, but the Bible, yes.' I smiled sadly. 'From my teens to my thirties I was an earnest seeker after reform.'

'You said Erasmus and Luther doubted Revelation was authentic? Why was that?'

'In ancient times there were many gospels, far more than the four we have in the Bible now, and countless Apocalypses, foretellings of how the world will end. But the ancient scholars who decided which were the authentic Christian texts inspired directly by God, rejected all the Apocalypses save the one we have, mainly because they believed the author was St John. But Erasmus and Luther cast doubt on that, because it was so different from the rest of the New Testament. In its violence and cruelty, its representation of Jesus as God's harsh judge, who *holds the keys of hell and death.*'

'Someone else holds them now,' Barak said. He blew out his cheeks, shook his head. He had never come across anything like this horror, and it had shaken him to the core. As it had me; but I had to act now, to tell Cranmer and the others, focus on that.

We both started as the door opened to reveal Cranmer's secretary.

He bowed. 'His grace will see you now, Master Shardlake,' he said. 'Only you, your man is to stay here.'

☦

CRANMER SAT behind his desk. Lord Hertford, Thomas Seymour and coroner Harsnet stood round him. Thomas Seymour was in a red silk doublet today, the sleeves slashed to show a vivid yellow lining; his brother in dull brown. All looked at me seriously, expectantly.

'What have you found, Matthew?' the Archbishop asked quietly.

I took a deep breath. 'My lord, I believe I know why Dr Gurney and my friend were killed. And a third who was killed in December.'

Cranmer leaned forward. 'A third?' His voice was horrified.

'Yes. And if I am right, there are four more deaths to come.'

Lord Hertford frowned, his eyes boring into mine.

Sir Thomas spoke. 'Come on then, man, spit out your tale.'

I told as concisely as I could how I had learned of Tupholme's death, how the manner of it had led me to the connection with Revelation. My auditors heard me in silence. I glanced at Cranmer's bookshelf. 'If you will check Chapter 16 of Revelation, my lord—'

'I know the New Testament by heart, Matthew.' He frowned, thinking hard.

Thomas Seymour laughed. A rich, booming sound that made Cranmer wince. 'I have never heard such a tale. The crookback lawyer's mind is addled by too much reading.'

Lord Hertford gave his brother a stern look. 'Remember where you are, Thomas, and watch your language.'

Cranmer seemed to have retreated into a brown study, his fingers toying with the big silver cross at his neck. When he sat up his expressive eyes were full of sorrow.

'I think Matthew could be right. These deaths do fit exactly with Revelation 16, even to their sequence. And in these times when every apprentice believes himself an authority on scripture – yes, a man who was mad and vicious enough could believe he was inspired to fulfil the prophecy – for Revelation is, above all, a prophecy of what must come to pass.' He gave a sigh that was almost a groan.

I looked at him. Was he talking of possession again, a man's soul taken over by the devil?

Hertford had pulled a Testament from Cranmer's shelf and was reading it. He nodded slowly. 'He is right, my lord. These murders fit the pattern of the vials of wrath too closely to be any coincidence. But we may take a little comfort.'

'Comfort? How?' Cranmer asked incredulously.

'If the killer's purpose is to fulfil these prophecies, the fact that the second victim was Lord Latimer's doctor surely has no significance.' He looked at Cranmer. 'This is not aimed at the proposed marriage.'

Cranmer nodded slowly. 'Yes, that follows. But the King would still be horrified beyond measure if he knew.' He glanced at Harsnet. 'I think he too might see the killer as inspired by the devil, and turn away from any possible involvement with the lady Catherine.' He smiled sadly. 'He is so superstitious; I have tried for years to persuade him out of such false thinking, but without success.'

'Would His Majesty necessarily be wrong to think this was inspired by the devil?' Harsnet's keen eyes darted round the room. 'Consider the blasphemous pattern the killer is following, how cunningly he planned these three terrible displays, his uncanny ability to carry the bodies over great distances.'

'The cottar's murder was also intended for display,' I said. 'But it was blamed on a woman he had thrown out.'

'Does that not speak to you of a man possessed?' Harsnet asked.

'Why are you gospel men always so ready to cry possession?' Thomas Seymour snapped irritably. 'We should be catching this man, not wasting time on these speculations. We cannot know what he is until then.'

For once I agreed with Seymour. 'Sir Thomas speaks true, my lord,' I said. 'Catching him remains our priority.'

Cranmer looked to me. 'Well, Matthew, where would you go from here?'

'We must find out if this Tupholme had any acquaintances in common with Roger and the doctor—'

'Fie, man,' Sir Thomas said impatiently. 'He was a cottar, a nobody, and the others were gentlemen.'

'Tupholme and Roger had both held radical reformist views, though in different ways both had abandoned them. Was that also true of Dr Gurney?'

'Yes,' Cranmer said. 'He – he had once been very radical, but recently he had become – disillusioned.' He frowned for a long moment, then looked at me. 'You think the killer may be seeking men who were once religious radicals but abandoned that position for one reason or another?'

'I fear so. And there is one place where radicals of all classes meet. In church.'

'The three dead men did not live near each other,' Cranmer said. 'They cannot have attended the same parish churches.'

'Sometimes radicals go to church outside their parishes,' Hertford said. 'Run private Bible-reading and prayer groups. And why should they not?' he added with sudden fierceness. 'When they are persecuted and driven underground for their beliefs.'

'Are you suggesting it was one of the godly people who did this?' Harsnet asked me, looking me straight in the eye.

'Not necessarily. But certainly someone who knew the reformers.'

Archbishop Cranmer buried his face in his hands. Everyone fell silent; Hertford glanced uneasily at Harsnet. I realized the Archbishop was caught in the middle, between his own reforming beliefs and the dangers the radicals presented to the very existence of reform. Lord Hertford, I thought, saw this, but Harsnet for the moment was too caught up in his own outrage. Sir Thomas did not care one way or the other.

Cranmer lowered his hands again and sat up straight in his tall chair, his face set hard. He looked at me.

'Matthew, the danger to me, to everyone in this room, grows by the hour. Some of my staff are still being questioned for heresy, though they will find nothing, for they are not heretics. More butchers are being arrested. Now there is a talk of a purge of booksellers. The Earl of Surrey is in the Fleet prison for Lent-breaking. And you will have seen that plays and interludes with a reformist slant are being made targets, their posters pulled down.'

'Yes, my lord.'

Hertford nodded in agreement. 'We are hanging on by our finger-tips.'

'Can you imagine what a gift to Bonner and Gardiner this would be, someone murdering radicals who have backslid in London? This horrid blasphemy would be meat and drink for his cause.'

'I found one clue at the scene of Tupholme's murder,' I said. I produced the badge from my pocket and laid it on Cranmer's table.

Lord Hertford bent to study it closely. 'A pilgrim badge. The wearer went to St Edward the Confessor's shrine in Westminster Abbey. I saw enough of these badges on people's coats before the shrines were done away with.'

'It can't have come from Tupholme, if he was a reformer,' Harsnet said.

'Nor from his woman,' Thomas Seymour added. 'I never heard of a Southwark whore that wore one of those.'

Cranmer took the badge, turned it between his thick fingers. 'So the killer dropped it. Perhaps it was torn from his coat as he struggled to tie that poor wretched cottar—'

'Hold fast,' Harsnet said. 'People don't wear pilgrim badges now. It marks you out as a Papist sympathizer.'

'Yes, it would be a defiant gesture,' I said.

'It could have been dropped deliberately,' Lord Hertford said.

'Yes, my lord,' I agreed. 'That is possible. But there may be another connection to the old religion.' I took a deep breath. 'Dwale was used to subdue at least two victims. And according to my friend Dr Malton, the only certain place dwale has been used in recent years is in the infirmaries of Benedictine monasteries. I wanted to ask you, my lord, whether I might make search among the Court of Augmentations records, to see what became of London's Benedictine infirmarians.'

Cranmer leaned forward. 'Could that be the explanation?' he asked eagerly. 'An ex-monk? A crazed, embittered papist making an example of men who were radicals once—'

'But is it not the radical godly men, not papists, who claim they understand the secrets of Revelation?' Again Sir Thomas surprised me with his perceptiveness.

'And perhaps these killings are to make an evil mockery of those very views,' Cranmer said. 'The papist church had its own students of Revelation, like Jonathan of Fiore.' His face lightened at the thought that the killer's religious motives might be conservative, not radical. He sat up, looked at us in turn. 'Master Harsnet, I want you to investigate whether the cottar had any links with the first two victims, especially through their religious affiliations. Matthew, look into the Court of Augmentations records. Edward.' He turned to Hertford. 'You are close to the King these days, I leave it to you to ensure no word of this comes near him.'

Hertford nodded. 'So long as no one here talks, I can do that.'

'And me?' Thomas Seymour asked.

'You, Thomas, keep your mouth shut,' his brother said.

Seymour reddened. Hertford turned to Cranmer. 'Well, so we investigate what has been done. But what of the future? If the lawyer here is right, and I believe he may well be, there will soon be a fourth killing.' He opened his Testament and read aloud: '*And the fourth angel poured out his vial upon the sun; and power was given unto him to burn men with heat of fire. And the men raged in great heat, and spoke evil of the name of God, which hath power over these plagues, and repented not.*'

'What will he do?' Cranmer said quietly. 'Where, and when?'

'Anyone could be the victim,' I said. 'Anywhere in London, a pious man like Roger or a man relapsed into sin like the cottar. We cannot know when he will strike, or where.'

'Then we cannot stop him?'

'Only if we catch him first,' I answered. 'And I think he will strike again before long.'

'Why so?' Harsnet asked.

'It seems Tupholme was found in January. Dr Gurney died in February, a month later. Roger died three weeks after that. A week ago. It would seem sensible to expect the fourth killing within the next fortnight.'

'What of the final three vials of wrath?' Thomas Seymour asked. 'What happens?'

Cranmer took a deep breath. 'The pouring of the fifth vial brings death to the sinful by darkness and great pain. That could mean death by any one of a hundred means. The sixth vial dries up the waters of the Euphrates, and I do not know what someone could do to simulate that. And when the seventh angel pours out his vial there are thunders and lightnings and a great earthquake.'

'My lord,' I said. 'There is one more thing I would ask, if I may. It could assist us.'

'Yes?'

'Dr Malton. He told me some of the old monastic infirmarians used dwale. He may know of them, even if he did not know them himself. I would like to take him into my confidence. He helped us over the dwale.'

'He's an ex-monk, isn't he?' Hertford asked sharply.

'Yes, but if Matthew says he will keep his confidence—' Cranmer gave me a long considering look – 'I will accept that. You may tell him, Matthew.'

Hertford gave me a dubious look, and Harsnet another. But Cranmer nodded.

There was silence for a moment, as we considered the horrors that might lie before us. Then Sir Thomas laughed. 'By Jesu, this killer would need devilish powers indeed to bring about an earthquake.'

'I am sick of your mockery, Thomas!' Cranmer turned on him

with sudden fierceness. 'We all know, or should know, that the devil may indeed be moving in this, with all his powers. But we must investigate this matter with reason.'

'You forget your presence here is only allowed because you are my brother,' Lord Hertford said. 'And the connection to Catherine Parr, about whose welfare you were so chivalrously anxious, seems to be gone. You are not needed. It was a mistake for me to involve you in the first place.' He shook his head. 'Foolish.'

For a moment fury flared in Thomas Seymour's face; then he stomped to the window like a sulky child. Cranmer turned back to us. 'Each of you knows what to do,' he said. 'Do it, with despatch.' He nodded in dismissal.

✝

OUTSIDE IN the corridor, Lord Hertford and his brother strode confidently away in opposite directions, but Harsnet lingered beside me. Barak was waiting, sitting on a bench a little way up the corridor. He came over and stood silently beside me.

'It seems we are to work together,' Harsnet said. 'You did well to find the link to that cottar, sir, and to the Book of Revelation. Though I pray you may be wrong about that.'

'It is indeed a fearful thought.'

'I am sorry if I spoke roughly in that meeting. You were right, we need reason to solve these dreadful crimes. But the idea that anyone who had studied the Bible could do such acts—' He broke off, shaking his head.

'The whole thing is monstrous. I have never heard of anything like it.'

'Nor I.' He looked at me seriously. 'Though I think we should have spent more time considering what sort of man this is.'

'You mean he may be possessed by a devil, who makes him do these things? Well, sir, I see it more likely that he is sick in his mind, and the sickness has driven him to a fanaticism the like of which has never been seen.' I spoke placatingly, but firmly. I thought of Adam Kite, gibbering on his knees in the Bedlam. And as Guy had said, madness may take many forms.

'And you think he may be killing people who have abandoned a biblical understanding of religion?' Harsnet looked agitated.

'I think it may be possible. I think he may be a man of radical religion, gone mad.'

'But have you ever heard of a man who was mad, yet could plan and execute such an ambitious scheme? Though the devil could. And if you are right, this is a blasphemy.'

'I confess I do not know what we are dealing with, sir, but I see no point in speculating now.'

Harsnet inclined his head; I could see he did not want to get drawn into argument, he wanted to keep good relations with me. I changed the subject.

'There seemed to be difficulties between Thomas Seymour and his brother.'

He nodded. 'Lord Hertford is a clever man, a great man. In the right circumstances he could be a great reformer, in religion and in righting social injustices too. His devotion to his family is his only weakness. Restraining his brother is hard.'

'Yes.' I thought, a truly strong man would surely not indulge his affections so far.

'Will you let me know what happens at Augmentations?' Harsnet asked. 'A note marked for my urgent and personal attention will reach me.'

'I will.'

'If I send a messenger, should he go to your chambers?'

'Yes, or to my home if I am not there. I live hard by Lincoln's Inn, in Chancery Lane.'

'Then we will speak again soon.' Harsnet nodded to Barak, bowed and left us. I looked at my assistant. His face was pale. 'He's right,' he said. 'This is – monstrous.'

The full horror of it all hit me. Tupholme's terrible death, Roger and Dr Gurney, all three killed with such planning and precision. 'There have been mad prophets before,' I said uncertainly.

'Reading Revelation scared me,' Barak said. 'It is so . . .' He struggled for the right word. 'Relentless. Like this killer.'

'You don't think he's possessed, as Harsnet does?'

'I don't know what he is.'

'Well, all I know is that I will find the killer of my friend. Now come, we are going to Westminster, to the Court of Augmentations.' I clapped Barak on his broad back, and led the way outside, striding with a confidence I did not feel, for whatever else he was, the man we hunted was surely a monster in human form.

Chapter Fifteen

A DAY LATER, I rode down to Guy's. It was Sunday, the first of April. It was another mild, sunny day; birds flew by with twigs and grass in their beaks, heading for the trees where the first dusting of pale green was spreading.

It was All Fools' Day, when people will play tricks on each other, but mercifully, although the streets were busy, nobody shouted out that my horse's tail was on fire or suchlike. People looked preoccupied; I had heard that two courtiers suspected of heretical leanings had gone to the Tower.

Barak and I had spent the previous day at the Court of Augmentations office, trying to find the records of infirmarians at the London Benedictine houses. Some senior clerk had ordered that all the records of the monks receiving pensions be reorganized, and the result was chaos. It was evening before we emerged, a good deal dustier, with three names, although the addresses were now held in a separate file and it would be Monday morning before that office opened.

As I neared Guy's I saw the bulk of the Old Barge over the rooftops, and felt a stab of guilt. I had not really tackled Barak over how he was treating Tamasin. He was expert at brushing off unwanted enquiries, and I feared, too, that if I tried to exert authority where his private life was concerned, I would only anger him again. I shook my head, for I did not see how I was to proceed.

When I turned into Guy's street I had the uneasy feeling that had come over me once or twice on the journey. As though I were being followed. I turned quickly in the saddle, but could see no one in the narrow street. I told myself that the hunt for Roger's killer was making me over-anxious. I reminded myself that I was due to go to dinner with Dorothy that evening, a prospect that filled me equally with pleasure and sadness.

I tied Genesis up outside Guy's shop, and knocked on his door.

He let me in, and I saw he already had another visitor, a tall, stout, rubicund man with a long grey beard. Like Guy he wore a physician's robe, but his was of the best cut. He had a long wooden wand in his hand, which he was pointing at the apothecary's jars that lined Guy's shelves. Young Piers had taken down a couple of the jars and was carefully measuring out quantities in a balance.

The stranger looked at me down a long beak of a nose. 'Perhaps you will allow me to complete my business before you advise your patient,' he said haughtily to Guy, who gestured me to take a seat, with an apologetic look.

I sat and watched as the fat physician pointed to another jar. 'A peck of the wormwood, and I'll take an ounce of antimony. Have you any ground cockerel's blood, sir?'

'I do not keep it.'

'A pity. It is a wondrous cure for headache.'

'Such wisdom,' Piers murmured. The physician stared at him, suspecting insolence, but the boy's smooth face was impassive. I could see, though, that Guy was repressing a smile as he wrote down the man's wants on a slate. Evidently his fellow-physician had consulted him in his other capacity, as an apothecary. The big man seemed one of those doctors whose strategy is to awe people with the arrogant confidence that often covers ignorance. I wondered why Guy tolerated him.

'That is all, sir,' his customer said. 'I will have it fetched tomorrow. How much?'

'A shilling.'

'You come cheap.' He brought out a fat purse and handed over the silver coin. Then he deigned to look at me. 'You are a lawyer, sir?' he asked. 'At which Inn?'

'Lincoln's Inn,' I replied curtly.

'I have a patient there. Master Bealknap, perhaps you know him.'

'I do. He seems ill and faint these days,' I added pointedly.

'Oh, I will have him well soon.' The physician seemed blind to the implied criticism. 'He needs more bleeding, that will soon restore him. I am Dr Archer, by the way. I have much experience in treating lawyers' ills.' He smiled condescendingly, then with a cursory bow to Guy, he restored his purse to his belt and left the shop.

'Who was that creature?' I asked.

Guy smiled wryly. 'Archer is a senior man in the College of Physicians. My status there is tenuous, I must put up with him. He is a great traditionalist, believes there has been nothing new in medicine since Galen, save for his own quack remedies. I let him come to get the ingredients for them. He is a man of influence, he likes to patronize me, and I am careful to undercharge him.' His voice was suddenly weary. He waved a hand. 'Let us forget Archer. Sit down.' He took a seat at his consulting table. 'How can I help you, Matthew? I see by your face this is no social call.'

I paused a moment before answering. Close to, I saw he looked tired, drained, and I felt reluctant to draw him again into the terrible affair of the murders; yet I needed his counsel. I fingered the pilgrim badge in my pocket.

Guy turned to Piers. 'Fetch us some wine, will you, my boy? You should not have mocked Dr Archer,' he added indulgently. 'Foolish as he is, he was suspicious.'

'I am sorry, master, but it was hard to resist.'

'Yes,' Guy answered. 'I know.'

'What shall I say if those men call again, selling oil from the giant fish caught in the Thames?' Piers asked. 'I know many of the apothecaries are buying it.'

'And claiming all sorts of magical properties for it, no doubt. Tell them to be on their way. And keep them outside, that stuff stinks.'

'That must have been them earlier,' Guy said after Piers had gone.

'I thought it was the local children knocking at my door and running away. They think it a good jest for All Fools' Day.'

'You are too soft with that boy, you know. Surely it is a dangerous thing to mock a man like Dr Archer.'

'Ah, but he is a droll lad.' Guy smiled again, then his face resumed its serious expression. 'What has happened, Matthew? Is it to do with Master Elliard?'

'Yes.' I hesitated again. What right had I to involve him in this? Then I thought, because he may help us. I met his gaze. 'It turns out that Roger was the third person to be murdered recently in a terrible, elaborate and apparently pointless way. But I think I know the reason, if you can call it a reason.' I told him about Tupholme and Dr Gurney, the link to the Book of Revelation, the possibility that the killer was seeking out apostates from radical religion. Guy's dark features seemed almost to lengthen and sag as I told him.

'I knew Paul Gurney,' he said when I had ended my narrative and sworn him to secrecy. 'Not well, but we met at a few functions. He seemed a quiet, scholarly man. No swagger to him, unlike Archer.' He shook his head. 'I can imagine him starting as a reformer, but disliking these ill-educated, self-righteous radicals now.'

There was a knock at the door, and Piers entered with a tray of wine. His handsome face was again impassive, but there was something intent in the expression in those large blue eyes that made me wonder if he had been listening at the door. I watched him as he laid down the tray and left the room, and let him see that I was watching.

'We found this at the site of Tupholme's murder,' I said when Piers had gone. I produced the badge. Guy turned it over in his long fingers, then gave me a keen look. 'You still think the killer is a Benedictine infirmarian? Because of this, and the dwale?'

'I think it possible.'

He studied the badge, then handed it back. He sighed deeply. 'You could be right. We do not know what has made this man what he is.'

'Barak and I spent yesterday at the Court of Augmentations,

tracing Benedictine infirmarians in London at the time of the Dissolution. The infirmarian who attended the nuns at St Helens is dead,
and the St Saviours man went to his family in Northumberland and
collects his pension there. But the Westminster infirmarian and both
his assistants are still in London. They collect their pensions at
Westminster. We won't have the addresses until Monday, but we
have names. The infirmarian is called Goddard, Lancelot Goddard.
He had two assistants, Charles Cantrell, a monk, and Francis
Lockley, a lay brother not in orders. Guy, have you ever heard those
names?'

'I told you, I did not know them. When I came to London I
was no longer a monk. And, Matthew, many ex-Benedictine monks
from elsewhere came to London after the Dissolution. What was done
to the monks was enough to drive men mad,' he added with sudden
bitterness. 'Torn from their homes and their lives. Thrown into a
different world, where the Bible is interpreted as literal fact, its symbols
and metaphors forgotten, and fanatics react with equanimity to the
blood and cruelty of Revelation. Have you ever thought what a God
would be like who actually ordained and executed the cruelty that is
in that book? A holocaust of mankind. Yet so many of these Bible-
men accept the idea without a second thought.'

'Bishop Bonner would destroy them just as cruelly.'

'Do you think I do not know that?' he answered angrily. 'I,
whose family was made to leave Spain by the Inquisition, loyal
Catholics though we were, because we had the taint of an Islamic
past?'

'I know. I am sorry.'

'So am I. Sorry for what the world has come to.' He leaned
forward, supporting his head with his hand for a moment, then
looked up. 'I am sorry, Matthew,' he said wearily. 'You came here
for my help.'

'No, I spoke insensitively. It is this matter – Guy, we spoke of
madness the other day. Harsnet thinks the killer is possessed, thinks
someone who was mad could not organize these murders so carefully,

so patiently. We think he lay out there in the Lambeth marshes for most of a cold, wet day.'

'What do you think, Matthew?'

'Possession is an easy cry to raise against the inexplicable. But these murders are so strange and terrible I do not know what to think. Even Barak is afraid. He has never heard of anything like them either.'

'I have,' he said quietly.

I stared at him.

'Obsession,' he said. 'It is a type of madness we did not discuss at the Bedlam. A man may have a strange, bizarre obsession in one part of his life. And yet seem normal, or pass for normal, in others. Obsessions have been known since Greek and Roman times. I had a case myself last year of a merchant who from his youth had had an obsession with collecting shoes. Men's shoes, women's shoes, old shoes past repair he plucked from dungheaps. He filled his house with them. Only his wife knew, and when she challenged him, he would say only that shoes came in useful. By the time she consulted me he was travelling all over London looking for them, neglecting his business.'

'But what has this strange story to do with this killer?'

'Bear with me, Matthew. I met with the merchant, and eventually he told me that when he was a child he had had no shoes. Somewhere in his mind he was frightened of that happening again. He had had his obsession so long he had almost forgotten how it started.'

'Did the knowledge help him?'

Guy shook his head sadly. 'No. He would not let it go, or could not. He was made bankrupt and ended penniless, where he began. He is probably dead now, he could not have borne the hard life of a beggar. And so, because of his obsession, that which he most feared came true.'

'A sad story.'

'And obsessions can take many forms. Love is the commonest. Someone convinces themselves that they must have the beloved, even if that person is utterly unsuitable, does not care for the lover at all.'

'Everyone has heard of cases like that.'

'And if a life can be dominated by fierce, twisted love, may it not equally be ruled by fierce, twisted hate?' He leaned back in his chair, fingering his cup, which he had emptied. 'It has happened before,' he added bleakly.

'Where? When?'

Guy hesitated again, then spoke very quietly. 'You should know why my studies once took a certain direction. When I was a young man in Paris, studying to be a physician, I fell in love.' He smiled. 'Oh yes, this brown, twisted old stick. I loved the daughter of a wine merchant, she was beautiful and clever, of Spanish origin, like me. The kindest person I ever knew. We were in love, and I wanted to marry her, but at the same time felt drawn to becoming a monk.' He looked at me, bleakly. 'And God decided the matter, or so I felt at the time. She was sitting by her fire one winter's night when a spark flew out and set her dress alight. She died of burns and shock the next day.'

'I never knew,' I said. 'I am sorry—'

'It was long ago. But for a while it made me deny God, deny any goodness working in the world. I raged. I had been studying diseases of the mind, and now I probed the darkest regions of that study with a sort of angry relish. That was my time of despair, but, as Aquinas tells us, that can be a step on the ladder of mystical love; in time, I felt God's love again, came back to the Church. Though in truth part of me still finds it hard to forgive Him, sinner that I am.' For the first time ever I saw tears in his eyes, and I realized that Guy was troubled, deeply troubled, by something. I opened my mouth, but he spoke over me.

'There was one case that was talked about in Paris when I was young. Though he had been dead then for sixty years, people still spoke of the Marshal Gilles de Rais when they wanted to curdle their blood.'

'Who?'

'He was a French knight and landowner. A successful military commander, who served with Joan of Arc against the English, to all appearances a normal man. But when he retired to his estates in Brittany he began abducting and murdering children in the most terrible and sadistic manner.'

'Children?'

'Yes. He did things I would not wish even to speak of. The local people knew what he did but he was a powerful man, beyond the law.' He fixed me with a bleak gaze. 'De Rais would get the local barber to come and style the hair on the heads of murdered boys that he had placed on stakes in his hall, and invite him to judge which looked the best. That is the type of thing he did.'

'Jesu.'

'Eventually, after five years, de Rais made the mistake of annoying the church in some dispute, and the local bishop stepped in at last. De Rais was tried and hanged for his crimes, which sent a wave of horror throughout the land when they were known. At his trial he said he had committed his crimes purely because they pleased him.'

'Dear God.' I remembered three years before, the case of a young boy I had encountered who had tortured animals and killed a beggar-boy shortly before his own violent death. I actually felt my skin crawl, as though some insect were on it.

Guy's look at me was bleak. 'I think there have been more monsters like this creature than we know.'

'Someone brutally killing people for no reason. Yet I have never heard . . .' I hesitated, frowning, as I recollected something from a long time ago. 'No, wait. I think there was a case . . .'

Guy leaned forward. 'Yes?'

'When we were students, we were given legal problems to solve, which involved looking up cases in the law books. We spent half our time delving through the dusty old books in the Lincoln's Inn library. I remember one of the students coming across a murder case from — oh, it must have been a hundred years ago — about a man who was executed for killing several young women. Where was it — in Norwich, I think.' I smiled wryly. 'There was nothing about the trial to create a legal precedent, but some lads passed it round because the trial report was full of gruesome detail. You know what students can be like.'

Guy smiled. 'But not you?'

'No. Coming to London from Lichfield, I thought there were more than enough gruesome things to see in the city, even then. I was more interested in finding new precedents to dazzle the benchers with. I will look for the case in the library.' I frowned. 'But I am not sure this man was such a killer as you describe. And even if he was, they must be rare indeed. How could anyone get away with it? How would the whole region where such a thing happened not turn all their energies to finding such a killer? From what you say, De Rais was a powerful man. Surely an ordinary person would be swiftly hunted down, even in a large city.'

'You know how difficult the detection of crime is, Matthew. In England, more than most of Europe. Each city and parish enfor⁄ cing the law through Justices of the Peace and coroners who are often corrupt, with the aid of a few constables who are usually stupid men.'

'And who investigate killings with little or no reference to what may be happening in neighbouring districts. Yes. I have been talking about these things with Harsnet and Barak. And how most killers who are caught are impulsive and stupid—'

'Whereas this one plans, obsessive as a lover, careful, meticulous, patient. He puts his whole self into his terrible work – the expression perhaps of a limitless rage.'

'And this man has chosen apostates from radical reformism.'

He must have an utter devotion to his twisted passions, above anything else in the world. He can have no conscience. In his world only he matters. And it is perhaps not so large a step from there to persuading yourself that God himself has set you the task you so enjoy. Bringing forward the good and holy work outlined in the Book of Revelation.' Guy's face was drawn. 'Obsession,' he said quietly. 'It is a wicked, wicked thing.'

'He is mad, then?'

'He cannot be sane as we understand the word. But it may be that his cleverness means he is able to pass himself off as normal, perhaps even work. Although I would have thought there must be signs. Such a gross distortion of the soul must leave outward signs . . .' He shook his head again, then fixed me with intense brown eyes full of pain. 'That pilgrim badge,' he said.

I took it out. 'What of it?'

'If we have learned anything about this man, it is how careful he is. He would not have simply dropped something as rare and controversial as a pilgrim badge from the Westminster Abbey shrine.'

'As Barak said, it may not have been him. One of the constables—'

'Would hardly be likely to carry a pilgrim badge.'

'So if the killer dropped it, he may have done so deliberately to mislead us?'

'Or to give you a clue. Perhaps that is part of his madness. But from the study of obsession, Matthew, a study I regretted making and which has haunted me ever since, there is one thing I am sure of. This man will not stop at seven. How could he, if killing has become the centre of his universe, the centre of a mind collapsed in upon itself?'

'But there are only seven vials of wrath—'

Guy nodded. 'But Revelation is a whole sequence of violent stories, one after another, layers of them. When this cycle is finished, he has many more to choose from.'

'Jesu.' I sat there feeling utterly drained, staring at Guy. A terrible thought occurred to me. Dorothy, like Roger, like me, was a lapsed radical. I told myself not to be so foolish; none of those murdered had been connected to each other and there was surely no reason why he should change his pattern and go after Dorothy. And she was a woman, whose opinions counted for less. Then my eyes widened, for I saw that behind Guy the door to his inner chambers was open, just a crack. Something glinting in the crack had caught my eye and now I saw it was another eye, staring back at me. For a second I was filled with terror. Had I been followed after all? Wordlessly, I pointed at the open door.

Guy turned, then before I could stop him he jumped up and threw it open. The boy Piers stood there, a large bowl in his hands.

'Piers.' Guy's voice was sorrowful as he stood over the boy. 'What are you doing? Were you listening to our talk?'

'I am sorry, master,' the boy replied humbly. 'I was bringing you the powdered henbane I had prepared.' He gestured at a bowl of powder he held. 'I knew you wanted it urgently. I heard you talking, was uncertain whether to knock.'

I knew he was lying, and I could see that Guy was not fooled either. In a moment the pain that had been deepening on his face throughout our talk turned to anger. 'Is this how you repay me after I took you in, when you were homeless and friendless after your old master died?' His voice rose, a note of real pain in it, then suddenly he broke off and looked at Piers, who had stepped back a pace and was clutching the bowl in both hands. Guy sighed, then reached out and laid a hand on the lad's broad shoulder. 'You must learn to curb your curiosity,' he said gently. 'The keeping of confidences, even secrets, is part of our trade.'

'I am sorry, master.' The boy cast down his eyes.

Guy took the bowl of henbane. 'Thank you, that was well and quickly done.'

Piers turned to go, but I called him back, standing up and looking at him with a stern gaze. 'Your master and I were discussing a matter of state. If you breathe one word of what you have heard outside these walls you will end in the Fleet prison or the Tower, and it will be me that makes sure you go there.'

'I heard hardly anything,' Piers answered quietly, somehow sounding humble and reproachful at the same time. 'But I promise to say nothing, sir. On my oath.'

'Be sure of that, boy.'

'Go, Piers,' Guy said wearily. The apprentice bowed and closed the door behind him.

'I have said you give that boy too much latitude, Guy.'

'That is my business,' he answered sharply, then shook his head. 'I am sorry, the terrible things we have been talking of disturb me. I will make sure he keeps quiet.'

'You must, Guy.'

He fell silent. I frowned. When he had criticized Piers I had seen that the boy met his gaze, not with humility but with a sort of cold challenge. It seemed to me that in some way I could not fathom, Guy was frightened of him.

Chapter Sixteen

I RODE BACK to Lincoln's Inn, the sun warm on my face, the breeze gentle for the first time that year. Normally I appreciated the spring, especially after a winter as hard as this last one, but the horrors I was labouring with seemed to make the brightness a mockery. I told myself I must not sink under this weight. My mind went back to Guy, how the terrible story of de Rais had struck him to the heart. My mind again turned to Piers and the strange sense that somehow Guy feared him. It was understandable that Guy should look for some sort of successor, even a memorial, in the boy. But I still felt he was using Guy, as a spoiled child will coldly manipulate an indulgent parent.

I rode under the great gate and into Lincoln's Inn, leaving Genesis with the ostler. First I went to Dorothy's rooms. Margaret, answering the door, told me that Dorothy had gone out, to see to the arrangements for Roger's funeral. Old Elias had accompanied her. I asked Margaret to send Elias to find me on his return, either in the library or my chambers.

I turned to the Inn library. I had much work to catch up on, there were more hearings at the Court of Requests tomorrow, but there was a piece of research I had to do first.

On Sundays Gatehouse Court was quiet, no one about. Then I noticed a black-clad figure walking towards me. It was Bealknap, coming across from his chambers. As he approached I saw he looked worse than ever: pale and feverish, eyes bloodshot. Even his short walk had set him breathing heavily.

'How now, Bealknap.' I felt sorry for him, he had only that

arrogant fool Dr Archer to care for him. At the end of the day he was still a suffering man.

'You have destroyed my business,' he hissed at me, scattering my charitable thoughts.

'What?'

'You could have helped me over that paper I did not file. You know I have been ill. But you would not help a fellow-lawyer, and now I have lost my best client. Sir Geoffrey Coleswyn hoped for profit from that holding. He will pass the word around among the landowners he knows.'

'For heavens' sake, man,' I said impatiently. 'It was your own fault. This is ridiculous.'

'I have built a reputation on my success in getting rid of bad tenants and squatters. The people you act for. Riff-raff, land-stealers, ne'er-do-wells. Sir Geoffrey will see I lose it—'

'I have no time for this nonsense,' I said. His pale, furious face aroused only my contempt.

'You will regret what you have done to me, Shardlake!' Bealknap was shaking, whether with rage or bodily weakness I could not tell. 'This time you have gone too far. You will regret it. I have made sure of that.'

'Bealknap, you sound like a demon in a mystery play.' I stepped round him, dismissing his absurd threats from mind as I walked on to the library.

'Just wait, master crookback!' he called after me. 'You will see!'

✝

The library had its usual hushed atmosphere, seated barristers leafing through law books with stern, concentrated expressions, while elsewhere students grubbed through cases with puzzled frowns. I went and looked over the high shelves. The law books were organized by year, and there were fewer of them for the last century. From the time printing came in, more and more books of law cases had been collated, but the books from the middle of the last century were still few, and handwritten. I found the volume I wanted, a yearbook from 1461. It was ancient and battered, the leather covers stained and in places torn. I took it to a desk in a secluded part of the library away from the windows, lit by candles.

The report on the case was a long one, as though the reporter, like my fellow-students, had revelled in the gruesome details of ripped-open bodies. It had indeed been in Norwich, in the summer of 1461, that a young man called Paul Strodyr had been arraigned, tried and convicted of the murder of nine young women over the previous five years. Six had been prostitutes, three were described as 'respectable young women'. Reading between the lines, it appeared that it was the death of the respectable women that had galvanized the city. There seemed to have been a tremendous hue and cry that had ended with Strodyr's cousin reporting that he had seen him covered in blood on the night of the final murder. After a guilty verdict was brought in he had admitted committing the crimes, and had raged against the evil of prostitutes, said that God desired them to be destroyed.

Several things struck me. The first was that Strodyr was not a man of status and power like de Rais, but a farm labourer. There was no evidence of obvious signs of madness – the reporter said that he was a cheerful, friendly young man who worked on the local farms. Apart from that the report was silent on details about Strodyr – he was sentenced to hang, but if he had said anything from the dock it was not recorded.

I put the book down and sat thinking. So Guy was right, there had been cases of apparently pointless mass murder before. In this case the murderer had been caught. But Strodyr's ordinary back-ground and the fact that no one seemed to think him strange only stressed the difficulties we faced in finding our killer. And in a city the size of London, perhaps ten times the size of Norwich then, how much harder to find a single man. I thought again of the murderous child I had encountered a few years before; if he had lived would he have been another Strodyr, another de Rais? I could see no way to tell.

✝

I WENT BACK to chambers and worked for a while. I jumped when the door opened and Barak came in. He looked tired and smelled of sweat, but was smiling.

'I have the addresses,' he said. 'And some news.'

I threw down my quill. 'On a Sunday?'

'I went down to Augmentations this morning. There were a lot of clerks there, trying to sort out the mess this reorganization has made. I managed to chivvy them into getting the Westminster records. I got the addresses and a register of payments with them.'

'Well done.' Yet I thought it sad that he should choose to work on Sunday, when he might be at home with Tamasin.

He sat down opposite me. 'The infirmarian himself has not been in to collect his pension since December. Just before the first murder, the cottar. His name is Goddard, Lancelot Goddard.'

'Did you get his address?'

'Yes. It is a poor street near the Steelyard. I've been down there—'

'You did not try to see him by yourself—'

'Of course I didn't,' he said impatiently. 'I asked around the neighbours. They said there had been an ex-monk that rented a house there since Westminster Abbey went down three years ago. He kept apart from the locals, thought he was a cut above the shopkeepers and the like who live there. He left in January, saying he had inherited a house from his mother. I went to the place where he used to live; it's boarded up. Then I went to see the landlord; he's in the next street. He said the monk was a good tenant, quiet and always paid on time. He confirmed the story of the inheritance, said the monk came to tell him he was going, left the landlord with a month's rent in hand.'

'What did this Goddard look like?'

'A man nearing forty. Distinctive. High cheekbones and a big mole on the side of his nose. Tall and well set up, dark hair.'

'What about his assistants?'

'I got their addresses. One, Cantrell, lives in Westminster still, the other out near the old Charterhouse. At a tavern, called the Green Man.'

'A tavern.' I raised my eyebrows.

'So it seems. That's Lockley, the lay brother.'

I nodded. As he was not a monk, he would not have got a pension. But a tavern was a far cry from a monastery.

'What do you think has happened to Goddard? It is strange he vanished in January. Do you think—'

'That he could be the killer? Hold on, Jack, there could be another reason he disappeared.' I looked at him seriously. 'He could be another victim.'

Barak shook his head. 'Sounds like he deliberately vanished. Failed to leave an address.'

'I must send a note to Harsnet. You did well,' I added. 'I will tell him.'

He leaned back in his chair. 'I needed to do something,' he said. 'To find something – something—'

'Something real? Amidst all this inexplicable horror?'

'Yes.'

'Well, you have found it.' I looked at his face, tired and anxious still. I would not tell him of Guy's theory or my studies, not yet, not tonight. 'You should go home, you look as if you have had enough for one day.'

'Ay.' He looked guilty. 'I told Tamasin I'd be back for lunch. I'd best go.'

I shook my head after he had gone. If I were his age and Tamasin my wife, I would not be spending Sunday afternoon harassing clerks in grubby archives. I turned my thoughts to Westminster Abbey. I remembered it had been one of the last monasteries to be dissolved. The King had not wanted the buildings destroyed as they housed the tombs of his father and other royal ancestors; he had squared the circle by turning the abbey into a cathedral. The former abbot had been installed as dean; he was known as one of Cromwell's agents inside the monasteries, working for its closure. His appointment afterwards had caused much cynical laughter.

I penned a long note to Harsnet and took it to the porter's lodge, telling him to have it delivered urgently. I looked out at Chancery Lane, the few passers-by, remembering the strong sense of being followed I had had earlier. As I returned I saw old Elias walking rapidly towards me; Dorothy was back. I walked with him back across Gatehouse Court, past the fountain, to Dorothy's, determinedly trying to clear my head of thoughts of Strodyr, of the other murderers. But with Roger perhaps the victim of such a man, that was not easy.

✝

THE MAID MARGARET let me in. Dorothy was sitting in her usual place before the fire, beneath the wooden frieze, still dressed in black. I was glad to see she was occupied, embroidering a dress with little flowers. She looked up with a smile, and I was glad to see a little colour in her cheeks.

'How are you?' I asked gently.

'Life must go on, must it not? The clock still measures out the hours, even with Roger gone.'

'Yes, it does.'

'Samuel is coming tomorrow. And I have arranged Roger's funeral for Tuesday.' She looked at me. 'A week today since he died.'

'I know.'

'I am trying to keep occupied. With embroidery, as you see. And I have supervised the preparation of a fine repast. To thank you, for all you have done.'

'It is little enough, Dorothy. I am sorry commitments do not allow me to take on any of Roger's cases. But Bartlett has brought me a list of lawyers who can, and they are all honest fellows.'

'Good. I shall need the money. The Treasurer came to see me

today, full of sorrow for my loss, but hinting they will be appointing a new Inn member now and he will want these rooms.'

'Have you enough to take a house? If not, I can—'

She raised a hand. 'No. Thank you, Matthew, but Roger was a prudent man, there is enough saved for me to live carefully. But I do not know where I shall go. Samuel suggested in his letter that I return to Bristol.'

'Will you go?' I found my heart sinking at the thought.

She hesitated. 'I do not know, yet. Is there any news?'

'We are making progress. I'm afraid that is all I can say.'

'Do you know yet why Roger was killed?' Her voice was no more than a whisper.

'No. But Dorothy . . .' I paused. 'We know of three men this man has killed now. All the victims of some terrible ritual. While he is at large, I think – I think you should not go out alone.'

'You think I might be in danger,' she said quietly.

'No. Only – it's as well to be safe.' Dorothy looked at me intently for a moment, then nodded. I felt suddenly fired anew with anger at what had been done to her and Roger.

A serving man appeared, bearing a large tray of meat with sweet-smelling sauces. I followed Dorothy to the table.

'There,' she said. 'A saddle of lamb. I am glad Lent is over. They say they are arresting butchers who sold meat then.'

'Yes.'

'I did not go to church today. I confess I cannot find it in my heart to feel anything but anger towards a God who could allow such an evil thing to happen to such a good man.' She looked at me. 'Do you think that a wicked thing?'

'No. I understand. I have not been either.' I sighed. 'Though I suppose one could answer that it is not God's fault if one of his creatures uses free will to commit a heinous sin.'

She smiled, an angry little smile. 'That is a reasonable answer. But reason has little to do with how I feel now. It would help if I could pray, but I am too angry.' She frowned. 'Perhaps in time.'

'Yes. When you feel ready.' I felt a hypocrite, for I prayed but seldom now myself, but I wanted to say the things that might best comfort her.

'You are understanding, Matthew,' she said quietly. We ate in silence for a while, enjoying the meal. She dabbed her lips with a napkin, then gave me a doubtful look. 'I have something else to ask of you. I hesitate, when you have done so much . . .'

'Whatever I can do, I will.'

'I have been thinking on Roger's idea for a hospital for the poor. He had barely begun the work when he was taken, but he had a list of subscribers. Would you take up the plan? It was something he wished to do so much, it would honour his memory.'

'I will, Dorothy. But not yet. Not till the case is solved.'

'I see you are tired. I should not press you. But – it would keep him alive, somehow.'

'A fitting memorial.' I smiled. 'We could name it the Roger Elliard Hospital.'

'Yes.' She shook her head. 'I sit and look at that frieze, study the wooden animals peering from behind the trees. We gave them names, you know, Peter the hart and Paul the rabbit and Simon the horse.'

'It is a fine piece.'

'I should get that corner properly repaired. I shall take it if I go to Bristol. There is so much of Roger in these rooms—' Suddenly she broke off, bowed her head, and began to sob gently. I rose and went round the table to her. Hesitantly, I took her shoulders. 'There now,' I said, gently. It came to my mind that this was the first time I had actually held Dorothy, something that once I had longed to do more than anything.

She reached out and took my hand, a smile coming to her tear-stained face. 'You have been so good, Matthew. What would I do without you?'

Her words and her touch sent a wave of feeling through me. I had to prevent myself from embracing her fully, kissing her. Something must have showed in my face, for she released my hand. I stepped away.

'I am not myself,' she said quietly. 'I am suddenly tired, today has been too much. Would you mind if I went to bed now?'

'Of course not.'

'I will take care.'

'Good. I am probably being overcautious.'

'Come and dine after the funeral. Samuel will be here. You have not seen him since he was boy.'

'Yes. I will.' I was suddenly tongue-tied. 'I – I should go.'

'Very well.' She wiped her face. 'There. All over now. But still I find it hard to compose myself.' She looked at me seriously. 'I need time.'

✞

OUTSIDE I LEANED against the stone wall, breathing deeply. I realized now what I had been hiding from myself: that the fact that Dorothy was single again had kindled old fires. I thought again of her warm shoulders, her hand on mine. Then I thought of Roger, dead in the snow. 'God forgive me,' I whispered to myself.

And then I saw, across the courtyard, a figure standing by the door of my chambers, now closed and locked. It was a woman, a small slight figure, and I realized with a shock of recognition that it was Tamasin. I ran across the yard, my robe billowing around my legs. She was huddled against the door. I saw to my horror that her face was puffy and swollen, one eye nearly shut, her dress torn and her coif askew. She stared at me, trembling.

'Tamasin,' I said. 'Dear Jesu, who has done this to you? Was it—' For an awful moment I thought it might have been Barak.

'I came to find Jack.' Her voice came thickly through swollen lips. 'We had an argument, he went out again. I could not stand being in that house alone: I kept feeling someone was outside, kept fancying I heard breathing at the door. I had to leave, I was going to your house if Jack was not here. All the way here, I thought someone was behind me.'

'Tamasin . . .'

She looked at me, a stare of pure fear. 'Then as I was about to turn in here, someone leaped at me, pulled me into a corner and began beating me—' She broke off, breathing heavily, though she did not cry.

'Who?' I asked. 'Who?'

'His voice was – strange – not like an ordinary voice. He said he knows you and Jack are hunting him, but you would not stop his mission. Master Shardlake, he knows your name, and Jack's. He knows where we live. Who is he?'

Chapter Seventeen

I UNLOCKED THE DOOR to my chambers and helped Tamasin inside. I guided her through the dark to a seat in my room, then returned to the outer office. I locked the door and then, with trembling hands, lit a taper from the embers of the fire. I took it through and lit the candles in my room. As the yellow light flickered into the corners I saw that Tamasin was sitting where I had left her, head sunk on her chest. She had pulled off her bloodstained coif and held it in her lap. I poured a goblet of strong wine and held it to her lips. Her teeth chattered. I felt fury towards whoever had ravaged her pretty face; and horror, as well, for an even worse fate might have befallen her.

I sat down opposite her. She took a couple of sips of wine, then she suddenly coughed and put her hand to her mouth. She brought it away with half a white tooth in the palm. She stared at it stupidly, still in shock. Her whole face was bruised, and she had a nasty cut on one cheek.

'Tamasin,' I whispered. 'I am so sorry.'

She looked at me through her swollen lids. 'Why? It is not your fault.' Her voice came thick and distorted.

I hesitated. 'How much has Jack told you of the work we have been engaged on?'

'Nothing. Only that it was a secret matter. I feared it was politics again.'

'It is something worse than that.' I rose to my feet. 'Tamasin, do you know where Jack is?'

She sighed wearily. 'His usual haunts, I expect. The Turks Head tavern by Newgate, or the Red Dog near the Old Barge. He missed lunch, he came back late and we – we had an argument. He stormed out again.'

Damn him, I thought. 'I am going to get the gatekeeper to send someone to find him, and Guy too. You need attention.'

She nodded. 'My face – hurts so much.' She looked at me. 'Do you know who he is, the man who attacked me?'

'I fear it may be the man we are seeking. He attacked you just outside the gate?'

'Yes. He leaped out between two houses. When he left me I managed to get up. I would have gone to the gatekeeper, but his lodge was dark; I came in, I thought I would be safe inside the Inn, and perhaps you might be working late . . .'

'I was at Mrs Elliard's,' I said. 'You are sure he said Jack and I were hunting him?'

'Yes.'

Sitting there, I felt my hair rise on my scalp. The killer knew who Barak and I were, that we were after him. But how?

'You said his voice was strange.'

'Yes. Harsh. Guttural. As though he were disguising it.'

'Thank God I was here tonight. Listen, Tamasin, I am going now, to rouse the gatekeeper. I will lock the door.'

'Take care, sir, he may be out there still.'

✝

I TOOK THE DAGGER I kept in my desk and slipped it into my sleeve. In the main office I doused the candles and stood for a moment looking through the mullioned window at Gatehouse Court. A few upper windows were lit. Dorothy's windows were all dark now. The courtyard was empty. I took a deep breath, transferred the dagger into my hand and stepped outside.

I crossed the yard rapidly. Ahead, the gatekeeper's lodge was dark. Either he or his deputy was supposed to keep watch all night, but I knew they often drank themselves to sleep. I took pleasure in banging on the door as loudly as I could. After a minute the gatekeeper opened up. An old soldier, a big, red-faced man, his breath stank of beer. I quickly told him a woman had been attacked and her attacker might still be around, ordered him to rouse himself and send his assistant in search of Barak and Guy.

Back in chambers I did what I could to help Tamasin, fetching water and a cloth for her to wash her poor ravaged face.

'Jack should have been with me,' she said. 'He should not have left me in fear.' Shock had been replaced by anger.

'Tamasin, you said you had feared someone was outside your apartment.'

'This last few days, when Jack has been out, several times I heard a footstep outside. Tonight I went up to the door to listen, and – I heard breathing, as though someone had their head right up against the door on the other side.'

'Did you tell Jack?'

'He said I was full of fancies. But tonight, listening at the door, I did hear a footstep, someone leaving. The outside door creaked. It was so silent then, I could no longer stand it, and I ran out of the house. It was foolish.'

I sat back. He must have been waiting outside, perhaps he waited outside every night. I felt a creeping horror again. He must have followed Tamasin to Lincoln's Inn. And he *had* been following me, I had been right there. Tamasin began to cry, softly, and I laid a hand on her arm. It seemed to be my job tonight to comfort innocent women tormented by this creature.

✝

BARAK ARRIVED half an hour later, rousted from the Newgate tavern by the gatekeeper's assistant. He rushed in, wide-eyed. 'What's happened? They said Tammy's been hurt!' He hurried over to his wife, but halted as she lifted her head and turned her ravaged, angry face to him.

'Yes, Jack,' she said. 'By the imaginary fellow outside our door, by my fancy, my phantasm.'

He turned to me. It was one of the few times I had seen him at a loss. I gave him some wine, sat him down and told him what had happened. All the time he kept glancing at Tamasin, who still sat looking at him fiercely. She was very angry.

'I never thought he could know where we lived,' Barak said to Tamasin. 'Or even who we were. How could I?' He turned back to me. 'And why do this? It's almost as if he was taunting us!'

'You know I thought I too was being followed,' I said quietly.

'Do you think this could be someone we know?' Barak asked.

'I hardly know what to think. Tamasin, did you see nothing of him?'

'No. He jumped out at me from behind. I closed my eyes when he started hitting me. He was very strong. When I fell to the ground he kicked me once and then said what I told you, that he knew you were hunting him, but you would not stop his mission.'

'That settles it. It was him.' Barak's face was ashen.

'Who?' Tamasin's voice was suddenly shrill. 'Who is it you are hunting? Who has he killed?'

Barak and I looked at each other. He nodded, and I told Tamasin the story of the three murders, the link to the Book of Revelation, the task from Cranmer. I did not tell either of them, though, of Guy's theory about compulsive killers, nor of my own researches into the Strodyr case.

'Oh my God,' she said when I had finished. 'Then why did he not finish me off, if he is seeking more people to kill?'

'I think you did not fit what he calls his mission. Revelation speaks of the fourth vial causing men to be scorched with fire.'

'So he wanted to threaten us?' Barak said. 'Warn us off?'

'I think so. Jack, you and Tamasin should move to my house. Tonight. There is safety in numbers. And I will ask Harsnet if he can send a man over, to keep watch. I will send another message.'

'That's a good idea, Tammy,' Barak said gently.

'Yes,' she answered bitterly. 'Leave it to your master to protect me.' She began to cry again. This was not like Tamasin; she was at the end of her tether. I nodded impatiently to Barak, and mouthed the words, 'Comfort her.'

But Barak was angry too now, at the insult to his manhood. 'That's not fair,' he said. 'If I'd known this man was real, but you've had so many fancies—'

It was the worst thing he could have said. She half rose. Injured as she was, I think she would have thrown herself at him, had a knock on the outer door not made us all start and whirl round. I went to open it. Guy stood there, his eyes wide. 'Matthew,' he said. 'A man came to call, with a garbled message about a woman attacked here.'

'Come in, Guy.' I sighed heavily. 'You have arrived at just the right moment.'

✟

GUY ATTENDED TO Tamasin. She had suffered bad bruising to her face, a broken tooth and a cracked rib. She would not be fit to go out of doors for a week, but I was relieved to hear that there would be no permanent damage apart from the tooth which had been broken off, fortunately at the side rather than the front of her mouth. Guy said he would send her to a tooth-drawer to have the remnants of the broken tooth extracted.

'I will fetch some stuff from the Barge,' Barak said, as Guy applied some soothing oils to Tamasin's face. 'Could you take Tammy to your house, sir?'

'I will.' I followed him out to the outer office. There I took his arm. 'If you do not comfort her,' I said in an angry whisper, 'accept your part in what has gone wrong between you, you will lose her.'

He shook off my arm and glared at me. 'Leave my wife's affairs to me,' he said thickly. 'What do you know of married life?'

'Enough to know you have a rare pearl in Tamasin.'

'I'll keep her safe,' he said. 'We'd best turn our minds to catching this man. Either he is someone we know, who knew we would be on the marshes that day and has found out where we live, or . . .'

'Or what?'

'Or maybe the devil's in it after all.' He turned away, threw open the door and went out.

☦

It was long before any of us went to bed that night. When Guy left I held a whispered conversation with him on the doorstep, telling him about the Strodyr case. He nodded sadly. 'It is what I expected,' he said.

I led Tamasin home. Barak arrived with baggage from the Barge, and I installed him and Tamasin in the room Tamasin had occupied when she helped look after me during my illness the previous year. My housekeeper Joan, who was fond of her, was horrified to see her face. When they were settled upstairs she took me aside.

'That poor girl,' she said.

'I know. I am sorry to involve you in my troubles again.' I had told Joan that Tamasin had been attacked by someone we were investigating, and that I had sent the gatekeeper to find some protection from Harsnet.

'Tamasin and Master Jack, they seem to be hardly speaking. After what she's been through . . .'

'I know, Joan. Between her anger and Jack's pride they have fallen out. We must try to bring them together.'

'But should we interfere, sir? Between man and wife?'

'I think if something is not done they may not be man and wife much longer.' I looked at Joan. She looked frightened and tired, and suddenly old. I remembered thinking she needed more help around the house, yet I had done nothing. I laid my hand on her arm. 'It will be all right.' I spoke with a confidence I did not feel.

☦

Harsnet responded to my messages with commendable speed. Not long after first light next morning a man arrived from him, a muscular fellow of around thirty, craggy-faced with keen eyes. He told me he was Philip Orr, one of the Westminster constables, and had agreed to take on the job of watching the house out of respect for the coroner, 'a good man and a godly one,' as he put it. Another hot-gospeller, I thought, but was nonetheless grateful to Harsnet for providing someone capable so quickly. The coroner had also sent a message by Orr; he wished to question Dean Benson of Westminster Cathedral at once about his former infirmarian and his assistants. He asked Barak and I to accompany him, saying he would meet us by the abbey gatehouse at eight thirty. The letter noted that I should have time to go on to Westminster Palace for that morning's hearings in Requests. I was grateful to him for considering that.

'He works fast,' I said to Barak as we walked down to the river to catch a boat. It was still mild, but drizzly, a light rain driven into our faces by the wind. The look Barak had given me when he came down to breakfast that morning left me in no doubt he did not want to hear any more about his marriage; Tamasin, still suffering from her injuries, had stayed in bed.

'Lord Cromwell trained his men well.'

'He is a religious radical. I hope that doesn't cloud his investigative skills.'

'He seemed sharp enough to me,' Barak replied. I did not pursue the point; he was in a mood to turn discussion into argument.

We walked from Whitehall Stairs to Westminster again, through more squally rain; I was glad the day's court papers were secure in the leather panniers Barak carried. Instead of turning left into New Palace Yard as usual, we went under the gatehouse of the former abbot's prison into Thieving Lane. The rain had stopped, and patches of white clouds moved across a blue sky, sending shadows chasing each other across the ground below.

The Westminster streets teemed with people. Well-dressed MPs were walking to Parliament from their lodgings, harried unmercifully by beggars and pedlars. Some of the Members had been here long enough to develop the trick of waving a hand in dismissal without looking if someone approached, but one man in a fine red cloak and jewelled cap was being mobbed by a group of pedlars. He had made the mistake of trying to argue with one, and seeing an opening the whole group had flocked round him like starlings round a dropped cake. 'No, no, I said I don't want any of that stuff!' he called plaintively as someone grasped his sleeve. He lost his temper and began shouting, 'No! No! Go away, damn you, and take your rubbish!' A pedlar thrust a copper necklace in his face.

Barak laughed. 'Some country gruff. They'll eat him alive.'

I jumped back as a long iron knife was thrust in my face. It was another pedlar, a tray of ironware tied round his neck. A tall grey-bearded man, smelling mightily.

'Have a care!' I snapped.

'Fine steel knives, the very best, sir!'

I shouldered him aside and we went on. Harsnet was already standing by the ancient gatehouse, wearing a lawyer's robe embossed over the heart with the royal arms, his hands clasped behind his back as he looked up Thieving Lane. He nodded as we approached. I began by thanking him for sending Orr to my house.

'The women must be protected. And if the rogue does try to gain entry we have a chance to catch him. Orr is a good man. I hope your wife is not too badly hurt, Goodman Barak.' His face softened with genuine concern.

'A bit of rest and she'll be all right.'

'But what exactly happened?'

I told Harsnet about the attack on Tamasin. He set his lips. 'How can that have happened? We must talk further after we have seen the dean.'

'And you, sir?' I asked him. 'Have the neighbouring coroners reported any – any horrific murders like our three?'

'None. And we are still in the dark as to how our killer got to know those men, why he chose them.' He sighed, then essayed a tired smile. 'Well, let us see what Dean Benson has to say. I told him to expect us. He will be at the former prior's house, which he has taken over.' Harsnet frowned; a reformer would disapprove of an ex-monk benefiting from the Dissolution.

'One thing,' I said. 'Have you thought, this last week, that someone might be following you?'

The coroner shook his head. 'No.'

'I fear I have. I think you should take care, sir.'

'I will. Thank you.' He drew a deep breath as he led the way under the gate into the old monastic precinct.

✝

THE OUTER COURTS of most Benedictine monasteries had long been places of commerce, but Westminster had been in a class of its own, partly because of its enormous size but also because of its ancient privilege of sanctuary. Those who were wanted by the law could move there and set themselves up beyond the reach of justice. Thus the house of God had been surrounded by villains evading retribution. The precinct was ringed with a mixture of fine houses and poor tenements, home to criminals of all sorts, all paying profitable rents to the monks. Most of the old privileges of sanctuary had been abolished by King Henry – one of his better initiatives – but the Sanctuary itself had survived the Dissolution, and debtors and petty thieves could still find refuge there. Some fugitives had spent a lifetime in Westminster Sanctuary, often living a comfortable life, doing business in London using lawyers like Bealknap as intermediaries, and going each Sunday to St Margaret's church, a fine, recently rebuilt building that domin-ated the northern part of the precinct.

As we passed the church, I noticed a little group standing outside, two of them clerics in white robes. 'Bonner.' Harsnet spat out the name. I recognized the feared Bishop of London, a squat, thickset, round-faced figure. He was laughing with the other cleric, perhaps the St Margaret's vicar. I studied the bishop who wanted to purge London of radicals.

'He seems cheery enough,' I observed.

'Vicar Brown is cut from the same cloth,' Harsnet said grimly. 'St Margaret's is still full of gold and candles and images; it was enough trouble to prise their relic of St Margaret's finger out of them. That porkling of the Pope would have us all back to Rome.'

'Yet Bonner was once Cromwell's man,' I said.

'Now Cromwell is dead the wolves cast off the sheep's clothing they adopted to keep in favour.' He glared at the bishop. 'God forgive me, I wish our killer would aim at Bonner, not good reformers. But the devil looks after his own.'

I looked at Barak. He shrugged. We walked past the huge old bell-tower, now converted into ramshackle tenements, then turned east, under the looming shadow of the abbey church, into the southern precinct, bordered by the great monastery walls.

Chapter Eighteen

Around the south precinct there were more houses, mainly poor tenements for pedlars and jobbing workers. Men were outside their houses loading carts with produce and otherwise preparing for the day. There was a smell of resin in the air, for there were many carpenters' yards at Westminster servicing the abbey and Westminster Palace. To our left a high wall separated off the inner precinct containing the monastic buildings; the gates that had once sheltered the monks' comfortable lives from the world stood open, though a guard with a pike stood outside. Harsnet told him who he was and we were allowed through the gateway, into a yard full of monastic buildings in the course of demolition or conversion. All around, workmen were sorting hammers and picks from their carts before starting their day's work. We walked to a large attractive house that stood amid the ruination in a little crocus-filled garden of its own. Harsnet knocked at the door.

A servant answered and bade us enter. Like Cranmer's secretary he asked Barak to wait in an anteroom, ushering Harsnet and me into an office furnished with rich hangings and dominated by an enormous oak table strewn with papers. I wondered if these things had come from the monastic buildings. The choir stalls covered with cushions standing against one wall certainly had. Outside the sound of hammering began.

The door opened, and a short man in white cleric's robes entered. We exchanged brief bows, and he walked to take a seat behind the table. 'Please, gentlemen, be seated,' he said in mellifluous tones, waving us over to the choir stalls.

I studied William Benson. The last abbot of the monastery, a monk who went over to Cromwell and had been put in the abbot's place to hasten the Dissolution. The deanery of the new cathedral was part of his reward. A stocky man nearing fifty, he had a plump, deceptively sleepy face, an air of contentment, ambition achieved.

'What can I do to aid the Archbishop?' he asked.

Harsnet spoke first. 'It is a most secret matter, sir. The Archbishop charges that nothing be said outside these walls.'

'Nor will it be. My duty is to obey my superior.' Benson smiled, looking between us with his sleepy eyes. 'You intrigue me.'

'I fear it is a very disturbing story,' I added, feeling I should stake some claim to authority.

Benson gave a throaty chuckle. 'I have laboured in God's English vineyard for many years. Nothing disturbs me now. Except that hammering,' he added with a frown. 'They are taking for ever to pull the frater down.'

Part of the house you ran for several years, I thought. I watched to see whether his detached expression would change as Harsnet briefly told the story of the murders and the prophecies in Revelation, but it did not, though Benson began toying with a gold ring on his plump hand, twisting it round and round.

'And you think the man may be a former monk?' Benson shook his head. 'I do not think that can be. Most of the brethren accepted the Dissolution quite happily. Six have become prebendaries here, under me.'

'How many monks were there at the Dissolution?' I asked.

'Twenty-four. Not all the older brethren were happy with what happened. But they were realists, mostly. All signed the surrender happily, except old Brother Elfryd who made it a condition that he should be buried in the old procession way when he died. His wish was granted,' he added with a little smile. 'He died soon after he left, and lies there now. Half a dozen of the brethren died soon after they left the monastery.'

'What of the infirmarian, Lancelot Goddard?' Harsnet asked. 'And his assistants? There were two listed at Augmentations.'

'And do you know if Dr Goddard used dwale?' I added.

'Used what?' I thought he answered a little too quickly, something sparked for a moment in his sleepy eyes. I explained what the drug was. 'This is very disturbing,' he said quietly. He sat thinking, busily working his ring. At length he raised his eyes to meet our faces.

'I do not know whether Dr Goddard used this dwale. I left the infirmary to him. He was very competent, I recall no complaints.' He paused. 'I will give you what help I can, gentlemen. But I think you are wrong. Whoever this – abomination is, I do not believe he is from here.'

'How well did you know Dr Goddard?' I asked.

'Not well.' He allowed himself a cynical smile. 'It is no secret I was appointed abbot with orders to bring Westminster to a peaceful dissolution. Which I did. The monks I noticed most were those who needed persuading, or pressing. Dr Goddard was not one of those. He was responsible for the monks' infirmary – looking after everyday illnesses, and caring for the old monks – and he also attended to those from the locality who came to the small infirmary we ran.'

'With his helpers?'

'Yes. Charles Cantrell in the monks' infirmary. Francis Lockley in the lay infirmary, for poor men of Westminster.'

'Was either qualified?' I asked.

'No. Cantrell was a monk, Lockley a lay brother who worked for us and lived here. Goddard trained them both.'

'What was Goddard like?'

Benson inclined his head. 'Not a companionable man. People thought him cold. He came from a well-off background and tended to look down on those of inferior origin. He accepted the Dissolution quietly, like the others. He spoke little in chapter.'

'He has disappeared from his lodgings,' Harsnet told him. 'Have you any idea where he might have gone?'

C. J. SANSOM

Benson shook his head. 'I am afraid not. He had been here a long time, I do not remember who his family were. And most of our records were destroyed.'

'Yes.' I knew that was true, most of the monastic records had been burned along with their illustrated books during the Dissolution.

'Anything you might know, sir . . .'

'He was infirmarian when I came. I remember hearing he became a novice when he was very young. He was around forty when the monastery closed.'

'He was a snob,' I said thoughtfully. 'They said that at his old lodgings. So he never really abandoned the standards of the outside world.'

Benson laughed. 'That was hardly uncommon among the monks. Their worldliness was one reason the monasteries had to go.'

'Do you know where he trained as a doctor?' I asked.

'He didn't. He would have learned on the job under the old infirmarian, as most did. I am afraid "Doctor" was a courtesy title. But he would have had a good training, lasting many years. Knowledge passed down through generations of infirmarians.'

'Like the dwale.'

Dean Benson inclined his head. 'Perhaps.'

'Was there a herb garden?'

'Yes. It is gone to waste now.'

'I wonder if he grew poppies.'

Benson spread his hands. His silk robe rustled. 'I do not know, sir. He may have done.'

'What sort of man was Dr Goddard to deal with?'

'Not difficult. Correct, self-contained.' He smiled. 'He had a disfigurement, a very large mole on the side of his nose. I think he was conscious of it, knew it detracted from his dignity. He would seem angry if people looked at it. Perhaps that warped his character. Some said he had no warmth towards the sick. But perhaps a doctor has to be detached.'

As you are, I thought. But yours is a politician's detachment. He hadn't cared about any of the monks, they were pawns in the game of Dissolution. Benson was hiding something, I felt sure.

He gave his thin smile again. 'I remember his assistant in the lay infirmary, Brother Lockley, used to mock Goddard, imitate his cold precise speech. Lockley often got into trouble for levity, though he performed his duties in the lay infirmary well enough.'

'And the other assistant?' I asked. 'Cantrell.'

'Ah, yes, young Brother Cantrell. Goddard trained him up, but he never seemed satisfied with him, I recall.'

'Goddard's old neighbours said that he had come into an inher- itance,' Harsnet said.

Benson pursed his lips. 'I have an idea his family had money, and lived near London. Somewhere to the north I think. You may be able to find out somehow.'

I doubted it. They said there were sixty thousand souls in and around London now. 'Are there no records at all left?' I asked.

'All gone,' Benson said, shaking his head. 'When the abbey closed, the Augmentations men told us to burn all our papers, our records and songsheets, even our books. Lord Cromwell wanted monasticism utterly exterminated, sir.'

'And you lost touch with your charges?'

'All except those who work under me now.'

'Those three men?' I asked. 'How were they built, how strong were they? Our man is strong, and clever too.'

The dean laughed. 'Then I think you may discount both the assistants. Neither showed any great brains and muscle still less. Lockley is a small round man in his fifties with a taste for the bottle. Young Cantrell was a tall and stringy fellow. I recall he had a huge Adam's apple in his thin neck, it was hard not to look at it. He had trouble with his eyes, I remember. He took to dropping things in the infirmary. Goddard found he was short-sighted and got him some glasses so he could do his work.' He raised a finger. 'I remember now, Cantrell lives in the precinct outside here, his father was a carpenter. I saw him some time ago in the street, with his thick glasses, and remember thinking he would have trouble carrying on his father's trade. Cut his fingers off likely as not.' He laughed. 'And you said the doctor was cold, I thought.

Harsnet looked at me. 'We should see those two men, Master Shardlake. Barak has the addresses?'

'He does.'

'Good. Then we will leave you, dean. But we may call on you again.'

'Of course,' Benson shook his head, gave a puzzled smile. 'You believe this man will commit seven murders? To fulfil the prophecy of the seven vials in Revelation?'

'Yes, sir,' I answered seriously. 'He has only reached the third vial. I fear the fourth must come soon.'

Benson shook his head again, then rose. 'Then I pray you soon catch him.'

☦

WE COLLECTED Barak and went outside. The hammering was louder. I turned to Harsnet.

'He was hiding something,' I said.

The coroner nodded. 'That was my thought too. But what?'

'He's watching,' Barak said quietly. Harsnet and I turned. The dean was at his window, staring out at us. He turned away, disappearing into the shadows of his room.

'It might be interesting to take a look around,' I suggested. 'At the chapterhouse, the infirmary buildings and garden.'

Harsnet nodded. 'Very well.'

We picked our way carefully over rubble and building materials, heading for the cloister. We passed a great pile of mattresses, perhaps from the dormitory.

'What did you think of Benson?' I asked Harsnet.

'A greedy careerist.' Harsnet frowned. 'It is sad Lord Cromwell had to use such people in the cause of reform.' He looked at me. 'It disillusioned many people.'

I wondered if Cranmer had told him that it had disillusioned me.

The three of us walked on, past where the old monks' dormitory was being demolished, men on the roof pulling off slates and casting them into the gutted interior of the fine old building. To our right, neglected and full of weeds, was what must once have been the abbot's formal garden. Next to it was an area where herbs had grown wild, neglected for three years. I recognized the distinctive stems and seed heads of poppies.

'So,' Harsnet said. 'Goddard did grow poppies.'

I looked at the desolation. 'Yes. And heaven knows what else.'

We walked back, through the din of demolition work, and entered the old cloister between the monastic buildings and the church. All at once it was quiet. Then another shower began, pattering on the roof of the walkway and hissing on the flagstones of the cloister yard within. Harsnet looked out over the cloister where the monks once walked, stroking his short greying beard. I wondered what he was thinking. Then he turned to me with an unexpected smile. 'There is a bench over there,' he said. 'Perhaps now would be a good chance to have a talk, in peace and quiet, before we go to visit the chapterhouse.'

'Yes. My head is fairly buzzing with all that has happened.'

The three of us went and sat down.

'I think Dean Benson knows more than he allowed,' I said.

Harsnet nodded. 'I agree. We will question him again, and soon. But I do not think he knows Goddard's whereabouts. He would realize it would not be wise to conceal that.' He shook his head, sighing deeply. 'And what is Goddard? Is he the man we seek, or another victim, or neither?' His west country accent was stronger, as it seemed to become whenever he spoke with emphasis.

'It is over two months since he disappeared. I think if he had been a victim he would have been found by now.'

'But where has he gone?' Harsnet frowned. 'The dean should have known. Had he no care for the monks he led?'

'He was just a political appointment,' Barak ventured. 'My old master made a lot of those.'

Harsnet looked at him and nodded. I was glad he seemed to respect Barak, did not try snobbishly to exclude him from our councils. 'Yes,' he agreed. 'That is true. But we must find him somehow.'

'And whoever the killer is, he has found us,' Barak added grimly. 'Found my wife.' He looked down and clenched his hands.

'I think he marked us that day out at the marshes,' I said. 'Somehow afterwards he found out who we are, me and Barak at least, and he has been following us ever since.'

'If he's been following me without me noticing he's a lot sharper than I am,' Barak said grimly. 'But that's not impossible.' He rubbed his face fiercely with both hands.

'I think that he knew Dr Gurney's body had been found and the matter was being kept secret,' I said. 'So he killed Roger in a way absolutely no one could miss. And then he spent his days waiting on the marshes for investigators to visit the scene of Dr Gurney's murder, with which Roger's would surely be connected, lying on that rush matting we found. To mark the men who would be pursuing him.'

Harsnet shook his head. 'But what sort of man could lie out on there for days on end? And then he lay for hours in the very depths of the marsh, lay there until it grew dark and we had to leave him. Such patience, such endurance, it seems – not human.'

I knew he was thinking of possession. I hesitated for a long moment, then told them both of Guy's theory about obsessive madness, about the cases he had mentioned and about Strodyr. Harsnet listened carefully, staring at me with those keen, sharp blue eyes. At the end he shook his head firmly.

'Those people, the Frenchman and that Strodyr, they sound to me as though they *were* possessed. As this man does. I am sorry, Serjeant Shardlake, but I do not trust Dr Malton. I feel he still cleaves to his old loyalties. And with Bishop Bonner showing as much mercy to Protestants as a butcher shows to the poor lambs at Eastcheap, you must forgive me if I am still dubious about his involvement.'

Barak turned to us, his eyes suddenly fierce. 'Whether he's possessed or mad, that doesn't answer the question of why the arsehole's pursuing us now, rather than us pursuing him.'

'Oh, we *shall* pursue him,' Harsnet said with grim determination. 'And we shall find him.'

'I wonder if we should be looking for him among the radical Protestant sects,' I said, looking Harsnet firmly in the eye. 'As well as churches with radical preachers and church congregations there are study groups, private meetings. Some have developed extreme doctrines – Adamites who believe we have regained Adam's primeval innocence, Arians who deny the Trinity . . .'

I expected Harsnet to disagree fiercely, but he nodded. 'Ay, persecution drives men inwards. When even a faithful man writing some godly matter in rhyme to encourage little children to read the word of God, like a friend of mine, may find himself in the Fleet prison . . .'

'And this man seems to think he has a mission from God to kill lapsed radicals.'

'Or wants us to think that,' Harsnet answered. He looked at me seriously. 'Perhaps the killer is really a supporter of Bishop Bonner's persecutions. If this got out it could only encourage them.'

'Either way, he knew the religious past of Dr Gurney and Tupholme and my poor friend Roger,' I insisted. 'The three had nothing else in common.'

Harsnet sighed, then nodded. 'Very well, I will see some enquiries are made.' He seemed to hesitate, then said, 'Have you thought, sir, that you may be a potential victim? You were once a radical, like Master Elliard.'

'Never as radical as he.' And yet I knew Harsnet was right, theoretically I was a potential victim, though Harsnet and Barak were not. I thought again, with a sudden chill, that Dorothy was too. 'Thous-ands in London fall into that category,' I added. 'Thousands.'

Harsnet studied me, as though he sensed my fear and was weighing up my courage. He gave the slightest of nods, then said, 'One thing we have to think about is resources. If we are to seek out Goddard, enquire among the sects, protect those who need protection, we need a body of men who will keep this matter secret. I command certain resources, but they are limited.' He took a deep breath. 'However, another has offered help to Archbishop Cranmer.'

'Who?'

'Sir Thomas Seymour.' He inclined his head. 'Ay, that was a surprise to me too. Do you know why Seymour first became involved?'

'His link to Catherine Parr?'

'Ay. He said he wanted to protect her interests as a chivalrous man, but there was more to it than that. When Dr Gurney was found dead he feared that he might be a suspect, part of a plot to drive the King away from the Lady Catherine. Archbishop Cranmer told me he was relieved when Tupholme was found, and the focus shifted away from her. But now he has offered to help us with trusted men from his household.'

'Why?'

Harsnet gave a mirthless laugh. 'Sir Thomas loves adventure. And he has a household full of young men of like mind.'

'That sounds possible, from what I've heard of him,' Barak agreed.

'He is a detestable rogue. But we must take help where we can. The Archbishop and Lord Hertford are so close to the royal court that something happening in their households would be noticed. But no one will notice, still less care about, a lot of comings and goings at Sir Thomas Seymour's.'

'Can he be trusted?' I asked dubiously.

'He has reason to keep his mouth shut. This matter should have gone before the King, he is already implicated in the secret. I think he is safe.'

'Well, sir, you know far more about matters relating to the royal court than I. I will trust your judgement.'

Harsnet bowed his head in acknowledgement. 'Thank you.' He hesitated. 'Whatever our differences in matters of belief, I am sure we can work together well.'

'Indeed, I hope so, sir,' I said, a little embarrassed.

'Perhaps you would come and dine with my wife and me one evening,' he added. 'We could get to know one another better.' The coroner reddened, and I realized he was actually a shy man.

'I should be pleased.'

'Good.' He stood up. 'And now, let us take a look at the chapterhouse. I expect it will be full of papist imagery.'

✟

WE ASKED a passing clerk where the chapterhouse was located. He pointed us to a heavy oak door some distance off. It stood ajar. We passed inside down a short passage into one of the most extraordinary rooms I have ever seen. It was enormous, octagonal, and lit by huge stained-glass windows. The floor was beautifully tiled. Brightly coloured, beautifully crafted statues of the Virgin and St Peter stood at the entrance, as though guarding the way in.

But what transfixed all three of us, so that we stood staring with open mouths, was that beneath the windows each wall was divided into panels, on each of which was painted, in bright colours and embossed with gold leaf, a scene from Revelation. There were scores of them, the whole story, in unsparing, vivid colour: St John, Christ in Judgement, the flaming pit of Hell, the beast with seven heads and ten horns, and the seven angels, pouring their vials of wrath upon a world red with torment.

Chapter Nineteen

W E STOOD IN SILENCE, turning on our heels to survey the great panorama of destruction. The unfolding story of the panels was interrupted, on one wall, by a Doom Painting showing the righteous ascending to Heaven while below the pale naked sinners were thrown into Hell. But even that image lacked the sharp colours and vivid scenes of the Revelation story. For the first time I felt its full power.

Barak went up to the panels to take a closer look, his footsteps echoing on the tiles. He stopped before a portrayal of a great beast with seven snake-like necks issuing from its powerful shoulders, at the end of each a snarling head crowned with either one or two horns. Before it, his head framed by a gold-leaf halo, stood the figure of St John, the witness of what was to come, his expression full of fear. I joined him.

'So that's what the beast with seven heads and ten horns looked like,' I said. 'I couldn't imagine it, somehow.'

The style of the paintings was that of two hundred years ago, the figures lacking the realistic fluidity we had achieved in these latter days. But it was vivid and terrifying nonetheless.

'The Westminster monks saw this,' I said quietly. 'Goddard, Lockley, Cantrell. Every day, in chapter. Yes, this could eat into a man's soul.'

'Lockley the lay brother wouldn't have come to chapter, would he?' Barak asked.

'A lot of other business would be done in the chapterhouse. He'd have seen the panels often.'

Harsnet joined us. 'The papists say we have given the Bible to people who cannot understand its message, who are driven to wild interpretations. But see, Master Shardlake, pictures may have the same effect. If this room had been slubbered over with whitewash like a good Reformed church, Goddard might never have had his mind turned. I think the devil came to him through these pictures.'

'If it is Goddard.'

'Yes, if. But he seems the most likely.'

I looked at him. 'Is this what the dean was hiding from us? Did he remember this panorama, perhaps the effect it had on someone?'

Harsnet set his lips. 'That we shall discover. Serjeant Shardlake, I will see the dean again tomorrow. Can you talk to those other two ex-monks, see what they know? Let us build up our knowledge before we confront Benson again.'

'I will,' I said. 'After court today, if I may.'

He nodded agreement. 'And I will send word to the Common Council of London, someone there may know of Goddard's family.'

'I should like to take a look at what is left of the infirmary buildings before we go.'

'Yes. We should do that.' Harsnet cast a last look of distaste round the chamber, then led the way out. I paused at a panel showing a grim-faced angel, winged and clad in white, pouring liquid on to an earth that was turned to fire. Agonized white faces pierced the flames.

'The fourth vial,' I murmured to Barak. 'Dear God, I hope we catch him before he butchers someone else.'

✟

OUTSIDE IN the cloister we asked another clerk where the old infirmary buildings were. He told us the monks' infirmary was demolished now, but that the lay infirmary which had cared for the poor of the parish lay a little distance off, through the old monks' graveyard. The rain ceased as we left the cloister and crossed a path through a grassy square dotted with headstones, some going back centuries. As with all the dissolved monasteries, the stones would soon be dug out, the coffins disinterred and the bones thrown into a communal pit.

The infirmary was a long, low building, apart from the main complex to safeguard against plague. The heavy wooden door was unlocked. Inside was a bare chamber, dimly lit by high dusty windows, nothing left but rags of cloth in the corners, marks on the walls where pictures and a large cross had hung, and an empty fire-grate with mouse droppings scattered around.

'Where do the Westminster patients go now?' I asked quietly, thinking of Roger's hospital plans. His face seemed to appear again before me, smiling cheerfully and nodding.

'They have nowhere,' Harsnet answered sadly.

We all turned quickly as the door creaked. Someone was trying to open it, slowly and stealthily. Barak put his hand to his sword as an extraordinary figure crept into the room. An old man, with a thatch of untidy fair hair like a bird's nest, thin and ragged, his cheeks fallen in. He had not seen us, and as we watched he took a long twig he had found somewhere and began poking at the rubbish in one of the corners.

'What are you doing here?' Harsnet's clear voice echoing round the chamber made the intruder start violently. He dropped his twig, clutched his hands together in front of his chest and stared at us in fear. 'Well?' Harsnet asked.

He cowered away. 'I – I washn't doing any harm, shir.' His voice was slurred, unintelligible, and at first I thought he was drunk. But then I realized that he was toothless. I also saw that he was actually a younger man, his sunken cheeks making him look older.

'You came here for a reason,' Harsnet went on. 'You're in the middle of the abbey precinct, you didn't just wander in.'

'I wash looking for my teeth,' he said, wringing his hands and backing away. 'I keep hoping I'll find them, in a corner. Shomewhere I haven't looked. Shomewhere at Westminster.' There was a look of baffled helplessness in his wide blue eyes, and I wondered if the fellow was an idiot.

'All right, but leave us,' Harsnet said more gently, evidently coming to the same conclusion. The man scurried out and closed the door behind him with the same slow, creaking motion, as though afraid of disturbing us further with the noise.

'What in Jesu's name was all that about?' Barak asked.

'Some poor beggar out of his wits,' Harsnet said. 'They are everywhere at Westminster, evidently they can even find their way in here. The guards should be told.' He frowned at Barak. 'And I would be grateful if you did not take the Lord's name in vain.'

Barak's eyes glinted. Far away, I heard the clock tower strike ten. 'I have to be at court,' I said. 'Barak, come quickly. I am sorry, master coroner, but we must go. I will report to you, once I have seen those two ex-monks.'

✝

WE WALKED BACK with Harsnet to the main gate and out into the busy precinct. It had come to life now, the shops busy, people milling around. Seeing us, a couple of pedlars hurried over. One carried a tray full of old jars, the stink of their contents reaching us from yards away. 'Oil from the great fish, masters,' he called. 'Full of magical properties!' Barak waved him away. A skinny hand clutched at my robe, and I half turned to see a ragged woman holding a pale, skinny baby. 'Feed my child,' she said. I turned away before she could meet my eye, remembering the stories that beggar-women would keep their babies hungry to arouse pity. Or was that just another story we told ourselves, to salve our consciences as we made these people invisible?

As we headed into the gate leading into Thieving Lane, I saw there was a melee outside one of the shops. A middle-aged man and his wife, both looking frightened, stood outside between two parish constables. Two more constables were heaving battered chests from inside the shop, while another rummaged through a third chest, set on the muddy ground. It seemed to contain a variety of outlandish costumes. The crowd that had gathered looked sour and hostile, and I noted the blue coats of several apprentices. A little gang of beggars had made for the crowd, scabby and scurvy, some breechless and wearing skirts of cloth. Among them were a couple of women, young perhaps but with leathery, weatherbeaten faces, passing a leather bottle between them and laughing.

'No books yet,' the constable searching through the chest said.

'We've no forbidden books,' the shopkeeper pleaded. 'All we do is supply costumes for plays. It's our livelihood. Please—'

'Ay,' the constable beside them said. 'For companies that perform John Bale's plays, and other heretical rubbish.' There was an angry murmur from the crowd. His colleague lifted sets of false whiskers from the chest, making one of the drunken women laugh wildly.

'They're bringing the purge to Westminster too,' Harsnet muttered angrily. 'That was what Bonner was doing down here.'

'I must get to court,' I said. I did not want to get involved in what could turn into a nasty scene. 'Let me past,' I said, trying to push my way through. But the growing crowd only pressed closer together as they shoved and pushed to get a better view of the scene, blocking the way to the gate.

Barak stood in front of me and began shoving a way through. On the outer fringes of the hurly-burly more beggars had gathered, working the mob with outstretched hands. A ragged youth stepped in front of me. 'Get out of my way!' I said irritably, shoving past him to the edge of the crowd.

'Yah! Hunchbacked crow!' he shouted.

Just as we pushed through the edge of the crowd I felt a sharp pain on my upper left arm. At the same moment, I heard my name spoken, faintly, a whisper. 'Shardlake.' I cried out and put my other hand to my arm. It came away covered with blood. Harsnet and Barak turned as I cried out. I lifted the sleeve of my robe, which was torn, to reveal a long rip in my doublet. Blood was seeping through it.

'I've been stabbed,' I said, feeling suddenly faint.

'Take off your robe,' Barak said briskly. His eyes darted over the crowd, but it was impossible to see who had done this in the melee.

I did as I was bid. Passers-by looked on curiously as Barak opened the rip in my upper hose wide, then whistled.

'That's some cut. Lucky he missed the artery.' He took his dagger and cut my ruined robe into strips. Then he wrapped the strips round my upper arm, making a tourniquet. The blood gushed faster for a moment, then slowed.

'That needs stitching,' Harsnet said. His face was pale.

'I'll take him to the courthouse, then send for Dr Malton,' Barak said. 'Can you help me?'

'It was him,' I breathed. 'I heard – my name spoken – just as he struck me.' I felt faint.

We staggered across New Palace Yard into Westminster Hall. My arm throbbed with pain, my clothes were red with blood. Harsnet spoke to the guard and I was helped into a little side-room where I sat on a bench, my arm held up on Barak's instructions.

'I'll go and fetch the old Moor,' he said.

'Go first to the Clerk of Requests,' I said. 'Tell him I have been injured, ask for today's cases to be adjourned. Then go to Guy. It's all right, the bleeding's much less,' I added as he looked at me dubiously. 'Hurry, now.'

'I will stay with him,' Harsnet said. Barak nodded and left.

'Did you see who it was?' I asked Harsnet urgently.

He shook his head. 'No. The crowd was so thick, it could have been any one of those wretched men come to watch those poor shopkeepers.'

'It was him.' I clenched my teeth at a sharp stab of pain from my arm. 'He went for Tamasin, and now he has gone for me. He sliced my left arm open. This is another warning.'

'But how could he know where you would be today? No one did surely, save me and Barak?'

'You did not tell Cranmer you were meeting me? Or the Seymours?'

'No. There was not time last night.' He looked suddenly frightened. 'Dear God, what powers has the devil lent this creature?'

My tired brain could see no rational way to answer him, to account for this man's ability to hound us unseen, to know where we were at every move. Suddenly I felt giddy. I closed my eyes, and I must have fainted for the next thing I knew someone touched my shoulder and I opened my eyes to find the boy Piers standing over me, staring into my face with a look of professional interest. Guy and Barak were beside him, Barak looking seriously worried.

'You passed out,' Guy said. 'It was the shock. You have been unconscious half an hour.'

I realized I still was lying on the bench in the little room; through the closed door I could hear the bustle and chatter of the courts; from a distance someone called for the parties in a case to come into court.

'You will be sick of the sight of me, Guy.'

'Nonsense. Let's have a look at you.' He undid the tourniquet. A deep gash, three inches long, ran below my shoulder. The red wound, standing out against flesh that was white from being held in the bandage, reminded me horribly of Roger's body, and my head swam again. 'Lie back,' Guy said gently, as his fingers probed the wound. 'I am going to put an unguent on it that hinders infection,' he said. 'Then we must stitch you up. It will be painful, I am afraid.'

'Do what is needed,' I answered, though my stomach churned. 'Barak, have you been to the court?'

'I told the office you were taken ill. The clerks went to the judge and he's agreed to stand your cases over.' Barak hesitated, then continued. 'Harsnet says perhaps you should stand out all of your cases till this business is done. Cranmer or Lord Hertford can smooth the path.'

'It might be a good idea. Some of them at least. Although I must attend Adam Kite's hearing on the fourth. That is too delicate a matter to hand to someone else.'

Guy was applying a thick paste to my arm. It stung. 'Let us get it properly clean before we stitch it. You will be in pain for a while,' he said. 'You will be tired too, as your body works to mend itself.'

He patted my arm. 'Let's stitch you up. Piers will do it. Do not worry, he has done it many times now. I will supervise.' The boy approached, delved in his bundle and brought out a thin, sharp needle to which black thread was already attached. 'Now remember,' Guy told him, 'slowly and carefully.' The boy put down his bundle and knelt beside me. He smiled. 'I will be gentle, sir,' he said quietly, then brought the needle down to pierce my flesh.

✝

Two hours later I was back home, lying on cushions in my parlour. Barak came in.

'Is it arranged?' I asked.

'Yes. The other Requests barrister will take some of the cases. But the clerks were sniffy about it. I think a message from Cranmer or Lord Hertford to the judge would do no harm.'

'I'll write a note to Harsnet. It was good of him to help you carry me over to Westminster Hall, not many coroners would have done that.'

'He's too full of his own rightness in religion for my liking. He really does seem to think the killer is possessed.' He shook his head. 'I almost begin to wonder if he could be right.'

'You, Jack, afraid of devils?'

'I know. But I can't account for this game of hoodman blind the bastard's playing with us. Attacking Tamasin, and now you, vanish-ing each time like some spirit of the air. And how does he follow us around without being seen?'

'I have been thinking on that, sitting here.' I sat up, wincing at a stab from my arm. 'The killer first murdered the cottar, and my guess is he thought there would be a mighty hue and cry when he was discovered. But everyone blamed the Welsh whore.'

'Yes.'

'Next he murdered Dr Gurney and left him in that pool. A dramatic killing of a prominent man, likely to cause widespread public horror. Perhaps, too, he thought someone would make the link to Revelation from the way Dr Gurney was killed. But Cranmer hushed it up.'

'So he hadn't made the stir he wanted.'

'No. So then he kills Roger. In a more public manner still. Then he waited for us on the marsh.'

'He would need to be as crafty and calculating as a fox. And patient as a cat.'

'And utterly committed to what he is doing. Remember how he hid out in the marsh when we chased him? But by then he had seen us, marked us. He follows you to your home and me to mine.'

'Without either of us noticing? Come on, I've followed people before today, for Lord Cromwell. It's not easy, especially if there's only one person doing the following. And if it is Goddard, he's supposed to have a great mole on the side of his nose.'

'I know. I haven't worked out yet how he does it.'

'And while we hunt him, he hunts us. And today in the crowd he took an opportunity.'

'Yes.'

'How the fuck could he have known we were at Westminster today?' Barak burst out.

I shook my head. 'Knew we were due at court, perhaps. But how would he know which court I worked at, the timetable?' I bit the side of my finger. 'Unless . . .'

'What?'

'Unless someone is helping him, telling him our movements.'

'Thomas Seymour?' Barak asked, narrowing his eyes. 'I don't trust him.'

'No. Seymour wants him caught. But I believe someone may be

helping him. That makes more sense to me than the devil giving him superhuman powers.' I sighed. 'I think he spends his whole life planning, waiting. Endlessly, obsessively, working toward the next time he will break free of all restraints and kill wildly. And make a spectacle, for that is what he likes.'

'That's the old Moor talking,' Barak noted shrewdly. 'In any case, here's another question. He's taking a hell of a risk, attacking you in public. But in that crowd he could have killed you. He could have killed Tamasin too.' His voice ended on a gulp, and I saw how the whole thing had harrowed him to the core. 'Why didn't he?'

'He wants me to withdraw from the case?'

'But they'd only appoint someone else.'

'Yes, they would.'

'It's almost as though the arsehole's taunting us. One thing's sure, you and I will both have to watch every step we take outside. Be glad we've got that man of Harsnet's in the kitchen.' He clenched his fists. 'I spot the bastard who's doing this and I'll kill him with my own hands.'

'No. We need him alive.' I shook my head. 'Is it Goddard, Barak?'

'I don't know.'

'We are so embroiled in the mystery and terror that it is tempting to clutch at any possibility.' I sighed. 'Whoever he is, I pray we catch him before someone else dies horribly.' I frowned. 'Before he shows us again how clever he is, for surely that is part of it.'

Barak's face was still clouded with perplexity and fear. To distract him I said, 'That crowd looked as though it could get nasty.'

'Bonner's after the player companies as well, then,' he said without much interest.

'As this morning showed, he could end by stirring up a hornet's nest. One the size of a city.'

'Ay. There could come a time when the sectaries fight back. Oh, a plague on both sides,' he added irritably.

'Indeed,' I agreed. 'Tell me, by the way, what do you think of Guy's assistant? Young Piers?'

'Didn't much like the look of him. Bit of a creeper and crawler, for all his pleasant manner and pretty face. He's clever, he sewed your arm up well. Trouble was, he looked as though he was quite enjoying it.'

'Guy would say he was learning the detachment of a medical practitioner.' I laughed wearily. 'Remember eighteen months ago, when you were hurt in that fall at York and found yourself an invalid? It is my turn now.'

He smiled.

'We have seen some troubles.'

'That we have.'

Barak still looked preoccupied. 'How is Tamasin?' I asked tentatively.

'Sleeping,' he said. 'She needs to rest. I—'

We were interrupted by a frantic knocking at the door, then urgent voices, Joan's and a man's. Footsteps sounded across the hall. Barak and I looked at each other.

'He's struck again,' I breathed.

But when the door opened it was Daniel Kite who stood there, his hair wild, breathing heavily.

'Sir!' he said. 'You must come! For the love of God, come!'

'What—'

'It's Adam, sir. He has escaped. He's got himself on top of London Wall, out by Bishopsgate, he's calling on the crowds to repent, to forsake the priests and come to God! They'll burn him this time!'

Chapter Twenty

I T WAS A MILE and a half to Bishopsgate, a painful walk through the London throng, my arm in its sling throbbing at every jolt. Daniel and Minnie strode on as fast as possible, Daniel with a set face, Minnie looking as though she would collapse at any moment. A gust of wind brought another squally shower, nearly casting my cap to the ground. I had donned my best robe and cap, for I guessed I might need to exert some authority at Bishopsgate.

Daniel had told me that a friend had arrived at his workshop an hour before to tell him that Adam was standing on top of London Wall, screaming out to the crowds that they must come to God for salvation. He had gone out there and seen his son haranguing a growing crowd; they had come for me because they had nowhere else to turn. I wondered angrily how Adam had escaped from the Bedlam. It struck me that this frantic preaching was something new. I had sent Barak to fetch Guy, with a pang of conscience at disturbing him again; yet he had come nearer than anyone to communicating with Adam, and if the boy could not be got down from that wall it might be the fire this time.

☦

As WE WALKED up All Hallows Street we heard the murmur of a crowd and shouts of laughter. A moment later Adam came into view. He was standing on top of the ancient, crumbling city wall, shouting down at the crowd which had gathered thirty feet below. Dressed in his filthy rags, his hair matted and his eyes wild, Adam looked like one of the wild country lunatics who escape their families and hide in inaccessible woods until they die of hunger. He was standing above Wormwood Street, perhaps fifty yards out from Bishopsgate Tower; somehow he must have got to the top of the gatehouse and clambered out. It seemed no one had gone out after him. The ancient city wall was wide but it was crumbling away in many places. Even as I watched, Adam dislodged a large stone with his feet, which crashed down to the crowd. 'Hey, there, look out!' someone cried. Adam almost slipped but managed somehow to regain his balance.

'You *must* come to Christ!' he bawled at them. 'You *must*, you must ensure you are one of the elect! The end is coming, the Antichrist is here! Please, you must pray!'

I saw Reverend Meaphon in the crowd, his face redder than ever. We shouldered our way over to him. Another cleric was standing beside him, a tall thin old fellow with a beaky-nosed face and thick white hair, well combed and clean. How well these radical preachers all seemed to look after their hair, a peacock trait above the sober clothes. Minnie clasped Meaphon's arm. 'Oh, sir, you came!'

Meaphon turned to me, and I saw the cleric was frightened. 'He has to be got down,' he said urgently. 'If he's taken I will be questioned, the whole congregation will!'

'And mine!' the other cleric said. 'I am William Yarington, rector of the next church to Reverend Meaphon's.' He spoke to me in tones of portentous seriousness, evidently assuming I was a radical sympathizer. 'Our truth, our true faith, is under threat from papists and backsliders as never before. That mad boy should have been kept shut away and secure, with someone to pray with him all the time.' He glared at Meaphon.

'He manages enough prayers by himself,' I snapped.

Yarington looked me coldly up and down, then turned away. He muttered something that sounded like, 'Another unbeliever.'

I turned to Meaphon.

'Have you tried speaking with him?' I asked.

'Yes, yes! I have ordered him down, told him to stop his shouting. I said he could put his parents in danger. But he won't listen.'

'If they find us here, if they associate me with him . . .' the white-haired cleric muttered and cast his eyes around, as though looking for escape, then fixed them again on Adam as the boy cried out that he was suffering for them all, like Jesus on his Cross.

'Word will get to Bonner soon. He'll be here!' Meaphon shook his head.

'It might be better for everyone if he fell and broke his neck,' the other cleric said.

Minnie had broken down again and was sobbing on her hus-band's breast. 'Do something, sir,' Daniel implored me. 'Please!'

There was a fresh gust of laughter from the crowd. Some wretch had brought a dancing bear to entertain the crowd and the little bruin, chained and muzzled and with strips of coloured cloth sewn into its ears, stared at the crowd in fear. Its keeper thwacked it on the nose, called 'Dance!' and the poor creature began to shift from leg to leg. The keeper put his cap on the ground for folk to throw pennies.

'Here!' someone called up to Adam. 'You dance too! Come on, give us a dance!'

Two middle-aged men in the robes of the Cutlers Guild were next to me. 'This is blasphemy,' one said angrily. 'The Common Council should be fetched, he should be imprisoned, punished for this display.'

'Someone's gone to Bonner's palace,' his fellow said in tones of grim satisfaction. 'He'll be punished all right.'

'You are right, brother!' someone called to Adam from the crowd. 'You have the spirit in you!' The crowd, I saw, was mostly good-natured, seeing this as a spectacle, a joke. But as with the costumiers' arrests, this could turn nasty.

I stepped to the front of the crowd, directly underneath Adam, and looked up at him. He had paused and was taking deep whooping breaths. He was, I saw, shivering. If he fainted . . .

'Adam,' I called. 'Please come down! Your mother is sore upset!'

He looked down at me, then shifted his gaze to the crowd. 'The world is ending!' he yelled. 'The Antichrist is here! If you do not deny Satan and come to Jesus you will all burn! Burn!'

'Speak, parrot, speak!' someone called out mockingly.

'Cure the hunchback's arm, like Jesus healed the sick! Give us a miracle!'

I felt an angry despair. There was no communicating with Adam, one might as well try talking to a brick wall. None of the hot-gospellers listened, they only ranted, and either you took what they said for God's word or in God's name they casually condemned you to eternal torment. Adam was mad but that was where his madness had grown from. The killer's, too, perhaps, not only declaring God's bloody verdict but implementing it too. I clutched my throbbing arm, feeling utterly helpless.

There was a murmur behind me. Some men were shouldering their way through the crowd. With a sinking heart I caught a glimpse of raised pikes. A moment later Bishop Bonner, in black robes and cap and surrounded by his guards, appeared. The crowd stepped away and he moved through, short and stocky and powerful, leaving me, the Kites and Meaphon exposed. The other minister melted into the crowd. Above us, Adam had started declaiming scripture, and I recognized a garbled paraphrase of Revelation: *The fearful, and unbelieving, and whoremongers and sorcerers, shall have their part in the lake that burneth with fire and brimstone . . .*

'Cease that blasphemy!' Bonner's thunderous roar silenced the crowd and made even Adam pause and blink. Close to, the face under the dark cap was round and jowly, the large dark eyes alive with anger.

'Papist!' someone in the crowd shouted out. Bonner stared round furiously, but in the close-packed crowd there was no way of telling who had spoken. The bishop turned his furious eyes on me. 'Who are you, lawyer? Are you of his family? And you—' His gaze turned to Meaphon, who quailed. 'Oh, I know you, sir, you are a leader of the mad giddy company of schismatics.'

I had heard of Bonner's rages; his anger was fierce and once roused did not abate. 'Heretic!' he shouted in Meaphon's face. The cleric flinched, his courage visibly draining. 'It's not his fault, sir.' Daniel Kite spoke up bravely. 'He was trying to talk Adam down. Our son. He is mad, sir, stark mad—'

'*God is the judge of all, Jesus will come with sword in hand.*' Adam had begun again. Bonner turned to the soldiers. 'You! Go up through the gatehouse, bring him down. If he falls, it'll be no loss.'

The soldiers approached the wall, but then paused, staring upward. There was a murmur from the crowd as three figures stepped through an upper window of the gatehouse on to the wall. Guy and Barak and Piers. They moved slowly along the wall towards Adam, Barak and Piers holding their arms out for balance but Guy, behind, walking straight, his robe hitched up so his feet would not stumble on the hem. The crowd fell silent; even the furious Bonner was quiet.

'Come, Adam,' Guy called. 'Remember me. Remember we talked?'

The boy stared at him foolishly, as though wondering how he had appeared there. Barak and Piers were almost next to Adam. They looked at him dubiously, I saw fear in both their set faces. If they tried to grasp Adam he could bring all three down. 'Why are you doing this?' Guy asked.

To my surprise, Adam answered him. 'I thought I could bring others to God, it would prove I was saved.'

'But not all who are saved can be messengers to the world.' Guy waved at the crowd. 'See, look at those people, you are not strong enough to convert that heathen crowd. It is no shame.'

Adam began to cry then, and sank slowly to his knees. Some lumps of old mortar, dislodged, pattered down on the crowd. Barak and Piers knelt carefully beside him, eased him to his feet and with difficulty led him back along the wall. They helped get the boy through the window of the gatehouse. Guy stepped in after them.

Bonner clicked his fingers and walked toward the gatehouse, the guard following. Daniel and Minnie stepped hesitantly after him. Meaphon hesitated a moment, then stepped backwards and disappeared into the crowd. I watched him go. Cowardice, or the realization that his presence now would only anger Bonner? Then I tensed. I felt someone watching me, caught the merest glimpse out of the corner of my eye. Someone with a beard. I whirled round. I saw a figure turn away into the crowd, a glimpse of a brown doublet. My heart thumped. Was it him, following again? I stood rooted to the spot, realizing my anxiety for Adam had made me careless.

'Master Shardlake, please, help us!' It was Minnie Kite's voice. I turned back to her.

✝

ADAM HAD emerged from the gatehouse on to the street. Guy and Barak each held one of his arms, for he was trying to drop to the ground again, his eyes were closed and his lips moved in silent prayer. The gatekeeper followed, looking anxiously at the bishop. Bonner planted himself in front of Adam, arms akimbo.

'This is a fine sight,' he thundered. 'What did you think you were doing, boy?' Adam ignored him, his eyes on the ground, praying even now. Bonner reddened. 'You had better answer, boy preacher, or you will find yourself in the fire like Mekins.'

'I don't know how he got up there,' the gatekeeper said. 'He must have sneaked up through the house. On my oath, sir, I don't know how he did it unless he's a sorcerer and can make himself invisible.' Bonner snorted.

'Slave of the Roman harlot!' someone shouted out from the crowd. Bonner turned again, frowning mightily. 'Traitor!' someone else called out. This time there was a murmur of approval from the crowd. The soldiers took a firm hold on their pikes. The mood was beginning to turn.

Daniel and Minnie had been looking on helplessly, an expression of mingled fear and distaste in Daniel's eyes as he stared at Bonner. Minnie, though, stepped forward. She fell on her knees before Bonner, grasped the hem of his robe. 'Please, sir,' she said. 'My son is mad. Sick in his mind. The Privy Council sent him to the Bedlam. He must have escaped. He can be sore cunning despite his scattered wits.'

Bonner was quite unmoved. 'I heard of that decision, Bishop Gardiner told me. The Privy Council was wrong. This display shows your son to be a wild heretic.' He glared round at us. 'I will shortly make matters so hot for you people, you will wish yourselves gathered into God.' He stared at Adam, his expression twisted with distaste. 'I shall begin with this slavering creature.' He looked round defiantly at the crowd; whatever else, Bishop Bonner did not lack courage.

I took a deep breath and stepped forward. 'Sir, he *is* mad,' I said urgently. I waved at Guy. 'This man is his doctor, he will certify it. I have been unhappy with the boy's security, his care at the Bedlam. The matter is before the Court of Requests.' I spoke loudly enough for the crowd to hear it; there was a constant murmuring now.

Bonner looked curiously at Guy. 'So you are Dr Malton,' he said. 'I have heard of you. The ex-monk.'

'Yes, my lord.'

'I heard you were a sound man among the physicians,' Bonner said. 'Why are you working with these heretics?'

Guy was at his diplomatic best. 'The Privy Council decided he was mad, my lord, not a heretic. I believe he is indeed mad and I hope he may be cured. Brought to his right thinking,' he added meaningfully.

One of the guards looked over the murmuring crowd, then leaned forward and whispered something to Bonner. He looked over at the crowd, then back at Guy and me. 'Very well,' he said. 'But I shall keep myself informed on his progress.' He turned to me. 'As for you, lawyer, make sure he is kept safely locked up. I might not be so accommodating next time.' He gave me a stern nod and walked away. The soldiers followed.

'Well done,' I breathed to Guy. He gave me a sombre look.

'I think he realized that if he were to burn a boy a doctor had certified mad, London would be even more against him than it was with Mekins. But he will not forget. Matthew, Adam *must* be kept secure.'

'Are we taking him back to the Bedlam?' Barak asked.

'Yes. Come on. It is a short walk. Let's see what Keeper Shawms has to say,' I added grimly.

Piers, who had hung back during the conversation with Bonner, now stepped forward and took Adam's arm, Barak taking the other.

We set off, the crowd staring after us, sorry to be deprived of their entertainment. Daniel and Minnie followed behind. They made no effort to talk to their son; they knew it would be useless.

☥

THE LONG LOW building that housed the Bedlam presented its usual bland face to the world. I knocked on the door and it was opened by the woman Ellen. She had cast off her coif and her dark hair was wild, her expression frightened. When she saw Adam her face flooded with relief.

'Oh God's mercy, you have him! Where was he?'

'Preaching to the multitude from the top of London Wall.' A group of anxious faces stared from the doorway of the parlour, including the woman who had exposed herself on my last visit.

'Oh Jesu.' Ellen leaned against the wall. 'I knew Adam would make another exhibition.'

'Where is Shawms?'

'Gone out, sir. I am here alone with the patients. One of the under-keepers is ill, sir, the other visiting his family in Kent. Master Shawms said he had to go out and he took our third keeper, Leaman, with him. I had thirty people to look after. I thought Adam was safe, I thought he was chained. He must have got out of the window, I came to his cell and he was gone—'

'Let's get him back in his room.' At Ellen's directions, Barak and Piers dragged Adam, still a muttering deadweight, to the open door of his chamber. Daniel and Minnie followed with Guy. I turned to Ellen.

'So Shawms left you alone?'

'Yes, sir.' She hesitated, then said quickly, 'I think he did it on purpose, I think he left Adam unchained so he would get out. He is the only one with keys to the chains.'

'When did you find Adam was gone?'

'An hour ago.'

'But did you not raise the alarm?' I frowned, puzzled. Why had someone as conscientious as Ellen done nothing?

She reddened and lowered her voice to a whisper. 'I may not go out.' She wrung her hands together, the gesture somehow full of the most terrible anxiety. 'I did not know what to do. The other patients were afraid. I think Shawms wanted Adam arrested and dealt with as a heretic. He wanted him out. And I would be blamed for letting him go. Oh, he is cruel man, a savage—'

'But why, Ellen? When you told me before you could never leave the Bedlam, I did not realize you meant you could not leave the building. Why?'

'Do not ask me, sir.' She gave me a desperate, pleading look. I began to wonder if this woman had perhaps done something terrible, that perhaps she was kept from leaving by order of the court. But then why was she given charge of the patients?

The main door opened and Shawms entered, another keeper at his side. When he saw me he smiled wickedly.

'Good day, master lawyer. How is your charge?'

'Safe in his cell,' I answered grimly. 'With his parents and his doctor.'

'Oh.' Shawms' face fell.

'He got out, as you planned, but we got him back safe.' I stepped up to him. 'Now, sir, listen to me. Your heartless plan to let him escape and blame this poor woman is discovered. I will raise what you have done with Archbishop Cranmer if anything like this happens again.' His eyes widened. 'Yes, I am the Archbishop's man. Do you understand?'

He gave me a savage look. 'I don't know how he got out,' he muttered. The other keeper meanwhile backed away and disappeared.

'You are a brute, a brute!' It was Minnie's voice. She and Daniel had appeared in the doorway of Adam's cell. Behind them I saw Barak looking grim, but Piers, just behind him, was smiling slightly. He was enjoying this.

'So take care, master keeper.' I looked at Ellen. 'And do not take it out on her. I do not know what hold you have on her that she cannot go out, but you will not make her your scapegoat.'

Shawms laughed then, throatily. 'Me got a hold on her? Is that what she told you?'

'She told me nothing.'

'I bet she didn't.' He laughed again, gave Ellen a look of cruel amusement, then stared round at the parlour doorway. 'Come on, you lot, there's been enough spectacle for one day.' The patients retreated before his advance, and Ellen flitted quickly past me, vanishing up the stairs.

With a sigh, I turned back to Daniel and Minnie, standing outside Adam's door. 'The doctor asked us to come out while he talked to Adam,' Daniel said. 'There's no hope for him, is there? With Bonner after him now?' The big man's whole body seemed to sag. 'God help me, out there I half wished Adam would fall, end his suffering.'

'No, Daniel, no,' Minnie said fiercely. 'He is our son.'

'Even Reverend Meaphon abandoned us.'

'*I* will not,' I said. The big stonemason nodded, but his body still slumped hopelessly. Shawms reappeared, jangling his big bunch of keys. 'He'd better be chained up again,' he said grimly.

'Must he, sir?' Minnie asked me.

'If he is not to escape again, I fear so.'

Shawms went into the cell. There was a metallic clinking, then Barak and Piers came out with the keeper. 'We'll leave you,' Barak said. 'You should go home, with that arm.'

'Ay. We can look for those – those people – tomorrow.' I chose my words carefully under Piers' curious eye. It struck me all at once that he was like a bird: a curious opportunistic predator in bright plumage. They walked off, Barak striding out firmly ahead, avoiding the company of the apprentice.

✝

INSIDE THE CELL Guy was kneeling, face to face with Adam, who had squeezed himself into a corner once again. Somehow he had once more gained the boy's attention, was whispering to him in soft tones. I stood watching.

'Did you really think if you converted people, you might be saved?' Guy was asking.

'Yes.' A whisper. 'But I was wrong. How could I save them, if I am not saved myself?'

'The dark angel told you that you were not saved. When did he tell you that?'

'It was in a dream. After I sinned.'

'How did you sin?'

'No.' Adam squeezed his eyes shut. 'No. I have sinned in all ways. No.'

'All right.' Guy laid a hand on his shoulder as the boy gave one of his dreadful, wrenching sighs. 'You must be tired, Adam. After all that running, and climbing.'

'Tiredness does not matter,' Adam muttered. 'I have to pray.'

'But tiredness saps the concentration. How can you pray well, then, or listen to God? Sometimes it is effortful to listen to Him. And what if you had fallen from that wall? You would have no more chance to pray.'

'I was afraid. I did feel I might fall. It was such a long way down.' And with those three sentences, the first I had heard from him that related to the real world, Adam's face seemed to clear, to slip into the lineaments of an ordinary boy, if a terrified one.

'I was afraid too, when I got up there,' Guy said. 'You step out on the wall and your head reels.'

To my amazement Adam smiled, a tiny watery smile. 'Yes, it does.' Then he frowned, checking himself. 'I have to pray,' he said.

'No, not now. You are too tired. With sleep, and some food later, you will pray better. Do not go to God too tired and weak to attend to him.' Guy leaned forward, his brown eyes boring into Adam's. 'There is still time, still time to be saved. But sleep now, sleep. Come, your eyes are closing.' The boy's eyelids fluttered. 'Closing. Sleep. Sleep.' He took Adam's shoulders and gently laid him on the floor. The boy did not resist; he was already asleep. Guy rose, wincing as his joints cracked. Adam did not stir.

'That was remarkable,' I said to Guy.

'It was easy. He was completely exhausted.' He looked at me. 'You too look tired to death, Matthew. And pale. How is your arm?'

'Sore. I should go to Daniel and Minnie—'

Guy laid a hand on my arm. 'I am worried about you, Matthew. All this is affecting you – this other matter.'

'He was there, Guy, today, in the crowd. The killer. I only caught a merest glimpse, but it was him. I know. He taunts me. I am too weak for this,' I burst out savagely.

'No. You will press on. I know you.' He spoke the words in a tone that was half comforting and half bleak. He looked sad.

'It is Roger's funeral tomorrow afternoon. Dorothy has sent me a note of the time.'

'You should go home now, rest that arm.'

'I know. Yet I fear that he will strike again, soon.' I paused, then went on, 'This is affecting me, Guy, not like Harsnet, who thinks we are dealing with a man possessed; nor like Barak, who has never come across the like of this before, and is frightened, thrashing about for an answer. It is the horror of it, it seems to seep into my bones somehow. Oh, I was content before Roger was murdered. Content for the first time in years. And now . . .' I shook my head. 'I think you are right about what he is, Guy; this is some strange and terrible form of madness.' I looked at him. 'You must have suffered mightily all those years ago, to be driven to such a strange and terrible course of study.'

'I did. I told you. And yet all study is worthwhile, observing things and trying to understand their hidden patterns. Medical books alone can become binds and fetters, as can the Bible in the wrong hands.'

'Do you think you understand the pattern of this killer's mind?'

He shook his head. 'No. It is too dark and too strange. With Adam Kite I am hopeful that I will come to understand, but this man – no.'

Again I saw how his thin face was lined with pain. 'You suffer now, too, don't you?'

'We all suffer, Matthew. We have to find our own ways through, with God's help.' He forced a smile. 'I thought young Piers acquitted himself bravely today. He volunteered to come with me, volunteered to go up on that wall with Barak. You see, you had him wrong.'

'I saw him smile as Minnie Kite railed at Shawms. He is not someone you should invest so heavily in.'

'He will learn compassion.'

I did not argue with him then. Yet I doubted what he said was possible. But it also seemed to me then that there was little hope in the world, and a man should not be blamed for clinging on to that which he could find.

Chapter Twenty-one

IT WAS LATE AFTERNOON by the time I left the Bedlam. I was exhausted, my arm hurt, and I had not eaten since breakfast. The sun was setting as I arrived home. Barak was waiting for me in the parlour; it was a moment before I remembered he and Tamasin had moved in.

'A message from Harsnet,' he said. 'He's still trying to trace Goddard. He wants us to meet him tomorrow night to report on those two ex-monks. Apparently he's attending the reopening of some church where the steeple fell down. St Agatha's, down by the river.'

'A radical church, no doubt.'

'It is. Someone I worked with under Lord Cromwell used to go there. The vicar is a man called Thomas Yarington. We met him earlier.'

'Did we?'

'He was the white-haired cleric that was with Meaphon. The one who melted into the crowd when Bonner appeared.'

'Oh, him.'

'The note says Sir Thomas Seymour's going to be there too.' He handed it to me. 'Harsnet invites you to dinner as well.'

The note was brief. 'All right,' I said. 'We will go and visit the ex-monks tomorrow, after court. There is a case I must attend myself in the morning, but the afternoon is free, until five, when Roger is buried.'

'Where's the funeral to be?'

'St Bride's. It is to be quiet, only friends and relatives. Samuel will be home now.' I massaged my arm. 'We can see the ex-monk who lives at Westminster first, then ride out to the other one – where is he?'

'Up at the Charterhouse, beyond Smithfield. Lockley, the lay brother.'

'I am going to get something to eat and then I must go to bed. How is Tamasin?'

'She's sleeping too. Her broken tooth has been hurting her. She's going to the tooth-drawer tomorrow.'

'Go up to her. I will see you in the morning.'

I went to the kitchen to get some food. Joan was preparing some pottage, and looked more tired than ever. I had to get her some more help. My stitched and bandaged arm was hidden under my doublet; I did not want to worry her even more than she was already.

'I'll bring you up some cold food, sir,' she said. Looking past her, through the open door to the scullery, I saw Harsnet's man Orr sitting at the table with the kitchen boy Peter. A little book open before them.

'He's teaching Peter to read,' I said.

'Yes, but it's all hot Bible stuff,' Joan answered disapprovingly. 'It'll give the lad nightmares.'

I went up to bed. In my room, I looked through the window. A beautiful spring evening, my lawn a pretty design of crocuses, daffodils beginning to break through. A world away from the turmoil and darkness around me. During the night I had a strange dream of someone whimpering and pulling at my injured arm. When I turned round it was Bealknap, looking weak and wasted. 'You could have helped me,' he said, pleadingly. 'You could have helped me.'

✝

NEXT MORNING Barak and I rode down to Westminster. I felt safer riding, above the crowd and better able to watch it. My arm throbbed, but much less than yesterday. I had to admit Piers had made a good job of his stitching. Barak had been unusually quiet at breakfast, and Tamasin had not made an appearance.

'It was brave of you to go out on London Wall yesterday,' I said.

'I feared young Kite might turn on us, throw us down to the street.'

'That is not the sort of madness he has.'

'Who knows what mad folks may do?'

I looked at him. 'He was there, you know, our killer. I caught a glimpse of him, turning into the crowd, when you were in the gate-house.'

'What did you see?'

'A glimpse of a brown doublet. He was tall, I think.'

'Might just have been someone in the crowd leaving.'

'I don't think so. I − I felt it. I feel he has me marked.'

Barak was silent for a moment. Then he asked, 'D'you think he's pretending to be a sectary somewhere, mixing with the radicals?'

'Ay, and garnering names of people to kill. The sectaries probably spend half their time cursing and criticizing backsliders.'

I spent the morning at court, and then we rode down into Westminster, moving slowly through the busy, narrow streets. A beggar came right up to me and I flinched away. 'On your way!' Barak shouted. 'It's all right,' he said, 'I had him marked.'

'Now I must look out for beggars, instead of avoiding their eyes all the time. An ironic justice.' I laughed bitterly.

We passed into the hive of activity that was the southern precinct. Barak looked round the buildings. 'The record said he lived on the same street as the White Oak Inn. See, it's over there.' He pointed to a small, two-storey house. It was in poor repair, the paint flaking from the frontage. On the other side of the house was a large double-door, locked and padlocked. 'Adrian Cantrell, Carpenter' was painted above it in faded letters. We looked at it. 'I thought all the ex-monks were offered church livings as well as their pensions,' he said. 'Yet neither of these two, Cantrell and Lockley, seems to have taken them.'

'Lockley was only a lay brother, he wouldn't have been offered a benefice. But Cantrell would. Quite a few did not take up the offer, though.'

'Maybe he got himself a wife.'

We crossed the muddy road.

I knocked on the door. There was no answer, and I was about to knock again when I heard shuffling footsteps from within. The door opened to reveal a gaunt young man in his late-twenties. He wore a scuffed leather jerkin over a shirt that was in sore need of a wash. His face was thin, framed by a shock of straw-coloured hair, and he wore wood-framed spectacles, the glass so thick his eyes were like blue watery pools.

'Are you Charles Cantrell?' I asked.

'Ay.'

I smiled to try and put him at ease. 'I have come on behalf of the King's assistant coroner. We hoped you might be able to help us with some questions. May we come in?'

'If you like.' The young man led us into the house, which had a sour, unwashed smell, up a dim corridor and into a parlour with only a table of rough planks and some hard stools for furniture. Through a dusty window we saw a yard, containing a small vegetable garden run to weeds, and a storage shed which must have been used by his father. I noticed Cantrell kept a couple of fingers against the wall as he walked, as though guiding himself. He waved us to the stools, sat down on one himself and faced us. His posture was slumped, dejected.

'I understand you were an assistant in the monks' infirmary at Westminster,' I said. 'Before the Dissolution. We are seeking information on your master, Dr Goddard.'

He screwed up his face in distaste. 'Is he dead?' he asked. For the first time, he seemed interested.

'No. But he needs to be traced, there are some enquiries to be made. We wondered if you might know where he was.'

Cantrell gave a short, bitter laugh. 'As though he'd keep in touch with me. He treated me like a louse. I didn't want to stop being a monk when they closed us down three years ago, but I was glad I'd never see him again.' He paused. 'Has he killed a patient? It wouldn't be the first time.'

'What?' I stared at him. 'What do you mean?'

Cantrell shrugged. 'There were one or two he sent to their rest before their time through bad treatment.' He paused. 'Goddard was a shit.'

'You know this for sure?' I asked.

He shrugged. 'There was nothing I could do, Abbot Benson wouldn't have listened to me. Besides – you didn't cross Goddard.'

'You were frightened of him?' Barak asked.

'You didn't cross him.' The boy swallowed, causing the prominent Adam's apple Dean Benson had mentioned to jerk up and down. He licked his lips nervously, and I caught a glimpse of grey teeth.

'We have spoken to Abbot Benson,' I said. 'He told us Goddard got you some glasses. You have problems in seeing?'

'Yes. He got me the glasses because I was useful.' I caught a bitter note in Cantrell's voice, though I could not read his expression properly; those swimming blue pools behind his lenses were disconcerting. 'He didn't want the trouble of training someone else up,' the young man continued. 'Not when the abbey was soon to go down.'

'How long were you a monk?'

'I entered the novitiate when I was sixteen. My father got me in, he did carpentry for the abbey. He didn't want me working for him, said I was clumsy. Though it was my eyes, of course.' Cantrell's voice had sunk to a sad monotone.

'How came you to work in the infirmary?'

He shrugged. 'Goddard wanted someone to train up and I was the only young monk there. I didn't mind, I thought it would be better than copying old texts, which is what I did before. They burned them all, when the house went down.' He laughed bitterly.

'Do you miss the life?'

He shrugged. 'I liked the routine, after a while I believed all they said, about our serving God. But – well – it was all wrong, so they say now, 'tis as futile to say Masses for the dead as throw a stone against the wind.' He paused. 'The world has gone all crooked. Do you not think so, sir?'

'Tell me about Dr Goddard,' I said. 'What he did that killed his patients.'

'I won't get into trouble?' he asked nervously.

'You will if you don't answer,' Barak said.

Cantrell considered. 'Dr Goddard was an impatient man. Some-times he used to prescribe what I thought was too much medicine, and the person would die. There was an old monk, too, he fell down some stairs and smashed his arm badly. It had to come off. Goddard used to do the operations himself, it cost money to bring in the barber-surgeon, and he gave the monk a big dose of some stuff that sends you to sleep; he slept through the operation all right but never woke up afterwards. Goddard said he must have given him too much. He said, at least he'd never have to hear his creaky whining again.'

'This medicine, was it called dwale?'

'Yes, sir.' He looked surprised that we knew.

'Surely if you thought the doctor was hastening people out of the world, you should have spoken.'

Cantrell shifted uncomfortably. 'I wasn't sure, sir, I'm no doctor. He would have talked his way out of it, and I'd just have got into trouble. And you don't know what he was like.' He hesitated. 'He would look at me sometimes as a man will look at a beetle on his table.' Then he laughed, uneasily. 'I'd be working away in the infirmary sometimes, not saying anything because he didn't like conversing with inferiors like me. Then suddenly he'd fly at me for some little mistake, nothing.' A strained, bitter smile flickered over his thin face. 'I think he did it just to make me jump.' He paused. 'What has he done, sir?' he asked again.

'I am afraid I cannot say. Your eyes, they are still weak?'

'Even with the glasses I can hardly see. They say the King wears glasses now.' He laughed bitterly again. 'I'll wager he can see better than me.' He seemed to slump further on the stool. 'When I left the monastery I went back to work for my father, but I was no good. After he died I gave up the business.' He looked at an inner door. 'That was his workshop. Do you want to see?'

I looked at Barak. He shrugged. I stood up.

'Thank you, no. But thank you for your help,' I said. 'If you think of anything that might help us, anything at all, I can be reached at Lincoln's Inn.' I hesitated, then added, 'I am sorry for the trouble with your eyes. Have you ever seen a doctor?'

'There is nothing anyone can do,' he said flatly. 'I will go blind eventually.'

'I know someone—'

'I have little faith in doctors, sir.' His mouth twisted in a sardonic smile. 'After my time with Dr Goddard. You understand.'

✞

OUTSIDE, BARAK shook his head. 'You'd send every sparrow that falls from a tree to the old Moor.'

I laughed. Then Barak touched my arm. 'Look, over there, that old woman's waving to us.'

I followed his gaze. An aged, respectable-looking goodwife in a white coif, carrying a basket in which a pair of dead rabbits lolled, beckoned to us from the other side of the street. We crossed over to her. She fixed us with a pair of sharp eyes.

'Were you visiting Charlie Cantrell?' she asked.

'What's that to you?' Barak asked.

'He's not in trouble, is he?'

'No. Helping with some legal enquiries, that is all.'

'He's a poor fellow, I don't think he stirs much from that house. His father died last year and Charlie inherited the house and business. I was a friend of his father. Adrian was that skilled with wood, he was always turning away business. Charlie can't do carpentry with his poor vision, now all he has is his monk's pension.' She looked between us, waiting for a reply, eager for gossip.

'You live nearby, goodwife?' I asked.

'Five houses down. I've asked Charlie if he'd like some help with cleaning, his house is filthy and he could afford someone else to do it out of that pension, but he won't have anyone there. I reckon he's ashamed.'

'Poor young fellow.' I looked at her stolidly, and seeing she was not going to get anything out of us she wrinkled her face at me then turned and walked off, the rabbits' heads hanging out of her basket, bobbing up and down.

'Nosy old bitch,' Barak said.

'Young Cantrell is not one of those who went from the Dissolu-tion to a better life.'

'Poor arsehole. Shouldn't think there was ever much go in him, even if he could see properly.'

'No. But he damns Goddard, more than ever.'

'Yes. Now all we have to do is find him.'

I sighed. 'Let's see what the other assistant can tell us.'

Chapter Twenty-two

WE RODE UP TO Smithfield through a countryside coming to life again after the winter, the cattle out in the meadows again after months indoors. In the fields men were ploughing while women walked behind pairs of shaggy-hoofed horses, casting grain from bags at their waists. I wondered what Lockley would be like. An ex-monk living at, perhaps running, a tavern was unusual, but with thousands thrown out of the monasteries there were many stories stranger than that.

We reached the great square of Smithfield. It was not a market day, and the big cattle pens were dismantled, stacked against the walls at the north end. To one side stood the great church of St Bartholomew's where, three years before, Barak had saved my life in the course of our first assignment together. Behind the high walls I saw all the monastic buildings had come down now. Nearby stood the great empty hospital, reminding me again of my promise to Roger. Only a few hours now to his funeral.

Barak turned to me, nodding at the church. 'Remember?' he asked.

'Ay.' I sighed. 'That was as dangerous a time as this.'

He shook his head. 'No. Then we were dealing with politicians. When they do villainy they have reasons. They don't kill in a mad frenzy.'

'As often as not it is only for their own power and wealth.'

'At least that's something comprehensible.'

We rode on, up Charterhouse Lane and under the stone arch leading into Charterhouse Square. This was a wide grassy area dotted with trees that covered the burial pits from the Great Plague of two hundred years ago. An old chapel stood at its centre. A ragged little group of beggars sat huddled outside. To the north, beyond a low redbrick wall, lay the buildings of the Charterhouse, whose monks had defied the King over the break from Rome. Most had been brutally executed as a result; Cromwell had masterminded that, along with so much else. These days the buildings were used for storage, apart from those which I had heard had been made into lodgings for the King's Italian musicians, whom he had recently brought over at great expense.

As with all the monastic houses, the monks had rented out land in their precinct. On this side of the square the dwellings were small and poor-looking, one- and two-storey wooden affairs, but opposite was a row of fine stone and brick houses. I had heard that the best one belonged to Lord Latimer, and now therefore to his widow Catherine Parr. I studied a large redbrick mansion with tall chimneys, the only house standing in its own drive. As I watched, a horseman in red livery galloped down the road fronting the houses and turned in at the drive, raising clouds of dust. More pressure from the King?

Barak brought me back to earth, pointing to a sign dangling over a narrow, ramshackle old building nearby. 'There's our place. The Green Man.' The sign showed a man clothed in vines, painted bright green.

As we dismounted outside the tavern the beggars came over to us. Maybe the chapel had been abandoned when the Charterhouse was dissolved, and they had taken refuge there. Thin, dirty hands clutched at us as we tied the horses to the rail outside the tavern.

'Piss off,' Barak said, waving a couple of the hands away as he tied up. After what had happened in the Westminster crowd we both looked warily at the pinched faces, the ragged, stinking clothes. There were several children. 'Here,' I called to a starveling lad of about ten whose head was half bald and red raw, his hair eaten away by some disease. 'Mind the horses and I'll give you a groat when I come out.'

'I'll do it better!' Other hands plucked at my sleeve. 'He's fucking useless,' another boy called out. 'Hairless Harry!'

'No,' I said, shaking them off. 'Him.'

We knocked on the tavern door and waited, ignoring fresh entreaties from the beggars. Footsteps sounded, and a woman opened it. She wore a stained apron over a creased dress and a white coif from which tendrils of black hair escaped. She was powerfully built, short and square, but her face showed the remnants of past beauty. Her grey eyes were sharp and intelligent.

'We're not open till five,' she said.

'We don't want a drink,' I answered. 'We are looking for Francis Lockley.'

She gave us a sharp, suspicious look. 'What do you want with him?'

'Some private business.' I smiled. 'He is not in any trouble.'

She hesitated, then said, 'I suppose you'd better come in.' She looked at our boots, messy with the mud of the southern precinct. 'Wipe your feet, I don't want that mess all over the floor. I've just cleaned it.'

We found ourselves in a medium-sized tavern, with whitewashed walls and tables and chairs scattered round a rush-strewn floor. The woman put her hands on her hips and faced us. 'Did you give money to those beggars?' she asked. 'They'll be hanging round half the day. They usually piss off to Smithfield about this time. I don't grudge the poor caitiffs the shelter of the old chapel but I don't want them pestering my customers.'

I had had enough of her scolding. 'Do you work here?' I asked pointedly.

'I own the place. Ethel Bunce, widow and licencee of this parish, at your service,' she added sardonically.

'Oh.'

'Francis!' she called loudly. A serving hatch in the wall opened, and a short, fat man with a bald head and a round piggy face peered out. He too wore an apron, and behind him I saw a large bucket where wooden mugs floated in scummy water.

'Yes, chick?' He caught sight of us, and immediately his eyes narrowed and he looked worried.

'These gents want a word. What have you been up to?' She laughed as she said this, but her look at us was as uneasy as the fat man's.

Lockley emerged through a side door. He was a little barrel of a man, a powerful physique run to seed, but still strong-looking. I wondered if that was why Mistress Bunce had taken him in. A widow might inherit a tavern licence, but would need a man to deal with difficult customers. Yet there was something loving in the look she gave Lockley as he sat on a stool beside her. I made a guess at why they seemed worried; they were living in sin.

'We are not interested in the domestic arrangements between you,' I said gently. 'We have come from the King's assistant coroner. We seek the whereabouts of the former Brother Goddard of Westminster Abbey.'

The reactions of the pair to the news were quite different. Mistress Bunce looked relieved that no one was after them over their sleeping arrangements. Lockley, though, narrowed his eyes again and pressed his lips together. I saw from the rise and fall of his chest that he was breathing hard. 'That old shit Goddard?' he asked.

'You did not like him?'

'Treated me like dirt. Because my father was a potman. As I am now,' he added, glancing up at the widow with a look that was hard to read. She laid a strong hand over his.

'You're more to me than that, sweet.'

I wondered whether to ask her to leave but guessed that anything Lockley told us she would get out of him later. 'You worked under Goddard in the lay infirmary, I believe,' I asked him. 'Helping him with sick people who came from Westminster town seeking help.'

Mistress Bunce's eyes narrowed. 'You seem to know a lot about Francis.'

'We are questioning the former monks who worked with God-dard. We have spoken with young Master Cantrell, and with the dean.'

He looked suddenly worried. 'What did they have to say?' he asked.

'That is confidential,' I said.

Lockley laughed, nervously. 'Young Charlie, eh? He had a bad time with Goddard.'

'Have you any idea where Dr Goddard may be now?'

Lockley shook his head. 'Haven't seen him since the day we all left the abbey. Nor wanted to.'

'You cannot remember where he went?'

'Didn't even say goodbye. Just told me to clear out the last patients and hand the key to the Treasurer as I was bid.' He hesitated. 'May I ask why you are seeking him?'

'We are investigating a death.'

'Whose?' he asked. His whole body seemed to tense again.

'I may not say. But tell me, do you know anything about Dr Goddard using a drug called dwale?' One of Lockley's hands was resting on the table and he clenched it.

'I knew Dr Goddard used something to make his patients sleep if he had to operate on them in the monks' infirmary. But he wouldn't have wasted anything like that on the patients in the lay infirmary.' He shrugged. 'He wasn't much interested in what went on there. He'd come in and look at people, give them a bit of advice or some herbs, set the odd broken bone. But mostly he left their care to me.' He looked me in the eye as he told the story, he had himself under control now.

I nodded slowly. 'Tell me more about what you thought of Dr Goddard.'

'He had a high opinion of himself. Though I daresay doctors are all alike in that. He could be very sharp and rude.' He leaned forward, smiling confidentially. 'He had a huge great mole on one side of his nose. Biggest I've ever seen. If anyone looked at it, he'd go red and try to cover it with his hand. It was a way to get a rise out of him if you dared, but he'd always be in a foul mood afterwards.' He looked at Barak and grinned anxiously. I knew he was keeping something back, but I had no evidence, nothing to confront him with.

'What was your background?' Barak asked.

'I was an apprentice to a barber-surgeon before I went to Westminster. Ten years I was there, then I worked with a barber-surgeon again afterwards.'

'I see,' I said. 'Young Cantrell did not like Goddard either.' I looked at him, remembering his worried look when I said we had spoken to Cantrell and Dean Benson. But he had regained some confidence now. 'Ay, Goddard gave that boy a hard time. He had a nasty sharp tongue. But Charlie Cantrell was always a wet fart.'

'I saw the infirmary yesterday. Empty now, of course. It looked a gloomy place.'

'It was. Conditions got steadily worse all the time I was there. Abbot Benson wanted the abbey to go to seed, to be closed. Cromwell paid him well. The old papist church was rotten,' he said with sudden fierceness.

'You are not one of those who still cleave to the old faith, then?'

'No.' Lockley frowned. 'But the barber-surgeon I worked for when I left was one of those hot-gospellers. They're even worse, puffed up because they think they have the keys to Hell and death.'

'So you came here, to me,' Mistress Bunce said, squeezing his hand. 'To find rest.'

Lockley did not respond to her gesture; instead he gave me an angry look. 'Maybe neither the radicals nor the papists have it right, maybe the heathen Turks do.' He laughed bitterly. I sensed something desperate, almost wild, about him then. He was not a man at ease in his mind.

Mistress Bunce laid her hand on his again. 'Now, chick,' she said warningly, casting us a nervous glance. 'He says things without thinking. You don't mean it, do you?'

A sudden rumbling came from under the tavern, and I felt the stone flags tremble. I looked up, startled. From somewhere far below came the sound of rushing water. 'What's that?' Barak asked.

Lockley smiled faintly. 'It makes new customers jump. They think the devil's coming up from Hell to get them. We're connected to the old sewer that was built to drain the Charterhouse. It runs under the cellar. The monks always did themselves well with their plumb-ing. Most of the buildings round the precinct are connected to their old sewer system, water flushes down from springs up at Islington fields.'

'Yes.' The widow took the chance to move the conversation away from religion. 'We have our own little room of easement that drains down there, and all the tavern's waste goes through a cellar hatch into the sewer. The only thing is, the watchman of the Charterhouse has to be reminded to open the lock gates under the old monastery, or the water builds up then rushes through, like just now. He's a drunk. But there's no one else lives there now, except those Italian musicians of the King's, and they're just stupid foreigners.'

Lockley gave me another challenging look. 'Ethel was here when the Charterhouse defied Cromwell, refused to accept the royal suprem-acy. Prior Houghton was taken out, hanged, drawn and quartered at Tyburn, his arm nailed to the door of the gate. You remember that, Ethel, don't you?'

'It was a long time ago,' Mistress Bunce said uneasily.

'Religious folks.' His face twisted with contempt and something more than that, pain. In his own way, like Cantrell, he was one of those who had suffered from the changes. He got up.

'Well, sir, we must get back to work. I am sorry I could not help you more.'

I hesitated, then rose too. 'Thank you, sir. If you think of anything else, please contact me. Master Shardlake, at Lincoln's Inn.'

'I will.' He looked relieved the interview was over.

'We may well call again,' I added lightly. His face fell. He was hiding something, I was sure.

'I'll see you out.' Mistress Bunce rose and accompanied us to the door. In the doorway she looked round to make sure Lockley could not hear, then lowered her voice.

'I'm sorry for his words about religion, sir,' she said quietly. 'Francis has had a hard time. He was used to life at the abbey. He found life outside hard, especially with that gospel-leaning barber-surgeon pestering him to join their faith. He started drinking, would come here and get drunk every night. That was when I took him in. I know drunks, I knew that love and care and something to do could help Francis.' She looked at me, her bossy manner gone, a tired and vulnerable woman. 'He doesn't drink now, but he says bitter things.'

'Do not worry, goodwife,' I said gently. 'I have no interest in Goodman Lockley's beliefs.'

'He's bitter he's ended up a potman, like his father was.' She looked at me, utterly weary. 'Strange how the world turns, isn't it, sir?'

✝

WE RODE AWAY from the tavern deep in thought. Barak broke the silence.

'He was hiding something, wasn't he?'

'I think he was. Something about Goddard.'

'I might have forced it out of him.'

'No. That's Harsnet's job. I'll tell him tonight.'

'I don't think the woman knows anything.'

'No. Poor creature. I don't think she gets much thanks for her care of him.'

'Maybe he'll order him in for some stiff questioning.'

'Yes.' I did not like the idea of the bitter, disappointed little man being treated roughly. But if he was hiding something we had to find out what it was.

We returned to my house. I was tired, my arm sore whenever I moved it. I could have done with an evening at home resting, but I was due at the chapel for the funeral. I wondered what Samuel would be like; I had not seen him since he was a toddler.

Tamasin was lying on a pile of cushions in the parlour when we came in. Her eyes were less puffy, but her features were still a mass of brightly coloured bruises and her mouth was swollen. She looked utterly exhausted.

'How are you, chick?' Barak asked with what sounded to me like forced cheerfulness.

'Sore. My mouth hurts.' Her voice was a mumble, and when she opened her mouth I saw her cheeks were padded with bloodstained cotton. I shuddered, and my tongue went to the gap in my own mouth, where two years before I had had a tooth snapped off by a torturer in the Tower.

'By Mary, it hurts,' she said. Barak went over and put an arm around her.

'Could have been worse,' he said. 'The tooth was at the side. You'll still have your pretty smile.'

'Oh, that's all right then,' she said sarcastically.

'I didn't mean—'

Tamasin looked at me. 'Do you know what the wretch said, the tooth-drawer? When he told me his fee would be five shillings, I told him it was too much. He said he'd waive the fee and give me ten shillings if I'd let him take out all my teeth. Said I had a good set and they'd make a good false set for rich folk.' She looked at me. 'He brought out these wooden blocks shaped like people's jaws, wanted to measure them against the size of my mouth. He said my mouth was a good standard size. I told him to forget it and get on with his work, that he was heartless to show me such things when I was in pain. I was surprised that Dr Malton recommended him.'

'He's lucky I wasn't there,' Barak said. 'The arsehole.'

'Though I suppose he did the job quickly enough, and with less pain than I expected.' Tamasin shuddered. 'Ugh. He was a vile man, his apron stained with blood, a necklace of teeth hanging over his shop-sign.'

'You should go to bed, Tamasin,' I said. 'Rest.'

'Are you going to Master Elliard's funeral, sir?' she asked.

'Yes. I must change. I am going to Dorothy's. I am accompanying her household. When I come back, Barak, we will have a quick supper then go to meet Harsnet.'

'I was thinking,' he said. 'This church. St Agatha's, Irish Lane. Isn't it the one where the steeple fell down a couple of years ago?'

'Yes. It's one of the reformers' churches. There is no need for you to come,' I added. I glanced meaningfully at Tamasin.

Barak shrugged. 'Harsnet said both of us in his letter. He might have things for me to do.'

I opened my mouth to protest, then closed it again. If I remonstrated with him in front of Tamasin that would only infuriate him.

'I'll be all right,' she said pointedly.

'That's good,' Barak said. 'You rest.'

I met Tamasin's eye. She looked furious.

✞

FOR THE FIRST TIME since Roger's death, Dorothy was dressed in her best. Beside her stood a slim dark lad of eighteen, handsome in his black doublet, whose resemblance to his father was so close it almost took my breath away. It was as though Roger had returned.

'Samuel,' Dorothy said. 'You will not remember Master Shardlake. You were but a child when we moved to Bristol.'

The boy bowed to me. 'I remember you, sir. You brought me a spinning top for my birthday. It was very brightly coloured. I thought it a marvel.' His voice was like Roger's, clear and a little sharp; though Samuel spoke with the flat vowels of the west country.

'Yes,' I said with a laugh. 'I remember now. You were five. You have a good memory.'

'I do for kindnesses, yes. I must thank you, for all you have done for my mother.' He laid a hand on Dorothy's.

'She has been very brave.'

'Is Samuel not the very image of Roger?' There were tears in Dorothy's eyes.

'He is.'

'It comforts me. Roger lives on in my son. But, Matthew, you hold your arm strangely. Have you done something to it?'

How observant she was. 'A careless accident. It is not serious. Will you stay in London long, Samuel?'

He shook his head. 'I must go back to Bristol next week, there is a cloth fair I must attend. I am hoping that when matters are – settled – my mother may come and join me there.'

'Oh.' I had not thought she might go so soon. The news disconcerted me.

'Time enough to think of that later,' Dorothy said. 'There are things to arrange. And I cannot leave everything to Matthew. Though he looks after me, he has been my rod and staff.' She smiled at me warmly.

'I do what I can,' I said, embarrassed.

'My son is engaged, Matthew,' she said quietly. 'What do you think of that? To a Bristol merchant's daughter.'

Samuel blushed.

'Congratulations,' I said.

'Thank you, sir. We hope to marry next year.'

There was a knock at the door. Margaret came in. 'The coffin is here,' she said quietly.

Dorothy shuddered, looked utterly bereft again. 'I will see them,' she said.

'Let me,' Samuel said.

'No. No. Let me go alone.' She squeezed his arm, then left the room, leaving Samuel and me alone. There was an awkward silence for a moment. The clock ticked. I looked at the wooden frieze, the botched repair in the corner catching my eye, then smiled at Samuel.

'Is there any more news, sir? Of the investigation?' he asked hesitantly. I realized it must be hard for him, suddenly thrust into a man's role by this tragedy. 'It eats away at Mother,' he continued, 'not knowing why my father was killed in that awful way. If he had been attacked in a robbery it would have been bad enough, but that terrible – display.' He looked at me anxiously. 'And you said she may be in danger.'

I thought, she has kept her word to me about not telling anyone about the other killings. She has not even told her son. 'It is only a precautionary measure,' I said. 'We are making progress, Samuel. I cannot say much now, but if it helps I may tell you that we believe your father was not killed from malice against him. I think he attracted the attention of – let us say, of a madman. I think you can tell your mother that much.'

'But why is it so secret?' the boy burst out. 'It worries Mother, though she will not say so.'

I hesitated, then spoke cautiously. 'There are politics involved. There was another murder like your father's. The victim was a man of some importance. Though that was not why he was killed, it was just this madman chose him too.'

'A lunatic.' Samuel frowned. 'Yes, anyone who killed a man as good as my father would have to be mad.'

'Roger was a good man, and a good friend. But do not press me now, Samuel, I have told you more than I should have already.'

He nodded slowly. 'Poor Mother. How they loved each other.' He laughed nervously. 'I used to feel left out sometimes, that was why I stayed in Bristol to make my own life. Yet I loved Father, he did so much for me.' Suddenly Samuel was a boy again, blushing and with tears in his eyes. 'Take care of Mother, sir. She says you and Margaret are her only true friends.'

'I will,' I said. 'I will.'

'I wish she would come back to Bristol with me, but she is stubborn.'

Dorothy reappeared in the doorway; pale, holding herself tightly. 'The other mourners are gathering outside. His friends, the servants. We must go.'

I took a deep breath and followed Samuel from the room.

Chapter Twenty-three

ROGER WAS BURIED; laid to earth in a peaceful corner of old St Bride's churchyard. All through the burial service, as the priest spoke of Roger being gathered to the Lord, all I could think was that he should not have been laid here for another twenty, thirty years. Afterwards I left Dorothy and Samuel to have some time alone together. I picked up Barak from my house and we rode south to our meeting with Harsnet.

✝

ST AGATHA'S CHURCH stood in a lane leading down from Thames Street to the waterfront. It was a mixed area, ancient crumbling wood-framed tenements gradually being displaced by newer, modern houses of stone. The church itself was small and very old, though looking up I saw it had a new lead roof and a pointed steeple. I remembered now hearing the story of the steeple's collapse in a storm two years before; two families in neighbouring houses had been killed. It was nearly dusk when we arrived, the sun slanting at a low angle, long shadows in the lane. At the bottom of the lane the grey river flowed; the wherries on the river just lighting their lamps. It was low tide and a stink of rot came from the rubbish-strewn banks.

A number of horses were tied to a rail outside the old wooden lychgate, where a little group of men in sober black stood. They turned as we approached, and one stepped out in front of us. 'Can I help you, gentlemen?' He was small, with a grizzled beard, in sober but well-cut clothes. He looked like a merchant or tradesman.

'We have been asked to meet Coroner Harsnet here,' I told him.

At once his expression changed and became friendly, almost servile. 'Ah, yes. He is here. With Sir Thomas Seymour. And Lord Hertford too, he has honoured us with his presence.' The church-warden swelled with pride. 'They do us a great honour by attending the reopening of our church. I am Walter Finch, at your service, churchwarden.'

Finch led us to the lychgate. 'Friends of the coroner,' he murmured to the others, who at once bowed low. We followed him through the churchyard to where more people, men and women, stood round a fire that had been lit against the far wall. A spit had been placed over the fire, and a small boar was roasting on it. The handle was being turned by two boys at each end, white aprons over their good clothes. Pig fat dripped into a large tray set underneath. The smell of roasting meat filled the air. 'Burn, Pope, burn,' one of the boys said, and the other laughed. I looked at the church. Only one of the three large windows was of stained glass; the glass in the others was clear.

Finch smiled at us. 'When the steeple collapsed two years ago it was a tragedy, it ruined the interior as well as the roof. We had to redecorate entirely. But sometimes the Lord brings opportunity through misfortune. We got rid of all the statues and other idols, emptied the side-chapels, replaced two broken windows with plain glass.' He smiled happily. 'This is how God means his house of worship to be, not stuffed with gold and incense. I would like to take the rood screen down, though that would get us into trouble. I would show you inside, but Reverend Yarington has the key. He isn't here yet.'

'I see.' I thought of the families killed in the collapse.

Finch winked at me. 'And if Bonner's men say it is too like a Lutheran church we may always say that we could not raise enough money to redecorate. The servants of the Lord must be as wise as serpents, as the book says.'

I looked around at the people in the churchyard. I guessed this had been a reformers' church for some time. These were the sort of folk who attended Meaphon's church, where the Kites went. There were merchants and guildsmen, and a smattering of people from the labouring classes who stood against the wall, looking uncomfortable. There were several clerics there; I saw Meaphon himself, talking earnestly to another merchant. He caught my eye, nodded briefly and looked away. I guessed he was uncomfortable at the way he had backed down before Bishop Bonner the day before. I wondered if the serpent's wisdom of these people would save them from Bonner when he moved against them. I recalled his squat, powerful form confronting me under London Wall, and suppressed a shudder.

Sir Thomas Seymour and Lord Hertford were standing with Harsnet, near the roasting boar, Harsnet talking earnestly to Lord Hertford. Sir Thomas was studying the company with a bored look. He raised his eyebrows when he saw us, and nudged his brother. 'Here's the crookback,' he said, not bothering to lower his voice.

'Master Shardlake.' Lord Hertford nodded to us as we approached. 'And this must be Jack Barak.'

'Yes, my lord.' Barak bowed.

'I remember my poor friend Thomas Cromwell speaking highly of you,' he said, a sad note in his voice. Hertford and his brother were dressed in their best, Lord Hertford in a crimson doublet under a dark cloak with a gold chain round his neck, Thomas in a yellow doublet with slashed sleeves showing a green lining, and a black cap with a bright emerald brooch pinned to it.

'Any news, Shardlake?' Harsnet asked.

I told him of my interviews with Cantrell and Lockley, my feeling Lockley was hiding something. He nodded.

'We'll talk to him again. And Dean Benson.' He gave me one of his stares. 'It looks like Goddard is our man, doesn't it?'

'It is too early to say, I think.'

'Yes, perhaps. I have been unable to find any trace of Goddard's family as yet. I am making enquiries among the guilds, and those who own land around the city.'

'But he was a monk for years,' Sir Thomas said. 'If his family are from near London they should be easy to find.'

'His family may have come here from somewhere else while he was a monk,' Lord Hertford said. 'Many people of wealth gravitate here, especially if they have a relative in London already, to increase their fortune. Or lose it,' he added. 'How is your arm, Serjeant Shardlake? Coroner Harsnet told me you were attacked.' He looked at Barak. 'And your wife, too?'

'Yes, my lord,' Barak answered. 'She got away with some bruises and a broken tooth.'

Sir Thomas clapped Barak on the shoulder. 'I would not have taken you as a married man, I thought you another young roisterer.'

'Not any more, Sir Thomas.'

'This affair could not have come at a worse time,' Lord Hertford said. 'Those butchers are still being questioned about Lent breaches. But they won't give Bishop Bonner any names, brave men.'

'I think this man is possessed,' Harsnet said.

'Whatever he is,' Hertford said, 'we must catch him.'

A serving man appeared at our side, offering us platters of roast pig. I looked over to the cooking fire. The pig was cooked through now and the serving men, wiping their brows, stepped away from the fire which still burned merrily, throwing up bright yellow sparks as the boar fat sizzled. Dusk was falling rapidly; beyond the houses to the south, the Thames shone a white colour now as the sun fell to the horizon.

'I can smell bad fish somewhere,' Barak said.

'So can I. It must be coming from the river.' And indeed the smell of roast meat was now unpleasantly mingled with a salty, fishy smell.

'Where is Reverend Yarington?' someone asked. 'He should be here by now.'

I winced as Sir Thomas grasped me by my bad arm. 'Harsnet says one of those ex-monks you saw lives on Charterhouse Square.'

'The lay brother, Lockley, yes. In a tavern there.'

He frowned. 'I know those houses and taverns built round the sides of the old precinct. The largest house there is where Lady Catherine Parr lives. I have visited her there.'

'Easy, Thomas,' his brother said. 'It is surely clear now there is no connection between her and the murders.'

'I would not have her near any danger.' Sir Thomas' expression was anxious. I wondered, is that because you love the lady, or because she is a wealthy widow who may still turn the King down?

'Is there any more news of the projected marriage?' I asked Lord Hertford in quiet tones. That was, after all, what had first brought the involvement of these people in all this.

He speared a piece of boar and transferred it to his mouth. He glanced at his brother, then said, 'The lady still refuses to give the King an answer, she says she needs more time.'

Harsnet grunted. 'That was the tactic Anne Boleyn and Jane Seymour used. Keep him dangling, it only makes the King more determined to get what he wants.'

'No.' Sir Thomas smiled, a flash of white teeth against his dark beard. 'Lady Catherine refuses because she does not want to marry him. As who would?'

'Keep your voice down,' Hertford snapped. 'Thomas, I trust you have not visited the lady again. If the King knew—'

'I haven't,' Thomas snapped back.

'I would like to go,' I said to Harsnet in a low voice. 'My arm throbs, I need some rest.'

He nodded. 'Of course. I will stay here.' He looked around. 'It is strange Reverend Yarington is not here. I am sorry you were hurt.'

'It is getting better.'

He smiled. 'Good. My wife and I look forward to meeting you tomorrow at dinner. And you will meet my children.'

'Thank you, sir. How many children have you?'

'Four. All healthy and obedient. And a good wife. You should marry, sir.'

'I do not think that is my lot.'

'You have no one, then?'

I thought of Dorothy. 'One may hope,' I said with a sad smile.

'Press your suit, Brother Shardlake. Tie the knot, like young Barak here.'

'Knot's the word for it,' he answered under his breath.

'Goodnight, sir.' I shook Harsnet's hand and turned to leave, Barak following. I frowned at him. 'That was a churlish thing to say. A knot indeed——'

Suddenly a woman screamed. 'The church! The church is on fire!'

Everyone stopped eating and talking. Through one of the windows, the surviving stained-glass one, a flickering light could be seen. It cast strange shadows on the darkened churchyard.

Reverend Meaphon was the first to step forward and grab the handle of the church door. 'It's locked!' he shouted. 'Who has the key?'

'Reverend Yarington!' Everyone looked around, but there was still no sign of the white-haired minister.

'Go to the vicarage!' someone shouted.

'He doesn't allow visitors to the vicarage,' the churchwarden said nervously, 'he is so afraid of anyone finding his copies of Luther and Calvin.'

'There's no time for that anyway. We have to get in and put out the fire.'

'Break the door down!' someone called.

Sir Thomas looked at the solid oak door, and laughed. 'You'd need a battering ram to break down that door!'

'There's a side door,' someone called. A couple of men ran round the church, but reappeared a moment later to say it, too, was locked. I looked at the window. The flames seemed brighter now.

The churchwarden Finch stepped forward. 'I've a key! I left it at home!'

'Then go and get it, you fool!' Harsnet said, giving the dithering churchwarden a push. Finch cast another horrified glance at the flickering light coming through the church window, then hurried away. Someone knelt down on the ground and started praying for the Lord to save their church, not to subject it to a second disaster.

Lord Hertford appeared beside us. He bent and spoke quietly to Harsnet. 'I think I should leave. There is nothing I can do, and there is going to be a scene here if the church is on fire.'

Harsnet nodded agreement. 'Ay, my Lord, that may be best.'

'I am staying,' Sir Thomas said. 'I want to see this.' His face was full of excitement. His brother frowned at him, then shrugged and walked swiftly away.

Harsnet was staring at the window. 'Look! The fire seems to be at one fixed spot,' he said in a low voice. 'And I smell no smoke.'

'And what's that noise?' Barak asked quietly.

Above the sound of the man praying to Heaven and the horrified murmuring of the rest of the congregation, a strange sound was faintly audible from the church. A series of muffled grunts, more animal than human.

'Dear Jesus, what is happening in there?' Harsnet asked, fear visible in his face in the dim light.

Finch ran back into the churchyard, a large key in his hand. There was a flurry of activity around the door. He unlocked it and threw it open. Half a dozen people dashed in. Then they stopped just inside. Someone gave a yell of terror. Sir Thomas Seymour lunged his way through the crowd, Barak and Harsnet and I following. We were hit by an awful stench of burning flesh, and something more: the rotting fishy smell Barak had noticed. Inside the doorway we all stopped dead at the horrific, extraordinary sight within.

✝

A MAN IN a white clerical robe was chained to a stone pillar in the nave and he was on fire, blazing like a human torch in the darkness though there was no fuel stacked around him, no visible reason why he should be burning. In the doorway someone fainted, and others sank to their knees and called out to the Lord. Barak and Sir Thomas Seymour went forward, Harsnet and I following. The heat from the burning man was so intense we had to stop seven or eight feet away. I shall never forget that dreadful sight. It was Reverend Yarington who was burning there, his clothes already charring, red burned flesh showing through, blood trickling into the flames with a sizzle. He stared at us in terrible agony, and I saw he was gagged, a cloth tied round his mouth with string. The sounds we had heard were his muffled howls.

He watched with bulging eyes the bulk of his congregation who stood horror-struck, until someone shouted, 'Water! Get water!' Three men rushed out of the church, and I saw Yarington's bulging eyes turn to follow them. But it was too late, it had been too late before we ever entered the church. Even as we watched, the flames engulfed Yarington's head. I gazed with horror as that proud head of white hair caught light, becoming a yellow halo for a second then vanishing with a hiss. As the flames began to rip his face apart, his head slumped forward, and the terrible grunting noise ceased.

'No smoke,' Harsnet said in a shaking voice beside me. 'No smoke and no fuel. This is the devil's work.'

The men who had run out returned with buckets of water and torches. They lit the plain whitewashed interior of the church, the black thing chained to the pillar. They threw the water over Yarington, and the flames went out with a sizzle and a hiss. Thin trails of smoke now began to rise from parts of the body. Sir Thomas Seymour stepped boldly forward and looked into the burned face. 'He's dead,' he said. He stepped back. 'Ugh, he stinks.'

I looked at Yarington's body slumped in its chains, the white clothes melted into burnt flesh. Someone turned away to vomit. Even Barak, whose stomach was of iron, looked pale. It was not just the sight, but the smell, roasted flesh mixed with that stink of rotten fish. I looked at the floor. There were spots of some thick liquid there. I bent and hesitantly put my finger to one of them, lifting it and sniffing hesitantly.

'Fish oil,' I said quietly. 'He was covered in fish oil, probably the oil from those great fishes that is being sold everywhere.' I turned to

Harsnet. 'That was the fuel.' I looked again at the face, though my stomach heaved. The gag was burned into his face now. The cottar Tupholme had been gagged. I guess that Yarington had been drugged, was unconscious when he was brought in here and chained to the pillar. He would have woken with a shock to find himself on fire.

Around us people were speaking in horrified whispers, clinging to each other, women crying. Harsnet looked at the body of the vicar, taking deep breaths. Quietly, he quoted from the Book of Revelation:

'*And the fourth angel poured out his vial upon the sun; and power was given unto him to burn men with heat of fire.*'

Barak walked over to the side door and pulled at the handle, confirming it was locked. Already I could see the familiar picture: Yarington overpowered somewhere, rendered unconscious, the killer using the vicar's own keys to lock them both inside the church, then escaping through the side door when poor Yarington was set alight, locking it after him.

'The killer knew we would be here,' I said. 'How could he know that?'

'Jesu, he's right,' Harsnet said. 'This spectacle was meant for us as well as the churchpeople. But it cannot be coincidence that we are here too. My vicar. My poor vicar.' Tears started to his eyes.

'Taunting us,' I said bitterly. 'Again. Playing with us, showing we are helpless.'

Someone stepped forward to try and loosen the chains, but when he touched the metal he pulled his hand away with a yelp. It was still burning hot. Meaphon stepped forward. He took off his cassock and threw it gently over Yarington's ruined head.

Harsnet looked round at the shocked congregation. 'Listen to me, all of you!' he said. 'I will investigate this outrage, the murderer will be caught! But until then say nothing – nothing – of what has happened here tonight! It would only give comfort to our enemies.'

There were murmurs from the crowd.

'Nothing, do you hear! If this news spread it could cause a panic.

We are all under threat enough!' Harsnet's west country accent was prominent. 'Finch, I make you responsible for people keeping silence until I return. Bring down the minister's poor body when the chains have cooled enough.' Harsnet turned back to Sir Thomas and Barak and me. 'Come,' he said quietly. 'All of you. We must see the Archbishop at once.'

Chapter Twenty-four

ARCHBISHOP CRANMER was with Lord Hertford when we arrived at Lambeth Palace. We were sent in, though again Barak had to wait outside.

The Archbishop looked dog-tired. He was unshaven, black stubble covering his sallow cheeks. Lord Hertford stood by his side. The Archbishop waved to us to sit.

'So there has been another?' Hertford said. I saw he looked afraid.

'Yes, my lord,' Harsnet replied. He told the story of what had happened at the church.

Cranmer sat silent a moment, then said, 'Poor creature. I pray that after his terrible sufferings he is now in Heaven.' He turned to Hertford. 'Each killing is more spectacular than the last. If this goes on, the whole affair cannot fail to become public.'

'Can it be kept quiet?' Hertford asked. His tone was sharp, his expression intent. He seemed more in control than Cranmer.

'I have spoken to Yarington's congregation,' Harsnet said. 'Sworn them to silence. I have left Reverend Meaphon in charge there. I will go back when I leave here, have the body removed and make the point once more that if Yarington's killing becomes known that can only benefit Bonner.'

'No public inquest again,' Hertford said.

'We are interfering with the course of the law,' Cranmer replied. 'But we have no alternative if we are to keep this quiet. Where will he strike next?' he burst out in sudden anger. 'And how was he able to get Yarington inside the church and make this terrible display without anyone seeing?' He looked at me.

'I think the killer did the same as with Dr Gurney and Master Elliard,' I said. 'Invited Yarrington to some meeting point, drugged him with dwale, used his key to open the church and tie him up during the day, then locked the door and waited until the gathering outside had started before setting light to the fish oil he had obtained.'

'It is just as well we were there,' Harsnet said. 'The sight of poor Yarington burning in the church, without any apparent fuel or smoke, made me think it was the devil's work. If we had not been able to calm the congregation somewhat I think they would be running through the streets crying the devil had done this. Though I'm not sure they would have been wrong,' he added quietly.

Hertford looked at me with a penetrating gaze. 'We have to stop him,' he said. 'Bonner and Gardiner are still questioning the courtiers and the Archbishop's staff that were taken last week. They have found nothing, but they will keep pressing.'

'That will not be enough for the King to act against us,' his brother said. 'And I hear the London butchers are all saying they cannot remember to whom they sold meat in Lent.'

For once Hertford nodded in agreement with Sir Thomas. 'That is true. And I think Bonner is hesitating to arrest too many people. He was booed at London Wall yesterday.' I looked at him. So they knew about that. Hertford continued: 'And the King will not be satisfied with evidence concocted out of half-truths and rumours to link you with the radicals. He loves you more than any man. Hold to that, my lord.'

Cranmer sighed deeply. 'That was what they said about Cromwell and Wolsey. Watch the King for me, Edward, watch who is going in and out of the Privy Chamber, who is whispering in his ear.'

'I will.'

There was a moment's silence.

'May I, my lord?' I reached across and took a blank sheet of paper from the Archbishop's desk. I had to try to make some order out of this chaos. Cranmer waved a hand in assent. I wrote quickly, the others watching in silence. Then I laid my work on the desk. They all leaned forward to see what I had written:

VIAL 1: *An infected sore*
Tupholme – Cottar – radical reformer turned sinner – January (killed December?)

VIAL 2: *Death in salt water*
Dr Gurney – Doctor – radical reformer turned moderate – February 20th

VIAL 3: *Death in fresh water*
Roger Elliard – Lawyer – radical reformer turned moderate – March 25th

VIAL 4: *Death by fire*
Rev. Yarington – Cleric – radical reformer – April 3rd

VIAL 5: *Death in darkness and great pain*

VIAL 6: *River dries up*

VIAL 7: *Great earthquake*

'He is speeding up,' Hertford said quietly.

'I think it is Goddard,' Harsnet said. 'Dean Benson and the man Lockley are hiding something about him, I am sure. I will have them questioned tomorrow. We should bring the men and subject them to stiff questioning in your prison, my lord.'

'No,' Cranmer said firmly. 'We are not questioning them about a religious matter. We cannot just pluck people off the streets of London with the atmosphere as it is just now.'

'And we are not sure it is Goddard,' I said. 'Not yet.'

'What picture have you formed of him?' Cranmer asked.

'By all accounts Goddard was a cold man. A good doctor but one who did not care about his patients. He was sensitive about a disfigurement he had – a large mole on his nose. But somehow, from what those who knew him say, I cannot see him having the savage rage of this killer.'

'Unless he is possessed,' Harsnet said.

There was silence for a moment. Then Cranmer said, 'If Yarington was still a radical reformer, he does not fit the pattern you have drawn.'

'So far as we know,' I said. 'There may have been more to him than met the eye. We should go to his house. If Yarington was as godly as he seems, then my idea that the killer is punishing backsliders from radicalism falls down. But if not, it narrows the field of possible victims.'

Thomas Seymour grunted. 'To every lapsed radical in London. How many hundreds is that?'

'Many,' I admitted. I rubbed my arm; the stitches were pulling.

Lord Hertford looked at my paper. 'According to Revelation the pouring out of the next vial will result in people gnawing their tongues in darkness, in great pain. That could mean anything.' He stroked his long beard, frowning.

'I'd still like to know how he will dry up a river as the sixth vial is supposed to do,' Thomas Seymour said scoffingly. 'Or cause a great earthquake like the seventh.'

'He'll find something,' I said. 'Something that fits.'

Cranmer turned to Harsnet. 'You have made no progress in tracing Goddard?'

'Not yet, my lord. I am enquiring of the Surrey and Kent and Sussex authorities as well. Discreetly.'

The Archbishop nodded. Then he looked at me. 'Matthew, you are acting for that boy in the Bedlam. Yarington's neighbour Reverend Meaphon is his parish priest, is he not?'

'Yes. He was there yesterday, when young Kite got himself on top of London Wall. So was Yarington.'

'Make sure that boy is kept safe, out of sight.'

'I will, my lord. It seems the warden at the Bedlam may have let him out deliberately, to try to get rid of a problem. He will not do so again. There is a hearing in Requests tomorrow, to ensure his care.'

Cranmer nodded, then looked at my arm. 'And you think the killer is following you, taunting you.'

'Yes.'

'Only you?'

'It seems so. Barak's wife was hurt too, but I fear that is because of her connection to me. He wants me to leave the case.'

Thomas Seymour laughed. 'You are being overanxious. Why should you matter to him?'

'I do not know,' I answered. I turned to Harsnet. 'Nothing has gone amiss with you?'

'No. Though working at Whitehall Palace I would be harder to get at.'

Cranmer drew a hand down his face. 'There is nothing to do but keep on with the hunt. See Dean Benson and the man Lockley again tomorrow. Where does Lockley live?'

'Out by the Charterhouse.'

Sir Thomas frowned. 'My lord, I have said I do not like the Lady Catherine Parr being so near to someone who may be involved somehow with these murders.'

'She is surrounded by servants,' his brother answered with a note of weariness. 'And she hardly fits the pattern of his victims. A woman of quiet sincere faith.'

'Nor did Yarington. But that didn't stop him going up like a Christmas candle tonight.'

'My lord,' Harsnet said. 'I think we should go to Reverend Yarington's house now. The churchwarden told me he lived in the rectory, a couple of streets away from his church, alone but for his servants. I told him not to send word what has happened.'

Cranmer considered a moment. 'Very well. Matthew, Gregory, go now to poor Yarington's house, speak to his servants, find what you can about his life. Take a couple of my guards, and if you think it worth holding any of the servants in custody have them brought back here quietly. Now, Matthew, before you go, I would see you alone for a minute.'

The others filed out, leaving me alone with the Archbishop.

'This terrible matter affects you, Matthew, does it not?'

I felt tears behind my eyes. The Archbishop could have that effect. 'Yes,' I answered.

'Because your good friend was one of the victims? And because the perpetrator follows you and mocks you?'

'Yes. And because I have never seen such—' I hesitated – 'wickedness before.'

'It preys on me, too. I have seen many men – too many – killed for political reasons. But this is different. I sense this man enjoys what he does.'

'I think that is so.'

'How could someone possibly do such things and believe they are carrying out God's will?' Cranmer burst out with sudden emotion. 'Is it some blasphemous mockery of religion, inspired directly by the devil? Gregory Harsnet believes so.'

'I do not know, my lord. I try not to think too hard on that.'

'Fire,' he said quietly. 'It is a terrible way to die. The heretics I have pleaded with, begged with to recant, I frightened them by telling them of the skin shrivelling, the fat melting, the hissing and crackling.' He closed his eyes and sighed. 'I would have saved them if I could, but the King is always adamant for the harshest punishments. Once it was Catholics he thought to persecute, but he is returning more and more to the old ideas in religion. A Catholicism without the Pope. And he gets harder to persuade each year.' He shook his head, closed his eyes for a moment, then gave me a sudden piercing look. 'Can you bear this?' he asked.

'Yes, my lord. I have sworn to avenge my poor friend. I will hold to that. I will find courage.'

He smiled wryly. 'Then so must I. Catherine Parr still holds out, you know, she will not give the King an answer. She is frightened, poor woman, hardly surprising given it is scarce a year since Catherine Howard went to the block. Yet I must urge her friends to persuade her to yield, for the influence she could have on the King.'

'She will be in danger.'

'Yes.' He nodded firmly. 'That is what we must all face, for the sake of Jesus' truth. He endured the worst horror of all, for us.' The Archbishop sat silent a moment longer; frightened, sad, compassionate, yet implacable. Then he bade me go. 'Solve this. Find him.'

✝

BARAK AND HARSNET were waiting for me in the corridor. Harsnet was pacing up and down, frowning. Barak sat on a chair, one leg jigging nervously. He looked impatient, angry, frightened. Harsnet looked at me curiously. 'He wanted a few words about the murders,' I said. 'They disturb him.'

'Does he too feel the devil is in this?'

'He does not know, nor do I. It is not a speculation that can profit us,' I added sharply. I turned to Barak. 'Come, we are going to Yarington's house.'

We went outside, where a couple of the palace guards joined us: big men in helmets with swords at their waists, for the Archbishop's palace needed guarding as much as that of any other great man of state. We went down to the pier and took the Archbishop's barge back to town, then walked up to Yarington's church through the city; dark and silent now, for it was past curfew, the constables raising their lanterns in the faces of late travellers. They bowed when they saw our fine clothes and the uniformed guards.

'I was scared shitless when I saw that man burning,' Barak said. 'That poor bastard burning like a candle, for a minute I really thought he'd been set alight by some supernatural power.'

'It was fish oil,' I said brusquely. 'This stuff about devilry does not help us.'

We reached the church, silent and empty now, the windows blank and dark. We walked a little way until we found a fine rectory, set in a wellkept little garden. Harsnet banged loudly on the door. Flickers of light appeared at a window as someone lit a candle, and a man's voice called 'Who is it?' through the door in a scared voice.

'We come on Archbishop Cranmer's business,' Harsnet answered. There was the sound of bolts being drawn back, and the door opened to reveal a small, elderly fellow, his scant grey hair disordered and his nightshirt tucked hastily into his breeches. His eyes widened with fear at the sight of the guards.

'Is it the master?' he asked. 'Oh, God, he hasn't been arrested?'

'It's not that. You men, stay outside,' Harsnet told the guards, then walked past the old man into a little hallway, doors and a staircase leading off. I followed. 'Are you his servant?'

'His steward, sir. Toby White. What has—'

'Why should he be arrested?' Harsnet asked sharply.

'They say Bonner will arrest all godly men,' he answered, a little too quickly I thought. I did not like the steward; he had a mean look.

'Who else lives here?'

The servant hesitated then, eyes darting rapidly between me and Harsnet. 'Only the boy, and he's abed in the stable.'

'I am afraid I have bad news, Goodman White,' Harsnet said. 'Your master died this evening.'

The old man's eyes widened. 'Died? I didn't know where he was, I was starting to worry, but – dead?' He stared at us incredulously.

'He was murdered,' Harsnet said. The steward's eyes widened. 'When did you last see him?'

'He had a message late yesterday afternoon. A letter. He said he had to go and see a fellow cleric. He didn't say where. I thought he must have stayed overnight.'

'What happened to the letter?'

'Master took it with him.'

Harsnet looked at me. 'Like Dr Gurney and your friend.' He turned back to the trembling servant. 'You knew he was going to the reopening of the church tonight?'

'Yes, sir. I thought perhaps he'd gone straight there.'

Harsnet stood silent a moment, thinking. I saw the servant glance quickly at the staircase, then away again.

'Perhaps we should look over the house,' I said.

'There's nobody here,' the servant said, too quickly. 'Just me.'

'If your master had forbidden books,' I said, 'we do not care about that.'

'No, but——'

Harsnet looked at him suspiciously. 'Give me that candle,' he said firmly. The old man hesitated, then handed it over. 'Stay here,' Harsnet told him. 'Barak, keep an eye on him.' The coroner inclined his head to me, and I followed him up the stairs.

✝

THE FIRST ROOM we looked into was a study, well-thumbed books lying among papers and quills on a big desk. I picked one up, peering at it to try to make out the title. *Institutes of the Christian Religion*, by John Calvin. I had heard of him: one of the most radical and uncompromising of the new generation of continental reformers.

Harsnet held up a hand. 'I heard something,' he whispered. He pointed across the corridor to another door, then marched across and threw it open. A shrill scream came from within.

It was a bedroom, dominated by a comfortable feather bed. A woman lay there, naked; a girl, rather, for she was still in her teens, smooth-skinned and blonde-haired. She grabbed the blankets and pulled them up to her neck. 'Help!' she shouted. 'Robbers!'

'Quiet!' Harsnet snapped. 'I am the King's assistant coroner. Who are you?'

She stared at us with wide eyes, but did not reply.

'Are you Yarington's whore?' There was anger in his voice.

'What is your name, girl,' I asked quietly.

'Abigail, sir, Abigail Day.'

'And are you the minister's woman? There is no point in lying.'

She reddened and nodded. Harsnet's face twisted in disgust. 'You seduced a man of God.'

A look of defiance came into the girl's face. 'It wasn't me did the seducing.'

'Don't you bandy words with me! A creature like you in a minister's bed. Do you not fear for your soul? And his?' Harsnet was shouting now, his face filled with anger. I had grown to respect and almost like the coroner these last few days but the terrible events of the evening were bringing out another side of him: the hard, implacable man of faith.

The girl made a spirited reply, her own fear turning to anger. 'Keeping body and soul together's been all I've worried about since my father was hanged,' she answered fiercely. 'For stealing a *gentleman*'s purse.' There was bitter contempt in her voice. 'It killed my mother.'

Harsnet was unaffected. 'How long have you been here?' he snapped.

'Four months.'

'Where did Yarington pick you up?'

She hesitated before answering. 'I was in a house down in Southwark where he used to come. We get many ministers down there,' she added boldly.

'They are weak men, and you tempt them to fall.' Harsnet's voice shook with anger and contempt.

This was wasting time. 'Did you ever hear of a whore called Welsh Elizabeth?' I asked her.

'No, sir.' She looked from one to the other of us, frightened again. 'Why, sir, why?'

'Your master is dead,' Harsnet said bluntly. 'He was murdered, earlier tonight.'

Abigail's mouth opened wide. 'Murdered?'

He nodded. 'Get some clothes on. I'm taking you to the Archbishop's prison. There'll be some more questions. Nobody will miss *you*,' he added brutally. 'And after this you'll find yourself whipped at the cart's tail as a whore, if I have anything to do with it.'

'It's only some questions about your master,' I said as the wretched girl began to cry. 'Come, pull yourself together and get dressed. We shall be downstairs.' I took Harsnet's arm and led him out.

Outside, he shook his head sorrowfully. 'The snares the devil sets to pull us down,' he said.

'Men are men,' I answered impatiently. 'And always will be.'

'You are a cynic, Master Shardlake. A man of weak faith. A Laodicean.'

I raised my eyebrows. 'That phrase comes from Revelation.'

Harsnet blinked, frowned, then raised a hand. 'I am sorry. I am – affected by what we saw tonight. But do you realize, if Yarington hadn't been keeping that whore he wouldn't have died tonight? He was killed for his hypocrisy, wasn't he?'

'Yes. I think he was.'

Harsnet closed his eyes wearily, then looked at me. 'Why did you ask about Welsh Elizabeth?'

'That was what the cottar Tupholme's woman was called. I wondered if the killer might have got his information through a whorehouse. About the two carnal sinners punished with death,' I added. 'It's clear now that Yarington did fit the pattern.'

'Yes he did.' Harsnet's face set hard. 'I'll find out what house she was at.'

'Be gentle with her, please. Nothing will be served by harshness here.'

He grunted. 'We'll see.'

✝

THE STEWARD TOBY was sitting in the kitchen, together with a scared-looking boy of around ten, ragged and smelling of the stables, with dirty brown feet. He stared at us, wide-eyed, from under a mop of brown hair.

'Who is this?' Harsnet asked.

'Timothy, sir, the stable boy,' Toby said. 'Stand up for your betters, you silly little shit.' The boy stood, his legs trembling.

'Leave us, boy,' Harsnet said. The child turned and scurried out.

'Well,' Harsnet said sarcastically. 'So much for there being nobody at home.'

'He paid me well for keeping her presence quiet,' Toby said, his voice surly.

'You connived at sin.'

'Everyone sins.'

'Who else knew?' I asked.

'No one.'

'People must have seen the girl coming in and out,' I said.

Toby shook his head. 'He only let her go abroad after dark. It was easy enough in the winter, she didn't want to go out anyway in the snow and ice. I wondered how he'd keep her secret now the days were getting longer, and spring coming. He'd probably have kicked her out soon.' He smiled sardonically, showing yellow stumps of teeth. 'He had a good excuse to keep folk away, his precious copies of Luther and that new one, Calvin.'

'How long were you with your master?' Barak asked.

'Five years.' His eyes narrowed. 'I was paid to be a loyal servant, not question my master's deeds. That's what I did.' He paused. 'How did he die? Was he robbed? You can't move in London for sturdy beggars these days.'

'No,' Harsnet answered noncommittally. 'You can't.'

Toby shook his head sadly. Yet I sensed he had had no great affection for his master.

'So he found the girl in the stews?' I asked.

Toby shrugged. 'I think he went there often. Funny thing, since he brought Abigail here you'd think he'd be happier, but he only ranted against sin more and more. Bad conscience, I suppose. Religious folk are mighty strange, I say. I just go to services as the King commands.'

'What about the boy? He must have known she was here.'

'I told him to keep his mouth shut or he'd lose his place. He wouldn't dare do anything – he's an orphan and he'd end on the streets if he was kicked out of here. Master kept her well hidden. If the churchwardens had found out he'd have been defrocked.'

'We have reason to believe whoever killed him knew he had the girl here,' I said.

Toby sat up, alarmed. 'I told you, I said nothing to anybody—'

'Then who else could have known?' Harsnet asked. 'Who came here?'

'If he had business to conduct he met people in the church. No one came into the house but me, I had all the cleaning of it. If I went out I left Timothy with instructions to tell callers to come back later. He's bright enough, he knew what to do.'

Harsnet got to his feet. 'You are coming with me, Goodman White. You and the girl can spend a night in the Lollards' Tower, see if you remember any more. Jacobs!' he called. One of the guards came in. Toby looked at him in fear.

'I've done nothing,' he said, his voice rising.

'Then you've naught to fear,' Harsnet replied, as the guard lifted the old man to his feet.

I rose. 'I think I'll question the stable boy,' I said.

Harsnet nodded. 'Good idea.'

I went out to a little yard at the side of the house. Candlelight winking through an open door led me to the stable. The boy sat there on an upturned bucket beside a straw mattress, leaning against the side of a big grey mare and stroking it. I saw a crude straw bed in one corner. He looked up, terrified, his dirty face stained with tear-tracks. I felt the softening I always did when faced with lonely, unhappy children.

'Are you Timothy?' I asked gently.

'Yes, sir,' he whispered. 'Sir, Toby says Master is dead. Did a bad man kill him?'

'I am afraid so.'

'What is happening to Master Toby?'

'He is going with the coroner. I would like to ask you some questions.'

'Yes, sir?' Soothingly as I had spoken, he still looked frightened.

Hardly surprising, a group of strangers clattering in at near mid-night.

'You know about Abigail, the woman who lives here?' I asked.

He did not reply.

'Were you told to keep it secret? It does not matter now.'

'Toby said Master would beat me if I ever mentioned her name. Master did hit me once, for swearing. But I wouldn't have told, sir, she was kind to me for all Toby said she was a great sinner. Sir, what will happen to Abby? Will she be all right?'

Not if Harsnet has his way, I thought. I took a deep breath. 'You told no one about her? You will not be punished for telling the truth.'

'No. No, I swear I didn't. On the Bible, sir, on the Bible if you wish. I told no one about her. I liked her being here. She was kind, sometimes this last winter she would give me pennies, let me sit by the fire indoors if Master and Toby were out, She said she knew what it was to be cold and hungry.' His eyes filled with tears again. I guessed he had had no kindness from Yarington nor from the steward. Only from the whore.

I sensed there was something more, something he was keeping back in his fear. But if I told Harsnet of my opinion, the boy would be dragged with the others to the Archbishop's prison. And some-thing within me rebelled at that, I could not do it.

'Master Shardlake!' Harsnet's voice called from outside, making the boy jump.

'I must go now, Timothy,' I said. 'But I will come and see you tomorrow. You will be without a place now your master is dead. Toby said you have no family.'

'No, sir.' He sniffed. 'I will have to go a-begging.'

'Well, I will try to find you a place. I promise I will come again tomorrow, and we will talk more, eh? For now, close the stable door and go to sleep.'

'I told the truth, sir,' he said. 'I told nobody about Abigail.'

'Yes, I believe you.'

'Did the constables catch the man who killed Master?'

'No. Not yet. But they will.'

I left the stable. Outside, I bit my lip. What if he ran away? But he would not, not with the prospect of another place. He knew something, and it would be easier to find out what it was once he had got over his initial shock.

'Master Shardlake!' Harsnet called again impatiently from the open doorway.

'Yes, I am coming!' Suffer the little children, I thought bitterly.

✠

I JOINED HARSNET, who had gone down the street and stood looking at the church with Barak.

'How did the killer know about Yarington's whore?' He sighed. 'I'll have the girl and that servant questioned hard, but I don't think they know anything. What about the boy?'

'He told no one about Abigail. I said I'd come and see him again tomorrow, when he's calmer. He will be without a place now. I told him I'd try and find him one.'

He looked at me curiously. 'Where?'

'I don't know yet.'

'I hope you can. Or if he lives he'll grow to be another beggar starving in the streets and threatening the peace.' He shook his head. 'I would they could be cared for, and brought to God.' His anger seemed to have passed.

'My friend Roger was starting up a subscription among the lawyers for a poor men's hospital.'

'Good,' he said. 'That is needed. Preachers too. The beggars are utterly devoid of the fear of God. I've seen that in my work.'

'They are outcasts.'

'So were our Lord and his disciples. But they had faith.'

'They thought a better world was about to come.'

'It will,' he said quietly. He smiled at me. 'I am sorry for my anger earlier. You will still come to dinner tomorrow?'

'Of course.'

'I wonder if Yarington had any family. I will find out from the servants.' He turned as the guards appeared in the doorway. Abigail and Toby slumped between them, looking terrified. 'I must go with them.' Harsnet bowed quickly, and walked away.

'I don't envy them,' Barak said as the two were led away.

Chapter Twenty-five

BARAK AND I walked back to Chancery Lane. I was bone-tired, the stitches in my arm tweaking and pulling.

'We should have a few hours' sleep when we get back,' Barak said. In the moonlight he too looked exhausted. 'There's Adam Kite's case tomorrow, then Smithfield with Harsnet, then the dean.' He groaned at the thought of it all.

We walked on in silence for a while. Then Barak said, 'That poor arsehole Yarington a lecher, eh?' He sounded almost back to his usual mocking self, perhaps glad to be dealing with ordinary human weakness again after the horror at the church.

'Yes. And the killer knew that somehow.'

'How?'

'I don't know. If we can find out, we may have him.'

'What will he do next?'

'It's impossible to say. As Hertford said, the fifth prophecy is vague.'

'What do you think those people are hiding – Lockley and the dean? They're hiding something.'

'Yes, they are. We must find out tomorrow.'

'Do you think they were part of some nest of sodomites? The monasteries were full of those filthy creatures.'

'I don't know. Lockley certainly didn't strike me as being inclined that way.'

'You can't always tell.'

'You sound as fierce against sin as Harsnet.'

He grinned. 'Only sins I don't feel drawn to myself,' he said with a flash of his old humour. ''Tis always easy to condemn those.'

We arrived back at Chancery Lane. 'I must go and see that boy Timothy first thing,' I said wearily. Behind a window I saw a lamp raised. Harsnet's man Orr, on watch.

'What if he makes a run for it in the night?'

'He won't run. I told you, he needs a new place.'

'And how are you going to conjure that out of thin air for him?'

'I have an idea. I will not let him down. Now come, I am too tired to talk more. We need a few hours' sleep, or we shall be seeing double tomorrow.'

✝

WHEN WE REACHED home I asked Barak to have me wakened no later than first light, and wearily mounted the stairs to bed. Exhausted as I was, I could not sleep. Lying in bed in the darkness I kept turning Yarington's terrible death over in my mind, trying to fit it into the pattern of the others. At length I got up, threw my coat over my nightshirt and lit a new beeswax candle. The yellow glow spreading from my table over the room was somehow comforting.

I sat at the table, thinking. I was sure the killer had been there when we got Adam down from London Wall. Yarington had been there too. Was that when the killer had decided that Yarington would be his next victim? No, that spectacle had been planned a long time, and Yarington's fornication with that poor girl had been known to the killer. But how, when the cleric had kept it so secret? It had not been a matter of common knowledge like Roger's and Dr Gurney's turning away from radical reform, or poor Tupholme's noisy affair with Welsh Elizabeth.

It was important to see that boy tomorrow, find out if he knew anything. I had not seen nearly enough evidence to be sure that Goddard was the killer. But if not Goddard then who was he, this man who knew about medicine and the law and mixed, or had mixed recently, with the radical sectaries? I wondered uneasily whether Harsnet was pressing the radical reformers enough for information; he would be far gentler with his own people than with Abigail.

The old law book was on my desk. I had borrowed it from the library. I opened it again to the case of Strodyr, smelling dust and ancient ink again. Strodyr too must have planned his killings with care, to go undetected for years. I read again how he refused to say anything at his trial but that he had often raged 'most obscenely' against the wicked trade of whores. Did our killer too somehow believe he was doing God's work, or was it all some terrible game? Or were both the same in his unfathomable mind? I remembered the German Anabaptists, who in overthrowing society in Münster believed that in their violence they were pushing forward God's will, bringing Armageddon about all the faster. Perhaps the killer believed each step was a symbolic fulfilment of the Revelation prophecies, that he would bring about the end of the world. I resolved to talk to Guy again. At last, I fell asleep.

☦

I WAS STILL deeply asleep when Joan knocked gently at the door. I rose slowly, my back stiff and sore, although my arm ached less. I decided to leave off the sling. I went to the window and looked out. The sky was lightening, clear and blue with light fluffy clouds. For the first time in several days I did my back exercises, grunting as I twisted and stretched. Then I dressed and went downstairs. I scratched at my stubbly cheeks, conscious I needed a visit to the barber.

In the parlour Barak, dressed in his shirt and upper hose, was already breakfasting on bread and cheese and wizened apples.

'Last year's apple crop is drying out quickly,' he said.

'I'll get Peter to open up a new barrel. They'll be fresher.'

'Is your arm better?'

'Yes, it is today.'

'Young Piers did a good job, then.'

I pulled the loaf towards me. 'Is Tamasin not up yet?'

'Just. She is getting lazy.' I looked at him and he reddened. 'Her bruises are going down, and her mouth is healing, but she still doesn't like to be seen. She'll be all right in another day or two. She's still furious about that tooth-drawer asking her to sell him her teeth.'

'She could have been killed that night,' I said seriously. 'And it happened because of our work. My work.'

Barak put down the remains of his apple. He was silent a moment, then said, 'I hate this job, chasing after this lunatic or devil-possessed man or whatever he is. I suppose I've been taking it out on Tamasin.' He shifted uncomfortably.

'Why?' I asked gently.

'Because she's there, I suppose. It's no way to treat your wife, I know.'

I asked quietly, 'Do you still want her for your wife?'

'Of course I do.' He glared at me, and I wondered if I had gone too far, but then he sighed and shook his head. 'I know I've been a churl, but—' he ran his fingers through his thick, untidy brown hair—'somehow you get into a way of behaving and it's hard to get out of it.' He sighed again. 'But when all this is over I've decided to leave the Old Barge and see if I can't find a decent little house for us to rent nearer to Lincoln's Inn.'

I smiled. 'That is marvellous news. Tamasin will be so pleased.'

'And I'm going to stay home more. Spend less time in the – er – taverns.' His hesitation made me wonder if Tamasin's suspicions had been right and he had been seeing other women.

'Have you told her?' I asked.

'Nah. I'll wait till things have settled down a bit.'

'But you should tell her now.'

He frowned. I realized I had gone too far. 'I'll tell her when I think it's right,' he said brusquely. 'I'll get dressed, then I'll tell Peter to get Sukey and Genesis saddled and ready.' He got up and went out.

His mention of Peter reminded me of my promise to the boy Timothy. I paused to eat some bread and cheese, slipped one of the wrinkled apples into my pocket and went to the kitchen. There I found Joan and Tamasin. Tamasin was sitting at the table, slicing vegetables for the evening meal. Her bruises were less puffy now, but still horridly colourful, red and black, and her face was still swollen. Joan looked up at me and smiled, but Tamasin put a hand up to hide her face.

Joan was washing, bent over a large wooden bucket. Her face, surrounded by her white coif, was red as she kneaded the wet fabric. I reflected with a pang of guilt that she was near sixty now. Her late husband had once been my steward, and when he died fifteen years ago I had kept her on as housekeeper. It was an unusual arrangement for a single man, despite the difference in our ages, but I had always liked her quiet, motherly ways. I had been going to ask her if she knew of any help that might be needed in the houses near by, but last night a new idea had occurred to me. 'I wonder, Joan,' I said, 'if you could use the help of another boy in the kitchen.'

She thought a moment. 'Peter has a lot to do, between the stables and helping me in here.' She smiled tiredly. 'But I do not know how he would take to having a second boy around.'

I smiled. 'This boy is younger than Peter. We would make it clear he is the senior. I need to talk to this other boy some more, though.'

'It would be good to have someone else, sir.'

'Then I will see what I can do today.'

'Thank you,' she said gratefully. She lifted the bucket of clothes in their dirty water and headed for the yard. Tamasin rose and opened the door for her, then returned to the table.

'Your bruises seem better, Tamasin.'

'They are still a dreadful sight, sir. But I suppose they will be gone soon.'

'How is your mouth?'

'I have little pain there now. That tooth-drawer was good after all.'

'Guy would not have recommended someone who did not know his work.'

'I still can't believe he offered to buy my teeth, take them all out. I'd be a hideous sight.'

Her tone was sad, drained of emotion. She looked at me. 'What happened last night? Jack would not tell me anything when he came in. Just told me to go back to sleep.'

'He would not have wished to worry you, Tamasin. I am afraid there has been another killing.'

Her eyes widened. 'Were you and Jack in danger?'

'No. No, we found the body.'

'Will this never end?' she asked. 'It is having a bad effect on Jack. On you too, sir, I can see that.' Then she gave a sardonic smile that made her seem years older. 'Or maybe I mistake the fact that Jack is tired of me for the effect on him of hunting this brute.'

'You still love him?' I asked directly.

'Yes,' she answered quickly. 'But I will not go on like this for ever, I will not be ground down to powder as some women are.'

I smiled. 'It was your spirit that attracted him to you in York, I know that.'

She ventured a smile in reply, but it still held a sardonic edge. 'Not my pretty face? Not that it is pretty now.'

'Your pretty face as well. And it will heal. Tamasin, perhaps I should not tell you this but I will. Jack still loves you. He knows he has not been behaving as he should. He has told me that when this is over he will move you out of the Barge, to a good house.'

'He said that?'

'Yes, on my honour. But in confidence, you must not tell him what I have said.'

She frowned. 'But why did he not tell *me*?'

'He only told me because I was goading him. You know what he is like.'

'Do I? I thought I knew him . . .'

'Give him time, Tamasin. I know he can be difficult but – give him time.'

She looked at me seriously. 'I will, but not for ever,' she said quietly. 'Not for ever.'

The yard door opened and Joan returned, holding the bucket to her hip. 'I had better go to the stables,' I said. 'Jack will be wondering what has happened to me. We have some visits to make this morning. Think of what I have said, Tamasin.'

She nodded and smiled. I went out to the stables, where Barak was talking to Harsnet's man Orr, who straightened his cap as I approached. I liked him. He was quiet, watchful, unobtrusive. 'A quiet night?' I asked him.

'Yes, sir.'

I looked at Barak, feeling a sudden rush of irritation. How could a man be so foolish as to go into a prolonged sulk – for that was how it seemed – with a woman of Tamasin's qualities? If it had been me and Dorothy – I suppressed the thought.

'Ready?' I asked brusquely. 'Then let's get going.'

✝

WE RODE BACK through the city to Yarington's house. The horses plodded along contentedly. When we reached our destination we tied Sukey and Genesis up outside and I feared for a moment the boy had run off after all. If so, my softness might have lost us vital evidence. But Timothy was in the stable, sitting on his bucket beside the horse. He had been crying again; there was a bubble of snot at one nostril.

'Good morning, Timothy,' I said gently. 'This is my assistant, Barak.'

He stared at us with frightened eyes.

'It's cold in this stable,' Barak said gruffly. Timothy would remind him of his own urchin childhood.

'I have a position for you,' I told the child. 'Working in my house. Kitchen and stable work. How would you like that?'

'Thank you, sir,' he brightened. 'I – I will do my best.'

I took a deep breath. 'There is a condition, though.'

'A what, sir?'

'Something you must do for me. You must tell me something. Yesterday you said that you told no one about Abigail?'

'No, sir. I didn't. I didn't.' But he reddened, squirmed uneasily on the bucket. The horse, sensitive to changes of mood, turned and looked at him.

'But there is something else, isn't there?'

He hesitated, looked between me and Barak.

'Come on, lad,' Barak urged.

'I promise you Abigail will come to no harm,' I added. 'But I think there is something more you did not tell me.'

Timothy breathed hard, the snot quivering at his nostril.

'Tell us, lad,' Barak said. 'Master Shardlake's house is warm. You'll like it there.'

'I watch people,' the boy blurted out suddenly. He pointed to a knot-hole in the stable door. 'Through there. I get tired of being in here all the time.'

'Master Toby did not let you out much?'

'Only to help clean the house. I'm sorry if it was wrong, looking.'

'What did you see?' I asked quietly.

'Tradesmen who called. The egg-man. The chimney-sweep, and the carpenter to repair the wooden screen when Toby knocked it over. But that was before Abigail came.'

'And after?'

'A man used to come and see Abigail sometimes. When the master was out and Toby had his day off. Toby didn't know about it.' He bowed his head.

'Who was he?' I asked.

'Don't know.' He shook his head.

'Did he come often?'

'A few times. This winter. When there was snow on the ground.'

'Was he a tall man, a gentleman?' I asked, thinking of Goddard.

'No, sir.' Timothy shook his head again. 'He was young.'

'How young?'

He thought for a moment. 'I don't know — maybe twenty.'

'What did he look like?'

'Taller than either of you. Strong-looking, like him.' He pointed to Barak.

'Fair or dark?'

'Dark. He was handsome. Abigail used to say he had a handsome face.'

'She talked to you about him?' I tried to keep a tremor of excitement from my voice.

'Not much, sir. I told her I'd seen him. She said the less I knew the less I could tell. She didn't like me knowing.'

'So he used to visit her secretly.'

'Yes.'

'Did she know him before she came here?'

'I don't know,' Timothy said again. 'Honestly, sir, I don't know that.'

'Was he in the reverend's congregation?' I asked.

'Don't know, sir. I only saw him because he came round the back door. When master was out. Please.' He began to look upset. 'Please, sir, I've told you all I know.'

'All right,' I said. 'Thank you, Timothy. Now come, you are coming back with us. Barak, take my papers on to court. I will join you there after I have delivered Timothy home.'

He looked dubious. 'Shouldn't you clear it with Harsnet, before taking him?'

'No. Timothy's master is dead, and I am buying his services.' I leaned close to Barak. 'And I want him kept safe at my house. He may be the only one that has seen the killer and lived.'

'Whoever he was trying to describe, it doesn't sound like Goddard.'

'No.' I nodded and looked at him. 'It doesn't, does it?'

Timothy had got to his feet. He laid a hand on the horse's flank. 'Please, sir, may I take Dinah too?'

'I am sorry, lad, no. We already have two horses.'

He bit his lip. I thought, the horse and Abigail are probably the only friends he has ever had. But I could not take another horse I did not need.

Barak reached out a hand. 'Come on, sniffly,' he said kindly. 'Let's get you home and safe.'

Chapter Twenty-six

I RODE ALONG slowly back to Chancery Lane, the boy trotting along at my side, one hand on Genesis' harness to avoid being separated from me in the crowded streets. I reflected that Harsnet would not be pleased at my news, certain as he was that Goddard was the killer. As of course he still might be, but we must find the identity of this man who had visited the prostitute. It was still early, the shopkeepers again opening up and throwing out any beggars they found in their doorways. One, a young man, had collapsed in the street and was being half carried by two others. Timothy looked at the scene then up at me, his face frightened. On impulse I halted and told him to climb up behind me.

We reached my house, and I could see from his wide-eyed expression that Timothy was overawed by its size. I led him inside and through to the kitchen, where Joan was working. I was pleased to see that Harsnet's man Orr was helping her, peeling potatoes. Joan exclaimed at the boy's dirtiness, gave him a bucket of water and ordered him to the stable to wash himself down. He went out obediently. Young Peter was in the kitchen and greeted Timothy with a surly nod. Joan frowned at him. 'You had better treat Timothy well, he is younger than you and in a new place. You should be pleased he will be doing some of the jobs you don't like. Now take him those old clothes of yours I looked out to cut up because they had got too small.'

'Yes, Mistress Joan.' Peter sidled out of the room. Joan smiled at me.

I smiled back. 'Degree matters for everyone, does it not? Even kitchen boys.'

'It's as much the fear of losing a place. So many beggar boys in London now, you can always find one cheaper than the one you have.'

'Yes. Such competition brings fear.' When this was over, I decided, I would hire a man, too, to help Joan. I could easily afford it.

I went upstairs to change into my best robe. Although the day was the warmest so far, I felt cold, and the stitches in my arm ached as I dressed. I ran over the arguments I had prepared for Adam's case, for the court to receive regular reports on his care, and for his fees to be met out of the Bedlam funds. I had arranged for Guy to be present to testify that Adam was so ill he needed the court's protection. As for his release, I felt there was no question now but that he was safest where he was.

Would he ever be cured, I wondered, or would he stay forever imprisoned in that terrible agony of soul? And what of the killer we were hunting? Did he suffer? My sense was that he enjoyed what he did, the meticulous planning and the cruel execution. Already, somewhere out there, he was planning his next killing. I had the part of the Book of Revelation that dealt with the seven angels off by heart now: '*And the fifth angel poured out his vial upon the seat of the beast; and his kingdom waxed dark; and they gnawed their tongues for pain.*' The seat of the beast, I knew, was supposed to be the lair of the devil. 'They gnawed their tongues for pain.' I shivered.

☦

BARAK WAS WAITING for me in the crowded vestibule of the Court of Requests. I looked around the familiar scene: the parties sitting round the walls watching the lawyers negotiating in the centre of the room. I recognized an elderly couple sitting with my fellow-pleader in Requests, Brother Ervin. Ervin gave me a curt nod; I had greatly added to his workload by standing out of most of my cases. I would lose money by this, I supposed, though that was the least of my worries; I had enough. The old couple, who were pursuing a claim against their landlord and had come all the way from Lancashire to find justice, gave me hurt looks. Daniel and Minnie Kite stood huddled together in the doorway with Guy, dressed in his physician's robe and cap. Barak and I joined them.

'Adam's not here, sir,' Daniel said anxiously.

'We are a little early. They will bring him.'

'Will they be gentle with him?' Minnie asked anxiously.

'This judge is a fair man. Is Reverend Meaphon not with you today?'

'He's been detained at a neighbouring parish. The minister there is sick.'

I was interrupted by a hard tap on my injured arm, which made me wince. I turned to find myself looking at a short, spare man in his forties, dressed in an expensive fur-lined coat, a silk velvet cap on his head. His thin face had the red puffiness and broken veins of a hard drinker.

'Are you here for that Kite boy?' he asked in a peremptory tone.

I bowed. 'I am, sir.'

'I am Sir George Metwys. Warden of the Bedlam. I am here at the request of Archbishop Cranmer.' He glared at the Kites and at Guy. 'I do not know why the Archbishop has interested himself in these people.'

'I am grateful for your attendance, sir,' I said smoothly. 'Perhaps you could indicate whether you will be opposing my applications. For Master Kite's welfare to be reported regularly to the court, and his fees to be paid from the Bedlam funds.' Paid by you from the profits you take from the paying inmates, I thought. You will have a little less to get drunk on.

'I won't be opposing,' Metwys grunted. 'I've had a hint from Cranmer's people. Though if I had my way—' He broke off as a rattling sound and then a groan echoed round the crowded chamber. Everyone turned round. Keeper Shawms, assisted by two stout under-keepers, was dragging Adam into the vestibule. His legs were chained together, and the keepers held him up by his stick-like arms. He was trying to sink to the floor to pray, groaning when they would not let him. Shawms looked red with embarrassment. Daniel Kite bit his lip and his wife let out a sob. Adam, his head bowed, did not even look at us as he passed. He gave off a foul odour.

I watched as the keepers manhandled Adam on to a bench and sat beside him. On either side people shuffled away, one man crossing himself. Somehow the spectacle of Adam's condition seemed more terrible in this familiar environment, than it had in the Bedlam or even when he was shrieking on top of London Wall. Minnie made a move towards him. Guy laid a restraining hand on her arm. 'Not now,' he whispered.

'What an exhibition,' Metwys said. He glared at Adam and his keepers. Shawms, seeing the warden, rose and bowed deeply.

We waited uncomfortably for a further half-hour. From where Adam sat there was a periodic clank of chains as he tried to lurch down on to his knees. Guy went over to try and talk to him but today he made no impression; he returned defeated.

Barak had been watching the scene fixedly. 'Jesu,' he muttered as Adam tried to lurch forward again. 'This is a nightmare.'

At last the usher appeared and called everybody into court. I went to the advocates' bench in the front and laid out my papers. Metwys took a seat at the back, away from Adam and his keepers. Barak and Guy and the Kites sat with Adam on a bench near the front. Judge Ainsworth appeared from an inner door and sat down on his bench. As he cast his eyes over the court Adam let out a groan. Ainsworth looked at me.

'I think we will take the case of Adam Kite first,' he said. 'Brother Shardlake?'

I outlined my applications. Ainsworth nodded slowly, then cast a sharp look at Shawms. 'This poor creature looks to be at death's door,' he said. 'Are you feeding him?'

Shawms rose, looking red and uncomfortable. 'Sometimes he will not eat, your honour. He has to be spoon-fed like a child, and sometimes he spits it out over the keepers.'

'Then you must redouble your efforts, fellow.' He turned to Metwys. 'Sir George, you are Warden. What say you to these applications?'

Metwys rose. 'I am willing to consent, your honour. I wish to discharge my responsibilities to the best of my abilities. But it is our rule that we only take people in the Bedlam who can be cured, and for a limited time.'

'But surely there are many who have been there for years, their relatives paying for their keep?'

I thought of the keeper Ellen, who had said she could never leave.

Metwys looked as if he might choke. 'Only when their relatives cannot care for them themselves.'

'And are rich enough to pay to be rid of them.' Ainsworth tapped his quill on the desk. 'I am minded to grant this order, though normally this would be a matter for the Court of Wards and Liveries. But I am concerned at how long this situation may last.' He turned to Guy. 'Dr Malton, you have been treating this boy. What do you say?'

Guy stood. 'Adam Kite is very sick, your honour. He has come to believe himself cast out of God's favour, for reasons I do not fully understand. Yet I believe that I can help him.'

'Then he is not some wild heretic?'

'No, your honour. Though I can see how his actions could be interpreted in that way.' He paused. 'From the point of view of public order he is best kept where he is. But I too would not want him to be left in the Bedlam indefinitely.'

'That would be a little unfair on Sir George Metwys' purse.' Ainsworth permitted himself a little smile, then looked again at Adam.

'Is there any point in my questioning him?' Ainsworth asked me.

'None, your honour. I doubt Master Kite is even clear where he is.'

'Yet you think he can be helped? How long do you think you will need?'

Guy hesitated. 'I do not know. But I am willing to treat him without payment.'

'Then I will make the order. Reports to me every fourteen days. Payments to be made from the Bedlam funds subject to review by me. Review hearing in two months.' He looked again at Adam. 'This boy is very young. Too young to be left to rot indefinitely in the Bedlam because in his madness he says dangerous things.' He turned to me. 'At law, if he is insane, he should be made a ward of court. Yet the Privy Council have not warded him. So at the moment he is in a state of legal nonexistence.'

'That is so, your honour.'

'At the Privy Council's will. But these, I suppose, are the times we live in.' He looked at me. 'Make sure he is cared for, Serjeant Shardlake.'

'I will, your honour.'

Ainsworth looked down at his papers, and I nodded to Barak. He nudged Shawms. The keepers manhandled Adam into the passage, and I walked out with Daniel and Minnie. Metwys followed at a distance.

Outside, Daniel and Minnie expressed their thanks. Guy offered to walk part of the way home with them. They nodded, turning sorrowful eyes to where Adam was being hauled through the door, followed by many curious looks. Barak and I left them on the courthouse steps. The rain had stopped, though the skies were still leaden.

'No sign of Harsnet,' Barak said.

'We'll have to wait.' I watched the receding figures of Guy and the Kites. Guy's tall head was bent to hear something Minnie was saying.

'By God, the old Moor will need all his skills.' Barak's voice was suddenly full of angry emotion.

I turned to him. 'The hearing today upset you?'

'Wouldn't it upset any human creature? Sometimes . . .' He hesitated.

'What?'

'Sometimes these days I feel that everywhere I look there is madness and darkness and devils.'

'We are bound to find the killer now, as we are to aid Adam Kite.' I spoke quietly, to myself as much as to him.

'Ay, and here comes the man of sure and certain faith to tell us where to go next.' Barak nodded to where Harsnet was approaching, his coat swirling round him as he shoved through the crowds around the court. He looked weary, exhausted.

'The girl's escaped,' he began without preliminary.

'Abigail?' I asked. 'The prostitute? How?'

'Asked to go to the jakes and slipped out through the window. It's on the first floor, she's lucky she didn't break her neck.'

'What about Yarington's steward?'

'Oh, he's safe in the Lollards' Tower. Whining creature. But there's no more to be got out of him.'

'I have some news at least,' I said. I told him what the boy Timothy had said. Harsnet thought hard for a moment, then shook his head.

'That might mean nothing. Abigail's visitor isn't necessarily the killer.'

'But who else would know Yarington was keeping a whore? Unless he had a history of it.'

'He didn't.' Harsnet shook his head. 'I've spoken to all the congregation. As far as they were concerned, Yarington was a man devoted to celibacy. It was only in these last few months he started being cautious about people coming to his house.'

'Any progress in finding Goddard?'

'I've asked the London city council and the coroners and sheriffs of Kent, Surrey and Middlesex to seek out a well-to-do family of that name, whose son went for a monk. Nothing. And I've put the word around so that questions are being asked among all the radical churches and religious groups.' He looked at me seriously. 'That is a delicate matter, it is fortunate I am trusted there. But no one so far knows anything of a man of Goddard's description.'

'Perhaps a handsome young man with dark hair, such as Timothy described, should also be asked for?'

'There could be hundreds such,' Harsnet said irritably. 'But I will ask,' he added more quietly. He looked at me. 'I am going to have to change our arrangements today. I am due to meet with Lord Hertford. Bonner is extending his search for butchers and performers of forbidden plays down to Westminster, but it's not his jurisdiction. We are going to try and stop him.' He looked across the courtyard to the Painted Tower, where Parliament was meeting, two guards in the red coats of the King's livery standing with pikes at the bottom of the steps. 'They are going to pass the Act forbidding Bible-reading to all but men of gentleman status,' he said quietly. 'The King has sanctioned it. Our backs are against the wall.' He sighed. 'I will have to leave you to go to Lockley yourself, Serjeant Shardlake, but say you have my authority and he'll find himself arrested if he doesn't cooperate. Let me know what happens. Can you meet me here again in three hours?'

'Yes. It might be worthwhile using the time to visit young Cantrell again,' I suggested. 'Though I don't think he knows anything more.'

'Yes. Anything. Anything that may help us, Master Shardlake.' He gave me a desperate, harried look, then turned to go.

'Should we cancel our dinner tonight?' I called after him.

He waved a hand. 'No, no, we have time for that.' Then he walked quickly away.

☦

WE RETURNED TO Chancery Lane. The streets were crowded now, and I felt nervous and vulnerable as we rode along. My arm hurt too. When we arrived home Philip Orr was sitting in the kitchen, repairing a broken box. 'No sign of anyone around that shouldn't be?' I asked.

'No, sir,' he said seriously. 'Thank the Lord. Just the usual beggars in Chancery Lane.'

'Hanging around up to no good, like the lawyers?'

He gave me a puzzled look. Like many of the radicals, he had little sense of humour.

'I expect you will be glad when this is over, to be able to get back to your normal work,' I said. I realized I did not know what Orr's usual work was.

He smiled sadly. 'Spending my days in this kitchen is restful compared to my normal duties, sir. I assist Master Harsnet in collecting the bodies of those who die. I take them to the storage place. And I ensure order in the court, and sometimes go and chase up witnesses who do not wish to appear.'

'Your master will be missing you, then.' I realized Harsnet had deprived himself in order to ensure our security.

'I have an assistant, he will aid him as he can.'

We set out again to Smithfield. 'Harsnet didn't sound like he's having much luck with his search,' Barak said. We had reached the country lanes now and relaxed our watchfulness.

'London and the neighbouring counties are a large area to scour. Sixty thousand people in London, they say, and more every year.'

'Ay. And the godly folk will be suspicious of questions, even from Harsnet.'

'That is what this man relies on. The anonymity of this heaving city. He could not do what he does in some country parish, or even a small town, without running a much greater risk of being caught.'

'Mad and possessed, Harsnet called him.'

'He is not possessed.' I decided then to tell Barak of the conversation I had had with Guy. As we turned into Holborn and passed the great houses of the rich facing the north side, I told him of De Rais and Strodyr. 'They did what they did for perverted pleasure, neither God nor the devil came into it.'

He nodded slowly. 'Well, that is true of most of the stronger urges men are subject to. If someone has a desire to beat whores, or sodomize boys, the urge seizes them and they have to follow it. Sometimes men who otherwise are quite normal.' He gave me a sidelong look. 'Lord Cromwell knew that, and took advantage of it with his spies in the brothels over at Southwark that cater to special tastes.'

'I know. Obsession,' I said quietly. 'A hidden, all-consuming obsession with violent killing.'

We passed through a busy throng at Smithfield, for it was market-day, and arrived at Charterhouse Square. There were only a couple of beggars sitting on the steps of the old chapel, two older men and an old woman who looked as though they could not move far. The others would be begging at Smithfield, I guessed. I wondered if they supported these old folk, shared the meagre charity they received.

There were a couple of other horses at the rail where we tied Sukey and Genesis up, and the tavern doors were open. Inside it was busy, a group who looked like Smithfield drovers sitting together. Three ragged, weatherbeaten men whom I took to be from the community of beggars sat at one table quaffing ale. Mrs Bunce and Lockley were busy, the latter moving among the tables and the former serving behind the bar hatch.

The clientele looked up curiously as we entered. Lockley caught sight of us, and exchanged a glance with the widow. 'We would like another word, sir,' I said loudly.

'Come into the back.' His tone was low and angry. The clientele looked on with interest as I followed Lockley into a back room, where a moment later Mrs Bunce joined us. It was a cheerless place, with a scored table and some stools the only furniture.

I decided it would do no harm to let Mrs Bunce remain; she might let something slip.

'What is it?' Lockley asked us. His manner today was one of angry hostility. He stood with his fists bunched and glared at us with those sharp, deep-set eyes.

'How now, potman,' Barak said sharply. 'That's no way to talk to a man on business for His Majesty's coroner.'

Lockley sighed, shrugged and sat down at the table. Mrs Bunce stood beside him. 'What do you want?' Lockley asked, more quietly.

'We have not found Infirmarian Goddard yet.'

'Pox on him.'

'Are you sure you know nothing about him that could help us?'

'I told you all I knew last time. Goddard wasn't interested in the lay infirmary. He sneered at me for my ignorance but let me get on with treating the patients. I had to do everything myself. So far as he was concerned the patients in the lay infirmary were just a nuisance.'

'And those in the monks' infirmary? The ones the young Cantrell dealt with?'

'Goddard had to take better care of them, or he would have had to answer to the community. He kept a close eye on young Cantrell. Made him get glasses when it was clear he couldn't see properly.'

'I told you before that we are investigating a death. We think it possible that Goddard may have murdered someone.'

'How?'

'I may not say. Only that it was a violent attack.'

I would swear that Lockley seemed relieved. He laughed contemp‑ tuously. 'Goddard would never attack anyone. He was a cold man, and a lazy devil, never there when you wanted him. And he had plenty of money, I know that. Why should he kill someone?'

I nodded slowly. 'Yes, I can see you believe that,' I said quietly. Then I looked him in the eye. 'But I think you are hiding some‑ thing. Something else to do with Goddard. I advise you to tell me what it is.'

Lockley clenched his fists harder on the table. Strong, solid fists, callused with years of hard work. His face grew red.

'Will you leave me alone!' His sudden exclamation startled me, and I saw Barak's hand go to the hilt of his sword. 'I know nothing – nothing! Leave me alone! All my life it's been nothing but pester,

pester, pester. The patients, Goddard, that wretched barber-surgeon and that church of his, saying I was damned. And you!' He turned round to Mrs Bunce and glared at her. Then he put his head in his hands and groaned. 'I don't know whether I'm coming or going.'

I looked at Barak, astonished by this childish outburst. Ethel Bunce's mouth set in a tight line, but I saw tears in her eyes.

'What are you hiding, Master Lockley?' I asked quietly. 'Tell us, and perhaps that will resolve your confusion.'

'He knows nothing, sir, I'm sure,' Mrs Bunce said. 'You should have seen the state he was in when I met him, given over to drink, spending the last of the money he had. Francis is not as strong as he looks—' Lockley jumped up suddenly, the chair banging on the floor behind him. 'Get out, both of you, get out!'

'You could find yourself arrested, and questioned in a hard place if you will not answer me,' I said quietly.

'Then do it, do it! I'm past caring! To hell with you all! I'm going back to my customers!' He started walking to the door. Barak made to step in front of him, but I shook my head. Lockley left, moving quickly for a fat man. Mrs Bunce hesitated, then looked at us beseechingly.

'Francis is not strong in his mind, sir,' she said. 'What he says is right, all his life he has been pestered by people who think they are better than he is.'

'So have most people,' Barak answered unsympathetically.

'But Francis can't take it, it affects him. I have tried to help him, but I think it has ended by him seeing me as another – persecutor. Though I'm not, I love him.' She looked at us bleakly.

'All right, madam, leave us,' I said.

When she had gone Barak said, 'We should arrest him.'

'We don't have the authority.' I sighed. 'We'll tell Harsnet what's happened. My guess is he'll send some men up tonight, when the tavern is closed.'

'Could he be our man?' Barak asked. 'Most people would be

terrified at the prospect of arrest, but he seemed hardly to care. His own woman said he is not quite right in himself.'

I shook my head. 'Running a tavern is a full-time job. He couldn't possibly have done what the killer has done without Mrs Bunce knowing. And I can't see him killing Roger or the others, I just can't see it.'

'You don't know.'

I looked at him seriously. 'If the killer was Lockley, do you think he would let us take him alive? No, let Harsnet deal with him.'

Chapter Twenty-seven

WE DECIDED TO ride back down to Westminster from Smithfield; it would take less time than riding the horses back home and catching a wherry. We rode along Holborn, right out into the countryside, taking a short cut over the fields to Drury Lane. A pair of hares were boxing in the field, jumping wildly about. 'Spring is truly here,' Barak said.

'Ay, yet I seem to feel cold all the time these days, as though winter has lingered on in me.'

✟

I FELT ANXIOUS as we rode down into Westminster, with all its noise and smells and danger. Under the old bell-tower in the Sanctuary we saw a group of gypsies had set up a stall, a piece of brightly coloured canvas showing the moon and stars with a table in front. Two were playing flutes to attract attention, while at the table an old woman was telling fortunes from the cards. Barak stopped to look, and indeed with their faces almost as dark as Guy's and their fantastic costumes of embroidered turbans and bright, trailing scarves, the gypsies were an arresting sight. These colourful newcomers to our shores were expelled by the King some years ago, but many had escaped and some had gravitated to the Sanctuary. They seemed to be doing a good trade, though a black-clothed man stood on the fringes of the crowd, waving a Testament and denouncing them for heathenish practices. The crowd ignored him; the Sanctuary was not a godly place.

'Come on,' I said, looking nervously over the crowds. 'I don't want to stop here, make a target.'

Barak nodded and pulled on Sukey's reins. We rode past the railing preacher. 'Woe to those who follow the ways of the devil!' he cried.

We rode down into the southern precinct. We had seen from the clock tower in Palace Yard that we were a good hour and a half early for our meeting with Harsnet. We turned towards Cantrell's house. Nearby a pack of wolfish dogs nosed and picked at a pile of rubbish on the corner. I knocked loudly on the door under the faded carpenter's sign while Barak tied the horses to the rail. I was unhappy at leaving them there but we had no choice and Sukey at least would neigh and kick if a stranger tried to untie her. Once again footsteps approached slowly from within, but this time they stopped before reaching the door and Cantrell's voice called out in timorous, cracked tones.

'Who's there? I am armed!'

'It is Master Shardlake,' I called out. 'The lawyer who was here before. What is the matter?'

There was a brief pause, then the bolt was drawn back and the door opened a few inches. Cantrell's thin face looked out; he peered closely at us from behind those thick spectacles that magnified his eyes. 'Oh, sir,' he said with relief. 'It is you.' He opened the door wider. I stared at a long piece of wood he held in his hand. On the end was a large smear of what looked like dried blood.

'Someone attacked me,' he said.

'May we enter?' I asked gently. He hesitated, then opened the door wide to allow us in. The sour, unwashed smell hit us again.

He led us into the bare parlour. A wooden plate with the remains of a greasy meal lay on the table, a pewter spoon black with dirt beside it. I saw the dirty window giving on to the yard was broken. There was glass on the floor.

Cantrell sat down on one of the hard chairs, facing us. We sat at the table. I avoided looking at the filthy plate. I saw rat-droppings in a corner. Cantrell's face looked strained and miserable, several spots coming out on his forehead beneath the greasy blond hair. He placed the stick on the floor.

'What did you want, sir?' he asked wearily. 'Have you found Infirmarian Goddard?'

'Not yet.'

'I told you all I know.'

'Only a few more questions. But what happened here? Is that blood on your piece of wood?'

'It was two nights ago. I couldn't sleep. I heard breaking glass downstairs. I always keep a piece of wood by the bed in case of burglars.'

'What would they steal?' Barak asked.

'Burglars wouldn't know there is nothing here. I went downstairs. It was dark but I saw the window was open wide. A figure was there, a man. When I came into the room, he just stood there. I don't think he saw the piece of wood. He said something and that let me know where his head was and I hit out.'

'The edge of that piece of wood is sharp,' Barak said. 'You seem to have done some damage.'

'Ay, I got him on the head. He groaned and staggered and I hit him again. Then he got out of the window again, stumbled away.'

'What did he say to you?'

'It was a strange thing for a burglar.' Cantrell frowned.

'What?'

'He said, "It is your time now." Why would he say that?'

I looked at him, appalled. Had Charles Cantrell escaped becoming the killer's fifth victim?

'Did you tell the constable?' I asked.

He shrugged his thin shoulders. 'What's the point? There are always burglaries in Dean's Yard. He won't try here again, though. I hope I hurt him hard, I hope he dropped in the gutter somewhere,' Cantrell added with gloomy viciousness.

I chose my words carefully. 'Was there anything you recognized about the man? Anything familiar about his voice?'

He stared at me with those half-blind, fishlike eyes. 'He was just a figure in the dark, a shape. I cannot see anything unless it is close to. Your face is just a blur from here even with my glasses.'

'Was he tall or short?'

'He must have been quite tall. I aimed high.' He thought a moment. 'There *was* something familiar about that voice. A sharp voice.'

'Could it have been your old master?' I asked quietly. 'Infirmarian Goddard?'

He stared at me in silence for a long moment. 'I – I suppose it could have been. But why – why would that old bastard attack me in my house? I haven't seen him in three years.'

'He would have known your father's house was near the abbey.'

'But why – what has he done, sir? You never told me last time.' There was an edge of shrill panic in Cantrell's voice now.

I hesitated. 'Could I see that piece of wood?'

'I won't get into trouble for this, sir? I was only defending myself.'

'I know. I just want to see it.'

Reluctantly he passed it over. I had noticed a few hairs among the blood. They were black. Like Goddard's; like the whore Abigail's unknown visitor.

'You dealt him a couple of good blows, by the look of it. But scalp wounds bleed a lot. He may have been more shocked and hurt than damaged.' I passed the stick back to Cantrell. His wrists were skinny, lumps of bone. I thought of Adam.

'You did not answer my question, sir,' Cantrell said.

I sighed. 'Infirmarian Goddard may be – deranged.'

'But why attack me?'

I looked at the broken glass on the floor. Yes, someone had broken in there from outside. Cantrell had not picked up the glass. I wondered whether with his poor vision he was afraid of cutting himself.

'Have you ever had anything to do with the radical religious reformers? The godly men.'

He was silent for a moment. Then he bowed his head.

'It is important,' I said. 'It may explain why you were attacked.'

'When I was a monk,' he said in a quiet voice, bowing his head as though ashamed, 'my father became a reformist. He joined a group that used to meet together at an unlicensed preacher's house, in the Sanctuary. When I left the abbey and came home it was all "You monks got what you deserve, you will go to hell unless you follow the true path of the Word."' I could sense anger in Cantrell's voice as he imitated his father's harsh, rough tones. 'I was losing belief in the old faith then. I let him drag me to some of these house meetings. There were only half a dozen in the group, they believed they had to prepare for the end-time, had a mission from God to find those he had elected to save and convert them. They were stupid, they only knew a few bits of the Bible that suited their arguments and didn't even understand those. Some couldn't even read. I had read the Bible for years, I could tell they knew nothing.'

'There are many such,' I said.

'Theirs was all idle talk and frantic babble.' Cantrell's voice was louder now, full of bitter anger. 'I only went to keep Father quiet. They kept saying they could save me, they would baptize me in the true faith.' He shook his head. 'My father was already ill when I came home, after he passed away I stopped going.' Cantrell looked up again, staring around the room. 'He had a growth.'

Cantrell's voice was quiet again. 'When he died I feared he might somehow still come back, to chide and rail at me. But he has not, there has been only silence in this house since.' He gave an exhausted sigh then and fell silent himself, lost in a world of his own. I looked around the room, at the filthy table and the broken window. Cantrell might be just about surviving from his monk's pension, but he needed help, someone to take care of him.

'How will you get the window repaired?' I asked. He shrugged. 'Perhaps the neighbours might help,' I suggested.

He shook his head fiercely. 'They're a nosy lot. The old shrew up the street used to come in. Tidying up, interfering with my things, telling me I needed to get married.' He laughed angrily. 'Perhaps I could find a blind woman and we could stumble around the house together. I hardly dare go out for victuals in case a cart runs me down.'

'What happened to this little religious group? Are they still active round Westminster?'

He shook his head. 'The vicar of St Margaret's heard there was some radical preaching going on. He got their leader arrested and the others fled. Last year.' A bitter laugh again. 'So much for their cleaving fast to the True Word. They ran like rats.'

So the fate of the group had become public. What had happened to them, I wondered. The members had probably become involved with other groups, other churches. Perhaps, somewhere among them, the murderer had mixed with them, where he heard Cantrell's name spoken of as a backslider. If the killer was Goddard, he would have recognized the name.

'Can you remember the names of the people in the group?' I asked. He gave me half a dozen. They meant nothing to me, but they might to Harsnet.

'But, sir,' Cantrell asked. 'What is all this to do with Master Goddard?' He blinked at me helplessly. I dared not tell him the whole story.

'I am not sure, Master Cantrell. But I think you may be in need of protection. I might be able to arrange for a guard to come to the house, stay here with you.'

Cantrell shook his head vigorously. 'No. I do not want anyone here. Criticizing and saying the place is filthy.' He looked at me again with those wide swimming eyes. 'If Goddard comes to me again, let him. You won't tell me why he's after me, but I care little if I live or die.'

I looked at Barak, who shrugged. I would try and arrange for a guard to be posted, just the same.

'Do you think me a great sinner,' Cantrell asked suddenly. 'Not to care if I die?'

'I think it a great shame.'

'What is death anyway? Afterwards it will be eternal bliss or eternal torment, one or the other, who may know which these days?' He gave a humourless cracked laugh.

'There is one last thing I would ask you,' I said. 'I have just been to see Francis Lockley again. I gained the impression there was something he was keeping back about Infirmarian Goddard. Something he did not want us to know about the man. Can you think what that might be?'

'No, sir. I had nothing to do with the lay infirmary. I only saw Francis when he came to see Master Goddard, to borrow some implements perhaps.' He shrugged, and I thought, he really does not care about anything, not even his own life or death.

✝

WE LEFT THE HOUSE, returned to the stink and the noise of Dean's Yard. 'He's in a bad way,' Barak observed.

'A state of deep melancholy, I would say. Not surprising given what is life has become, and the condition of his eyes.'

'He could pull himself together a bit. Accept some help. Imagine not caring if you lived or died, but caring if someone thought your house was filthy.'

'When we see Harsnet, I will see if I can arrange a guard. I could not bear to see Cantrell tortured like the others.' I did not think the killer would return to Cantrell now his victim had been alerted, but I could not be sure. 'There is one more piece of information we have,' I said. 'We are now looking for a man with an injured head.'

We led the horses across the road to the gate in the abbey wall. Barak nodded to the guard. There was still an hour before Harsnet was due. I felt a need to be alone for a while. 'Barak,' I said, 'see if you can find somewhere to stable the horses. I am going to take a walk inside the precinct. I will meet you back here in an hour.'

'Are you sure that's safe?'

'I shall be within the precinct. It is guarded. I will see you soon.' To settle the argument I turned away from him, nodding to the guard. Recognizing me, he opened the door in the wall to let me through. I stepped again into the precinct of Westminster Abbey.

✟

INSIDE, I PICKED my way through the maze of rubble to the old cloister. All was still and quiet. I walked the ancient flagstones, looking out at the deserted inner courtyard, thinking. I had picked up clues, but they only seemed to deepen the mystery. Was it Goddard we were looking for, or the young man who had visited Abigail? And why had the killer chosen Cantrell to be the fifth victim, as it looked likely that he had? If it was Goddard he would know the lad would be unlikely to be able to help himself. I felt an uncharacteristic satisfaction at the thought of Cantrell bringing that piece of wood down on his assailant's head. I thought how Cantrell, like Meaphon, had a peripheral link to me. I shook my head. It was dangerous and foolish to imagine that the killer was somehow focused on me as an audience. Had the killer not gone out of his way to try and terrorize me into dropping the case? Yet I could not prevent a clutch of fear at my heart at the recollection that I fitted the pattern of a man who had turned away from radical religion.

I realized how weary I was. I decided to take a walk through the ancient Westminster Abbey church, to calm myself. As I paced slowly I saw that the door to the chapterhouse stood half open, and heard voices from within. Hesitantly I walked across. To my surprise, I heard the sound of hammering. I stepped into the vestibule.

A group of black-robed clerks were carefully removing thick rolls of yellow parchment from old chests, laying them on the tiled floor. Workmen, some on ladders, were putting up heavy wooden shelves along the walls. One by one, the maroon-framed scenes from the

Apocalypse were being hidden from view. As I watched, a heavy nail was driven through the body of the seven-headed monster.

One of the clerks, a tall young fellow, looked up at me enquiringly. 'Are you from the Rolls House, sir?'

'No – I was just passing, I heard the hammering. Of course, I remember now. The chapterhouse is to be made into a repository for state documents.'

He nodded seriously. 'The paperwork of state just grows and grows, we have to put the ancient documents somewhere.'

I looked at the walls. 'So the old paintings are being covered up.'

He shrugged. 'The windows too, I hear. Well, 'tis all old monkish stuff. What are those little pictures anyway? They're not very good.'

'That is the Apocalypse of St John. The story of Revelation.' At my words one of the clerks looked up, and a workman stopped hammering. The clerk who had spoken to me walked over to the wall, studied a painting of the Great Whore uneasily.

'Is it?' he asked. He thought a moment. 'Well, the end-time should not be portrayed in crude pictures like these.' Another gospel man, I thought.

I left them, following the cloister walk to the door to the abbey church. The church was deserted except for black-robed attendants walking slowly to and fro, their footsteps echoing on the stone flags. The great hushed space, stripped now of all its images and ornaments, was lit dimly by a grey light from the high windows. The monks had prayed here for centuries, now all was stillness, silence. There was only one guard, by the door, and he was asleep. There was nothing of value left to steal; the King had it all.

I walked up to Henry VII's chapel where the King's father lay. There the great vaulted shrine was still in place, the white stone bright in the light from the large windows, contrasting with the dimness of the abbey. I returned to the nave, and walked among the old royal tombs.

I found myself in front of the sarcophagus of Edward the

Confessor, naked stone now. I had seen it in the days before the Dissolution, magnificently framed by rich gold and silver statues and images reflecting the glow of a thousand candles. There had been crutches and walking sticks piled there too, for the tomb was believed to have the power to cure cripples. I remembered that one of the tomb's first cures was supposed to be a hunchback. All nonsense, but nonsense of such power.

I became aware of a group of people nearby, grouped before a bare stone altar adorned only with a cross. Four stout men in livery, holding their caps in their hands, while their other hands rested on their sword-hilts. In front of them a woman knelt on the stone floor, her head bowed. She was beautifully attired, in a red silk dress with black cuffs inlaid with gold leaf, and the hands which she held in front of her, palms pressed together in an attitude of prayer, had jewelled rings on each finger. Her black hood was inlaid with pearls. One of the guards, seeing me looking, shot me a warning glance that said I should not approach. Then the woman lowered her hands with a sigh, and I saw it was the Lady Catherine Parr. She rose to her feet, her dress rustling. The expression on her face was similar to the one she had worn at her husband's funeral, closed in and worried, but as she stood up her face relaxed, the small mouth settling into a mild, gentle expression as she smiled at her guards. She nodded, and they began walking away.

They were halfway to the door when there was a sudden disturbance. I saw a ragged little man was praying before one of the tombs, and no sooner had I registered his presence than he got up and darted out before Lady Catherine, throwing himself to his knees in front of her. I started forward out of some instinct to protect her but her guards had got there first. One of them pointed a sword at the man's throat. Lady Catherine stood with a hand to her breast, shocked and frightened. The man raised his head and I saw it was the mad beggar whom Barak and I had encountered in the infirmary, talking about looking for his teeth.

Then another figure stepped from the shadows with a drawn

sword. It was Sir Thomas Seymour, dressed in a dark blue doublet with jewels to match. Lady Catherine turned pale.

'Are you safe, my lady?' Seymour asked.

'Quite safe, Thomas,' Lady Catherine said. She frowned. 'Put down your sword, you foolish man.' She looked down at the beggar.

'Good lady,' the wretched man burst out. 'I cannot find my teeth, I cannot eat, please, my lady, make them give them up to me!'

'You madwag,' the guard said, still holding his sword to the beggar's throat. 'What do you think you're doing, accosting Lady Catherine?'

'My teeth – only my teeth—'

'Let him go,' Lady Catherine said. 'He is out of his wits. I know nothing of your teeth, fellow. I see you have none. But if they are gone, they are gone. Mine will go too one day.'

'No, good lady, you do not understand—'

'We should have him taken in charge, my lady,' the guard said.

'No,' she answered firmly. 'He cannot help himself. Give me a shilling.' The guard lifted his sword, delved in his purse and brought out a silver coin. Lady Catherine took it, then bent and handed it to the man, who still stared up at her with beseeching eyes. She smiled, a gentle smile that reminded me of Dorothy's, though their faces were quite unlike.

'There, fellow, go and buy some pottage.'

The beggar looked from Lady Catherine to the hard faces of the guards, then rose to his feet, bowed and scampered away. Sir Thomas was still standing there, a faint look of amusement on his face. Her guards looked away as Lady Catherine took a step towards him. 'Thomas,' she said, her voice quivering. 'You were told—'

'A servant in your household said you would be coming to the abbey today,' he said. 'I wanted merely to see you, watch you from a distance.' He looked serious. 'But when I saw you might be threatened, I had to draw my sword.' He put his hand on his heart. It seemed to me an actor's gesture, but Lady Catherine's face flickered with emotion for a second. Then she said quietly, 'You know you must not try to see me. It is cruel of you, and dangerous.' She cast a worried look around, her eyes resting on me, still standing at some distance. Sir Thomas laughed. 'The crookback will say nothing, I know him. And I bribed the attendants to stay away from this part of the church for a little while.'

Lady Catherine hesitated a moment, then gestured to her guards and walked away rapidly. Her men followed. Sir Thomas gave the tiniest of shrugs. Then he turned to me.

'You won't say anything, will you?' His tone was quiet, but with a threatening undertone. 'Not to my brother, or Cranmer?'

'No. Why should I wish to be involved?'

Seymour smiled, white teeth flashing in his auburn beard. 'Well judged, crookback.' He turned and walked away, his steps loud and confident.

Chapter Twenty-eight

I REJOINED BARAK at the gate to Dean's Yard. He stood with the horses, looking watchfully over the crowds going to and fro. I told him about my encounter with Catherine Parr and Thomas Seymour.

He raised his eyebrows. 'He's taking a risk meeting her in Westminster Abbey, if the King's told him to leave her alone.'

'I don't think Seymour intended to talk to her. I think he just wanted her to see him in the shadows, know that he had not forgotten her.'

'He doesn't strike me as the lovelorn type.'

'No. But I think she may be. Where he's concerned, at least.' I shook my head. 'She struck me as an intelligent, good-hearted woman – what could she see in a man like Seymour?'

'A bedmate? She's had one older husband, and another in prospect if she marries the King.'

I shook my head. 'Her expression while she was praying seemed fearful, desperate—'

'Sounds like the Lady Catherine really made an impression on you.' Barak grinned wickedly.

'Don't be stupid. It was just – she seemed to have something good and honest in her, that you don't often see in ladies of the court.'

'Nor anyone else there, for that matter—' Barak broke off. 'Watch out, here comes Harsnet. I take it we are saying nothing about Seymour being in the church.'

'No. That's not our business. We know now these killings have nothing to do with Catherine Parr.'

I watched as Harsnet walked across Dean's Yard with his

confident stride, looking neither right nor left. The beggars and pedlars did not approach him; perhaps they knew who he was and that he could arrest them on the spot. I had heard they had their own body of knowledge. 'Good afternoon,' Harsnet said. He looked more cheerful than before.

'A good meeting?' I asked.

He nodded. 'We are going to be able to stop Bonner spreading his persecution down here. Westminster is well out of his jurisdiction.' He fixed me with his keen eyes. 'What news from Lockley?'

I told him of my suspicion he was still keeping something back, and of the attack on Charles Cantrell.

'I'll have Lockley taken in for questioning after we've seen the dean,' he said. 'What about the wife? Should we take her too?'

'No. I do not think she knows anything.'

'And young Cantrell attacked?' He looked across the yard to the run-down carpenter's shop. He frowned. 'But why in God's name does Cantrell not want someone posted at his house?'

'He says he does not care if he is attacked again. I am not sure he is quite in his right mind.'

'How so?'

'He is half blind, he was thrown out of Westminster Abbey and then saw his father die. He has suffered much.'

'Yet his father and his friends seem to have offered him salvation. I know some of those groups have more wild enthusiasm than deep faith. Yet they are on the right path.' Harsnet looked at me earnestly.

'Whether they are or not, Master Cantrell joined this conventicle and then withdrew from it. That would be enough for our killer to believe he deserved death.'

'I'll arrange for a guard. I'll have one posted there whether he likes it or not.' He sighed. 'But I'm running out of men. I'll have to speak to Lord Hertford, see if he can supply anyone. What were those names that Cantrell gave you?'

I gave Harsnet the names of the group Cantrell's father had

belonged to. He rubbed his chin. 'I've heard of one or two of those. I will ask around my contacts.' He took a deep breath. 'And now, let us see what we can get out of Dean Benson.'

✝

THE DEAN WAS in his study again, in the fine house set amidst the warren of half-demolished and half-converted monastic buildings, labouring over papers. The sound of hammering and sawing was louder today, and his plump face was irritable. When we were shown in he gave us a look of hostile enquiry, bidding us sit down with a patrician wave of the hand.

'I see by your expressions this matter is not resolved,' he said. 'I confess I found the insinuation of involvement from ex-monks from Westminster distasteful.'

'It's more than distasteful,' Harsnet replied sharply, causing Benson to raise his eyebrows. 'There has been another murder, and we can find no trace of Goddard or his family. No trace at all.' His manner was steely, he looked the dean squarely in the eye. Benson frowned.

'And do you know of any direct connection between Goddard and these killings?' he asked smoothly. 'Beyond the suspected use of dwale, and the pilgrim badge? That's little enough to go on.'

'Maybe. But we need to find him.'

'I have told you all I know. I have no idea where Goddard is.'

'Master Shardlake here has been talking to the lay brother who worked in the public infirmary. Francis Lockley.'

The dean grunted. 'Where is Lockley now? Somewhere there's a bottle, I'll warrant.'

'Never mind that,' Harsnet countered sharply. 'The point is we believe he knows something about Goddard, and is hiding it.'

'I do not think he knows Goddard's whereabouts,' I said. 'But he knows something.'

'Well, I do not.'

'I am having Lockley brought in for questioning,' Harsnet said.

'What is that to do with me?' Benson's look did not change, but one plump hand slid across the desk to a quill. He picked it up and began fiddling with it. 'Be very careful how you deal with me,' he went on. 'I have important contacts. I have the gratitude of the King himself for the way I brought Westminster Abbey to a peaceful surrender. I am dean now, I have the responsibility for this great church and its royal tombs.'

'We are hunting a murderer,' Harsnet said. 'Someone who has brutally murdered four people and already tried to murder a fifth.'

'And I tell you again, it has nothing to do with the abbey.' Impatience entered his voice. 'God's bones, man, I knew Goddard. I used to talk to him, he was one of the few monks in this place with any intelligent conversation. But all he ever cared about was his comfort and his social status. The idea of him killing people to fulfil some prophecy in Revelation is – ludicrous.'

'If a man is possessed by the devil,' Harsnet said quietly, 'it does not matter what he was like before. He will be consumed by the desire to do the devil's bidding.'

Benson stopped playing with his quill. 'Possession.' He laughed cynically. 'Is that what you think? That idea will get you nowhere.'

'I saw the wall paintings telling the story of the Apocalypse in the chapterhouse,' I said. 'They are being covered up now, behind shelves and documents.'

'Yes, that was my idea to use the chapterhouse to store surplus records. We have plenty of space in the precinct now. What of it?'

'The monks must have seen those paintings hundreds of times. So must you. I do not think one could look at them day in, day out, and not think about the story they portrayed.'

He shrugged. 'I used hardly to notice them, except to think what poor quality the paintings were.'

'They could still affect a certain type of man.' I met Benson's gaze. He stared at me fixedly for a moment, then pointed his quill at me. 'I know who you are now. I have been trying to think why your name is familiar. You are the lawyer the King mocked at York two years ago. What was it he called you? A bent spider? I heard that story when he returned. People said he compared you to some big Yorkshire fellow you were with. It went down well with the Yorkers.'

I did not reply. 'You are no man of God, sir,' Harsnet said quietly.

Benson turned to him, suddenly angry. 'I am a realist. In the end people like me cause less trouble in the world. When I was a young monk, I saw the system was corrupt and rotten. So I made myself known to Lord Cromwell – there was a realist, if ever there was one – and he gained me the post of abbot. And I made sure this house made a quiet surrender, with no opposition and no scandal, because the King would not have wanted that in the royal resting place. He intends to be buried there one day. And he will be angry if you make a scandal now. So be warned. You may get more than an insult from him the next time.' Benson stood up, indicating the interview was over. I saw from Harsnet's expression that he would have liked nothing better than to take the dean in for questioning himself. But Benson was right, he was a powerful man, and in the absence of any evidence Harsnet had to proceed cautiously. I thought he had not handled the dean well, making his hostility so obvious.

✝

OUTSIDE THE HOUSE, Harsnet turned to me. I could see that he was battling with anger. 'Did you believe him?' he asked.

'I think he, too, is hiding something. But either he believes it is immaterial to our investigation, or he thinks himself safe because of his powerful contacts.'

'His contacts wouldn't protect him if he were hiding information about a murderer four times over.'

'No.' I paused. 'At least, they shouldn't.'

Harsnet set his lips tight. 'Let's see if Lockley says something that will help us put Benson under a bit of pressure. Now I must find a couple of constables and pick Lockley up. I will see you tonight at six, Serjeant Shardlake.' He bowed and strode away.

'I don't envy Lockley,' Barak said.

'No.' I looked back at the dean's house. 'A realist, Benson called himself. Well, he is. I should think, like most of the monks who helped Cromwell, his motives were money and power. I wonder if he ever thinks about the monks who were thrown out, I wonder if his conscience ever pricks him.'

'Didn't look to me like he had one.' Barak winced slightly as a huge block of stone crashed down from the refectory. He looked around the demolition work. Then he laughed.

'What's so funny?'

'That arsehole Benson going on about how he became dean of this place. Look at it. He's master of a heap of rubble.'

'He still runs Westminster Abbey church under the King's favour,' I said seriously.

Barak looked over at the huge church. 'So Henry wants to be buried there,' he said quietly.

'The sooner the better,' I said, more quietly still.

✝

HARSNET LIVED at the top end of Westminster, in a row of fine old houses in King Street, just down from the Whitehall Palace gatehouse where pennants flew, outlined against the clear blue sky, the setting sun reflected in the tall gatehouse windows. I turned to Harsnet's front door, which had a brightly polished knocker in the shape of a lion's head. I wondered what dinner with his family would be like, but even more I wondered what Lockley had told him.

I knocked at the door and a manservant ushered me into a large parlour. Gold plate shone on the tall wooden buffet, and a wall painting showing the journey of the Magi to Bethlehem covered one wall, with camels and caravan-trains picked out in soft, pleasing colours.

Harsnet was there with his wife. The coroner looked neat and spruce in a black velvet doublet, his beard newly trimmed and showing flecks of grey in contrast to his dark hair. But he had a worried, preoccupied look. His wife was a small round-faced woman, in a brown dress of good quality, with fair hair and bright eyes full of curiosity. She had been sitting on a pile of cushions, embroidering. She got up and curtsied to me.

'Elizabeth,' Harsnet said, 'allow me to present Serjeant Matthew Shardlake, who is working with me on an assignment of – some difficulty. There are some things we should talk about after our meal,' he added. He gave me warning look, and I realized his wife knew nothing about the murders. So I would have to wait for news of Lockley.

Elizabeth spoke in a high, pleasant voice. 'I hardly see Gregory these days, and when I do he looks tired out. I hope you are not responsible for all the work he is doing, sir.'

'Indeed not, madam. I am only his fellow-toiler.'

'Gregory speaks well of you.' I looked at Harsnet, a little surprised for I had thought he would have scant respect for someone not of his rigid faith. He smiled uncomfortably, and I realized again that he was a shy man.

'I have not thanked you properly for sending your man to my house,' I said. 'He is a good fellow, and gives the women a sense of security.'

Harsnet looked pleased. 'I knew he would give good service, he is a member of my church.'

Elizabeth invited me to sit at a table covered with a bright embroidered cloth. 'I hope you like roast mutton, sir,' she said.

'It is one of my favourite dishes,' I answered truthfully.

She rang a little bell, and servants brought in a large dish of mutton and bowls of vegetables. I realized this was the first time I had been out to dinner since that last night at Roger and Dorothy's. Samuel would be gone by now, she would be alone again. I would visit her tomorrow.

The door opened again and a maid ushered in four children, two boys and two girls, ranging in age from perhaps four to ten, hair combed tidily, the younger two in nightshirts. 'Come, children,' Harsnet said. 'Meet Master Shardlake.' The children went and stood obediently beside their father; the two boys bowed to me, the girls curtsied. Harsnet smiled. 'The boys are Absalom and Zealous, the girls Rachel and Beulah.' All Old Testament names, except for Zealous; one of the strange names the radical reformers gave their children now, such as Fear-God, Perseverance, Salvation. The two little girls stared with scarce-concealed interest at my back; the younger boy had his head cast down, but the elder, Zealous, had a surly, angry look. His father laid a hand on his head.

'I hope you have learned well from your beating,' he said seriously. 'To take Our Saviour's name in vain is a great sin.'

'Yes, Father,' the boy said, quietly enough, but his eyes looked angry still. Harsnet dismissed the children, watching as they left the room, then shook his head sadly. 'I had to strike Zealous with the cane for swearing when I came in,' he said. 'An unpleasant part of a father's duty. But it had to be done. I was unaware he knew such words.' He was silent again for a moment, that preoccupied look on his face again.

'Children can be a trial,' Elizabeth said, 'but they are a great comfort, and they are the future.' She smiled at me. 'My husband tells me you are not married.'

'No,' I answered briefly, reaching for another slice of mutton with my knife.

'Marriage is a state to which man is called by God,' she said, keeping her eyes fixed on me.

'So your husband has said,' I answered mildly. 'Well, God has not called me.' I turned to Harsnet. 'You said you had been assistant coroner six years. Where did you read law, sir?'

'At the Middle Temple. Then I worked in Lincolnshire, where my parents came from, for some years. Then the Northern rebellion came six years ago. I raised a troop of men against those papists. Though we had no fighting. They surrendered to us immediately.'

'In Yorkshire it was a different story,' I said.

'By God's grace the rebellion was put down there too. But afterwards I had a message to see Thomas Cromwell. You knew him too, I think.' Harsnet fixed me with that penetrating stare of his.

'Yes, from his early days as a young radical.'

'He was in the days of his great power then. He said he had marked me as a man of ability, asked me to take the post of the King's assistant coroner, the old one having just died.' Harsnet sighed. 'We were happy in Lincolnshire, we did not wish to move, and although the post carries a good salary, like all royal appointments, money has never been our main concern in life.'

'Lord Cromwell was not a man who could be easily refused.'

'Oh, I did not wish to refuse. He told me the post meant one more man of faith at court.'

'He works himself to death, Master Shardlake,' Elizabeth said. 'But we must all play our part as God wills.' She smiled, and I wondered if that was an oblique reference to my single state.

'You said you are thinking of starting a hospital for the poor,' Harsnet said.

I was glad of the change of subject. 'Yes, it was Roger Elliard's idea. To take subscriptions from the members of Lincoln's Inn, perhaps from all the Inns of Court, to fund a hospital for the poor and sick. When I have enough time I intend to start work on the matter.'

He nodded agreement. 'That would be a fine thing. Between these four walls, the King has no interest in spending any of the money gained from the monasteries on replacing their hospitals with something better.'

'No,' I agreed. 'Building palaces is all that interests him, and war with France now the Scots are beaten.'

Harsnet nodded in agreement. 'Ay, and all for vainglory.'

'Gregory . . .' his wife said uneasily.

'I know, my love, we must be careful. But to return to the hospital, Serjeant Shardlake. I would like to help you when your project gets going. I still have contacts at Middle Temple. Where would you build it?'

'I confess I have not thought. Though there is no shortage of land in London since the monasteries went down.'

He nodded. 'Somewhere central. That is where they all gather to beg. We see how they suffer every day. And suffering and uneducated as they are, they lie under a great temptation to doubt God's providence and care.'

'They could be taught the Bible in the hospital,' Elizabeth added.

'Yes.' Harsnet nodded thoughtfully. 'After their bodies have been mended.'

We had finished the meal now. Harsnet caught my eye. 'If you will excuse us, my dear,' he said to his wife. 'Serjeant Shardlake and I need to talk. Shall we go to my study, sir?'

I stood up and bowed to Mrs Harsnet. 'Thank you for that excellent repast, madam.'

She inclined her head in acknowledgement. 'I am glad you enjoyed it. Think, sir, if you were to take a good wife for yourself, you could have such a table every night.'

✝

HARSNET LED ME to his study, a small room whose main item of furniture was a paper-strewn desk. On one wall was a large fragment of stained glass enclosed within a frame, a design of red and white roses with golden leaves on a dark background in between. It had a pleasing effect, lightening the room. 'That came from the old nunnery at Bishopsgate,' he said. 'I thought it a pretty design, and there are no idolatrous representations of saints to spoil it.'

'It is pretty indeed. But, sir – what of Lockley?'

His whole neat, erect posture seemed to sag as he sat down, waving me to a chair opposite him. My heart sank as I realized there was more bad news to come.

'He's gone,' Harsnet said bleakly. 'Made a run for it. When my men arrived at the tavern they found the Bunce woman in a great state. Lockley had gone out to make an order at the brewer's three hours before and never come back. She said he'd been on edge ever since you came.'

'Well, that proves he was hiding something.'

He had laid a hand on the table, and he suddenly clenched it into a fist. 'Lockley gone. He could be the killer.'

'I don't think so. I don't think he is clever enough, apart from anything else. No, it's some secret to do with those connected with the abbey infirmaries. Barak speculated that there might have been some sodomites there, but I doubt that too.'

'I would bring Dean Benson into custody here and now, but that is not so easy. I have an appointment with Lord Hertford tomorrow, I will see what he can do. He will not be pleased,' he added.

'We do not have much luck.'

'And the killer does. Perhaps that should not be a surprise. With the devil inside him, everything he does succeeds. He seems invisible, untouchable.' He looked at me with an intense, haunted gaze.

'He failed with Cantrell,' I said. 'Would the devil have allowed that?'

Harsnet stared at me, suddenly stronger and harder again. 'I know you do not believe the killer is possessed, sir. But how else can you explain someone doing such wicked, evil things? For no possible personal gain.'

'He must gain something. In his disordered mind. I think he has an insane compulsion to kill. He would not be the first.'

'Madness? If you are to justify that definition, sir, if it is to be more than just a word, you must tell me in what ways his mind is disordered, how and why he is mad.'

'I cannot,' I admitted. 'I can only tell you that there have been similar cases in the past.'

'When?' he asked, surprised.

I told him about Strodyr and De Rais. When I had finished he spread his hands, gave me a sad smile.

'But surely, sir, those are further examples of possession rather than madness as we know it. Whatever that ex-monk Dr Malton may say.'

'Perhaps there will never be an explanation for such men as these.'

'But surely possession is an explanation,' Harsnet said. He leaned forward. 'Acts that make sense only as a wicked mockery of true religion.'

'True religion?' I asked quietly. 'Is that how you would describe the Book of Revelation?'

'How else?' Harsnet spread his hands wide. 'It is a book of the Bible, and all of the Bible is God's word, telling us how to live and find salvation, how the world began and how it will end. We cannot pick and choose which parts of the Bible to believe.'

'Many have doubted whether the Book of Revelation is inspired by God. From the early church fathers to Erasmus in our own day.'

'But the church fathers did accept it. And Erasmus remained a papist. Not a true Bible man. The Book is Holy Writ, and the devil has entered this man to make him blaspheme.'

I did not reply. Harsnet and I would never agree. To my surprise, he smiled suddenly. 'I see I will not convince you,' he said.

I smiled back. 'I fear not. Nor I you.'

He looked at me, not in a hostile way but with compassion. 'I am sorry my wife was so insistent about the virtues of the married state. Women these days will say what they please. But she has a point. Matthew, I may call you Matthew—'

'Of course—'

'I have watched you with interest this last week. Working together gives one a chance to weigh up a man. You are clever, and a moral man.'

'Thank you.'

He looked at me earnestly. 'You were a successful lawyer, who was close to Thomas Cromwell in his early days. You could have been one of the commissioners appointed to do away with the monasteries, I think.'

'I did not want that job. It called for more ruthless men than I.'

Harsnet nodded. 'Yes, a moral man. But a moral man should surely not lack faith.'

'I shared my law chambers once with a good man, a man of the new faith. He left to become a preacher on the roads. I think he is still out there somewhere. I often think of him. But then I have known good men who cleaved to the old faith too.' I looked at him. 'And evil men of both.'

'I think you are uncertain, you are indeed what the Bible calls a Laodicean.'

'Laodicea. One of the churches St John of Patmos criticized in Revelation. Yes, I am uncertain.' I let a coldness enter my voice. I did not want this conversation, I did not want Harsnet trying to convert me in his patronizing way, but I did not wish to be rude to him. His compassion was sincere, and I had to work with him.

'Forgive me,' he went on, 'but do you not think perhaps the state of your back makes you bitter, resistant to God? I saw how it affected you when Dean Benson mentioned the King's mockery of you at York. Sadly that is the sort of thing some men will remember, to throw in your face.'

Now I felt anger. He had gone too far. 'I was a hunchback when I was a man of faith,' I said firmly. 'If I am a doubter now, a Laodicean as you say, it is because for ten years I have seen men on both sides who talk of the glory of God yet harry and persecute and kill their fellow men. By their fruits shall you know them, is not that what the Bible says? Look at the fruits of religion in these last ten years. This murderer has many examples of cruelty and violence to inspire him.'

Harsnet frowned. 'The agents of the Pope show true religion no mercy, and we have to stand fast. You know what Bonner is doing. I do not like hard measures, I hate them, but sometimes they are necessary.' A tic flickered on his cheek momentarily.

'What do you believe, Gregory?' I asked quietly. 'Like Cranmer, that the King has been appointed by God to supervise the doctrine of the Church, that all should be in accordance with his will?'

'No. I believe the true Christian church should be self-governing. No bishops, nor ceremonies. As it was in the early church, so it should be at the end. I believe the end-time is coming,' he concluded.

'Yes. I thought you might.'

'I see the signs, the strange things everywhere in the world like those great fish the waters threw up and the persecution of Christians. The Antichrist is here and he is the pope. This is no time for half-measures.'

'I believe the Book of Revelation was written by a false prophet,' I said. 'Who repeated his dreams and fantasies.'

I thought Harsnet would burst out angrily but the compassionate look remained on his face. He sighed heavily. 'I see you believe what you say, Matthew. And I can see things from your point of view. Believe me, I do not like the things I sometimes have to do, like the way I had to conduct that inquest.' The tic fluttered again on his cheek, twice. 'I prayed hard that day. And I believe that God answered me, confirmed that I must keep the truth of poor Elliard's death secret. I never act without praying, and God answers, and then I know that I have taken the right path.' He smiled. 'And in the end I answer to him, not to mortal men.' He looked at me with passionate seriousness. 'I too doubted when I was young, I think we all doubt then. But one day when I was praying for enlightenment I felt God came to me and it was as if I wakened from a dream. God's love for me was clear, as though my mind had been washed clean.' He spoke with passion.

'I thought I felt the same, once,' I said sadly.

'But it was not enough?'

'No.'

Harsnet smiled. 'Perhaps that time will come again. After this horror is over.' He hesitated, the shyness showing through again. 'I would like to be your friend, Matthew,' he said. 'I am a loyal friend.'

I smiled. 'Even to Laodiceans?'

'Even so.'

I shook his hand. And I wondered whether at the end of this trail of horror, I would regain my faith, or he would lose his.

Chapter Twenty-nine

IT WAS DARK when I rode back along the Strand, weary after the long day, past the houses of the wealthy that lined the road from Westminster to London. Gentle yellow candlelight flickered in their windows, lighting the road dimly. There were few people about after the London curfew, but as always these days I was watchful.

The air was still mild, but damp, and looking up at the sky I saw the stars were hidden by cloud. We were going to have rain. The stitches on my arm pulled painfully. Tomorrow if time allowed I would go and see Guy and ask when I might have them out. I wanted to talk to him again too, about Adam Kite and about what sort of creature the killer might be. The conversation with Harsnet had remained in my mind; I did not believe the killer was possessed, but was unsure that I really had any better idea *what* he was. And I did not know when he might strike again, or where.

When I entered the house Harsnet's man Orr was sitting in the hall, reading a Testament.

'All quiet, Philip?' I asked him.

'Yes, sir. I walked up and down the street a few times, made myself seen. Just the normal traffic. A lot of legal men, a pedlar with his cart crying his wares most of the morning.'

'He's a long way out. I shouldn't think he'd get much passing trade here.'

'So many workless men have gone for pedlars these days, they are getting everywhere.'

'True.' I passed inside, glad Orr was there. I liked his solid conscientiousness. His presence would be a deterrent if our dreadful visitor thought of doing more damage to us.

Inside, all was quiet. I headed for the stairs, then paused on the bottom step as I heard something faintly from behind the closed kitchen door. A woman crying. I walked quietly across and opened the door.

Tamasin was sitting at the table, weeping. A hard, wrenching sound, full of deep misery. Joan was sitting beside her, an arm round her shoulders. Looking past them to the window I saw the two boys, Peter and Timothy, standing outside in the yard, their noses pressed against the pane. I gestured at them and they turned and fled.

'What has happened?' I asked.

Tamasin raised her head and looked at me. Her bruises were almost gone, but her face was red and streaked with tears. I realized it was a long time since I had seen it looking normal.

'It is nothing,' she said.

'Of course it is something.' I heard the impatience in my voice.

'Just a disagreement between her and Jack,' Joan said.

'He came back drunk an hour ago,' Tamasin said bleakly. 'Crashed into our room and gave me foul language for reply when I asked him what was wrong. I will not stand for much more of this,' she said with sudden fierceness.

I frowned. 'Then I will see him. I will not have him drunk in this house.'

I left the room and went upstairs, angry with Barak, and myself too. I had offered to help her, yet had achieved nothing.

I found Barak in his room, sitting on a stool by the bed. When he looked up his face was red, too, but with drink. 'Don't you start,' he said.

'I'll start where I like in my own house. Is this how you keep your promise to make things up with Tamasin?'

'None of your business,' he muttered.

'It is my business if you upset her. Where have you been?'

'Drinking with some old mates. In town.'

'You never used to get drunk like this. Why now? Still because of the lost child?' I added more gently.

He did not reply.

'Well?'

'I am sick of this business,' he said. 'Sick to the heart, if you must know. He could strike again tonight. We have nothing, nothing but bits and pieces of information.'

'I know,' I replied, more quietly. 'I feel the same. But you have no right to take it out on Tamasin.'

'I didn't.' His voice became truculent again. 'I came in here and she started going on at me for being drunk. I told her to let me be and when she didn't I called her some names. She doesn't know when to let me alone.'

'You could have told her what ails you.'

He looked at me. 'What? Tell her the man who attacked her is still free, we know fuck all and are waiting for him to kill again? Perhaps attack us again? I hate being so powerless. I wish we could get at him.' He shook his head.

'I think you should sleep this off,' I said. 'And when you wake up, apologize to Tamasin. Or you will lose her.'

'Maybe one of Harsnet's devils has entered me,' he said bitterly.

'Ay, from out of a bottle.' I closed the door, leaving him.

☩

STRANGELY, I SLEPT WELL that night, as though my expression of anger and frustration at Barak had released something within me. It began raining heavily as I prepared for bed, drops pattering against the window the last thing I heard. I woke early; the sky was still cloudy, but the rain had stopped for now. It must have gone on all night, for there were large puddles on the garden path beneath my window.

The rest of the house was still quiet; Barak and Tamasin did not seem to be up and I wondered if they had managed to mend things between them at all. From Barak's frame of mind last night, I doubted it. It had felt strange to berate him, for a long time now I had looked on him as a friend rather than a subordinate.

Until some news came from Harsnet's enquiries, and his efforts to put pressure on Dean Benson, there was plenty of work awaiting me at Chancery Lane. First, though, I would visit Dorothy. I wondered how she was faring without Samuel. I wished I had some news of Roger's killer for her. I heard Joan's voice in the kitchen, talking to Orr, but I did not wish to become embroiled in a discussion with her about Tamasin and Barak, and I did not feel like breakfast either, so I left the house quietly. I walked the short distance up Chancery Lane to Lincoln's Inn. The road had turned to mud and I was glad I had put on my riding boots.

At Lincoln's Inn the working day had begun, black-robed lawyers stepping to and fro across Gatehouse Court with papers under their arms, the fountain splashing under the grey sky.

Margaret answered the door to Dorothy's rooms. She told me her mistress was at home, going through papers. 'How is she?' I asked.

'Trying to get back to a normal life, I think, sir. But she finds it hard.'

Dorothy was in the parlour. She still looked wan and pale, but greeted me with a smile. 'You look tired,' she said.

'This hunt.' I paused. 'He is still at large. It has been nearly two weeks now, I know.'

'I know you will be doing all you can.' She rose from the table, wiping her quill and setting it by the papers. 'Come, this wretched rain has stopped. Will you take me for a walk in Coney Garth? I need some air.'

'Gladly.' I was pleased to see she could give mind now to such ordinary things. 'You will need boots, the ground is wet.'

'I will get them.'

She left me in the parlour. I stood by the fire, the animals peering at me from the undergrowth on the wooden frieze. Dorothy returned, dressed in a black cloak with a hood and high walking boots, and we went out of doors and crossed Gatehouse Court. Lawyers nodded to us, their stares a mixture of curiosity and discomfort. I noticed Dorothy still resolutely avoided looking at the fountain.

We walked into the bare heathland of Lincoln's Inn Fields. The murderer had escaped this way after killing Roger. Nearby was a long hillock, the sides dotted with rabbit holes, where students would come to hunt their dinner later in the season. We followed a path that led to the top of the hillock, the ground drier there. Dorothy was silent, thoughtful-looking.

'Samuel will have arrived in Bristol by now,' I said.

'Yes. He very much wanted me to go back with him.'

'He also said you would not be driven away from your home.'

'No, I will not. I will stay here until the killer is caught. And there is business I must finish here. Master Bartlett has kindly made a summary of monies due to Roger for his cases. And I am not lonely. Many kind people have visited.' She smiled sadly. 'You remember Madam Loder, who was at the dinner last month. She called to see me two days ago. I had no sooner sat her down on some cushions and handed her a glass of wine then she leaned forward and those false teeth of hers fell out on her lap.' She laughed. 'Poor woman, she was very embarrassed. She is going to have some firm words with the tooth-drawer who prepared the denture.'

Her words reminded me of Tamasin's experience. I wondered whether Mrs Loder ever thought to wonder where those teeth of hers came from.

'Are you still taking care not to go out unaccompanied?' I asked. 'It is only a precaution, but I think it is as well.'

'Yes.'

'Will you stay in London, do you think, or go to Bristol? In the long run?'

She sighed. 'I think it would be hard for me to buy a house in London. But perhaps in Bristol I could.' She raised her eyebrows. 'Treasurer Rowland has sent a message; kindly worded, but he made it clear he wants me out of our rooms as soon as possible now.'

'He is a heartless man.'

She shrugged. 'There is a vacancy at the Inn now, he will want to fill it.' She gave me a searching look. 'Samuel would like me to move back to Bristol permanently. But it is not just obstinacy that makes me stay. It is too early to decide on something like that.' She sighed. 'It is hard to think clearly. Everywhere the empty space of Roger's absence follows me. It is like a hole in the world. Yet do you know, I realized this morning that I had worked for half an hour without thinking of him. I felt guilty, as though I had betrayed him.'

'I think that is how grief is. The hole in the world will always be there, but you begin to notice the other things. You should not feel guilt.'

Dorothy looked at me curiously. 'You have known grief too?'

'There was a woman I knew who died. In the plague of 1534. Nine years, but I still think of her. I used to wear a mourning ring for her.'

'I did not know.'

'It was after you and Roger went to Bristol.' I looked at her. 'Dorothy, may I ask you something?'

'Anything.'

'The business you feel you must stay for. Is part of it waiting for the killer to be caught? Because I do not know when that will be.'

She came to a halt, turned and laid a hand on my arm. Her pale face, outlined by the black hood, was full of concern. 'Matthew,' she said quietly. 'I can see this dreadful thing is burning you up. I am sorry it was me that set you on this hunt. I thought officialdom did not care. But now I know they are seeking this man, I want you to leave the matter to them. This is having a bad effect on you.'

I shook my head sadly. 'I am bound tightly into the hunt for him now, bound into those official chains. He – he has killed again.'

'Oh no.'

'You are right, Dorothy, the horror eats into me, but I have to see it through now. And I have involved others too. Guy, Barak.' And even if I was willing to leave the killer alone, I thought but did not say, would he leave me? 'Do not be sorry,' I continued. 'We think we may know who the killer is. We will catch him. And one thing we are certain of now is that Roger was a chance victim, in the sense that the killer could equally have chosen someone else.'

'That is little comfort, somehow it makes it worse. But it has happened, I must bear it. Nothing will bring Roger back.'

I smiled at her. 'You are so much calmer now. Your strength is helping you.'

'Perhaps.'

'Do you feel God helps you in your grief?' I asked impulsively. 'Succours you?'

'I pray. For help in dealing with what has happened. Yet I would not ask God to take away my grief. It must be borne. Though I cannot understand how God would allow a good man to be destroyed like that. That is what I mean by his being a chance victim making it worse.'

'I suppose one could answer the killer is an evil man, who has turned from God and all that is good. And God allows us the free will to do that.'

She shook her head. 'I have not the heart for such speculation these days.'

We walked on in silence for a little. Then she said, 'You have much courage, Matthew, to do this hateful work.' She smiled at me. 'For anyone it would be bad, but you – you are affected by things.'

'It has affected Barak too. And Guy, I think.'

'Are you sure you cannot give it up?'

'No. Not now.'

We had reached the edge of the little escarpment and stood looking out over Lincoln's Inn Fields, towards the more distant fields of Long Acre. Clouds in varying shades of grey raced across the sky, promising more rain.

'Do you remember when we first met?' Dorothy asked suddenly. 'That business of Master Thornley's paper?'

I smiled. 'I recall it as though it were yesterday.' Thornley had been a fellow student who studied with Roger and me twenty years before. The three of us shared a little cubby-hole of an office at the Inn. It had been a summer evening. I had been sitting working with Roger when Dorothy had called, with a message from her father, my principal, about a case the following day where he required my assistance. Scarcely had she told me when Thornley had burst in. 'He was such a fat little fellow,' Dorothy recalled. 'Do you remember? He had a round red face, but that evening it was white.'

I remembered. Thornley had been set a fiendishly complicated problem in land law, one on which he had to present a paper on the morrow. 'The story he told us.' I laughed aloud at the memory. 'He would be unable to present his paper because his dog had eaten it. The lamest excuse in the world, yet that time it was true. Did you ever see that dog?'

'No. It lived in his lodgings, did it not?'

'A great big lurcher he brought up from the country. He kept it in that tiny lodging room of his in Nuns Alley. The beast chewed all the furniture to shreds, then started on the contents of his open workcase. Those chewed-up fragments of paper he pulled from it. Some of them still wet with dog-spittle, the ink all run.'

'And we helped him. You sorted out all those torn bits of paper, as Thornley and Roger and I copied out the exercise again. Some of it was illegible and Thornley had to cudgel his brains to remember what he had said.'

'Roger filled in some of the blanks for him.'

'And next day Thornley presented it, and was praised for the precision of his answer.'

'What became of Thornley? I never saw him again after we qualified.' I looked at her. 'Was that the first time you and Roger met?'

'Yes, it was. But it was you I came to see that day.'

'Me?'

She smiled gently. 'Do you not think my father could have got a servant to deliver his message? I offered to bring it round so that I could see you.'

'I did not realize,' I said. 'But I remember noting that you and Roger got on very well, and feeling jealous.'

'I thought you were not interested in me. So when I met Roger—'

'So you came to see me,' I said quietly. Something seemed to pull at my heart. I looked out over the greens and browns of the flat landscape 'How little we know each other,' I said at length. 'How easy it is to make mistakes.'

'Yes,' she agreed with a sad smile.

'Recently – I am not even sure I know Guy as well as I thought.' I hesitated, full of confused emotion, then looked at her. 'I hope you do not go to Bristol, Dorothy. I will miss you. But you must decide.'

She lowered her eyes. 'I feel I am a burden to my friends.'

'Never to me.'

She stared out over the fields. There was an awkward moment of silence. 'We should go back,' she said quietly. She turned and led the way, her skirts rustling on the wet grass. I feared I had embarrassed her. But I knew then, amidst all my trouble, that if she stayed, then after a decent period I would seek to gain her hand. I felt in time her old feelings for me might be resurrected. Perhaps they were budding already, or why had she recalled that story? And I had a sudden certainty that Roger would have approved.

☩

RECOGNITION OF my feelings for Dorothy, which perhaps had never really gone away in the intervening years, and the thought that there might be some hope for me in the future, cheered me. Amidst all the danger and confusion it was something optimistic to hold on to. And then, going across the courtyard from Dorothy's to my chambers, I saw Bealknap again. He was walking across Gatehouse Court, stooped and bent, and I saw that now he needed the aid of a stick. His head was cast down and I could have avoided him, but I did not do so. I remembered my meeting with his physician in Guy's shop, the man's confident talk of bleeding and purging.

Bealknap looked up as I approached. His face, always thin, was skeletal now. He glared at me, an expression full of spite and malice. I remembered how in the days of his health he would never look you straight in the face.

'I am sorry to see you with a stick,' I said.

'Leave me, get out of my way.' Bealknap grasped the stick tighter, as though he would have liked to strike me with it. 'You will end by regretting the way you have treated me.'

'At the Court of Requests? I had to do that. But believe it or not, I do not like to see anyone ill.' I hesitated, fought a sudden urge to walk away. 'I met your doctor some days ago,' I said. 'Dr Archer.'

His eyes narrowed with suspicion. 'What has my physician to do with you?'

'He was at my friend Dr Malton's premises when I called there. He mentioned you as a patient he had at Lincoln's Inn. He sounded like a great old purger.'

'So he is. He bleeds and purges me constantly, he says my body is badly disordered and keeps producing bad humours which must be forced out.' He put a hand to his stomach and winced. 'He has given me a new purge to take now. The lax comes on so quick it plucks my stomach away.'

'Some doctors think of nothing but purging. Have you thought of getting a second opinion?'

'Dr Archer was my father's doctor. What would going to a second doctor serve except – confusion? And expense. Archer will get me right in the end.' He looked at me defiantly. It surprised me that Bealknap, of all people, should place his trust in a physician who was clearly making him worse. But a man may be as cunning as a serpent in one sphere of life, and naive as a schoolboy in another. I took a deep breath, then said, 'Bealknap, why do you not go and see my friend Dr Malton? Get another opinion?'

'That brown Moor? And what if Dr Archer found out? He would stop treating me.'

'Dr Archer need not know.'

'Dr Malton would want paying in advance, I imagine. A new fee for him.'

'No,' I said evenly. But if Bealknap went to Guy, I would pay him myself rather than leave Guy to chase him for payment.

Bealknap's eyes narrowed into a calculating look. I could see he was wondering whether he could get a free appointment out of this, and thus to his strange way of thinking score a point against me.

'Very well.' He spoke aggressively, as though accepting a challenge. 'I will go. I will hear what he has to say.'

'Good. You will find him down at Bucklersbury. I am seeing him tomorrow, shall I make an appointment for you?'

His eyes narrowed. 'Why are you doing this? To find some profit for your friend?'

'I do not like to see anyone brought low by bad medical treatment. Even you, Bealknap.'

'How can laymen know what is good or bad treatment?' he muttered, then turned and walked away without thanks.

I watched him go, his stick tapping on the stone flags. Why had I done this, I asked myself. I realized that if Guy was able to help Bealknap, which was at least possible, it would be me who in a way would have scored a point against my old enemy. And given myself a sense of virtue, too. I wondered if that was partly why I had offered to help him. But if we never acted except when we were certain our motives were pure, we would never act at all.

Chapter Thirty

For the rest of the day I worked steadily in my office. The rain began again, coming down heavily all afternoon. Barak was there too; in no mood for conversation, occasionally wincing, probably at the pains in his head after his drinking bout; so far as I was concerned, he deserved them. Towards evening a rider came from Cranmer's office summoning me to a conference at Lambeth the following afternoon. I reflected there could have been no dramatic developments or he would have wanted to see me at once. It must be our lack of progress he wished to discuss. I went to bed early; it rained heavily again in the night and I woke a couple of times to hear it pattering on the roof. I thought of the killer, out there somewhere. He could be watching the house now, for rain and cold meant little to him. Or he could be sitting in some room, somewhere in the vast city, listening to the rain as I was, while heaven knew what thoughts went through his mind.

Next morning was fine and sunny again, the warmest day so far. The spring was moving on. Sitting at breakfast I saw Tamasin walking on her own around the garden, pausing to look at the crocuses and the daffodils. She walked back towards the house and sat on the bench next to the kitchen door. I went outside to join her. Her bruises were quite gone now, her face strikingly pretty once again. But she looked preoccupied. She half rose as I approached, and I waved her to stay seated.

'Is that bench not wet?' I asked.

'It is kept dry by the eaves. Your garden is beautiful,' she added wistfully.

'I have had a lot of work done here over the years. How is Jack this morning? I think he did not go out again last night.'

'No. He still had a sore head.' She took a deep breath. 'But he has apologized. He said what he told you, that when this business is over he will move us to a little house somewhere. Perhaps even with a garden. He said it would give me something to do. I wish he had told me first.'

'Would that cheer you?'

'I would like a garden,' she replied in a flat tone. 'But I doubt we could afford that.'

'Perhaps it is time I reviewed his salary.'

'I am surprised you do not dismiss him, after how he has behaved in your house,' she said with cold anger.

'We have all been under great strain, Tamasin.'

'I know.' She looked at me seriously. 'But the troubles with Jack began long before this, as you know.'

'He knows he has done wrong, Tamasin. When all this is over, and you are settled somewhere else, things will be better. You will see.'

She shook her head. 'You know what a sharp tongue he has. He has sulked and got drunk and insulted me before. Then he is sorry and says he loves me, then he does it again and says he is sorry again and so it goes on. It is our lost child that has driven us apart.'

'There are worse husbands,' I said quietly. 'He does not beat you.'

'Am I to be grateful for that?'

'Give him time, Tamasin.'

'Sometimes I think, why should I bear this? I even think of leaving, only I have nowhere to go.' She bit her lip. 'I should not burden you with this, sir.'

'Only you have no one else.' I looked at her seriously. 'For what it is worth I think you should remember Jack is under great pressure now.'

'I used to admire his adventurousness, at the same time as I wanted him to settle down. After this I think he will be only too happy to live a quiet life. But will he want to live it with me?'

'I believe so. I am sorry; it was I who involved him in all this. Because my friend was killed.'

She looked at me. 'How is his widow?'

'She is strong. But the weight of grief still lies full on her.'

Tamasin gave me a searching look. I wondered if she had divined something of my feelings for Dorothy. I rose. 'I have to do some work, then go to Lambeth Palace.'

'The Archbishop?'

'Yes.'

'Take care, sir,' she said.

'And you, Tamasin. You take care too.'

I left her and went round to the stables. I decided not to take Barak with me. Left alone together, perhaps he and Tamasin might be able to talk more. I would have been reluctant to walk to Westminster alone, but felt safer on my horse, though I had not had that sense of someone following me lately. I felt sorry for Tamasin, sorry for Barak too now. I thought again of Dorothy. Doubts came into my mind; my feelings for her might have lain dormant all these years, but there was no reason she should ever feel as strongly. Yet perhaps, in time – I told myself I must wait and see how things developed over the months to come.

Young Timothy was in the stable, scraping dung-laden old straw into a pail. A batch of new straw stood by the door. Genesis stood in his stall, looking on placidly. I was glad to see the horse was at ease with the boy.

'How are you faring, Timothy?'

'Well, sir.' He smiled, a flash of white teeth in his dirty face. It was the first time I had seen him smile. 'Master Orr has been teaching me and Peter our letters.'

'Ah yes, I saw him with Peter. It is good to know them.'

'Yes, sir, only—'

'Yes.'

'He talks about God all the time.'

I thought, and you will have little time for God after your experiences at Yarington's. 'You and Peter are getting along?' I asked, changing the subject.

'Yes, sir. So long as I leave him to his work, and stick to mine.'

'Good. You seem to have made friends with Genesis.'

'He is an easy horse.' He hesitated. 'Do you know, sir, what became of Master Yarington's horse?'

'I am afraid not. Someone will buy him.' Timothy looked crestfallen. 'I do not need another horse,' I said. 'Now come, saddle Genesis for me.'

I rode out, thinking how sad it was that the child's only friend had been Yarington's horse. But I drew the line at buying it for him. The stable was not large enough, apart from anything. I pulled aside hastily to avoid a grey-bearded pedlar pushing a cartload of clothes. Waifs and strays, I thought. And beggars and pedlars. Everywhere. The hospital — when this was over I must set to work on the hospital.

✝

THE RIDE TO Westminster Stairs took longer than usual, for the streets were waterlogged and one or two were flooded. I heard people saying the Tyburn had overflowed in its upper reaches, flooding the fields. I noticed a printer's shop, closed and shuttered, and wondered if the owner had been taken away by Bonner's men.

When I arrived in Cranmer's office at Lambeth Palace the atmosphere was tense. All the men of power who had involved themselves in this grim quest were gathered. Harsnet stood near the door, looking downcast. Lord Hertford stood opposite, stroking his long beard, anger in his prominent eyes. His brother, Sir Thomas, stood next to him, arms folded, looking grim. As usual he was dressed in bright, expensive clothes: a doublet in a bold green, the arms slashed to show a vermilion silk lining. Cranmer sat behind his desk in his white robe and stole, his face severe.

'I hope I am not late, my lord.'

'I cannot stay long,' he said. 'There are matters I must attend to.'
He looked drawn and anxious. 'Among them trying to persuade the
Privy Council to allow me to have Dean Benson in for questioning
without saying why.' He laughed bitterly. 'When most of them would
rather have *me* arrested than him.'

Hertford looked at me. 'We have been asking Coroner Harsnet
how it is he cannot find this Goddard despite all the resources we
have given him.'

'It is easy to disappear in London,' I said. Harsnet gave me a
brief, grateful nod.

'But this man must have antecedents.' Hertford slapped a hand
violently on to his desk, an unexpected gesture that made us all start.
'He must have come from somewhere before he joined the abbey, or
did he spring from the earth like some demon from Hell?'

'I do not believe his family are from within London,' Harsnet
said. 'I think they may have come from the nearer parts of Middlesex,
or Surrey or Kent. It must be near enough for him to ride into
London. I am still making enquiries with the officials of all those
counties, but it takes time.'

'Time is what we do not have,' Cranmer said. 'There are still
three more vials to be poured out, three more murders to come, and
with each it gets harder to conceal what is happening.' Cranmer
looked at me sternly. 'Master Harsnet says you think there may be
another suspect. Some young man who visited Yarington's whore.
The whore who escaped,' he added, with a sidelong look at Harsnet.
They were blaming him for everything: the lack of progress, the escape
of the whore and Lockley's vanishing.

'The fact he knew Yarington kept a girl in his house makes this
visitor a suspect,' I said carefully. 'But there is nothing to link him
to the other murders. Yet all the evidence against Goddard, too, is
circumstantial.' I glanced at Harsnet again, then back at the Archbishop. 'My lord, the man we seek is very clever. He seems to have
made killing his life's mission.'

'More like a man possessed by the devil than a madman,' Lord Hertford observed. Was he, too, of Harsnet's way of thinking, I wondered.

'We do not know what he is,' I answered.

'Something new,' Sir Thomas said. 'Well, the world is full of new things.' He gave a quick, cynical half-smile. I thought, this is like an interesting puzzle to him. 'Maybe we should leave this man to fulfil his prophecy,' he said. 'Concentrate on covering up the murders. When he has completed the seven he will stop, surely. Perhaps he thinks the world will come to an end then. When it does not, perhaps it will be too much for him. Perhaps he will kill himself.'

'I do not think someone so devoted to killing could stop,' I said quietly.

'I agree,' Cranmer said. 'And how can we allow these outrages to continue?' He turned again to Harsnet. 'How many men do you have at your disposal, Gregory?'

'Four.'

'And you are circulating the names Cantrell supplied amongst the radical brethren?'

'Yes.'

'And now we need to find Lockley as well as that girl Abigail.' Cranmer considered. 'You need more men. People who are competent to make these enquiries. I dare not take men from my household, there are spies there now.'

'I need to be careful too,' Lord Hertford agreed.

'Perhaps I can help,' Sir Thomas said. 'I have a household full of clever young men, and a good steward. I can lend you a dozen if you like.'

His brother and Cranmer exchanged glances. I could see that they were wondering how far he could be trusted. I wondered why he had made the offer. Perhaps for him this was an adventure now, the Turkish war on a small scale. Hertford hesitated, then nodded.

'Very well, Thomas,' Cranmer said. 'If you could make some

men quietly available that would help us greatly. But they must come under the direct supervision of Coroner Harsnet.'

Seymour looked at the coroner. 'My men are to be placed under the orders of a clerk?'

'If you want to be involved, yes,' Lord Hertford told him bluntly.

Sir Thomas met his gaze for a moment, then shrugged.

'I will use them well,' Harsnet said. 'I can send them to the constables of all the villages round London – from Barnet and Enfield to Bromley and Surbiton – to find whether the name Goddard is known.'

The Archbishop looked at Harsnet. 'Perhaps I should have set this in train before, given you more resources.'

I looked at him with respect; it was unheard of for anyone in power to admit a mistake. Harsnet nodded in gratitude.

'And you, Matthew,' Cranmer added, 'keep thinking, keep puzzling it over. That is your role. And keep yourself and your household safe.' He put his hand to his mouth, kneading his lower lip between his finger and thumb. 'What will he do, do you think, when he has poured out the seven vials?'

'Find a new theme for murder,' I answered. 'There are plenty in Revelation.'

✝

CRANMER CLOSED the meeting shortly after, asking the Seymour brothers to stay behind. Harsnet and I walked together along the dim passageways of the Archbishop's palace.

'These new men will be a great help,' he said.

'Yes,' I agreed. 'Cranmer understands how hard you are working,' I added.

'He is always most loyal to those who serve him. Yet I feel I let him down, letting the whore escape then losing Lockley. I let the steward go, by the way. He knew nothing more.'

'We all make mistakes, Gregory.'

He shook his head. 'I should have served him better. Particularly with all the strain he is under now. You saw how troubled and afraid he is.'

'No evidence of heresy has been found among his associates who were arrested?'

'No. There would be none to find. The Archbishop is too cautious to hire men whom the papists would call heretics.'

'Then perhaps he will be safe. His enemies cannot go to the King without evidence.'

'They will not give up easily. And things are going badly in Parliament. The Act to prevent women and common folk from reading the Bible is progressing fast. But Christ and his saints will nevertheless win the final victory, for so we are told.' His tone became intense. 'The persecuted church is the true church.' He gave me a piercing look, suddenly the hot-gospeller.

'What news on Catherine Parr?' I asked to change the subject.

'Still she will not agree to marry the King. They say she thinks on the fate of Catherine Howard. Better to think on God's will, the chance she has been given to influence the King.'

'How can we ever be sure what God's will is?'

He smiled, his severe mood gone as quickly as it had come. 'Oh, but one can, Matthew. If one prays. As one day you will understand, I am sure of it.'

✠

I RODE BACK along the riverbank to London Bridge. I passed the spot where we had found Dr Gurney's body. In the distance I could see the squatters' cottages where Tupholme had been mutilated and left to die. That day the river sparkled in the spring sunshine, the beds of reeds behind the path soughing gently in a light breeze. I wondered if I would ever be able to appreciate the beauty of the vista again.

I crossed the river at London Bridge and rode into town through the crowded streets. Though feeling much safer on horseback, I still looked around warily as I rode along. On the corner between Thames

Street and New Fish Street a pair of beggars sat underneath the new clock tower they were building there, no more than steps and scaffolding as yet. Two sturdy-looking young men in ragged clothes and battered caps, they sat staring out at the crowd. A woman sat between them, also dressed in rags, her head cast down. As I passed, she looked up, and I saw that she was beautiful, a young maid no more than sixteen. She met my eyes with a desolate look. I thought of the tooth-drawers, who would pay to destroy her face.

The taller of the two young men saw my eyes meet hers. He stood up and took a couple of steps towards me.

'Don't you eye up my sister!' he shouted in a country accent. 'Think you're fucking wonderful in your fine robe, don't you, fucking hunchback! Give us some money, we're starving!'

I moved the horse along, as fast as I could through the crowds. My heart thumped as I heard the beggar try to follow me through the crowd, a shower of insults and demands for money at my back. People turned and stared back at him. 'It costs money to look at normal people, bent-back!' I looked over my shoulder. The beggar's friend had taken his arm and was pulling him back to the clock tower, afraid of attracting the constable. I moved on, glad the encounter had not taken place at night.

✝

THE FOLLOWING MORNING I rode down to Guy's shop. I tied Genesis up outside and knocked at his door. Holding the reins had made my stitches pull again; I would be glad to have them out.

Guy himself opened the door. To my surprise he was wearing a pair of wood-framed spectacles. He smiled at my astonishment. 'I need these for reading now. I am getting old. I used to take them off when visitors called, but I have decided that is the sin of vanity.'

I followed him inside. Seeing his magnified eyes behind the glasses reminded me of Cantrell; I wondered how he was faring, stumbling about his miserable hovel.

Guy had been sitting at his table. The big anatomical volume lay open there, revealing more gruesome illustrations. A quill and ink pot stood next to it; Guy had been making notes on a piece of paper. He invited me to sit. I took a stool at the table. Guy sat opposite me. He gestured to the book, which I had avoided looking at.

'The more I study this text the more I realize it changes every-thing.' There was excitement in Guy's voice. 'All the old medical books we have been reading for hundreds of years, Galen and Hippocrates and the other Greeks and Romans, they have so much wrong. And if they are wrong on anatomy, may not everything else they say be called into question?'

'Beware the College of Physicians if you claim such things. To them those books are Holy Writ.'

'But they are *not* Holy Writ. They are the works of men, no more. And they have become binds and fetters, no one may question them. At least in your sphere of study there are developments, changes. The law progresses.'

'Mostly at the pace of an old tired snail. But yes, it does.'

'I begin to see these old medical texts as no more than an infinite chaos of obscurities.'

'You could say that about the law, too. But yes, we take so much ancient knowledge for granted,' I said. 'Like the Book of Revelation. Yet people need certainties, more than ever in these disturbed and disoriented times.'

He frowned. 'Even if those certainties bring hurt to them and others. Do you know, I heard a tale the other day at the Physicians' Hall of one of those end-timers, who thinks Armageddon is almost upon us, who broke his leg and refused to have it treated, though the bone was sticking through the skin and it would become infected. He said he was certain the Second Coming would take place before he died. He thought his broken leg a test from God. It is a paradox. Revelation,' he said. 'How it has dominated Christian imagery. I believe that many people thought the year 1000 was the end of Time, and stood on hills waiting for the end of the world. What an evil book it is, for it says that humanity is nothing, is worth nothing.' He sighed, shook his head, then managed a sad smile. 'How is your arm?'

'The stitches pull. I would like to have them out.'

'It has only been five days,' he said doubtfully. 'But let me look.'

He smiled warmly when I removed my robe and doublet, and showed him my arm. It looked almost mended.

'Piers did a good job there. And it has healed well, you're a fast healer, Matthew. Yes, I think those may come out. Piers!' he called out. Evidently the boy was going to cut them out as well as put them in.

'He is doing so well.' Guy's face brightened. 'He learns so fast.'

There was much I could have asked but I held my tongue. Instead I told Guy about Bealknap. 'He went to Dr Archer complaining of weakness and nausea, and he has been purging and bleeding him so that there is little of him left. I feel he may die.'

Guy looked thoughtful. 'I am afraid he would not be the first patient Archer killed with his treatment. He is the most traditional of traditionalists. Yet I ought not to take another doctor's patient.'

'Bealknap wants a second opinion. He begins to realize Archer is doing him harm. He started with fainting and a bad stomach; I think he is quite ill now.'

'Bealknap. I remember that name. He has done you harm in the past, has he not?'

'Yes. He is the greatest rogue in Lincoln's Inn. In fact, I will pay your fee, otherwise you will have to battle for it. I imagine he is making Archer wait for his money.'

'You would help an enemy?'

I smiled. 'Then he will owe me a moral debt. I would like to see how he deals with that. Do not think my motives are of unalloyed purity.'

'Whose are?' He looked sad, then smiled at me. 'I think also you do not like to see suffering.'

'Perhaps.'

The smile faded from my face as the door opened and Piers

entered, neat in his blue apprentice's robe, the usual bland respectful expression on his handsome face. Guy stood and touched his arm.

'Piers. Your patient is here. Take him through to the other room, would you?'

Piers bowed. 'Good morning, Master Shardlake.'

I rose reluctantly and followed him out. I had hoped Guy might come to supervise, but he stayed with his book. In the treatment room, with its shelves lined with more apothecary's jars, its long table and its racks of fearsome-looking instruments, Piers smiled and gestured to a stool beside the table. 'Would you bare your arm, sir, then sit there?'

I rolled up my shirtsleeve again. Piers turned and looked over Guy's instruments. I stared at his broad, blue-robed back. When Guy had praised him just now I had seen a haunted look in his eyes, almost as though he were trying to console himself with the boy's skill. But what was he hiding?

Piers selected a small pair of scissors, opened and closed them experimentally, then turned to me with a deferential smile, though I thought I saw cold amusement in his eyes. I watched apprehensively as he bent and snipped the black stitches. He did it gently, though, then took a pair of tweezers and slowly pulled out the broken threads. I sighed with relief when it was over, the constant pulling sensation of the last few days gone. Piers looked at my arm.

'There. All is healed. It is wonderful how Dr Malton's poultices prevent wounds from becoming infected.'

'Yes, it is.'

'There will be a scar of course, it was a nasty gash.'

'You are learning a lot from Dr Malton?'

'Far more than from my old master.' Piers smiled. 'He was one of those apothecaries who believed in exotic herbs prepared in consultation with astrological charts.'

'A traditionalist?'

'If I might dare to say it, sir, I think he was not quite honest. He had the dried-up body of some strange, large lizard with a long tail in his shop. He would cut bits off, powder them up and get people to take the powder. Because the lizard was so strange, patients thought it had some great power.' He gave a cynical smile that made him look older than his years. 'People always believe in the power of the strange and unfamiliar. It is good to be working with Dr Malton now. An honest man, a man of reason.'

'Your old master died, I believe.'

'Yes.' Piers fetched down one of the jars. He opened it, and I caught the sickly smell of the ointment Guy had used before. Piers put some on the end of a spatula and touched it to my arm, spreading it gently. 'It was the smallpox killed him. The strange thing was, he did not dose himself with any of his own remedies. I think he did not believe in them himself. He simply took to his bed and waited to see if the pox would kill him. Which it did. There, that is done, sir.'

I found Piers' even, unemotional tone in talking of his master's death distasteful.

'Had he family?'

'No. There was just him and me. Dr Malton came and did what he could for him, but the smallpox takes its own path, does it not? Sometimes it kills, sometimes it disfigures. My parents died of it when I was small.'

'I am sorry.'

'Dr Malton has been father and mother to me to since I came here.'

'He said he is going to help you train to become a physician.'

Piers looked up sharply, perhaps wondering why I was asking taking such an interest. He knew I did not like him.

'Yes.' He hesitated, then said, 'I do appreciate all the kindness he has shown me.'

'Yes, his kindness is of a rare sort.' I stood up. 'Thank you for seeing to my arm.'

Piers bowed. 'I am glad it is better.'

I left the room. He did not follow me. I remembered him listening at the door when we were talking of the murders. I thought, Guy might be kind, but you are not. You are cold and calculating, like a predatory animal. You have some hold over my friend, and I will discover what it is.

✝

NEXT DOOR, Guy was still reading his book. He offered me a glass of wine and asked to look at my arm. He nodded with satisfaction. 'Piers has done a good job.'

'I do wonder if he possesses the human sympathy one would hope for in a physician.'

'He has had little chance to develop it. His parents died when he was young. And my late neighbour, Apothecary Hepden, worked him hard and taught him little.'

'He told me about his death. He seems to have thought little of him.'

'Yes, Piers can speak harshly. But I believe he has the capacity for sympathy, I believe I can teach it to him.'

'He says you are a father and mother to him.'

'Did he say that?' Guy smiled, then his expression turned sombre.

'What are you thinking?' I asked gently.

'Nothing.' He changed the subject. 'I have been to see Adam Kite again. You know, I think there is improvement. That woman keeper, Ellen, she works hard with him. She forces him to eat and clean himself, tries to pull him away from his obsession with constant prayer.'

'Did you know she is a former patient, and is not allowed to leave the precinct?'

'No.' Guy looked taken aback. 'That surprises me.'

'She told me herself.'

'She is gentle with Adam, but very firm. It has had an effect. The other day he even talked of normal everyday things for a minute. He said the weather is getting warmer, he did not feel so cold. But still I cannot get him to explain why he feels such a sense of sin. I wonder what brought it on.'

'What do his parents say? I saw you leave with them after the court hearing.'

'They say they have no idea. I believe them.'

'Thank you for doing this. Adam cannot be – easy to work with.'

Guy smiled sadly. 'He touches me, yet intrigues me too. So like you with Bealknap, my motives are not all pure.'

'I ought to visit Adam again.'

'I am going to see him again tomorrow morning. Would you like to come?'

'Very well. If I can.'

'You do not sound as if you want to.'

'I find it distressing. He is in such pain. And religious madness makes me think of the man we are hunting, and who has been hunting me.' I looked at my arm. 'How can he believe that what he is doing is inspired by God?'

'Have we not seen enough these last years to know that men may do cruel, wicked things, yet believe they have communion with God? Think of the King.'

'Yes. Belief in God and human sympathy can be very different things. Yet the killer is something different again. That obsessive savagery.' I looked at Guy. 'He still has three murders to commit. And if he succeeds, I, like you, do not think he will stop. I told Cranmer so today.'

'No. Such a momentum would have to be carried forward. Till he is caught, or dies.'

'How will he feel if he pours out the seven vials of wrath and the world does not end?'

'There have been many in these last years who thought they knew when the world would end. When it does not they go back to Revelation for the clues they have missed. And that is easy. It is not a story in sequence but a series of violent narratives giving alternative ways in which the world will finish. So they find a new formula.'

I nodded slowly. 'Does he suffer, I wonder?'

'The killer?' Guy shook his head. 'I do not know. My guess would be the acts of killing are a sort of ecstasy for him, but perhaps, that apart, he lives in a world of pain.'

'But he conceals it — he is able to live a normal life or something like it. Without standing out.'

'Yes. I think among the many things he is, he is a good actor.'

'Is it Goddard?' I shook my head. 'I don't know. Harsnet still thinks he is possessed.'

Guy shook his head. 'No. He is an obsessive, and all obsessions come from some maladjustment of the brain. Not the devil.' He set his lips. I thought, why are you sure?

We were silent for a moment. Then I asked, 'What happens after the vials are poured out? In Revelation. What comes next?'

Guy rose and went to his bookshelf. He brought down a New Testament and turned to Revelation.

'The seven vials of wrath are in Chapters 15 to 16. Already before then there has been another version of the end of the world, disasters coming when the seven angels blow their trumpets.' He turned the pages with his long brown fingers. 'Hail and fire, a mountain falling into the sea. But there is not such concentration on the torments of men as there is in the story of the seven vials. Perhaps that was what attracted the killer.' He paused, turned the page. 'The judgement of the Great Whore comes after.'

'When I read them, those passages seemed more obscure than most. Who is the Great Whore meant to be?'

Guy smiled sadly. 'It used to be thought she symbolized the Roman Empire, but now the radicals say she represents the Church of Rome. And after that, war in Heaven and Jesus' final victory.'

He passed the book across to me. I had studied the passages about the seven vials to exhaustion, but now I read on, aloud. '*I saw a woman sit upon a rose-coloured beast, full of names of blasphemy, having seven heads and ten horns.*' I remembered the painting of the creature in the Westminster chapterhouse. '*And the woman was arrayed in purple and rose colour ... And upon her forehead was a name written, Mystery, Babylon the*

Great, the Mother of whoredom and abominations of the earth ... and the beast that was, and is not, even he is the eighth, and is of the seven, and shall go into destruction ... her sins have reached into heaven, and God hath remembered her iniquities.' I put the Testament down with a sigh. 'I can make little sense of it.'

'Nor I.'

We both jumped violently at a loud hammering on the door to the street. We exchanged glances. As Guy crossed to open it, the inner door opened and Piers came in. I wondered whether he had been listening outside again.

'Who is it?' Guy called out.

'It is I, Barak!'

Guy threw open the door. I caught a glimpse of Sukey, tied to the rail beside Genesis. She was breathing heavily, Barak must have ridden here fast. There was no sign of drunkenness about him today, he was sober and alert, his expression hard and serious. He stepped inside.

'There has been another killing,' he said. 'There's some strange mystery about this one. Dr Malton, sir, can you come with us?'

Chapter Thirty-one

'WHO?' I ASKED.

Barak glanced at Piers. Guy turned to the boy. 'Would you fetch my horse to the front of the house?' he asked. Piers hesitated for a moment, then went out. Barak looked between us. His face was set hard.

'It's Lockley's wife.'

'He has killed a woman?' Guy gasped.

'Sir Thomas sent a man round to keep guard at the inn. He was too late. He found her lying on the inn floor. She's been mutilated. The message said something strange, something about poisoned air. We're to join Harsnet there at once.'

'What about Lockley?'

'I don't know.'

Through the window I saw Piers leading Guy's old white mare round to the front. We went outside.

'May I come too?' Piers asked Guy as we mounted.

'No, Piers, you have studying to do. You should have done it last night.' The apprentice stepped back, an expression of angry sulkiness momentarily crossing his face.

'How much does that boy know about what has been happening?' I asked Guy as we rode quickly up the street.

'Only that there has been a series of murders. He could not fail to see that,' Guy added with a touch of asperity, 'as he has been helping me at the autopsies. He knows he must hold his tongue.'

'You know he listens at doors,' I said. Guy did not reply.

✝

WE RODE ON rapidly, up to Smithfield and on to Charterhouse
Square. The square was deserted except for two men standing at the
door of the inn, under the sign of the Green Man. One was Harsnet
and the other was a tall man carrying a sword, who was coughing
into a handkerchief. I saw some of the beggars standing by the chapel,
looking on from a distance but not daring to approach. We pulled
up and tied the horses to the rail next to Harsnet's. Guy went over to
the tall man. 'What ails you?' he asked quietly.

The man lowered his handkerchief. He was in his twenties, with
a neat black beard. He stared for a moment at Guy's dark face, then
said, 'I do not know. I came here two hours ago. I knocked but
could get no answer.' He coughed violently again. 'The shutters were
all closed so I broke in. There is a woman lying on the floor, she's –
mutilated.' He spluttered noisily. 'There's something in the air in
there, it's poisonous, it burns at my throat.'

'Let me see,' Guy said. He gently opened the man's mouth and
looked in. 'Something's irritated your throat,' he said. 'Sit down on
the step, try to breathe easy.'

'It was horrible. Like something grasping to take your breath.'

I looked at the door: the lock was smashed. The guard had pulled
it shut again when he came out.

'Have you been inside?' I asked Harsnet.

'No. I looked in – one sniff was enough; it's like this fellow said,
like something trying to rip your throat out.' He looked at Guy.
'How do you come to be here, sir?'

'I was with Dr Malton when the message came,' I said. 'Dr
Malton may be able to help us. Guy, what do you think can have
happened to the air?'

'There is only one way to see.' He pulled a handkerchief from his
pocket, held it to his nose and threw the door wide open. I took a
step back as something sharp and stinging caught my nostrils. Guy
went in. With the shutters drawn the interior was dark. I made out a
large pale shape, spotted with darker patches, lying under the open
serving hatch. A body.

Guy stepped rapidly to the shutters, throwing them open. A draught of fresh air was immediately drawn into the room with the light. We looked in from the doorway. I saw the tavern was in chaos, overturned chairs and tables everywhere. The pale shape under the serving hatch was indeed Mistress Bunce, lying face down on the stone floor. Her coif had been removed, revealing her long dark hair. Her dress had been pulled up to beneath her armpits, and her underskirt torn off; it lay bundled up under one of the tables. Her plump, pale body was half naked, her arms tied behind her with rope.

'Shit.' Barak breathed.

I saw red weals at her wrists where the poor woman had struggled to free herself, but the knots were tight. There was another piece of cloth lying beside her face, something dark red on top of it.

'Dear God, what has he done to her?' Harsnet breathed. I saw his hands were clenched tight.

Guy crossed to the body and stood looking down at it. Quickly, he crossed himself. Harsnet, watching from the doorway, narrowed his eyes at the gesture. 'It is safe to come in,' Guy said quietly. 'The fumes are dispersing. But put handkerchiefs to your noses and mouths, take shallow breaths.'

Harsnet and Barak and I drew out our handkerchiefs and stepped cautiously inside. 'What was that stuff?' Barak asked.

'Vitriol,' Guy answered. 'In a very powerful concentration.'

We looked down at the body. The white flesh on the trunk and legs bore big red marks that looked like burns. To my horror, half the woman's posterior had been burned away, leaving a huge, monstrous red wound. Yet there was no blood around her, only a pool of colourless liquid.

'What is this vitriol?' Harsnet asked Guy. The air was much clearer, but there still a faint harsh tang. 'For God's sake, what did he do to her?' His voice rose.

'Vitriol is a liquid that burns and dissolves everything it touches,' Guy answered grimly. 'It is well known, alchemists make it up frequently to dissolve stone. They think it has special powers because gold is one of the few things it cannot destroy. It must have taken hours to do this, using repeated applications.' Then Guy did something I had never seen him do before, no matter what awful things he had to look upon. He shuddered violently.

Harsnet bent to the liquid under the body. 'What's this?' He put out a finger.

'Don't touch it!' Guy shouted, and Harsnet quickly stepped away. Guy took a spatula from the pocket of his robe and touched it to the liquid. There was a faint hiss and it began to smoke. 'Vitriol,' he said. 'See how it has eaten into the wood. It has even marked the stone flags.'

'If it's so poisonous,' I asked, 'how did he manage to wait here for hours?'

'I suspect it was night, and he had those large shutters giving on to the yard open. Even so he would need to keep going over to the window.'

Barak was looking through the serving hatch. Cups and pewter goblets stood on a draining board; more lay in the washing bowl. It seemed the killer had come just after the tavern closed; perhaps he had been a late customer.

'Janley!' Harsnet called. The guard entered reluctantly, staring with horrified eyes at the mutilated corpse. 'Search the rest of the building,' Harsnet ordered. 'Go on!' Reluctantly, his hand on his sword, Janley opened a door to the inner chambers and stepped through.

'Was it Lockley?' I breathed. 'Is he the killer?'

'Perhaps Lockley's been killed too. Perhaps he's in another room,' Barak said. He wiped his brow, he was sweating.

'*And the fifth angel poured out his vial upon the seat of the beast.*' I quoted from the Book of Revelation, the chapters we all knew now. '*And his kingdom waxed dark; and they gnawed their tongues for pain, and blasphemed the God of Heaven for sorrow and pain of their sores, and repented not of their deeds.*' Guy bent and, very carefully, turned the brutalized body over.. He let out a groaning sigh. I made myself look at Mistress Bunce's face. The lower half was covered with blood. I will never forget the eyes, wide open, bulging from her face in her last horror and agony. Guy felt her jaw, then took out his spatula and gently touched the piece of cloth beside her face, and the red thing on top of it. He took a corner of the cloth and covered it.

'What . . .' I asked.

'It is her tongue. He gagged her with this cloth while he tortured her. Then at the end he removed it. To fulfil the part of the verse that talks of gnawing tongues. He pulled out the tongue and snapped her jaw shut on it.' He touched the slack face. 'Yes, he broke her jaw doing it. At some point after that she died; her heart probably gave out.'

'What sort of creature could do this to a woman?' Harsnet asked, incredulous.

'She's not the first person he's tortured to death,' Barak said. 'The cottar was cut up and left to die. But this is even worse.'

'When the Bible talks of the seat of the beast,' Harsnet said, 'it means the place ruled by the devil, not a human – a human rear. This is like some hideous blasphemous joke. A devil's jest.'

We all turned as Janley returned through the inner door. 'There's nothing,' he said. 'The rest of the house looks normal.'

'Did Lockley do this?' Harsnet asked.

Barak looked at me. 'Begins to seem like he's the killer after all.'

'I still can't see it. I could see him having knowledge of dwale, but what about the legal knowledge that letter to Roger demonstrated? I wouldn't have said Lockley was someone who could write a proper letter.'

'Then where is he?' Harsnet burst out. The terrible scene had unnerved him deeply.

'Lockley vanished and Mrs Bunce dead,' I said quietly. 'Goddard vanished and Cantrell attacked. The three who worked at the Westminster infirmary.'

'Surely Goddard attacked the other two,' Harsnet said.

'It could equally be that Lockley attacked Goddard and Cantrell. Goddard's body could be hidden somewhere.' I shook my head.

'That woman didn't work at the infirmary,' Harsnet said. 'She wasn't even a religious woman, from what you told me.' He glanced at the terrible corpse, then turned to Janley. 'For God's sake, cover her up!' The young man took his handkerchief and laid it over Ethel Bunce's ruined face. He looked green. The awful wounds below still lay exposed. Guy stood, fetched the undershirt from where it had been thrown by the killer and covered them.

'You are from Thomas Seymour's household?' I asked Janley.

'Yes. I am his Master of Horse.'

'I'll warrant you didn't expect a horror like this.'

'No, sir. I was sent to guard a tavern.' He laughed then, a little hysterically.

I turned to Barak. 'I think we should give this house a full search. Come on, let's start with the living quarters.'

✝

WE WALKED UP the narrow wooden staircase. There were two bedrooms. The one where Lockley and Mrs Bunce slept together had a cheap truckle bed. There was no other furniture save a large chest full of women's clothes. 'Poor bloody bitch,' Barak said as he searched through them. 'I think Lockley killed her. It can't have been Goddard.'

'Why not?'

'Because he would have had to reconnoitre the tavern, find out their routines and whether anyone else lived here. I can't think of any way to do that other than coming in as a customer. If it was Goddard, Lockley would have recognized him and told us, surely.'

'That makes sense,' I said. I looked at the cheap, worn dresses and large underclothes that Barak had laid on the bed. The violation of the last privacy of the poor woman downstairs felt like a further humiliation of her. 'Come, put those back. Let's see what's in the other room.'

The second bedroom contained broken chairs and other odds and ends, and another chest, locked with a padlock. I set Barak to picking it, a skill he had learned in his days working for Cromwell. After a couple of minutes, he heaved the lid open, to reveal men's clothes this time, but at the bottom there were a number of small wooden boxes.

Barak took out the boxes and began opening them. One contained two pounds in assorted coins, another some cheap jewellery. But the next contained something very different, a wooden block with a hinge, in the shape of a human jaw. There were holes where teeth could be placed.

'What the hell is this?' Barak asked.

'A block to set dentures in,' I said quietly. I took it from him. 'Remember Tamasin told us the tooth-drawer showed her one. They set teeth in those sockets and fix them in people's mouths. There's an old barrister's wife at Lincoln's Inn who has dentures, but she can't get a block to fit properly, they keep falling out.'

'Maybe she could try some of these,' Barak said. He had opened the remaining four boxes and all contained denture blocks in different sizes. 'What's he got these for?' he asked incredulously. 'Lockley wasn't a barber-surgeon, was he? He worked for one, and left.'

I turned the ugly wooden things over in my hands. The blocks had never been used to house teeth, there were no traces of glue in the tooth-holes. Pictures in my mind came together, some pieces of the puzzle fitting together at last. 'No,' I said quietly. 'He wasn't. I think he was something quite different. Now I understand, now I see what they were being so secretive about. Come, we have to go to Dean Benson, now. Bring those boxes.'

I led the way downstairs. Guy and Harsnet had both sat down at a table marked with the round rings from a hundred goblets of beer. Harsnet looked agitated, Guy drawn and sad. Janley stood by the window, staring out on the tavern yard. Harsnet looked up. 'Anything?' he asked.

'Yes,' I said. 'We need to go to the dean—'

I broke off as there was a sudden loud rumbling noise and the flagstones trembled beneath our feet. Harsnet's eyes widened. 'What in God's name is that?'

'This place is connected to the old Charterhouse sewer system,' I said. 'They must have opened the sluice gate over there. It happened when we came here before. We ought to investigate that cellar. There'll be a way down somewhere.'

'I'll help Goodman Janley look,' Barak said. He laid the boxes of teeth on the counter.

I glanced over at the body. 'What will you do with it?' I asked Harsnet.

'Store it in my cellars at Whitehall. With Yarington.' He gave me an anguished look. 'And keep quiet.'

I nodded.

'Why did you say we must go to the dean?'

'I think I know what he has been holding back.'

'We've found the cellar.' Barak called from inside the house. 'There's a metal hatch in the hallway.'

'We ought to see what's down there,' I said. I went into the stone-flagged hallway, Harsnet following.

Barak had raised the hatchway and stood looking down. There was a ladder. Cold air came from below. Janley appeared with a lamp, a lighted candle inside. Barak took a deep breath. 'Right, let's have a look.'

'Be careful,' I said.

But there was nothing to see in the cellar. The candlelight showed only bare stone flags, barrels stacked against the walls. Barak and Janley found another hatch there, leading down to the sewers. Janley opened it and we caught a whiff of sewer smells.

'Should we go on down?' Janley asked, peering nervously into the darkness.

'No,' Barak said. 'Listen.' There was a sound of rushing water, faint then suddenly loud as someone up at the Charterhouse opened the sluice gates to flush more excess water through. The building shook again, and a rush of vile-smelling air was pushed upwards into the cellar and out through the hatchway to where we stood.

'That's a lot of water,' Barak called up.

'With all the rain the ponds at Islington are probably full to overflowing,' Harsnet said.

Barak and Janley climbed back up and we returned to the main room. Guy rose from his knees by the body, rushes and dust clinging to his robe. He had been praying.

'What is Benson holding back?' Harsnet asked.

'I'll tell you on the way. We—'

There was a knock at the door, faint and hesitant. We looked at each other. Harsnet called, 'Come in!' and the door opened. An elderly couple stepped nervously inside. Both were small and thin, grey-haired, poor folk. They looked at us and then at the thing on the floor. The woman let out a little scream and ran back outside. The man turned to follow but Harsnet called him back. Through the open door we saw his wife standing trembling on the steps.

'Who are you?' Harsnet asked him roughly.

'We lodge next door,' the man said in a thin voice. He rubbed his hands together nervously. 'We heard all the noise, we wondered what was happening.'

'Mistress Bunce has been murdered. Master Lockley has disappeared. I am Master Harsnet, the king's assistant coroner.'

'Oh.'

'Please bring your wife inside. We wish to question you.'

'She's upset,' he said, but Harsnet's look was unyielding. The old man went outside and brought his wife back. She clung to him, avoiding looking at the body.

'We think this happened last night,' I said. 'After the tavern closed. Did either of you hear anything?'

The old man stared at Guy, his dark face and long physician's robe, as though wondering how he had appeared there.

'Last night?' Harsnet repeated impatiently.

'There was a lot of noise at closing time.'

'When was that?'

'They shut at twelve. We were in bed, the noise woke us. It sounded like tables going over. But you get rough people in this tavern now, beggars from the chapel when they have any money. We knew Francis had gone. Ethel has been in a frantic state, asking everyone round the square if they had seen him. She liked to rule the roost, poor Ethel.' He looked around the room, then down at the covered body. 'Did some drunkard kill her?'

'Yes. You heard nothing later on in the night?'

'No'

The woman began to cry. 'Oh please, let us out of here—'

'In a minute. How well did you know Mistress Bunce and Goodman Lockley?'

'We've lived next to the tavern for ten years. We knew Master Bunce before he died, he kept a quiet house. He was a godly man.'

'What do you mean?' I asked.

The neighbour looked between us nervously. 'Only that he belonged to one of the radical congregations. If you talked to him for any length of time he would always bring the Bible and salvation into it.'

'Yet he kept a tavern?' Harsnet sounded incredulous.

The old man shrugged. 'I think he was converted after he bought it. It was his living. And as I say, he kept it very orderly. No swear-ing or fighting.'

'And he kept it closed Sundays,' his wife added. She looked at the covered body and crossed herself. 'Ethel had a hard time of it, a woman trying to run a tavern alone.'

'When did she take up with Lockley?'

'Francis? He came about two years ago. First as a potman, then they got together.' She shook her head. 'I've sometimes thought Eddie Bunce must be turning in his grave, Ethel taking up with an ex-monk.'

'She didn't try to bring Master Lockley into her husband's congre-gation?'

She shook her head again. 'No, we never heard any more about Bible truth after Eddie died, and the tavern began opening on Sundays. She must have left the church.'

'Got a noisier type of customer in,' her husband added gloomily.

Harsnet and I exchanged glances. So Mistress Bunce was an apostate from a radical congregation, like the others.

'Which church did Master Bunce go to?' Harsnet asked.

'Clerkenwell. Those radicals had better watch out, with Bishop Bonner after them.'

'Did Mistress Bunce have any living relatives that you know of?'

'No, sir. We didn't know them well.' He looked at the body again. 'She was decent enough, Ethel, though Francis could be a grump. Even if they did live in sin.'

'We would like to go to the funeral,' his wife said.

The old man looked at us. 'Please, sir, what do you think happened? We only ask because we wonder if we are safe. If there are robbers about.'

'You are not in any danger,' Harsnet said. 'But that is all I can tell you till we investigate further. In the meantime, this is to be kept quiet. You tell no one Mrs Bunce is dead. It could hamper our investigation.'

'But how——'

'You *will* keep quiet. I order it in the King's name. A guard will remain here for now. Thank you for your help,' he concluded in a tone of dismissal.

✟

HARSNET SHOOK his head after the old man led his wife away. 'Poor old creatures,' he said. 'Come then, Matthew, if we are to go to Westminster now. I want to know what you have puzzled out. Janley, stay here, secure that door and keep enquirers away. I will arrange for the body to be removed.'

'Can I go home?' Guy asked.

'Yes,' Harsnet answered shortly. He still did not like or trust Guy, it was clear. With most folk it would have been his colour, but with Harsnet I was sure it was his religion.

✟

WE ALL STEPPED outside, relieved to be out of that dreadful place. We stood on the step, looking out at the wide square. On the other side, in the distance, we saw a coach surrounded by four riders pull into Catherine Parr's courtyard.

'A visitor for Lady Catherine,' I said. 'Perhaps it is the Arch-bishop.'

'If it is, God speed him. True religion needs her help,' Harsnet answered. He walked down the step, and unhitched his horse from the rail. I made to follow, but Barak touched me on the arm.

'What is next?' he asked. 'What happens when the sixth vial is poured?'

Guy answered. 'Revelation talks of great waters being dried up. The Euphrates.'

'How's the arsehole going to make a killing that symbolizes *that*? Dry up the Thames?'

'He'll find a way.' I answered grimly. 'Whatever it is, it will be some other method of torturing another poor soul to death. Jesu knows what.'

Chapter Thirty-two

GUY RODE BACK to Smithfield with us. There he turned left into town, bidding us farewell. 'Shall I see you at the Bedlam tomorrow morning, Matthew? I am going at nine o'clock.'

I agreed to the rendezvous, then watched him for a few moments, a lonely figure in the country road, his stoop noticeable as he rode away.

'Now, Matthew,' Harsnet asked. 'What is it that you have worked out? What are in those little boxes that Barak is carrying?'

I told them what I believed. Lockley had been keeping secrets, the dean too, and perhaps Cantrell.

'Maybe we should talk to Cantrell first,' Barak suggested. 'See if he can confirm it.'

'We can talk to him afterwards,' Harsnet answered grimly. 'I want to confront the dean directly.'

'You could go home, Jack,' I said. 'See Tamasin.'

He shook his head. 'No, I want to see the end of this.' He looked at me, and I saw that like Harsnet and me, he had been deeply shocked by what had been done to Mrs Bunce. 'I wish we could have saved her,' he said.

✝

WE RODE DOWN to Westminster. It was a Saturday; Parliament and the courts were shut, there were fewer people around. Shopkeepers and pedlars eyed us as we passed, and one or two called out, but we ignored them. In the Sanctuary we passed a big cart loaded with planks of newly cut wood, the resin smell sweet in the foul town air.

The cathedral doors were closed but we heard the sound of hymn‑singing from inside, the choir no doubt preparing for service.

'I wonder where the dean is,' I said.

'We will go to his house.'

We rode on to Dean's Yard, passed under the wall into the abbey courtyard and once again tied up the horses outside the pretty old house standing amidst the chaos of building works. Enquiries of the steward revealed that Dean Benson would be occupied in the cathedral all day. Harsnet sent a message asking him to attend us on a matter of urgency which might involve his personal safety. 'That'll bring him,' he said as the steward hurried away, leaving us sitting in the entrance hall.

In a short time we heard footsteps approaching up the garden path. The dean entered. He was breathing heavily; he must have hurried over as soon as he got the message. He looked at us angrily. 'What in the name of Heaven has happened now?' he demanded. 'Why do you say I am in danger?'

'May we speak in your office?' Harsnet asked.

'Very well.' The dean sighed and led us down the corridor, his cassock rustling. After a few steps he turned, staring at Barak, who had followed us, carrying Lockley's boxes. 'And you propose to bring your servant to an interview with me?' he asked me haughtily.

'Barak comes too this time,' Harsnet said, looking the dean hard in the eye. We had agreed this beforehand. 'He has something to show you.'

The dean looked at the boxes Barak carried, shrugged and walked on.

Once in his office, Harsnet told the dean of Ethel Bunce's murder, Lockley's disappearance, and the attack on Cantrell. 'So you see, dean,' he said. 'The killer seems to be focusing his attention now on those associated with the infirmary.'

'Why should that endanger me?' The dean looked at the boxes on Barak's lap and took a sudden deep breath. I saw that he guessed what they might be.

'There was a connection between you and them,' I said. 'More, I think, than the mere fact that you had overall authority over the monks' infirmary and the lay hospital. I think that is what you have been hiding.'

Barak opened the boxes, revealing the dentures. From the way the dean's eyes widened and he sat back in his chair I knew my suspicions were right.

'Let me tell you what I think happened,' I said quietly. 'Goddard used to administer dwale, a powerful and dangerous soporific, to render people unconscious for operations. Meanwhile a fashion came in among the rich for wearing false teeth set in wood. The teeth are usually obtained from healthy young people, preferably as a complete set. Master Barak's wife recently had to have a tooth removed, and the tooth-drawer suggested he pull out the lot, offering to pay her well for them.'

'Is there some meaning to this story?' the dean asked angrily. But his eyes kept going back to the boxes.

'I do not know how often you visit the abandoned parts of the old monastery now, but I have twice encountered a beggar who keeps sneaking into the premises, asking anyone who will listen if they know where his teeth are – he has not a tooth in his head. He is mad, of course, but I wonder what drove him so. Something that was done to him here? Perhaps his teeth were removed, under dwale? Perhaps they were checked for size against one of these boxes we found in Lockley's chest. One of the reasons the tooth-drawers find it hard to get people to volunteer their teeth, even for high sums, is the pain involved. But destitute folk who came here to have their illnesses treated could be offered a dose of dwale to make the process itself painless.'

There was silence in the room. A loud hammering began somewhere outside, making the dean jump. He took a deep breath. 'If Goddard and Lockley, and Cantrell for all I know, had some scheme going in the infirmary, I knew nothing of it. And what has that to do with your hunt for the killer?'

'We need to know all, dean. And from the way you looked at those boxes it is clear this is not news to you.'

A second hammer joined the first. The dean closed his eyes. 'That noise,' he said quietly. 'That endless noise. How am I supposed to be able to think?' He opened his eyes again. He looked between the three of us, then took a deep breath.

'I congratulate you, Serjeant Shardlake. Yes, you are right. Back in 1539, four years ago, I learned Goddard was inviting patients in the lay hospital to sell their teeth. The fashion for false teeth was coming in then, and he had made an arrangement with a local barber-surgeon in Westminster. A man called Snethe, at the sign of the Bloody Growth. He buys teeth, and other things as well from what I hear.' He took another deep breath and then continued. 'Lockley worked with Goddard. By then, everyone knew the monasteries had no future and many of the monks tried to protect their financial security in various ways. That was the way Goddard chose, so he could preserve his status if the monastery closed. Lockley, I imagine, spent his share on drink.'

'How did you learn about this?'

'Young Cantrell told me. He worked in the monks' infirmary and had little to do with the lay hospital, but he learned what was going on, he heard Goddard and Lockley talking one day. Goddard told him to keep it quiet or he would suffer for it, but Cantrell suspected that one or two of the people Goddard and Lockley renderd unconscious for their teeth never woke up.'

'Cantrell,' I said. 'He was terrified at the mention of Goddard's name.'

Benson continued: 'I had been told by Lord Cromwell to seek out any scandals that might be going on, for use if we needed to put pressure on the monks to surrender.' He looked at us again. 'Yes, and all of you worked for him too, so you have no cause to be righteous with me. He told me to let what they were doing continue, so that we could spring a trap if need be, make a scandal of it. But his preference was for the monastery to be closed quietly and peacefully, *without* scandal, because that is what the King wanted. And that is what I achieved.'

'Did Goddard know Cantrell had informed on him?'

'No. I never told him I knew.'

'So more people could have died?' Harsnet said.

'Perhaps. I was under the Lord Cromwell's orders. As all of you know, one did not defy those lightly.' He leaned forward, regaining confidence now. 'And the King would not like to hear a scandal about Westminster, even now. I obeyed Lord Cromwell because he had all the power then, though I had no sympathy for his extreme radicalism in religion. But I knew he would go too far and his enemies on the Council would bring him down. Which is what happened. And now we are going back to more sensible ways.'

'So you swung with the wind,' Harsnet said.

'Better swinging with the wind than swinging in the wind, as many have.' Benson pointed a stubby finger at the coroner. 'The King knows nothing of this, does he? This killer you are seeking? I have been making soundings – oh, very discreetly, do not worry. The King would not be glad to hear Archbishop Cranmer had been keeping things from him, not at this time when there are so many voices raised against him.' He turned to me. 'Your search does not go well, does it? You seem to be caught up in a nasty tangle, master crookback. You would not want to annoy the King a second time.'

Harsnet turned to me, ignoring Benson. 'Where does this leave us? Is the killer some demented ex-patient of theirs?'

'I doubt it,' I said. 'They were poor, helpless folk. Yet there is some link, there has to be.'

'It's Goddard,' Harsnet said. 'He is choosing victims he knows.' He looked at the dean. 'You've told us everything?'

'All, now. On my oath as Dean of Westminster.'

'I know how much that is worth, sir,' Harsnet replied, his voice full of contempt.

Benson glared at him, then turned to me 'Am I safe?' he asked.

'I do not think you are at risk,' I replied. 'All five victims so far were associated with radical religion and moved away from it. But you, I think, were always a time-server,' I dared to say.

'A practical man, as I told you before, master crookback.'

✝

OUTSIDE THE HOUSE Harsnet shook his head.

'We are no further forward,' I said.

'At least we know how ruthless, and indeed cruel, both Lockley and Goddard could be. Why could Benson not tell us earlier about that scheme? He knows he is safe,' he added bitterly.

I did not reply. It occurred to me that the aggressive way Harsnet had tackled the dean from the beginning had not helped. He had been ruled by his dislike of the man. Sometimes dealing with political creatures one must dissemble and pretend friendship, as they do.

'And why didn't Cantrell tell us about this either?' he asked.

'Too afraid, I should think. It didn't do him much good telling Benson. We had better go and see what he says now. We can leave the horses here.' I pointed to the door in the wall, leading to Dean's Yard. 'There, that is where he lives. Though "exists" might be a better word.'

We went out and crossed the road to the tumbledown shop. 'I see no guard,' Harsnet said.

'Knowing him, he may have refused to have one.'

'Then he must be made to.'

'There I agree.'

We crossed the road and knocked at the door. After a moment Cantrell opened it. 'It is you, again, sir,' he said without enthusiasm. He peered at Harsnet through his glasses. 'Who is this?'

'I am the London assistant coroner,' Harsnet said, mildly enough. 'Master Shardlake is working with me. We wanted to see how you fared. We hoped to see a guard at the house.'

'He is out the back.'

'May we come in?'

Cantrell's shoulders sagged wearily as we followed him down the musty corridor to the parlour, Harsnet leading the way. The place still smelled of unwashed skin and bad food. We went into the dirty little parlour. I saw the window to the yard had been repaired. Outside a burly man wearing a sword sat on an old box, eating bread and cheese. Cantrell gestured at him. 'He insisted. I don't want a man in the house. He can stay out there.'

I looked round the parlour. There was a broken dish on the floor by the table, pottage leaking into the floorboards.

'My dinner,' Cantrell said gloomily. 'I dropped it when you knocked. I tried to put it on the table, but missed.'

'You should get your eyes seen to,' I said. 'Remember I said I know a physician who would see you for no fee.' I would pay Guy's fee, I decided. If I could do it for Bealknap, I could do it for poor Cantrell.

Cantrell stared at me. I wondered what his eyes looked like exposed, what disease ailed them. He was silent a moment, then said, 'I am afraid, sir. Afraid he will say I am going blind.'

'Or he may say new glasses would help you. Let me make an appointment.'

'How long will I have to have that man here guarding me?' he asked sullenly.

'He may be needed for some time yet,' Harsnet said. 'I have to tell you that Francis Lockley has disappeared and the woman he was living with has been killed. The man who broke in here – could it possibly have been Lockley?'

Cantrell stared at us, his mouth falling open with surprise. 'No, it wasn't Francis. He was short, and the man who broke in here was tall. Dr Goddard was a tall man.'

'With a large mole on the side of his nose, Serjeant Shardlake said?'

'Yes.'

'And with a cut on his head after you thwacked him with that piece of wood,' Barak added approvingly.

'I don't know, I don't know,' Cantrell said with sudden petulance. 'Why do you all have to come here, asking me questions? I do not understand what is happening. I just want to be left alone, in peace.'

Harsnet looked at him without speaking for a moment, getting his attention. 'We have just been to see Dean Benson,' he said. 'He told us about the wretched scheme of Goddard and Lockley's, extracting patients' teeth under dwale. He told us you reported them to him.'

'Why did you not tell me?' I asked.

Cantrell sank down on a stool, a gesture of utter weariness. 'Is that why Dr Goddard is after me?' he asked. 'Because I told?'

'Dean Benson never told Goddard about that,' I said. 'But why did you not tell me?'

'Much good it did me when I told on him the first time. I always suspected Dr Goddard guessed what I'd done, though he never said anything. His tongue seemed harsher than ever after that.' The young man sighed deeply. 'It does no good, trying to do right. It is better to be left alone.' He looked up at us with those huge swimming eyes behind his glasses. 'It wasn't just patients they took teeth from, you know. Word got around among the beggars and pedlars that there was money to be had with no pain for young folks with good teeth. Many healthy folks came to the infirmary.' I thought suddenly of the attractive young woman I had seen yesterday. 'Dr Goddard could pick and choose. I was always surprised nobody in authority knew, all the beggars did. But no one takes notice of beggars, do they?' He relapsed into silence, staring at the floor.

'I will have a word with the guard.' Harsnet looked at Cantrell, shook his head, then went out of the back door. He spoke briefly with the guard, then returned.

'There's been nothing suspicious while he's been here. But he's unhappy at not being allowed into the house. He even has to sleep in the shed which is full of old carpenter's junk. Why will you not let him in, Goodman Cantrell?'

'I just want to be left alone,' Cantrell repeated. I feared he might burst into tears. I put a hand on Harsnet's arm, and he followed me out of the parlour. I turned in the doorway and spoke to Cantrell. 'I will speak to my physician friend. I will arrange an appointment for you.' He did not reply, just sat looking at the floor.

✝

OUTSIDE, HARSNET SHOOK his head again. 'The smell of that place. Did you see how dirty his clothes were?'

'Yes, he is in a bad way. Poor creature.'

'Going the same way as Adam Kite, by the looks of him,' Barak said.

'I will help him if I can,' I said.

'You would help all the mad folks in London. They will drive you as mad as they.'

'Serjeant Shardlake merely wishes to help,' Harsnet said reprovingly. I rubbed my arm at a sudden twinge from my wound. 'How is your arm?' Harsnet said. 'I forgot to ask.'

'Much better. But I have just had the stitches out. I hope that guard knows his business. I don't want to lose Cantrell too.'

Harsnet looked at me. I could see that like Barak he thought I was getting too involved in the troubles of the young ex-monk. 'He's competent enough. He is the last man I have. If we need any more we will have to rely on Sir Thomas Seymour.' He sighed heavily. 'In the end it will be as God wills.'

✝

HARSNET RETURNED TO his office at nearby Whitehall, and Barak and I rode home along the Strand. It was late afternoon now and the shadows were lengthening.

'What the hell happened in that tavern last night?' Barak asked. 'Is Lockley the killer, and killing his wife part of his plan? If that were so, surely he would leave her to the end, as the seventh victim, not reveal his identity now?'

'I cannot see him as the killer. He does not have the fierce, cold intelligence the killer must have. Unless he is a good actor. Guy says the killer must be acting most of the time, to be able to pretend to be normal.' I shook my head. 'But how could Lockley know anything about the law, enough to prepare that letter for Roger?'

'I don't know. I can't see it being Goddard either, though. It doesn't feel right, somehow.'

'I agree. Dr Goddard sounds more and more like a man obsessed with status and money, not with religious feeling.'

Barak grinned sourly. 'Unlike our pure brother, coroner Harsnet.'

'He's not so bad. He has some good qualities.'

'He'd like to convert you. Make you a godly man too.' He snorted. 'How could anyone believe in a merciful God after what we've seen in that tavern?'

'I suppose some would say that God gives man free will and if he abuses it that is his doing, not God's.'

'Try telling that to Mrs Bunce.'

☩

AS WE TURNED into Chancery Lane I remembered that I had agreed to see how Adam Kite was faring. And I must ask Guy to see Cantrell. I could understand the young man's fear. What if Guy told him he would end wholly blind?

We took the horses round to the stable, then went into the house. As soon as I opened the door, Joan came hurrying down the stairs. 'Dorothy Elliard's maid Margaret has been round with a message,' she said.

'Has something happened to her?' My heart was suddenly in my mouth.

'No. She's all right. But she has a Master Bealknap in her lodgings. He collapsed on her doorstep. Margaret says he's at death's door.'

'Bealknap?' I asked incredulously. 'But he barely knows Dorothy.'

'That was the message, sir. It came half an hour ago. Margaret asked you to go over there as soon as you returned.'

'I'll go now.'

I opened the door and hurried back down the path, walking rapidly round to Lincoln's Inn, where candles were being lit in the windows as darkness fell. Margaret let me in, her plump face anxious.

'What is going on?' I asked.

'I heard a knocking at the door early this afternoon, sir, and when I answered I found this man in a barrister's robe collapsed on the doorstep. The mistress got the cook to put him to bed. He said you knew him—'

'I'm in here,' Dorothy called from the parlour.

'I'd better go back to him, sir,' Margaret said. 'He's in a bad way.' She hurried away with a rustle of skirts. I went into the parlour, where Dorothy was standing by the fire, studying the discoloured section of the wooden frieze.

'I must get this section redone. It was so poorly repaired, it irritates me now I spend so much time sitting here.' Her face was pale, and I sensed she was making an effort to stay calm. 'Thank you for coming, Matthew.'

'What has happened? Why is Bealknap here?'

'Margaret found him collapsed on the doorstep. Asking for help. She called me. He was lying there white as a sheet, gasping for air.' There was a slight tremble in her voice. I realized the sight must have brought back the memory of Roger, lying by the fountain. Damn Bealknap, I thought.

'Margaret said you've put him to bed.'

She spread her hands. 'What else could I do? He said he was dying, asked for my help. Though I barely knew him, and liked him no better than you did.'

'He knew a woman would not turn him away.' I frowned. 'I will go and deal with him.'

'Matthew,' Dorothy said quietly. 'Do not be too harsh. I think he is very ill.'

'We'll see.'

✝

THEY HAD PUT Bealknap in a bedroom; from the schoolboy-sized tennis racquet on a wooden chest I guessed it was Samuel's old room. Margaret was leaning over the bed, trying to get Bealknap to drink something from a cup. He lay in the bed in his shirt. I was shocked by how bad he looked, his face against the pillows as pale as death in the light of the candle on the bedside table. He was conscious, though; he stared at me with wild, terrified eyes.

Margaret turned to me. She looked distressed. She, too, had seen Roger's corpse. 'I'm trying to get him to drink some weak beer,' she said.

'Leave us,' I said gently.

She put down the cup and left the room. I looked down at Bealknap. It was a strange thing to see him so close up, and so helpless. His disordered yellow hair was thinning, a large bald patch at the crown. Some of the drink Margaret had given him had spilled around his mouth. He looked utterly helpless, and his frantic stare showed he knew it.

'Why have you come here?' I asked quietly. 'You know what this household has suffered.'

'I knew — Mistress Elliard — was still here.' His voice was faint, his breath rasping. 'I knew she was kind. I have — no one else — to help me.'

'Anyone would help a fellow barrister in a state of collapse.'

'Not me. Everyone hates me.' He sighed, closed his eyes for a moment. 'I am finished, Shardlake. I cannot eat, the food just passes through me. Dr Archer said the last purge would wear off, but it has not. And I bleed sometimes, I bleed down there.'

I sighed. 'I will arrange for Dr Malton to come and see you here.'

'I think it is too late. My vision blurs, I feel faint all the time.' With a great effort, he pulled a skinny hand from beneath the covers and grasped my wrist. I tried not to flinch at the unexpected gesture. 'I have never believed in God,' he whispered, still fixing me with his agonized gaze. 'Not since I was a child. The world is a battleground, predators and prey. The rules and conventions of the law only disguise the fact. But now I am frightened. The Catholics say if you confess your sins and repent at the end, God will receive you into Heaven. I need a priest, one of the old type.'

I took a deep breath. 'I will have Dr Malton fetched now, and he may know a priest who will confess you. But I think, Bealknap, with proper treatment you may come round. I will send Margaret back in.' I tried to rise, but he still held me fast by the wrist, his grip surprisingly strong.

'You believe, don't you?' he asked.

I hesitated. 'I have no – certainty. I have not had for some time.'

He looked surprised. 'I always thought you did. All your concern for rules and ethics, the way you always looked down on me, I thought you were one of the godly folk.'

'No.'

'Then why help me now? When you hate me? I have done some hard things to you. Because you looked down on me as though I were a louse, not a man.' A brief flash of anger in the pale eyes.

'You are still a fellow human being.'

Bealknap seemed to think for a moment. He bit his lip, showing long yellow teeth. Then he said, 'The priest may not come – in time. At least I can tell you about one sin, tell you what I did. Though I do not know why he asked—'

'What do you mean, Bealknap? You are making no sense.'

He closed his eyes. 'Near two weeks ago. After you lost me the case involving that marsh cottar. The next day a man called at my Chambers. His name is Colin Felday.' He paused for breath. 'He is a solicitor, he hangs around the Westminster Sanctuary looking for clients and I am one of the barristers he brings them to. Not a –

respectable man, one of those you would disapprove of.' He tried to laugh, but the cracking sound turned into a cough. He opened his eyes again, full of fear and pain. 'He said he had a client who would pay good money for information I could give him about you.'

'What sort of information?'

'Anything I could give. About your work habits, where you lived. Even about what sort of man you were. About your man Barak. I told him you were a starchy prig, bitter about your fate as a hunchback. I said you were a persistent lawyer. Like a damned terrier dog. And no fool.' He tried to laugh again. 'Oh, no, never that.'

I stared down at him. This was the killer, it must be. This was how he had found out about me; this solicitor had perhaps written to Roger at his instruction. 'Who is Felday's client?' I asked sharply. 'What is his name?'

'He said he could not tell me that. Only that he wished you no good. That was enough for me.' His eyes were full of anger now. This might be a confession, but I saw there was no real contrition. Only terrible fear at the prospect of death.

'I think Felday's client has killed five people,' I said. 'I have been hunting him. And he has been hunting me. He sliced my arm open, and hurt Barak's wife badly.'

Bealknap's eyes slid away. 'I didn't know that. No one can blame me for that.' I smiled wryly at the reappearance of the old Bealknap; somehow I knew then he would survive.

'Where does Felday live?' I asked.

'Some cheap lodgings by the cathedral. Addle Hill.'

'I will have Guy fetched here,' I said quietly. 'And I will ask about a priest.' Bealknap nodded weakly, but did not open his eyes. His confession had exhausted him, or perhaps he could not meet my eye now. I left him, closing the door quietly behind me.

✝

DOROTHY WAS sitting in her chair by the fire, Margaret on a stool opposite her. They both looked drained. 'Margaret,' I said. 'Could you bear to go back and sit with him? I think if he gets some liquid into him that would be good.'

'Is he going to die?' Dorothy asked bluntly after Margaret left the room.

'I do not know. He thinks he is. I am going to have Guy fetched here. Bealknap wants a priest too, one who can confess him.'

She gave a mirthless laugh. 'Bealknap never struck me as a believer in the old ways. Or in anything save lining his pockets.'

'I think for him it is a sort of insurance.' I shook my head. 'He is a strange man. It is known he has a massive chest of gold locked away in his chambers. But no wife, nor friends, only enemies. What drove him to be so?'

Dorothy shook her head. 'Who can say? Well, I hope he lives. I would not want another death here. Thank you for coming, Matthew.' She smiled. 'Margaret and I – we did not know what to do. Somehow we could not think.'

'That is hardly surprising in the circumstances.'

She got up. 'At least let me give you some supper. I'll wager you have not had any.'

'No. There is something I must do urgently.'

'About these killings?'

'Yes. A possible lead.'

She came over to me, and took my hand. She looked down at it. 'You have been through so much. You look more tired than ever.'

'I think we may be near the end of the trail.'

'Seeing that man Bealknap lying on the doorstep, so white, it brought everything back. When I first saw Roger's body.' Suddenly she burst into tears, bringing her hands up to her face. I forgot myself, and took her in my arms.

'Oh Dorothy, poor Dorothy . . .'

She looked up at me with her tear-streaked face. Looked into my eyes. And I felt if I kissed her now, she would respond. But then she blinked and took a step back. She smiled sadly. 'Poor Matthew,' she said quickly. 'Running from pillar to post to help me.'

'Whatever I can do, at any time.'

'I know,' she answered quietly.

I bowed and went out. On the front doorstep I paused, suddenly overcome with emotion. She did feel something for me, I felt that now. I looked out over Gatehouse Court. It was dark, only a few lights at the windows. I took a deep breath, and began walking briskly homeward. I would send Peter to fetch Guy. Barak and I had another mission now, to find Felday. My heart, already beating fast, beat harder and my legs shook a little at the thought that perhaps at last we had found our route to the killer.

Chapter Thirty-three

I WALKED RAPIDLY back to the house. As I stepped inside I felt suddenly faint. I stood with my back against the door for a moment, taking deep breaths. Then I climbed the stairs to Barak and Tamasin's room. I knocked, and Barak's voice bade me enter.

They made, at first sight, a peaceful domestic scene. Tamasin was sitting at the table, sewing; Barak was lying on the bed. He looked relaxed, but then I noticed a slight frown on his brow, and one foot jiggled up and down.

'Jack,' I said, 'I am afraid I need you for a while.'

'Not another,' he said, his eyes widening.

'No.' Tamasin looked at us with anxious eyes. I smiled reassuringly. 'It is all right. We need to go on an errand.'

'What's happened?' Barak asked as we walked back down the stairs. He seemed glad to be called to action now he knew we were not going to gaze at another tortured victim. I told him about Bealknap's confession about the solicitor Felday. 'You go drinking with some of the jobbing solicitors,' I said. 'Do you know him?'

'I've had him pointed out to me,' Barak answered. 'Thin, sharp-faced fellow. Gets most of his clients from the Westminster Sanctuary, he's well known down there.' He looked at me seriously. 'My friends said he will do anything for money. And they're no angels.'

I paused at the bottom of the stairs. 'We must go and see him now. If this client of his is the killer – and who else would be asking questions like that about us? – we can identify him at last.' I hesitated in the doorway. 'I wonder, should we fetch Harsnet?'

'We should get to Felday at once,' Barak said. 'Take our chance now.'

'Yes. It is the best opportunity that has come our way yet.'

Barak's face set hard. 'So that's how the arsehole knew where I lived, and he would have been told you work at the Court of Requests. He's probably been following us around.'

'So much for supernatural powers granted by the devil. Nothing supernatural about getting a crooked solicitor to get information from a crooked barrister. And he must have money, if he can afford to set a solicitor and a barrister as spies.'

'We still don't know how he's been able to follow us unseen.'

'We soon will.'

'What are you going to do about Bealknap?'

'Send Peter to fetch Guy. Let's find him.'

'I'd leave that old arsehole to rot.'

'Not in Dorothy's house. Come on.'

I went to the kitchen. Philip Orr was seated at the table, a mug of beer in his hands, a stool creaking under his weight as he talked to the two boys, Timothy and Peter, who were sitting at his feet. 'And then the King entered the city,' he said dramatically. 'You've never seen anyone like His Majesty. A huge man, taller by a head than all the courtiers and servants who followed him. Jewels glinting in his cap and on his doublet. And beside him Queen Anne Boleyn, that was later found to be such a wicked strumpet—' He stood hastily as we came in. The boys too scrambled to their feet.

'Sorry, sir,' Orr said. 'I was just telling them about my time as a city constable—'

'That is all right. But I have a job for Peter to do. Come,' I said to the older boy, 'I will write a note. I want you to take it down to Bucklersbury, quick as you can.' I looked at Timothy. 'Is it not time you were abed?'

'Yes, sir.'

I had been pleased to see Peter and Timothy side by side. There was a new sparkle in Timothy's eyes, that had been so dull before.

'Goodnight, then,' I said. Peter followed us out. I went into the parlour, hastily scribbled a note to Guy and gave it to him. He hurried off. 'Right,' I said to Barak. 'Let us see what good Master Felday has to say for himself. Addle Hill's not far. Bring your sword.'

✝

We walked quickly along Fleet Street to the city wall. The guard there, seeing my lawyer's robes, let us through. The huge bulk of St Paul's Cathedral was no more than a vast dark shape ahead of us. It was a dark night; the moon hidden by clouds, and I smelt more rain in the air.

'You and Tamasin made a peaceful-looking scene just now.'

'I'm trying to behave. But it's hard with this business constantly knocking round my head.'

'It will come right.'

As we turned into Carter Lane we saw a commotion ahead of us. Two constables had a ragged-looking man by the collar. 'I only want to sleep in the doorway,' he said. 'It's going to rain again.'

'Then get wet!' The constables poked him with the end of their staffs, sending him staggering into the street. 'Be gone, mange-hound!' The vagrant turned away and the constables, hearing our footsteps, turned to us. 'I am a barrister visiting his solicitor,' I said as they held up their lanterns. They bowed and let us pass.

Addle Hill was a long street leading down towards the river. At the top the houses were large old four-storey buildings with overhang-ing eaves, most of them dilapidated-looking. Built on Thames mud as they were, many had settled and shifted with the years and some looked ready to topple over. A woman peered at us from a doorway, then melted back into the darkness.

'Good few whores round here,' Barak said quietly.

'No one else about, though. We're going to have to knock at a lot of doors to find him.'

A group of figures was approaching up the street, some carrying lanterns, conversing quietly. A man and woman left the group and, calling goodnight, went into one of the houses. 'We can ask these folk,' Barak said.

'Excuse me,' I said, stepping into the path of the group. An old man at their head raised a lantern. I saw that he, and the people behind him, wore dark clothes and were carrying Bibles. They must be on their way back from some meeting. I asked him if he might know where a solicitor named Felday lived. He shook his head, but a young man stepped forward. 'I know him,' he said. He took in my lawyer's robe. 'Is he instructing you, sir?'

'I have some business with him.'

'He is not well esteemed among his neighbours,' the young man said censoriously. He was no more than twenty. 'He is known as unscrupulous and irreligious.'

There was a murmur of agreement within the group. I frowned at the young man. 'My business is my affair,' I answered sharply. 'Now, will you have the Christian charity to tell me where he lives?'

The young man shook his head sorrowfully, then pointed down the hill. 'Half a dozen houses down, on the right, the house with the blue door.'

'Thank you,' I answered brusquely and stepped out of their way. The group moved on. 'He spoke irreligiously, Thomas,' one of them said loudly enough for me to hear. 'Talking lightly of Christian charity.'

Barak looked after them. 'More godly men,' he said. 'They never miss a chance to tell off someone they think less pure than them.'

'They're bold, walking about in a group like that after dark with Bonner after them all.'

'Probably hoping to be martyrs, like half these godly folk.'

I took a deep breath. 'Right, let us find Felday.'

✞

THE HOUSE we had been directed to was less shabby than the rest; the blue door recently painted. I tried the handle but it was locked.

I knocked several times before the door was answered by a woman in her thirties. She smiled at us. 'Yes, sirs?'

'We are seeking Master Felday.'

The smile turned immediately to a scowl. 'You and several others,' she said. 'He's not been in for days. I keep having to answer the door to people looking for him.'

'Perhaps we could go to his rooms. Where are they?'

'First floor, on the left. And tell him when you find him that if he goes away again, to let people know. It's not a neighbour's duty to answer the door every five minutes.' She delivered her last words to our backs as we hurried up the stairs.

There was a wide landing on the first floor, two doors leading off. The layout was similar to the Old Barge where Barak and Tamasin lived, only larger and cleaner. We knocked loudly on the left-hand door. There was no reply. Barak tried it. It was locked.

'Where's the arsehole got to?' he asked. 'Think he's skipped?'

'I don't know.' I hesitated for a moment, then said, 'Break it down.'

He looked at me. 'You sure? That's breaking and entering.'

'We have Cranmer behind us if anyone complains.'

'We should get some light first. I'll go and ask that woman for a candle.'

He went back down the stairs while I looked at the closed door. I wondered if part of the killer's deal with Felday – for I was sure the killer was his client – was that he should make himself scarce for a while, in case I managed to follow the trail back to him. If so, I would find him.

Barak returned, carrying a candle. 'I think that woman downstairs is a high-class doxy. She asked if the lawyer wanted to visit her. I told her you'd think about it.' He grinned, but I sensed the anxiety behind his clowning.

'She'll be disappointed, then. Give me the candle, let's get inside.'

Barak took a step back, then kicked hard and expertly at the lock. The door flew open with a crash, banging against the wall. Inside, darkness and an unexpected breath of cool air. I cupped a hand before the candle-flame to protect it.

'There's a window open somewhere,' I said.

'If he's gone away maybe he left the window open to air the place. It's a bit whiffy.' Barak drew his sword and we stepped carefully inside. There were several doors leading off the hallway. One was half-open; that was where the draught of air was coming from. Barak drew his sword and with the point gently pushed it fully open.

Inside I made out a wall lined with shelves. Under the open window was a large desk, and my hand tightened on my dagger as I saw the figure of a man lying slumped across it. He wore a white shirt. One of his arms lay on a little pile of papers; the corner of the top page waved up and down in the light breeze.

We went in. Barak prodded the prone figure lightly with his sword-tip. He did not stir. I brought the candle over and shone the light on the man's head. He was young, no more than thirty, with thick brown hair and a thin, handsome face, the features delicate. His eyes were shut, his expression peaceful. He looked as though he had fallen asleep.

'It's Felday,' Barak said.

Something moved in the room. We both jumped round. Barak pointed his sword at a corner. Then he gave a tense bark of laughter as we realized the edge of a brightly coloured wall-hanging had been caught by the breeze.

'Jesus, my heart was in my mouth there,' he said.

'Mine too.'

He went over to the window and closed it, then used the candle to light a lamp that stood on a table. Then he took the man gently by the shoulders and lifted him upright in his chair. It was hard work, because his shirt-front was a mass of blood which had flowed on to the table and congealed there. Barak laid down his sword and ripped the man's shirt open. I winced at the sight of a large stab-wound in his chest, right over his heart.

'At least this poor fellow died quickly,' Barak said quietly. 'A stab to the heart, he wouldn't have known what hit him.' He looked at me. 'Is this the sixth victim?'

'No,' I said quietly. 'This killing was quickly and simply done. Not like the others. And I see no symbolic linking to waters drying up.'

'You mean someone else killed Felday?' Barak asked, astonished.

'No, I think it was our killer,' I answered quietly. 'But not as part of his sequence. I think Felday was killed in case we found our way to him, or in case he talked.' I sighed. 'Bealknap told Felday I was persistent.' I looked at poor Felday. 'I think the killer came to visit him, calling on him as a client to his solicitor. They were probably sitting talking across the table when he thrust the dagger in his heart.' Sure enough, an empty chair was positioned opposite where Felday sat. I looked again at the solicitor's oddly peaceful face. 'By the sound of it Felday was an irreligious man. Just as well for him; if he had been an apostate from the godly men, he would no doubt have been incorporated into the sequence, and he would have died slowly and dramatically.' I began prowling round the room. 'He didn't want Felday found quickly. That's why he left the window open, to keep the room cool and prevent the smell of death going through the house too quickly.'

'I'd say he's been dead a few days,' Barak said. 'He's rotting, you catch the smell close to. God, the bastard is clever.'

'Come,' I said. 'Help me. I want to go through the desk and all these papers. See if there is some sort of clue. A note, a receipt, anything.'

For an hour we searched the solicitor's office, and the rest of the neat, well-appointed little dwelling. Outside heavy rain started again, hissing on the cobbles and dripping from the eaves. But among all the papers we found nothing, only an empty square of dust on one of the shelves where some papers had been taken, probably Felday's notes for his spying work. The trail had gone cold.

Chapter Thirty-four

WE RETURNED HOME. I sent a message to Harsnet, then ate a gloomy dinner on my own; Barak did not want any. Felday's death, coming so soon after Mrs Bunce, was almost too much to bear.

I was almost pleased to have an interruption later that evening, when one of Roger's clients called in a state of great anxiety. It was Master Bartholomew, who had organized the interlude at Lincoln's Inn. That was barely three weeks ago, though it seemed an eternity. Two of the actors he employed in his company had been arrested a week before, for possessing forbidden plays by John Bale. While he himself steered clear of religious controversy, Bartholomew found that many of those he worked with now did not wish to be associated with him; such was the climate of fear developing in London.

'My costume supplier won't let me have any costumes for my next performance, and a carpenter who was to build the scenery has pulled out. It is a performance of *The Castle of Perseverance*, at the Lord Mayor's house next Thursday. They are breaching their contracts, is there nothing I can do? Normally I would have gone to Master Elliard, but since his death . . .'

I told him he could sue, but not in time to save his performance. He could only try persuasion. Master Bartholomew left, gloomy, but less panicked, to try again with his contractors. In the doorway he looked out into the rain that was teeming down again, and raised the hood on his coat. Then he turned to me. 'Is there no progress on finding Master Elliard's killer, sir? I heard the inquest was adjourned for the coroner to investigate.'

'I fear there is no news yet.'

He shook his head. 'Nor ever will be, perhaps. That's what happens if you don't catch a murderer quickly. You never catch them.'

He left. I thought, if he or any of the citizenry knew the true story, what a panic there could be in this anxious city.

✝

NEXT MORNING I rode out early to the Bedlam. I had passed a disturbed night, constantly waking to the sound of the rain, and was in a tired and worried frame of mind as I rode along, Genesis taking careful steps in the muddy streets. Felday's death still preyed on me; if I had not become a focus of the killer's attention he would not have died. But then if he had not been so crooked, he would not have died either. I had had no reply from Harsnet yet, and I had left a message at home saying where I was going.

I had received a brief note that morning from Dorothy. Guy had visited Bealknap, and judged that with care and rest he should recover, though any more purging and bleeding might well kill him. 'Your doctor friend advises he stay here some days, until he is stronger,' Dorothy concluded. Reading between the lines I guessed she would rather he had not.

The sight of the Bedlam gates ahead brought me back to the present. As I rode through the yard, I saw two familiar figures come out. It was Daniel and Minnie Kite, Daniel's large arm round his wife. He looked thoughtful, though Minnie looked more settled. They glanced up as I approached, and I pulled Genesis to a halt.

'Good morning,' I said. 'You have been visiting Adam?'

'Yes, sir,' Daniel said.

'I am meeting Dr Malton here shortly, he is making one of his visits.'

Minnie's face lightened. 'He is a good man. I believe he is helping Adam. He says it will take a long time, but I think my son is somewhat better.'

Daniel nodded. 'Sometimes now he will pay us a little attention.

Stop praying, just for a short while. And he will eat too. I wonder —
I wonder whether he may be able to follow me into my trade after
all.' He looked at me almost pleadingly, so I could supply an
answer.

'Perhaps one day,' I said noncommittally.

'But I'm not sure it ever was the work Adam wanted.' Minnie
looked at me. 'I do wonder if my son is angry with us for some
reason. The way he still treats us.'

'If you wait a little, Dr Malton will not be long. You could talk
to him.'

They looked at each other dubiously. 'Perhaps we—' Minnie
said, but her husband shook his head.

'No, chick. We must go to service. In these days, we must show
our support to our preacher.' He looked at me again, and something
had closed up in his face.

'How is Reverend Meaphon?' I asked neutrally.

'He is very worried, sir. These are days of persecution.' He looked
at me. 'We fear in our church that one of our neighbours, Reverend
Yarington, has been arrested. He has not been seen for days. None of
his congregation will say what has happened, but Reverend Meaphon
is sore distressed. He says Christian folks must stand together against
the devil in these days, and he is right.'

'Then I will leave you. Shall I ask Dr Malton to call upon
you?'

'Yes, sir,' he said. 'That would be kind.'

They left me. I wondered at how even Minnie seemed to be
putting her church before her son now. If Adam had become angry
with her in the past, perhaps that was why. Everything was polarizing.
Last week a traditionalist priest had been arrested for pricking his
finger and letting drops of blood fall on to the holy wafer in an effort
to prove to his congregation that the bread indeed turned into the
body and blood of Christ on consecration.

✝

I tied Genesis up outside the long, low asylum building and knocked at the door. Keeper Shawms answered; at the sight of me he frowned, then forced his expression into a semblance of a smile. 'Master Shardlake,' he muttered.

'Good day. I am meeting Dr Malton here.'

He stood aside for me to enter. 'He ain't here yet. But Ellen is with Kite. He is getting the best of care.' Shawms' voice was respectful, but there was a nasty look in his eyes.

'Good. The first report to the court is due in a week. I shall want to see it before it is sent. How is Adam?'

'That black doctor says he is improving, though I can't see it. He and Ellen like to get him out of his chamber, have him sitting in the parlour. But it upsets the other patients.'

'I am sure you cope.'

I had been aware of muffled shouting nearby, and now a door opened and the fat keeper Gebons appeared, red-faced. 'His Majesty is in a fierce state, sir,' he told Shawms. 'Wants his crown mending. Can you settle him?'

Shawms sighed heavily, brushed past Gebons and threw the door of the chamber wide. Inside I saw the old man who believed he was the King, sitting on his commode in his patchwork robe. The paper crown on his head had had an accident, several of its points were flattened. 'You will repair my crown!' he shouted, waving a fist. 'You are my subjects and you will obey me!'

Shawms grabbed the paper crown from his head and crushed it in a meaty fist. 'That for your crown!' he snapped. 'One day you will babble so far you will not be able to pull your tongue in again. Now be quiet, or no lunch.' The fat old man seemed visibly to shrink into himself, then buried his face in his hands and began to weep. Shawms left him, slamming the door behind him.

'There, that's shut him up,' he told Gebons with satisfaction. 'Now, Master Shardlake, we are busy, as you see. I will leave you to go to Adam's chamber.'

The door of Adam's room was open. Ellen was seated on a stool opposite him. Adam was still chained; there must be no repeat of what had happened at London Wall. 'Come, Adam,' Ellen was saying, 'take the spoon and feed yourself. I am not going to put it into your mouth like a little baby. Come on.' She put on a babyish voice. 'Goo-goo, ga-ga.'

To my surprise, Adam responded to her gentle mockery with a smile, quickly suppressed. He sighed, but took the spoon and bowl, and under Ellen's watchful eye he ate the pottage.

'Well done, Ellen,' I said. 'I have never seen Adam smile before.'

She got to her feet and made a little curtsy. 'I did not see you, sir.' She blushed.

'I am meeting Dr Malton here.'

'Yes, I knew he was coming. I try to make Adam laugh. I have not quite managed that, but I got a smile as you saw.'

'Yes.' Adam was now eating as fast as he could. He ignored me.

'I hear the King has proposed legislation forbidding women to read the Bible,' Ellen said.

'Yes, that is right. And uneducated folk.'

She smiled sadly. 'Everything is going back to the old ways. Well, perhaps that has to be, it is the new ways that brought poor Adam to this pass.'

I looked at her, wondering whether it was because of some religious nonconformity that Ellen was not allowed to leave the Bedlam. But she had spoken with detachment. I looked again at Adam's chained leg. 'Ellen,' I said quietly, 'I do not know why it is you may not leave the Bedlam, but if I can help you in any way I would be pleased.'

She gave her sad smile again. 'Thank you, sir. But I am happy enough.' Yet her expression was sad. I thought, how can such an intelligent woman bear to spend her whole life in this place, second-hand news her only knowledge of the world outside?

Adam, having bolted down his pottage, curled himself over and began to pray. 'Heavenly father,' he whispered. 'Forgive me, I have sinned against the light. The light—'

'I will let him pray a little now he's eaten,' Ellen said, 'until Dr Malton comes. That is another of his ideas, to bargain with Adam, allow him some time to pray but insist he does other things too.'

'Is there any change in him?'

'A little, I believe. But it is hard work. He woke yesterday saying he believed the birds singing outside were crying out against his sins.'

'This is harrowing work for a woman, Ellen,' I said. 'I could not do it. It must be hard for you, spending all your time with these folk. None of them can be easy.'

She frowned a little. 'Who is easy in this world?'

I realized I had offended her. There was a moment's awkward silence. 'I saw Adam's parents,' I said. 'They say he has made some progress.'

'Yes. I think his father feels helpless, it is sad to see that big man standing there, totally at a loss for what to do.'

'But no more difficulties from Keeper Shawms?'

'No.' She smiled again. 'Thanks to you, sir. He lets me take Adam into the parlour to mix with other patients now. Dr Malton says it is important for Adam to have other people around him, to try and take his attention from that doleful world in which he has set himself.'

'Shawms says Adam still upsets the other patients.'

'Less than he did. They call on him to be quiet, to stop praying. That is no bad thing for him.' She smiled sadly. 'Everyone here can cope with everyone else's problems. But usually not their own.'

'No indeed,' said a voice from the doorway. Guy came in. To my surprise he had a copy of the New Testament under his arm. He looked tired and I felt guilty for sending him running off to Lincoln's Inn the night before. 'How is Bealknap?' I asked.

'Dr Archer should be arraigned for assault,' he said. 'Apparently Master Bealknap had gone to him with no more than a prolonged stomach ache. He was not eating and so had grown weak. All Archer's bleeding and purges have done is make him weaker yet. I am not surprised he thought he was dying. I have prescribed good food and bed rest for a week, then he can go to his chambers and hopefully look after himself.'

'Good. Thank you.'

'I fear Mistress Elliard was not pleased when I said he should be under someone's care just now.'

'Dorothy still finds it hard to cope. Finding Bealknap collapsed on the doorstep reminded her of Roger's death.'

'She is a charitable woman. I am afraid I played on that a little. But Bealknap is my patient now, I must put him first.'

'I suppose so.' Damn the wretch, I thought.

'I said I would visit him again tomorrow evening, see how he goes.'

'Did you bring a priest?'

'No. He does not need that. Bringing one would only set him thinking his end was upon him again.'

'Come to dinner at Lincoln's Inn tonight after you have seen him. As a reward for your trouble. And I will give you Bealknap's fee.'

Guy smiled. 'He is a strange man. He answered all my questions about his symptoms readily enough, for he was in great fear. But after I told him he was not going to die he hardly said a word more. Gave me no thanks, nor you.'

'That is Bealknap. I will tell you later,' I added grimly, 'about something he has done.'

Guy raised his eyebrows. Turning to Ellen, he asked, 'How is Adam?'

'He has had some breakfast. Even gave me something like a smile.'

'Then we make progress.' Guy went over to Adam and touched him gently on the shoulder. The boy ceased his frantic whispering, sighed and raised his bony head. 'I need to pray, Dr Malton. I have had no time to pray.'

Guy sat on his haunches to face him. I envied the suppleness of his limbs. 'I brought the Bible again,' he said quietly. 'I thought we could go through some passages. To read the book is as important as prayer in the eyes of God, is it not?'

'I will go and see to the other patients,' Ellen said. 'Cissy is mopish again, she will not do her sewing.'

'Thank you for all you are doing,' Guy said.

She curtsied and left us. I watched her go, her long brown hair swinging round her shoulders under her coif. I turned back to Guy, who had the Bible open and was struggling to engage Adam in conversation.

'If you read the gospels, you will see that Jesus does not want his followers to suffer unnecessarily. He wants them to live in the world, and more than anything to live together in harmony; not to cut themselves off as you have done.'

'But God *does* test his people, test their faith. Look at Job. He tested him and tested him.' Adam banged a skinny fist on the stone floor.

'Is that what you feel? That God is testing you?'

'I hope so. It is better than being cast out. To suffer in Hell for ever and ever. I am afraid of Hell, so afraid. I read in Revelation—'

'Read the four gospels, Adam. You will see that none who repents is rejected. Look at Mary Magdalen—'

But Adam shook his head fiercely then, bent right over and began to pray again, his lips moving soundlessly. The vertebrae stood out on his skinny neck. Guy sighed, then stood up. 'I will leave him be for a few minutes,' he said. 'That is our bargain.'

'Guy, your patience is as bottomless as the sea.'

'I am following the trail of a mystery. Trying to understand things by looking at Adam's reactions.'

'You would not leave him the Bible to read?'

'Oh no. He would look for all the passages about damnation and being cast out for sin, and clasp them to his heart. I wonder what started this. It is often something terrible that has happened in the real world that causes mad people to withdraw into a world of their own.'

'His mother still thinks he is angry with her and Daniel.'

'I think perhaps that is part of the story, but not all.' He looked over at Adam's crouched figure, stroking his chin.

'What inner world has our killer made for himself? I wonder.' I looked at Guy. 'He has killed someone else.' I told him what Bealknap had done, and about the murder of Felday. I spoke in a whisper, that Adam should not hear, but he was so lost in prayer I doubt he would have taken any notice had I spoken normally.

Guy stood thinking for a moment. 'The killer's world will be very different from poor Adam's. I think he is in a state of obsession and self-glorification so strong it can never be mended. You know, Matthew, there are few obsessives in the Bible. Certainly none in the New Testament.'

'What about St John? What about the Book of Revelation?'

'Christianity would be better without that book. It preaches nothing but cruelty and destruction. It teaches that the destruction of human beings does not matter, is even to be rejoiced over. It is evil. No wonder it is the book the killer chose.' He sighed. 'Matthew, I should spend some time with Adam. We will talk more tonight.' He smiled. 'I think his care is assured. Shawms and his master Metwys are afraid of the court.'

'Guy, 'I said hesitantly. 'Can I ask another favour?'

'Of course.'

I told him about Charles Cantrell's eyes. 'Yes I will see him,' he said. 'I cannot say what ails him till I see him.' He looked at me seriously. 'It may be simple, or he may indeed be going blind.'

'Then better he should know.'

I left Guy to try and counsel Adam. I was not sorry to go. On the way out I looked into the little parlour. Ellen was sitting with the patient Cissy, trying to make her sew properly, as earlier she had tried to make Adam eat. Cissy sat slumped in her chair, her eyes unfocused. 'Take the needle,' Ellen was saying. 'It is such a pretty blouse.' I thought there was something almost saintly in her patience. I was sure she heard me come to the doorway, but she did not look up.

☦

THAT NIGHT I had Joan prepare a rich chicken stew. Guy arrived at six, on time as usual, and we sat to our meal. Tamasin had told me Barak had gone out drinking with his friends again. She sounded weary and angry. It was not a good sign. As we ate I told Guy more about Felday.

'So you had to encounter yet another body.'

'Yes. It is affecting Barak hard.'

'How are he and his wife?' I had told Guy something of their problems.

'I tell myself once this nightmare is over, Barak will make it right with her again. God knows,' I burst out in sudden vehemence, 'it has taken over all our lives. I was going to take some time this afternoon to work up the subscription list for Roger's hospital, but I found it hard to concentrate.'

'You will do it.' He looked at me. 'That will please his widow.'

'Yes.'

'She will need time to set herself in order, Matthew,' Guy said. 'Much time, strong though she is.'

'I know.' I smiled wryly; he had guessed my feelings. I looked at him. 'How long a wounded soul takes to mend. And Adam, can he ever mend?'

'I think so. With the help of Ellen, who is putting much effort into his care, I think he can be brought back to the world. I will untangle how he was set on this terrible path, I am determined. As for time?' He spread his hands. 'Six months, perhaps a year. But I will bring him back to the real world, where we must live if we are to stay sane.' He spoke with sudden passion.

'That sounded heartfelt.'

He nodded, slowly and heavily. Then he looked at me and said,

'I am far from being as sure and certain of things as I might appear, Matthew.'

'You said that once you had the time of despair.'

'Yes.'

'And now? You are troubled again?'

'Yes. Yes, I am.' He paused, then sighed, a sigh that was half a sob. 'Not about God or his goodness, but about what I am.'

I took a deep breath. 'Has this got something to do with Piers?'

He gave me a piercing look, but did not answer.

'Has he some hold over you, Guy?'

'No. Or at least, not in the way you mean.' His face was suddenly anguished. 'He was so tractable when he came, did everything to help me. But now he goes out roistering in the evenings at will. And yes, you were right, he listens at doors when I am consulting with patients. And I thought—' He broke off, resting his head on a tightly clenched fist.

'Thought what?'

When Guy spoke again, it was in broken, fractured tones, head bowed. 'I am fifty-seven years old, Matthew, an old man. I was a monk for thirty years, and I have been out in the world again for five. When you become a monk you take vows of poverty, chastity and obedience. If you take your vows seriously — and I know not all the monks did, you saw that for yourself when we met at Scarnsea — you separate yourself off from earthly passions. That is not something to do lightly. I told you of the woman I loved when I was young.'

'Who died.'

'Yes. And that I was angry, bitterly angry with God. I felt he had taken Eloise from me to drive me to the cloister.' He shook his head. 'I went from that anger to doubting God's goodness, doubting whether the picture of God given by the Church was even true at all, whether the savages of the New World had it right in believing God was a cruel and vengeful being who demanded human sacrifice. As I felt Eloise had been sacrificed. In my medical studies I started looking at diseases of the mind, that matched my view of man and God as flawed and lost.'

The passionate anger that had come into his voice was like nothing I had ever heard from him before.

He nodded, then smiled gently. 'But that was the nadir, Matthew, that was the lowest point I reached, perhaps that God allowed me to reach, for I was very near despair. I continued to pray. I did not want to but I felt it was important; oddly enough it was an anchor to the real world, which was slipping out of focus for me. And one day I heard a gentle voice that seemed to say, "I did not take Eloise out of the world. Why should your life be more important than hers?" And that gentlest of chidings showed me that all along, without even thinking of it, I had been assuming my scholar's life was more important to God than hers, that he would snuff hers out as a ploy to get me into the cloister.' He sat back. 'There. When God gently chides our arrogance we may be more confident it is truly Him talking to us, than when people come from prayer puffed up with righteousness.'

'Amen to that.'

'After that, my bitterness slowly left me. Yet now I am disturbed and uncertain in my mind again. It is strange we should be hunting an obsessive murderer just now. When I am again prey to disturbing feelings, and yes, this time they are about Piers.' He hesitated, then said, 'I have wondered if my feelings for him are honourable.'

So that was it. And Piers, I knew, would use that. 'What do you think?' I asked gently.

He shook his head sadly. 'I am not sure. When I first met him, when his old master was dying – and that old fraud did not treat Piers well, by the way – it was his intelligence that struck me, intelligence that was being wasted. But I noted his fair form and face, and when he came to my home I found I had feelings that were new and strange to me.'

I could think of nothing to say. Selfishly, I thought, Guy is my rock. Do not let him crumble now.

'Oh, I have pondered on it deeply,' he said, 'and prayed too. And you know what I think? I think what I want, perhaps have always wanted, is a son. To educate, to exchange ideas with, to come and visit me when I am past working. In the cloister there was always company, but in the outside world I am so often alone. That is why many ex-monks suffer so.'

Guy looked at me, his face full of sadness. 'Have you ever felt that, Matthew? The need for a child, or some substitute for a child?'

'Oh, I collect waifs and strays,' I answered. 'I suppose I always have. The children Timothy and Peter, young Cantrell. Barak and Tamasin are my waifs and strays in a way. And there was old Master Wrenne.' I sighed. 'And my assistant Mark, that you knew at Scarnsea.' I looked at him. 'Even if one's motives are honourable, one can choose the wrong people to be one's – I do not know – substitute children.'

'Yes.' He hesitated and took a deep breath. 'Piers – he – he flirts with me.' Guy bit his lip. 'The way he smiles, the way he touches me gently sometimes, he is inviting me to something. And part of me, I fear, would follow. He knows that, knows how to use it if I am angry with him. I fear he has raised something in me I did not know was there, something more than this urge to be a father to him.'

'Guy, in a way it does not matter what your feelings are. It matters more what Piers is. He is cold, calculating, exploitative. I have seen how he listens at doors, seen his wheedling and his arrogance when he is with you.'

Guy put his head in his hands. 'Something else has happened now,' he said. 'I have noticed that money has been going missing. Small amounts from my purse, here and there, but it adds up to several pounds now.'

'You must get rid of him,' I said quietly.

'Cast him out, I that took him in?'

'You took a viper to your bosom.'

'Did I? Or is Piers disturbed, not well in his mind, that he takes my money? He has no need to steal, I give him enough.'

'Get rid of him.'

'Do you think Piers is one of those who prefers men to women?' he asked suddenly.

'I do not know. But I think he is one who would use any trick to gain advantage.'

Joan came in then with the next course, and we fell silent. Not until he was about to leave did he say, 'I will pray about this, Matthew. I will not talk to Piers yet.' He shook his head. 'I cannot believe he is as bad as you think. He has a good mind.'

'And a bad heart.'

When Guy left I returned to the parlour and sat thinking of the loneliness so many men carry in this divisive, fractured age, and the ruthless people who would exploit it.

And then another thought took shape, one that sent a chill down my spine. We had been talking of Piers as cold and intelligent and ruthless. He knew about our hunt for the killer. He listened at doors, and he had seen the bodies of the slain. But I shook my head. It was impossible; he worked for Guy, and the killer had freedom to come and go as he pleased. And it could not be Piers who followed us. No, Piers was no killer. In an odd way, he was too selfish, too coldly sane. My mind was in a fever. I would be suspecting Joan or Tamasin next. Was it truly Goddard? And if not him, who? Who?

Chapter Thirty-five

ANOTHER DISTURBED NIGHT; a ghastly dream in which I found myself back on that dark icy morning when I entered Lincoln's Inn to find the two students standing by the ice-covered fountain. But in my dream, when they turned to face me, one slipped away into the darkness. The other was Piers. He reached in and turned the body over, and it was Guy lying there with his throat slashed. I woke with a gasp to the sound of heavy rain lashing at the window, and then my heart jumped with horror, for footsteps were ascending the stairs. I exhaled with relief as I recognized Barak's steps. He must have been out late again.

✝

IN THE MORNING it was still raining, and I saw that large puddles were spreading on my lawn. As I dressed I looked across to the wall that divided my land from the old Lincoln's Inn orchard. Water would be coming in from there as it had two years before. The ground was becoming saturated.

In the parlour Barak was sitting at the table, looking dubiously at a plate of bread and cheese.

'I heard you come in late last night,' I said.

'Went out drinking with some friends.'

'Again?' I reached for some bread. 'Could you not take Tamasin out one night?'

He fixed me with a blear-eyed look. 'I needed to get out for a drink. I'm fed up of hanging around waiting for some new horror to happen.'

'Where is Tamasin?'

'Still in bed, snoring. She woke up when I came in last night and went on at me, so she's catching up on sleep.' I realized their reconciliation was not working out. His expression made it quite clear he was not going to talk about it.

'Guy was here to dinner last night,' I said.

'Tell him all about us, did you?' Barak needled.

'He told me about some troubles of his own. Money has been going missing. He thinks it is Piers, but cannot quite bring himself to believe it.'

Barak gave me a penetrating look. 'When I saw the old Moor with Piers, he seemed to think the sun shone out of his arse.'

'He wanted someone to care for, to teach. But he is beginning to see what Piers is really like.'

'Are you sure?' I wondered whether he had read between the lines, guessed Guy's feelings were not so simple as that.

'Yes. But he will not accuse him yet. And Piers can be – persuasive.'

'How about if we were to pay a visit to young Piers, put a bit of pressure on him? We could see how he reacts and take it from there.' He smiled briefly. A hard smile.

'You mean when Guy is not there?'

'He's not going to let us do it when he is there, is he?'

I hesitated, then said, 'I know Guy will be out this evening, he is going to see Bealknap again. Knowing his habits he will go after supper, probably around seven.'

'We go to Bucklersbury then?'

I nodded agreement. 'We only talk to him, though. Nothing rough.'

'Even if he's not a thief, he's an eavesdropper and a nasty bit of work. Won't do any harm if we put some salt on his tail.'

'All right.' I finished my bread and cheese, and got up. 'We must go,' I said. 'I had word last night. Harsnet has called a meeting to discuss the latest development. At Whitehall this time, not Lambeth Palace.'

Barak got up quickly. 'Yes. I need something to *do*, or I will end up as mad as Adam Kite.'

✝

WHEN WE REACHED WHITEHALL, it was to learn that Lord Hertford and Sir Thomas Seymour were both with the coroner. Barak was forbidden to attend the meeting, told to wait on a bench outside Harsnet's room again. 'I am sorry,' I whispered to him as the guard knocked on the door.

'I'm getting used to it, common fellow that I am.' Barak gave one of his sardonic grins, stretching out his legs, his boots muddy from riding through the streets. The guard frowned; a respectful demeanour was expected within the royal palace. From within, Harsnet's voice called me to enter. I took a deep breath and opened the door.

Harsnet was sitting behind his desk. Lord Hertford stood by the wall. Both looked grave. Sir Thomas Seymour lounged against the wall beside his brother, an angry look on his louche, handsome face. As always he was dressed like a peacock, a doublet in bright blue today, a cap with a huge feather in the band.

'Close the door, Matthew,' Harsnet said. 'And come over here. I do not want anyone overhearing us.'

'Barak is sitting outside, but he is safe.'

'No one is safe at Whitehall just now,' Hertford said. 'The very walls have ears.' He turned his penetrating gaze on me. 'We were to meet at the Lambeth Palace, but His Grace the Archbishop has other concerns today.'

'Not more bad news, my lord?'

'Not from the courtiers that were arrested. They are going to have to let them go. But Bonner is tightening the screw further on the London radicals. Early this morning the bishop's men and the London constables arrested eight men for possession of unlawful books, together with three printers and a bunch of apprentices for acting unlawful plays. By Jesu, they're keeping the London constables busy. The Archbishop is trying to find whether any of those arrested have associations with him.'

'Is there any danger of that?' Thomas Seymour asked.

'He thinks not.'

'The King has always loved him,' Harsnet said quietly.

'The King was close to Anne Boleyn, and Cromwell, and Wolsey,' Thomas Seymour said bitterly. 'Yet he destroyed them all. He has never truly trusted anybody, nor ever will.'

'Quiet, Thomas,' his brother said severely. 'Things are not so bad as that.' He looked at Harsnet, then me. 'Yet if this were to come out now – that the Archbishop has launched a secret hunt for a madman who is killing lapsed radicals because the Book of Revelation told him to – it would be very dangerous. And the longer it goes on, the harder it becomes to conceal. Have you learned nothing more, Gregory?' he asked Harsnet with sudden passion.

'I wish I had. I have been working day and night. None of the radical groups know about Goddard. There is no trace of him in London or the neighbouring counties. It is as though when he left his lodgings he vanished into the air.'

Lord Hertford turned to me. 'And you found the killer had been using a lawyer as his agent, but now he has killed the lawyer too.'

'He has.' I told him the story of Bealknap and Felday. When I had finished he stood pulling at his long beard anxiously, almost tugging it. Outside, rain slashed against the window.

'So there have been five murders linked to the vials of wrath. Two more to go. And this man Felday killed along the way. We must catch him.' Hertford turned to his brother. 'Judging by your news, the King is determined to marry Catherine Parr, however long she keeps him waiting.'

'What news, my lord?' Harsnet's head jerked up.

'My brother has been appointed Ambassador to the Regent of the Netherlands.'

'Because the King fears Lady Catherine may still have a mind to marry me,' Sir Thomas said. Angry as he had looked, he shifted his stance, swaggered lightly.

'We cannot be sure that is why you were chosen,' his brother said. 'And if it is, think yourself lucky the King is sending you on an ambassadorship, not to the Tower.'

'Perhaps.' Sir Thomas looked at me curiously. 'You, sir. Someone said the King made mock of your bent back, when he was at York two years ago.'

I took a deep breath. 'He did, sir.' Who had told him that story, I wondered.

'He would not get to York now,' Seymour said. 'He is so fat he can hardly walk. He has ulcers on both legs now. When they are bad he has to be taken around the palace in a wheeled chair. They say when the ulcers leak the smell as you enter the Privy Quarters would stun a bull. When you leave here, Master Shardlake, if you hear the squeaking of wheels in the corridors, I should run as fast as you can in the opposite direction.' He laughed bitterly.

Harsnet shifted uneasily in his chair. Lord Hertford shook his head. 'Your indiscretions will be the death of you one day, Thomas. But it is true the King's health worsens every month. He cannot live many years longer. And then, if a queen sympathetic to reform were in place, ready to assume the regency for young Prince Edward . . .' He spread his hands.

I thought, they have planned for this marriage, looking years ahead. How deeply my hunt for Roger's killer had become entangled in court politics.

'When do you go abroad, Sir Thomas?' Harsnet asked.

'I do not know. A few weeks, perhaps.'

Harsnet nodded, his face expressionless, though I guessed that, like me, he would rather Sir Thomas and his careless tongue were gone tomorrow. But we badly needed the support his household could give.

I jumped at the sound of a loud knock. After Sir Thomas' words, a shiver of fear seemed to pass through the room, but Lord Hertford called out in a firm voice, 'Come in.'

Barak entered. He knew when to be humble, and bowed his head under Hertford's glare. 'I am sorry to interrupt you, my lord, but the guard from Lockley's tavern is here. Janley. They have found him.'

'Alive?' Hope came into Harsnet's face.

'No, sir. Dead.' Barak looked around the company, took a deep breath. 'In the old Charterhouse. The manner of his death shows he is the sixth victim.'

Lord Hertford seemed to slump. He put a hand to his brow.

'Who knows?'

'Nobody who matters, my lord. Yet.'

'Shardlake, Harsnet, go there now.'

'I wish to go too,' Sir Thomas said.

'Very well,' Lord Hertford agreed. He looked between us. 'He has made us all dance, has he not? And now again. Will we ever have him dancing as he should, at the end of a rope?'

Chapter Thirty-six

T HE RAIN CONTINUED during our long ride to the Charter-house. I was constantly blinking water out of my eyes as Sir Thomas, Barak, the guard Janley and I rode together; the others listening as I shouted questions to Janley about what had happened there. We rode as fast as we could along roads that were turning to quagmires, mud spattering our horses and our boots.

'The Charterhouse watchman came running over to the Green Man this morning,' Janley told us. 'The place is empty but for him and the Bassano family, the King's Italian musicians; they've turned some of the old monks' cells into accommodation for them.'

'No one else lives there?' Sir Thomas asked.

'No, sir. The place is used to store the King's hunting equipment and tents and costumes for the masques. The watchman's known as a hopeless drunkard. Apparently he used to spend most evenings in the Green Man getting sow-drunk; Lockley and Mistress Bunce often had to put him outside at closing time. One of his duties is to open and close the lock gates in the old conduit-house, keep the water flowing on through the cellars of the houses in the square. He would forget and the locals had to go over and remind him.'

'Do the locals know about this?' Harsnet asked.

'No, sir. The watchman came running over an hour ago, babbling about floods and a dead man in the conduit. He knew I was some sort of official guard. He said it was Lockley. I sent him back and rode to the coroner's office, which I'd been told to do if anything happened.'

'You've managed to keep the truth of what happened to Mrs

Bunce a secret?' I glanced at Janley, noticing the man looked tired and strained.

'Ay. I've told everyone who called it looks like Lockley came back, murdered her and fled. I've hinted it was about money. A lot of neighbours and old customers have called round.'

'Good. Well done.'

'I'll be glad to be gone, back with my family. I keep thinking of that poor woman lying there. Especially at night.'

'She was only a tavern keeper,' Sir Thomas grunted. 'Be thankful it wasn't someone more important, it would be harder to cover up what happened.'

✟

WE ARRIVED AT Charterhouse Square and followed the path between the trees covering the ancient plague pit. We rode past the deserted old chapel. The door was closed; the beggars would be out seeking alms in the town. We drew up at the small gatehouse set in the long brick wall of the dissolved monastery. There was a rail for horses there and we tied our animals up. Sir Thomas frowned at the mud on his fine netherhose.

Janley knocked loudly at the door. Shuffling footsteps sounded and a thin middle-aged man with a red face and a bulbous, pock-marked nose opened it and peered at us with frightened eyes.

'I've brought some people to see the body, Padge,' Janley said gently.

The watchman looked at us uncertainly. 'They'll have to climb down to the sewer. I don't know how you'll get him out. He's fixed to the lock gates somehow, blocking them. He's naked. It's horrible. Why has someone done this? Why?' His voice rose.

'Leave it to us, matey,' Barak said soothingly.

We followed the watchman through the gates, past the ruins of the old monastic church with the windows out and the roof off, and found ourselves in a large, square, grassed courtyard. In the centre stood an octagonal, copper-roofed building, with taps on the sides.

That had to be the old monastic conduit, fed by the streams from Islington, where the monks had drawn their water and which then went on to drain the sewers under the houses in the square. Round the sides of the yard stood the old monks' cells, little square two-roomed houses, each with a small patch of garden behind, water dripping from the eaves. This would have been a peaceful place once. The monks of the Charterhouse had lived secluded lives in their cells round the central square, an architectural pattern unique among monastic buildings. The cells had stout wooden doors secured with padlocks. To our left was a larger building, the doors open. I saw figures within.

'I've put the Bassano family in there,' the watchman said. 'They came into the gatehouse earlier, gabbling away about being flooded out.' He pointed to the conduit and I saw that water was seeping and bubbling up between the flagstones surrounding it. A section of the grassy square between the conduit and the cells on one side was waterlogged. Still the rain pelted down on us. The watchman wiped his face with a trembling hand. 'I went to look at the conduit-house where the lock gates are, and saw a body jammed in front of them. I leaned over the rail and saw his face, saw it was poor Francis.'

'Stopping the waters of the Euphrates,' I said quietly. 'Master Padge, did you hear anything last night?'

'No. A man has to sleep,' he added in a truculent mumble.

'Not if he's a watchman,' Sir Thomas said sharply. 'Where are the Italians?'

Padge led the way to the building with the open door. It had evidently been the monastic chapter house, for there were benches round the wall as there were at Westminster Abbey. But this was a far smaller, more austere room. Most of the space was taken up with chests and wardrobes; to store the costumes for the masques, no doubt. Two huge suits of armour stood beside them, and half a dozen enormous jousting lances were stacked against the wall. A little group of people had found space on the benches and sat huddled together, looking scared. They were swarthy, dark-haired; four men and three women with children in their laps. All were clutching musical instruments, lutes and tabors and even a harp. I saw the men's doublets and the women's dresses were soaked through.

'Does anyone speak English?' I asked.

One of the men stood up. 'I do,' he said in heavily accented tones.

'You are the Bassano family, the King's musicians?'

'Yes, sir.' He bowed. 'I am their servant, Signor Granzi.'

'What has happened to you?' Sir Thomas asked. 'You look like a lot of drowned rats.'

'We woke this morning to find the floors of our quarters in water above our feet,' the Italian said. 'The ground goes downward from that conduit. Water was coming into our rooms. We had to rescue our instruments. We came here, then called the watchman. What is it, sir? We heard the watchman cry out.'

'Nothing to worry you.'

'Did any of you hear anything strange last night?' I asked. Master Granzi consulted the other in their strange, musical tongue, then shook his head. 'No, sir. We were all asleep.'

Sir Thomas grunted. 'Come on, Padge. Take us to where you found the body.' He pushed the watchman out into the rain; a born bully.

As we crossed the courtyard Harsnet fell into step beside me. 'Those musicians perform before the King. If they learn there has been a killing here it will be a fine bit of gossip to tell around the court. They must not find out what has happened.'

'I agree.' Was that what the killer had intended?

'We'll say it was an accident.'

'Padge is a drunk. He'll talk in his cups.'

'I'll take him with us when we leave,' Harsnet said. 'Keep him somewhere safe and put one of Sir Thomas' men in here for now. I'll square it with the Court of Augmentations.'

Padge led us back to the gatehouse. He had appropriated one room, a truckle bed on the floor. The room stank of beer. There was a fire burning in the grate, and he lit three lamps from it. He passed them to Barak, Janley and then me.

'We'll need these, sir,' he said and led the way back to the outer courtyard. We followed him, heads bowed against the rain, into a low, square building standing on its own. In the centre of the stone floor was a large square opening, protected by a low railing. An iron ladder bolted to the side led down into a brickwork shaft streaked with green lichen. A large wheel stood off to one side.

'I left the lock gates slightly open last night,' Padge said. 'After all the rain there is a lot of water coming through and it needs to drain. When I came this morning I thought to open them fully with the wheel but they were stuck fast. I looked down the shaft and – you will see.' The hand that held his lamp began to shake.

We all went to the rail and looked down, holding our lamps out over the shaft. It went down twenty feet. At the bottom, on one side, a pair of heavy wooden gates about eight feet high was set into the brick wall. They were slightly open, enough to let a trickle of water through. My eyes widened as I made out the body of a naked man at the bottom of the gate. His posture was strange, he was spreadeagled against the wooden gates, limbs outstretched. His face looked upwards, merely a white shape in the gloom, but I could make out that it was Lockley.

'The body's fixed to those gates somehow,' Padge said.

'Did you go down to look?' Sir Thomas asked. Padge shook his head vigorously.

'We'd better see. Barak, Harsnet, come with me. You too, Shardlake – if you can climb down ladders,' he added with a nasty smile, a flash of white teeth in the gloom.

'Of course I can,' I replied sharply, though I did not relish the prospect.

Sir Thomas swung easily over the railing and began his descent. Barak and Harsnet followed. I made up the rear, grasping the slippery rungs hard.

At the bottom we found ourselves standing on wet brickwork

that sloped down to a central channel where the water ran off down an archway into darkness. We looked at the lock gates, rendered speechless by what we saw there. The naked body of Francis Lockley had been laid out at the bottom of the gates and then nailed to them, like some terrible mockery of the Crucifixion, his hands nailed to one gate and his feet to the other. Big, broad-headed nails, driven in to the hilt. The gates could not be opened without ripping them out, and that would require more force than the weight of the water and turning of the wheel above could provide. I saw there was a mass of dried blood on the back of his head, but little sign of blood flowing from the terrible wounds. Lockley had at least died quickly. I guessed if he had been drugged with dwale and left to wake in the darkness there was the risk that he might live long enough to talk to a rescuer. The killer had put his safety before his sadistic cruelty. Nonetheless the savagery was unspeakable.

A loud creak from the gate made us start back.

'There's a lot of water backing up there,' Barak said anxiously.

'How in hell did the killer get him down here?' Sir Thomas asked.

'Dropped him down, I'd guess,' Barak said. 'Then climbed down the ladder.'

The gates creaked again. 'I think we should get out,' Barak said with sudden urgency. 'With the rain there's more water building up behind there all the time. Those nails are driven in fast, but at some point they'll give way.'

'You're right,' Sir Thomas agreed. 'Let's leave.'

We climbed the ladder again. Janley and Padge were sitting on stools on either side of the gloomy little room. We just stood there for a moment, shocked and overwhelmed by the latest murder. Then Harsnet said, 'I have to get out of here.' We followed him out into the courtyard. The rain seemed to be easing off.

'It will be a hard job getting Lockley out,' Harsnet said quietly. 'And as you said, Barak, a risky one. We will have to block the gates in some way while we remove the body, bring it up on ropes.'

'I will go and arrange that now,' Sir Thomas said. Even he appeared subdued. 'With some men of my household I can trust to keep their mouths shut. We cannot wait.'

'No.' Harsnet agreed. 'Not just the musicians' instruments but all the King's possessions that are stored here will be flooded out. But I do not understand how he got Lockley into the precinct, how he knew where the conduit-house was.'

I looked around. 'If he was hanging about the vicinity he could pick up that the watchman was a drunk,' I said quietly. 'Easy enough to get in here at night and explore the buildings to see if they would suit his purpose, which I guess he had already worked out.'

'If he talked to the watchman, the drunken old sot may remember him,' Sir Thomas said, his eyes lighting up with excitement.

'I doubt he did.'

'Why?'

'Because Padge is still alive. He should be questioned, certainly, but remember the killer has already murdered one man who could have led us to his identity.'

Harsnet nodded. 'Then we must question the tavern customers again. Ask them if a stranger has been asking about the Charter-house.'

I nodded to the chapel. 'The beggars too, perhaps.'

'Ay. Someone may have asked one of them for information in return for a groat. It's possible.'

Sir Thomas looked at me. 'Do you think there is any significance in the last two murders being round the Charterhouse?' he asked. 'Because do not forget, Lady Catherine Parr lives across that green. And the killer may know something of the layout. Dr Gurney was staying there when he was killed. That's three out of six murders now with a connection to Charterhouse Square.'

'I do not think so. I think he deliberately chose Lockley and his wife because he knew of their past somehow. Dr Gurney's presence on the other side of the square is surely a coincidence.'

'He must be strong to have got the body in here from outside,' Barak said.

'He brought my friend Roger Elliard's body across Lincoln's Inn Fields and into the Inn. Assuming he killed Lockley before he got here, I imagine he did the same. Lockley was a small man, like Roger, but fat. Yes, he must be very strong.'

'Shall we look around?' Barak asked. 'See if we can find where he got in?'

'Yes. We cannot get any wetter.'

We turned to go, but just then three figures walked under the gatehouse arch, like us muddy from riding. Barak's hand went to his sword-hilt, but I recognized the leading figure as Dean Benson, swathed in a heavy coat. He indicated to the two retainers who accompanied him to stay where they were. They stood in the yard, rain dripping off their caps. Benson came up to us. His plump face was anxious.

Harsnet stepped forward. 'What are you doing here, sir?' he asked.

The dean wiped his face with his sleeve. 'I have ridden halfway across London in the rain looking for you, sir. Your servant at Whitehall wouldn't tell me where you were at first, I had the devil's job to get it out of him. Can we please go inside, I am covered in mud—'

'Pox on the mud!' Sir Thomas Seymour said brutally. 'Who are you and what do you want?'

Benson thrust his chest forward. 'I am William Benson, Dean of Westminster Abbey. And who are you?'

'Sir Thomas Seymour, brother of Lord Hertford.'

'Seymour?' The dean frowned, and I could see his mind making connections. *So the Seymour family were involved in this—*

'What do you want, sir?' Harsnet asked again.

'We should go inside. What I have brought here should not get wet.'

Harsnet hesitated a moment, then led the way back into the conduit-house. Janley and Padge bowed as the gentleman of the church entered. The dean looked round him, puzzled. 'What is going on in here?'

'Never mind that for now,' Harsnet said. 'Please, tell us why you have come.'

Benson delved in his pocket and pulled out a piece of paper. 'This was pushed under the front door of my house just before dawn. My steward brought it to me.' He handed the paper to Harsnet. We gathered round the coroner. The paper was folded, Dean Benson's name and the words *MOST URGENT* written on it. Harsnet opened it. Inside was written, again in block capitals:

LANCELOT GODDARD
KINESWORTH VILLAGE
BY TOTTERIDGE
HERTFORDSHIRE

We stared at the simple, stark message, the address. 'Hertfordshire,' Harsnet said quietly. 'I did not think to make enquiry so far.'

'I've been to Totteridge village,' Barak said. 'It's at the bottom of that little finger of Hertfordshire land that sticks down towards London. It's a couple of hours' ride away.'

'You say this was pushed under your door,' Sir Thomas said. 'You didn't by any chance write it yourself?'

'Of course I didn't,' Benson snapped.

'The killer knew we were about to find the sixth victim,' I said quietly.

'And now he is giving us his address?' Harsnet said incredulously. 'He is surrendering?'

I took the piece of paper. I felt reluctant to touch the writing, the killer's writing. 'No. That would be to abandon his mission. And Goddard may be the victim, not the killer. The killer may not be inviting us to this village to surrender. It could be to show us the seventh killing. The last. The great earthquake that will signal the end of the world.'

✝

THERE WAS SILENCE for a moment. The dean looked between us, puzzled. 'There has been a sixth death? Who? Here?' He looked around, then his eyes fixed on the shaft.

'Down there,' I said quietly. 'Your former lay brother, Francis Lockley.'

The dean looked at the hatch, then stepped away, his face white. 'Dean,' Harsnet said. 'Go back to your house and stay there should we need you again. And tell nobody. You have seen now that the Seymour family is involved in this, how high this matter reaches.'

'What are you going to do?' Benson asked.

'Take steps,' Harsnet said noncommittally.

'Get out, you're wasting time,' Thomas Seymour said. 'Or do you want me to take you down to get a proper look at what's down that hatch? It's not pretty.'

The dean shrank away. He looked round us again, then turned and went out. He called to his retainers to follow him, and we listened to their footsteps on the wet flagstones dying away.

Harsnet looked round at us. 'We should ride up to Totteridge now,' he said. 'Sir Thomas, can you get some men—'

'I'm not sure we should do that,' I said urgently. 'It is what he would expect. We could be riding into a trap.'

'But if Sir Thomas can get some men,' Barak said, 'and we can ride there in force—'

'The hunchback's right,' Seymour said. 'This creature's got something waiting for us up there. It would be better for me to send a couple of trusted men up to that village, my steward and another man, an ex-soldier, who was with me in Hungary. They can spy out the land, find out whether Goddard lives there, make contact with the local magistrate. They can report back tonight. Coroner Harsnet, you

432

should tell the Archbishop what has happened, then I will report to him personally as soon as I have news.'

'We should storm the place,' Barak pressed.

'Let's see the lie of the land first,' Seymour said 'We can go to that village in force tomorrow.' He looked at the coroner. 'But we shall need the Archbishop's approval.'

Despite his insulting behaviour towards me, I looked at Sir Thomas with a new respect. He had been an ambassador with a fighting army in Hungary, he was thinking strategically.

'I should go with your men,' Harsnet said.

'No, Gregory,' I said. 'There is every chance that the killer will recognize you, given how he has been following us. It may be possible for Sir Thomas' men to make enquiries without showing who they are.'

'You think this man's possessed by the devil,' Seymour said. 'We have to show as much cunning as he does.'

Harsnet frowned. 'We need reliable men,' he said after a pause.

Seymour laughed. 'Do not worry, coroner, my steward is reliable and sober. He even goes to church on Sundays when I do not need him to organize some hunting.'

Harsnet looked at me. I nodded. 'Very well,' he said reluctantly.

Seymour looked at the watchman, Padge. 'And I'll get someone to replace him and keep people away. You'd better keep him safe somewhere for a bit, ply him with drink. His big ears have been flapping all this time.' The watchman gave him a bitter look, but dared say nothing. 'Janley should go back to the tavern,' Seymour concluded. He grinned at us suddenly. 'The chase is on, gentlemen, the hunt is nearly over.'

✞

WHEN HE HAD LEFT, Harsnet ordered Janley and the watchman to remain in the conduit-house and asked Barak and me to step outside. Mercifully the rain had ceased and a weak sun was trying to penetrate the clouds.

'You suggested there might be a trail, Barak?' Harsnet said. 'Shall we see? Then I must go and report to the Archbishop.'

Harsnet was silent, thoughtful, as the three of us went through the outer gate, following the wall that bounded the precinct. A gate led us into an orchard, reminding me again of the aftermath of Roger's death at Lincoln's Inn.

Barak led the way through the long grass around the trees. My shoes and netherhose were getting a further soaking from the grass. 'Can't see anything,' he said. 'Everything is sopping wet. No, wait, look there.' He pointed to the ground. A single long line ran through the grass. It had left a heavy impression.

'What is it?' I asked.

'A wheelbarrow,' Barak said. 'Wherever he was hiding Lockley, he must have had some distance to bring him. This is how he did it.'

'But a man carrying a body in a wheelbarrow would be noticed.'

'Not if he had a cover over it. I wonder where this leads.' He began following the thin line through the orchard. The trail led us back towards Aldersgate Street. It followed a gap in a hedge and disappeared in the short grass of a pathway round a field. Barak looked towards the distant road.

'The time and care he takes,' Harsnet said. 'He must have killed Lockley them come back for Mrs Bunce, and kept Lockley's body somewhere before putting him into the conduit yesterday.'

'And what he did to Mrs Bunce must have taken most of the night,' I said quietly.

'How could he overcome both of them?'

'Perhaps somehow he got them both to take dwale. Perhaps he came in late and persuaded them to take a glass of beer with him. He is clever enough for anything,' I added bitterly.

'And now he wants us to go to that village,' Barak said.

'Yes.' Harsnet looked at me. 'I think you are right. The seventh vial will be poured out somehow in that Hertfordshire village. I should have gone with them.'

I admired his courage, but could not agree. 'The chance to make some enquiries by stealth could make all the difference.'

Harsnet nodded reluctantly. 'What will he do?' he asked, his voice full of tension. 'Who will the seventh victim be? Is it to be one of us, a stranger, or someone else from the abbey? He is probably already dead, another body waiting to be found.'

'Or is Goddard himself the victim? Someone should check young Cantrell is safe,' I asked.

'Ay, not bludgeoned and carted off somewhere in a wheelbarrow.' Barak's tone was suddenly savage. The strain showed in his face again. He turned to me.

'What nightmarish bloody thing is he going to do this time? How will he make the earth quake?'

Chapter Thirty-seven

W E WALKED BACK to where Sukey and Genesis stood out-side, cropping the long grass growing against the outer wall. I looked back at the gate where Prior Houghton's arm had been nailed; I almost fancied I could make out a red outline on the wood. 'So much violence these last ten years,' I said quietly. 'Per-haps the wonder is that more people have not become obsessed with killing.' My first sight of poor Lockley's naked, crucified form at the bottom of that hatch came back to mind. I seemed to see Roger's face less and less often now, as though the later horrors had crowded it out.

'Where now?' Barak asked. 'Go home and wait for further instruc-tions?'

'No. Let us go and visit Master Piers now. See if he has been stealing. We may be called to Hertfordshire later.'

'What if the old Moor is there?'

'Then we make some excuse. And I wish you would stop calling him that.'

'There's no ill meant. I'm sure he's been called worse. Want a hand into the saddle?'

✝

WE RODE OFF. A little group of half a dozen beggars had gathered on the chapel steps. All had something wrong with them, two carried crutches and the others had pale, sickly-looking faces. The balding boy who had held the horses the day we first visited Lockley and Mrs Bunce was there. Perhaps they had been inside, drawn out by the activity round the Charterhouse gate. Now they began walking and limping towards us, crying for alms. 'Out of the way!' Barak called. 'We're on urgent business.'

We rode on. 'Hope Harsnet arranges to question them,' Barak said. 'They may know if someone was asking about the Charterhouse.'

'He will. He is conscientious and thorough.'

'Bit of a plodder, though, isn't he?'

'He doesn't have much imagination, I grant you.'

'Pious hot-gospeller.'

I smiled. 'You've never liked him, have you?'

'Neither did you, at the start. Remember that inquest he fixed?'

'He's better than most of the men who work at the King's court. He's got some principles, some humanity. Maybe he's been a bit slow at times, but he's never faced anything like this.' I looked at Barak seriously. 'None of us have.'

'You're right there. You know what scares me most of all?' Barak asked suddenly.

'What?'

'The way every killing seems to be planned to show us the killer is cleverer than we are. He presents them to us like trophies. Yarington, Mrs Bunce, Lockley. The three killings that have happened since we got involved.'

'I know. He tried to stop me acting, by attacking Tamasin and then me. But when that failed he turned to — as you say, showing he could outwit us.'

'But why?' Barak asked. 'Why?'

'I do not know. Perhaps it is part of his madness.'

'And now he gives us his address,' he said incredulously. 'That's mad.'

'He gave us *an* address. I am still not persuaded it is Goddard. Surely he would have been known among the sects, at least by description. With that mole on his face they say he has.' I sighed. 'I keep asking myself, is there anyone else it could be?' I laughed, hearing a touch of wildness in my own voice. 'Do you know, I even considered the possibility that Piers might be the killer.'

Barak shook his head. 'What the killer does takes so much time and planning, how could Piers do that while working full time for Guy? And Piers doesn't have anything to do with religious groups, I'd doubt he has any religion at all.'

'I know. It's a crazy idea. I've got to the stage where I'm clutching at straws.'

'Because you don't believe it is Goddard?'

'I'm just not sure.' I winced, another slight pull on the reins making my arm hurt.

'You all right?'

'Yes. Just my arm. And I'm cold.'

'The sun's come out.'

'I know. But I feel cold so much of the time now.'

✝

BARAK AND I left for Guy's house shortly after half past three. The apothecaries were working in their shops at Bucklersbury; through the window next to Guy's a man in a long robe could be seen, pouring powder into a large apothecary's jar. We tied the horses up outside. Barak spoke to me quietly. 'Will you let me take the lead in questioning him?'

'Do you think I will be too soft with him? I promise I will not.'

He looked at me seriously. 'I think a bit of rough questioning from me might throw him, take him off balance.'

I thought a moment, then nodded. 'All right.'

He knocked loudly on the door. We heard footsteps, then Piers opened the door, carrying a candle. He looked at us in surprise. 'Dr Malton has gone out, sir.'

'We know. It's you we've come to see, young cock,' Barak said cheerfully, shouldering his way inside. I followed him in, giving Piers a thin smile. I saw that either Piers or Guy had been experimenting:

the table at the end of the room was crowded with flasks and vials of liquid.

'Cut anyone up today?' Barak asked.

'I was upstairs, studying. I do not understand.' Piers voice was quiet, his expression subservient, but there was anger in his eyes as he turned to me. 'Why do you allow your man to talk to me thus, sir?'

'I have some questions. Barak can ask them as one loyal servant to another.'

'I hear Dr Malton has had some money go missing,' Barak said. 'Know anything about it?'

Piers' expression did not change. 'I have heard nothing. Surely if Dr Malton has had money missing he should talk to me himself.'

'Ah, but Master Shardlake here is his attorney.'

Piers' eyes flicked between Barak and me, disoriented by the rapid-fire questions. 'I cannot believe Dr Malton has authorized you to question me like this,' he said.

'But here we are. Stealing is a capital offence.'

The boy's eyes narrowed. 'I have done nothing. I shall tell Dr Malton about this. He will not be pleased with you.'

'It was he who told us about the missing money,' I said.

'Where is your room?' Barak asked.

'Up the stairs. But you have no permission to go in there. I have rights as an apprentice!' His voice rose now, his face reddening.

'Tough.' Barak turned to me. 'Shall I go look in his room?'

'I will go. You stay here and keep an eye on him.' I stared at Piers. He was frightened now.

The boy stepped back, blocking the inner door with his sturdy form. 'No! You have no right!'

Barak drew his sword and used the blade to edge him away from the door. Piers watched with set lips, breathing hard, as I passed through. I mounted the narrow, gloomy staircase. Guy did not trust servants among his equipment; there was no one else in the house. On the upper floor I saw a door was open.

Guy's precious edition of Vesalius lay on a desk, open at a picture of a skeleton dangling from a gibbet, in the posture of a hanged man. Piers had been engaged in drawing a copy of the revolting thing, a quill was lying on the table. It was very well done.

I searched the room. Among volumes on the bookshelf dealing with medicine and herbs I found a copy of the Black Book, the summary of the most lurid cases of sodomy and fornication that Crom-well's agents had found eight years before in their investigation of the monasteries. Many copies had been sold to prurient readers. There was a chest containing clothes, some of surprisingly good quality. I explored the bed, turning over the mattress, and there I found a small leather bag. Inside was a collection of silver coins, totalling over a pound: far more money than an apprentice was likely to have. I took it, left the room and returned down the narrow staircase.

Piers was standing against the table, Barak facing him with his drawn sword. As I entered the room I held up the bag. 'Money,' I said.

'So, my pretty, you *are* a thief,' Barak said grimly.

A change came over Piers' face. It took on a hard, calculating look. Now, I thought, the mask is gone. 'I could say some things about that old blackamoor if I chose,' he said in a voice that was suddenly sharp as a file. 'Like how he prostrates himself before a big old cross in his bedroom, worshipping idols. How the priest he goes to is known as a secret papist. How he is a pederast, how he makes me commit immoral acts with him.'

'That is a lie!' I shouted angrily.

'Perhaps it is. But part of him would like to. I have seen enough of him to know he would look embarrassed and uneasy at such an accusation. You are a lawyer, imagine how that would look to a jury. Him being an ex-monk. Sodomy is a hanging offence as much as theft. If I lose all I will make sure he loses as well.' He looked at me grimly.

'Nasty little arsehole, isn't he?' Barak said.

Piers' next move was so sudden it took us unawares. He reached behind him to the table, grabbed a flask of liquid and threw the contents in Barak's face. Barak gave a loud yell and stumbled backwards, dropping his sword as he raised his hands to his face. Piers ran to the door, threw it open and fled into the night. I heard his footsteps disappearing into the warren of streets that made up Bucklersbury.

I ran to Barak and gently pulled his hands from his face, dreading what I might find. His eyes were red and weeping, but there were no other marks and I caught the sharp sweet smell of lemons.

'My fucking eyes,' he groaned.

'I'll get some water from the kitchen. I think it's just lemon juice, you'll be all right.' I hurried out, coming back with a pail of water and a cloth. I squeezed water into his eyes. 'Blink, you idiot,' I said roughly.

After a thorough wash the pain in Barak's eyes subsided, although they remained bloodshot. 'What's Guy experimenting with lemons for?' he asked. 'They don't come cheap.'

'Some cure, I suppose.'

'That little rat will be miles from here by now.'

'Yes. I think our best course is to stay here until Guy comes back.' I sighed. I was not looking forward to his return.

✝

He came in an hour later, his eyes widening with surprise at the sight of us sitting in his shop, Barak still dabbing his eyes with a cloth.

'What has happened?'

I told him, leaving out Piers' threats against Guy. When I had finished he sat down on a stool. He looked bereft. He sat thus for several minutes, then rose slowly to his feet. It seemed to me that he had aged ten years. 'Let me look at your eyes, Barak,' he said wearily. He took the candle and peered into them. 'You have been washing them. Good. It was only something I was working on with lemons, a poultice.' Then he turned to me, and his voice was as I had never heard it, trembling with anger.

'You should have come to me first. You should not have gone behind my back.'

'I thought it best for us to confront Piers.'

'You thought I would obstruct you.'

I had no answer. 'I have just been to see Bealknap,' he said. 'He is better, as I thought, complaining Mistress Elliard's servants do not empty his piss-bowl often enough. I took that ridiculous man on as a patient because you asked me, just as I involved myself in your hunt for this killer. And this is how you repay me. I thought you trusted me, Matthew.'

'I did not feel you could see Piers clearly. And this was urgent. And he is a thief, Guy.'

'And now he has gone.'

'I am sorry. What can I say?'

'Nothing.' He lowered his head, the damp cloth clutched in his hands. There was a silence that lasted only a few moments, but felt like an hour. Then I said, 'There has been another killing.' I told him about Lockley, and the note giving Goddard's address.

He looked at me. 'There is nothing I can do, is there?'

'No.'

'Then I wish you luck in Hertfordshire.' Guy gave me a look that was stony, almost contemptuous. 'I will not have Piers prosecuted if he is caught,' he said. 'I will not see an eighteen-year-old boy hanged for stealing a little money, as the law prescribes.' He picked up the bag of coins from where I had put it on his table, slipping it into his robe. 'There, your evidence is gone. And now I would like you to leave, Matthew. I hope you find Goddard.' His look said that his involvement in the affair was over.

'Guy—'

He raised a hand. 'No. Please go. I have an appointment to go and visit Adam at the Bedlam.' He gave Barak a sudden hard look, and I realized he was wondering if I had told my assistant about his confusion about Piers.

'I have not—' I began.

'Go, Matthew, please.' His cold, angry tone struck me to the heart.

Barak and I left the shop. As we untied the horses Barak asked curiously, 'What is it you haven't told me?'

'Nothing. Private matters of Guy's.'

We rode away in silence. I almost groaned aloud at the thought of the harm I had done to our long friendship.

Chapter Thirty-eight

W E RODE HOME. The streets were thronged. Most of the city
constables seemed to be on patrol, together with several guards
in Bishop Bonner's livery. Many people gave them hostile or frightened
looks. I thought of those who had been arrested, of the danger to
Cranmer. I wondered what the godly men were doing, keeping out
of sight, probably, waiting till the storm died down. But this latest
persecution would only encourage them to see themselves as martyrs.
It occurred to me that Harsnet, as a royal official and a radical, might
himself be in danger. Or would the protection of Cranmer and Lord
Hertford be enough?

I was exhausted; at home I went up to bed and slept for several
hours, then had a gloomy dinner on my own, Barak and Tamasin
staying in their room. Seymour's men must have reached Hertfordshire
by now. I went to bed early. In the morning there was still no word.
Barak joined me at breakfast.

'What's happening?' I said.

'Maybe Seymour's men are dealing with Goddard quietly up
there,' Barak said seriously.

I shook my head. 'They should tell us,' I said. A thought struck
me. 'Where is Tamasin? Is she missing breakfast again?'

'She's still abed.' Barak looked at me seriously. 'She's guessed somehow that there's been another killing, but I didn't tell her where I went
yesterday. She's getting mopish, she just lies in bed. She looked so – sad.'

'Why is it you can no longer communicate, do you think?'

'I don't know.' As so often, he changed the subject. 'You're not
going to report young Piers, then?'

'No.'

'What is it between him and the old Moor?' Barak looked at me curiously.

'I think the need for someone to care for, and to pass on his knowledge to, is so strong that it has taken him over. But in the end it does not matter. At least now he is rid of that boy. I hope he has escaped, gone somewhere far from London.'

'If he has any sense he will have. He'll know that if he's tried for theft, he'll hang.'

I stood up abruptly. 'I am going to the Bedlam,' I said. 'Guy said he was going to visit Adam there. I will try and talk to him, make him see sense.'

Barak looked dubious. 'He's pretty angry,' he said.

I almost said, attend to your wife, she is angry too, but bit back the words. 'I can't let it rest like this.'

'Do you want me to come?'

'No. No, I'll go alone.'

He gave me a worried look. I could see he was concerned that the strain was becoming too much for me; his own face looked strained enough. I put my hand on his shoulder.

'I'll ride,' I said. 'I'll be safe. Send word if there is any news from Hertfordshire.'

☩

I REACHED Bishopsgate without incident. But as I rode through the gates into the Bedlam yard I heard an unexpected sound: a woman screaming and sobbing in dreadful fear. For an awful moment I feared the killer had misdirected us again and the seventh killing was to be here, now. Then I saw that a woman was hammering and banging on the closed doors of the Bedlam building, screaming to be let in. A little crowd of passers-by had gathered, some laughing at this latest example of the antics of the mad. I wondered why no one came to open the door. Then, as I rode up to the crowd, I saw that the woman was the keeper Ellen. I dismounted and hastily tied Genesis to the rail.

Ellen took no notice of the crowd. She had flattened her whole body against the door as she screamed in what seemed an extraordinary terror. 'Let me in, Master Shawms! Please! Please!' I elbowed my way through the crowd and laid a hand on her shoulder. 'Ellen,' I said quietly.

She did not look round. She went rigid and seemed to press herself even more tightly against the door. 'Who is it?' she whispered.

'It is I, Master Shardlake. What on earth is the matter?'

'For pity's sake, Master Shardlake, make him let me in.' And with that her knees gave way and she slid down the door, still pressing herself against it, sobbing wildly.

I banged on the door. 'Shawms!' I shouted. 'Open this door! What is happening?' I heard voices whispering, just inside. And from further back in the building I heard people shouting, and thought I heard Adam's voice among them.

A key turned and the door opened to reveal Shawms, the big keeper Gebons behind him. Gebons was frowning; Shawms looked angry. As soon as the door opened sufficiently Ellen threw herself inside and flattened herself against the opposite wall. She stood there, breathing heavily. A gaggle of patients stood in the open door of the parlour, their expressions fearful. The old woman Cissy took a couple of shuffling steps forward, hesitantly stretching out an arm. 'Oh, Ellen,' she muttered. 'Poor Ellen.'

I saw that the doors of all the patients' rooms were shut. I heard the man who believed he was the King demanding his subjects behave themselves, while from down the corridor the one-time scholar was banging himself against his door with loud thuds. Between them I heard Adam's voice calling to God to help Ellen, save good Ellen.

Shawms shut the front door in the faces of the curious onlookers. 'What are you doing to these people?' I demanded.

He looked as though he would have liked to strike me, but kept his voice calm. 'Ellen there needed a lesson. Thanks to you she has taken over the welfare of Adam Kite and makes so bold as to tell me how he should be treated. Now she is moving on to the other patients, demanding that drivelling old dolt Cissy be released into the care of her family.' He glared round at the old woman, who shrank back into the doorway. 'As though her family wanted the trouble, any more than Ellen's family want her.' His voice rose. 'Have you not yet grasped what this place is, Master Shardlake? It is a rubbish-heap, where people of wealth leave their mad relatives. We may have our charity cases and sometimes people even get cured, or pretend they are to get out. But mostly it is a rubbish heap, one that generates gold for Warden Metwys as rubbish generates rats.'

'Ellen is a member of your staff even if she was a patient once. What in the devil's name have you done to her?'

Shawms laughed then, right in my face. 'Is that what she told you? Ellen is still a patient, she always will be. I have given her some of the duties of a keeper, for she is good with the patients, if too soft with them.' He looked at her. 'But sometimes she gets above herself, and I have to remind her of who and what she is by putting her outside.' He turned to Ellen, who was still holding herself rigid against the wall, breathing heavily, her eyes averted from the closed door. 'That is her madness,' Shawms continued brutally. 'She can't bear to go outside, says the world sways and rocks and will swallow her up. She's been like that ever since she was set on by a gang of youths down in Sussex where she comes from, and they made a woman of her before her time. Ain't that so, Ellen?'

Ellen forced herself to stand away from the wall. She clasped her hands in front of her. 'Yes, Master Shawms,' she said calmly. She looked from him to me, her long face filled with shame. 'So now, Master Shardlake, you know all about me.'

I felt great pity for the poor woman, but knew instinctively that to show it would be the worst thing I could do.

'It does not matter, Ellen,' I said quietly. 'Listen, poor Adam is distressed. Will you come with me and help him? You are better with him than anyone. If you feel able.'

She gave me a grateful look. 'Yes, of course,' she said quietly, and began walking steadily down the corridor, feeling for her bunch of keys. I turned to Shawms. 'I hope Adam is not too disturbed by this incident; I should have to report it to the court.' He gave me a vicious look. As I turned away Gebons gave me a look of something like admiration.

I joined Ellen at the closed door to Adam's room. 'Ellen!' he cried from within. 'What have they done to you?'

'It's all right,' Ellen called. 'I am here.'

'Has Dr Malton not arrived?' I asked her.

'No, sir, he was expected but is not here.' Ellen's voice and manner were almost normal now, just a little shaky, as though her earlier wildness had been a dream. She opened the door. Within, Adam was standing as near to the door as his ankle chain would allow him. His face was red, his frantic expression turning to relief as Ellen entered.

'Are you all right?' he asked her. 'You were screaming.'

'Yes, Adam. Do not disturb yourself, sit down.' I saw a stool had been brought into the room. The boy hesitantly sat down on it. 'It was Dr Malton's idea to bring that in,' Ellen told to me. 'Make him sit instead of crouching praying on the floor.'

For the first time, I realized, Adam had shown concern for someone else. Then he turned his wasted face to me, and said something I did not understand.

'My concern for Ellen was honourable, sir, please say you saw that it was so if you are asked. I was not sinning again, even in thought. It was not like the wicked reverend's woman.' Then his thin face twisted into an agonized rictus and he would have sunk to his knees had not Ellen held his shoulder. 'Come, Adam,' she said. The boy put his head in his hands and began to cry.

And then the connection came to me. His vicar, Meaphon, was friends with Reverend Yarington. Timothy had described the boy who had visited the prostitute Abigail as tall and dark. Adam was tall and dark and his mother had told me that once he had been good-looking, until this desperate obsession had reduced him to skin and bone.

I stepped forward. 'Adam, does the name Abigail mean anything to you?'

At that the boy wriggled out of Ellen's grasp and crouched against the wall, staring at me in horror. 'My sin is discovered,' he whispered. 'Oh God forgive me, do not strike me down.'

'Sir, what are you doing?' Ellen asked indignantly.

'Turning a key which must be turned,' I said. I knelt down beside Adam, making my voice calm. 'Adam, you came to Reverend Yarington's house once with a message from your own vicar, did you not?'

He looked at me with terrified eyes. 'Yes.'

'Abigail saw you and invited you in. She felt the need for a young man. She taught you things you had thought on but not experienced yet. Am I right?'

'How can you know that?' he whispered. 'Has God marked you as the instrument of my punishment?'

I smiled gently. 'No, Adam. Yarington's stable boy saw someone from the stable. I just realized it might be you. That is all. Abigail has run away and I needed to find her in connection with a case.' I must not tell him Yarington had been murdered.

'That is my great sin,' he said. 'I knew if my parents and the church found out they would cast me away, for I have lost my place with the elect.' Adam looked at me. 'You will not tell my parents, sir?'

'No. I promise.'

'I was wax in her hands,' Adams said. 'Jesus, my shield, seemed powerless. She must have come from the devil.'

'She was only a poor woman. Helpless herself, in the power of that hypocrite Yarington.'

'Yes. He is a hypocrite.' He nodded frenetically. 'I knew I should tell my parents, the church – I turned to God for guidance but could feel nothing, nothing. Has He abandoned me?'

'I am no theologian, Adam. But one thing is for certain, you have not abandoned Him. Only sought to reach Him in the wrong way, perhaps.'

It was too much for the boy, he buried his face in his hands and began weeping again. I stood up painfully, my knees creaking. I turned to Ellen. 'I must leave now. The information Adam has given me is important. For a – a case. I do not know when Dr Malton may come. May I leave Adam with you?'

A bitter look crossed her face. 'Do you mean, am I safe to leave him with?'

'No – I—'

'I am safe enough,' she said starkly. 'Unless I am made to go out.' She took a long breath. 'Most of the time I am sane.'

'I know I leave him in good hands with you.'

Her face coloured. 'Do you mean that?'

'I do. If Dr Malton comes, please tell him what Adam said. And tell him – tell him I tried to see him.'

'I see from your face this is something serious,' Ellen said. 'Is Adam in trouble?'

'No, I swear he is not.' I smiled at her. 'You are a good woman, Ellen. Do not let a bullying pig like Shawms make you think otherwise.'

She nodded, tears coming into her eyes. I left the room, my brain racing. So it was Adam who had visited Abigail. He was the dark-haired boy I had been seeking. I wondered suddenly if Ellen was indeed safe to leave with Adam, her terrible panic had shaken me. But no, I thought, apart from her strange malady, she is all too sane, saner than many of the thousands on the streets of London.

Chapter Thirty-nine

I RODE HOME in thoughtful mood. I could not face the morning crowds in the streets, and took the roads north of the city wall. It felt safe there too; there was no one around. The quiet made it worth passing by the stinking Houndsditch, where despite the injunctions of the Council people still dumped dead dogs and horses. I thought about Adam, how easy it was to forget that those who became mad were once ordinary people. I could see now that Adam's bone-thin, tragic face could have been handsome, once, how he could have been, as his father described him, a carefree romping lad. Such a boy would be seen by those in his church as one to be controlled, disciplined, frightened with Hell. And how well that had worked. I thought too of Ellen, her tragic story and what she might have been like before her terrible experience.

I turned into Chancery Lane from the north; it was at once busier. I was still deep in thought. I was brought sharply to myself by a shout of 'Look out, there!' I saw a pedlar directly in front of Genesis, holding a three-wheeled cart full of trinkets. As I jerked the reins I glimpsed a ragged coat, its tatters dragging in the dirt, and a filthy face framed by thick grey hair and a bushy beard.

'Ye'll have me over, ye'll pay if ye break my goods!' he muttered over his shoulder as he hauled his cart out of the way. I steadied Genesis, who had almost stumbled, and placed a hand on his flank to reassure him as I rode on. By the time I could glance back, the pedlar was almost up to Holborn. I rode on past Lincoln's Inn Gate to my house. It was still only half past four.

As I went upstairs to change out of my riding clothes I reflected that one aspect of the mystery was solved at least; the boy who had visited Yarington's house had been locked safely in the Bedlam all these weeks. It looked as if was Goddard after all. But why had he sent us his address?

I took down my Testament, and turned to Revelation:

> And the seventh Angel poured out his vial into the air; and there came a great voice out of the Temple of Heaven, from the seat, saying, it is done. And there followed voices, and thunders, and lightnings; and there was a great earthquake, such as was not seen since men were on the earth, so mighty an earthquake and so great.

I sat back in my chair. Every killing had been a simulation, a cruel parody, of what the seven angels had done to the sinful multitudes in Revelation. He had used the body of poor Lockley to dam a stream to symbolize the drying up of the Euphrates by the sixth vial. But as Barak had said, how could even he make the earth quake?

As I laid my Testament on my desk it fell open again, at an earlier page. A passage caught my eye. Paul's first letter to the Corinthians:

> And though I have the gift of prophecy, and understand all mysteries, and all knowledge; and though I have all faith, so that I could remove mountains, and have not charity, I am nothing.

I wondered if the killer had ever read that passage. If he had, it would have made no impression; it would not have chimed with his terrible urge to violence, he would probably not have noticed it. I closed the book feeling further despair at what men had made of their God.

✝

I WENT DOWNSTAIRS. As I passed the parlour I saw Tamasin, arranging some twigs dusted with early blossom in a vase. Her face wore an expression of pensive sadness. She saw me and smiled.

'I thought these would make a pretty display. I took them from the garden, I hope you do not mind.'

'They will remind us that it is spring. Where is Jack?'

'He has gone over to Lincoln's Inn to see how Skelly is getting on alone.'

'I should go there.' I hesitated. I looked at her seriously. 'Tamasin, we may be nearly there. We have located the house of the man that we think is behind all this, near Barnet. Sir Thomas Seymour has organized a party of men to go there and take him. We may have to go there tonight.'

'You have the murderer?' she asked.

'We are fairly sure who he is.'

'So Jack may be off adventuring again,' she said.

'Tamasin, he hates this. As I do, who brought him into it.'

'You are right,' she agreed. 'He fears this creature you are hunting.' Then she spread her arms wide in a despairing gesture. 'But I can give him no comfort. When I try to talk to him seriously he calls me nag or scold.' She sighed wearily. 'So the same pattern just goes on and on, like a donkey turning a waterwheel.'

'Tamasin—'

She raised a hand. 'No, sir. You mean well and I thank you. But I am talked out.' She curtsied and left the room.

Still restless, I decided to walk up to Lincoln's Inn to see Dorothy. If Bealknap was better, perhaps I could shame the rogue into returning to his own lodgings. But when I arrived Margaret said that Dorothy had gone out, to settle some accounts.

'It is good she is attending to business again,' she said.

'Yes.' I raised my eyebrows. 'How is my brother in the law, Master Bealknap?'

'He is a great complainer. You would think he owned this place and I were his servant.'

'Perhaps I could see him?'

'I will see how he is.' Margaret went inside, returning a minute later, red-faced. 'He says he does not wish to see you, sir. He feels too poorly. I am very sorry, but without the mistress here I cannot—'

'Of course. I think I can bear not seeing him.' I wondered if Bealknap was still ashamed of giving Felday information about me; of course he did not know that Felday was dead. 'Will you tell your mistress I am sorry he is such trouble?'

'Yes, sir.'

I walked away. For the first time in nearly a month I stopped and looked at the fountain. The water plashed peacefully into the great stone bowl. I thought, how did the killer get to know that Roger had once been a radical reformer years ago? As I stood there looking at the water, something stirred in my mind, something I had heard the day I went to Yarington's house and spoke to Timothy. What was it? It nagged at my tired brain as I walked home, adding to my general sense of unease.

✞

I WENT ROUND to my chambers, but Barak had just left. I followed him home; he was eating some bread and cheese in the parlour.

'Thanks for keeping an eye on the work,' I said.

'How did you get on with the old— with Dr Malton?'

'He was not there.'

'Do you want some food?'

'No. I am not hungry.' I looked at him seriously. 'I think you should go to your room, see Tamasin. She is in an unhappy humour.'

He sighed and nodded. In the doorway he turned. 'By the way, Orr said that pedlar who's taken to frequenting Chancery Lane is becoming a bit of a nuisance. He's called twice this last couple of days trying to sell trinkets, asking for one of the women of the house.'

I stared at him. 'Wait,' I said quietly. 'Close the door.' I was breathing hard with the thought that had come to my mind. 'This pedlar, is he a ragged greybeard?'

'Ay. Him that has been round here for days.'

'And carries his things in a three-wheeled barrow.'

'You don't think – but he's an old greybeard. And half the pedlars in London push three-wheeled carts.'

'But what a way to follow us, observe us unnoticed. Barak, is this what he has been doing? Is it him?'

'He's in Hertfordshire.'

'He's concentrated our attention there. Fetch Orr,' I said. 'Then go to the end of the front garden and see if the pedlar's in sight. Don't let him see you.'

Barak gave me a doubtful look, but hurried away. Orr appeared a minute later. 'What was that pedlar selling?' I asked.

'The usual stuff. Bits of cheap jewellery. Brushes and pans. I told him to be off.'

'Pedlars do not usually waste time on second calls if they have had no luck the first time.'

'He asked for the woman of the house. Perhaps he thought he could wheedle Tamasin or Joan into buying something. When he called he kept looking past me, into the house.'

Barak returned. 'He's coming down Chancery Lane from Aldgate. He'll be here in a minute.' He frowned. 'You're right, there's something odd. He's just pushing his cart down the street, not stopping at any houses or accosting passers-by.'

'I think he may be the killer,' I said quietly. 'What better way to go around unnoticed, follow people, listen to conversations, than pass yourself off as a ragged pedlar whom people will notice only to avoid, part of the refuse of mankind none of us wants to see.'

'But he's an old man,' Orr protested.

'I'm not sure he is,' Barak said. 'He walks like a younger man. And have we not recently passed Palm Sunday, when people dress up as the old prophets and false beards are ten a groat?'

'Jesu, have we got him?' Orr breathed.

'Shall we try to take him now, we two?' Barak asked him.

Orr nodded. 'He seems unarmed.'

'Let's do it now,' Barak said. 'We must hurry, or he'll be past us and into the throng of Fleet Street.'

I stood up. 'I'm coming too.' I spoke with more bravado than I felt. 'And if when we take him he proves to be a devil with forked horns under that beard and flies off over Holborn then we will know Harsnet was right.'

'I'll get my sword. Is yours in your room?'

'Yes.' It had lain there years; lawyers did not wear swords.

'Mine's in the kitchen.' Orr left, his face grimly determined. I looked round my parlour: the tall buffet displaying my plate, my prized wall-painting of a classical hunting scene. I realized how much it meant to me, the room at the centre of my life. I set my lips and went to fetch the sword from my room. As I went out to the landing, buckling on my scabbard, Barak's door opened and he stepped out. 'This is urgent, woman!' he called over his shoulder. 'We've got him!' He thundered down the stairs. Orr was already standing by the open door. Tamasin rushed out of her room, her face furious. She grabbed my arm. 'What in Heaven's name is happening? Will someone tell me?'

'We think the killer is outside,' I said. 'We think he is disguised as a pedlar. This is our chance, we must go.' I ran hastily downstairs. Orr and Barak were already outside. I caught a glimpse of Joan standing in the kitchen doorway, the two boys clinging to her skirts.

✝

THE SUN WAS low in the sky, the house casting long shadows across Chancery Lane. From the gateway I saw the pedlar had now passed my house, trundling his cart on down the gently sloping street. The three of us ran pell-mell after him. Lawyers and clerks passing by stopped and stared. As we splashed through a puddle I saw a blob of mud fly out and hit the coat of Treasurer Rowland, who had pressed himself against the wall to avoid our rush. I felt a momentary stab of satisfaction.

'We'll look silly if it's just some old pedlar,' Orr said. I had not breath to answer.

As we ran up behind him the pedlar heard us coming and turned, pulling a brake on one of the rear wheels of his cart. As Barak had said, he moved quickly for an old man. I caught another glimpse of a grey beard, wild hair, bright eyes in a dirty face. Then he turned to run.

Barak jumped him, grasping his ragged collar. Most men would have toppled but the pedlar stayed upright and seized Barak's arm, preventing him from reaching his sword. Orr grabbed at the grey beard, but it pulled away from his face with a ripping sound, opening a red gash on the man's cheek and hanging lopsided over his mouth. He ignored it. Then his knee came up between Barak's legs and Barak doubled over with a gasp. The pedlar jumped for his cart, thrust his hand to the bottom and pulled out a large sword, sending a heap of cheap bangles flying. He stood at bay against the cart; Orr and I, swords drawn, had him pinned against it. I became aware that we were surrounded by a whole crowd of passers-by, looking on from a safe distance.

I tried to get a look at the pedlar's face. The bushy grey hair obscured his brow, and blood from where his beard had been torn off was running from his left cheek into the wig. Something struck me as odd about the colour of his long nose, and I realized that like the beard it was a fake, and what I had taken for a dirty face was in fact caked with actor's make-up. Only the blue eyes, glittering with hatred and excitement, were real.

The pedlar made a sudden jump, striking out at me. More by luck than judgement I managed to parry the blow. Then Barak, face pale with pain, jumped to my side. He thrust at the pedlar's sword-arm, but a sudden shout from the side of the road distracted him and he missed.

'Stop this melee!' Treasurer Rowland was yelling at us as though we were a group of frolicking students. He disoriented us for a second. The pedlar took his chance and thrust his sword at Barak, catching him on the forearm and making him drop his sword. Then he jumped aside and ran at a man in the crowd, a law student who had dismounted from his horse to watch and held his animal by the reins. The pedlar slashed at his cheek with his sword, then dropped it on the ground as the boy screamed and put his hands to his face. The pedlar jumped into the horse's saddle, kicked at the horse and in a second he was racing back up Chancery Lane towards Holborn. The poor student lay writhing and screaming on the ground as Barak held his bloody arm and cursed. I thought of commandeering a horse from the street and making chase, but by the time I had done that the killer would be long gone. I turned wearily back to the scene around the cart.

Barak had received only a small flesh wound but the poor student was badly hurt, a slash across the nose and cheek that would scar him for life. It was a miracle the blow had missed his eyes. Treasurer Rowland ordered him taken back to Lincoln's Inn. Then he turned to me, furious, demanding to know why we had attacked a pedlar. Telling him it was the man who had killed Roger Elliard shut him up.

The crowd slowly dispersed, and Barak and Orr and I were left with the cart. We looked through it but there was nothing there but trays of pasteboard jewellery, some cloths and dusters and bottles of cleaning-vinegar for silver.

'Big enough to hide a body,' Barak observed. He took one of the cloths and wound it round his arm to staunch the blood dripping to his fingers.

'This is how he followed us, no doubt listening to our conversations. I don't remember any greybeard pedlar with a cart in the crowd when I was struck, but he may have other disguises.'

'Was it Goddard, sir?' Orr asked.

'With that false nose and hair and the blood on his face, who can say?'

'I saw no sign of a mole,' Barak said. 'If it's as big as people say, it'd be hard to hide.'

'Why was he here?' Orr asked.

'Perhaps to observe comings and goings. Perhaps to frighten us again, or even to do something to the women.' I thought a moment, then delved into the cart and pulled out the half dozen bottles of cleaning-vinegar. One by one I emptied them into the bottom of the cart. The contents of the fourth made a hissing sound and began to sear the wood.

'Vitriol again,' I said. 'That is why he has been calling at the house. This was meant to be thrown at Tamasin or Joan.'

☦

THE THREE OF US walked slowly back home. The cart we left where it was. It could tell us nothing more. I threw the fake beard inside it.

Joan was standing in the doorway. She looked frightened, and her eyes widened at the sight of Barak's arm. 'What happened?' she asked, her voice trembling.

'The man who attacked Tamasin and me was outside,' I said. 'He got away.' I looked at her wrinkled, worried face. I could not bear to tell her what might have happened had she, rather than Orr, opened the door to the pedlar. 'It's all right now. Where are the boys?'

'I told them to stay in the stable.'

I nodded wearily. 'They can come out now. Goodman Orr, thank you for your help.'

He nodded and followed Joan into the kitchen. Barak leaned against the banister, his face pale as shock caught up with him.

'I'd have had him but for that gabbling old arsehole Rowland,' he said fiercely.

'Yes, I think you would.'

'I can't tell Tammy about the vitriol. I can't even bear to think of it.' He sighed. 'She can't go outside until this is over. I'll tell her.'

'Why shouldn't I go out if I want to?' I looked up to find Tamasin at the top of the stairs, looking down at us. She must have heard Barak's final words. She looked at his arm. 'What the hell have you done to yourself now?' Her voice was sharp with anger and panic. I realized I had never before heard her swear.

'The killer was outside. We almost caught him, but he got away. This is nothing, just a scratch. Get some water and bathe it for me, would you?'

'But why do you say I can't go out?' Tamasin called down.

'He may still be around.'

'He's been around these last three weeks. Will you tell me what has happened?'

'I think you should tell her,' I said to Barak under my breath. 'She can bear it.'

'I can't. I can't bear such a thing might have happened to her because she is my wife.' He took a shuddering breath.

'What are you muttering about now?' Tamasin called down.

'Will you do as I say, woman?' Barak called up the stairs. Holding his arm, he strode up to where Tamasin stood, her expression a mixture of anger and perplexity. He walked past her into their room. She followed. The door slammed behind her.

Outside, the rain started up again, pelting hard against the windows.

✝

I WAS PREPARING to get ready for bed, looking out of the window at the rain and wondering if they had repaired the gates at the Charterhouse, when there was a knock at my door. I opened it to find Barak there.

'News from Harsnet?' I asked.

'No.' He was in his shirt, his right sleeve rolled up and his forearm bandaged. On the bare skin above the bandage I saw other scars, relics of old sword-battles. He looked very tired. 'May I come in?' he asked brusquely. 'I need to talk.'

I nodded assent, and he sat down on the bed. He was silent a long moment, then shook his head. 'She is angry because I will not let her go out of doors and will not tell her why.'

'You should tell her about the vitriol.'

He shook his head. 'I could not tell her that something so awful might have happened to her. Just the thought of him doing that to her face—' He broke off and I saw tears in the corners of his eyes.

'Come, you know how strong she is. That is what you first liked about her at York. Do you remember?'

'But I am her husband now. I should be able to protect her.' And then he added, 'I should be able to give her a child.' He was silent a few moments again. 'I know it is supposed to be the woman's fault when a child dies just after it leaves the womb, but who knows anything any more these days? What if the fault is mine? All I wanted was to provide for her, keep her safe, give her a family. Carry on my father's old Jewish name. And I have been able to do none of those things.' He stared bleakly at the door. 'I love her, I have never felt for any woman what I feel for her and God knows I have known plenty.'

'Perhaps that is the problem,' I answered gently. 'You built a fantasy of how married life would be, and find hard the reality of a union which heaven knows has been blessed with little luck. But that is the fault of neither of you. If only the two of you could talk freely.'

He gave me a sidelong look. 'For one who has always lived alone you are a shrewd old bird, aren't you?'

'Easy enough to see the problems in others' lives. I have made the opposite mistake with Dorothy. I have said too much to her too soon.'

'Ah, I wondered what was happening there.'

'Nothing is happening. And if you tell anyone else about it, I will have you out of Lincoln's Inn faster than a crow can fly,' I added jestingly, to relieve the tension. Barak smiled and nodded.

'Talking of crows,' he said, 'you don't think you may have competition from Bealknap? Maybe he is not ill at all, and seeks to rouse her pity.'

'Bealknap would only be interested in a woman if she were made of gold and could be melted down.'

We took refuge in brief laughter, then Barak said seriously, 'Will you be able to make it up with the old Moor?'

'I do not know. I will try. As you should with Tamasin.'

He rose with a sigh. 'I ought to go back to her. Thank you,' he added.

'Jack,' I said. 'Do you remember once at York you told me you were torn between your old adventurous, rake-hell life and settling down. You chose to settle down with Tamasin, you made your choice. To move from a life of self-reliance to sharing. You have much courage, now you must have the courage to open yourself to her.'

He paused at the door. 'There are different types of courage,' he said gloomily. 'Few have them all in good measure.'

✢

THE RIDER FROM Lambeth Palace called after midnight, when we had all gone to bed. I was not asleep, however, for lying in bed I could hear muffled shouts from Barak and Tamasin's room; they were arguing again. The sound stopped suddenly at the loud knocking on the front door.

Barak and I were told to come immediately to a conference with Archbishop Cranmer. We dressed quickly, fetched the horses and rode through the darkened city to Whitehall Stairs, where a large boat was waiting to ferry us across the Thames. It had stopped raining and bright moonlight shone down on the silvery, deserted river.

We were led to Cranmer's office. As Barak and I arrived outside another clerk approached from the opposite direction, Harsnet beside him. The coroner too looked as though he had just been roused from his bed.

The Archbishop was sitting behind his desk. His face was strained, great bags under his eyes. Lord Hertford was not present but Sir Thomas Seymour was, gaudily dressed as usual, his arms folded across his chest and a look of excitement on his face.

I told them of the incident with the pedlar. 'You could not see who he was?' Harsnet asked quietly when I had finished.

'No. He was well disguised.'

'Goddard had a large mole on his face,' Cranmer said.

'I did not see it. But he was caked with make-up.'

Cranmer sat considering for a moment. Then he turned to Sir Thomas. 'Tell them the news from Hertfordshire,' he said.

'I found Kinesworth easily enough. It's just a small village, a mile from Totteridge. The local magistrate knew all about the Goddard family. They lived in a manor house just outside the village. They were wealthy once, but Goddard's father was a drunk and lost it all. Their estates were sold by the time the father died thirty years ago. Goddard was still a boy then. He and his mother holed up in the house; apparently she was a woman of good breeding and ashamed of what had happened to the family. When he was old enough Goddard went to Westminster Abbey to be a monk. The old woman lived on at the house alone as a recluse until she died a few months ago and Goddard inherited it.'

'That was when he moved out of his London lodgings,' I said. 'That was where he went.' I took a deep breath. 'Is he there now?'

'Apparently he comes and goes. He was seen riding out to London yesterday. We waited all day to see if he would come back, but there was no sign until well after nightfall yesterday. Then smoke was seen coming from the chimney of the house.'

'So he's there,' Cranmer said.

'He could have been the pedlar on that timescale,' I said. 'Our encounter with him was at dusk.'

'Yes.'

'Then let us take him,' Sir Thomas said, his voice full of excitement.

'Wait a moment. What else do the locals say about him?' asked the Archbishop.

'He is known as unfriendly, does not mix at all with the local people. He doesn't come into the village, gets supplies sent to him. The house is just about falling down.'

'He has money then?' Harsnet said.

'Some at least.' I thought of the beggars who had come to sell their teeth.

'Did you see the house?' Cranmer asked.

'I went to look at it, from a safe distance. That was easy enough; it's surrounded by trees. It's a manor house, probably impressive once but decayed-looking. All the shutters were closed. It's got an overgrown garden surrounding it, woods all around. And here's an interesting thing,' Seymour paused. 'After his mother died Goddard dismissed the few old retainers she had left. It caused much resentment in the village.'

'So he is quite alone there?' I asked.

'Yes. I left a man to watch the house secretly, and rode back here with my steward.'

'This magistrate,' Harsnet asked. 'Can he be trusted?'

'I believe so. He seems capable enough.'

'You did not tell him I was involved?' Cranmer asked sharply.

'No, my lord. Only that this was a secret matter of state.'

Cranmer nodded. He turned to Harsnet. 'Sir Thomas has suggested we send a group of armed men to ride there now, break into the house.'

'Then let us do it.' The coroner laughed bitterly. 'After all the questions I asked in London and the neighbouring counties, and came up with nothing. If only I had gone that little bit further.'

'You did all you could,' Cranmer said. He turned to Sir Thomas. 'How many men can you provide?'

'A dozen, my lord,' he answered confidently. I could see he was enjoying being the centre of attention. 'Under my steward, Russell. All young men, strong and sporty. That is the type of man I like to have serving me.' He smiled complacently.

'What will they be told?'

'Only that some men of the court are hunting a villain, and we want their help to catch him.'

Cranmer looked round the room. 'I think this is what we must do,' he said. 'End this matter now.'

'After that note,' I said, 'that must be what he is expecting us to do. This is tied in with the killing of the seventh victim.'

'I know,' Cranmer said quietly. 'But what else can we do but go there in force?'

I had no answer. 'I want you to go with Sir Thomas' party, Matthew,' the Archbishop continued. 'It seems that for the killer you are connected to his mission. That is all the clearer after the pedlar's attack.' He looked at me sternly, perhaps expecting argument, but I only said, 'Yes, your grace.'

The Archbishop turned to Seymour. 'Mark this well, Thomas,' he said firmly. 'This is not sport. If it goes wrong and the King finds what we have been doing it will not only be me who suffers. Curb your enthusiasm for adventure. And remember that if Goddard is caught he must never be brought to trial. The matter will be closed, quietly and secretly. Tonight.'

Sir Thomas flushed, but nodded. 'I understand how important this is, my lord,' he said haughtily.

'Good. And thank you for what you have done so far. Now, what is happening at the Charterhouse?'

'My men have got Lockley's body out, but the gates won't open any further. They're jammed somehow. My brother is sending an engineer to look at the problem.'

'And I have been questioning the beggars,' Harsnet said. 'There was one who came there a few weeks ago, he stayed in that chapel they use as a shelter. He was very keen to learn all he could about the Charterhouse and about the tavern, though he never went there.' He looked at me. 'An old man, with a dirty face, thick grey hair and a beard. The other beggars didn't like him, I think they sensed he wasn't what he pretended to be.'

Seymour laughed. 'The man's a genius. The King should take him in his service as a spy.'

'His skills come from the devil,' Harsnet said.

'When did that matter?'

Cranmer turned to Barak, who had been standing quietly by the door. 'I want you to help Sir Thomas organize his men into an armed party,' he said. 'You worked for Lord Cromwell, you have useful experience in such matters.'

'Yes, my lord.' Barak bowed. I wondered if the Archbishop wanted Barak to make sure Sir Thomas organized things properly, and did not tell his men too much. From the hard look Sir Thomas gave him, I guessed he wondered the same.

The Archbishop stood up. 'I pray you can end this horror,' he said. As we turned to leave he looked to me and I saw commiseration on his face. Well, I thought, I set myself on this path the morning I found poor Roger.

✝

WALKING DOWN the corridor I fell into step with Harsnet.

'Will this be the end, Matthew?' he asked quietly.

'I do not know.'

'You are right to be cautious. I feel we are riding into the devil's jaws.'

'We will have many men.'

'I don't trust Seymour. He is an adventurer.'

'He is. But he has shown skill in this. His military experience is showing.'

'Perhaps.' Harsnet was silent for a moment, then said, 'I saw Lady Catherine Parr ride into her house in Charterhouse Square this afternoon, attended by her retainers. She has much land in the north, but stays on in London. It must be because she is still considering the King's proposal.'

'She will not be able to go without the King's leave. In a way she is trapped here.'

'She must marry the King,' he said with sudden passion. 'If reform is to survive at all. And we must stop Goddard,' he added. 'By any means we can.'

We stepped outside. Sir Thomas stood on the wharf by the raft, lights at his back from the smoking torches carried by the three boatmen standing in the boat. 'To my house,' he said. 'To fetch my men and horses.' As he stood with his arms on his hips, master of the scene, in his pose he reminded me of the King. I shuddered.

Chapter Forty

A LITTLE OVER an hour later, I sat on my horse outside my house. The moonlight shone on the puddles of a deserted Chancery Lane. The horses were nervous at being out at such an unaccustomed hour. I was tired and my injured arm ached.

Sir Thomas Seymour had gone to his house in the Strand to make ready for the journey to Hertfordshire. As Chancery Lane was en route, he had agreed that I should leave a message for Tamasin and Joan that we would not be back until late in the day. I had asked Barak if he wanted to write his own note for Tamasin, but he had shaken his head.

The sound of jangling harnesses approached from the direction of the Strand. A crowd of over a dozen men, all wearing swords, rode quietly up to me. The moon cast a pale light over them. A tall man in his thirties was in the lead, Harsnet and Barak beside him. The men accompanying them were all young, strong-looking, some with an air of suppressed excitement about them. All were dressed in sober, dark clothes. I realized Sir Thomas was not there.

'Ready?' Harsnet asked.

'Yes.'

He nodded to the tall man. 'This is Edgar Russell, Sir Thomas' steward.'

I nodded at the man, who bowed briefly in the saddle. I was glad to see that he had a serious, authoritative look about him.

Barak looked at the blank windows of my house. 'Everyone asleep?' he asked.

'Ay. I've left a note. I said you were sorry you wouldn't see Tamasin until tomorrow.'

'Thanks.'

'Where is Sir Thomas?'

Barak smiled. 'He's gone to fetch Dean Benson out of his bed and bring him up to Hertfordshire. He'll join us there.'

'Why?'

'So he can identify Goddard for certain, if we find him.'

Barak's horse Sukey pawed at the ground. Barak looked at me, full of suppressed excitement. 'Ready?'

'Ay.'

'All right, girl,' Barak said to the horse, then turned to the steward. 'Come on then, let's go and catch this arsehole.'

'There is no need to swear,' Harsnet told him reprovingly.

'Arsehole isn't swearing. Swearing is taking the name of God in vain.'

Some of the men in the entourage laughed. Russell turned in his saddle. 'Quiet, there,' he hissed, and the noise subsided. I was glad to see the steward seemed to have these men under control. 'We must go on now if we are to get there before dawn,' he said to me.

I nodded. We rode up Chancery Lane, the horses' hooves and the jingling of their harnesses sounding loud in the still night.

'What happens when we arrive at Kinesworth?' I asked Harsnet.

'There is an inn just outside the village we will use as a base. The innkeeper is a godly man, and a friend of Master Goodridge, the magistrate. We will set men in the woods that surround Goddard's house before dawn, and go in and take him when the sun comes up.' He leaned in closer. 'The steward Russell is a good man. He has these men under close authority. He was in Hungary with Sir Thomas, he knows warfare. It was he insisted all the men wore dark clothes to attract less attention.'

We rode on through the dark and silent roads, no sound but disturbed birds, the cattle dim shapes in the meadows. It was monotonous and once I almost dozed off in the saddle. It was still dark when Russell raised a hand for us to halt. We had come to a small country inn set back from the road. Lights were burning inside. We dismounted quietly.

'Magistrate Goodridge is inside,' Russell said. 'Coroner, Master Shardlake, come inside. Someone will take your horses. You too, Barak,' he added with a smile. 'We need all the practical minds we can get.'

Inside was a long low room set with tables, which no doubt functioned as a tavern in the evenings. It made me think of Lockley and poor Mistress Bunce. A fire burned in a hearth set in the centre of the room in the old way. Its warmth was welcome after the long cold ride.

A man of around sixty was sitting at one of the tables, a hand-drawn map before him. He rose to greet us. He had a tanned, swarthy complexion and sad penetrating eyes. An experienced and competent country magistrate, I guessed. He introduced himself as William Goodridge.

'What is the plan?' Harsnet asked.

He bade us sit and, indicating the map, said, 'That shows the house. It's a mile out of the village. There is lawn on all four sides, the grass is long and unkempt. Beyond that, the house is surrounded by woods.'

'An ideal layout to set watchers,' Russell said appreciatively.

'The house looks big,' I said. 'How many rooms are there?'

'About a dozen, as I recall. Old Neville Goddard was a hospitable man, I remember going to feasts and celebrations there when I was younger. But he could not control his drinking. His wife handled him badly too, she was a shrew.'

'Do you remember young Goddard?' I asked him.

He nodded. 'A surly, sulky young man. Clever but something – I don't know – effete about him. He had a great air of superiority for someone whose father drank himself into debt. I'm not surprised he went for a monk after Neville Goddard died, rather than stay with that termagant of a mother. All their lands were gone by then, to creditors. When the old woman died and Lancelot Goddard appeared again we hoped he might do something with the house, which she had left to fall to rack and ruin. But he comes and goes, talking to nobody.'

'And he arrived when yesterday?'

'I'm not sure, but there was smoke coming from a chimney when Master Russell and I went to look last night.'

'He never comes to the village? What about church services?'

'No. We are mostly reformers here, perhaps he does not find our ceremonies papist enough. There's a lot of gossip about him, as you may imagine, but people here are nervous of him.'

'The man we are after has a religion all his own,' I said grimly.

'You are sure he is still there now?' Harsnet asked.

'Oh, yes. The man I have watching sent a message half an hour ago saying there were lights at a window.'

Russell stood up. 'I hear horses. Somebody is coming.'

We all turned to the door as it opened, and Sir Thomas entered with four more armed servants. Dean Benson was with him as well, wrapped up against the cold in a heavy dark coat, looking miserable and afraid. Like Russell's men, Sir Thomas' new servants were soberly dressed, but Sir Thomas himself wore a cap with a red feather, a doublet sewn with little pearls and silk gloves.

He smiled at the company. 'Well,' he said. 'We are all here now. The dean here took some persuading, but he came.' He made a mock bow to Benson. 'Perhaps we can promise you some excitement.' The dean did not reply, but gave him an angry look. Sir Thomas laughed. He strode towards the map, studying it with professional interest. The steward explained the layout of Goddard's house. Sir Thomas thought a moment then turned to the company. 'We shall go in as soon as it is light. We have sixteen men now, a goodly number.' He looked round the room. 'Are you ready to storm this villain's citadel?' he asked.

'Yes, Sir Thomas!' The reply came in a chorus. Harsnet and I exchanged glances. These men did not realize what they might be facing.

The magistrate called the innkeeper and asked him to prepare some breakfast. It was only bread and cheese but it was welcome after the long journey. As we breakfasted a man came with a message that smoke was still coming from Goddard's chimney.

'All night?' I asked.

'Yes, sir.'

'That's strange,' Russell said.

'He's waiting for us,' I said quietly.

✝

AFTER WE HAD eaten there was nothing to do but wait for dawn. We all fell silent. Dean Benson sat by himself, pretending to read a book that trembled in his plump hands. Some of Sir Thomas' men closed their eyes to catch a little rest while they could; Barak too. I was too tense; I sat instead and looked out of the window. At length the light began to change, the sky outlined in dark grey instead of black. I heard the birdsong begin, a few cheeps at first then growing louder. Russell looked enquiringly at Sir Thomas. He nodded, and stood. Men who were awake nudged their dozing comrades. I could feel the tension rising around the room.

'Time to go in,' Sir Thomas said. 'Come, all of you, look at this plan.'

When we were all gathered round the table, Sir Thomas pointed with a gloved hand at the rough-drawn map. 'I'll post eight men around the house, in the woods. The rest go into the house, with me. And you, young Barak.' He turned to where I stood, the first notice he had taken of me. 'Also you, master crookback, I want you to go in too. Goddard has shown great interest in you.'

'Very well,' I said quietly. My heart raced.

'Coroner Harsnet, come with us, but I do not want you to go into the house. Magistrate Goodridge, I would like you to lead us there. You know the way. Dean Benson, you can keep your fat little rump on this chair here.'

The dean's shoulders sagged with relief.

Outside, a couple of pails had been set in the yard. They were full of mud. At Russell's request we all blackened our faces with the stuff, that we might not be seen while we were watching the house. As we went outside I heard the steward suggest to Sir Thomas that perhaps he should cover his fine clothes with a cloak. He acquiesced with a sigh, putting on a cloak fetched from the innkeeper. As I blackened my face I saw him look at the rough material with disgust. I thought, how many men of high estate are protected from their foolishness by their servants. Sir Thomas scowled as he caught me watching him. I thought, why does he dislike me so? Perhaps I offended his ideals of what a man should be and should look like, as once I had offended the King.

☨

WE SET OFF along the country lanes as the sun rose over the fields, revealing trees dusted with the light green of new leaves. A woman passed through a cattle meadow with pails hanging from a shoulder harness, milking the fat kine that gave the village its name. Wood-smoke rose from some of the poor houses dotted along the lanes, but no one was out ploughing or sowing yet. The woman stared in astonishment at the troop of armed men.

'There'll be gossip in the village soon,' Barak said.

We arrived at length at a stretch of woodland. The house was set in a little hollow in the middle; we caught a glimpse of it before descending into the trees. In the early light I saw an old manor house of white stone. A plume of smoke rose from one of the tall brick chimneys. Russell whispered to his men to move through the wood as quietly as possible.

We moved slowly forward to the edge of the trees, and found ourselves looking across a stretch of long, unkempt grass that had once been a lawn, to the house. All the windows were shuttered. But for that thin plume of smoke from a chimney the place looked abandoned; ivy and streaks of green mould half covered the walls. Russell disposed his men among the trees with whispers and gestures. Around us the birds were singing loudly. Russell's air of military efficiency and the numbers we commanded made me dare to hope that perhaps we might prevail.

'What is Goddard doing in there?' Harsnet, next to me, whispered.

'Whatever it is, we have him trapped now, surely,' Barak said.

'We shall see before this day is out,' Harsnet answered grimly.

'If we catch him, Cranmer wants him killed, doesn't he?' I asked. 'That was what he meant when he said the matter must be closed tonight.'

'Do you think he is wrong?'

'It goes against the things I believe.'

'I do not like it either; I am a man of the law too.' He looked at me. 'But how could we bring him to trial, let out the fact that the Archbishop and the Seymours have been conducting a private hunt? And he is an unclean creature, such as should be quietly destroyed in the dark.'

I glanced over to where Sir Thomas, Russell and Magistrate Goodridge were deep in quiet conversation. 'We are all pawns in a political game, Master Harsnet,' I said with sudden feeling.

'But who moves the pieces? Some would say the King, but I say God moves his servants, to his greater purposes.'

'God's stratagems,' I said. 'Many people get hard use from those, Gregory.'

Chapter Forty-one

WE TURNED AS Russell walked quietly towards us. 'We are ready to go in,' he said. 'Sir Thomas, me, Barak, Serjeant Shardlake, and six others. Ten men. We'll rush the house, break in, then two groups of two search upstairs, another two groups search downstairs. The rest of the men will stay in the woods, ready to catch him should he flee.' He looked around him.

Sir Thomas appeared. 'I will lead,' he said. He took a deep breath, then marched out of the trees towards the house, stepping quietly and carefully. We followed silently. Sir Thomas reached the lawn, stepping out into the thick grass. Then we all jumped as a great tumult of sound erupted at his feet and a host of white shapes darted up from the grass. Sir Thomas let out a cry, and behind him came the whistling sound of swords being drawn from scabbards. Then Barak laughed. 'It's geese,' he said. 'A flock of geese!' I saw that twenty angry birds were flying away over the grass, honking angrily.

Sir Thomas stood where he was, staring at the house. Nothing happened, but the strutting courtier looked suddenly vulnerable out there alone.

'This is dangerous,' I said to Barak. 'Those geese were set to warn of intruders, it's common enough in country places. He knows we are here now.' I looked at the blank, shuttered windows. 'We've lost surprise.'

Russell stepped out of the wood to join his master, waving to the rest of us, and we all loped through the grass and up to the front door. It was covered by a porch whose planks were rotted with damp, but the door itself looked strong enough.

'Kick it in,' Sir Thomas said brusquely, nodding to a large young man. He stepped forward and drew back a booted foot. Before he could launch a kick, Barak stepped forward quickly and grasped the handle. The door opened, smoothly, on well‑oiled hinges.

'He's making it easy for us,' he said.

We gathered round the doorway, looking in. With the shutters closed the interior was dim in the new dawn. I made out bare floorboards with old dry rushes on them and heavy, dusty furniture. Sir Thomas shouldered his way through and stepped inside. I thought, he does not lack courage. We followed him in, our eyes darting around fearfully.

We were in a large old entrance hall, a big wooden screen at the far end. On either side of it, two staircases ascended to a first‑floor balcony with rooms leading off. Behind each of the two staircases a hallway led to further ground‑floor rooms behind.

Sir Thomas walked to the heavy old wooden screen, pointed his sword into the space behind it, then threw it over. It hit the floor with a bang, raising great clouds of dust. Behind it there was nothing but a shabby old wall‑hanging. The great crash had resounded through the house but as its echoes died away there was a resumption of deep silence, broken only by men coughing from the dust.

Russell spoke, rapping out orders. 'You two, up that staircase. You two, the other one. I'll take the left‑hand doorway with Brown.'

'Master Shardlake and I will take the right‑hand doorway,' Barak said.

'Very well. Master Harsnet, Sir Thomas, please be ready to help secure any rat that comes running out.'

Harsnet nodded soberly. Sir Thomas smiled and laid a hand on his scabbard. 'I'll be ready to deal with him.' I realized he meant to kill him; Goddard would not get out of here alive.

Men began running to the steward's directions, their swords drawn. Footsteps echoed on the stairs. I followed Barak towards the right‑hand doorway. Barak spoke, his voice a murmur. 'I saw a faint light down here,' he whispered. 'Now I will get him.' He gripped his sword firmly in his uninjured arm.

He was right. As we passed into a dusty hallway of shuttered windows, I saw that a door at the far end was half open. A dim red light came from inside, flickering softly. It must be the room where the fire was lit. I felt heat wafting out. Then a tinkling of breaking glass sounded, and we became aware of another sound within the room, a low continual hissing, like a disturbed adder.

'What in God's name is that?' I whispered. I stared at Barak, wide-eyed. 'What's going on?'

'I don't know.' Barak hesitated, then walked steadily on, his sword held before him. He reached the doorway and stood listening for a second. The hissing was louder now. With a backward glance at me, he pushed the door open. We stared in, at a scene that might have come from Hell itself.

The room was large, probably the master bedroom. In one wall a large fireplace was set, and a fire burned brightly there, making the room stifling. Straight ahead of us was the only furniture in the room, an ornate, high-backed chair, such as a high official might use. A man was sitting there, dressed in the black robe of a Benedictine monk, the hood raised over his head. The face was middle-aged, with high cheekbones. The man stared straight at us, flames reflected from the fire dancing in his eyes. There was a large mole on one side of his long nose, a red gash across one cheek. Goddard stared at us. His lips were drawn back into a terrible, triumphant smile. One arm rested on the chair-arm, the other hung over the side. Beneath it lay a smashed lamp: that must have been the tinkling sound we heard. The candle within it still burned on the floor, on top of a thin trail of grey ash-like stuff. The ash led to a hissing, sparkling fire that was running quickly down a trail of dark powder to two large barrels under the shuttered window. It was at the far end of the room; we might not reach it before it burned down. I saw the shutters were not quite closed.

For once I reacted quicker than Barak, who seemed transfixed by

477

the sight of the gunpowder trail. I grabbed his arm, twirled him round and shouted, 'Run!'

We fled the room, back down the corridor. Sir Thomas, Russell and Harsnet stared at us. 'Get everybody out, now!' I yelled. 'There's gunpowder, he's going to blow up the house!'

I heard footsteps running towards us from all over the building. Those in the hall were already running for the door. Barak and I followed, with huge strides, almost leaping.

Then I felt a hot heavy impact at my back. It blew me off my feet as though I was a doll. Everything round me seemed to quiver, though strangely I heard no sound. My last thought before losing consciousness was, he did it, he made the earth quake.

Chapter Forty-two

WHEN I WOKE my first terrible thought was that I was dead and had been sent to Hell for my unbelief, for all around me was smoke, lit from behind by fire. Then I saw white circular lights moving in the smoke. One approached and for a dizzy moment I feared to see a demon, but the shape resolved itself into Harsnet's face, looking shocked and streaked with smoke-marks. He knelt beside me and I realized I was lying on my side on damp grass, and then that my back was bare, for a chill breeze wafted across it.

'Stay still, Master Shardlake,' Harsnet said in soothing tones. 'Your back is burned, not badly but the village healing man has been, he has applied some lavender to it.' I became conscious then that my back hurt; at the same time the echo of a distant, tremendous explosion seemed to sound in my ears. I realized that Harsnet's voice sounded strangely muffled.

I sat up, shaking my head. A blanket half covered me and I pulled it round to cover my bare back, a movement that hurt it, making me wince.

'I said that was the first thing you'd do when you woke up,' a voice beside me said. I turned to see Barak beside me, his lower half also covered with a blanket. Other men were lying in similar positions all over the long grass of the lawn. I turned my neck painfully. Behind me, at the far end of the lawn, the Goddard house was ablaze from end to end, flames and smoke belching from the windows and from the collapsed roof.

'He had gunpowder,' I said, clutching Harsnet's arm. 'He was in there, he lit the barrels—'

'Yes,' the coroner said gently. 'It is over. The back of the house has collapsed and the rest is burning fast. You saved our lives, sir, by calling out to us.'

'Did everyone get out?'

'Yes. But several others were injured by the blast. One of Sir Thomas' men was thrown through the air and landed on his head. He is likely to die. A doctor has been sent for from Barnet. You worried us, sir, you have been unconscious over an hour.'

'Are you hurt?' I asked Barak.

'Came down with a bit of a bang, like you. Think I've cracked a couple of ribs.'

'Why is there a blanket over your legs?'

'The explosion blew my hose off. Your robe was blown to tatters too, and your doublet.' He spoke lightly, but looking at his eyes I saw the horror in them that he probably saw in mine.

'It is all over,' Harsnet said quietly. 'He poured out the seventh vial, and made the earth shake. He killed himself doing it, probably thought he would be taken up to Heaven.' His mouth set. 'But now he will have found himself in Hell!' He hesitated. 'We think the seventh victim was you.'

'How did he know I would be here?'

'He knew you were at the centre of the investigation,' he said. He grasped at his left shoulder and winced; he had been hurt too. 'You said yourself he would know a large party of men would come here. You would probably be with them. That fuse must have been set slightly too long, or everyone in that part of the house would have been killed. He didn't care how many died,' he added bitterly. 'Ah, there is the doctor.'

I saw Sir Thomas and Russell, with a man in a physician's robe, walking among the wounded on the lawn.

'The men are being told Goddard was an alchemist,' Harsnet went on. 'That we were after him for conducting forbidden experiments, and he blew the place up by accident. Half the local villagers have turned out; Sir Thomas' men are keeping them to the other side of the woods.'

'Why would Goddard kill himself, just at the culmination of his great scheme?' I asked. 'Surely if he thought it would bring about Armageddon he would want to see it.'

'Who knows what went on in his mind? I think he was possessed after all, Master Shardlake, and now the devil has gathered his soul.'

Harsnet's voice still sounded muffled. I hoped my ears had not been permanently damaged. I lay back on one elbow, exhausted. 'Would you like me to fetch you some water?' he asked.

'Please.' When he left me, I lay down in the long grass, wincing at the pain that spread across my entire back. Then I sat up again, drawing the blanket round me, and looked at the burning house. There was a crash and a cloud of sparks as the last of the roof caved in. I turned to Barak.

'It's not over,' I said.

'But we saw him, that was Goddard, the mole on his nose and the cut on his cheek from where Orr ripped off his fake beard. He set a trap, he had plenty of warning with the geese and then us crashing in to set the fuse so it would blow us all to kingdom come.'

'But it didn't. We all got out.'

'Only just.'

I sat up slowly, rubbed a hand across my face, felt giddy for a moment. 'Did you see the window above those gunpowder barrels? The shutter was open slightly. There could have been someone else in there, who lit the fuse and got out. What if the fuse was timed so that whoever saw him would be able to get out of the room and testify the killer was himself dead?'

'But he was sitting there grinning at us. We saw him. Sit down, please.'

'What if Goddard wasn't the killer? What if the seven vials are only a stage in some larger pageant? The next stage of which he can go on to untroubled if he is believed dead?' I stood up, unsteadily. Barak grabbed at the blanket.

'Lie down. You've been unconscious an hour.' But I planted my feet on the grass and called out to Sir Thomas' party, my voice sounding to me as though it was coming from under water. Barak plucked at my blanket again. 'If you tell Sir Thomas we haven't got the killer after all, he'll be furious. He's in a bad enough state as it is.'

But I stepped away as Sir Thomas and Russell approached with the doctor. Sir Thomas looked subdued.

'Well, Shardlake,' he said. 'Here's a spectacular end to your hunt. You got out.' He looked at me accusingly. 'One of my men is like to die.'

'I am sorry for it. But I am not sure Goddard was the killer,' I said. 'I think there was someone else in that room, who may have got away.' I turned to Russell. 'Did any of your men hear or see anything in the woods after the explosion?'

'Your brains are addled,' Sir Thomas said angrily, and the doctor, a thin elderly man with a long beard, looked at me sharply. But Russell nodded slowly.

'Yes. Just afterwards one of my men saw something moving through the woods, said it looked like a man. But it was chaos there, the light almost gone, everyone shocked by the explosion and animals panicking and running to and fro in the shadows.'

'A deer,' Sir Thomas said. But from the look Russell gave me I could see he doubted too.

✝

A HEADQUARTERS had been set up in the stables behind Goddard's house. I got Russell to help me there, then fetch the man who had seen something. He was another of Sir Thomas' young servants, keen and sharp. 'I was sure it was a man that darted past me,' he said. 'It was just a glimpse, a figure darting between the trees, but I would swear it moved on two legs, not four.'

I was sitting on a bale of hay, Barak beside me. He looked at the young man and then at me. 'God help us. If not Goddard, then who is the killer?'

'I do not know.' I turned to Russell. 'The back of the house did not catch fire?'

'No. It collapsed in the explosion. Anything left of Goddard will be under there.'

'I would like the rubble cleared, and Dean Benson brought here to identify anything that is left of Goddard.'

'He won't like that,' Barak observed. 'He is still here, but he's been told Goddard blew himself up.'

'Sir Thomas wants this matter closed, sir,' Russell said in a warning tone.

'Perhaps if it is put to him that we need to ensure the killer is not still at large, and if he refuses and someone else is killed it will not reflect well on him.' I smiled at the steward. 'I am sure you are used to putting uncomfortable things to your master diplomatically.'

The young man ran a hand to his thatch of blond hair. Like everyone else he was dirty and dishevelled. 'I'll do what I can.'

'And I will tackle Harsnet,' I said.

✝

I HAD COME to have respect for Harsnet's acumen, but when he came into the stables, rubbing the shoulder he had hurt when the explosion blew him over, my suggestion horrified him.

'We can't do that,' he said. 'All on the word of what a servant thought he saw in the dark. We'll have trouble with Dean Benson, and Sir Thomas will be furious. He dislikes you already, Master Shardlake. He is not a good man to make an enemy of.'

'I have made greater enemies than him.'

Harsnet shook his head. 'It is over. Goddard ended it on his own terms but he did end it. Our duty now is to tell the Archbishop so, urgently.'

I looked at him. 'I know everyone would like it to be over. I wish I could believe that myself. But we cannot always believe what suits us.'

✟

THE STEWARD Russell turned out to be a better persuader than me, and an hour later those of Sir Thomas' men who were uninjured were dismantling the pile of rubble that was all that remained of the rear wing. Russell worked with his men. The explosion had thrown much of the stonework outwards, but part of the roof had collapsed straight down on to the interior of the house. I stood watching as the slates were lifted. Beside me was a frowning Sir Thomas. Harsnet stood at a little distance, occasionally shaking his head. Beside him Dean Benson sat on a lump of brickwork.

'Wherever he goes,' Barak said, 'that old arsehole always finds somewhere to sit down.' He stood beside me nursing his ribs, which the doctor had tied up with bandages.

To my relief, my hearing seemed to be clearing. 'Yes.' I looked out over the ghastly scene. Of the big old house nothing remained but a few skeletal walls within which rubble still smoked. The workmen cast nervous glances at the nearest wall, lest it collapse. On the lawn dazed figures wrapped in blankets still sat, looking at the burned house where they had so nearly died. A cart had arrived from Barnet and the more badly injured were being loaded on to it, supervised by the doctor and Magistrate Goodridge.

A shout from Russell made me turn round. Sir Thomas and Harsnet joined me in scrambling up the rubble. He was pointing at something by his feet. I saw that he had uncovered a severed arm wearing the tatters of a monk's robe, the hand undamaged and ghastly white. A moment later a man lifted a slate and jumped back with a cry. Underneath we saw a severed head, barely recognizable, for it was covered in thick dust. Sir Thomas, quite unaffected, took a handkerchief and began cleaning dust from the ghastly thing.

It was the man who had been sitting in the throne-like chair. The eyes had been blown out, leaving empty red sockets, but I recognized the mole on the nose, the slash on the cheek. Astoundingly the head was still smiling and then, fighting a rush of nausea, I saw why. Tiny nails had been hammered in to hold the mouth open, run through the flesh into the jaw. I looked up at Harsnet. 'This man was dead when we entered that room,' I said.

Seymour bent and picked up the head with no more concern than if it had been a football. I remembered the ghastly story of the cart full of Turkish heads in Hungary. He carried it, a little blood still dripping from the severed neck, to where Dean Benson sat. The cleric jumped up, his eyes wide with horror. 'Is that a—'

'A head, yes.' He held it up. 'Whose?'

'That is Lancelot Goddard,' Benson said, and collapsed in a dead faint.

✠

EARLY IN THE MORNING of the next day, Barak and I sat at breakfast. The journey back from Kinesworth had been uncomfortable for both of us, we had gone to bed early and slept late. I had tossed and turned uneasily, for pressure on my back brought pain from my burns. Putting my hand behind me, I could feel blisters rising.

'How are your ribs?' I asked.

'Sore,' he replied with a grimace. 'But they're only bruised, not cracked. I've had worse.'

'Is Tamasin joining us for breakfast?'

'I don't know. I left her dressing.' He sighed. 'Sometimes I wonder if she thinks I get these knocks to spite her.'

'Are you still on poor terms?'

'Probably. When we got back I tried to tell her I just wanted to sleep, but she wanted to know everything. I was too tired to talk,' he added. 'Too worried, too, because this isn't over.'

Before leaving the remains of Goddard's house, Harsnet and I and Sir Thomas Seymour had held a conference. It was clear now that Goddard had been a victim, not the perpetrator, of the killings. I wondered whether he, too, after leaving Westminster Abbey had

485

flirted with radical Protestantism, but drawn back and thus had qualified to became the seventh victim. The killer was still on the loose, and we had no idea who he was, or where he would strike again.

'Who *is* the bastard?' Barak asked. 'How did he get to know all these different people and their religious affinities?'

'At least we know how he got to us. By watching and spying as a pedlar. By the way, that gash on poor Goddard's head was on the wrong side of his face. The killer put it there to encourage our belief we were facing the killer in that room.'

'He slipped up there,' Barak said.

'It's the first time he has.'

'How did he get to Goddard? How did he find out where he lived?'

'Heaven knows. The magistrate said Goddard hadn't been seen for a few days. I'll wager the killer got into the house and tied him up, then sent that note to Dean Benson. And set up his greatest ever display.' I clenched my hands into fists. 'Who is he? Where is he now?'

'We're back to square one.'

'And without any idea where he will strike next. But one thing I am sure of. He will not end it now.'

'Do you think he will come after you?'

'I don't know. Why not just blow the house up with us all in it?' I sighed. I wished I could have consulted Guy. I had heard nothing since our quarrel. I would not have been surprised if Piers had returned, wormed his way back in with my friend.

I pushed my plate aside and stood up, wincing at the pain from my back. 'I should go to the Bedlam today. Shawms should have his report ready for the court and I want to look it over, and see Adam. And Dorothy later. I expect Bealknap is still there.'

'Are you all right to go out?' Barak asked.

'I can't sit around here. I will go to Chambers and try to do some work after I have seen Dorothy. I—'

The door opened and Tamasin came in. She wore a plain dress and her blonde hair was unbound, falling to her shoulders. She looked between us with a hostile glance. 'You have both been in the wars, I see,' she said.

'Where is your coif?' Barak asked. 'Your hair is unbound like an unmarried woman.'

She ignored him, and turned to me. 'Jack says you haven't caught him.'

'No,' I said. I added quietly. 'We have to go on searching.'

'He's killed eight people,' Barak said, impatiently. 'Nine, if Sir Thomas' man that was injured in the explosion dies. Seven of them in horrible slow ways.'

'We have to go on,' I said.

Tamasin sat down opposite her husband. She looked him in the eye, with an expression that was somehow both angry and sad. 'It is not what you're doing now that makes me angry with you. It is what you've been like since our baby died.'

Barak looked at me, then back at her. 'You shouldn't be talk- ing of this in front of someone else. Not that you haven't already, I know.'

'I talk in front of someone else because you won't *listen* when we talk alone.' Tamasin's voice rose to a shout and she banged a hand on the table, making us both jump. 'Do you ever think what it's been like for *me* since the baby died? Do you think a day passes without it all coming back to me, the day he was born? You weren't there, you were out drinking. Yes, that was when that started—'

'Tamasin—' Barak raised his voice, but she raised hers higher.

'The pain, the awful pain, I never felt anything like it. You don't know what women bear. And then the midwife telling me the baby was all twisted round in my womb, she couldn't bring him out alive and I would die unless she broke his little skull. You didn't hear that crack, it wasn't loud but it still sounds over and over in my head. Then she lifted him out and I saw he was dead – anyone could see he was dead – but still I wanted so desperately to hear him cry, hear him cry . . .' Tears were rolling down her face now. Barak had gone pale, and sat very still.

'You never told me,' he said.

'I wanted to *spare* you!' she cried. 'Not that you spared me. Coming back drunk, always going on about your son, your poor son. My son too.'

'I didn't realize it had been like that,' Barak said. 'I just knew he was born dead.'

'What in God's name did you think it was like?'

He swallowed. 'I've heard – that when a baby is twisted in the womb like that it can stop a woman having others. We—'

'I don't know if that's why there have been no others!' Tamasin shouted. 'Is that all you care about? Is that all you can say to me?'

'No, no, Tammy, I didn't mean—' Barak raised a hand. He should have gone up to her, taken her in his arms and comforted her, but he was too shocked by her outburst. All he seemed able to do was raise that hand. Tamasin stood up, turned round and left the room.

'Go to her,' I said. 'Go to her now.' But he just sat there, helpless, shocked. 'Come on,' I said more quietly. 'After all that we have been through, surely you can pull yourself together to comfort your wife.'

He nodded then and stood up, wincing at a stab of pain from his cracked ribs. 'Poor Tamasin,' he whispered. He stepped to the door but as he did so the front door slammed. Joan was in the hall. 'Tamasin's just gone out,' she said. 'I told her we weren't supposed to go out alone, but she just ignored me.'

Barak went past her. I followed him outside. We could see no sign of Tamasin. We went to the gate and stood looking up and down the road. A moment later Barak's horse Sukey went past the gate at a canter, Tamasin sitting side saddle. She must have gone to the stables. Barak called after her, but she disappeared down Chancery Lane, riding fast towards Fleet Street.

✞

TWO HOURS LATER, I was tying Genesis up outside the Bedlam. Barak had ridden out to try and find Tamasin, but she had disappeared into the crowds. We had no idea where she might have gone; she was an orphan, alone apart from Barak. She had had a few friends from her days as a very junior servant in Queen Catherine Howard's household, but Barak said she seldom saw them now. I realized how utterly, dreadfully lonely she must have been these last months.

Barak had gone off to see if he could still trace any of her friends. It seemed her outburst had shocked him into realizing fully what his behaviour had done, and he was full of contrition. I prayed that if he found her he would not retreat behind his defensive armour again. It was something he had to do alone, so I had ridden out to see Adam.

Hob Gebons let me in. He took me to Shawms' room, where the keeper produced a paper on which was written a report to the court saying that Adam was eating, was kept secure and received regular visits from his doctor. It struck me as being too well written for Shawms to have done it.

'Did Warden Metwys help you with this?' I asked.

Shawms gave me a surly look. 'I'm no hand at writing. I didn't come from some rich educated family.'

'I'll see how Adam is today. If it is still as you say I will approve the report.' I paused. 'Has Dr Malton been to see him?'

'Can't keep him out of the place.'

'Is he due today?'

'He comes and goes when he pleases.'

'And Ellen, how does she fare? I hope you have not been tormenting her again?'

'Oh, she's behaving herself now. 'Hob!' he called, and the fat warden reappeared. 'Visitor for Adam Kite. He's had more callers in a month than most patients get in five years.'

Gebons led me to Adam's cell. He was alone, chained as usual, and to my surprise he was standing looking out of his window, into the back yard. 'Adam,' I said quietly. He turned, then as soon as he saw me he slid down the wall, bent over and began to pray. I went and joined him, kneeling with some difficulty; it hurt my burned back.

'Come on, Adam,' I said. 'It is me. I will not harm you. You were not praying just now.' A thought struck me. 'Do you do this so you do not have to talk to people?'

He hesitated for a moment, then gave me a sideways look. 'Sometimes. People frighten me. They seek to hunt out my sins.' He hesitated. 'You did not tell my parents what – what I did with that Jezebel?'

'You mean the girl Abigail? No. I will say nothing, nor will Guy. We have a legal duty to keep your confidence. But your parents love you, Adam, I have seen that they love you.'

He shook his head. 'Always they used to criticize me, tell me to be quiet, respectful in my behaviour. They told me of the perils of sin. They know I am a sinner.'

'Are they not just repeating what Reverend Meaphon tells them?' I asked.

Adam sighed deeply. 'He is a man of God. All he wants is to bring people to salvation—'

'Your parents want more. They want you to return their love. I know your father wants you to go into the business with him one day.'

'I do not know. They say a son going into his father's trade can undo his reputation.' He hesitated, then added, 'And I do not want to be a stonemason, I do not like the work. I never have. That is another sin.' He shook his head.

'My father was a farmer, but I had no interest in it. I wanted to be a lawyer. I do not think that was a sin. Does not God give us each our own calling?'

'He calls us to be saved.' Adam screwed his eyes shut. 'Father, look down on me, look down and save me, see my repentance—'

I rose slowly to my feet. I frowned. Something in what Adam said had rung a bell. And then I made the connection with what

Timothy had said about visitors. I had spent so much time thinking about who the boy was who had visited Abigail that I had missed the rest of what the boy had said. I found I was trembling, for I realized that Adam had accidentally given me the answer. If I was right, I knew now who the killer was. It shocked me.

I jumped as the door opened, and Ellen came in with a tray. She coloured when she saw me there. 'I am just bringing Adam his food, sir,' she said. 'As a good servant should.'

'You have been much more than that to poor Adam, Ellen.' I took a deep breath. 'I would like to talk to you again, Ellen, but now I have to go — something urgent I must attend to. But I thank you again for Adam's care. I will see you soon.'

She gave me a puzzled look. With a quick bow, I walked rapidly away, past the door of the man who thought he was the King, and who called to me to walk sedately near the royal presence. First I had to go home and talk to Timothy. Then I had to see Dorothy, for if I was right it was she who might hold the last piece of the puzzle.

✝

AN HOUR LATER I was knocking on her door. I had stopped first at my house. Timothy was frightened to be questioned about Yaring‑ton again, and although he could not give me the name I was looking for he gave me a description, which if it did not prove my suspicions at least did not disprove them. It was enough to send me hurrying round to Dorothy's, barely pausing to ascertain from Joan that Barak had not yet returned.

Margaret the maid answered the door. 'Is Mistress Elliard in?' I asked.

'She has gone downstairs to have a word with Master Elliard's clerk about some payments due to his estate. Some clients have not paid because they know Master Elliard is dead. They think they can get away with it.' Her voice with its Irish lilt rose indignantly. 'And they say lawyers are wicked!'

Impatient though I was, I smiled at Margaret. She had been a tower of strength to Dorothy these last weeks, had probably helped her, been closer to her, than anyone. 'You feel much for your mistress, do you not?' I said.

'She was always good to me, patient of my clumsy ways when I started. And Master Elliard. It used to warm my heart to see how loving they were to each other.'

'Yes, they were.' It struck me that a week ago Dorothy would not have gone down to check on Roger's fees with the clerk, she would have sent me. The thought made me sad, and I chided myself for selfishness. 'She's coming back to herself,' I said.

'Yes, sir. Slowly. But it would help if she didn't have that wretched cuckoo in the nest.' She lowered her voice, inclining her head to the room Bealknap had taken over. 'He is running the servants ragged with his demands, and now he has rediscovered his appetite he is eating Mistress Elliard out of house and home. He is a guest, but the cost—'

'Then I will make an end to it,' I said grimly. I crossed the landing. The cloth of my shirt chafed against my raw back. Before this weekend I would have taken it to Guy to treat; but now there was no one, for I hated anyone else seeing my bent back. I took a deep breath, and shoved open the door of the chamber where Bealknap lay.

He was asleep, lying on his back and looking tranquil as a baby, a shock-headed baby with a fuzz of yellow stubble on its cheeks. His face, I saw, had regained both colour and flesh. A tray with a plate, empty save for drops of gravy and some chicken bones, lay on the floor. I looked down on him, then kicked the bed violently.

Bealknap started awake and stared at me petulantly with his pale blue eyes. He clutched the coverlet with his bony hands. 'What do you mean, coming in here and kicking the bed?' he asked. 'I am a guest.'

'A guest who constantly troubles his hostess's servants, and runs up great bills for food.'

'Dr Malton said I must stay here another week,' he answered indignantly. 'I have been very ill, I am still recovering.'

'Rubbish. Guy would never say that without consulting Mistress Elliard. *He* has manners. *He* is a gentleman.' I kicked the bed again.

'Why are you so angry?' He thought for a moment, then frowned, his eyes sliding away. 'Was it because of that solicitor I told you about? I am sure he was only making enquiries for some client, about a case.' He struggled to sit up. 'You cannot report me for it. I told you about it while in fear of death, I was temporarily *non compos mentis.*'

'I wonder if you have ever been anything else.' I looked at him. He was so caught up in himself he probably did not even see the effect he was having on this grieving household. I leaned over him, and said, 'Either you get yourself dressed and take yourself back to your own chambers this afternoon, or I will ask Mistress Elliard to come round to my house tomorrow, and while she is out I will send Barak here to turf you out in your nightshirt. Margaret will let him in and she will keep it quiet, do not doubt that.'

Bealknap gave a nasty smile. 'Oh yes, I see now. You would like to have Mistress Elliard to yourself. That is what this is all about.' He gave a wheezy laugh. 'She'd never be interested in an ugly old hunchback like you.'

'I'll tell Barak to roll you in some puddles when he kicks you out. And you make sure some money is sent over to Mistress Elliard from that great chest of gold you have.' At those words, he looked outraged. 'She is a poor widow now, you wretch. Two gold half-angels should cover it. I will ask her later if she has had it.'

'I am a guest, guests do not pay.' His voice thrilled with indignation now.

Outside, I heard the door open and close again. Dorothy had come back.

'Out, Bealknap,' I said. 'This afternoon. Or take the consequences.' I kicked the bed again, and left the room.

✝

Dorothy was in the parlour, not standing or sitting by the fireplace from which she had stirred so seldom since Roger died, but by the window looking out at the fountain. So she can do that now, I thought. I realized it was days since I had seen her, since that almost-kiss. I feared she might be out of sorts with me, but she only looked weary.

'Bealknap will be gone by this evening,' I said.

She looked relieved. 'Thank you. I do not wish to be uncharitable, but that man is unbearable.'

'I am sorry Guy suggested he stay here. I feel responsible—'

'No. It was me that let Master Bealknap in. Dr Malton came and saw him yesterday. Bealknap said he was told he should stay here another week—'

'Lies.' I shifted my position slightly, and a stab of pain went down my back. I winced.

'Matthew, what is the matter?' Dorothy stepped forward. 'Are you ill?'

'It is nothing. A slight burn. A house caught fire, up in Hert-fordshire.' I took a deep breath. 'We thought we had the killer, thought it was all over at last, but he escaped.'

'Will this never end?' she said quietly. 'Oh, I am sorry, I see you are tired, and hurt too. I am so selfish, caught up in my own troubles. A foolish and inconstant woman. Can you forgive me?'

'There is nothing to forgive.'

Dorothy had moved back to her favoured position, standing before the fire, the wooden frieze behind her. I studied it as she poured liquid from a bottle into two glasses and passed one to me.

'*Aqua vitae*,' she said with a smile. 'I think you need it.'

I sipped the burning liquid gratefully.

'You are so kind to me,' she said. She smiled, sadly, her pretty cheeks flushing. 'When we last met – I am sorry – my mind is all at sixes and sevens, my humours disturbed.' She looked at me. 'I need time, Matthew, much time before I can see what the future will be without Roger.'

'I understand. I am in your hands, Dorothy. I ask nothing.'

'You are not angry with me?'

'No.' I smiled. 'I thought you were angry with me, over Beal-knap.'

'Just irritated by him beyond measure. We women get cantankerous then.'

'You will never be that, if you live to eighty.'

Dorothy reddened again. The light from the window caught the frieze, showing up the different colour of the poor repair. 'It is a shame that discoloured patch draws the eye so,' she said, shifting the conversation to mundane matters. 'It used to annoy Roger terribly.'

'Yes.'

'The man who originally made it was such an expert. We contracted him again after that corner was damaged, but he was recently dead. His son came instead. He did a poor job.'

I took a deep breath, oddly reluctant to say what was in my mind.

'The carpenter and his son. Do you – do you remember their names?'

She gave me a sharp look. 'Why does that matter?'

'One of the killer's other victims also had a carpenter come to repair a damaged screen.'

Dorothy went pale. She clutched at her throat.

'What was their name? The father and son?'

'Cantrell,' she said. 'Their name was Cantrell.'

Chapter Forty-three

I RAN BACK to my house to fetch Genesis, then rode faster than I had for years, down Fleet Street and past the Charing Cross to Whitehall. My burned back throbbed and jolted with pain, but I ignored it. People stopped and stared and once or twice had to jump out of my way. I would have brought Barak, but Joan said he was still searching the streets for Tamasin. She looked upset; I knew she was fond of them both.

I managed to convince the guards at Whitehall Palace that my business was urgent. Harsnet had been in his office that morning but had gone over to the Charterhouse. Someone was sent to fetch him while I waited in his office. A servant lit a fire for me, giving me curious looks as I paced up and down.

It felt as if I waited an age. All the time I thought of what fresh horrors Cantrell might wreak. My first thought had been to go to his house myself with Barak, but even had Barak been at home he was still suffering from his injuries. I thought briefly of taking Philip Orr, but I did not wish to leave Joan and the boys unprotected. And this needed more than one man.

At last, in the early afternoon, Harsnet arrived. He looked utterly worn out. I had sat in the chair behind his desk but rose painfully to my feet as he entered.

'What has happened, Matthew?' he asked wearily. 'Not another killing?'

'No.' He looked relieved.

'I am sorry to fetch you back—'

'There are problems at the Charterhouse,' he said. 'The engineer

496

has repaired the mechanism of the wheel that opens the lock gates; it jammed when the watchman tried to open them with Lockley down there. But there is so much water backed up now he fears if he opens the gates its force could knock the doors off their hinges and set a flood running round the cellars of Charterhouse Square, all the way to Catherine Parr's house.' He looked out of the window; it was a sunny day again; I had hardly noticed. 'At least the water level hasn't risen any more in the Charterhouse quadrangle.' He sighed.

'I think I know who the killer is,' I said.

He stared at me. I told him about the work Cantrell and his father had done at Roger's house and Yarington's. His eyes widened, he leaned forward. When I had finished he stood in thought.

'We should act now, coroner,' I said.

'But Cantrell's eyes?' he said. 'He is half blind. We have seen him. And according to the guard there he never goes out.'

'What if his eyes weren't as bad as he pretended? One may have difficulty in reading what is written on a jar yet see well enough to murder. And what better disguise than near-blindness? Where better to hide than behind those great thick lenses? And he never lets the guard into the house. He could get out without his knowledge.'

'And he knew Lockley,' Harsnet said. 'And Goddard. And now, we know, Roger Elliard's and Reverend Yarington's houses. And he could have learned of people who had left the radical reformers' circles when he was with his father's group.'

'Westminster is only a step away,' I said.

'I know where the constables live,' he said, decisive now. 'I could get two or three of them and we could go round there now.'

'Before he strikes again.'

'You think he will?'

'I have always thought so, Master Harsnet.'

'I agree. He is too tight in the devil's grip for him to let him go.'

✟

497

WE WALKED QUICKLY down to Westminster. I chafed with impatience as I stood under the great belfry in the busy square, waiting while Harsnet went to find the constables. At length he reappeared, with three sturdy young men carrying staffs and wearing swords. Westminster was a rough place and the constables there tended to be young and strong.

We gathered in a circle. Harsnet told the constables we were hunting a suspected murderer, and he was dangerous. Then we walked down to Dean's Yard. A little group of prostitutes standing talking in a doorway faded away at the constables' approach. Harsnet lifted a hand to knock at Cantrell's door. I stopped him.

'No, leave two men here and we will go round the back and talk to the guard.'

'Very well.'

Taking one of the constables, we stepped into the noisome little lane running alongside the house, our footsteps echoing against the narrow walls. The constable pushed open the gate to Cantrell's yard.

It was empty, the door to the little shed shut. I went with Harsnet to the grubby rear window of the house and looked in. The tumbledown parlour inside was empty. The constable, meanwhile, opened the door of the shed. Then he laughed. We joined him and looked in at the sight of Cantrell's guard sprawled on a heap of dirty sacks. He was fast asleep, and the smell from him told that he was drunk. The constable kicked him. 'Wakey wakey,' he said cheerfully. The man stirred, groaned and opened his eyes to find Harsnet glaring furiously down at him.

'Is this how you guard your ward?' he snapped. 'The Archbishop shall hear of this.'

The guard struggled to sit up. A dripping tap caught my eye, set in the side of a large barrel. I lifted the lid and saw it was half full of beer. 'He's made sure there was temptation in his way,' I said.

'Where is he?' Harsnet asked the wretched guard. 'Cantrell? Is he in?'

'I don't know,' the man mumbled. 'He makes me stay out here.

He won't let me *in*, sir. That's the problem. He's not normal,' he added sulkily.

'You speak truer than you know, churl.' Harsnet turned away. 'Come on, let's get in the house.'

We wasted no ceremony. At a gesture from Harsnet the constable smashed the recently repaired window to smithereens, and one after the other we stepped through. The drunken guard had staggered out into the yard and stood watching us, his face crumpling as he realized he was probably out of a job.

Inside, nothing but silence. 'It's like Goddard's house again,' Harsnet whispered. I noticed the bloodied piece of wood, which Cantrell said he had used to see off his assailant, propped against one wall. I wondered which of his victims he had struck with that.

'Let's get those men in from the front and search it,' I said.

The constables were sent to look through the house. I told them to disturb nothing. They returned minutes later to confirm the place was empty.

'Let's see what we can find,' I said to Harsnet.

There was nothing in the parlour, nor in the miserable-looking kitchen next to it, only dirt and pieces of bad food in a cupboard. We turned to the door that led off the parlour, which Cantrell had said had led to his father's workshop. It was a stout oak door and it was firmly locked. It took two of the constables to break it down. Inside it was dark, the shutters drawn over the windows. In the lights from the parlour I saw stone flags, some sort of cart against one wall. We all hesitated for a moment on the threshold, then I stepped in and walked across to the window. I removed the bar across the shutters and opened them, light and noise from the street spilling in.

There were three large wooden chests against the wall. And I recognized that pedlar's cart. I went over and touched the handle. Here he had carried his trinkets in his guise as a pedlar, and bodies too, unconscious or dead. I was suddenly full of anger, anger at what Cantrell had done and at myself too. 'I was a fool,' I said quietly.

'Why?' Harsnet asked. 'He made fools of us all.'

'For allowing myself to be so easily deceived, to see Cantrell as he wanted to be seen, as another of life's victims.'

'We must look in these chests,' Harsnet said quietly.

'I'll take this one. You take that.' I lifted the lid of the nearest chest, dreading what might be within. It was a pile of disguising clothes, tattered robes, fake beards and wigs too — a whole wardrobe.

'Those must have cost money,' Harsnet said, glancing over.

'Some of them look old and well worn.' I pulled out a colourful patchwork coat. 'This is Joseph's coat of many colours. I've seen others like it at disguisings. He wouldn't need all of these.'

The chest Harsnet had opened contained bottles and jars of herbs and drugs, wrapped in rags. I opened them carefully. One stoppered bottle contained a thick, bitter-smelling yellow liquid. I lifted it out. 'I think this is dwale.'

'Where did he get it?'

'Made it, I would think, from Master Goddard's formula.' I took another bottle, sniffed the contents carefully, then tipped a few drops on to the ground. The vitriol hissed and spat.

'There can be no doubt now,' Harsnet said.

'No.'

'Where did his raging fury come from?' I asked.

'It came from the devil,' Harsnet said flatly. He looked at me. I shook my head.

'That would make it simpler, I suppose. Easier to bear.'

'Perhaps it *is* simple. You have thought too much on this man.'

'I have had cause to. He killed my friend.' I bent and opened the third chest, and we looked inside. There, under some cloths, lay a large flat wooden case. I recalled seeing something similar at Guy's. I opened it, then stepped back with a gasp.

Inside the box, neatly laid out, were knives of different sizes, a little axe and even a small cleaver. Trays contained little hooks and pins, and pliers and tweezers of various sizes. The cleaver and some of the knives had blood on them, and a foul smell rose from the box.

'Goddard's surgical equipment,' I said.

'As I said, possession by the devil.' Harsnet turned aside, his mouth twisting with disgust.

✝

WE WENT UPSTAIRS. There were two bedrooms. One, which had been stripped bare of all furniture except an old bed, I guessed had belonged to Cantrell's father. The other was his. There was an old truckle bed, and another chest, old and scarred, and a table with a large, heavy copy of the Bible in English set on it. The chest contained some of the poor clothes we had seen Cantrell wearing, and a rickety table and stool.

Harsnet had opened the Bible. 'Look at what he has done here,' he said quietly. I went over to him. He had opened the Testament at the Book of Revelation. The wide margins were filled with notes in red ink, in handwriting so tiny it was virtually illegible, though I made out words like *vengeance, punishment, fire,* etched in thickly and underlined. Turning over the pages I saw that all the passages dealing with the consequences of the angels pouring out the seven vials of wrath were likewise underlined: *a noisome and grievous sore, the rivers and fountains of water ... became blood, they gnawed their tongues for pain.*

'What a blasphemy.' Harsnet's voice trembled as I had not heard it tremble even at the worst things we had seen. I picked up the Bible and flicked through it. Passages here and there, like the destruction of Sodom and Gomorrah, were also marked, but virtually none of the New Testament apart from Revelation and, I realized, only a part of Revelation: the seven vials of wrath and then immediately afterwards the chapter on the judgement of the Great Whore.

'Look at the underlinings here,' I said. 'More even than in the passages about the pouring of the vials. Does this give us the clue to what he means to do next?'

'That book is tainted,' Harsnet said. 'Polluted.'

'The Great Whore. Who does he think she is?'

'She is symbolic of the Pope and Babylon of Rome,' Harsnet said. 'We know that now.'

'St John of Patmos did not when he wrote this book.'

'That is what he foresaw,' Harsnet said firmly. 'It is quite clear to those who study well.'

'That is not what Cantrell saw. No, he will have someone closer than the Pope in mind.'

Harsnet was silent for a moment. Then he turned to me. 'Where is he now, Matthew?' he asked quietly. 'I confess I am afraid.'

Footsteps sounded on the stairs and one of the constables appeared.

'There is an old woman downstairs says she knows Cantrell,' he said.

I looked at Harsnet. 'The neighbour.'

We went downstairs to find the old crone who had spoken to me the first time I visited Cantrell standing on the doorstep, peering round the large constable who stood in her way. She smiled a toothless grin when she recognized me.

'Ah, master lawyer, sir. We spoke before. I saw something was going on. Has anything happened to Charlie?' Her eyes were alive with curiosity.

'He is not here. We are seeking him.'

'In connection with a crime,' Harsnet added grimly. 'What do you know about him?'

'I live a few doors down. I was friends with Charlie's father, till he got religion and was too pure to speak to the likes of me. What's Charlie supposed to have done?' she repeated, trying to peer round us into the house again. She shook her head. 'He's not up to doing anything serious, he's a poor weak creature.'

'What is your name?'

'Jane Beckett.'

'Come, Jane,' I said. 'I want to ask you a couple of questions.'

'So you want to talk to me this time.'

The old woman wrinkled her nose as I led her into the parlour. She followed me into the old workshop, and now sadness did cross her face. 'Look at this place now,' she said. 'So sad and empty. Adrian kept it so neat, and it was always full; he never lacked work.'

I opened the chest full of clothes. 'Do you know where these might have come from? There are a lot of them.' I picked out the coat of many colours.

The old woman nodded. 'Ah, yes, those are Adrian's. He built up quite a collection. He used to work for the stage companies. Got contracts to build the sets for open-air performances. Built one at Hampton Court once, for a disguising before the King. He used to lend out costumes as well.' She looked at me. 'He was a good businessman, you know. These things are worth money, they shouldn't be left lying here.'

'Did Adrian ever take his son to the performances?'

'Charlie? Yes, when he was small. He used to love them. It was the only time you saw him happy. If it was something local a lot of the neighbours would go. I think Charlie wanted to be an actor, but he didn't have the skill for it, or anything else, so he went for a monk instead.' She laughed contemptuously, then turned back to me and said seriously, 'But Adrian had such skill, he could make pulleys that could make wooden dragons he built move across the stage as though they were real.' She stroked the coat with a skinny hand, then replaced it in the box. When she looked up her eyes were sharp with curiosity again. 'What's he done then, useless Charlie?'

'Never mind that,' Harsnet said.

A thought struck me. 'How did Adrian Cantrell die?'

'Fell down the stairs one night, according to what Charlie said. Broke his neck.' She laughed bitterly. 'Still, according to that hot-gospelling religion he believed in, he's gone straight to Heaven. What're those things in that chest? Those aren't Adrian's.'

I steered her away from the instruments and led her back outside;

she was clearly disappointed that I would not tell her more. In the doorway I asked her, 'That cart in the workshop? Was it Adrian Cantrell's?'

'Ay. He used to take things to customers in it.'

A thought struck me. To get from Westminster up to Hertfordshire, Cantrell must have a horse.

'What became of his horse?' I asked.

'I thought Charlie must have sold him.'

'What did it look like?'

She shrugged. 'Brown, with a white triangle down its nose.'

'You never saw him going in or out of there with a horse and cart?'

'Him that can hardly see?' She snorted. 'No. I saw him going out to buy something once or twice, shrinking against the wall, feeling his way along it.'

'Ever see him go out at night?'

She laughed. 'I shouldn't have thought that was very likely. Anyway, I got to bed early and lock my doors. It is not safe around here. Look, sir, what's this all about—'

'It doesn't matter. Thank you.' I gently closed the door on her and turned to Harsnet. 'So he learned about acting,' I said quietly. 'Perhaps even as a boy he needed to act to appear like a normal man. I wonder if he killed his father. I wonder if that was when he learned what he truly wanted to be.'

'Such speculation does not get us anywhere,' Harsnet said.

'No. You are right.'

'What about that horse?' Harsnet asked.

'He must have one.'

'Can he see to ride?'

'I begin to think he has greatly exaggerated that eye trouble of his. He has to be able to ride to get to Goddard's house.' I turned to the stairs. 'I want to have another look at his Bible, those underlined passages. See if I can wring some meaning from his scribblings.'

'I'll come up with you.'

Harsnet was too blinkered to give me any serious help. 'No, thank you, Gregory. I work best alone.'

✞

I CLIMBED the stairs again. It was strange to sit at Cantrell's desk, beside his bed, the room silent apart from the noises from the street. I sat down, held my head in my hands and bent over the book. Like a lawyer trying to get inside an opponent's mind through the text of an affidavit, I searched for what Cantrell might see here, what final enemy was to be destroyed. My mind tumbled and turned the words of the short chapter. '*I will shew unto ye the judgement of the great whore ... with whom the kings of the earth have committed fornication...*' On to where the angel said she would explain her mystery to the saint: '*And the beast that was, and is not, even he is the eighth, and is of the seven, and goeth into perdition.*'

I thought, after the seven vials the next victim will be the eighth; like the seven, but different somehow in kind. The most important victim because, after her judgement, Armageddon comes at last. I thought furiously. Was a woman his victim? It would have to be a woman to symbolize the Whore. Fornication with the kings of the earth. For Cantrell surely it would have to be a Protestant woman who had backslid, like poor Mistress Bunce that took up with the ex-monk Lockley. I thought, fornication, a king, the eighth. A woman who had not yet abandoned true religion but who would surely be seen to do so if she were to marry a religious conservative. '*The beast that was, and is not, even he is the eighth.*' King Henry VIII, who had been a reformer himself but was so no longer. Not the King, but a woman who would be his wife.

I stood up. I looked out of the window into the yard. The drunken guard had sat down on an upturned pail. I went back downstairs. I turned to face Harsnet. I made myself speak steadily.

'I think—' I said, 'I think he means to kill Catherine Parr.'

Chapter Forty-four

I STOOD BEFORE Archbishop Cranmer's paper-strewn desk. The prelate stared at me intensely, and I felt the force of the powerful mind behind those blue eyes. Around the desk, also looking at me, were both Seymour brothers. Harsnet and I had just finished telling them of our visit to Cantrell's house. We had gone immediately to Lambeth Palace, and the Seymours had been summoned to meet us there.

'Then it seems Cantrell is the killer,' Cranmer said quietly. 'Have you left men at his house?'

'The three constables,' Harsnet replied. 'They are hiding in the house and in the shed in the back yard. If he returns they will surprise him and take him.'

'But what if he does not?' Lord Hertford asked. As ever, he came straight to the point. 'What if he is even now pursuing his eighth victim?'

'We must send a squad of men to Catherine Parr's house at once,' Sir Thomas said. 'To ride to her succour, ensure she is protected. I already have men at the Charterhouse—'

'No.' Cranmer's voice was firm. 'What would the King think, if he learned there was a mob of your men in Catherine Parr's house? Dear God, if anything happens to her . . . The arrested courtiers are starting to be released; there was no evidence against them. And Bonner is frightened of arresting more people in London; he is starting to fear popular resistance. I have been with the King this afternoon, he has assured me of his trust. But what if something happens to Catherine Parr now, after I have concealed so much from him?'

'We cannot be sure Shardlake has the truth,' Hertford said.

'Cantrell could have built any one of a hundred fantasies around the story of the Great Whore.'

'Yes,' Cranmer agreed. 'He could. But I know Revelation, and I think Matthew could be right. We will send men of my guard to her house, tell some story of a threat from a dangerous burglar that I learned of.' Decisive now, he called for his secretary. Speaking rapidly and urgently, he told him to fetch the dozen best men from the palace guard, and at the same time order the river barge to take fifteen horses across the river.

The secretary looked confused for a moment. 'A dozen men, my lord? But that will leave the palace almost unguarded.'

'I don't care! Just do it!' It was the first time I had seen Cranmer truly lose his temper. 'Get the sergeant to choose the men, go to the landing stage yourself and arrange the horses. I want the best animals, ready for riding in twenty minutes!' Lord Hertford reached over and touched him gently on the shoulder. He nodded, and continued more quietly. 'And most important, I want a fast rider sent now to Lady Latimer's house in Charterhouse Square. He is to say a gang of burglars has designs on the house. The steward is to lock all the doors and windows, keep Lady Catherine safe until my guards arrive. Go now, do it!'

The secretary fled. Cranmer turned to Harsnet. 'Gregory, I put you in charge of this. Matthew, you and Barak are to accompany him.'

'Yes, my lord.' Barak was waiting outside. I had sent a message home before riding to Lambeth, and he had ridden across. He had traced Tamasin to the house of one of her friends, but she had refused to see him. He was in a turmoil of anger and contrition.

I winced at a sharp stab of pain from my back. 'What is wrong?' Cranmer asked.

'I was burned, at Goddard's house. Not badly.'

'You have borne much, Matthew, I know.' He gave me a hard, serious look. 'I hope Lady Catherine's steward has some sense. It is not over yet,' he said.

✝

WE DONNED our coats and hurried downstairs, through the Great Hall and out into the palace gardens, picking Barak up on the way. It was evening now, the sun setting behind stretches of white cloud, turning them pink. I shivered.

'Where are those men?' Harsnet said impatiently.

'The sergeant will have to gather them together,' Barak said.

Harsnet turned to me. 'Are you fit to ride to the Charterhouse, Matthew? With your burns?'

'I have been in this from the start. If this is the end I wish to be there.'

There was a sound of hoofbeats and jingling harness, and a rider shot out of the palace gates. 'There goes the messenger,' Barak said. A moment later a dozen armed and helmeted men appeared round the corner of the house, led by a sergeant. They had discarded their pikes and were armed with swords. They looked puzzled at this sudden change to their routine; they were used to patrolling the palace grounds, not chasing across London. But they were all strong-looking fellows, and the sergeant had a keen look about him. He was a tall man in his thirties, with a hawk nose and keen eyes. He approached Harsnet.

'Master coroner?'

'Yes.'

'Sergeant Keeble, sir.'

'Are your men ready to ride?'

'Yes, sir. We're to go to Charterhouse Square, I'm told.'

'Yes. Come, I will explain on the way to the landing-stage.'

'Cantrell's had a full day to get into Lady Parr's house,' Barak said to me quietly. 'And what's the betting he spied out the place carefully before?'

'Surely Lady Catherine is well guarded. Given her importance now.'

✝

THE ARCHBISHOP'S secretary had done his work; when we reached the river the barge was waiting, and on the London side we found a group of horses ready.

We then rode fast and hard to the Charterhouse as dusk deepened to darkness. The jolting movement set my back on fire; the muddy country road made riding all the more difficult. In the fields on either side of us startled cows blundered away. We rode on through Smithfield, into Charterhouse Square. On the corner stood the Green Man, now boarded up. We rode across the grass of the square and stopped outside the Charterhouse Gate. A little way off a group of beggars stood in the open doorway of the old abandoned chapel. They stayed where they were, watching; they were not going to approach a group of armed men. Sir Thomas drew his horse to a halt. 'We should make a search of the area first, I think,' he said. 'If we rush the place and he is near by, he might escape. I want him caught this time.' He ended with a hard look at me, and spurred his horse towards the gate of the Charterhouse. The gate was opened and we rode into the Charterhouse precinct.

Sir Thomas' steward Russell emerged from the conduit-house. Seymour told him what had happened. 'I suggest sending three or four of the Archbishop's men on foot to search the area,' Sir Thomas said. 'If he is hanging around and we send everyone looking round the square, we could alarm him and he might run. Shardlake, Barak, you should stay out of the way for now. He knows you.'

Again his strategy made good sense. Three of Cranmer's men were sent to reconnoitre; the rest of us stayed in the courtyard. A man in a stained smock emerged from the conduit-house and came over to us, wiping his hands on a rag. 'I've done all I can, Sir Thomas,' he said. 'I sent a man over to Islington Fields. The streams up there have overflowed, there is quite a lake of water. It is backed up behind the lock gates down there.'

'We cannot leave things as they are, master engineer,' Harsnet said.

'If we have no more rain the water up at Islington will start to drain slowly into the ground and the pressure on the gates will subside. Then we could open the gates in a few days. Let us hope the wet spell is over.'

Sir Thomas grunted. 'I want to leave this place. What if someone from Augmentations makes one of their unannounced visits and finds the Charterhouse full of my men, just across the road from Catherine Parr's house? It will get back to Richard Rich and he will tell the King. Come, master engineer, show me.' He marched off to the conduit-house, the engineer and Russell following. I smiled sardonically at Harsnet. 'Sir Thomas is going to tell the expert how to do his job,' I said.

The coroner sighed. 'He's right. We don't want Rich finding things amiss here, learning that the gates were blocked up by the body of a crucified potman.'

'No.' I looked over at the conduit-house, candlelight outlining the half-open door. 'I have come up against Rich before. He would do anything for his own advancement. Like most of those at court.'

'The Archbishop at least is different,' Harsnet said. 'He is a man of principle, a good man. The hope of all of us who wish to see reform preserved.'

I looked at him curiously. 'Yet he believes God has chosen the King to be his representative on earth. Your school of thought allows for no intermediary between man and God.'

'He is all we have. And Lord Hertford, of course.' Harsnet smiled to himself. 'If Lord Hertford ever came to rule this land ... but for now the Archbishop is our rod and staff. I would do anything to protect him, anything.' He spoke with fierce emphasis.

We turned at the sound of approaching footsteps. The three Archbishop's men had returned. They went into the conduit-house, and a moment later Sir Thomas and Russell emerged and hurried over to us.

'Master Shardlake,' Sir Thomas said. 'You said Cantrell's horse had a distinctive white mark on its face. Shaped like a triangle.'

'Yes. So the old woman said. Otherwise it is all brown.'

'There is a horse answering that description tied up on the common behind the houses. No sign of an owner.'

Harsnet took a long, shuddering breath. 'So you were right,' he said. 'I am sorry I doubted you.' He turned to Sir Thomas. 'We should get the Archbishop's men together. The time for concealment is past. We must get to Catherine Parr's house now.'

'I will lead them,' Sir Thomas said.

'I do not think that is wise, sir,' Harsnet said. 'You should not be seen there.'

'The coroner is right, sir,' Russell said quietly.

Sir Thomas hesitated, then nodded. He glared at Harsnet and me. 'You had better not make a mess of this,' he said coldly. 'If anything happens to Lady Catherine, I will see you pay with your heads.' He turned and stalked off.

'Arsehole,' Barak muttered when he was out of earshot.

'It's just bluster, sirs,' Russell said quietly. 'He can't do anything without his brother's permission.'

✝

WE WALKED FAST through the wooded square, emerging in front of the large houses on the eastern side. Lord Latimer's mansion was large, three storeys high, set back from the road in its own grounds. Lights shone at several of the large, diamond-paned windows. As we walked down the gravel path, the front door opened and a man emerged carrying a lantern; he approached Harsnet. He was middle-aged, full-bearded, with an anxious expression. Lord Latimer's arms, a grey shield with a red diagonal cross, were stitched prominently on his doublet.

'Master coroner?' he asked.

'Yes. Is all safe?'

He nodded. 'We've searched the house. There's no one here. We've told Lady Catherine there are robbers about, tried to get her to stay in her room, but she wants to take charge.'

'She doesn't know what she's facing,' I said.

'He's around somewhere. I can feel it,' Barak muttered. He looked into the deep shadows cast by the house. There were trees and bushes against the inner wall; plenty of space for Cantrell to hide.

'What do you mean?' The steward looked at me sharply. 'I thought it was a gang of burglars?'

'It's one man we're after.' Harsnet looked into the steward's eyes. 'An assassin, a madman. Lady Catherine must be told she is in real danger.' The man's eyes widened. 'How many entrances are there to this house?'

'Two. This one and the one for tradesmen at the back.'

'Have you had any visitors today?' I asked.

'A messenger from the King came with a note for Lady Catherine.' The steward hesitated. 'She's been rather agitated since.'

'Where is she?' Harsnet asked him quietly.

'In her rooms on the first floor.'

'All right,' he said. 'Now go, tell her she must stay there. Two of you men, accompany him, guard her.' Two men joined the steward and they ran back inside. Harsnet turned to the others. 'I want six men patrolling the outside. Everyone else, inside with me.' As the men moved to his orders I had to admire his ability to command, his decisiveness. He led the other four, and Barak and me, into the house.

We entered a large hall, the walls covered with expensive tapestries of Greek and Roman gods in woodland settings. Before us, a wide staircase led upstairs, the Latimer arms held by a pair of brightly painted wooden lions at the foot. Several doors led off the hall. One at the back was open, a couple of frightened-looking pages looking out. 'Get back in there,' Harsnet ordered. They hastily disappeared. We looked up as the steward clattered down the stairs. I was pleased to see he looked calmer now, his face intent.

'Lady Catherine has said she will remain in her rooms. But she would like to see you, master coroner.'

Harsnet took a deep breath. 'Very well.'

'What will you tell her?' I asked.

'That we have word of an assassin, no more.' He turned to the steward. 'Make sure all the servants are accounted for.'

The man nodded and disappeared towards the servants' quarters. Harsnet took a deep breath and mounted the stairs. Barak and I were left with the four remaining men, who fingered their sword-hilts uneasily.

'Is it true then, sir,' one asked. 'There is a madman after Lady Catherine?'

'It seems so.'

After a few minutes Harsnet returned looking sombre. 'Lady Catherine will stay in her rooms,' he said quietly. 'She is a fine lady, she received me most courteously and calmly. But I could see she was afraid.'

The servants' door opened and the steward reappeared. 'All the servants are present, sir. They are in the kitchen, all save Lady Catherine's waiting-women, who are with her. They've been told there are burglars. They're scared, sir.'

'Have you had any deliveries today?' Barak asked him.

'There are deliveries most days. The cook would know.'

'Then let us ask him,' Harsnet said. 'Good thinking, Master Barak. You men, stay here.' He looked at the steward. 'Go to your mistress. She should have you with her.'

We passed through the servants' door, following a stone-flagged passage into a large kitchen. Half a deer was roasting on a range, a boy turning the spit and another ladling juices over it. A large group of frightened-looking servants sat round a large table.

'Where is the cook?' Harsnet asked.

A fat man in a stained apron stepped forward. 'I am, sir. Master Greaves.'

'What deliveries have there been today?'

He nodded at the spit. 'George and Sam brought that deer over from Smithfield. And the coalman came this morning. He brought a new load, we put it in the cellar.'

'Where do you get your coal?' I asked.

'A man up at Smithfield. Goodman Roberts. He's been delivering for years.'

The freckle-faced lad turning the spit looked up. 'He sent his new assistant this week,' he ventured. 'And last week. I let him in.'

I exchanged a glance with Barak. 'What was he like?' I asked the boy.

'I didn't really see his face, sir, it was so black with coal-dust. He looked like he'd been rolling in the stuff.'

'Was he tall or short?'

'Tall, sir, and thin. He took the coal down to the cellar in the hall, as usual. I told him where it was last week.'

'Did you see him come out?'

The boy shook his head. 'Master Greaves sent me to the larder to peel some turnips.'

The cook looked worried. 'I can't be there to receive every delivery—'

'Did *anyone* see the coalman's boy leave?'

Heads were shaken round the table. 'You should have gone with him to the cellar, James,' the cook chided the boy. 'There are valuable things in this house—'

Harsnet interrupted him. 'Take us to the cellar.' He turned to me. 'Could it be him?'

'From the description, yes.'

'But how could he get hold of the coal—'

'By watching deliveries to this house, then dealing with Goodman Roberts as he dealt with the solicitor,' I answered grimly. I turned to the cook. 'Hurry, now.'

'I'll fetch the men.'

✝

THE COOK LED the way back to the passage outside, halting before a wooden trapdoor set with an iron ring. Harsnet went to collect the men he had left in the hall and returned.

'What is down there exactly?' Harsnet asked.

'Flasks of wine and barrels of vegetables, and the coal. And there's another trapdoor there, leading down to the sewer passage.'

'Part of the Charterhouse system?'

'Yes, sir. We're the last house in the system, after the water runs through our sewer it empties out into a stream that runs past the house. There is a large iron grille set into the wall where the water goes out. No one could get in or out that way.'

'Do you think he could be down there?' Harsnet asked.

'I doubt it. He'd be trapped.' I nodded agreement. 'No, if he is in the house my guess is it will be somewhere with an escape route.'

'We should do a thorough search,' Harsnet said. 'Two of you men search the house. You other two go down there and search the cellar, and the sewer.'

'The sewer is dry,' the cook said. 'There's something wrong with the mechanism up at the Charterhouse.'

'I know.'

Torches were fetched, the hatch was opened and Cranmer's men climbed down to the cellar. I glimpsed a large chamber full of barrels, a big pile of coal. The men looked behind the barrels, thrusting their swords into the coal lest anyone was hidden there. Then they turned to the trapdoor. 'It's bolted on the outside,' one of them called out. 'There can't be anyone down there.'

'Look nonetheless.'

They opened the trapdoor; cold air and a filthy smell wafted up to us. 'Go down,' Harsnet ordered. They descended, and shortly after I heard the sound of booted feet on iron rungs again, and someone called, 'No one!'

One of the men Harsnet had sent to search the house returned. 'There's no one here, sir.'

Harsnet and I looked at each other.

'Perhaps he got out of the house when Cranmer's messenger arrived and the search started,' Barak suggested. 'Knew something was up.'

Harsnet nodded gravely. 'If so, Lady Catherine is going to need to be carefully watched for some while. You four men, search the house once again. Please. Every nook and cranny.'

We returned to the hall. 'I am going to see the steward again,' Harsnet said. He left Barak and me alone in the hallway. Barak headed for the stairs.

'Where are you going?' I asked.

'Thought I'd join the search.' He smiled sadly. 'Take my mind off other things.'

'I'll join you.'

✝

WE MOUNTED the wide staircase. Above was another broad cor-ridor, and facing us a pair of wide doors, half open, two guards standing just inside. A blonde young woman in a fine dress of red velvet was looking out nervously. One of Lady Catherine's ladies, I guessed.

As we approached I saw a pair of inner doors was open. I glimpsed a bed draped with rich hangings and bright tapestries. Beside it, Harsnet and the steward were talking to a woman. I recognized the tall, shapely form and the striking, slightly severe face of Catherine Parr. Then she turned and stared back at me, and her dark eyes widened with fear. I realized she did not remember me from the day I saw her at Westminster. She thought this strange-looking man might even be the killer.

'You should not be looking in there!' the lady-in-waiting said, scandalized.

'I – I am sorry,' I stuttered. 'I did not mean—'

She slammed the door in my face.

Barak gave me a look of commiseration.

'You weren't to know—' he began. Then he broke off at a sudden yell from outside the house.

'Fire! Help! Fire!'

Chapter Forty-five

HARSNET RAN OUT of Lady Catherine's rooms. He stared at me for a moment, then we all ran to the nearest window, through which the glow of flames could be seen in the darkness. He shouted at Lady Catherine's steward, hesitating in the doorway to her chambers, to stay with his mistress.

Across the lawn, a large wooden summerhouse was well ablaze, flames at all the windows and smoke drifting across the grass towards the house. Guards and servants ran to and fro, carrying buckets of water. Discipline had vanished in face of the ever-present terror of fire.

'What is he doing?' Harsnet breathed.

'He's trying to distract us,' I said urgently. 'Fetch the sergeant, get those men back in the house!'

The coroner looked at me for a moment, then turned and ran down the stairs. Barak opened the window and leaned out. The summerhouse was blazing from end to end, there was nothing to be done for it and it was far enough from the house for the flames not to spread. As we watched, Harsnet ran outside, calling everyone back. I turned to look at Lady Catherine's closed doors. 'If he is trying to get everyone away from her, he has failed. Come!'

We hurried down the stairs. The movement jarred my back again, and I clamped my mouth shut against the pain. Through the open front door we saw guards running, the sergeant bawling at them to watch the doors and windows. The acrid stink of smoke drifted into the building.

'This is chaos,' I said. 'There is always panic when there is a fire. As Cantrell knows.'

'Is he still outside?' Barak asked.

'He may have come back in after starting the fire.'

Barak did not answer. I turned to him. He raised a finger to his lips, pointing to the half-open door of a room behind us.

'There's an open window in there,' he whispered. 'I can feel a breeze.'

He drew his sword; I did the same with my dagger. Barak stepped back, waited a second, then kicked the door wide open. We lunged inside.

We were in a storeroom, stacked chairs and tables and a heap of large cushions lying against the walls. The room was empty, but one of the three windows giving on to the lawn was half open. Barak jerked back the door lest anyone be hiding behind it, but there was only the blank wall. He slammed it shut again, then started thrusting with his sword under the stacked chairs and tables. I crossed to the window, coughing in the smoke-filled air. In the moonlight I saw the summerhouse collapse in a great flurry of sparks, the few men still on the lawn jumping back. I remembered the smoke at Goddard's house, that terrible impact on my back. Then I heard, behind me, a metallic clatter and a thud.

I whirled round. Barak was lying on the floor, his forehead red with blood, his sword beside him. Standing over him, the pile of cushions he had been lying under scattered around him, was Cantrell, in one of his old shabby smocks. He was carrying the piece of wood he had shown me at his house. He wore no glasses, and now I realized what the old woman had meant about his strange eyes. They were large, pale blue, with a dark heaviness in them such as I had never seen in human eyes before. It was as though, while he looked at me, he was also looking inward, at a terrible, exhausting vision. But he did not squint or peer; there was little wrong with his vision. He had been exaggerating his shortsightedness to deceive us, and his acting had been good.

I reached for my dagger; but Cantrell was quicker. In a single fluid movement he bent, picked up Barak's sword and thrust it at my throat. His clumsiness had been another act. I glanced frantically down at Barak; but he was unconscious, or worse.

'The Jew cannot help you.' Cantrell's voice was low, thick with gloating pleasure, quite different from his previous dull tones. He threw his club down on a cushion, keeping Barak's sword in his other hand held at my throat, the sharp point pricking at my skin.

'Now I have you,' he said. 'God has delivered you to me. I knew setting the summerhouse on fire would make everyone run about like ants!' He laughed, a childlike giggle that somehow chilled me to the bone.

'Catherine Parr is well guarded,' I said, trying to keep my breathing steady.

'I thought you would all think it had ended with Goddard, the pouring of the last vial.' He shook his head, his expression serious now. 'But of course the devil knows Catherine Parr is the Great Whore that was foretold. The devil told you the truth, didn't he? She will be well guarded now.' He frowned, looking for a moment like a thwarted child, then smiled again. 'But the Lord has delivered you to me. To remove an enemy and strengthen my hand.' He looked down at Barak's prone form a moment, stirred him with his toe and smiled at his own cleverness. Barak's face was white. I prayed he was still alive. I could hear voices outside, but dared not call, for Cantrell would slash my throat in a moment.

'Kneel down,' he hissed releasing the pressure of the sword a little. I hesitated, then knelt on the wooden floor. The burned skin of my back stretched agonizingly with the movement. A splinter dug into my knee. Cantrell pulled something from his pocket. A small glass vial, half-filled with yellowish liquid. Still holding the sword to my throat, he unstoppered it and held it out. 'Drink this,' he said.

I looked at it fearfully, knowing what it was. Dwale. His prelude to torture and death. 'You will never get us out of this room,' I said. 'The whole house is in uproar.'

'Drink it! Or I cut your throat and then the Jew's.' He pressed the sword to my neck, I felt a sharp pain, then blood trickling down my neck.

'All right!' I took the vial. It smelt of honey, he had mixed the evil stuff with nectar. I looked at it. My hand trembled. I thought, if I refuse and he kills me now, at least my death will be quick. But Barak would certainly die too. By drinking it I could live a little longer, and the instinct to do so is always powerful. I lifted it to my mouth. My throat seemed to constrict, I feared I would not be able to swallow it down, but I gulped once and it was gone. I wondered how long the dwale would take to have effect. Perhaps someone would come before it did. But immediately I felt strange, as though my body was enormously heavy. I tried to take a breath, but could not. Then everything slipped away.

✝

I WOKE IN DARKNESS, to a cesspit smell that made me retch and gasp. My body felt thick and heavy. A stab of pain shot down my back. I realized my wrists were bound in front of me, my ankles tied as well. I was propped up in a sitting position, my back against a brick wall, my legs on a rough, slimy floor. There was a light to one side. I turned painfully towards it. A lantern containing a fat bees-wax candle showed the ordure-smeared floor of a low, narrow brick passage. Cantrell sat cross-legged beside it, looking at me with a brooding gaze, his eyes glinting as they caught the light. He was near, four feet or so away. Barak's sword lay at his side.

I realized I was very cold, and shivered. The motion made the little wound at my neck sting.

'You are awake?' Cantrell asked in a neutral tone.

'Where are we?' I asked. My mouth was terribly dry, my voice came as a croak.

'In the sewer. Under the house.'

I looked round. There were long, narrow alcoves in the brick-work; they must connect to the lavatories above. Behind me, the passage stretched away into darkness. Ahead, as my eyes grew accustomed to the gloom, I made out the shape of a large metal grille, a patch of moonlit sky beyond. The thick iron mesh was broken in a few places, metal spikes sticking out at odd angles, but leaving barely space to put an arm though. We were trapped. Beyond the grille I heard the sound of running water; it must be the stream into which the sewer drained.

'I hid us under those cushions,' Cantrell said quietly, almost conversationally. He smiled. 'People came in, but they thought we were gone out of the window. They were all in such a panic, thinking of nothing but protecting the Whore. I got you down here when the house was quiet.'

'And Barak?'

'Still hidden under the cushions. They'll find him.'

'Is he dead?'

Cantrell shrugged. 'I don't know. It doesn't matter.' He frowned then, lapsed into his own thoughts.

'Why am I still alive?' I ventured after a few minutes.

He frowned. 'Don't distract me,' he said angrily. 'You distract me, damn you.'

I was silent again. The candle burned slowly down. Cantrell sat brooding. After a while he sighed, and turned to look at me again with his heavy, merciless gaze. 'You stopped God's plan,' he said. 'I don't know what to do.' He shook his head. 'I didn't complete the sequence, that is why I failed.'

'I don't understand.'

He put a hand to each side of his face. 'My head spins. Ever since God first spoke to me, so many messages, so many thoughts.' He sighed, a long groaning sound. 'God told me to set that fuse to give you time to escape, so you would think Goddard had done it all, but Goddard was not an apostate from true religion so the prophecies were not fulfilled – *you* are the apostate the seventh vial must be poured out on, the devil's agent too, you have to die, still, in a great earthquake.' He was talking fast now, gabbling to himself rather than to me. 'For the prophecies to be fulfilled, for me to be able to kill the Great Whore. I see it now.' He looked at me. 'But I cannot think how to do it, down here, and I cannot get you out alive.' He turned and pointed a skinny finger at me. 'I knew you were the devil's man when you came to where I left Dr Gurney. I marked your bent back, which is a sign of a twisted soul, I learned you were an apostate from true reform. You looked sad, lost. I recognized that in your face when I first saw you by the river. And I thought, yes, that is how a man possessed would look.'

I wondered with a shudder if he had rambled on like this to Tupholme, or Mistress Bunce, as they died in slow agony. The shudder turned into a bout of shivering, for I was cold, frozen. I had felt cold for weeks but nothing like this. Cantrell did not seem to care how cold it was.

'I'll have to get you out alive, later,' he said. 'Find some way to kill you.' I felt a wave of relief. So there was to be no torture and death down here at least, unless something in his buzzing, burning mind told him to kill me. I flinched as Cantrell reached into a pocket and pulled out a large, narrow pair of tweezers. He held them up and smiled.

'Don't think of rescue. They've no idea we are down here. After I hauled you down I used these to move the bolt back into position from below. There was just enough space, the hatch is a poor fit. I studied it when I came last week, the first time I acted as the coalman's boy.' He looked at his hand, where a piece of ordure from the floor adhered. He wiped it on his tunic, wrinkling his nose. 'This is a disgusting place.' He gave me a look that chilled me to the bone. 'It's your fault I'm stuck down here.'

He was silent for a while then, frowning with concentrated thought. He was mad, I knew. There was something in his complete self-obsession that reminded me of Adam Kite in his worst phase, but there was something very different too, something wild and savage that I did not begin to understand. I knew that at any moment he might jump up and kill me. But he stayed quiet, thoughtful. After a while he spoke suddenly. 'Goddard treated me badly. That hard tongue of his. He regretted it when I hammered nails into his jaw before I drugged him.' He smiled. 'How surprised he looked when he woke up, after I broke in and knocked him unconscious. He was another that thought I was stupid. He learned different.'

My back burned and the ropes chafed at my wrists and ankles as I listened to him. He was talking without even looking at me now. 'When they closed the monastery, put me out in the world, it made my head spin. Helpless, like a tiny boat in a great storm. Yet it was all meant by God. The day came when I heard his voice, and knew that it was his, that he had chosen me.' He looked at me then and smiled transparently. He seemed to notice how uncomfortable I was for the first time, and cocked his head slightly. 'Are you in pain?' he asked. 'Does your back hurt?'

'Yes.'

'Think what it will be like for you in Hell. They are all there already, your friend Elliard and the others. Perhaps the devil will choose to make you wield a pickaxe for ever and ever among the flames, breaking up stones, your bent back an agony of pain. For ever and ever.' He smiled. 'To purge the enemies of the Lord.'

I thought I caught a sound, back up the passage. I strained to hear. If they came quietly and took him by surprise I might be saved. But it was nothing. The silence that followed seemed to go on for ever, broken only by disjointed remarks from the madman facing me.

'The solicitor Felday said you knew Elliard,' Cantrell said at length.

'Yes. He was my friend.' I took a deep breath. 'That was when I decided I would find you.'

'No, no. That was the devil.' Cantrell shook his head vigorously, then suddenly was on his feet, grasping the sword. 'Do not deceive me!' He knelt before me, and again the sword touched my throat.

'Admit the truth,' he demanded. 'Say you are possessed by the devil. Say he is in you.'

And then I heard it. Far away. A metallic clunk. A creak. A faint rushing sound. I understood and my heart sank. They were opening the doors up at the Charterhouse that held the water back. They knew or suspected that we were down here, and they were going to drown us both like rats. I remembered Harsnet saying he would do anything to protect the Archbishop.

'Admit the devil is in you.' Cantrell's face was full of rage now. I did not know what to say. Would admitting or denying the accusation make him more likely to kill me?

'I cannot think,' I said. 'I am confused . . .' I thought feverishly, if I could get to the nearest alcove when the water came, wedge myself in somehow . . .

'The devil struggles inside you. Come, admit it. I command you in Jesus' name.' He twisted the sword point, opening a new cut in my neck.

Then came a violent blast of cold air and a roaring, crashing sound. Cantrell whirled round. In the light from his candle I saw a wall of water and foam filling the entire tunnel, rushing down on us. I thrust myself sideways, into the alcove. Cantrell had no time to make a sound before the flood sent him spinning away. I saw him go, arms outspread, as though he was flying.

✟

THE VERY FORCE of the flood saved me, for I had rolled far enough into the alcove for the backwash to slam me up against the far end. I twisted amid the rush of water, thrust out my bound legs and made contact with a side wall, pressing my back into the other wall at the same time. The pain was excruciating but I knew I must not slip or I too would be swept away. The water swirled around me, tugging at my clothes, nearly pulling me from my lodgement. My legs shook, the lump at my back scraped agonizingly against the bricks, burned skin peeling away. But I held on. The rushing water rose over my neck, over my face. My hair streamed out as some nameless stinking thing slid past my nose. My lungs burned and I felt my head swim. Is this the end? I thought. Does it end like this?

A great sucking sensation nearly dislodged me once more. It was the water ebbing. My head was suddenly in the open. I took a huge gasp of air. The water swirled down below my chest, then rushed away and was gone with a last rushing boom. Only a trickling sound remained, and loud drips falling from the ceiling.

I let myself tumble to the ground, shouting in agony as I landed on my shoulder, jarring it. I was a mass of pain, shivering with cold, wet through and stinking. And my hands and feet were still bound. I rolled out of the alcove, into the passage. And I thought, if I have survived, Cantrell might have too.

☦

A FAINT HALF-LIGHT coming through the dripping grille lightened the gloom. It was dawn, we had been here all night. I stared round frantically. Where was he? And then my heart leaped into my mouth as I saw him. He was sitting up against the grille, facing me.

I groaned. I was too weak to fight any more, even to think. But Cantrell stayed unmoving. I stared and stared through the gloom, trying to see if he was breathing. Once or twice in the seemingly endless time that followed he appeared to move. Then I heard shouting from beyond the grille and saw lights moving there, then several men jumped into the ditch in front of the grille, tramping through stream-water. They held their torches up, exclaiming when they saw Cantrell sitting there with his back to them. But by the light of their torches I saw now that he was impaled, one of the broken metal rods sticking right through his head, brains and blood smearing his face. He must have been thrown against it by the full force of the flood. His eyes were open and he looked astonished, angry. In his last seconds he must have realized that he had failed. I found it strange that during the night I had felt no sense of evil passing.

A guard bent to the grille, a key in his hand. It was hard to get it open.

'The lawyer's here!' he called. 'Alive!'

A new figure bent and entered the tunnel. Harsnet came up to me and held a torch to my face. I met his gaze.

'Is Barak alive?' I croaked.

'Yes.'

'You would have drowned me.'

He looked sad, but not ashamed, his face stayed set. 'We guessed you were down here.' Harsnet spoke slowly, his west country accent strong. 'There were marks on the bolt on the hatch, we wondered if he had somehow closed it from below. I feared that with the powers he has he might have got away in these tunnels, even if I sent a dozen men after him. It was the only way to be sure he died, the only way. I'm sorry, Matthew.'

Chapter Forty-six

THREE DAYS LATER an unexpected visitor arrived at my house. I was still in bed, recovering from my ordeal, when a flustered Joan appeared to say that Lord Hertford himself had called. I told her to show him up. I knew I should have made the effort to rise and receive him in the parlour, but I was too weary.

Lord Hertford wore a plain, fur-lined coat, a grey doublet beneath. I thought again how different he was from his brash, gaudily dressed brother. He had struck me before as a man of deadly seriousness, but today he was relaxed, giving me a friendly smile before sitting in the chair by my bed. I thought, today he is the politician.

'I am sorry I must receive you here,' I said.

He raised a hand. 'I was sorry to hear of what you suffered in that sewer. And at Goddard's house before. We would never have got Cantrell had you not realized Goddard's killing was intended to mislead us. Catherine Parr would be dead by now.'

I sighed. 'I am sorry we could not get him sooner. Nine victims killed, including the solicitor and the innocent coalman that we found dead.'

'Lady Catherine knows you saved her,' Lord Hertford said quietly. 'She knows, and is grateful.'

'You told her about Cantrell?'

'Not the whole story. But that there was a killer on the loose, and he wanted her for a victim. Harsnet had to tell her that to keep her in her chambers. She saw you that night, you know, for a moment. She thought you were the killer.'

'I wondered whether she did.'

'I told her you had saved her. She would like to receive you to thank you. She is a lady to remember favours a long time.'

'I am honoured.' Indeed I was, but at the same time apprehensive that someone else near the summit of the court had taken notice of me now. I looked again at Lord Hertford. He was smiling, he was happy.

'I do not know when she will send for you. She will have many calls on her time these next few months, for she has consented to marry the King.'

'She has?'

'She has accepted that it is God's will.'

'When will it be?' I asked.

'Not till full summer. The King plans to have Bishop Gardiner marry them.' He laughed. 'How he will hate that, marrying the King to a reformer.'

'But why *is* the King marrying her?' I had to ask. 'When his own sympathies grow ever more strongly against reform?'

'She has attracted him for some time. Since before her husband died. And he is old, and ill, and lonely.'

'His sixth marriage. Will she survive, do you think?' I could not help the question.

'It will be as God ordains. The Parr family can look forward to high places at court now. They are all reformers. And Archbishop Cranmer is out of danger.'

'He is?' I was glad to hear that at least.

'Yes. The King realized Gardiner's accusations about his staff amounted to nothing. He has set a commission to investigate the matter – and put Archbishop Cranmer himself at the head of it. Gardiner's plot is unravelled. And Bishop Bonner's campaign against the godly men of London has likewise uncovered little that even he could call heresy. People are being released. They will have to be careful for a while. But the tide is starting to turn again in our favour.'

'What of Dean Benson?'

'Back at his post, told by the Archbishop to keep his mouth tight shut.'

'If he had stopped Goddard and Lockley using the dwale to get those beggars' teeth, lives might have been saved.'

'We could not afford to make a scandal about that now. Think of what might come out if we did.' He looked at me steadily for a moment, fingering his long beard. 'You have proved your worth, Master Shardlake. Would you work for me as once you did for Lord Cromwell?'

'Thank you, my lord, but all I want is a peaceful life. My work at the Court of Requests. Trying to organize a hospital for the poor subscribed by the Lincoln's Inn lawyers.'

'My brother Thomas is shortly to leave England, to take up his position as ambassador to the Spanish Netherlands. I know he was cruel to you. I am sorry. You would not have to see him again.'

'I can take jibes. I have taken enough in my life. That does not matter.'

He inclined his head in acknowledgement. 'I too am keenly interested in bettering the lot of the poor. It has been harsh indeed in these last years. I may be able to help you with your plans. My patronage could be useful to you in many ways, as your skills could be to me.'

'I am sorry, my lord, but I'm not fitted for a public life, for the harsh decisions people feel they must make.'

He gave me a long, hard look, then nodded.

'Well,' he said quietly. 'You been through much of late. You need time to recuperate. But think of what I have said.'

'Coroner Harsnet would have drowned me,' I said. 'I thought he might visit me, but he has not.'

'I am sure he did not decide lightly to open those gates.'

'I am sure he decided it was God's will. Were the houses in the square flooded?'

'Some were, yes.'

'How was Harsnet so sure we were down there?' I asked curiously.

'The bolt in the hatch leading to the sewer had not been closed properly, though Cantrell thought it had. We could see someone had gone down there. But Master Shardlake, if Harsnet and his men had come down there after you, Cantrell would surely have killed you before they reached him.'

'There was a chance of that, yes. But Harsnet must have known that letting that great flood go would kill both of us. It was sheer chance I managed to press myself into an alcove, and that the water level fell before I drowned.'

'The coroner felt it was necessary.'

'My lord, it is these necessary things which those who work at Whitehall do, that mean I will remain a lawyer.'

He got up, defeated for now. I wondered if he would be back. He was an ambitious man; he was building up a network of people under his patronage. A principled man, too, as Cromwell had been. But Lord Hertford, capable as he was, would never be another Cromwell, for he indulged weaknesses, like his affection for his brother.

'How is your man Barak?'

'He is all right. He was struck a nasty blow, but his head is thick.'

'I would like to see him before I go. To thank him, from the Archbishop too.'

I called Joan to fetch Barak. He arrived looking pale, hollow-eyed. He bowed deeply to Lord Hertford, who thanked him for all his efforts. 'I have been trying to persuade your master to work for me,' he said. 'There would be a place for you, too, as his assistant. I could promise you an exciting life. See if you can persuade him.' Lord Hertford rose, bowed deeply to both of us and left the room. As his footsteps faded down the stairs, Barak turned to me. 'Persuade you my arse,' he said. 'I've lost enough myself this time.'

'I know,' I said sympathetically.

We had returned from the Charterhouse to find Tamasin's things gone, a note for Barak. The old friend she had gone to when she left had been employed in the late Queen Catherine Howard's privy kitchen. Tamasin had been working with her, helping to prepare the sweetmeats Queen Catherine loved, when Barak and I met her in York two years before. Barak had refused to show me her note, but had told me Tamasin had been offered her old job; now the King was to marry Catherine Parr a new Queen's Household was to be established and the chamberlain was looking for experienced servants. Tamasin had taken the post, and the accommodation at Whitehall that went with it. She said she felt she and Barak needed time apart, and asked him not to contact her. He had been struck to the heart, and it had taken much persuasion to prevent him from going down to Whitehall. He had agreed to wait a little before contacting her, though now she was gone he realized he wanted her with him more than anything.

'Can we get back to work soon? he asked. 'I need something to occupy my mind.'

'In a few days, Jack. First there are two people I must go and see.'

✝

BY THE END OF the week I was up and about again, albeit still stiff and sore. I sent Barak to inform the Court of Requests that I could return to work the following Monday, and he returned with a sheaf of new cases. It was a pleasure to read them, to feel my old life returning. But on the Sunday before I went back to work I saddled up Genesis and rode into town.

It was to Guy's that I went first. It was the twenty-second of April, four weeks to the day since Roger died and the horrors began. I rode through London on a quiet, peaceful spring Sunday. Even the grimy city felt clean and bright, the greys and browns of the streets relieved by patches of green from the trees in the churchyards, for the mixture of warm weather and rain we had had recently had brought fast growth everywhere.

I had guessed Guy would be home on Sunday afternoon, after going to church in the morning, perhaps studying. I had heard nothing from him in ten days, though I had sent him a note from my bed saying the killer had been discovered and was dead.

As I tied Genesis to the rail outside Guy's shop, my heart was full of trepidation. What if he rejected me, told me our long friendship was over? I stepped to the door of the shop, and was surprised to find it was ajar. I heard voices coming from the back room, voices I recognized. I entered the shop quietly, treading carefully towards the half-open inner door. I saw Guy's copy of Vesalius lying shut on the table.

Piers' voice from the inner room was low, but sharp as a file. 'You old black bastard, if that lawyer reports me for theft I could fucking hang—'

'He won't—'

'How do you know? And now I'm reduced to being a beggar, living among the lowest dregs, running at the sight of a constable—'

'No one is hunting you, Piers.' Guy's voice sounded unutterably weary. Then he added, 'Why did you steal from me?'

'Why not? Apprentices get paid a pittance and I worked my balls off for you.'

'You could have asked for more.'

'I wasn't going to stay with you, anyway. I was going to find another position and the money would come in useful.' He laughed, cruelly. 'I was sick of your pathetic whining about how I should have more sympathy for people.'

I stepped silently to the inner door, wishing Barak was with me.

'I tried to teach you some moral sense,' I heard Guy say, his voice near breaking. 'To be a good man.'

'While I did your dirty work, cleaning up the mess left when you opened up stinking bodies. And I knew you would like to open up my body, my arse anyway—'

'Never . . .' There was distress in Guy's voice now.

'I want money. I want all you have. Then you will write me a reference, I am going north to find a new place.'

'I will give you money, Piers. But a reference, never.' Guy's answer was firm.

'Then I'll cut your heart open, see if your blood is brown like your face—'

I drew my dagger from its sheath and pushed the door wide open. 'No, Piers,' I said quietly. 'That you will not do.'

I saw that Guy was sitting on a stool, his back against the wall. Piers held a long knife to his chest. The boy's face, so often mild and expressionless, was red and twisted with anger. It was also smeared with the dirt of the streets; the handsome well-dressed apprentice looked very different now. His eyes widened with fear as I entered, then narrowed again as he saw I was alone.

'Not got your bodyguard with you today, hunchback?' he asked. 'I'll do for you as well, and it will be a pleasure.'

'No. If you strike at Guy, I swear to God you will not leave here alive. Guy is right, you are under no threat. He took back the silver you stole and which I found; there is no evidence against you. Go now, get out of here and never come back. I promise you that is the best offer you will get this side of the grave.'

I felt utterly focused, full of cold anger. Having faced Cantrell, this nasty little creature seemed like nothing. My tone and the way I stared firmly into his stony, lifeless eyes must have made an impression, for Piers lowered his knife.

'Step away from the door, then,' he said.

'Throw the knife down first.'

He hesitated, then laid it on Guy's workbench. I stood away from the door and he walked past me, into the shop. There he bent quickly, lifted the copy of Vesalius and ran out of the door. His footsteps disappeared up the street. Guy took a long, shuddering breath.

'Thank you,' he said. 'I am not sure that he would have killed me, I do not think he had the courage for that. But I am glad it was not put to the test. Thank you.'

'He has your Vesalius.'

'Yes, he will get a good price for it. Well, I shall put the money he stole and you returned towards buying another.'

'I was not sure if it was wise to come,' I said. 'I am very glad I did.'

He nodded. I saw his brown hands, lying in his lap, were shaking. 'Piers knocked at the door an hour ago,' he said slowly. 'When I answered he pushed his way in, then drew his knife and brought me in here. Always when he worked for me he would smile, be quiet and deferential. But his face and voice today – the coldness, the anger.' He shook his head. 'I am sorry I did not contact you, Matthew, but I was still angry. You should have come to me first. I would have agreed to his being questioned, you know.'

'I am sorry.'

Guy smiled faintly. 'Well, I think today you have more than made up for it.' He lifted a hand. 'Take that stool there,' he said. 'I do not feel quite able to get up yet.'

When I had seated myself he looked at me silently for a long moment. Then he asked, 'Cantrell is dead?'

'Yes.'

'Tell me what happened, how it ended. If you feel able to.'

He sat listening as I told him about the siege of Goddard's house, my realization that Cantrell was the killer; the desperate hours in the sewers underneath Catherine Parr's house.

'I had not realized you had been tested so terribly,' he said quietly when I had finished. 'And you must let me look at your back before you leave.'

'I would be grateful. It still pains me. What was Cantrell, Guy? He killed seven people to fulfil the prophecy of the vials of wrath, two more along the way and, perhaps, his own father too. I think of him at Roger and Dorothy's lodgings, repairing that frieze, perhaps alone with her. Managing to seem like a normal human being. It chills my blood. I have been lying in bed, thinking and thinking, and I cannot fathom why he did those things. At the end he seemed confused, deranged, wild – not the calculating creature I expected. But he was not possessed, he genuinely believed he was doing God's work.'

'I do not know what he was,' Guy said quietly. 'I wish I did. No more than I know who Gilles de Rais truly was, or Strodyr. Some wild disturbance happened in their minds, made them less like humans than ravening beasts. Perhaps one day study will enable us to understand those darkest corners of the human mind which they inhabited. Perhaps not.'

'Yet I feel that Cantrell was connected to the blast of wild, brutal fanaticism that is sweeping through the land; so that England devours its own children. It gave him, at least, an excuse for what he wanted to do.'

Guy nodded sadly. 'We are in the middle of a bitter conflict between two religions. It has driven men to extremes, to the impious arrogance of believing they alone can comprehend the vast mysteries of Scripture, let alone the mind of God. Such people are incapable of understanding even their own minds, for they confuse their own needs, for certainty or power, with God's voice speaking to them. I am only surprised that more are not driven to stark madness. I try in my poor way to follow the much harder path of humility. Facing squarely the terrible mysteries of suffering and cruelty in God's world, doubting whether through prayer you have understood God's will or his voice or even his presence. Yes, I believe humility is the greatest human virtue.'

I shook my head. 'I think I am beyond belief. I have had to read the Book of Revelation over and over in this last month. It appals me. I read its cruel barbarous message and I despair.'

'No,' Guy said firmly. 'Do not despair, Matthew. Do not let Revelation curse your life too. And now, let me have a look at your poor back.'

✞

I left Guy's with a sense of peace, a fragile contentment, but peace nonetheless. Guy had rubbed fresh oils into my burns, and my back, too, was easier. And so I rode back to Lincoln's Inn, where I had an invitation to visit Dorothy. To her also I had sent a note from my sick bed, saying Charles Cantrell was dead. She had replied asking if she could come and visit me, but I did not want her to see me ill in bed so requested that I might visit her when I was better.

Margaret opened the door and welcomed me in. 'Your guest has finally gone,' I said with a smile, for in her note Dorothy had said Bealknap had left.

'Yes, the afternoon you came, in a great hurry. He barely stopped to thank the mistress.'

'For Bealknap to give thanks to anyone would for him be like having teeth pulled. Do you know if he has sent any money across?'

'Not him.'

'I did not think he would. I must do something about that.'

Dorothy was in the parlour. The first thing I noticed was that the wooden frieze was gone, the wall bare. Dorothy had abandoned mourning and wore a high-collared grey dress with pretty red piping on the collar and sleeves. She smiled at me, then came and took my hands. 'Matthew,' she said. 'I have been worried. You look tired, but thank God, not ill as I had feared.'

'No, I am tougher than people think. You got rid of the frieze?'

'I had it burned in the kitchen yard. I watched while the flames took it. The cook boys thought I was mad but I did not care. That creature touched it, but for it he would never have come here, would never have chosen Roger as a victim.'

'No. It was a terrible mischance.'

'What made him kill all those innocent people?'

'I have just been discussing that with Guy. It is a mystery to us both. Perhaps it is better left so; it is no good thing to dwell on for too long.'

'Were you there when he was caught?' she asked.

'Yes. But do not ask more, Dorothy. The matter is to be kept secret.'

'I will thank you to the end of my days for what you did,' she said. 'I wanted Roger's murderer caught and punished and you have done that for me, and for him, at great cost.' She released my hands and stepped away, then clasped them together in front of her. I guessed she had something important to say.

'Matthew.' She spoke quietly. 'I told you a while ago that I did not know what my future would be. I am still uncertain. But I have decided to go and stay with Samuel in Bristol, for a month or two at least. Roger's affairs are pretty well settled, and now his murderer is dead I need some time for reflection, some peace. I leave on Tuesday.'

'I shall miss you.'

'It will be only for a while,' she said. 'I will come again in June, to visit, and by then I will have decided whether to stay in Bristol or come back here and rent a small house in London. I know now I will be able to afford that. Bristol is full of merchants, Samuel will become one himself before long, and I confess a fear that, worthy people as they doubtless are, I may find myself a little – bored.'

I smiled. 'They do not have the sword-sharp wit and questing intelligence of lawyers. That is well known.'

'Exactly,' she said. 'And here I have good and interesting friends. And now, Matthew, stay to dinner and let us talk of pleasant things, the old days before the world went mad.'

'I would like nothing better,' I said.

Epilogue

The King and Catherine Parr were to be married that day, and in the larger London streets bonfires were being erected, together with spits for the roasting pigs which would be distributed later from the royal kitchens at Whitehall. As Barak and I rode along Cheapside I tried to block out a memory of Yarington burning in his church. Small boys were running up and down, bringing wood for the fires and hallooing excitedly at the prospect of the feast to come, their faces red on the hot summer day. The beggars had gone from round Cheapside Cross, moved on by the constables that they should not spoil the celebrations.

A month before, Lady Catherine had summoned me to the house in Charterhouse Square. She received me in a parlour hung with gorgeous tapestries, two ladies-in-waiting sewing by the window. She looked very different from the last time I had seen her. She was dressed now in the richest finery, a dress of brown silk embossed with designs of flowers on its wide crimson sleeves, a necklace of rubies at her throat and a French hood set with pearls covering her auburn hair. She was tall, and her mouth and chin were too small to be pretty, yet she had tremendous presence; a welcoming presence despite the rich formal clothes. I bowed deeply. 'My congratulations on your betrothal, my lady,' I said.

She nodded slightly in acknowledgement and I saw the stillness in her, the stillness of one who has placed herself under firm control, who must stay controlled now to fulfil the role she had accepted on that great, terrible stage, the royal court.

'I know you saved my life, Master Shardlake,' she said in her rich voice. 'And suffered great risk and privation in the process.'

'I was glad to, my lady.' I wondered whether Cantrell, had he seen her close to, would have realized how different she was from his frantic imaginings. But no, I thought, he would not, he could not.

She smiled, a smile of gentle warmth. 'I know Lord Hertford has been to visit you, to ask you to return to the world of politics. He has told me of your reluctance. Well, that is something I can understand. I want you to know, Master Shardlake, that I will never make demands on you, but if ever you need a friend, or a favour, or anything that it will soon be in my power to grant, you have only to ask.'

In all my years of involvement on the fringes of the court no one before had ever offered a favour without demanding something in return. 'Thank you, my lady,' I said. 'You are very kind. I shall remember your words with gladness in my heart.'

She smiled again, though her slim, richly draped body remained still and tense. 'I shall be watching you from a distance, Master Shardlake, not to demand service but to present aid if it is ever needed.' She extended a delicate hand heavy with rings, and I bent and kissed it.

✝

'SIX WIVES the King's had now.' Barak's words dragged me from my reverie. 'We can't even get one between us.'

'Do not give up on Tamasin, 'I said. 'I believe there is still hope there.'

'Don't see it.' Barak shook his head. 'But I'll keep trying.'

He had been several times to the kitchens at Whitehall Palace, to ask Tamasin to come back, begging her forgiveness. She had given it, but she would not come back to him, not yet at least, though she promised she would remain loyal to her marriage vows, no matter how many servants and courtiers showed an interest in her. I wondered whether she was making Barak realize that she was that rare if troublous thing, a woman determined that any relationship she had should be one of equals.

As for me, the nature of my own disappointment was different though it still bit deep. Dorothy had not returned to London. A few weeks ago, she had sent me a letter explaining that she had bought a small house in Bristol, near her son and his fiancée. Her letter ended:

As for us, I realize what you have felt for me, the old feelings that perhaps were always there but which returned after Roger died. You behaved honourably, Matthew, being yourself you could do no other and I believe your determination in hunting down Roger's killer was done for him as well as for me.

Yet I know now that I will never marry again; nor should I: the twenty years that Roger and I had together before that evil creature took him were, I know, blessed with a happiness that is rare among married couples. Any other marriage could only be a pale shadow, and that would be fair on nobody.

Forgive me, and come to visit us.

I had not actually asked her to marry me, yet I would have, she had divined that. I would not go to Bristol, not for a time at least; that would be too hard.

We passed the top of Bucklersbury, and I thought of Guy down at his shop. Our friendship was restored, though I felt a new reserve in him sometimes, and wondered if he would ever trust me fully again.

'Any more subscriptions for the hospital?' Barak asked me.

'A few. I wish I had more encouragement from Treasurer Rowland. He has never forgiven me for being curt with him when he stopped you catching Cantrell that time. It is a problem. If he would send a circular encouraging the Fellows to give, they would put their hands in their pockets, each to show himself more generous than his brothers.'

Barak shook his head. 'So the poor continue to suffer, because a puffed⁄up old arsehole resents being spoken to roughly. Well, it was ever thus.'

'I am afraid you are right.'

'One day the poor will take things into their own hands,' he said darkly; then smiled sardonically. 'Have you tried asking Bealknap for money?'

We both laughed then. Since my return to Lincoln's Inn Bealknap had studiously avoided me; he would vanish through doors or round corners at my approach. He was fully restored to health, and back to all his old ways. He had of course sent Dorothy no money, nor had he paid Guy's fees for the treatment that had saved his sorry life. Yet embarrassment, perhaps even a sense of guilt, led him to go to these lengths to avoid me. It was becoming a running joke round Lincoln's Inn that Bealknap was terrified of Brother Shardlake. He could have solved the problem in an instant by coming to me with some money for Dorothy and for Guy's fee, but Bealknap would suffer any humiliation, look any sort of fool, rather than part with any of the gold he kept sitting uselessly in his chambers. Now, indeed, I pitied him.

We passed under Bishopsgate Bridge. 'Well, here we are,' Barak said dubiously. 'I don't know how you think a visit here is going to cheer us up.'

'Wait and see,' I said as we rode under the Bedlam gate, into the precinct of the hospital. We tied up the horses and I knocked at the door. Barak looked along the length of the building, anxiously, as though some lunatic might lean from the windows and shriek at him, rattling his chains. But the house seemed quiet today. The big keeper Gebons opened the door, bowing to me. Since my confrontation with Shawms over his locking out of Ellen, Gebons seemed to have developed a respect for me.

'Are Goodman Kite and his wife here yet?' I asked.

'Ay, sir, they are. They are all in the parlour, with Ellen.'

'Come, then, Barak. This is what I wanted you to see.'

I led the way into the parlour. The scene there today could have come from any peaceful domestic home. Adam and his father sat at the table playing chess. Sitting watching him, Minnie Kite had a look of happy repose that I would not have believed possible four months ago. Beside her, Ellen sat knitting, a look of pride on her long, sensitive face. The old woman Cissy sat next to Ellen, also knitting, though sometimes stopping and staring into space with a look of desperate sadness, seeing something not here in the room.

'Well done, Adam.' Minnie laughed and clapped her hands as her son reached out and checkmated her husband.

As we entered, the company rose to greet us, but I bade them sit again. 'I have brought my assistant to see you, Adam,' I said. 'You may remember him from the court hearings. Master Barak. He helped me prepare your case.' Barak bowed to the company.

'I have beaten my father at chess for the third time running,' Adam said. Then he fell silent for a second. 'Is it the sin of pride to take such pleasure in it?' He looked at Ellen.

'No, no, Adam. How many times have we told you, it is no sin to take pleasure in the little diversions God has given us in this hard world.'

Adam nodded. He was still much troubled by fears of sin, but accepted – most of the time – that whether one was saved or damned was ultimately knowable only to God. His parents feared what would happen when he left the Bedlam and learned of Yarington's terrible fate, which the congregation had been encouraged to blame on Catholic fanatics. But Guy believed that Adam ought to leave soon, return to the world, face up to the things it contained. His parents remained as radical as ever in their religious views, but because they loved their son they had agreed with Guy that his fragile mental state meant the subject of religion must be treated gently. Bishop Bonner had unintentionally done the family a favour with his persecution of radicals in the spring; Reverend Meaphon had taken a living in Norwich, far from the tumults of the capital, and had gone in May. A new vicar had been appointed; a time-server with no deep belief, a harmless man.

Daniel Kite rose from the table. 'Come, son, shall we take a walk around the yard? I thought we might take ourselves as far as the Bishopsgate today.'

'Yes, all right.' Adam got up. His mother too rose and slipped her arm through his. I stepped away from the table. Adam turned to me with a nervous smile. 'Master Shardlake, when we come back, will you tell me more about life in the law?'

'I will, with pleasure.' On my last couple of visits Adam had shown some interest in his legal position, even expressing indignation when I told him he could not be freed without the agreement of the Privy Council. It was a world away from the days when nothing was real to him save his desperate struggle with God.

Adam glanced past me to Barak, and reddened slightly. 'I remember seeing you at court, sir,' he said.

'Ay, that's right.'

'I was in a bad way then,' the boy said quietly.

'That you were.' Barak smiled, though he still looked uneasy with Adam, and with this place.

We watched from the open front door as father and mother and son walked slowly across the yard, talking quietly; Ellen stood a little behind us, afraid as ever to step too close to the world out/side.

'Adam's parents care for him,' she said. 'They are not like those families that abandon their troublesome relatives here.' There was a note of bitterness in her voice; I looked at her and she forced a smile. I wished I knew the details of her story but beyond what Shawms had told me of the attack on her when she was a girl I knew nothing; she would not say, and I would not pry.

'This sudden interest of Adam's in the law is a new thing,' I said. 'He's a bright lad.'

'Who knows, one day he may make a lawyer?'

'Ay. I will give him Barak's place, and train him up. He will come cheaper.' Ellen laughed.

'Exploiting the mad, I call it,' Barak said. Then he turned to me.

'He certainly looks different from the last time I saw him. But there is still something . . .'

'Fragile?' Ellen asked. 'He has a long journey to make yet. But I believe he will complete it. One day.'

'So there you are, Barak,' I said. 'Madness is an illness, and sometimes, like other illnesses, it may be treated.' I thought, but did not say, that he had been so damaged he might well slip back at times, though I hoped never to the terrible state in which I first found him. Could he ever fully recover? I did not know.

Barak stepped outside and bowed to Ellen. 'I ought to get over to the Old Barge. I have things to pack. And some of Tamasin's things to sort out. She said I could take them over to her new lodgings. Better make sure I've got everything.'

'I will see you at Lincoln's Inn tomorrow morning.'

'Ay. Couple of tricky cases coming up.'

I sensed he was glad of the excuse to leave. He untied Sukey and rode away, raising his cap to the Kites as he passed them at the gate.

'Your assistant is moving house?' Ellen asked.

'Yes, he and his wife have separated. It is sad, he could not bear to stay in their old lodgings. He has taken a room near Lincoln's Inn. They may get back together in time, there is still a great bond between them. I hope so.'

'The papers requesting Adam's release go to the Court of Requests this week?' Ellen asked.

'Yes, on Thursday. If the judge agrees to the request it will be forwarded to the Privy Council. I believe they will grant it.' I knew they would, for Cranmer had written to me, promising he would see the matter through.

'Is he ready?' Ellen asked. 'There are still times when I go into his room and find him sitting, or worse kneeling, on the floor. Still times when he fears his damnation.'

'Guy believes it is time for him to leave, to *engage* with the world as he puts it. Under continual care from his parents, of course, and

Guy will visit him frequently. He cannot be certain Adam will not relapse, but he believes he will continue to make progress. And that the time when he might make some mad display is past. I hope he is right,' I added quietly.

'I shall never see him again,' Ellen said bleakly. I turned to look at her. She had retreated a couple of steps away from the open door.

'That is sad,' I said seriously. 'When you have done so much to help him. Guy says that without your persistence, your understanding of him, he doubts Adam would have made anything like the progress he has. The Kites would be glad to have you visit him, I am sure.'

'You know my situation, sir,' she said quietly. 'Please do not press me.'

Shawms appeared from his office, gave us a dirty look as he passed between us. When he had gone Ellen said, 'Will you do something for me, sir?' She spoke quickly, reddening, and I guessed she had had to screw up her courage to ask.

'Whatever I can, Ellen.'

'Will you come and visit me sometimes, when you have time? I love to hear what is happening in the outside world, I did not know the King was getting married again today until you told me. Everyone here is so locked inside their own worlds . . .'

'I would rather you made some venture into the outside world, Ellen. Come, will you not take just a few steps outside? You can hold on to my arm. Is it so hard?'

'Harder than you realize.' And indeed the very suggestion made her shrink back against the wall. 'Sir, there are those here like Adam who may be cured, with the help of good friends and those who love them. But there are others, like me, whose best hope of sanity lies in accepting their – disabilities.'

I looked at her. 'I will make a bargain with you, Ellen. I will come and see you, whenever I can, and tell you all the news. But I will also ask you to consider ways in which you may deal with your – difficulty, perhaps even overcome it. I would never make you go outside unless you were prepared to try, but equally I will never let the subject go.' I smiled. 'Is it a bargain?'

'You drive a hard deal, sir, like all lawyers.'

'I do. Will you agree my terms?'

She gave a small, sad smile. 'I will. And thank you for your care.'

Just then, a great clamour of bells began to ring across the city. We looked out through the open doorway, into the sunlit yard, listening to the joyful clamour. Out there, in a chapel in a palace, the King had finally married Catherine Parr.

HISTORICAL NOTE

The spring of 1543 brought another round in the struggle for power between religious reformers and reactionaries which dominated the later years of Henry VIII. Although Edward Seymour, Earl of Hertford, had begun his rise to power, the pre-eminent figure among the reformers remained Thomas Cranmer, whose close personal relationship with the King kept him in his key position as Archbishop of Canterbury. Part of his success was probably that, unlike Cromwell or Wolsey, he did not try to dominate the King.

Nonetheless, the return from abroad of the arch-conservative Bishop Stephen Gardiner led to attempts to unseat Cranmer with the assistance of London's Bishop Bonner. Religious radicals were hunted in Cranmer's households both in Cambridge and London, but nothing serious was found against him. The King frightened Cranmer by telling him, 'I know now who is the greatest heretic in Kent,' but turned the tables on Gardiner by appointing Cranmer himself to head a commission to investigate the allegations against him. I have largely followed the account of the attack on Cranmer given in Diarmaid MacCulloch's *Cranmer* (London 1996). It was probably autumn, rather than in the spring as I have indicated, that Cranmer found himself out of the woods.

Early 1543 also saw major attacks on Protestantism in Parliament and through a renewed campaign against radicals in London by Bishop Bonner. The Parliament of that year brought in strong anti-reformist legislation, notably forbidding the working classes and women to read the new English Bible, which under Cromwell's aegis had been placed in every parish church. I am very grateful to the librarian of St John's College, Cambridge, for allowing me to see their copy of the 1539 Great Bible, which may have belonged to Thomas Cromwell himself. I have used its phraseology in quoting from the Book of Revelation, though I have modernized the Tudor spelling. Susan Brigden's *London and the Reformation* (Oxford 1989) was an invaluable source for the campaign against the 'sectaries' in London, which included a manhunt for those who had broken the rules on eating meat in Lent. Her book portrays a London increasingly divided between radical and conservative parishes; the radicals, with their view of themselves as persecuted saints, often comforted themselves in the belief that Revelation foretold their eventual victory against the 'Beast' of Rome. Many believed then, exactly as Christian fundamentalists do today, that they lived in the 'last days' before Armageddon and, again just as now, saw signs all around in the world that they took as certain proof that the Apocalypse was imminent. Again like fundamentalists today, they looked on the prospect of the violent destruction of mankind without turning a hair. The remarkable similarity between the first Tudor Puritans and today's fundamentalist Christian fanatics extends to their selective reading of the Bible, their emphasis on the Book of Revelation, their certainty of their rightness, even to their phraseology. Where the Book of Revelation is concerned, I share the view of Guy, that the early church fathers released something very dangerous on the world when, after much deliberation, they decided to include it in the Christian canon.

Catherine Parr married Henry VIII in July 1543 following several months' courtship. Queen Catherine herself admitted years later that, unlike any of his previous queens, she had resisted the idea of marrying him. Partly at least this was because of her affection for Sir Thomas Seymour. It is uncertain whether Catherine Parr was already a reformist sympathizer by 1543; I think that she was, for otherwise she would have come to a sophisticated reformism only after marrying a King whose increasingly anti-reformist sympathies made such a religious position dangerous. That does not seem to me to make sense.

Tudor views of madness were more varied and more sophisticated than one might imagine. As with all branches of medicine, views of mental illness were based on the theory of imbalances between the 'four humours' of which the human body was made up. Thus, for example, the advice to the melancholic to eat salad because of its cold and wet properties. But there is also much evidence of 'common-sense' remedies, such as encouraging the 'melancholic' or 'mopish' (as upper-class and lower-class depressives were respectively called) to get out of the house, take the air, listen to music and enjoy cheerful conversation. I do not think Guy's solutions would have been unusual, although his interest in the subject of mental illness would have been. On the other hand, both Catholics and Protestants would often see the more florid types of mental illness as evidence of possession; Catholics tended to prescribe confession and appeal to sacred images, Protestants prayer and fasting. Occasionally, as happens to Adam Kite in the book, a mentally unstable religious obsessive could find himself in danger of being accused of heresy and burned at the stake. For early modern views of medicine, I found Roy Porter's *A Social History of Madness* (London 1987) a very useful introduction, while Michael MacDonald's *Mystical Bedlam* (Cambridge 1981) gives a fascinating picture of an early seventeenth-century therapist. His practice included cases of 'salvation panic' such as that from which Adam Kite suffers, and which seems to have been a new phenomenon brought about by Lutheran and Calvinist notions of God's predestined division of humanity into the saved and the damned. It has reappeared often during fundamentalist campaigns in the centuries since – the first great Awakening in eighteenth-century colonial America featured several notable suicides by people who had come to believe they were irrevocably damned.

As for care for the mentally ill, this was rudimentary and only accessible to the rich, like all medicine. Foucault has seen the emergence of mental hospitals in the eighteenth century, when people working in industrial environments could no longer look after mentally ill relatives at home, as 'the great confinement'. This assumes, however, that pre-industrial societies looked after the mentally backward and mentally ill better. While this may be true to some extent of those with low intelligence, who might be cared for at home, there are too many accounts of those with severe mental illness being chained up at home or abandoned to live and frequently die in uninhabited regions ('the wild men of the woods') for us to believe that life for the mentally ill in early modern Europe was anything other than precarious and grim.

The Bedlam, originally founded in the fifteenth century as a hospital for London's mentally ill, was one of the very few hospitals for those with mental problems in Europe. It has earned a grim reputation, not least because of the image of people visiting the Bedlam to laugh at the antics of the chained-up lunatics as a weekend diversion. This did indeed happen, but not until Stuart times. Little is known about the Tudor institution except that it housed perhaps thirty inmates, that they were usually kept there for a year (though some stayed for much longer), at the end of which they were discharged whether cured or not, and that it was a paying institution, which meant that most of the inmates came from the wealthier classes. There may have been some serious attempts at treatment at this time in the hospital, but the fact that the wardenship was used as a source of profit, and the grim conditions prevailing at most such 'privatized' institutions at the time, argue in favour of a more neglectful regime. But we do not know, so I have had to invent.

For background research, I had to read a number of books on serial killers. What struck me forcibly was that while there are certain common patterns that appear in the lives of these people, few exhibit all of these features, and there is still no real understanding of what turns some people down this terrible path.

The case of Gilles de Rais is, unfortunately, historically true. Strodyr, however, is an invention – I have been unable to find any verifiable references to serial killers in medieval England. Of course, given the lack of any real detection process at the time, that does not rule out there being any. I am grateful to James Willoughby for helping me by looking at the records of one possible case, which however turned out to be a *canard*.

On a somewhat lighter note, John Woodward's *The Strange Story of False Teeth* (Routledge 1968) was very helpful, although I disagree with his view that this sixteenth-century French fashion did not gain any popularity in England.

As usual, where historical dates are known I have tried to adhere to them, but although Vesalius' book referred to in the text was published in 1543, its appearance in England was probably a little later.

All the London churches mentioned in the text are fictional.

ACKNOWLEDGEMENTS

Once again, I am very grateful to Mike Holmes, Jan King, Roz Brody and William Shaw for reading the book in manuscript form. Thanks to Frank Tallis for discussions on the history of mental illness and its treatment. My agent Antony Topping once again read and commented most perceptively on the draft, as did my editor at Macmillan, Maria Rejt. Thanks to Mari Roberts for her copy-editing, to Frankie Lawrence and Rebecca Smith for their typing, and to Will Stone for research into the history of the doctrine of squatters' rights.